QUICUNQUE VULT

BY
KEIRA
MICHELLE
TELFORD

www.venaticpress.com

QUICUNQUE VULT

(kwi-kuun-kway vult)
An Explanation of the Words

The Victorians are known for their colorful language and love of euphemisms, driven by the compulsive need to conceal vulgarity wherever they saw it (or feared that it lurked). For example, a person whose job it was to collect dog feces off the street was called a 'pure collector.' Not even the slightest mention of poop.

Of course, sex was by far the biggest offender of their delicate sensibilities. People didn't even have sex, they had 'connexion.' A penis wasn't a penis, it was a 'burning machine,' and a woman's vagina wasn't a vagina, but a 'lubricious channel.' Her pubic mound was a 'hairy paradise,' and her breasts were her 'charms.'

When it came to prostitution, the sin of all sins, their language became even more inventive. While a common and polite word for a low class prostitute driven to the work out of necessity was simply 'an unfortunate,' there was a whole gamut of far more creative—and much less courteous—terms employed. In no particular order: Toffer (a high-class prostitute), wagtail, bobtail, pinchcock, tart (a late Victorian corruption of the slang 'jam-tart,' meaning an attractive woman), receiver general, drab (a nasty, sluttish whore, according to *Grose's Dictionary of the Vulgar Tongue*), doxy, cyprian, paphian, fallen woman, loose woman, harlot, bunter (half beggar, half whore), dollymop (a part-time prostitute), wench, stroller (a prostitute who works the streets), strumpet, fille de joie, lady of easy virtue, and a fucktress.

Among these and others there was also: Athanasian wench and Quicunque vult. Why? Because sometime during the fifth or sixth century, the Athanasian Creed (so named after a fourth century bishop called Saint

Athanasius of Alexandria) was written. It opened with the phrase:

Quicunque vult salvus esse, ante omnia opus est, ut teneat catholicam fidem.

In English, this is translated to mean:

Whosoever wishes to be saved, before all things it is necessary that he hold the catholic faith.

In the early nineteenth century, the opening words of this creed—Quicunque vult, meaning 'whosoever wishes'—were used interchangeably with the term 'Athanasian wench' when referring to: A forward girl, ready to oblige every man that shall ask her (*Grose's Dictionary of the Vulgar Tongue*, 1811). And that is how the title of this book came to be.

A NOTE FROM
THE AUTHOR

This book is written in the language of the time and uses terms that some people might find offensive. The author would like to make readers aware of that, and apologizes in advance to anyone who is disturbed by such terms.

In addition, there is a somewhat liberal use of expletives throughout. This is due to the fact that the Victorians viewed various medical and anatomical words (vagina, penis, sex, pregnancy, etc) as vulgar, and therefore these terms were only to be used by medical practitioners. In everyday language, the middle and upper classes would shroud everything in layers of euphemism, but the working classes (who are the primary focus of this book) were apt to use more basic language (cunt, prick, fuck, etc). In keeping with this, the characters you are about to meet use whichever terms are most befitting of their individual backgrounds.

Lastly, it should be noted that the meanings of some words have changed over the course of the last century. Perhaps most notably, the term 'gay' did not yet have any connection to same-sex attractions. In the late Victorian period, 'gay' was a word frequently applied to prostitution. For example, a prostitute may be called 'a gay woman,' a brothel might be a 'gay house,' and prostitution is sometimes referred to as 'the gay life.' If you have 'turned gay,' then you have resorted to prostitution.

In addition, a 'bully' was a sort of pimp often employed by brothel-keepers to ensure that customers always paid up and that the girls weren't harmed. Occasionally, these bullies would operate outside of the brothels, targeting prostitutes who walked the streets. In this case, they would offer the girls protection in exchange for a small (or not so small) slice of what they earned.

THE MORAL OF THE WHITECHAPEL MURDERS

"NOT HALF ENOUGH IS BEING DONE FOR THE WRETCHED"

"The veil has been drawn aside that covered up the hideous condition in which thousands, tens of thousands, of our fellow creatures live in this boasted nineteenth century, and in the very heart of the wealthiest, the healthiest, the most civilized city in the world. We have all known for many years that deplorable misery, gross crime, and unspeakable vice—mixed and matted together—lie just off the main roads that lead through the industrial quarters of the metropolis. The daily sins, the nightly agonies, the hourly sorrows that haunt and poison and corrupt the ill-fated tenants and sojourners in these homes of degradation and disease have been again and again described with more or less truth and force by our popular writers; but it is when some crime or accident, more than usually horrible, has given vividness and reality to the previously unrealized picture, and that we are brought to feel—what our keenest powers failed to adequately to conceive before—how parts of our great capital are honeycombed with cells, hidden from the light of day, where men are brutalized, women are demonized, and children are brought into the world only to be inoculated with corruption, reared in terror, and trained in sin, till punishment and shame overtake them too, and thrust them down to the black depths where their parents lie already lost, or dead to every hope or chance of moral recovery and social rescue. Then comes a terrible crime, bringing a revelation that fills every soul with horror, and makes us ask why sleeps the thunder, and how these things can be?"

-- The Morning Post, September 12, 1888
Reprinted in the Pall Mall Gazette

CHAPTER 1

Tuesday, March 1, 1887

TAKING HER PUNISHMENT, MARY JANE BRACES HERSELF against the wall of a dank, filth bestrewn alley, the rough brickwork scraping her palm, the damp clay covered with moss and grime. Eyes closed, she dips her head and grits her teeth, trying to disengage her mind from the violent, unrelenting assault on her body.

Every brutal stab feels like a searing hot blade piercing her skin, driving into the core of her being, and they come in quick succession, harder and fiercer with every thrust. Then, it happens. Her possessor growls, plunging the unwelcome lance into her abused flesh one last time, ramming it deep and pulling her back on it, impaling her to the hilt. There, he finds his release.

"Aye, that's it, love." Mary Jane forces sweetness into her voice, all trace of the Irish lilt she had as a child lost long ago, having been corrupted by her exposure to the world beyond the close-knit Irish enclave in which she was raised. "Finish up."

Spent and out of breath, the stout, mustached man behind her slackens his grip on her hips and withdraws his withering prick. Sated for tonight, he tucks himself back into his trousers and adjusts his woolen waistcoat as Mary Jane, her skirts bunched up in one hand, fishes a silk handkerchief out of her pocket and plugs the entrance to her body, mopping up his seminal deposit as gravity takes effect.

Turning to face her last customer of the night, she feigns satisfaction and curls her immodestly crimson-colored lips into a smile. He's a nice enough young man who—rather than sheathe himself in a prophylactic and dull the pleasure of their congress—insisted on checking her cleanliness by inspecting her privities at close range with a lighted match prior to the commencement of rutting. He flatly refused to conduct the operation face to face and muttered the name Susan throughout, but she'd be happy to take his money again.

"Told you I was worth a few bob." She winks.

"You are that." He chuckles, straightening his worn bowler hat, the grease-stained rim frayed and ragged. "I've no complaints."

In short order, he promises to see her again, bids her goodnight, and begins the short journey home to his wife, leaving Mary Jane alone in the darkened passageway to George Yard Buildings: a model lodging house near the north end of a narrow back alley in Whitechapel, in the East End borough of Tower Hamlets.

Here, the gaslights are extinguished at eleven o'clock of an evening, leaving the narrow covered footway cloaked in shadow, granting those in her profession some small amount of privacy in which to conduct their nefarious nightly affairs with little risk of interruption.

Indeed, much of the East End is filled with such nooks and crannies, creating a veritable warren of side streets, empty courtyards, and gloomy, unlit passages running between and through the countless tenements and lodging houses scattered about this iniquitous quarter, and Mary Jane knows every inch of it.

She's lived in Whitechapel for several months, taking her customers wherever convenient. If they can't afford to pay for a room and a bed—or if they're too fuddled or impatient to care—she'll see to their business in the nearest secluded hideaway, seldom having to stray outside the Wicked Quarter Mile: the vice-filled slum streets bounded by Crispin Street and Bell Lane to the west, Brushfield Street and Church Street to the north, Brick Lane to the east, and Wentworth Street to the south.

On account of her relative youth, fresh complexion, and abundant personal attractions, she never has to go far to find a man willing to part with his hard-earned coin. She's a sought after commodity, and moreover, since she's known for catering to certain peculiar letches of men—primarily, employing the use of her mouth or breasts for the purpose of sperm-drawing—her liberal carnal talents have earned her a reputation as being a harlot of the finest degree. Not that there's a tremendous amount of competition.

By and large, the women of vice in this area are past their prime, having turned to the work on account of suffering the loss of a husband or two and being no longer able to care for their children. Their faces are already worn by poverty, a number of them stricken with disease. In most cases, they tumbled down the social ladder in fits and starts, winding up in the East End slums when the last rung finally rotted out from under them. Others simply had the misfortune to be born into poverty. They were raised to accept their lot in life, prepared from the earliest age to sacrifice their virtue to meet their basic needs. For them, vice is a necessity.

Then, there are the pleasure seekers. Perpetually shackled to the streets, they're blind to the worries of the future, their eyes turned only to the next glass of gin, rum, or some other numbing intoxicant. Their course in life could likely have been averted, had their appetites for drinking and fucking not driven them into this state, enjoying everything to excess, with no sense of moderation or decency.

The invasion of strange men between their thighs is no great hardship for them, but that's not the case for Mary Jane. The sordid act brings her no pleasure. A man's article provides not the slightest bit of satisfaction, save for ensuring the payment of her rent, the luxury of regular hot meals, and the ability to purchase a few decent clothes.

Preparing to be on her way, she settles the ruffles of her flounced satin skirts, smoothes the layered pleats over her derrière, and straightens her low-cut satin bodice, adjusting the artificial violet she always wears

13

pinned to the left side of her breast, an inch or two above her heart. Once she feels suitably arranged, she hugs a self-crocheted maroon crossover shawl around her shoulders and emerges from the beveled archway of George Yard Buildings, slipping unseen up the alleyway and onto Wentworth Street. From there, weary and fatigued, she makes her way north, back to Thrawl Street, where she rents a solitary room in a crowded lodging house.

This single-lane street of dubious reputation is lined with three-storey buildings, most of which could be considered the lowest class of doss-house. During the day, children play in the gutters, their bare feet squelching through the dirt and muck of rotting garbage, picking through the organic waste in search of an apple core, or a piece of orange peel—anything that, in their desperation, might be considered edible.

As if that weren't sufficiently foul, Thrawl Street becomes altogether more unwholesome after nightfall. When the public houses kick out, the pavements fill with gin-soaked men and women staggering drunkenly homewards, crooning out-of-tune songs half-remembered from childhood, or initiating quarrels of the most aggressive and profanity-laden variety.

The plaintive cries of hungry infants ring out up and down the street, drowning out the hiss of the gaslights, and a frowzy old woman with a sunken face sits in the gutter, sobbing. She was recently expelled from Wilmott's Lodging House for lack of the fourpence needed to procure herself a bed for the night, and she's not alone.

Any who fail to come up with their bed money are left to their own. These shelter-less souls—a majority of whom sealed their own fate when they mindlessly drank, smoked, or fucked away the last of their coin—have little choice but to huddle in doorways, snatching what few precious moments of sleep they can. In so doing, they chance being awoken with a strong kick and the glare of an unsympathetic policeman's lantern before being made to move on to other streets and other doorways, where this rough treatment may soon be repeated.

Next door to Wilmott's, on the corner of George Street—which cuts through Thrawl Street north-south—is Cooney's Good Lodgings, the name being somewhat delusive.

This building, with its soot-blackened walls and filthy yellow canvas blinds, is the place Mary Jane very much reluctantly calls home. From the street, it looks mean. The heavy sash windows are stiff and uncooperative, many of them no longer functional, and some window panes have been broken out to ventilate the stuffy, noxious rooms. On the inside, it looks worse.

A din of laughter, crude execrations, and booze-fueled joviality is emanating from the communal kitchen as Mary Jane steps in from the cold, but she ignores all, greets the stout doss-house deputy—a homely woman in charge of collecting bed money—and heads straight for the rickety wooden staircase.

The steps are so steep and narrow that safely navigating them while under the influence of gin is a nigh impossible task. The uneven rises alone require a certain focus and concentration that those bleary-eyed bed-seekers stumbling home from the nearest drinking dens simply do not possess, requiring them then to crawl up on all fours, scrambling from one step to the next like poorly coordinated mountain goats.

Hiking up her ankle-length skirts so as not to trip, Mary Jane—in full possession of clear vision and proper equilibrium—nimbly negotiates three flights and reaches her floor unscathed, the hallway dimly lit by a few dirty paraffin lamps. While a vast proportion of lodgers at Cooney's are night boarders, paying only a few pence for a bed, a small number of private rooms are rented on a weekly basis to those who can afford to pay the whole fee in advance.

For the most part, families occupy these lodgings, pooling their resources to put a few measly scraps of food on the table and make the rent—which is three shillings and up, depending on the room. Mary Jane is in the minority here, being able to earn enough on her single income to keep the wolf from the door without the need

to share her space. In this respect, she is, one might dare to say, lucky.

Propping her foot on the wobbly, splintered banister railing, she flicks her skirts over her knee—all three layers, consisting of a silk petticoat, a flannel petticoat functioning as an underskirt, and a flounced emerald-colored, cotton-backed satin outer skirt—and fishes her room key out of her scuffed black leather boot.

As she unlocks her door, an argument in the neighboring room—recently vacated by an elderly couple who were evicted for non-payment of rent—is escalating. A man's voice can be heard berating a woman, calling her the vilest of all names. The woman retorts by calling him a brute and threatening to find herself a better man more deserving of her good nature.

Glad that she remains, for the time being, unbound to any man, Mary Jane enters her dingy room and tries to ignore the racket.

Her private sanctuary is small, but sufficient for her needs. The claustrophobic, eight-by-eight space contains little in the way of furniture, but—on account of being located above the kitchen, and thus utilizing the same chimney—she is fortunate enough to have her own fireplace. It's a privilege that costs her an extra sixpence in weekly rent, but allows her to be more self-sufficient and keeps the chill of winter at bay.

The modest furnishings are all the property of the lodging house, including a three-quarter size bed that dominates one wall and a small table pushed up beneath a window that's permanently stuck open a good five inches. She doesn't even own the bed linens.

There's also a tin bath—which she makes use of for quick washes between visits to the public baths—a small cupboard, a washstand, and two wobbly chairs, over which are draped various articles of clothing: a corset; a chintz skirt; a woolen pilot coat; a ruddy brown-colored linsey-woolsey frock; and a fitted black velvet jacket, the collar and cuffs trimmed with fur, the pockets trimmed with silk braid. Other garments are folded on top of the cupboard, including two pairs of woolen over-the-knee stockings—one red, one white—and the garter elastics to

hold them up, one white silk chemise, an embroidered silk camisole, and a lavish red satin corset with a black lace trim around the bust.

Beside them, a little wicker basket contains a plain cloth pouch holding an outlandish sampling of beauty products: some colored nail powder and an emery board; a jar of red lip paste; a jar of French rouge, and a feather puff to apply it; some eye paint; a pair of tweezers; two small tubs of beeswax—one pink-tinted salve for her lips, and one uncolored for her eyelashes; and a little face powder to cover the occasional blemish. Also in the basket is a hairbrush, a ceramic jar containing an orris-root-based dry shampoo powder, a small bottle of lemon juice—squeezed by her own hand—and a handful of seldom-used hair clips and pins.

In defiance of style and social conventions, Mary Jane prefers to wear her waist-length hair loose, sometimes pinning back the front sections to prevent her thick, auburn-colored mane from falling in her face, or otherwise braiding it to prevent it from becoming too tangled on poor weather days. Proud of her eye-catching locks, she detests fixing her tresses up, despite the fact that she's well above marriageable age. For the same reason, she rejects the wearing of a bonnet or a hat, even in the rain. In any case, these tricks not only make her appear younger, but are also part of her advertisement. Only a woman of loose morals would dare to go about with her head so uncovered, her hair so unrestrained, her lips so red, and her chest and shoulders—her *décolletage*—so exposed.

Endowed with generous proportions, Mary Jane began donning risqué outfits reserved for eveningwear, no matter the time of day, during her short stint working in a West End gay house, and has since seen no need to part with the aesthetic. This, among other things, ensures that she stands out among her class, her undeniably striking qualities helping to secure the exorbitant fees she charges for her services.

While many of the very youngest and prettiest in this district consider themselves fortunate if they get to pocket a shilling or two for each connection—some even

17

being willing to accept a brand new silk handkerchief in lieu of payment, knowing it can be sold on for a half-crown—Mary Jane seldom lets a man inside her for less than three.

Counting her money tonight, she smiles to herself. She's pocketed a little over seven shillings in the course of five hours, her earnings far exceeding the amount she'd be bringing home were she employed in some respectable job. In consequence of which, she need only work five days a week in order to keep herself above the poverty line, and when she can stomach putting in longer hours to earn a little extra, she's even able to save.

After concealing much of her takings in a lockbox stashed beneath the bed—leaving the paltry sum of a few pennies in her pocket—she proceeds to clean herself up. First, she plants her foot on the seat of a nearby chair and pulls the wadded up, semen-drenched hanky from her sex, then she fishes three more used hankies out of her pocket. Two of these were used to wipe her hands following manual stimulation. One was used to wipe the accumulated gunk and grime from underneath an uncircumcised customer's foreskin before she'd accept him in her mouth, her examination not only ensuring that he was as clean as he could be, but also that his genitalia showed no signs of disease or infection.

She shudders at the thought.

Setting all four hankies on the edge of the washstand, next to a small supply of prophylactic sheaths, she retrieves a full-to-the-brim ewer from the shelf underneath and pours a few inches of water into the porcelain basin, then proceeds to fill a small tin cup with the same. When the cup is three-quarters full, she adds some vinegar from a bottle in the cupboard and swirls the mixture around before drawing a measure of it into a slender glass douching syringe.

Though less astringent than some other questionable concoctions she could use, the vinegar serves its purpose. She squats above her chipped porcelain chamber pot, inserts the five-inch syringe into her vaginal canal, and pushes down on the glass plunger, injecting the solution into the depths of her body to swill out the dregs of

mucilage left behind by her last customer, as well as somewhat sanitizing the orifice. She does this twice.

Remaining in a squat, she then fumbles her long fingers inside herself, dislodging and tugging free a rubber diaphragm used to prevent any seminal fluid from traveling up into her womb. With that contraption removed, she douches twice more—once with the vinegar solution, once with pure water—and piddles, completing her clean-up with a quick scrub down using a bit of soap, thereby eliminating the unpleasant stench of vinegar from her privities.

That chore complete, she rinses off the diaphragm and the syringe, and gives the hankies a quick scrub in the basin before wringing them out and draping them over a curtain wire strung across the ceiling: a makeshift washing line. All the while, the domestic argument next door continues to escalate, resulting in the sharp slap of a backhand meeting a cheek, followed by the soft thud of a woman falling to the floor.

Having been on the receiving end of a male violence more times than she cares to think about, Mary Jane pities the poor creatures who so often have no choice but to suffer daily beatings for the sake of remaining with the man who pays their way in life. Today, she's thankful for her independence, no matter the cost to her dignity.

With the last of the water in the ewer, she tackles the thoroughly unpleasant task of brushing her teeth. Her toothbrush, made of carved wood and boar hair bristles, is old, and losing more bristles by the day. Many of them find their way between her teeth and stick there, resulting in more aggressive brushing to dislodge them, which invariably concludes with her spitting more hairs.

The tooth powder itself, at sixpence a pot, is something of a luxury—albeit an objectionable one. It's a concoction of chalk, cuttlefish bone, a dash of soap, and tincture of myrrh, with peppermint oil added as a breath sweetener. When mixed with water, the resulting paste is gritty and quite revolting. More often than not, she swills away the taste with a bedtime cup of tea, and to that end, she drains the basin back into the ewer, snatches up a teapot and cup from her cupboard, and stuffs two small

tins into her pocket: one containing tea leaves, the other holding a scant quantity of sugar.

Were she in the mood for it, she would light her own fire and have her drink in peace. A cheap copper kettle hangs from a hook above the hearth for just that purpose, but she hasn't the patience to get a fresh fire going. Instead, she checks her appearance in a tarnished and cracked mirror beside the door—inspecting her lightly rouged cheeks, her red lips, and the subtle dusting of black powder on her eyelids—then makes her way downstairs to the communal kitchen, holding the ewer in one hand and the teapot in the other, the cup wedged under her arm.

On any given night, the kitchen—a long room cluttered with a disorganized hodgepodge of tables and benches, an open fireplace and stove occupying one end— can be crammed with five to twenty people. Some come here to smoke, others seek the warmth of the open fire. A majority are regular boarders with whom Mary Jane is on nodding terms.

There being no sense of decorum in a lodging house of this variety, table conversation is generally of the lowest kind. Even the women—many of whom earn their wages on the streets—join in with the men, making use of the crudest language, their vulgar tongues plenty loosened by drink. However, besides a small gaggle of the usual boisterous characters, there's one new face tonight.

A young girl, no more than sixteen years of age, is standing by the fireplace, keeping her distance from the group. Her waist-length chestnut hair is unbound: a testament to her youth and purity. Two thin braids at the front are pulled back and tied behind her head, keeping it from her face, which is angled to the floor, obscuring her dainty features.

Too slender for the bodice of her hand-me-down linsey frock, a cotton sash is fastened around her waist, cinching it in. Darned in several places, the calf-length skirt—which only a girl of her age is able to wear without any loss of respectability, for it daringly exposes her ankles—is a patchwork of mismatched fabrics, some scraps torn from curtains, others from bed sheets.

20

The cuffs of her over-sized bodice are rolled up, her pale hands clasped in front her, her nails short and brittle. She's trying not to fidget. No more than five-foot-two, her scuffed ankle boots would afford her an inch more in height, were the soles not almost worn through.

As Mary Jane makes her way to that end of the kitchen, stepping over dropped crusts of bread, cockroaches, and other vermin, the girl peers up, watching her approach.

The air is thick with tobacco, and plumes of smoke are billowing from the coke fire, the chimney half-clogged and in dire need of sweeping. Placing her cup and teapot on an unoccupied table, Mary Jane flings open the back door and tosses the contents of the ewer out into the pitch black courtyard. In doing so, she lets in a gust of cool, much needed air, fetid though it is on account of the nearby privies, which have been backed-up for the last week.

Leaving the door open, she searches for a kettle amongst the jumble of cutlery, pots and pans, and various other cooking utensils all stored haphazardly on some sloping shelves beside the stove. Upon finding the dented, tarnished copper vessel and giving it a brief inspection for cleanliness—a scrutiny which it barely passes—she traipses warily into the courtyard, armed with both it and the ewer, and finds her way to the water pump by little more than guesswork, since the gaslight hasn't been lit once in over a fortnight.

By the time she returns to the kitchen with the ewer replenished and the kettle full, the girl by the fireplace is being harassed by an inebriated old soaker known only by the name of Roger. He has a reputation for driving his prick up anything willing, and his plaid trousers are already unbuttoned, one hand tucked inside as he leers over the girl's shoulder, trying to get his other hand around her skinny waist.

Adopting a scowl, Mary Jane sets down the ewer and kettle and intervenes. "Let the dear lass alone." She gives him a smack and shoves him away. "She don't want your filthy mitts all over her, I'm sure."

Roger stumbles backwards into a table, reaching out for anything to steady himself on, but only manages to grab a fistful of Mary Jane's skirts. Toppling clumsily onto a bench, he yanks her down with him, dragging her onto his lap.

"Fair Emma!" He beams a crooked smile, the tip of his swollen priapus poking through the gaping hole in his trousers. "How much for ya?"

"I'm done for the night." Mary Jane wrests herself free. "And even if I weren't, I wouldn't give you the time of day, never mind a touch."

Undeterred Roger digs through his pockets, coming up with thruppence and slapping it on the table. "Look here, I got some coin for ya."

"Ain't you generous?" Mary Jane laughs, turning her attention back to the kettle. "You'd best set your sights elsewhere, you cheap bastard. I've still got standards."

An older woman sitting next to Roger, dozing in an alcohol-induced stupor until now, perks up at the sight of the coppers.

"Waste not, want not." She snatches them into her greedy palm, drops them into her pocket, and hikes up her skirts. "It's been a good long while since I've had a poke."

Roger grunts something unintelligible and pulls out his rigid cock as she pivots to face him and straddles his lap, hovering over him until she receives permission to dock. He's not fussy when sober, never mind drunk, and in any case, neither one of them could be considered a particularly attractive specimen of the human species.

"That's it, love." She reaches down and helps to angle his article inside her, tiring of waiting for him to locate the correct part of her anatomy. "Get it well in there."

With a wiggle of her wide hips, she sinks down on him, making him groan as his turgid pipe slides into her sopping, well-used hole.

"Ooh, you're a big one!" she exclaims happily. "Nice fat prick for me."

Bracing herself against the table, she works her love-trap up and down his shaft, her mouth held open in silent

awe of his girth, which surely must be something of inhuman proportions to be capable of satisfactorily filling her to any great degree.

Widened by her advancing years and several full-term swellings, she wears no corset, for one could not possibly be made to contain her. Having birthed a steady stream of infants during her married years, her commodity, too, is in a sorry state of affairs. Even at some distance, Roger's cock can be heard sloshing in her, his pre-ejaculatory fluid mingling with her own juices and the lingering sediment of customers previous.

"Bloomin' heck, Em." She yowls at the sagging, tobacco-stained ceiling. "You oughta curse ye-self for not taking this one. He's got a fine poker on him, so he has." She bounces harder and faster. "I think he's gonna bring me over." She shoves a hand up her skirts and tickles the flabby flesh of her outer sex. "Ooh, yessir, I'm coming over."

Mary Jane chuckles to herself, her silver teardrop earrings swaying from side to side, the center-set cheap paste gems glistening in the firelight, shimmering as real emeralds might.

Careful to give the copulating pair a wide berth, she takes the discolored kettle to the hearth and hooks it over the raging fire, the angry flames licking at the very bottom of the scorched copper. As she bends to do so, she catches the reserved teen stealing more than a fleeting glimpse at her generous cleavage.

Intrigued by the attention, she stays bent forward a few seconds longer than strictly necessary, allowing the girl a proper eyeful.

"Good evening to you." She smiles warmly, attempting to harness the girl's hazel eyes with her blues. "I don't reckon as I've seen your face here before."

Instantly embarrassed, the girl's already rosy cheeks turn a deeper shade of red and she hugs her arms across her chest, dipping her shamed gaze to her feet. Overwhelmed by the bawdy ruckus surrounding her, the laughter and execrations of half-drunken men and women now punctuated by the primal grunts of a carnal act that's nearing its inevitable completion, she finds

herself utterly incapable of offering Mary Jane a reciprocal greeting. All she can do is stare, aghast, as Roger gropes the plump woman's massive breasts, clutching at them over her tattered dress.

"Go on, then." The woman unbuttons her bodice, baring her drooping, stretch-marked mammaries. "Get yer paws on me bubbies and have a good feel."

Intent on making use of all that's offered to him, regardless of its quality, Roger engulfs as much of her breast meat as he can, pulling and tugging on her distended nipples, pinching them between his fingers.

"C'mon, you fat fucker." She rubs her clit with violent determination, jouncing harder on his leaking prick. "Go off in me!"

Beneath her, he groans, his engorged tool swelling all the more before erupting into her cavernous depths, spewing his offering into her ravaged womb.

"That's the way," she encourages him, grinding on his lap. "Fill me up good. You ain't got nuthin' to worry about."

That's an assurance of some questionable worth. While it may be true that her breeding years are well behind her, enabling her to enjoy men without the need for precaution, disease in this city is rampant. Any number of revolting ailments could be working their way through her body, doing their damage in any number of as yet unseen ways.

Repulsed by the thought, the girl by the fireplace pivots to face the hearth instead, only to come face to bosom with Mary Jane. Stifling a whimper of surprise, she tilts her head up, awed by the height of this buxom stranger.

Indeed, at five-foot-seven, Mary Jane is as tall as most men, and she towers over the petite young girl, quite disarming her.

"Sorry." She plucks a dishcloth from a hook on the wall behind the girl's shoulder. "I didn't mean to startle you." She folds the dishcloth over several times and lifts the boiling kettle off the fire. "Fancy a cup of tea?"

24

CHAPTER 2

THE TEEN GIRL IN THE RAGGEDY DRESS LINGERS AT THE periphery of the room, watching Mary Jane prepare tea. Too shy to accept the tempting offer of a hot drink, she remains at her post beside the fireplace, looking more forlorn by the minute.

In the periphery of her vision—the open door giving her a lamentably clear view—the slatternly whore squats in the courtyard. With her back against the brick wall and her skirts pulled up around her hips, she clenches her pelvic muscles, squeezing out Roger's libation.

"Look at this lot!" She grins, indicating the puddle of semen between her legs. "He comes in bucket loads, that one!"

As she remains crouched there, her doings illuminated by the light from the kitchen fire, another string of thick, mucilaginous goop evacuates from her deepest recesses, a mingled slop of her own spend and Roger's abundant contribution. That proves to be the final straw for the young girl.

Now regretting her choice to decline the tea, she takes a few hesitant steps forward, making her way to a reclaimed church pew not far from the fire. On the table in front of it, Mary Jane warms the teapot with a splash of hot water from the kettle before retrieving her tin of once-used tea leaves from her pocket and dumping a healthy measure into the ready pot.

"Are you all right, my darling?" She looks up as the girl approaches, hoping to solicit further interaction. "Sure you don't want a cuppa?" She pours hot water over the leaves. "There's enough here for us both."

The girl clings to the end of the pew. "I ain't got nuthin' to give you for it."

"I ain't asking for nothing," Mary Jane forges on, undeterred by the girl's continued diffidence. "Now"—she wipes her hands on her spotless white apron, worn to protect her satin skirt from the grime of everyday living— "while this steeps, help me fetch up the other bits and bobs."

Stepping on the seat of a wonky wooden chair for extra height, she rummages through the ramshackle shelves, displacing the odd cockroach and passing items down to the girl as she finds them. First, a tea strainer. Next, a small creamer jug.

Though she's not sure if it's attraction or curiosity that has the adolescent's interest so keenly piqued, she's well aware that the teen's eyes are on her all the while, pinned to her every move, and she can't resist playing it up for her audience. Adding extra flourishes here and there, she flicks her long, wavy hair over her shoulder, adjusts her bodice, and runs her hands over her posterior, as if wiping dust off her palms.

Enjoying herself far too much, her fun nearly backfires when she stands on her tippy-toes to reach the top shelf and props her knee on the back of the chair, causing it to wobble precariously. With one leg shorter than the others and the floor uneven, the unstable piece of tat threatens to tip over, and as she grips one of the shelves for support, considering how embarrassing it would be to end up in the infirmary over such a clumsy attempt at flirtation, she feels a pair of steadying hands slip around her hips.

After taking a moment to regain her poise, she looks down, finding herself held securely by her young admirer, her dignity saved.

"Thank you." She plucks a cup off the nearest shelf and plants both feet firmly back on the floor, hooking a finger under the girl's chin to tilt her head up, making a

firm bid for eye contact. "You're very sweet. What do I call you?"

The girl meets Mary Jane's subtly painted sapphire eyes briefly, flashing a demure smile before dipping back into her own space as soon as the provocative older woman releases her to do so.

"Eva," she mumbles. "Eva Sullivan."

"That's a pretty name." Mary Jane fingers a stray wisp of hair out of Eva's face. "A pretty Irish name for a pretty Irish girl, if that's not too improper for me to say." She strokes the back of her fingers lightly across one of Eva's pinkening cheeks. "Am I making you blush?"

"With a fury." Eva keeps her head angled away, growing increasingly self-conscious. "Am I to call you Emma?"

"If you like," Mary Jane answers curiously, withdrawing from her. "Other people do." She turns her mind back to the task of tea-making. "Care for some milk?"

She gives the creamer jug a cursory once over, dislodging a dead woodlouse she finds in the bottom of it before wiping it on her apron and declaring it fit enough for purpose.

Milk here is stored in the cellar, where it keeps for a few days without turning sour, and is made readily available to regular boarders and renters along with some cheap bread and the occasional bit of cheese. It's not much in the way of a perk, and the bread's no doubt tainted with alum, plaster, or ground animal bones to enhance its whiteness, but it's better than nothing.

Feeling vulnerable and not wanting to be left alone, Eva accompanies Mary Jane out into the hall and down a set of narrow, twisted stone steps, using only a single paraffin lamp for light. Emerging at the bottom of the cobwebby passage, she's shocked to find the room teeming with life. Three pigs are penned up in one corner, feeding from a trough of slop. Beside them, a small gaggle of ducks are waddling back and forth in their cramped coop, quacking at the squawking chickens housed on the other side of the damp, bitterly cold, dirt-floored room.

"Eggs and meat," Mary Jane explains, answering Eva's unspoken question. "It's the most efficient way to keep in good supply." She dangles the paraffin lamp on a hook suspended from the low ceiling. "They'd probably keep a cow down here n'all if they could."

With barely more than five feet of clearance, Mary Jane has to stoop to make her way about the room. Placing the creamer jug on a narrow workbench, she investigates a small pantry cupboard containing bits of cheese and other perishables, and pulls out a covered jug of milk, filling the creamer with its day-old contents.

Behind her, Eva covers her nose with her sleeve. "However can you bear it?" she asks, her voice muffled by the fabric. "It reeks worse than the privy!"

"You grow accustomed to the smell after a while," Mary Jane assures her, replacing the jug in the cupboard. "I've had a whiff of some human beings what has a worse stench about them than this. Honestly, only when you've had a bloke's crusty prick in your mouth do you truly appreciate the cleanliness of pigs."

Eva grimaces, feeling her stomach churn. "I couldn't never ..." She shakes her head vehemently. "Not never." She glances at the pig pen. "I'd sooner kiss a pig square on the chops than suck on a fella's nasty doodle."

"Really?" Mary Jane keeps her back to Eva a moment longer, delving for something in the cupboard. When she pivots to face the teen a few moments later, she's holding a fat, slightly upwards-curved smoked sausage at her groin. "You don't find this tempting?" She aims her meat at Eva, waggling it from side to side. "You wouldn't give me a lick?"

Eva's pale cheeks flush the deepest shade of red, her jaw flapping. "I ain't never seen such a thing!" She covers her face with her hands. "Oh, lummy!" Despite her discomposure, she peeks through her fingers, more intrigued than she is unnerved. "In any case, I wouldn't know how," she confesses her inexperience. "Not even in jest."

"And that's precisely as it should be." Mary Jane tosses the sausage back into the cupboard. "A girl of your tender years ought quite rightly to be ignorant of such

vulgar things, yet so many are ruined by undeserving, cunt-struck, fuck-hungry boys before they even know what they're about." She speaks plainly and with passion, reflecting sourly on her own misspent youth. "Purity gone. Innocence gone." She shakes her head, banishing a memory. "You've done well to avoid the trouble a standing prick so often causes."

Eva's hands fall away from her face, her expression turning solemn. "Is it truly awful?" She wrinkles her nose. "I can't say as I have any partic'lar inclination to acquaint me-self with a man's privities in that manner." She pauses. "Or in any manner, point of fact."

Mary Jane regards her closely, rolling those words over in her mind. "P'raps we have something in common, then?"

"Aye, p'raps," Eva answers halfheartedly, not entirely sure that she understands.

"Well, let's get on." Mary Jane breaks into a smile regardless. "Our tea's getting cold."

Creamer jug in hand, she snatches the paraffin lamp off the hook and leads the way back up the gloomy steps to the kitchen, Eva hot on her heels.

"Looks like you've found ye-self a leech," someone remarks snidely, squinting at Eva through gin eyes. "Best shake it now, before it gets attached."

Seeing the smile drop from Eva's face, Mary Jane plants the creamer on their table at the back of the room, close to the fireplace, and squeezes the teen's arm.

"Pay them no mind." She slides into the reclaimed pew, patting the space beside her. "Sit with me, please."

Forcing a weak smile, Eva sinks onto the pew, cautious not to sit too close for fear of drawing further criticism from the room. Not that Mary Jane appears even remotely concerned. Humming an old Irish tune, she dribbles a small measure of milk into each cup, then pours the steaming tea over the strainer.

"Here you are, my lovely." She sets a cup in front of Eva. "Sugar?" Without waiting for confirmation, she pulls the small sugar tin from her pocket and taps a sprinkling into Eva's drink, then her own. "I hope it's to your taste."

Eva remains quiet, her mood dulled by the snarky commentator.

"This place ain't so bad really." Mary Jane drapes her arm across the back of the pew behind the teen, trying to perk her up. "Most folks are harmless enough."

"Most?" Eva peaks an eyebrow.

Mary Jane leans closer, sliding a hand over Eva's shoulder, pleased when she feels no sudden burst of tension in her muscles, nor any indication that she dislikes the advance.

"See him?" She directs Eva's attention to a white-haired man smoking a pipe at one of the benches. "He's a lecherous oaf, but he'll do you no ill. The poor old codger barely knows what day it is half the time. This one"—she points to a fubsey old woman passed out over one of the tables—"she's got a mouth on her what could put sailors to shame."

Eva giggles, warming her hands on the teacup. "What about that 'un?" She nods to a spreeish young Irishwoman in the midst of a song and dance with an invisible partner, her skirts hitched up so as to avoid tripping, her cheap cotton stockings puddling around her ankles.

"That's Lushy-Loo." Mary Jane cringes, watching the woman trip over her own feet. "The dear old thing's all sweetness when she's got a drop in her, but keep well clear of her when she's dry."

"Fair enough." Eva takes a sip of her tea. "And what about you?" She peers up at Mary Jane. "What ought I to know of you?"

Struggling to interpret the question, Mary Jane hesitates, the silence between them only broken when two male boarders stagger by, both rather the worse for drink.

Not paying close enough attention to his surroundings, the weaker of the pair stumbles over one of the many Cooney's Lodging House cats and plummets to the floor by Eva, his pipe smashing on the stone and cracking one of his front teeth. Dazed by the fall, he groans and rolls onto his back, spitting out the broken

30

nub of his pipe and a shard of his tooth, his upper body angled awkwardly beneath the tabletop.

Disturbed by his proximity—and the distinct odor of urine about him—Eva shuffles closer to Mary Jane, brushing shoulders with her, soliciting protection.

"You'd best not be looking up her skirts, you dirty old bastard." Mary Jane glowers down at him. "Take so much as a peek at her quim and you'll have my fists to answer to."

"Oi-oi, watch out." The other man chortles, kicking at the disgruntled, hissing cat before heaving his poorly-coordinated friend off the floor. "Looks like our Fair Emma's got her dander up tonight, and she's proper handy with her mauleys."

"Hook it, both of you." Mary Jane flashes both men an obscene hand gesture and they saunter off, swaying unsteadily, clinging to one another for balance.

Once they've vacated the room, Mary Jane expects Eva to retreat to the other end of the bench. Instead, the unsettled teen remains close, quietly sipping her tea, not seeming to mind having Mary Jane's arm wrapped around her shoulders.

Assuming she wants comfort and security, and more than happy to be the one to provide it, Mary Jane rubs her thumb over Eva's collar bone.

"Is this your first time in a doss?"

Eva nods, gulping down more tea. "Me, my mam, and her new bloke. We got a private room, but they booted me out for a bit 'cause they was going at each other."

Mary Jane would like the opportunity to get to know Eva better, but their conversation is cut short when a much older woman in a shabby dress ornamented with an artificial violet slides onto the bench opposite them.

"She's a new one." The aging lodger indicates Eva with a tip of her head, her straggly gray hair spilling out of a bun. "Very pretty she is, too." She flashes Mary Jane a grimy grin, her teeth yellowed from chewing tobacco.

"It ain't like that," Mary Jane grumbles under her breath, slipping her hand off Eva's shoulder and returning it to the pew. "Whatchu want?"

"Got any to spare?" The woman rubs her hands together, eyeing the teapot.

Before answering, Mary Jane inspects Eva's cup, finding it empty but for the dregs. "Are you done, love? Or you want more?"

Eva nods to the former and shakes to the latter, so Mary Jane slides the empty cup across the table toward her acquaintance.

"Help yourself, old duck."

"You're a good 'un, Em." The old duck pours a cup of tea, draining the contents of the teapot. "Ain't many like you about." She fixes Eva with a smirk. "Our Em's been treating you nice, has she? I 'spect she has."

Mildly perplexed by the old duck's queer smile, Eva opens her mouth to answer, but stops short when the woman jerks her knee beneath the table, smacking hard into the warped wood and almost spilling her tea.

"Ow!" She rubs her shin, pouting at Mary Jane. "No need to get rough wi' me. I was only teasing the wee young thing."

"Well, don't." Mary Jane finishes the rest of her tea, unamused. "I already said it ain't nothing like that."

Still confused—both at the question, and why it ought to spark violence—Eva's brow creases. "Ain't nuthin' like what?"

Saving Mary Jane from having to explain herself, something small, furry, and warm brushes against Eva's ankle beneath the table.

"Eww!" She swings her legs up onto the pew as a rat bolts out from under the table. "Did you see that?!" She shifts sideways, tucking her knees up. "It was a rat!" She scoots up the bench, pressing herself against Mary Jane, her back to the older woman's breast. "Where'd the rotten beast go?"

"I don't know, but you'd best keep an eye out." Mary Jane feigns seriousness. "There could be more about, and the cats can only eat so many."

Right on cue, another Cooney's Lodging House cat—black as soot from tip to tail—jumps up onto one of the other tables, a fresh catch twitching in its mouth.

"Is there honest more?" Eva looks about from left to right, as if expecting an ambush.

"Most definitely." Mary Jane creeps her hands around Eva's tiny waist. "In fact, here comes another one!"

With that, she targets the unsuspecting teen's ribs and armpits with tickles, making her squeal—first in horror, then delight—her limbs flailing.

"Stop, stop, stop!" Eva giggles uncontrollably, trying fruitlessly to fend off the good-natured attack, finally toppling backwards into Mary Jane's lap. "Mercy! Please, mercy!"

Granting her respite, Mary Jane suspends her assault. As the giggles subside, she cradles Eva in her arm, supporting her neck and shoulders. The hand previously driving the playful molestation now rests across Eva's taut stomach, fingers splayed over her midsection.

Half fearing the truce may only be temporary, Eva clamps her hand over Mary Jane's, holding her in place, finding her skin soft and cool, her fingers long and slender. Somehow, this shocks her. She'd imagined someone of such a position in life to have the rough hands of a woman whose years have been spent at hard graft, but this woman's skin is unblemished by labor, or by the harshness of the summer sun, which is seen to darken and speckle the exposed flesh of the seasonal hop-picker year after year.

Frozen in place, she remains locked in Mary Jane's eyes, incapable of breaking the magnetism, even when she hears the old duck cackling at their antics. In the end, it's Mary Jane who looks away first, fearing that her simmering passions may soon become too apparent.

"Come on." She rubs Eva's back, heaving her upright. "Let's get you off to bed."

CHAPTER 3

MARY JANE LEADS THE WAY UPSTAIRS, EMPLOYING EVA TO carry the cup and teapot while she holds the heavy, water-filled ewer to her chest, her skirts clasped in her fist. Three steps up, however, they're halted by the lodging house deputy.

"Oi there, child." The woman flags Eva down. "Yer mam says you ain't to go back to the room tonight. We're up to the rafters as it is, so you'll have to bundle with another. Number twenty-four, the bed is. Like it or lump it. Ginger'll show ya."

"Ginger?" Eva looks around, seeing no-one else.

"Aye, that's me." Mary Jane kicks a dead rat to the edge of the staircase. "Come now."

She starts up the steep, crooked steps, leaving Eva to follow at a much slower pace, her footing not so assured on this unfamiliar terrain.

"I thought your name was Emma?" Eva catches up to her on the first-floor landing, a single paraffin lamp casting a pale brassy glow around them.

"Nah, and it ain't Ginger, neither." Mary Jane stops in front of an open doorway, the door itself long gone. "Most go by nicknames here."

She enters the cramped sleeping quarters beyond, checking each bed for the number matching the one assigned to Eva by the deputy, which is no easy task given

that some of the numbers—painted onto the floor at the foot of the beds—are so worn they're barely legible.

The beds themselves are little more than narrow cots, and there are five crammed into the eight-by-eight space. The makeshift mattresses—filthy palliasses made from sacking stuffed with wood shavings—are set upon rusted metal frames bought for cheap from the local infirmary when they upgraded to better. What passes for pillows are little more than muslin pouches stuffed with rags, and the blankets are coarse woolen sheets stamped with 'Stolen from Cooney's Good Lodging House, Thrawl Street,' lest an unscrupulous boarder should make off with them and attempt to sell them for a few coppers or a hot meal.

Worse yet, the walls are moving. At first glance it might well be thought a trick of the light, with shadows dancing on the blistered wallpaper, or highlighting craters in the crumbling plaster, but a closer look soon dispels the notion. This room has vermin.

Cockroaches scurry from one crevice to another in search of food, and as Eva trails behind Mary Jane, she crushes one beneath her boot, its insides splurging through the floorboards. The beds, too, appear alive—some more so than the women in them. Lice swarm around the palliasse seams, scurrying out for their nightly blood feed.

In one of the beds, a woman groans then passes gas, the foul odor expelled from her bowels adding to the already pungent stench of unwashed human bodies, stale booze, and halitosis. Compounding these vile emissions, the bed sheets are only washed weekly, and since tomorrow is laundry day, the linens are ripe with the accumulated fetor of the prior six days.

Upon finding the bed in which Eva is meant to sleep, Mary Jane bunches up her skirts and lifts her foot, prodding at the sleeping woman therein with the toe of her boot, avoiding all contact with the infested bedding.

"This young girl is said to doss here," she announces unapologetically, rousing the frail old woman from her slumber.

Her wrinkled face and arms are marked with excoriation, the various abrasions and scabs resulting from the excessive itching caused by repeated exposure to her nightly louse visitors. One such scab has recently torn open, and as she rolls over to make room for Eva, her blood smears over the sweat-stained sheets, three young lice tumbling from the folds in her nightgown.

That does it. Feeling bile rise into the back of her throat, Eva bolts from the room. Leaning over the banister railing on the landing, she gasps for breath, willing herself not to vomit onto the floor below, the teapot and cup clutched to her chest, worried that she might drop them.

"I shan't go back in there." She sobs, hearing Mary Jane exit the room behind her. "I'd sooner sleep out here. Even in the gutter, come to that."

"Oh, darling." Mary Jane rubs her back. "Are you opposed to the idea of bundling?"

Eva shakes her head, sniffling. "Not in principle."

"No need for such dramatics, then." Mary Jane heads for the second flight of stairs. "I have a private room, and I'd be so bold as to say that it would be rather preferable to a night spent on these old boards." She taps her boot on the greasy, blackened floor, coming to a stop when she realizes she's not being followed. "Unless it's the thought of sharing a bed with another woman what displeases you?" She doubles back a few paces.

"I'd say it very much depends upon the woman in question." Eva meets Mary Jane's eyes, then glances back inside the room. "And to some degree, the bed."

"Well, what say you to me?" Mary Jane ventures. "Might you like to sleep with me?" She pauses. "I have a full can of insect powder, and I use it liberally."

Eva's stomach turns upside down, a small flutter of excitement rippling through her. "You would really do that?" She wipes her teary cheeks on her sleeve, her tears stemming. "Invite me to your bed?"

"I just did, didn't I?" Mary Jane cocks her head in the direction of the stairs. "So shall we?" She leads the way up two more flights.

On the third floor, all has fallen relatively silent, the violent argument replaced by the repetitive thud of a headboard bashing against the wall and the occasional oath. At her door, Mary Jane props her foot on the doorjamb and flicks her skirts over her knee, fishing her room key out of her boot. As she does so, she catches Eva peeking, the teen's rapt fascination divided between her breasts and her upper thigh. It pleases her, but it doesn't last. Upon realizing her interest has been noted for the second time, Eva averts her eyes and sucks on her bottom lip, a fresh blush coloring her cheeks.

"It's all right to look," Mary Jane assures her, straightening up. "I shan't mind. I'm rather used to being gawped at." She takes a step closer, smiling invitingly. "Sometimes, I even enjoy it." She winks, turning the key in the lock and pushing open the door.

Despite receiving such unequivocal permission, Eva keeps her eyes downturned, finding the floor a much safer target for her attentions.

When they get inside, Mary Jane heads straight for the cupboard to set down the ewer and light a farthing dip, bathing the room in the soft glow of candlelight, the curtains permanently drawn to keep out the dust kicked up by the hooves of passing horses. Meanwhile, Eva casts her eyes over Mary Jane's few personal belongings, including the corset laid out on one of the chairs. Drawn to it, she trails her fingers over the worn pink satin, following the lines of the concealed whale boning and the center front busk, imagining the article fitted tightly to Mary Jane's body, hugging the curves of her hips and waist, supporting her ample bosom.

Unaware that she's being watched, she slides her hand up the garment, feeling the way it's been tailored, molded, and cinched to suit Mary Jane's specifics. Fascinated by the outward sweep of the bust gores, shaped as they are to accommodate Mary Jane's full chest, the decorative stitching not only beautifying the garment but also adding extra structural support, Eva lays her hand over one of the rigid cups. Her own corset has significantly less flare in its shape, her petite breasts

requiring little in the way of propping up. But Mary Jane's ...

"You know what I am, don't you?"

Mary Jane's voice startles her and she snaps her hand away, taking a half step back and bumping into her hostess's chest.

"Aye," she murmurs softly, her breathing heavy. "The way you look ..." She catches Mary Jane's reflection in a mirror above the washstand, captivated by the daring use of rouge on her cheeks and the carmine paste on her lips. "The way you dress ..." She turns her head to the side, taking another peek at Mary's Jane's décolletage, her laced-up breasts framed by her emerald bodice. "You're ..." She thinks of a nice way to say it. "Gay."

A second passes. Self-conscious about the prolonged contact, Eva breaks away and places the teapot and cup on the table, spotting the collection of silk hankies dangling on the curtain wire where Mary Jane left them to dry.

"It don't bother me, if that's what you're getting at." She roams her eyes over the many and varied contraceptive devices next to the basin on Mary Jane's washstand, and on the shelf beneath it. Unfamiliar with such accoutrements, she picks up the glass douching syringe and ponders its shape, trying to determine its purpose.

"If you don't know, it's probably best not to ask," Mary Jane warns her, smiling apologetically. "My name's Mary Jane, by the way. Mary Jane Kelly. Some people who know me by that name call me Em, which others misconstrued for Emma. That soon became Fair Emma, on account of my complexion and my ... well, my rather pleasing attributes, to be blunt."

"You never cared to correct 'em?" Eva replaces the syringe where she found it, at the same time spying several birch rods peeking out from under the washstand, but not daring to question what they might be used for.

"I s'pose I've never yet seen the point." Mary Jane plumps down on the bed and removes her boots, sitting casually with her knees apart and her skirts pulled up, the way no lady ought to. "Most have no need to know who I

truly am. It don't make no difference to the customer, nor to the casual acquaintance I pass on the street."

"What about Ginger?" Eva admires Mary Jane's rich, auburn tresses. "Did you get that one 'cause of your hair?"

"Could be," Mary Jane acknowledges the possibility. "Or it might have something to do with that." She directs Eva to a small row of empty ginger beer bottles underneath the table. "I've been known to have a wee partiality for the stuff."

At that moment, following a brief post-coital lull, a plate smashes in the neighboring room and the fighting starts up again. As an irate Irishwoman bellows "I'll knife ya!" at the top of her lungs, Eva flinches.

"Is that your mam?" Mary Jane supposes, catching a hint of shame on her cheeks.

Eva nods, picking at a loose thread on her sleeve. "It weren't like this when my dadda was around, but he's dead now. Gin took him."

"I'm sorry." Mary Jane prepares the bed for occupation, flinging back the covers and plumping the pillows. "Have they been on the ran-tan tonight?"

"Like every night, just about." Eva sighs, sinking into one of the chairs. "This new bloke ain't so bad some of the time, though. He's helping me get sorted with a job."

"Oh, aye?" Mary Jane unbuttons her bodice, releasing herself inch by inch. "What doing?"

Eva watches her intently, following every flick of her wrist, her movements smooth and elegant, the bodice slipping off her shoulders as it if were made of the finest silk, exposing a fitted, embroidered cotton and lace cap-sleeved under-bodice beneath.

"Flower girl," she says at last, remembering she was asked a question. "Not artificial ones, like what you're wearing, but real ones. He's gonna take me down Covent Garden Market tomorra and lend me stock money so as I can get me-self started. He says he knows people what works there."

"Is that so?" Mary Jane's jaw tightens, laying her bodice on the tabletop. "And you're sure that's all he's got in mind for you?"

Eva pulls a face. "What's that to mean when it's at home?"

"Those Covent Garden girls have been known to supplement their income through other, less respectable means," Mary Jane explains delicately, unfastening her white apron and folding it next to her bodice. "And you look as though you're of that age."

"What age is that?"

"The age where innocence is clinging on by a thread, and all about there are plenty men who'd seek to strip you of it. Am I right?"

Eva nods, turning her gaze back to the floor. "I ain't never had connection with a man."

"Nor should you have to." Mary Jane brings her hands to Eva's chin, cupping her face and raising her head up. "Don't go wrong." She strokes the teen's smooth cheeks, admiring her youthful innocence. "Don't go wrong as I have. This ain't the life you want, believe me."

"Was you a flower girl?" Eva wonders, curious to know if Mary Jane's warnings are born of personal experience. "Is that how you turned gay?"

Mary Jane's hands slip away and she retreats to the washstand, shaking her head. "I didn't need London to show me to the bad." She pours a little water into the basin. "By the time I got here, I'd already found it on my own."

"Where's you from, then?" Eva pries. "You ain't from the East End, I knows that."

"How?"

"You talk too proper. You put it on good, but you ain't born of these parts."

"True enough," Mary Jane admits, but doesn't expound upon it.

"I'm from Camden," Eva volunteers then, hoping she might encourage Mary Jane to share, and also wishing she had a more exotic story to tell than that of being a first generation Irish Londoner. "St. Pancras is where I was born, but we moved to Bethnal Green soon after my dadda died and we ran short of coin. I ain't never been out of London, and I surely ain't never been to Ireland,

but my mam's from County Cork. She come over in fifty-four, when she was just a nipper."

She leaves a lull for Mary Jane to fill.

No such luck.

"What about you?" she prods lightly. "Where's home?"

"Elsewhere," Mary Jane answers elusively, washing all trace of artificial color off her face. "I was born in Limerick, though."

Eva's confusion deepens. "How comes you don't sound like it?"

"I've moved around." Mary Jane brushes out her mane and fixes it in a loose braid. "And three years ago, when I was first in London, I worked at a gay house in the West End. Them places only take on the best class of whore, don't you know?" She affects an upper class accent, then slips seamlessly back into a coarser tongue. "Turns out any sort of otherness ain't a bit conducive to work in those parts, so I had to talk proper."

"The West End?" Eva grins, awestruck by the thought of it.

"Aye." Mary Jane smirks, charmed by her childish wonder. "You couldn't get near me for less than ten bob in them days, and it was at least a quid for full connection—not a penny under. Course, the house took half of that."

"A whole pound?!" Eva's eyes widen. "You must've been a right toffer!"

"Indeed I was." Mary Jane chuckles, tossing her the brush. "And very much in demand."

"I can imagine," Eva comments absently, working the brush through her own tresses.

The words escape before she has a chance to think about how they might sound, and as soon as they hit the air, she feels a now familiar heat rising into her cheeks. She doesn't have any time to formulate an apology, though. With a swoosh, Mary Jane unbuttons her under-bodice and peels it off, revealing a pale lilac corset.

Darned in multiple places where the whale boning has worn through the old satin, it's nothing extravagant. At least, not anymore. It tells of a life lived far removed

from the East End streets, the faded floral design and lace flourishes reminding Eva of those decadent garments she's seen in shop windows, imported from France. Such finery as she could never afford.

Losing herself in a daydream, imagining how the corset must've looked before so much wear and washing, it takes her a moment to realize that Mary Jane isn't wearing anything beneath it, her modesty barely protected.

"Oh, Lordy! Your diddeys!" She gawks at Mary Jane's bulging breasts, round and full, almost spilling out from their satin confines. "I ... you ... holy buggering shite." Flustered beyond all capacity to speak coherently, she hides her eyes behind her hands. "I didn't realize you was so unrigged! Where's the rest of your bloody underclothes?"

Mary Jane bursts into hearty laughter. "Your natural charm don't half come out when you're taken by surprise." She wanders to the cupboard and unhooks the corset from the steel busk at the front, saving her from having to untie and retie the lacing at the back. "I don't always wear my chemise on account of it getting in the way of my line of work." She lays the corset down next to the stockings and pulls on her off-the-shoulder silk shift, its cap sleeves and hem decorated with white lace, its deeper neckline designed for pairing with eveningwear. "You can look now." She spins to face her guest.

"Is that silk?" Eva pores over her.

"Aye." Mary Jane runs her hands over her hips. "It was gifted to me by one of my friends, as were my petticoats, one of my corsets, and various other sundries." In case Eva doesn't completely understand, she elaborates. "That is to say, these things were compliments from a very generous customer who sees me regular and happens to be not short of a few bob."

Eva lets that thought settle, especially mulling over the use of the word 'friend,' but doesn't fixate on it. "You don't wear no nightgown?"

Mary Jane shrugs, unconcerned. "I don't presently possess one."

Her skirts and petticoat come off next, revealing a pair of long, shapely legs, there being not a stitch on her in the way of drawers.

"No drawers, neither!" Eva's jaw slackens in disbelief.

Amused by her incredulity, Mary Jane cracks a wry smile. "Now those would *definitely* hamper my ability to do my work, don't you think?" She removes her teardrop earrings with care, laying them in a little ceramic pot on top of the cupboard.

"Them's so pretty." Eva eyes the gems from afar. "I ain't never had no jewels."

"They ain't real." Mary Jane taps her fingernail on one of the fake emeralds. "Colored glass. No worth."

"All the same." Eva's no less taken with them. "I ain't never had so much as a piece of old brass to wear, and them do look so lovely on you."

Entranced, she watches Mary Jane sit on the bed and start work on her patterned woolen stockings, easing off the thin elastics holding them in place above her knees before rolling them down one by one, exposing her smooth alabaster skin all the way to her colored toenails. Like her neatly trimmed fingernails, they're tinted dark pink and buffed to a pearly luster. Delicate. Alluring.

She has to look away. Even witnessing the simple act of Mary Jane flicking her skirts over her knee to pull her room key from her boot had been a sight erotic beyond all measure. Neither the naughty French postcards her older brothers used to stash underneath their floorboards, nor the full nudity of her father's favorite paphian could compare to that flash of smooth, pale thigh above Mary Jane's stocking. How she wants to drop a kiss there, tasting the salt of Mary Jane's skin, bringing her face to the hallowed place where the perfume of her femininity is strongest ...

"Are you planning on spending all night in that chair?" Mary Jane cuts into her daydream. "Or are you getting in here with me?" She pats the palliasse.

Jolted back to reality, Eva finds Mary Jane already in bed, her petticoat and skirts draped over the edge of the table, her stockings on top. Rising, lightheaded and half

44

in a daze, she reaches for the top button of her bodice, then hesitates, looking sheepishly about the floor.

"Do you have to piddle?" Mary Jane guesses.

Eva nods, wringing her hands. "I should've done it in the privy afore I come up."

"Don't be daft." Mary Jane pulls the chamber pot out from under the bed. "Here you are, love. Do your business."

"All right, but don't listen." Eva drags the pot to the back of the room, where Mary Jane can't see, then squats, humming a tune to obscure the sound of her piddling.

When she's done, she puts the lid on the pot, drapes a towel over it, and banishes it to the far corner. "You sure it's all right for us to sleep together?" She approaches the bed. "I shan't mind if you wants me to make me-self a place on the floor."

"Get unrigged and come to bed already," Mary Jane insists, propping her head on the heel of her palm, her elbow resting on her pillow. "If I didn't want you in here with me, I daresay I wouldn't have tendered the invitation in the first place."

Her confidence bolstered by that, Eva begins to shed the layers, aware that Mary Jane's eyes are trained on her as she peels off one garment then the next, their roles now reversed. By the time she's down to her chemise and split drawers, she's shivering.

"I'll keep you warm." Mary Jane welcomes her to the bed, careful not to ogle her svelte body, silhouetted as it is through the sleeveless white cotton shift.

"I ain't never shared a bed with no-one but my sister and that," Eva confesses, wriggling under the covers, not sure what the proper etiquette might be for sleeping so inappropriately clad with a woman who is, after all, a complete stranger.

"This ain't no different," Mary Jane assures her, blowing out the candle on the cupboard and casting the room in shadow. "Ain't nothing wrong in it."

"I know." Eva rolls onto her side, aiming her bum at her new sleeping partner. "Even if there was," she feels compelled to add, "I can't say as I'd let it trouble me."

While cogitating on the meaning of that statement, Mary Jane tries to get comfortable in the three-quarter size bed. There's not a lot of room at the best of times, and managing to find a cozy spot without crowding her timid bedmate soon proves problematic. Used to sharing her bed with lovers, she's not entirely sure where her limbs ought to go, and in the end, only one solution presents itself.

"May I put my arm around you?"

After a second's hesitation, "Mm-hmm."

The answer doesn't sound entirely convincing, but eager to move her back away from the cold, damp wall, Mary Jane nonetheless shuffles a few inches closer and slips an arm around Eva's tiny waist, feeling a reflexive tightening of muscles as she does.

"Has no-one ever held you like this before?" she asks, trailing her hand over Eva's midsection, trying quell the unchaste feelings stirred in her by the young slip of a girl who would surely balk at such lascivious attentions. "You feel tense."

To that, she gets no response.

Unfamiliar with the adult world of sexual intricacies and utterly ignorant of the concept of flirtation, Eva has difficulty knowing what to make of Mary Jane's kindness. In pursuit of more definitive answers, she turns onto her back, engaging her directly.

"Can I ask you summink?"

"Of course." Mary Jane rubs her hand over Eva's flat stomach, suspecting what might be coming and fearing that it may well result in a rapidly evacuated bed. "What's wrong?"

Eva's brow furrows in thought. "What was that woman on about? Your friend in the kitchen, I mean. When she were asking if you was being nice to me."

"Well"—Mary Jane considers her answer carefully— "I s'pose she thinks I'm inclined to behave generously towards you because she knows I rather enjoy the company of women."

"Oh." Eva works that over in her mind.

A hollow silence invades.

When the inexperienced teen offers up nothing further, Mary Jane starts to pull away, resigning herself to sleeping awkwardly against the wall, thinking she's made her bedmate feel uncomfortable, but then ...

Eva grabs her hand, preventing her withdrawal. Rolling back onto her side, she tugs Mary Jane's arm around her middle, tighter than before.

"Goodnight," she mumbles drowsily, snuggling against Mary Jane's body, aligning them from head to toe and keeping hold of her hand. "I'm glad to have met you."

Her heart warmed by the gesture, Mary Jane presses a light kiss on the side of Eva's head. "So am I, love." She curls up behind the chestnut-haired beauty, sharing her warmth, detecting not the slightest bit of tension in her body. "Sweet dreams."

CHAPTER 4

Wednesday, March 2, 1887

AT THE CRACK OF DAWN, MARY JANE WAKES UP TO THE rare, but not unfamiliar—and certainly not unwelcome— sensation of a woman in her arms. Eva is draped across her chest, cheek to breast, sound asleep, her hair tumbling from an unraveled braid.

Mary Jane runs her fingers through that lush mane, silently admiring her young bedmate until she begins to stir, murmuring softly.

"Morning, love." Mary Jane kisses the top of her head.

Imagining herself to be resting on a pillow, Eva yawns and nuzzles her face against Mary Jane's breast, only realizing her mistake when her lower lip grazes a prominently stiff nub protruding from the warm, soft mound.

Suddenly wide awake, she recoils. "Oh, Lordy! I didn't mean to ..."

"It's all right." Mary Jane won't hear an apology. "I weren't complaining. As things go, there's far worse to wake up to than a nice cuddle."

Upon sitting, Eva gazes down at Mary Jane. Her chemise is pulled tight across her chest, the outline of her breasts visible beneath the silk even in the shadowy blue first light of day, both nipples rigid and aimed at the ceiling.

Contemplating what it would be like to suck one of those rubbery protuberances into her mouth, pinching it between her teeth and coaxing it to swell more, Eva's lip tingles with the memory of its brief kiss with Mary Jane's body.

Aware that she's staring, and afraid that her own nipples are visibly stiffening, she breaks off the fantasy and clambers out of bed. "I must get ready for work."

Mary Jane rolls over and watches her get dressed. "The deputy serves breakfast in the kitchen for tuppence. Are you hungry?"

"Aye, but I ain't got tuppence." Petticoat and corset-clad Eva digs in the deep pockets of her dress, pulling out a few fluff-covered peppermint humbugs and a farthing.

Resigning herself to waking, Mary Jane yawns and flings back the covers. "I do."

She pads across the room and dons her clothes, starting with her stockings and petticoat. Thinking nothing of it, she then peels off her chemise and tosses it onto the bed, stretching her arms above her head as she traipses half-naked over to the cupboard to retrieve yesterday's lilac corset.

Getting an unexpected full frontal view of topless Mary Jane knocks Eva for six. She doesn't know where to look. The only breasts she's ever had occasion to see in the flesh—apart from her own, which she once spent fifteen minutes pondering in the mirror, wondering if they were ever going to get any bigger—have been those of her mother and sister, and neither pair was particularly spectacular. Not like the women in the French postcards belonging to her brothers. Not like Mary Jane.

Instead of looking away, she keeps her eyes on the seemingly nonchalant display, committing it to memory, feeling a faint glimmer of disappointment when the corset all too soon robs her of the view.

Continuing with her morning routine, Mary Jane uncaps the glass jar of lemon juice she keeps on top of her cupboard—a natural deodorant—and dabs a hanky into it, rubbing some of the juice under both arms before putting her under-bodice on over the corset.

50

"Want some?" she offers the dumbstruck teen.

Eva nods, meeting her by the cupboard. "My mam always puts sodium bicarbonate in hers, but it gives me a terrible rash."

"This won't hurt you." Mary Jane dabs another corner of the hanky into the lemon juice and lifts one of Eva's arms, rubbing it into her pit.

Eva squeals, twitching and jerking in Mary Jane's grasp. "Tickles!"

"Some tickles can be nice." Mary Jane does the squirming teen's other arm, her lips curling into a deliciously wicked smile. "I give the best tickles."

Rather hoping that's intended to be a euphemism of some sort, Eva quivers in Mary Jane's experienced hands, making no attempt to conceal her blush. "Like the tickles you gived me in the kitchen?" she asks innocently.

"No," Mary Jane replies softly. "Not quite like those."

The rest of their morning grooming routine takes a good fifteen minutes, every step peppered with extended moments of mutual admiration. As Eva sits to roll on her stockings, Mary Jane moves in behind her and brushes her tousled locks, braiding the silky mop for her so that it won't get in the way while she's working.

There's face washing and teeth brushing, plenty of laughter, and by the time both women make it down to the kitchen for breakfast, they're in high spirits, despite the early hour and the frosty chill of the spring morning.

Taking their place in the breakfast line—behind a growing number of market porters and casual laborers about to head out to earn an honest day's pay—Eva's stomach growls, excited by the promise of nourishment, the scent of smoked fish and freshly-brewed tea invading her nostrils.

"Got a wolf in your belly?" Mary Jane gives Eva's bellybutton a poke. "Not to worry, we'll soon have you sated."

Eva giggles, then flinches, distressed by the breakout of a fight in the corner of the room as one teenage boy thumps another in the ribs and instigates a scuffle to determine who should get the last slice of buttered bread.

For want of security, she clutches a fistful of Mary Jane's skirts, comforted by her mere presence.

"Keep close to me, love." Mary Jane takes her by the hand, weaving their fingers together. "No-one will bother you if you're with me." She rubs her thumb over the back of Eva's hand. "I'll keep you safe."

Eva believes that.

As they near the front of the line, Mary Jane digs in her pocket for fourpence, scraping the crusty remains of something that might be spermatic fluid off one tarnished penny before showing the amount to the deputy and dropping the coins in the collection tin held by a bored six-year-old boy sitting cross-legged on the serving table.

"Since when's you up this early?" The deputy scoffs at her, pouring two cups of tea.

"Since I woke up with this beautiful young woman in my arms and offered to buy her breakfast as a token of my gratitude for a wonderful night."

Mary Jane leaves that statement entirely open to interpretation, knowing the deputy will be quick to make assumptions, and curious to see how Eva will react.

Sure enough, both of the deputy's eyebrows go up. Her eyes flit to Eva, then back to Mary Jane. "When I said for you to show her to bed, I didn't mean yours, you queer old goat."

Though Eva turns the deepest shade of scarlet, she shows no inclination to disabuse the deputy of the erroneous notion that something indecent may have occurred. Accepting her plate of buttered bread, cheese, and smoked fish with one hand and her cup of tea with the other, she mumbles some inaudible thanks and follows Mary Jane to a small table at the edge of the room, but doesn't immediately sit.

Setting down her breakfast, she rifles through her pockets and dumps the contents out on the tabletop: the humbugs, the fluff, and the farthing. "It's all I got to give you."

"Put that lot back in your pocket." Mary Jane yanks Eva into the chair next to her. "I don't need it, nor want it." She slouches forward and makes herself comfortable,

propping one foot on the edge of Eva's chair and resting her elbow on her raised thigh, her legs relaxed and apart, her skirts pulled up over her knees so as not to restrict her movement.

It reminds Eva of the way her father used to sit at the fireplace, smoking his pipe and reading the daily newspaper before bed. Indeed, a quick glance around the room reveals several men of all ages adopting similar postures, their gender being under no great pressure to conform to any exacting standards such as those so staunchly applied to members of the fairer sex. Standards which Mary Jane seems apt to flout at every given opportunity.

In contrast, Eva sits with her back straight and both knees together, just as she was taught. For a split second, she ventures to move her knees away from each other, testing out the sensation, but it feels perilously risqué and she snaps them back together twice as fast.

"Eat," Mary Jane encourages her, noting that she's yet to dig in. "Or are you afraid of what I'll want in return?" She tears off a chunk off her own portion of somewhat stale whole wheat bread and butter, washing it down with a sip of lukewarm tea.

"Not at all afeared." Eva picks at the crust of her bread. "Just ... not entirely sure."

"Well, I like you." Mary Jane fingers a wayward lock of hair away from Eva's eyes, moving it behind her shoulder. "And I liked having you with me last night." She lets her hand glide down Eva's back. "It was nice."

"I reckon I like you n'all." Eva knows her cheeks are aflame again, not used to being on the receiving end of such open affections, no matter how mild.

"No need to fret about it, then." Mary Jane pats Eva's back before retreating into her own space. "I don't expect nothing from you."

Happy with that answer, Eva starts to eat. She begins gracefully, nibbling at her breakfast like a mouse, but hunger soon overcomes her. She devours her fish and one piece of bread in a few mouthfuls, then starts work on the second slice.

Watching her, Mary Jane breaks into a broad smile. "Not so ladylike now, are we?"

"You must think I'm such an oinker." Eva covers her mouth, speaking with it stuffed full, her cheeks pink with embarrassment. "But I didn't have no supper."

"Take your fill." Mary Jane nudges her own plate over. "Help yourself to mine n'all if you want. I can always get more later."

That gives Eva some pause for thought. "Will you be working tonight?"

"Some." Mary Jane nurses her spider-cracked cup, her smile fading. "A few hours usually gets me what I need."

Unable to look her in the eye, Eva asks, "How much is it?" She swills down the rest of the bread with her tea. "For you, I mean. To be proper up you." She swallows hard. "I'm curious is all."

Mary Jane's cunt pulses at the thought of being penetrated by Eva. It's been a while since she's had any meaningful intimacy. That is, being tailed for pleasure not money. The kind of fucking that makes her shiver. Resolving to rectify that situation as soon as possible, she puts those thoughts out of her head for the time being and turns her mind back to the question at hand, raising an eyebrow at Eva's money on the table.

"A lot more than a bloody farthing," she teases, not really in the mood to discuss her work in any serious detail.

"Oh, lummy heck." Eva finishes Mary Jane's portion of fish and wipes her mouth with the back of her hand, staring into her lap, utterly mortified. "I weren't suggesting ..."

"I know, love." Mary Jane pats her thigh. "It's thruppence for a look. More for ... more. I ain't cheap."

Eva ogles her breasts, appreciating how they heave inside her bodice with every draw of breath. "Thruppence a look? You'd put me in the bloody poorhouse." She grins, feeling less self-conscious by the minute. "I can't stop looking at you. I ain't never seen a woman with such personal assets."

"You're one to talk." Mary Jane lays a hand on her waist. "You're sweet and beautiful, and you're gonna have fellas lining up for you before you know it."

"I hopes not." Eva snorts, not in the least bit perturbed by the physical contact.

"No?" Mary Jane keeps her hand in place, lightly caressing Eva's ribcage. "Why's that?"

Eva gets no chance to respond. A stout man in his mid-thirties with a thick mustache appears in the kitchen doorway and looks around the room, causing Eva to leap to her feet and Mary Jane to recoil.

"There you is." His beady eyes find Eva, then fall upon the empty plate in front of her. "Where'd you get the coppers for that?"

"I gave 'em to her." Mary Jane stands up, not only matching his height, but exceeding it by a clear inch. "She was hungry."

He looks her up and down, knowing full well what she is. "In exchange for what?" he asks, his eyes fixed to her chest, not her face.

"Nothing untoward." She clenches her jaw.

He grunts, disbelieving, and snaps his fingers at Eva. "Time to go." He motions for her to come. "Grab yer coat."

"Thank you for buying me breakfast." Eva scoops her farthing and humbugs off the table, holding her palm open to Mary Jane. "Are you sure you don't want—"

"Quite sure." Mary Jane closes her hand around the pocket dregs. "And you're welcome, love. Any time."

While Eva dashes upstairs to fetch her coat—a gray woolen pilot coat—Mary Jane follows the impatient man into the lobby.

"Flower girl, eh?" She crosses her arms. "What inspired that, then?"

"Is that your business, whore?" He turns his back on her.

"You know what game they'll drag her into." She grabs him by the sleeve of his jacket and spins him around. "Is that what you want for her? A life such as mine."

"I ain't got no love to spare for the child, and she has to make her way in the world somehow. Any case, rent needs paid, and I can't say as I'm fussy how." He jerks himself free. "Now you'd best not touch me again, bitch."

"Or else what?" Mary Jane dares him to lay a hand on her.

His fist twitches and he looks as though he might give it a try, then he catches sight of something behind her and thinks better of it.

"Let's be off," he barks, storming out of the building.

Eva, having witnessed the tail end of their heated discourse, descends into the lobby with an empty basket on her arm and a concerned frown on her face. "Is everything all right?"

Mary Jane takes her firmly by the shoulders. "Don't you do nothing bad. You understand me?" She glances outside, making sure the angry mustache is out of earshot. "If you're short of money, and he pesters you for it, come to me and I'll see you right."

"Why?"

"'Cause I ain't gonna sit back and let a delightful young girl like you end up on the wrong path. I hope you want better for yourself than that n'all."

A moment passes. Eva's eyes drop to Mary Jane's lips, a thought crossing her mind ...

"Get coming here!" the mustache bellows from the street. "Let the whore alone!"

Wincing apologetically, Eva starts to leave, but only gets a few paces before stopping and retracing her steps. Impulsively, she drops her basket on the floor and flings her arms around Mary Jane's neck, standing on tiptoe to press a chaste kiss on her cheek.

"Thank you," she whispers, holding Mary Jane tight, murmuring happily when she feels Mary Jane's arms sweep around her middle.

But it doesn't last long. Not wanting to provoke the irate mustache any more than necessary, she breaks away, snatches up her basket, and darts off, turning back once in the doorway to flash Mary Jane a sheepish smile before disappearing into the street.

Following Eva's departure, Mary Jane returns to her room and to her bed—though not to sleep. She works out some of her tension with a few soft tickles, then begins her day afresh, her body well-prepared for whatever punishment might be thrust at it.

Having only to take a handful of men a day, she can afford to be picky, thus much of her morning and early afternoon is spent leisurely, window shopping and taking coffee with friends. Proper friends, that is. Her work begins in earnest in the late afternoon, when she shoos a gaggle of tarts away from the Ten Bells public house on Commercial Street, where she picks up much of her trade.

As soon as she walks in, those harlots sober enough to retain their good sense know to make themselves scarce, lest they risk a hair pulling or a fist. Any fuck-worthy man found in any Commercial Street pub from the Golden Heart to the Princess Alice is Mary Jane's for the taking, as they well know, since that's her regular patch. Only if she passes them up, or they fail to produce the required coinage, may the cheaper paphians swoop in to fight over her leavings.

This being her first port of call, she orders up a small glass of gin and casts her eyes around the room. That's usually all it takes. With a smile and a nod, she'll invite a man to approach, her cool manner more reminiscent of the now extinct breed of courtesan once found prowling the Argyle Rooms, rather than that of a common pinchcock.

Once a bargain's been struck, she'll leave with him. Depending on the service about to be rendered, they'll either go to his private rooms, the nearest alley, or the Ringers' Buildings, where a room and a bed can be had at the rate of one shilling per hour.

Owned by Walter and Matilda Ringer, the proprietors of the Britannia—an unlicensed beerhouse on

the corner of nearby Dorset Street—the rooms in the building next door are let out to all manner of dubious tenants, including a pair of spinsters who occupy the top floor and run something of a casual bawdyhouse. Though they specialize in the prostitution of underage girls, they always keep a few rooms spare, should any of the local harlots seek to bring their amours in from the cold. For a fee, of course.

Fortunately, Mary Jane has no need of a bed today. The shillings and pence come easy, and by early evening, she's made her minimum without having to accept the intrusion of a cock in her body. This is often the way. As word spreads that a young, full-bosomed cyprian is willing to drop to her knees and take a prick in her mouth—an act considered so dirty and wicked that many a woman would be insulted and repulsed by the mere notion of it—men line up, shillings in hand, keen to experience the novelty of a different orifice for their pleasure.

All this she does in a quiet courtyard beside the Ringers' Buildings, and now she's ready to call it a night. Before she slinks back to Thrawl Street, however, she exits onto Commercial Street and spots three young boys loitering in front of Spitalfields church, gawping at her. Two of them are shoving the third in the back, urging him in her direction and shouting words of encouragement when he takes his first steps.

"What can I do for you, love?" She welcomes his approach by slackening the maroon shawl around her shoulders, showing him her décolletage.

The short, skinny boy takes off his cap and wrings it in his hands, not brave enough to make eye contact with her, nor daring enough to gawk at her chest. "I ... it's my birf'day."

"Oh, aye?" Mary Jane runs her eyes over his three-inches-too-short trousers and tattered shirt. "And how old might you be?"

"Sixteen." He counts the years off on his fingers to be sure. "My bruvvas said it's time I had knowledge of a woman."

Mary Jane looks over at the two other boys. "Them's your brothers?"

More nodding.

"Come on, then." She takes his hand and leads him a short way down a nearby side street, pulling him through a covered passageway and into a tiny courtyard lined with tenements, inside which an old coster's barrow is stored in an alcove by the washhouse.

By the time they get back there, the boy is sprouting a proud erection.

"Now"—Mary Jane hops up on the end of the barrow—"it's thruppence to have a look whilst you fetch your mettle, or sixpence for me to toss you off. For a shilling, I'll give you *minette*, which means I'll use my mouth. Or, if you've got three bob on you, you can put it up me. So what's it to be?"

"Three bob?!" He looks horrified.

"Hey, I used to be worth a quid back in the West End, so count yourself lucky."

The boy digs in his pockets, pulling out a thruppenny bit and two pennies.

Mary Jane feigns disappointment. "Well, it looks to me like you've got yourself a choice to make. You can either have a quick peep, then go back out there to your brothers and tell 'em you've stuck it up me, hoping they believe you, or I could be generous and give you a discount toss, on account of it being your birthday and all. In that event, we can walk out of here together, and I'll let your brothers know you're the best fuck this side of the Thames. Whatchu think?"

He hands over the coins.

"Good lad." Mary Jane pockets the money and turns him around, hitching up her skirts and positioning him between her legs. "Let's see what you're hiding in here." She reaches for the buttons on his trousers, unfastens them with practiced hands, then does the same for his drawers, soon releasing his perfectly average, nothing-to-be-ashamed-of erect cock. "Ooh, look at that nice big prick." She wraps her hand around it, giving him a couple of quick tugs. "Big and hard for me."

She squeezes her thighs around him, stroking his chest with one hand as she strokes his pipe with the other, her chin resting on his shoulder, whispering in his ear.

"That's it." She puts on her best sultry voice, encouraging him to close his eyes and lean into her. "Let me take care of you, my sweet boy."

She works his rigid shaft up and down, his inexperience and overexcitement apparent when he starts to leak within only a few seconds, the dam threatening to break much too soon.

Taking pity on him, she slows down and tries to make it last, intent on giving him his money's worth as well as providing a memorable experience, but he only manages to hold back a few more minutes before his legs start buckling beneath him.

"Are you ready to come?" she whispers, swirling her thumb around the tip.

He nods, trembling.

"All right, then." She finishes him off, her hand squelching in pre-ejaculatory fluid, moving harder and faster until she feels his priapus swell and pulse. "Let it out, boy."

Grunting, clutching at her knees for support, his hips jerking reflexively, he climaxes, his copious release splattering on the nearby wall.

"Well done," she praises him, milking every last drop out of him before pulling a hanky from her pocket and wiping her hand. "Worth it?" She hops off the barrow, crouches in front of him, and cleans off his still semi-erect pego, feeling it fatten again in her hands.

"I wish I had three bob," he whines.

"I'm sure you will one day." She tucks him away, fastening his buttons for him. "And when that day comes, you know where to find me." She winks, scooping his hand into her own. "Now, let's brag to your brothers."

As promised, she walks him right up to his waiting siblings and gives him a light peck on the lips. "Thanks, love." She grabs his crotch, then turns to the other boys. "This lad's got the biggest cock I've ever had in me, and he don't half know how to use it."

60

With that, she leaves, grinning to herself as the impressed brothers take it in turns to pat him on the back for a job well done.

About to make her way home, she spots a familiar face heading for the Britannia. The curvaceous, raven-haired woman—her closest friend and frequent drinking partner—is nineteen years old and voluptuous in every respect. Her long, frizzy hair is scruffily pinned up, much of it trapped beneath her bonnet, save for a mess of untamed curls falling about her face.

It's been a while since they've been lushing together, and even longer since they've shared a bed. Given that, and the fact that her throat could well use the lubrication, she decides to follow her friend into the pub. At the very least, she'll get to enjoy an evening of drunken revelry. At best, she'll get to fulfill her earlier resolution to have a decent fuck.

CHAPTER 5

EVA SITS IN THE DARKENED HALL OUTSIDE HER MOTHER'S room in Cooney's Good Lodgings, watching a large, fat beetle waddle along the floor, trying to squish itself into any crevice it can find.

All is quiet inside the room, the nightly melody of fornication and anger long since subsided. She could very well let her herself back in and reclaim her makeshift mattress on the floor, trying to draw warmth from her thin woolen blanket while, less than ten feet away, her mother and mustached lover sleep together on the room's only bed, but she'd rather not. Instead, she chooses to stay put, waiting for Mary Jane's return, hoping for another invite to her sheets. Unfortunately, when Mary Jane does finally make it back to Thrawl Street, she's not alone: she's in the company of another woman.

Heavily intoxicated, she and the short, dark-haired woman—who's carrying a half-drained bottle of gin— tumble into the building in fits of laughter, each whispering for the other to be quiet. Heading up the stairs, their ascent less than smooth, they totter and trip, using the grimy walls and the wobbly banister rail to steady themselves, pausing every now and again to trade kisses with one another, whispering filthy secrets and bawdy promises.

Between the smacking of lips and half-mumbled proclamations of lust, Eva gathers that the other woman's

name is Maria. She looks somewhat worse off than Mary Jane, wearing only a plain blue dress and a dirty white apron, ornamented with nothing more than a lopsided and disheveled artificial violet, but she has a pretty face and considerable attractions.

Adjusting her position to get a better vantage point, Eva spies on the giddy pair as they reach the first-floor landing and top-heavy Maria takes a spill, her foot catching on the lip of a wonky step, causing her to lurch forward.

Rather than help her friend, Mary Jane's instinct is to save the booze. She wrenches the precious bottle from Maria's hand before a single drop spills and holds it protectively to her chest, guffawing at Maria's graceless collapse.

"Whore," Maria grumbles playfully, righting herself and giving Mary Jane's bum a hard slap. "See if I help you the next time you're down on your knees."

Mary Jane snorts, taking a sip of the gin. "I've been on my fucking knees all damn day, my lovely. I didn't see no-one stepping in to give me relief." She grabs Maria by the hand and pulls her up the next flight of stairs.

When they get to the second-floor landing, more girlish laughter ensues. The bottle passes back and forth between them several times, then Mary Jane backs Maria against the wall and drives a hand up her skirts, probing her sex.

"I need you tonight," she growls, hooking her arm under Maria's knee, lifting her leg up and wide, spreading her open. "I ain't had a woman in days."

Weak to Mary Jane's forceful advances, Maria does little to object. "You naughty wench." She gasps, feeling three of Mary Jane's fingers plunging inside her. "Get me into bed afore I gush all over."

Grinning, Mary Jane eases her sex-coated digits free and licks them clean, leading the way up the final few steps to the third floor. Here, she falters, the grin fading from her crimson lips when she spots Eva sitting on the floor.

Her mood mildly subdued by the unexpected sight of the young teen, fearing that this inadvertent display of

uninhibited prurience might put an end to their burgeoning friendship, tears prick her eyes. Biting them back, she wipes her sticky hand on her apron, lifts her skirts, and props her foot on the banister, struggling to fish her room key out of her boot. Maria, however, remains blissfully unaware of their audience.

"Give us your bubbies." She sweeps her arms around Mary Jane's waist and makes quick work of unfastening her clothing, reaching in to grope her breasts.

"Oi, watch it." Mary Jane slaps her hands away. "We ain't alone."

Confused, Maria separates herself and takes a look around, scowling when her eyes fall upon Eva. "Oh, look at you, you little peeper." She plants her hands on her hips. "Enjoying the free show, are we?"

Keen to shut Maria up before her mouth does any damage, Mary Jane grips the key firmly in her hand and hastens to get it in the lock. After several failed attempts, her bleary eyes rendering the simple task inordinately difficult, she succeeds in getting the door open and swiftly manhandles Maria through it.

"Go on in." She gives her a shove, closing the door behind her. "I'll be right there."

Trying—but largely failing—to compose herself, she then presses her back against the wall and slides to the floor, crouching in front of Eva, not realizing that she's topping off this evening's repertoire of lewd behaviors by flashing the teen her bare cunt.

With her knees crooked and her skirts bunched up, Eva has a most perfect view of her shaved womanhood. The peachy lips of her sex, plump and smooth, are flushed with arousal, slightly parted to reveal a glimpse of the pink, moist flesh hidden within, her skin glistening with anticipation.

When she realizes she's indecent, she makes some halfhearted effort to push her skirts down between her legs, covering herself. "Oops! You don't wanna look at that old hat, I'm sure." She lolls her head against the wall, sighing. "Oh, if only you did ..." She squints at Eva, trying to focus, her eye paint slightly smudged. "Wanna know a secret?"

Eva nods, not at all sure what might be about to spill from her lips.

"If you wanted to look at me"—Mary Jane heaves herself forward onto her knees and crawls across the creaky floorboards to the petrified teen, smashing heads with her in an attempt to whisper in her ear—"I'd let you."

Her breath is hot and she reeks of rum and gin, her lips grazing Eva's earlobe and her chest thrust into Eva's face. With her bodice and under-bodice both undone, her corset is the only thing containing her breasts, but thanks to Maria's drunken manipulations, its effectiveness has been somewhat diminished.

Eva can see the hint of a dark pink circle of skin peeking out above the satin, one breast threatening to break free, and she eyes it with bated breath, willing the fabric to slip.

But no such luck.

"I wouldn't charge you, neither," Mary Jane goes on, bursting into another fit of giggles, oblivious to her escaping bosom. "By the way"—she almost topples over, nuzzling her face into Eva's hair, very nearly poking the teen in the eye with one of her earrings—"Maria won't be here long." She hiccups. "So if you need a place to sleep, you can let yourself in after she's gone. I'll leave the door on the latch." She breathes in deep. "Mmm, you don't half smell pretty." She plants a sloppy kiss on Eva's head. "Like lavender and marigolds."

Using the banister rail for support, she pulls herself upright and stumbles into her room, the door slamming behind her. A moment later, a flurry of giggles is followed by a groan of pleasure, the bed creaking and protesting under the weight of two adult bodies.

At first infrequent and quiet, the moans soon increase in rate and intensity. Succumbing to curiosity, Eva repositions nearer Mary Jane's door, eavesdropping on the passionate tryst.

"Oh, Mary," Maria mewls. "Use your tongue ... lick me ... gamahuche me."

Jealous but conflicted, aware of a pleasant warmth spreading through her abdomen and growing stronger every minute, Eva keeps listening.

"Don't stop," Maria begs, her cries becoming ever more frantic. "I'm almost coming." She wails. "Almost ... almost ... oh, Gawd in heaven!"

Overcome with a desperate need to know what Mary Jane could possibly be doing to generate such cries of ecstasy, Eva gets down lower on the floor and peers through a three-inch split in the wood panels of the door, straining to see what's going on inside the candlelit room.

There's no nudity on display, but the scene is tantalizing enough without it. Mary Jane is kneeling on the floor beside the bed, her face buried between Maria's thick thighs, using her mouth in a way that Eva never knew possible.

"Mary ..." Maria grips the back of Mary Jane's head. "Mare, Mare, Mare ... here it is ... it's coming on ... oh!"

With that, she lets out a howl, the likes of which Eva's never before heard. She appears to convulse, her entire body in spasms, then she settles. In the ensuing stillness, the air filled only with faint whimpers and heavy breathing, Eva turns away from the scene and presses a hand to her chest, feeling her pounding heart beneath, her southern anatomy pulsing and throbbing.

But that was just round one. After a brief recovery period, more giggling precedes the rapid squeaking of the bed and the onset of more moaning. Now confused as much as she is intrigued, Eva takes another look through the hole.

She's never known the business of human coupling to last longer than a few minutes before arriving at an abrupt and sticky conclusion, her meager knowledge of the carnal act gleaned only from sharing a single-room dwelling with her shamelessly lewd mother since early childhood. This is strange and unusual territory, although the position she finds Mary Jane in with Maria is a familiar one.

Completely unrigged, Maria is on her knees on the bed, bent forward and clutching the headboard, adopting the same position most often assumed by Eva's mother

during coition. Behind her, Mary Jane—naked but for a pink ribbon tied around her waist and thighs—is assuming the role of the male, holding Maria's hips and slamming into her over and over again, every pelvic thrust meeting her raised rump with the harsh slap of skin against skin.

Eyeballing the pair from behind, unable to see the point of connection, Eva's inexperience in such matters renders her incapable of fathoming how or why such an act might be pleasurable, yet it undoubtedly is. On the receiving end of Mary Jane's vigorous labors, Maria cries out every time their flesh meets, and when Mary Jane breaks rhythm to grind against her in small, circular motions, she lets out a throaty growl.

Distressed by the intensity of her own lusts, Eva moves away from the peephole and closes her eyes, taking several calming breaths, trying to ignore the seemingly never-ending cycle of female sexual gratification on the other side of the door.

Time passes. An hour or two ticks by, and she starts to doze, her mind drifting into the realm of fantasy. In her dream, she's in bed with Mary Jane, both of them disrobed. That in itself would not be so shocking, except for the fact that Mary Jane has a certain physical endowment not natural to the female form. And what an endowment it is! From her sex protrudes a large erect cock, the fat purple head oozing pearly droplets of excitement.

"Look how stiff you make me," she says, kneeling on the bed, languidly stroking her engorged priapus.

As she works her fist up and down the thick shaft, she squeezes more pearls from the tip, using it to make her whole prick wet and slippery, precisely the way Eva would see her brothers fetch their mettle late at night.

Stirred by the sight, Eva lies down and spreads her legs, almost without conscious thought, silently offering her purity up for Mary Jane to take.

She never thought it possible to feel the way she's heard other girls of her age and younger confess to feeling, desiring to have a prick up them, their wombs flooded at the climax of a man's lust. Indeed, until

meeting Mary Jane, she'd never had so much as a truly unchaste thought. Not like the other girls.

In the most extreme case, she knows of two sisters who colluded to take their mother's lover in secret one afternoon, eager to explore the sensations of connection for themselves. In the bedroom, they pulled up their skirts and showed him their commodities, pleading with him—oh, not that it took much pleading!—to frig their virgin cunts.

This he did without objection, probing each of them in turn, the bulge in his trousers growing larger and larger until his rigid piercer made such a tent that the strain of the restricting fabric caused him some pain, relief from which could only be—no doubt!—attained by setting the thing free.

Gleefully, the girls did watch as he took out his sturdy prick, biting their tongues to prevent themselves from begging for it like a pair of wicked whores in the making. They did touch it, though. Amidst snickers and blushes, they took it in turns to feel its stiffness, the smoothness of the skin, and then to lick the tip and taste the salty discharge issuing forth from it.

The more they licked, of course, the more they were rewarded with his copious secretions, which they lapped up like dogs at the water bowl. Experimenting with different combinations of hand and tongue, they soon found they could coax even more from the tiny slit by massaging the fat pipe just below the crown—and that they did.

All fun must come to an end, however, and soon enough, he felt his release nearing. Cautioning them of this fact, he waited patiently as they whispered back and forth, concocted a plan, then laid on the bed and lifted their skirts again, baring themselves to him for the second time.

They wanted to see him finish, they said, and urged him to stimulate himself until he splattered their young bodies with his muck, the finale of this encounter leaving them with their excitements piqued and an unquenched thirst for amorous congress.

Predictably, as the days went on, despite their best attempts to cool their newly heated passions, they found themselves increasingly incapable of quelling their lusts, and as one might well expect, they went on to fuck the man.

Waiting until their mother was suitably preoccupied outside the home, they invited him to their bed, which they'd shared since birth. Happy to be of service, the willing man—the opportunistic man!—drove his prick into one, fucked her till the point of release, then withdrew and fucked the other. Oh, how the pair fought over who should to get his spunk inside them first.

In the end, it was decided that the oldest ought to receive him in the first instance, followed by the youngest an hour later, and both were pleased to relate how they could feel him coming up them, his hot pipe spewing his seminal offering into their wombs. And he must've been potent, or they must've copulated like dogs in the ensuing weeks, for both girls fell with child within a few months of their sexual awakening—their mother, too. All three women now with swelling bellies and the fella nowhere to be found.

For Eva, hearing of this sordid affair did little to arouse her interests in the opposite sex. In fact, it served only to make her ever warier of the dangerous potential of the male organ, towards which she's never felt any particular attraction. Yet here she is, with her legs wide apart and Mary Jane kneeling between them, positioning herself for penetration, a perfect replica of the virile member throbbing at her groin.

More than ready to be deflorated, Eva whines as Mary Jane rubs the swollen prick-tip up and down her labia, smearing her cleft with the white fluid of pre-fuck. Then, she feels pressure as Mary Jane angles the bulbous head of the unsheathed instrument through her folds and pushes at the entrance to her body.

"Are you ready, my love?" Mary Jane whispers, forcing the head of her cock through Eva's virgin slit. "Do you want me?"

"Yes," Eva coos, gazing into her eyes. "I want you."

As the words leave her lips, Mary Jane enters her. She feels the heat from Mary Jane's shaft burning up inside her, her body stretching to accommodate its girth, every inch of her filled. Then, Mary Jane starts to move.

Lying on top of her, their bodies pressed together, she fucks slow and deep for a good long while, then hard and fast, stabbing her priapus into Eva's depths in short, sharp, rapid thrusts, driving herself toward the inevitable conclusion of their coupling.

Throughout, Eva feels her insides tingle with the most curious sensations, pressure of a different kind building somewhere deep in her core—and she's not the only one whose release is beginning to crest.

"I need to come," Mary Jane whispers between thrusts, her rhythm breaking. "It's so close upon me." She groans, her struggle to maintain a steady pace becoming ever more apparent. "May I do it inside?"

"Yes," Eva pleads, gripping Mary Jane's bum. "Wet in me! Pray do!"

At that moment, Mary Jane floods her womb with a torrent of hot cream ... and she wakes up with a jolt, shuddering uncontrollably, her muscles twitching, her privy parts racked with contractions. Momentarily concerned, disoriented, and lightheaded, she thrusts a hand up her skirts and inside her drawers, finding her girl parts drenched.

Jerking back her hand, she stares at the white, webby fluid coating her fingertips, not at all sure what to make of the dream, nor of her peculiar, violent reaction to it. She can feel her heartbeat pounding in the most unusual place, her breathing shallow and irregular, her head spinning. Mary Jane's room has fallen silent now, and as she entertains the thought of peeping through the crack once more to see if her neighbor's amatory late night visitor is gone, the door swings open and Maria slips out, slinking quietly down the staircase.

As soon as she disappears from sight, Eva gets up and tries the door, expecting Mary Jane, in her drunken state, to have forgotten to leave it on the latch, but it pops open with a gentle shove. Inside, Mary Jane is asleep on the bed, half-covered in tangled bed sheets, her chemise

bunched up around her upper thighs, exposing the lower swells of her pale buttocks.

Tiptoeing in, Eva locks the door behind her and walks over to the bed, sidestepping an empty gin bottle that's been abandoned on the floor beside a crumpled heap of Mary Jane's skirts, the rest of her clothing flung haphazardly over the table.

Not wanting to rouse a softly snoring Mary Jane, she strips to her chemise, pulls back the covers, and slips into the bed as gently as possible, blowing out the guttering farthing dip on the cupboard as she sinks into the sheets.

Facing the wall, curled into a ball, Mary Jane murmurs, but doesn't wake. Once she settles again, Eva snuggles up behind her, placing a hand lightly on her side, exploring the womanly curve from the dip of her waist to the swell of her hip. When she gets to that hip, her fingertips brush the hem of the chemise and she edges further, stroking Mary Jane's silky thigh before reaching around her shapely body.

The dream still playing on her mind, she creeps her hand over the soft flesh of Mary Jane's belly and moves lower, beyond her abdomen, finding the smooth mound of her motte.

She keeps going. Of course, logically, she knows there's nothing out of the ordinary lurking in Mary Jane's most private place, but she just needs to feel ...

Stirring again, unaware of who's in bed with her, Mary Jane snatches up Eva's wandering hand and places it on her breast, holding it there, causing Eva to take a sharp draw of breath. Unable to grasp the entire breast—her small hand not big enough for the task—Eva gives it a light squeeze, fondling the firm orb and feeling the nipple stiffen against her palm.

In response, Mary Jane extends a hand behind her, fumbling around Eva's hip and under her chemise, grabbing her bare rump.

"You want fucking?" she mumbles groggily.

Eva freezes, afraid that Mary Jane will turn over and realize her mistake, but thankfully, after a few seconds of silence, her grip slackens and she drifts back to sleep, snoring once more.

CHAPTER 6

Thursday, March 3, 1887

MARY JANE WAKES UP WITH A GROAN, WINCING AND clutching her forehead. Feeling the presence of a warm body behind her, cuddled up to her, she rolls onto her back, curious to know who her bedmate is. She vaguely remembers bringing Maria home and engaging in several rounds of intense and energetic fuckery that continued without respite until they were both exhausted and passed out. Beyond that, the details are blurry.

Her temples pounding, her body punishing her for the overindulgence of booze, she lifts her head and squints at the tangle of limbs draped over her. There's an arm flung around her middle, bent at the elbow, a hand lightly cupping one of her breasts. Further south, there's a leg crooked over her thigh, the knee tucked up under her chemise and pressed to her crotch.

It's not Maria, she knows that much. The proportions are all wrong. And that can only mean ...

"Eva," she whispers under her breath, moving a flop of deep brown hair away from the face on the pillow beside her, unveiling Eva's delicate, youthful features.

Coming properly to her senses, her mind acclimating to consciousness, she notices something tickling at her upper thigh: a soft thatch of curls. Ever so gently, her breath held tight in her lungs, she lifts the covers and peeks beneath, finding Eva's chemise rucked up around her waist, her drawers absent and her untamed, untouched mount bared.

"Oh, my good Lord." She marvels at the sight of a full triangle of dark, bushy pubic hair, temporarily hypnotized by it until Eva squirms and shifts, roused by the draft.

Not wanting to be caught peeping—or for their accidental entanglement to be a source of embarrassment for the demure teen when she wakes—Mary Jane drops the covers and nudges Eva's knee away from her core. Unfortunately, her efforts have no remedying effect. Instead of moving away, Eva nestles closer, clenching her hand around Mary Jane's breast and wiggling her hips, rubbing herself on Mary Jane's thigh.

Biting back a whimper, Mary Jane plucks Eva's hand off her breast and turns onto her side, separating their bodies. "Good morning, my sweet." She kisses each of Eva's fingers in turn. "How long have you been in my bed?"

Eva shrugs, yawning.

"I'm sorry I weren't in a better state last night." Mary Jane keeps hold of her hand. "I must've seemed a right mess."

"S'all right. It ain't your fault." Eva steals back her hand and grabs the hem of her chemise, forcing it down. "I shouldn't impose on you."

"It's no imposition."

"All the same." Eva rolls away, tucking her chemise between her thighs, shamed by her careless indecency. "I oughtn't ..."

Her words trail off, tendering nothing elucidating and leaving Mary Jane to hazard a blind guess as to the nature of her discomfort.

"I'll understand, you know." She retreats a few inches, giving Eva more space in the bed. "If what you saw last night makes you uncomfortable with me."

"No, it ain't like that." Eva spins back around, shaking her head emphatically. "I swear it ain't." She clutches a handful of Mary Jane's chemise. "Not even a bit. Honest."

Perplexed by Eva's contradictory emotions, but reluctant to push her for clarification for fear of adding to her confusion, or inadvertently pressuring her into

making a premature declaration of her feelings, Mary Jane treads lightly, easing the conversation forward.

"So you still want to sleep with me, then?" She pries Eva's hand off her chemise and coaxes it around her waist instead.

"I reckon I'd be with you every night if you'd have me." Eva shuffles closer, sweeping her hand onto Mary Jane's lower back and resting it where the smooth inward curve of her spine gives way to the sensuous rise of her buttocks.

"Really?" Mary Jane fusses over her, moving strands of coffee-colored hair away from her face. "You'd like to be my little bed warmer?"

"Uh-huh." Eva nods. "I'd pay you board n'all," she offers quickly, lest Mary Jane should think her a sponge. "I could cook and clean and see to your washing. My mam says I'm proper good at all that."

Detecting a certain seriousness behind that casual proposal, Mary Jane probes deeper. "You don't enjoy living with your mam?"

"Him, more like it." Eva shudders, covering her chest with her free arm. "I don't care for the way he looks at me. Like I'm a turkey, or a piece of roast beef."

Mary Jane knows that look: as though he wants to gobble her up. He's keen to be the first one to taste her flesh; to tear into her tender meat; to take what he wants and get his fill before passing her on to the next in line.

Worried that he might've already tried to take a bite or two, she forces herself to ask, "Has he ever ... ?"

Eva shakes her head, moved by the genuine concern in Mary Jane's damp eyes.

"Good." Mary Jane plants a kiss on the end of her nose, summoning a smile. "I don't want no-one touching you." Realizing how possessive that sounds, she corrects herself, feeling a rare, self-conscious blush blooming on her cheeks. "Not unless you want them to, that is."

Eva drops her gaze, feeling her stomach tighten, a knot forming at the thought of Mary Jane being touched by all and sundry. "You let men at you all the time."

"Aye"—Mary Jane's forced smile fades—"but I ain't got nothing left to protect."

Privately mourning all that she's lost—virtue, chastity, dignity, and more—and cursing those who guided her, in her naivety and desperation, to take the first wrong step, seduced as she was by the lure of domestic independence and want of a good wage, she lets a heavy silence creep in.

"I wish I was like you," Eva says then, breaking it.

"No, you bloody well don't." Mary Jane laughs, rubbing her tired eyes and smearing yesterday's eye paint all over her cheeks. "Ain't nothing good about me."

"You take care of yourself," Eva contends defiantly. "You does whatever you want, and you don't need no fella to bring coin in."

"Is that whatchu think?" Mary Jane recognizes some of her former self in Eva's grand declarations. "P'raps it seems that way in some lights, but the truth is, I ain't got a penny to my name and I rely on fellas more than anyone."

That subdues Eva's advocacy somewhat, but not entirely. "Still," she presses on, "I bet you can pocket my whole day's wage in less than an hour."

Realizing she's yet to inquire about Eva's first day in her new occupation, Mary Jane perks up and throws on a fresh smile, ignoring the teen's attempt to engage her in a wage comparison. "How did you get on yesterday?"

Eva doesn't look impressed. "A hansom nearly ran me down in Westminster, some half-fuddled toff spat on my carnations, and I only brung home two and six. You prob'ly get nearly that much for a quick knee-trembler down some stinky alley."

Mary Jane looks apologetic, her brow creased with sympathy. On a good day, five or ten minutes in a slimy alleyway would not only match Eva's takings, but exceed them by sixpence.

A disgruntled scowl sets in on Eva's face. "Is it more?" She pouts. "You're telling me your quim goes for more than a half-crown?"

"A thruppenny upright is more like a three bob upright for me, if I'm lucky," Mary Jane begrudgingly admits. "I told you I weren't cheap."

"I know, but gorblimey!" Eva makes a face. "I didn't think ... I mean, what do they get for that? Do you give 'em a song and a dance n'all? Not that I don't imagine you're worth a good few bob—you surely are—but who round here can afford you?"

Not many, Mary Jane thinks, glad of as much. "My flesh commands top coin. I'm young enough, clean, and I ain't bad to look at, but it won't always be that way. I'm reaching the end of my best years."

"How old?" Eva scrutinizes her face, unable to see past her superficial beauty. "Twenty summink?"

"Let's say two and twenty. Sounds about right to me." Mary Jane winks. "Come twenty-five or thirty, my worth will decrease year by year till I'm taking men for thruppence or a glass of gin, just like all the other worn-out old bunters you see traipsing up and down Commercial Street night and day."

Tears pool in Eva's eyes. "Don't say such things."

"Why not? It's true." Mary Jane forges on, setting her mind to deter Eva from the wickedness of the street. "Most who fall young find a way to scratch and claw their way out of this life long before they hit their decline, but those who don't ..."

"You ... ?" Eva fails to articulate the question.

"I've tried." Mary Jane thumbs an escaping tear away from her cheek. "Every attempt has left me worse off than the last."

"Is that why you ain't a West End toffer no more?"

Mary Jane nods. "This is the first time I've ever promenaded myself on the streets. I was always tied to a house and a bawd. First, there was one in the West End, then two more down Ratcliffe way, by the docks. Early on, I thought I'd best secure my future by selling myself to one man instead of many—be that as a mistress or a wife—but nothing worked out quite the way I imagined."

She pauses to caress Eva's face. "When things fell apart for me the last time, I came here, to Thrawl Street. I reckoned I could hardly do much worse if I went off on my own, so instead of binding myself to another man, I've been trying to put some money by." She bops Eva's nose with the tip of her finger and quirks a smile. "Not

much, but whatever I can. I have a fancy to set myself up somewhere. Elsewhere, I mean—not London. A little coffeehouse somewhere quiet. Whatever the case."

"You'd like that?" Eva's heart is gladdened by her optimism.

"I can pour a nice cuppa, and I ain't bad at baking a cake, neither." Mary Jane grins. "In the meantime, thank God for these." She grabs her ample breasts and jiggles them at Eva. "Worth their weight in gold, they are."

"I believe it." Eva giggles, coloring up. "I love the way you look." She roves her eyes over Mary Jane's body as her hand—resting limply near Mary Jane's hip all this time—slips southward, spurred into action by such playfulness. "And I don't just mean your diddeys," she goes on, gliding her hand over Mary Jane's rump. "I love all parts of you in equal measure."

Exploring the older woman's well-formed curves, she caresses a deliciously rounded buttock for a few seconds before running her hand up, following the shapely swell of Mary Jane's hip into the dip of her waist.

In a district where many women, stricken by the insidious disease of poverty, are either emaciated and under-nourished, or over-fattened on the daily and excessive consumption of beer, Mary Jane's robust, comely figure is pleasantly proportionate. Her healthy, statuesque form not only alludes to a background of good-living—telling of a life far removed from the East End, where she was free from deprivation and food was in fair enough supply—but also highlights her ongoing ability to sustain it.

"You're all womanly and that." Eva worships her, traversing the contours of her stomach and abdomen. "So soft." She swoops upwards, trailing over Mary Jane's ribs and settling at the underside of her breast. "So beautiful."

Feeling uncharacteristically brave, she swipes her thumb over the dark pink circle visible behind Mary Jane's silk chemise, arousing the nipple and causing it to stiffen as Mary Jane lets out a soft, appreciative sigh.

Immediately, she retracts her hand. "I'm sorry." Her cheeks burn. "I ought not do things like that. I know it ain't proper."

"Whoever's told you such nonsense?" Mary Jane reaches for her hand, plucking it from the neutral space between them and coaxing it back to her breast. "It ain't no crime, so please don't be sorry. I like your touch." She presses her hand over Eva's, encouraging her to play with the nipple, making it fully erect. "Do you like the way my body responds to you?"

Eva nods, teasing the rubbery nub with her fingers. "You have such lovely diddeys." She grabs the whole breast, fondling it without reservation. "You're just the prettiest woman I've ever seen, and that's for no doubt."

"I s'pose you ain't never looked in a mirror, then." Mary Jane smiles, eyes half-lidded, her passions ignited by Eva's tender ministrations. "You're the most delightful creature I've ever had the good fortune to cast my eyes upon, and you may touch me wherever you please."

As Eva circles her puffy areola, giving the nipple a gentle tug, Mary Jane groans, unable to smother her pleasure before it escapes. Tilting her head back, her eyes closed, she clutches at the hem of her chemise, grappling with the temptation to snatch up Eva's hand and whisk it to her core. In doing so, the silk shift rides up a few inches, threatening to expose her commodity, and Eva's eyes wander, her hand soon straying southward.

"Oh, my good Lord Jesus Christ, yes," Mary Jane mewls at the ceiling, feeling Eva's tentative fingers making their way across her midriff. "What I wouldn't give to—"

SLAM!

A door bangs closed, followed by the heavy, stomping footsteps of the mustached man in the hallway outside Mary Jane's room.

"Where are ya?!" he booms, bashing repeatedly on Mary Jane's door. "Are you in there with that whore?!"

"Shite!" Eva jerks her hand away from Mary Jane's body and scrambles out of bed, horrified to see how light it already is outside. "I'm late! He's gonna rage at me."

"I hope she's giving you lessons!" He thumps his fist on the door again, making it rattle on its hinges. "Oi!" More thumping. "Are you pair listening to me?!"

"Leave it out, will you?!" Mary Jane returns fire on him, bellowing at the top of her lungs. "She's coming already!"

"Aye, I bet she fucking is!" he barks back, pounding his fist into the door once more for good measure. "I wants her downstairs in two minutes, or I'm coming in there and dragging her out by her ear!"

Eva rushes to get her clothes on, managing to acquaint Mary Jane's hairbrush with her ruffled mane just enough to get it under control before diving back onto the bed to say goodbye.

"Will I see you later?" she hopes.

"I'd like that very much." Mary Jane smiles up at her. "May I buy you supper?"

"Aye, you may." Eva relishes the novelty of being asked such a thing. "I dunno what time I'll make it back, though. He's told me not to bother showing my face until my basket's empty, and I was out past dark yesterday."

"What if I can't wait that long?" Mary Jane juts out her lower lip.

"Then you can buy me dinner instead." Eva leans forward and gives her a lingering peck on the cheek, letting it land near the corner of her mouth.

This time, not caught off-guard by the gesture as she was yesterday, Mary Jane kisses her back. "Where will you be?" She runs her thumb over Eva's lower lip, gazing at her soft mouth.

"I start off down by St Paul's, working my way through the City and up Moorgate." Eva recalls the previous day's route. "I daresay I'll be around Finsbury Square and the Artillery Ground by mid-afternoon."

"All right, my love." Mary Jane plants another quick kiss on her. "Now be away with you before your mam's bloke comes back and has another rant." She gives the teen a light shove off the bed, leaning over to spank her bum before she gets out of reach.

That elicits a squeal of delighted surprise, and Eva leaves the room with a grin plastered on her face, thrilled to be the recipient of Mary Jane's interest.

In the wake of her departure—the door barely closed behind her—Mary Jane rolls onto her back and drives a

hand to her core. Being with Eva is swiftly becoming a torture of the sweetest kind, and following their impromptu morning fondling, her skin is slick with lust, her clit swollen and hard. It takes only a few short strokes before her legs are trembling.

Once relieved, she falls asleep, only waking several hours later when there's a knock on her door. Knowing it can't be rent day, she hesitates to answer, but the knocking persists.

"Who is it?" she grumbles. "Whatever you want, I ain't got it."

"It's Missus Sullivan," a faint female voice in the hall replies. "Eva's mam."

Her chest tightening apprehensively, fearing that she's about to be warned off, Mary Jane slips out of bed and opens the door to a diminutive Irishwoman with a bun of unkempt brown hair and a worn face. She looks nothing like the Missus Sullivan of Mary Jane's imagination: a burly, boisterous woman with a hefty set of lungs and thick fists.

Far from that, this woman is thin and frail. Her third-hand clothes hang limply off her shoulders, and there's not an ounce of meat on her. To Mary Jane's eye, she has the look of a woman with a strong predilection for laudanum, a potentially fatal side-effect of which is the suppression of appetite.

She might've been beautiful once, but that time has long since passed. Though not quite forty, she has deep lines on her brow, her features prematurely hardened by the conditions of her life. Being a heavy drinker in addition to all her other woes, she's got a permanent tremor in her hands. An old clay pipe is clasped in one of her palms, though there's not enough tobacco left in it to smoke. All major vices accounted for.

"You's Mary Jane?" the haggard woman asks, squinting, one of her eyes puffy and blackened from a recent beating.

"Aye." Mary Jane leans on the doorjamb, her arms folded, anticipating unpleasantness.

"My littlin spoke to me of you last night." Missus Sullivan's lungs crackle when she breathes. "She says you've been sweet to her."

"I've been looking out for her if that's whatchu mean." Mary Jane defends herself against an inferred accusation. "A girl of her age don't belong in a place like this unguarded."

"As if we got a choice about that." Missus Sullivan cackles, baring several gaping holes where her tobacco-stained teeth have been knocked out. "She oughta be getting off on her own, but I can't shift her out 'cause she don't want the same as others. You know my meaning? She won't even so much as look at a boy, never mind take to one, and I'll be damned if I can't make no sense of it."

Mary Jane listens quietly, letting the poor woman unburden herself.

"Billy—him's my fella—he reckons I gave her my breast too long and that's the cause of it. She prefers to mix with her own, see? I had her on my dairy till the wee thing was well in her second year 'cause I didn't wanna get another in me." She presses a hand to her concave abdomen. "She was the last of my lot, thank the good Lord. Had 'em all back-to-back, I did, but I s'pose that's what I get for enjoying a poke as much as I do."

She pauses to scratch at her head, picking a stray louse off her scalp and cursing at it before flicking it over the banister rail. Meanwhile, the smell of tobacco draws Mary Jane's attention into her neighbor's room, finding a uniformed sailor sitting on the foot of the bed, lighting a pipe. That seems to bring Missus Sullivan back on course.

"Got any French letters?" she asks abruptly. "Only he won't do it wivout a sheath, and I ain't got the time to run and get none."

Not the money, more like, Mary Jane thinks.

"I didn't know you was gay," she comments absently, expressing no judgment.

"I ain't." Missus Sullivan plants her hands on her hips, affronted. "It's my day off, and I pick up a bit extra where I can, that's all." She huffs, settling her dander. "Now do you got one or not? Just the one'll do. I'll swill it out if need be."

Nodding, Mary Jane pads across her room and retrieves a single French letter from her small supply on the washstand. "Here you go." She hands the rubber prophylactic over. "Aught else?"

"Got any baccy?" The woman raises her pipe, trying her luck.

Mary Jane shakes her head. "Sorry. Not my vice."

Accepting that, Missus Sullivan turns her gaze to the floor. "I'll pay for the thingamabob in a few days." She plucks another louse off her head. "After rent and that."

Doubting the likelihood of ever seeing so much as a farthing, Mary Jane releases her from the debt before it becomes one. "Don't fret about it."

"Ta, deary. You is a nice one, just as Eva says." Missus Sullivan takes a step back toward her room, then vacillates, working something through her addled mind before letting the words out. "She's becoming dreadful fond of you, you know."

"That's all right." Mary Jane smiles. "I'm fond of her n'all."

"Well, just you be careful with her. She gets attached, bless her." Missus Sullivan's mind veers off on another tangent. "I've told her it ain't no good to keep having such fancies, but she won't be put right. Bessie—her's my sister—she says I should send her into service. Says she needs some discipline and that'll do the trick. 'Cause you ain't the first she's clung to, see? She's been hanging on skirts all her life, but you's the first one what hasn't given her a sharp kick. Once they realize what she's about, they don't want nuthin' to do."

"Are you coming back here, woman?!" The sailor grows impatient. "What am I waiting for?!"

"I'm coming, I'm coming," Missus Sullivan mutters, turning back to Mary Jane one last time. "Don't tell no-one about this, eh? Billy'd murder me if he found out."

Mary Jane shakes her head. "Not a word, I swear."

Mumbling more thanks, Missus Sullivan shuffles back inside her room. Minutes later, Mary Jane gets herself dressed with the background accompaniment of a squeaking bed and a continual string of compliments addressing the sailor's virility and the size of his cock.

CHAPTER 7

MARY JANE HUMS A MELANCHOLY TUNE TO HERSELF, HER legs dangling over the side of a stack of crates in an abandoned warehouse on the verge of ruin, waiting for the young man in front of her to dig through his pockets, scrounging up coppers. Upon exhausting his search, the scruffy laborer drops a mere thruppence into her open palm.

"Is that it?" She rolls her eyes, pockets the coins, and lifts her skirts, tucking them up around her belly as she reclines against the wall, bringing her knees up and spreading herself for him.

He groans at the sight of her, fumbling to get his already stiff cock out of his trousers, and she guesses he won't last much over two minutes. To speed him along even quicker, she increases the visual stimulation at measured intervals, gauging the level of his excitement by the rapidity of his breathing and the speed of his fist.

First, she opens her legs wider, causing her plump labia to part, baring some of the inner pink. Then, she uses her fore and middle fingers to pull her delicate folds open, exposing the hidden slit. When the novelty of that wears off, she brings her other hand into play and dips her middle finger inside herself, swirling it around, her pleasure only half-feigned as she builds up to a triumphant fake climax designed purely to make him spill—which he does.

His release found—her job done—he tips his cap to her and leaves. Not ten minutes later, she's back in the warehouse with another customer, and this one gives her a shilling. For that, she gets down on her knees and fishes his prick out of his trousers, holding her breath so as not to be overwhelmed by the stench of his unwashed genitals.

As per her usual routine, she pulls a clean hanky from her pocket, ready to wipe him down and give him a quick inspection, looking him over for any signs of disease before she accepts him into her mouth, but she never gets that far.

When she wraps her hand around his shaft and moves his foreskin all the way back to give the unveiled cockhead a sharp pinch, he spontaneously erupts. With a grunt, his hips twitch, his prick throbs, and he spends on her face, his seminal libation splurging all over her cheeks, nose, mouth, and eyes.

Dropping his disgraced, dribbling cock, she spits his salty muck onto the ground and wipes a dollop off her right eyelid, grimacing up at him. "Really?"

Red-faced, he apologizes profusely and buttons himself up, tossing a few more coins at her before scurrying off, no doubt vowing never to return.

Weary already and the day less than half gone, her busiest hours yet to come in the evening, Mary Jane wipes her face off on the hanky and wanders back to Commercial Street.

Passing trade comes easy to her. She can be as picky as she likes, and is tempted to turn the next gent away when he hands her a shilling for minette. She can still smell the last fella's mucilage on her skin, her stomach churning at the thought, but since she'd far rather have a prick in her mouth than in her cunt—where it's apt to be altogether more dangerous—she steels herself for the continued punishment regardless of her disgust.

Somewhat warily, she takes him to an alleyway behind the Ten Bells and drops to her knees, releasing his cock from his pants. Fearing another accidental misfire, she promptly moves her face out of range, but his wrinkled tool flops out only semi-erect.

Satisfied that she's in no imminent danger, she whisks out another hanky and proceeds to examine him from root to tip.

"Whatchu doing?" He peers at her over his rotund belly, wondering why he's yet to feel her sweet mouth around his pego.

"Just having a look."

Undeterred by his obvious annoyance, she spits on the hanky and gives him a quick wipe down before squishing the soft, purple head.

"Oi! Watch it!" He smacks her hand away. "I ain't got no pox!"

Assured that he doesn't—there being not the slightest hint of unusual discharge or any abnormally foul odor—she gives the tip a gentle kiss, leaving a smear of crimson lip paste on it. "Calm down, old boy. I don't wanna get clapped, that's all."

Without further delay, she takes the crown between her lips and fists the base, trying to coax him hard. After five minutes, she takes a breather and stretches her jaw, then goes back at it, but his prick refuses to stand. In the end, her jaw aching, she gives up.

"Why's you stopping?" He scowls at her.

"'Cause I've been on my knees for a good quarter hour and the only thing getting stiff is my jaw." She spits on the ground, banishing the taste of him from her mouth, and wipes her hand off on a hanky. "Come back when you get it working."

"Fine." He puts himself away and upturns his palm. "Where's my money?"

"Ha!" Mary Jane guffaws. "Is my time worth nothing?"

Incensed by her laughter, the disparaged swell grabs a fistful of her mane and yanks her off the ground, jerking her head to the side so that she has no choice but to look up at him, like a dog submitting to its master.

"I want my money, you thieving little fucktress," he growls.

Matching his anger, her eyes narrowed and her lips taut, not even remotely intimidated, Mary Jane seizes his cods, squeezing them hard. "Hands off, arsehole."

He releases her and crumples to the ground. "Bitch!"

Unfazed by the insult, Mary Jane storms out of the alley and heads in the direction of Thrawl Street. Thoroughly fed up, and in no mood for pleasantries, she doesn't even break stride when one of her regulars—an eighteen-year-old boy who's in the habit of seeking her out at least twice a week—chases her down, making a concerted effort to hamper her progress.

"I'm not taking any more just yet." She dodges around him.

"Aww, come on, Miss Em," he persists. "I've got a whole shilling on me this time." To prove it, he pulls the coin from his pocket and flashes it in front of her face.

"I've had just about enough of that for the time being." Mary Jane ruffles his sandy hair, softening to him. "Maybe later, though. And maybe see if you can get your hands on another two bob before then, eh?" She slips a hand around the back of his neck and tugs his face to her breast. "I'd rather have a nice poke." She finds an erection tenting his trousers and gives it a quick stroke. "Wouldn't you like to get your prick up me?"

He groans into her cleavage. "Oh, I do, I do, Miss Em. I loves your quim."

"Off you trot, then." She gives him a push. "Go find me some coin, boy."

On a mission to get inside her by the end of the day, he dashes off, ready to beg, borrow, and steal for the privilege, leaving her to walk the rest of the way home chuckling to herself. Past experience tells her there's very little chance of his making up the deficit by this evening, and he'll be so impatient to have his pleasure that he won't want to wait to accrue it.

Indeed, in the few months they've been acquainted, he's only been able to get up her three times. More often than not, he has to settle for a sly rub: a service in which the customer gets to thrust his prick along the valley of her sex instead of inside her. Though the act is so named because many an unscrupulous whore has been known to lodge a man's instrument there, nestled in her copiously oiled-up folds so as to trick him into thinking he's in the proper channel, many now embrace this intercrural

coupling as a legitimate service in its own right, offering it as a cheaper alternative to full coition. If Mary Jane's luck holds, she'll manage to get through the whole day without having to give up anything more.

Locking herself in her room at Thrawl Street, she removes her diaphragm—not needed thus far—and cleans herself, scrubbing every inch of her face and brushing her teeth twice, determined to eradicate all trace of her recent activities.

Eager to meet up with Eva, she then hurries through the rest of her routine, painting herself up and giving her used hankies a wash before emptying her pockets of French letters and some of her money. Allotting a modest portion for savings, she stores one shilling in the lockbox beneath her bed—thus removing the temptation to spend it—and drags out a wicker basket, inspecting it for wear and tear.

Having been used as a makeshift laundry hamper for the last several months, it's half-filled with an assortment of dirty linens and harbors a faint odor of feet. After dumping the linens out onto her bed, she lines the basket with a clean piece of muslin cloth repurposed from an old curtain—saved in case it should come in useful—and sprinkles it with a dash of lemon juice, freshening it up.

Happy enough with her efforts, she retrieves two bottles of ginger beer from the cupboard, along with the remains of a crusty loaf and a block of hardening cheddar cheese, and proceeds to make two sandwiches. It's not enough, but it's a start.

Before leaving, she places all in the basket, drapes a woolen blanket over it, and gives herself a brief appraisal in the mirror, instantly regretting the largely unconscious decision to apply so much color to her face.

Making a few minor adjustments to her appearance, she puts on her fitted black velvet jacket and buttons it all the way, thus concealing her immodesty. Though she opts to leave a dusting of rouge on her cheeks and the sooty powder she routinely uses to darken her eyelashes and brows, she wipes away all trace of red lip paste with a washcloth. Not entirely satisfied with that, she then dabs

some tinted beeswax on her lips instead, giving them a glossy sheen and only the faintest hint of color.

Her spirits now well lifted—the finishing touches made—she fixes her shawl around her shoulders and sets her mind to pick up some rashers of bacon, two sausage rolls, two apples, and some celery on her way to Finsbury Square, which is little more than a fifteen minute walk from Thrawl Street.

Arriving in the designated area on the cusp of two o'clock, picnic basket on her arm, she finds Eva right where she said she'd be. She's engaged in discourse with a boy of her own age, but not for the purpose of selling him flowers. The boy—a boot-black by the looks of it, his ill-fitting clothes smeared with mud and shoe polish—is wringing his cap in his hands, twisting it all around, betraying his shyness. Not far off, his younger brother, no more than ten years of age, sits curbside, minding his upturned wooden box, brushes, and rags: the tools of a boot-black's trade.

Soon to be too old for the work, the boy must train up his sibling before moving on to labor of a manlier sort, the transition from boyhood to adulthood then complete, excepting one more important milestone: the obtainment of a wife.

That's where Eva comes in, Mary Jane imagines, eyeing them from the other side of the street, her sightline broken intermittently by throngs of ladies and gents, the frequent passing of carriages, and one chock-full sixty-person tram car drawn by two large stallions.

Fully prepared to stand by and wait for their business to conclude before making her presence known, she hovers by the tramway, disinclined to interrupt, but Eva has no such reservations. She's been keeping a keen lookout for Mary Jane, and leaps on the first opportunity to pull away from her unwanted suitor.

"Begging your pardon, but I must go," she cuts him off mid-sentence. "My friend's here."

Leaving him no pause for objection, question, or entreaty for her to remain, she darts into the street, weaving her way through foot traffic to reach Mary Jane. As she gets closer to her target, she breaks into a broad

smile, her chest heaves, and her cheeks color with anticipation. Behind her, the lovesick boy slinks away with his tail between his legs, his advances rebuffed, his prospects for courtship looking increasingly gloomy.

"Am I barging in?" Mary Jane fears, watching the young boot-black resume his work, not wanting to upset some pre-existing relationship, nor to impede any opportunity Eva might have to cultivate a bond with someone willing to take on the role of future provider, should she be inclined to do so.

"No, you bloody well ain't." Eva rises onto her tippy-toes and wraps an arm around Mary Jane's neck, dropping a soft kiss on her cheek. "I've been so giddy all day thinking of you."

"Me, too, darling." Mary Jane sweeps her into an embrace, holding her close. "I haven't been able to think of anything else."

For those with keen powers of observation, something as simple as a hug can be a most telling thing. A woman with no amorous intentions is apt to lean forward into the embrace, projecting her rump outwards so as to limit bodily contact, thereby meeting the other party with a light kissing at the breast and nothing more. When a woman is desirous of intimacy, on the other hand, there's no such rear projection. Instead, the body remains entirely in line with itself until the last moment, whereupon she may tuck her pelvis forward, ensuring full connection from groin to breast—as Eva does now.

Even when the hug breaks, she's loath to separate herself. Leaving her arm hooked around Mary Jane's neck, she arches her back and angles her upper body away, keeping their loins mashed snugly together.

In response, Mary Jane tightens her grip around the teen's waist, recognizing in her the first subtle hints of sexual want. No longer seeing a confused, curious girl, but a young woman sharing her own tastes and passions, she makes an advance and moves in, tilting her head and pressing a chaste, fleeting kiss directly on Eva's lips.

Overcome by the gesture, Eva swoons, swaying unsteadily on her feet and clutching at Mary Jane's

shoulder for support, her legs weak and threatening to give out beneath her.

"Steady, love." Mary Jane holds her upright. "Breathe."

Recovering but slowly, Eva takes in a lungful of air, her vision clearing as her senses return to her, equilibrium restored. "Do that again. Oh, pray do."

"I dare not, lest you should faint on the tramway." Mary Jane rubs noses with her instead. "Are you ready to eat?"

"I'm half-starved." Eva peers down at Mary Jane's basket. "Whatchu brung?"

"I thought you might like to accompany me on a picnic." Mary Jane peels back the edge of the blanket, revealing a peek of the basket's contents. "It's not much, but I hope you'll like it."

"I'll love anything you give me, I'm sure." Eva smiles, slipping her hand onto Mary Jane's waist, excited by the prospect of being courted. "Where shall we go?"

"I know a place." Mary Jane drapes her arm around Eva's shoulders, bringing them side by side and tighter together. "Somewhere quiet."

She leads the way further north alongside the tramway, up to Old Bunhill Fields Burial Ground. Filled to capacity, the cemetery's been disused for over twenty-five years, the last burial having taken place in 1860. Now a public park, complete with gardens, seating, paths, and walkways, it's a tranquil spot amid the bustle and commotion of inner city life.

"This way." Mary Jane takes Eva's hand and pulls her off the path and over the grass, navigating the uneven ground among lichen-covered monuments and trees, ultimately selecting an isolated spot behind a large altar tomb.

Here, she lays down the woolen blanket in the shade of a tree and sits with her back to the tombstone, the picnic basket by her side.

"Sit." She pats the spot next to her, urging Eva to settle close.

"No-one's ever took me on a picnic afore." Eva scoops her dress under her bum and lowers herself

92

gracefully onto the blanket, setting her half-empty basket of flowers to the side.

"Well, I'm glad to be your first." Mary Jane slips off her shawl and folds it beside the basket, then reaches for the top button of her velvet jacket. "Do you mind? I'm a little warm."

Eva shakes her head. "I've no objection."

Glad of that, Mary Jane frees herself of the cumbersome, tight-fitting garment and folds it on top of the shawl, pleased when Eva's gaze drops to her chest.

"Thirsty?" She swipes a bottle of ginger beer out of the basket and hands it over.

"This is a first n'all." Eva inspects the offering, struggling with the cork, her fingers slipping as she tries to get a decent grip around it.

"Give it here." Mary Jane reclaims it. "You're far too dainty for your own good." She clamps her teeth around the cork and yanks it out with a satisfying pop, spitting it into the basket as she passes the bottle back.

Eva takes a sniff of the contents before putting it to her lips and taking a small, tentative sip, coughing when it hits the back of her throat for the first time.

"You've never had ginger beer before?" Mary Jane uncorks her own bottle, giving it the same treatment before taking a few quick gulps.

Eva shakes her head. "Never had no booze. My mam forbid it, scared we'd all take after our dadda in that way." She gives the beer another try. "We only had milk or tea. If we couldn't afford tea, we just had water what'd been boiled over the fire. She don't trust it straight from the pump."

"Well, I hope I'm not corrupting you," Mary Jane teases, rooting in the basket for food. "I don't want to get done for the moral degradation of a minor."

"I just turned sixteen," Eva declares proudly. "That's plenty old enough."

"So I'm allowed to corrupt you a little bit?" Mary Jane passes her one of the sandwiches.

Not knowing what to say to that, Eva accepts the unevenly cut sandwich with a smile and devotes her full attention to it, demolishing the whole thing in a matter of

a few short minutes. Next, she starts on the bacon and sausage, and finishes with the apple and celery, both of which help to clean her teeth.

As they eat, a comfortable silence sets in. While Eva sits in a most proper fashion, with her legs tucked sideways, keeping her knees and ankles together at all times, not an inch of her white cotton stockings bared, Mary Jane pulls her skirts up, propping her ginger beer between her red-stockinged knees as she eats, her legs crossed at the ankles.

Indeed, it's becoming quite apparent that Mary Jane is wholly unconcerned by the exhibition of that which ought to be kept private. Not that Eva has any complaint to lodge. At every flutter of the wind, Mary Jane's skirts—petticoat and all—ruffle, revealing fleeting, tantalizing glimpses of her milky thighs, and Eva's eyes are riveted there, willing the wind to kick up time and again.

Aware of the attention and seeking to encourage it, Mary Jane finishes her sandwich, brushes off her hands, and plucks her ginger beer from its resting place. Nursing it in her lap, she crooks the leg nearest Eva, causing her skirt to crumple further up her thigh, independent of the wind's intermittent and unreliable interference.

Feigning ignorance of her state of indecency, she leans against the tombstone, sucking back a healthy amount of the ginger beer. "That young lad I saw you with," she inquires then, curious to know more of what she inadvertently interrupted. "Does he wish to pay court to you?"

"Nah." Eva scrunches up her nose, the very thought displeasing her. "I think he had half a mind to walk out with me once, but I ain't never been interested. And I ain't never led him on, neither," she's quick to add. "Where we used to live, up Bethnal Green, I'd get paid to watch all the nippers in our street and round about. Only a farthing a head, but some days I had twenty of 'em all around me, dawn till eve, and that's almost a tanner. Anyway, Jimmy used to come and hang about, making a right nuisance of his-self, bringing me flowers and trinkets and that. I ain't never asked for none of it." A small trace of guilt seeps onto her face. "He did bring me

a sausage roll once, and I scoffed that down mighty quick, but if he thinks that means I'm keen on him, or that I've made him any promise, then he's gone barmy."

Mary Jane chuckles. "You might have to get used to receiving attention of that sort, I'm afraid." She lays her hand on Eva's thigh, feeling that she garters above the knee, unlike most girls of her class. "You're going to attract interest from all quarters, whether you want it or not."

"Ain't there no way to make it stop? What's I s'posed to say?" Eva's brow furrows with concern. "I daren't tell my mam this, but some fella come up to me on Fleet Street yesterday and starts asking me all sorts of bawdy things. First, he asks me if I'd let him kiss me. I says 'no, sir, I ain't that way, sir,' then he asks me if I've ever been felt. I tells him I ain't never had a man, and he offers me a sovereign—a full sovereign, would you believe that?!—to go with him to a room down the Strand. He says he'll show me what it's all about, and promised not to take up more than an hour of my time."

Mary Jane cringes. Not only was the swell trying to despoil her, but he was insulting her in the process. Sure enough, a sovereign—twenty shillings, no less—is a fine amount of coin, especially to a poor girl, but it's a pittance for a virgin who can be verified *intacta*. Such girls have been known to fetch twenty pounds or more.

"Promise me you won't never be tempted." Mary Jane repositions, shifting sideways to face Eva, resting her shoulder on the lichen-covered, weather-worn limestone. "And next time some toff approaches you with such a vile offer, you tell him you have someone watching out for you. Say he's a real brute of a fella with a jealous temper, and if he sees someone taking liberties, he'll fly up and baste him. Or I will. I'll find him and cut his cods off just for looking at you."

Eva shuffles closer. "It gives me flutters to hear you say such things. If I told my mam what happened, she'd baste me for not taking the sovereign."

"She'd never?" Mary Jane is openly dismayed. "Ain't she worried about you ruining yourself?"

"Ruining me-self for what?"

"Well, a husband I s'pose." Mary Jane finishes her ginger beer, tossing the empty bottle into the picnic basket. "Not that you should have to take one if you don't want to, but many women do. If not for pleasure, then for security."

That piques Eva's curiosity. "Have you ever been so inclined?"

"Once, when I was about your age," Mary Jane answers slowly, as if deciding how much she wants to disclose. "Of course, that was before I knew myself."

"You married?"

Mary Jane nods. "So the story goes, but I have no husband. Not anymore."

"And you've no desire to take another?" Eva pushes onward.

"Not if I can help it." Mary Jane picks absently at a blade of grass. "There is someone who would yoke me if he could. He was a regular friend of mine from my Ratcliffe days, and by that I mean he was one of my best customers." She coaxes a wandering ladybird onto the tip of her finger. "I left my last gay house to take up with him in Bethnal Green, but it didn't work out."

"You couldn't love him?"

"Love?" Mary Jane raises both eyebrows. "Now that's a luxury seldom to be found in such dealings, even when the two parties are compatible in matters of attraction."

"So what was it, then? Did he not treat you good?"

"He knocked me about once, and that was once too often. I left him only a few months ago." Mary Jane's tone conveys no hurt, only annoyance. "In any case, he ain't right for me in that way." She pauses, watching the ladybird take flight. "No man is." She turns her eyes back to Eva. "You do understand that, don't you?"

Eva chugs the last of her ginger beer before answering, hoping to draw some courage from it, but even then, all she can summon is a nod.

Lightheaded from her first taste of alcohol, weak though it is, she closes her eyes, staving off another spell of faintness. In the next moment, Mary Jane's palm is pressed to her cheek, turning her head.

Eyes still shut, she senses Mary Jane moving toward her, and she knows what's coming: a kiss. Longing for it, but so terrified to receive it, she takes a sharp draw of breath, mewling like a kitten as their lips bump together, and then ...

She jerks away in a panic, breathing rapidly, almost hyperventilating. Feeling as though she might retch, she leans over the edge of the blanket and hangs her head, waiting for her queasiness to pass. As she does, she brings her fingertips to her mouth, touching where Mary Jane's lips made brief, delicious contact with her own.

Rejected and confused, Mary Jane pulls back, slumping against the tombstone and tucking her heels to her bum. "Forgive me." She resists the urge to reach out and offer Eva comfort, lest the gesture should be unwelcome. "I've been drawn to you since I first laid eyes on you. I thought you knew that, and I thought you felt the same."

"Oh, but I do." Eva snaps out of her stupor and swivels around, scooting her bum into the crook of Mary Jane's lap, her back against Mary Jane's thighs. "I truly do."

"Then why such fright?" Mary Jane asks, her voice tremulous, barely louder than a whisper. "Whatever you feel, it's all right." She puts on a brave face. "I shan't be upset with you, or angry. If you don't want me in that way, you need only say."

Eva wriggles closer, coaxing Mary Jane's hands onto her waist. "Have you ever wanted summink so much that the thought of it turns your tummy all upside down?" She fixes her eyes upon Mary Jane's chest. "That's how I feels when I'm with you. All topsy-turvy like."

"There's no need for you to be so anxious." Mary Jane wraps her arms around Eva's middle, scooping her into an embrace, much relieved by her confession. "I shan't bite."

"But I ain't never been kissed in the proper way." Eva pins her gaze to Mary Jane's mouth. "What if I don't do it right?"

"Oh, my darling. Is that your only worry?" Mary Jane cups her face. "Close your eyes," she coaches the

performance-conscious teen, moving in. "Let me show you."

Eva does as she's told.

"Now wet your lips for me." Mary Jane hovers a hair's breadth away, her breath tickling Eva's mouth.

Trembling from head to toe and barely breathing, Eva runs the tip of her tongue over her lips and rubs them together, moistening them.

"There's nothing to be afraid of," Mary Jane assures her, registering her lingering apprehension. "I won't ever do anything to hurt you. I promise."

With that, she presses her lips ever so gently to Eva's. It lasts but a few seconds. Once certain that Eva isn't going to succumb to another attack of timidity, she repeats the action, this time applying more pressure. When that, too, is reciprocated, she gets bolder.

She nudges Eva's lips apart with her own and pinches them between hers. As soon as that kiss breaks, she instigates another. And another. Wrapping one hand around the back of Eva's neck she lies the teen down on the blanket, cradling her head, kissing her still.

Though Eva's dress rucks up around her thighs, she keeps her knees together, aimed skyward. Making no advance to part them, Mary Jane leans over her young companion, caressing her body. Their lips still locked together, kissing more feverishly than before, she runs a hand up Eva's outer thigh, under her dress but over her drawers.

As that wandering hand comes to a rest on Eva's hip, squeezing and kneading, the chaste teen whimpers and squirms. She can't help but think back to her dream, recalling how it felt to have Mary Jane on top of her and inside her, loving her and fucking her.

Feeding off Eva's evident arousal, Mary Jane glides her hand inward, from hip to motte, and burrows her way inside the folds of Eva's split drawers.

"I want to feel you," she whispers, dragging her fingers through Eva's thick curls before teasing her fingertips between the teen's closed thighs, halting at the apex of her cleft, seeking permission to continue.

Overcome with desire, Eva relaxes her legs, the tension in her muscles dissipating. She's about to welcome another's hand on her sex for the first time, but then heat courses through her body, starting at her core and radiating outward, accompanied by the same abdominal pressure she felt when Mary Jane's dream form spent inside her.

All of a sudden, she breaks her lips away from Mary Jane's and her body stiffens. She dips her head, her eyes squeezed shut, and tries to suppress a shiver, convulsions seizing her insides.

"What's wrong?" Mary Jane looks down at her, feeling her shudder. "Did you just … ?"

"I dunno what's the matter with me." Eva feels a trickle of moisture seeping along the valley of her treasure and shoves Mary Jane's hand away, frightened she might feel it. "I dunno what it is." She scrambles to her feet, tears brimming in her eyes. "I'm all wrong."

"Darling." Mary Jane tries to hold her back. "I'm so sorry. Please don't go."

Eva slips from her grasp.

"Will you see me later?" Mary Jane tries in vain to prevent her from departing so hastily.

Offering no reply, Eva snatches up her basket of flowers and leaves, never looking back.

CHAPTER 8

IT'S GETTING LATE, AND HAVING NO MORE NEED FOR COIN—despite spending a few pence more than she ought on drink—Mary Jane is about to head for home when one of her regular customers accosts her leaving the Ten Bells.

"It's not our time, is it?" She frowns at him. "Have I mixed up my days?"

She normally meets him once a month, whenever he can afford the pleasure. Like many of her 'special' customers—those whose particular kinks and letches demand some form of unique service for which she can charge far above her average rates—he usually sends notice by mail, which she collects regularly from a post office on Whitechapel High Street. In this manner, the pleasure of her company can be booked up to a month in advance, but occasionally, desire and impatience outweigh financial responsibilities.

"I've a great need of you," he says, grabbing her hand and imploring her to follow him.

"All a sudden?" She giggles, amused by how even the meekest of gentlemen can be so easily undone by the demands of an unsatisfied cock.

"It's been brewing." He drags her down Commercial Street, leading her in the direction of the Ringers' Buildings, where their assignations usually take place.

101

"Don't pull me along!" Mary Jane clutches her skirts and picks up her pace, trying not to lose her shawl in her effort to keep up with him.

He's a nice enough man, though she knows next to nothing about him. He always comes to her clean, freshly bathed, for which she has great appreciation. Sometimes, she's seen him dropped off in a brougham—a private one-horse carriage—so she knows he has access to money, but she suspects it's his wife's. That he's married is one of the few facts she's learned of the man she's been instructed to call William.

Many women, Mary Jane's sure, would consider him handsome. He's in his thirties, with a well-groomed mustache and neatly combed hair. He has strong shoulders and arms, as if bred for hard labor, but his hands are soft. She fancies he married above his class, and fearing disgrace and the loss of his fortuitously acquired position, he dare not permit her to know the truth of him. Not that it matters.

He pays a shilling for privacy, as he always does, and in no time at all, they're inside a small room furnished with a double bed and a washstand. The sheets are changed once daily, which is better than never, and some raggedy towels are provided so that they might be laid on the bed to capture the spillage of any fluids. In particular, the blood of deflorated virgins.

Despite a seemingly inescapable musty odor, the rooms here are bearable. The floral wallpaper is faded and peeling, and the floorboards are warped and splintered, but the beds are in relatively good shape, and the Britannia is only a stone's throw away. If you allow her to keep the change, one of the young girls employed here will happily run down to fetch you a pail of ale, or a jug of ginger beer—whatever your pleasure.

Overall, there's little to complain about, providing you avoid using the room at the end of the hall. That one, Mary Jane well knows, has a peephole in the wall.

The peephole is positioned to give a perfect view of the bed, and for the exorbitant fee of ten shillings—plus a one shilling surcharge per peep—you can rent the room on the other side of it for a few hours and spy on any

number of unsuspecting couples. Every time one couple leaves and another enters, you rack up another shilling, thus the peeping room is the most lucrative in the house—and Mary Jane's been on both sides of it.

One of her regulars likes her to fellate him while he watches, and he gives her a running commentary from beginning to end. Between bouts of oral stimulation—for he can go three times before his prick refuses to stand—he lets Mary Jane peep. He enjoys hearing her comment on the different paphians who come and go, some of whom she recognizes, others she doesn't.

For the most part, you see nothing more than harlots carrying out their daily business. Rarely, you get to see a married man with his wife's maid. Once, Mary Jane saw a man bugger himself with the handle of a wooden spoon while an old, flabby tart put her mouth to work on him.

Thanks to that peephole, she knows plenty of what her competition gets up to. She knows who consents to being socratized, who practices the art of minette, and who likes to be gamahuched, though all would vehemently deny such things if asked.

On the opposite side of it all, she has a regular who likes to see her receive other men. Impotent since a work injury permanently damaged his back, he hasn't been able to sustain a cock-stand for years, but he still enjoys the titillation. If it can be so arranged, he prefers to be in the same room, watching the operations at close range, but if no willing male can be found, he'll settle for watching through the peephole.

Out of a genuine liking for the man—who's never been anything but gentle and somewhat pitiful—Mary Jane makes sure to always give him a good show. Knowing the room as well as she does, she positions herself at the best angle for his viewing pleasure, often strips nude without being asked, and puts extra effort into her grunts and groans, feigning the utmost delight.

His has a letch for men with mammoth-sized cocks, so despite it hurting her and feeling altogether quite unpleasant, she'll sometimes lure in the baker's son. Even if he can't afford it, she shams lust and pays for the room

out of her own pocket, trusting that her faithful voyeur will reimburse her when all's said and done.

If it's been prearranged to do so, she'll make an excuse to leave the room as soon as she's received his wetting—often by claiming that she needs to wash, there being no water in the ewer—and she'll steal into the next room. Lying upon the bed, legs akimbo, she then lets her voyeur see the man's abundant sediment trickle out of her.

Sometimes, he'll grope her, which is a luxury permitted to only a few of her specials, and he has a particular passion for it. He likes to paddle his fingers in her, feeling the warm spunk splurging around his digits, perhaps wishing it was his. Once, he ate it out of her, which she only let him do for an extra shilling and the novelty of having a man do such a thing.

It was the one and only time she's ever let a man lick her commodity, though she's been asked plenty. In an attempt to keep her work separate from her private enjoyments, she won't often allow men to touch her in any way that she likes to be touched by a woman. Only her specials, on very rare occasions—and for extra money down, of course—are permitted the pleasure of using their hands upon her.

Then, there are men who never want to touch her at all. Men like William. He only wants from Mary Jane what he cannot get from his wife, and thus has never laid so much as a finger on her—which suits her perfectly.

Their meetings always begin with the shedding of clothes, he stripping naked, and she divesting herself of everything but her boots, stockings, and corset. That done, she lies on the bed and toys languidly with her sex, her legs wide apart.

"Does it please you to look at me?" she coos softly, seeing his priapus stiffen.

He's never seen his wife's notch. A prude to her core, she only consents to their connection in a darkened room while she's wearing her chemise or nightgown, thus an unrestricted view of Mary Jane's fresh, young cock-trap is enough to get his prick standing.

Kneeling between her legs for a prime view, he enjoins her to frig until she spends—the pleasure generated by her own hand entirely genuine—then he has her dip inside herself, probing deep into her canal.

When her fingers are sufficiently wetted, she pulls them out and offers them to his mouth. He licks them clean—his only taste of female spendings—then drops onto all fours, presenting his posterior.

"Do it," he begs. "I want it now."

Obediently, Mary Jane slides off the bed and delves in the pockets of his great coat, pulling out a strap-on leather dildo and a French letter. After tying the dildo on, she sheathes it in the French letter and slathers it with pomatum from a jar on the bedside table.

Once prepared, she hands him a towel to lay on the bed beneath him, ready to catch his pleasure when it comes, and gets onto her knees behind him, giving his rump a hard slap before spreading his cheeks.

Relishing these antics, grinning all the while, she eases the tip of the phallus into his rectum. Once through the sphincters, it pops in and glides easily up his passage and he moans, wrapping his fist around his oozing tool.

She'd be lying if she said she didn't find some thrill in the reversal of roles. He likes it rough, so she holds his hips and thrusts violently inside his fundamental orifice, glad that she has someone to take out her frustration on.

Nearing his crisis, he fists his throbbing erection, growling out obscenities. "Cunt ... bugger ... fuck ..." He starts to tremble. "I'm coming ... fuck ... buggery ..." With a howl, he erupts copiously onto the towel.

Out of breath, Mary Jane slows to a stop. When he's completely done, she withdraws and pulls off the soiled French letter, turning it inside out in the process. Dumping it in the nearby chamber pot, she doffs the dildo and starts getting dressed.

Flopped onto his back, sated, his wet pipe deflating, William points to his trousers, indicating where money is to be found. "Left pocket."

Claiming one gold sovereign, Mary Jane thanks him, wishes him a good night, and leaves, their transaction complete. She intends to go straight home, but gets no

further than the Britannia when she spots a well-dressed male figure standing in the porch of the Queen's Head public house on the corner of Fashion Street, less than two hundred feet away.

He doesn't move. He looms there, eyeballing her from the stoop, the lower part of his face illuminated by the porch gaslight. Everything from the nose up is hidden in the shadow cast by the wide brim of his hat.

In the breast pocket of his jacket, a red silk handkerchief protrudes, and Mary Jane recognizes him by that alone. It's Joseph Fleming, her former keeper.

Even though she can't see his eyes, she feels him looking at her, his cold stare causing a chill to ripple from the base of her neck to the bottom of her spine. They parted on bad terms, and she's not in the mood to fight. Avoidance is the best strategy, but he's effectively barring her path to Thrawl Street.

Keen to put some distance between them, she considers taking the long route home, but that would have her cutting through Itchy Park: a disused graveyard attached to Spitalfields church. Homeless people sleep there at night, knowing there's very little chance of being disturbed by the local policemen, and every square inch is infested with fleas and other vermin—hence the unflattering name. It's an unlit patch of dead grass and withering trees, the old gravestones splattered with urine and feces.

From there, she'd have to walk alone through a dark alley bisecting two rows of single-room dwellings beside the rag store, hopefully unseen. Dashing quickly across the next street, she'd then have to pass along another gloomy passage among yet more tenements before emerging onto Flower and Dean Street.

Moving swiftly past the low lodging houses that occupy almost every building in this warren, and avoiding the rotting trash littering the gutters, she'd turn onto George Street and make the final sprint home. Assuming he didn't follow her.

It's too much to bet on, so instead of running the risk of engaging him, she turns in the opposite direction and retreats to the Ten Bells. Greeted by a series of

enthusiastic jeers and whistles, she makes her way through the crowded, smoke-filled room and orders herself a gin. Whether it's her fifth or sixth of the day, she's not quite sure, and as she reflects on that, a pair of hands slips around her waist.

Reacting instinctively, she jabs her elbow behind her, striking her assailant, and pivots free as the grip on her waist slackens. Prepared for a fight, her fist is clenched as she spins around, intending to thump whoever has dared to take liberties with her person.

But it's not an overenthusiastic fella.

It's raven-haired Maria.

"Fucking Christ!" Mary Jane gives her a shove instead of a punch, knocking her into a bar stool. "I could've walloped you."

"You bloody well did!" Maria clutches her upper arm where Mary Jane's elbow struck. "Just for that, you can buy me a drink."

Gin heals all wounds, and one glass soon becomes three. Maria and Mary Jane settle at a small table in the corner, keeping as much to themselves as possible, Mary Jane fighting off the advances of drunken men at intervals, but accepting the drinks as and when they come to her.

Sitting with her legs crossed at the knee, not giving half a fuck for propriety, she passes the time gossiping with Maria, hoping that Fleming gets bored and wanders off before she gets drunk and forgets why she came into the pub in the first place. Though that could take a while. She's developed a fairly good tolerance for hard liquor, unlike Maria, who's already feeling the effects of the gin.

"Want some company again tonight, Old Mare?" She sinks her head onto Mary Jane's shoulder, angling for an invite into her bed. "I'm in the mood for it. I've had a rotten bloody day."

"Really?" Mary Jane cocks an eyebrow. "What's a shite day like for a laundress? A bloke semenalized my face earlier. How would you like that? I'd rather have soap in my eye than the contents of a man's ballocks."

Becoming increasingly spoony, Maria snuggles closer, rubbing Mary Jane's thigh beneath the table.

"Take me home and I'll lick you clean." She brings her mouth to Mary Jane's ear, whispering, "Everywhere."

Laughing, Mary Jane picks Maria's hand off her lap. "I can't. I ain't exactly free." She swirls her gin in her glass, her nipples tingling, remembering what it felt like to wake up with Eva all over her, half nude. "I've been sleeping with someone."

"Since when?" Maria pulls a face at her, giving her thigh a slap. "If I recall, we had a jolly spree last night. What changed?"

"I kissed her."

"Kissed who?"

"My neighbor's daughter." Mary Jane smiles, contemplating the taste of Eva's lips. "Nothing else has gone on, mind. The dear girl ain't ready for that." She sucks back more of her gin, wishing she hadn't been so greedy when she had Eva in her arms. "She's young and ... unsullied."

"And you're sweet on her?"

Mary Jane groans, slumping in her chair and pressing a hand over her heart. "She's so beautiful. She makes me ache."

"That's where she makes you ache?" Maria cocks an eyebrow. "You know what that means, duntcha? You've only gone and caught yourself some feelings."

"Mary Jane?!" A woman's shrill voice cuts through the ruckus. "Where's Mary Jane?!" she screeches. "Is that Emerald pinchcock in here?!"

"Oh, shite." Mary Jane downs the rest of her drink.

Maria peers through the smoke-filled room at an irate Irishwoman bellowing in the doorway. "Who the flamin' hell's that?" She screws up her face.

"My girl's mam." Mary Jane stands up and straightens her skirts, hoping she looks at least somewhat presentable. "You looking for me, Missus Sullivan?"

Missus Sullivan jabs a finger at her, then at the front door. "You get yer pretty arse out there now, afore I drag you out by yer hair!"

Assuming Missus Sullivan's come to give her an earful for trying to get inside her virginal daughter's drawers, Mary Jane bids Maria a swift goodnight and

steps compliantly out onto the street, apologizing profusely.

"I didn't mean to upset Eva." She glances in the direction of the Queen's Head, relieved to see the front stoop vacated, Fleming nowhere in sight. "I swear, I would never do anything to—"

"Listen here." Missus Sullivan cuts her off, wagging a disapproving finger. "I'm sure as I dunno what's gone on atween you and my littlin, but that girl's gone mad as a bag of weasels over you. All I've bloody well heard is 'Mary Jane this' and 'Mary Jane that,' and then I comes home to find her sat in the hall outside your door, bawling her eyes out, saying you's never gonna speak to her again."

Mary Jane feels a pang of heartache in her chest. "That's not true."

"Whatever the daft fool's gone and done to make you dull on her, just put that out of your head and give her another go."

"Whatever *she's* done?" Mary Jane's heart breaks a little more.

"Aye." Missus Sullivan clasps her hands together. "I'm begging you to go easy on the lass. She ain't never had no-one return her affections afore. All her siblings growed well up and got married and whatnot—except the one what died—but she ain't never had no prospects where that's concerned. All her fancies turned on her. One boxed her ears, another poked fun. The last one dragged her by her hair all the way home and told me she was of a wrong sort. Said I ought to have her put away, she did." The scrawny woman huffs. "Then you comes breezing along, has her in your bed, makes such sweet love to her—so she says—and puts all fresh ideas in her head, then you vanishes off down the pub at the first quarrel."

For all that Missus Sullivan looks half-dead, she's full of fight for her daughter. She gesticulates wildly, expressing her distress, and her screeching voice carries halfway down the street, announcing their private affairs to everyone within earshot.

"There weren't no quarrel," Mary Jane sets her right, fielding a few strange looks from a group of passersby. "It was a misunderstanding."

"All the better, then." Missus Sullivan points in the direction of Thrawl Street. "Now you get your cunt lickin' arse home and tell her she's forgiven."

Nodding compliantly, Mary Jane starts walking. "Has she had any supper?"

"Why? You buying?"

CHAPTER 9

MISSUS SULLIVAN CLUTCHES A FISH AND CHIP SUPPER protectively to her chest—as if fearing that Mary Jane might change her mind and try to take it back from her—and pushes open the sloping, warped door to her cramped, squalid, windowless room in the Thrawl Street lodging house.

After depositing two more portions of fish and chips on the table in her own room and lighting a couple of candles, Mary Jane brushes her hands off on her apron and accepts Missus Sullivan's invitation inside, finding Eva curled on a pile of rags on the floor, crying hysterically into the tattered linen.

Sparser even than Mary Jane's room, this one—dimly and unevenly lit by a single oil lamp hanging from the ceiling—has no fireplace and only one chair. The table is splintered and cracked, one broken leg propped up on a copy of the Bible, and the bed—somewhat shabbier than Mary Jane's—has dirty sheets, the bloodstained palliasse never washed since one of the room's previous occupants died there in childbirth. To prevent bedbugs crawling up from the floor, all four bed legs are standing in rusting cans filled with coal oil.

Further in and Mary Jane has to breathe through her mouth. The stench of human feces is ripe, the chamber pot not emptied after someone's bout of explosive diarrhea during the night, flies swarming around it.

Kneeling at Eva's 'bedside,' she grasps her skirts in her fist, not wanting any of her clean clothing to touch but a single stitch of anything for fear of picking up a wandering louse or flea, or some other such livestock.

"Eva," she coos, placing a hand on Eva's hip. "Darling, it's me. Do stop crying."

Sucking in air in fits and starts, unable to catch her breath, Eva gasps and sputters and rolls onto her back, another flood of tears set off the instant she looks up at Mary Jane and finds no hint of animosity for her earlier behavior. Certain that she's undeserving of such goodwill, she snatches up the older woman's hands and lavishes them with sloppy kisses.

"Forgive me," she wails, smearing snot and tears onto Mary Jane's skin. "Please forgive me, Em."

"Now, now, love. That's enough." Mary Jane tugs her hands free and fights to get them under Eva's armpits, heaving the uncooperative teen into an upright position. "Up you get." She rises to her feet, using all her strength to hoist Eva up with her. "It's time to go."

"Where?" Eva sniffles, coughing and wheezing, half choking.

"To my room, silly billy." Mary Jane backhands tears from her streaked cheeks. "I dunno about you, but I could use a bit of a cuddle." She puts on a broad smile, affecting more cheer than she feels. "You fancy that?"

"And heaps more besides." Eva sinks into Mary Jane's breast, sobbing softly.

"Hush now." Mary Jane holds her, kissing the top of her head, stroking her tresses. "There's no use for all this sadness." She separates herself so that she might look upon Eva's face. "Whilst we stand here dithering, our supper's getting cold."

Eva snivels, peering up at her for confirmation of the offer, not trusting that she heard it correctly.

"Of course, that's assuming you still want to spend the night with me." Mary Jane hopes to tease out a smile. "Do you, my darling?"

"Oh, Em!" Eva grips Mary Jane in a vise-like hug. "I wanna be with you. I do!"

Mary Jane flashes a look at Missus Sullivan. Gauging her reaction to this unrestrained demonstration of affection, she detects nothing but the faint sigh of resignation and disappointment that she's sure all mothers must feel when their grown children—the product of their sacrifice and hard labor—deviate from the paths expected of them.

"Come on, then." She urges Eva out of the room and into the hall. "Let's be having you." At her own door, she gives Eva's derrière a light pat, spurring her through, pleased when she catches the beginnings of a smile tugging at her lips.

Before she takes a step to follow, however, she's held back by Missus Sullivan.

"You'll treat my littlin right, won't ya?" she frets, grabbing hold of Mary Jane's arm.

"Always," Mary Jane assures her. "I swear it."

"Be patient wiv her and that. She's a timid one, but she warms nice." Missus Sullivan lets go, patting Mary Jane's sleeve to smooth out the creases caused by her clenched hand. "She'll please ya, I know she will. I've always thought she'd make someone a nice little wife." Her mind drifts, her eyes turning vacant. "Take care now, deary." She shuffles off, disappearing inside her room without saying a single word more.

Perplexed by the odd manner about her neighbor, Mary Jane returns to Eva. She's seated at the table, slumped forward, staring at the floor, her eyes puffy and red. Though remaining bedraggled and forlorn, her tears have stemmed and her breathing has normalized, the wheezing and blubbering subsided.

Not wanting to trigger any more hysterics, Mary Jane focuses on the distraction the food provides and goes straight for it, opening a package of fish and chips in front of her. "Do you want some bread?" She licks grease off her fingers and wipes her hands on her apron. "I just bought a fresh loaf."

She turns away from the table to fetch it, but barely has a chance to reach the cupboard before Eva comes up behind her and seizes her, locking her into another frantic hug.

"Heavens, you squeeze so!" Mary Jane steadies herself on the cupboard. "I shan't need to wear a corset anymore. Not if you keep clinging to me like this. Whatever's got into you?"

"I'm so sorry, Em," Eva rasps, her throat dry and raw. "Honest, I am."

"You don't have nothing to apologize for." Mary Jane pats Eva's arms, urging her to loosen her grip. "Now ease up, love."

Far from doing so, Eva strengthens her hold. "You ain't cross with me?"

"Not a bit." Mary Jane tries and fails to wriggle free.

"Well, I ain't gonna be a fool like that again." Eva presses her cheek to Mary Jane's shoulder. "I love you, and I don't wanna muck nuthin' up."

Mary Jane falls still. "You love me?"

"Uh-huh," Eva murmurs softly. "I'm mad for you, I truly am."

At a loss as to what to think, or how to rightly respond, Mary Jane pries Eva off her. "Come now." She spins to face her eager devotee. "Let's eat."

With hunger momentarily taking precedence over all else, Eva doesn't object. She reclaims her seat at the table and scoffs every scrap of food presented to her by Mary Jane, swilling it all down with a shared bottle of ginger beer. It quiets her for a few minutes, but as soon as the bottle runs dry and her meal's reduced to crumbs, her woes return.

"I don't wanna lose you," she mumbles, her voice cracking. "I knows I acted all queer earlier." She refers back to their spoiled picnic, still fearful that her erratic behavior might've irreparably altered the dynamic between them. "I dunno what come over me."

"It's all right." Mary Jane flattens and folds the newspaper used to wrap their fish and chips, saving it for fire lighting material. "I'll hear no more apologies from you. It was my fault." She pushes the newspaper aside and flicks up her skirts, propping one foot on the crossbar of her chair, her thighs casually parted. "I misread you dreadfully. I thought you were ready for

physical pleasures, and that was entirely my mistake. You did nothing wrong."

"You didn't misread nuthin'." Eva swivels to face her. "I *am* ready." She wriggles her bum to the edge of the chair and hikes up her skirts, determined not to be behindhand with Mary Jane again. "Please, Em. I ain't never felt the way I feels when I'm with you." She throws her legs open. "I want you to have the first of me. I do!"

Recognizing in her the last vestiges of a child impatient for full womanhood, Mary Jane dives forward and forces Eva's knees together, preventing her from baring her drawers. "For goodness sake, love, stop!" She keeps her hands where they are. "Be sure of what you're doing before you go giving yourself up."

"This is what I want," Eva insists.

"Is it?" Mary Jane sighs. "To be frank, I'll be damned if I can make heads nor tails of what you want, and I doubt you can, either. One minute you're swooning for me on the street, pleading for my kisses, and the next minute you're running from me. Then I find you crying over me, and now you're professing love for me all a sudden. My darling, if you're confused—"

"I ain't confused," Eva maintains adamantly. "I fancy you, I knows I do." Fresh tears prick her eyes. "I can't keep my mind off you—nor my eyes for that matter—and I dunno what to do 'cause I ain't never felt this way afore. Not like this."

"Then why did you run away?"

"Because I thought my womb was falling," she blurts out, immediately feeling self-conscious. "My mam says that happens to lustful women, and I ain't half been having some proper wicked thoughts these past few days."

"Wicked thoughts?" Mary Jane shakes her head. "No, no, no, darling." She takes Eva's hands in her own. "A fallen womb is an affliction of gay women. It's a weakness in the female body caused by the overuse of quack remedies taken to force our monthlies on, on account of our being caught in the family way too often, or to cure a pox of some kind. We put our bodies through such torture for the sake of keeping healthy or

unencumbered." She clasps Eva's tiny mitts in her lap. "I promise you, it's not something that arises for want of a fuck. If it were, all women would be destined to suffer the same fate."

Eva giggles. "All women want to be fucked?"

"Aye." Mary Jane smirks. "A few hoity ones might pretend they don't, but they do," she whispers, as if disclosing some big secret. "It's a natural want."

Eva thinks about that for a moment. "I wanted it with you today, I really did." She colors up, smiling sweetly. "I felt so lewd, and so randy. I wanted you to have me." Her smiles fades. "Then I come over all funny and ruined it."

Mary Jane rubs Eva's hands, soothing her. "Can you describe these feelings to me?"

"I dunno." Eva nibbles anxiously on her lower lip, doing her best to recall the unusual sensations. "I went all shivery, my insides went all squeezy, and I got right dizzy and thought I were gonna conk out. I ain't never felt my heart beating so hard atween my ears and elsewhere—in the oddest of places."

"Oh, my love. I knew it!" Mary Jane's eyes brighten. "I felt you quiver in my arms. You spent! It's nothing bad. It's the pinnacle of a woman's pleasure."

Eva shakes her head, frowning. "That don't make no sense. That can't be it."

"Why not?" Mary Jane's excitement dulls.

"'Cause you wasn't even touching me down there." Eva clenches and unclenches her thighs, remembering the feel of Mary Jane's hand on her motte. "Not proper anyway. And the first time I had such a peculiar turn, you wasn't even real."

"Come again?" Mary Jane arches an eyebrow. "This has happened before? When?"

"I had a dream about you," Eva confesses shyly. "A lewd one."

"Oh, aye?" Excitement returning, Mary Jane leans closer. "What was I doing?"

Eva keeps her eyes down. "I think you can imagine."

"I dare not." Mary Jane holds Eva's hands to her chest, letting them graze the upper swells of her breasts. "Pray tell me. And do be explicit."

"You was ... oh, lummy." Eva takes a deep breath, preparing to divulge all. "You was having me, and just the thought of your doodle being in me—"

"My what now?"

Eva makes a face, wishing she'd kept that part to herself. "You had a doodle. Ignore that bit. Anyway, when you spent up me, that's when I woke up all squeezy and damp. I put a hand to my grummit and it was all sticky."

Happy to take credit for Eva's first orgasm even though she wasn't present for it, Mary Jane beams broadly, exuding a little pride. "That's what happens when a woman comes. It's perfectly normal."

"So there ain't nuthin' wrong with me?" Eva doesn't seem quite convinced.

"Oh, my love." Mary Jane fawns over her. "Not at all. Have you never given yourself a tickle before?"

Eva shakes her head. "I ain't never thought to put a hand to me-self in that way. Does it give the same pleasure? To tell the truth, I didn't even know what pleasures two women could have together until I heard you with your friend Maria."

"You listened?"

Thinking it best to leave out the peeping, Eva nods. "I knows I shouldn't have."

"It's nothing to be ashamed of." Mary fingers her long, dark mane. "Did you enjoy listening to us? How did it make you feel?"

"Jealous." Eva nuzzles her cheek against Mary Jane's hand. "Is Maria your ..." She stops abruptly, not sure what word to use. "Is she yours?"

Mary Jane shakes her head, keen to clarify the nature of their acquaintance. "We've entertained one another here and there, but I'm not bound to her. If that's been troubling you, then you needn't worry." She kisses Eva's cheek. "I shan't have her again." She flicks Eva's hair over her shoulder. "Not if you truly want to take up with me."

"So it'll just be the two of us?" Eva hopes.

117

Mary Jane nods, moving nearer and tucking her head to Eva's neck, planting a single velvet kiss just below her ear. "I promise."

She follows that kiss with another ... and another, working her lips from Eva's jawline to the collar of her dress and back again, nipping at her skin, careful not to leave a mark, save for a few smears of her rose red lip paste. Sliding her chair closer, she parts her legs on either side of Eva's and keeps the kisses coming, cradling Eva's neck in the palm of her hand.

"Em ..." Eva lolls her head to the side, relying on the support of Mary Jane's hand, giving her unfettered access to every inch of available skin.

"Mm-hmm." Mary Jane nibbles on her earlobe. "Are you feeling randy again, my darling?" She runs a hand up Eva's thigh, stopping just beyond her garter.

Eva nods, whimpering.

"So am I." Eager for more intimate contact, but afraid to make the same mistake twice, Mary Jane hesitates to explore further. Instead, she plucks Eva's hand off her lap and guides it up her skirts. "Have you ever felt a woman before?" she asks, but she knows the answer, moving Eva's hand ever higher. "Do you want to touch me?"

Pouncing on the invitation, Eva fumbles her hand over Mary Jane's smooth mound and between her silky labia, driving through her drenched folds and probing the entrance to her body.

"Your grummit's ever so wet." She gasps, her fingers gliding along the cleft. "Is it always this way?"

Mary Jane shakes her head. "Not nearly so much."

"Why is it now?"

"Because I'm with you." Mary Jane stifles a groan and reaches for Eva's hand. "Feel this here." She aims the teen's exploratory fingers at her swollen clit.

"What is it?" Eva swirls her fingers around the hardened nub, investigating its rigidity.

"It's the center of a woman's pleasure." Mary Jane struggles to concentrate, dropping her forehead onto Eva's shoulder with a moan.

"Can I feel inside?" Eva moves her hand lower, intending to dip two fingers into Mary Jane's slit, but her progress is halted by a slamming door and a shocked shriek.

CHAPTER 10

"OH, YOU BEAST!" MISSUS SULLIVAN CRIES OUT NEXT DOOR. "No! You won't have me!"

A scuffle ensues, but it's not long before Missus Sullivan's protests give way to the primal grunts of a man rutting on his mate, these carnal sounds accompanied by the repetitive thud of a headboard smacking against the wall.

"That's it, you randy brute!" Missus Sullivan changes her tune. "Give it a good shove. Get it right up me!"

Eva grimaces, withdrawing her hand from between Mary Jane's legs. "I'm sorry, I can't. Not with all that business going on."

"I quite understand." Mary Jane pulls back, her own arousal impossible to maintain. "At least they came to terms quick this time. Has it always been this way?"

Eva shakes her head, inspecting her sticky fingers. "She was teetotal until my dadda died. Then my sister left, my brothers followed, and things went bad for us. It was just me with her then, and I tried taking care of her, but she prefers the company of a fella."

"So I've noticed," Mary Jane mutters under her breath, wondering where Missus Sullivan disposed of the French letter she used with her sailor. "What is it they're always fighting over anyway? Money troubles?"

"He don't earn enough. Not since he lost his regular job down the docks and turned to casual labor." Eva

ponders her sex-slathered fingertips, flicking her tongue over one to get a taste of Mary Jane's fluids. "He don't got no work at all sometimes, and my mam only earns a few shillings a week charring. She'd do more, but she's been in terrible pain these last few years. It's on account of her tight-lacing, so she says, but she reckons fellas prefer the form of it so she won't stop. Anyhow, she takes laudanum for the pain it gives her, but the med'sin don't half make her sleepy."

Judging by Eva's nonchalance, Mary Jane guesses she has no idea of the seriousness of her mother's condition. Still, she does nothing to disabuse her, seeing little point in causing her any more worry. Laudanum addiction plagues many a good woman—the pain that accompanies the withdrawal confirming their perceived need of the medicine, and so perpetuating the cycle—and it's certainly not a suitable topic of conversation for this time of night.

"If I was of a mind to take up with another bloke, I'd be sure to get myself one what could keep me in coin," Mary Jane says then, rising to begin her bedtime grooming routine.

"I thought you said you didn't want one?"

"I said I won't take no husband," Mary Jane corrects her, "but I ain't entirely opposed to the thought of making myself someone's mistress, just for a short time." She runs her hairbrush through her mane. "Think of it this way: he pays my rent, buys my food, and keeps me how I need to be kept. It's always seemed to me that selling myself to one man beats selling myself to many, and I could still keep some of my special customers on the side, but only the ones what pays well for my services. I could save more that way. See?" She pulls the sovereign she earned earlier out of her pocket, showing Eva the gold. "Another year or so, and I reckon I could have a pretty penny saved up if I didn't have no expenses."

Eva admires the coin, having never before seen any denomination above a shilling. "What must you do for this?"

"It's probably best you don't ask." Mary Jane has no intention of giving her the specifics. "Some of my best customers have rather unusual bedroom tastes."

Eva's limited imagination takes off, thinking immediately of the most vulgar thing she's ever heard whisperings about. "Did you let him go in the back way?"

"Hish! No!" Mary Jane smacks her lightly with the backside of the hairbrush. "That's still virgin, thank you very much, and I've no desire to be socratized."

"What then?" Eva hands the coin back, trading it for the hairbrush, curious to know if the man's letch has anything to do with the birch rods she peeked underneath Mary Jane's washstand two nights ago.

"Well, let's just say that his back way ain't so virgin. Will that suffice?"

"Sodomite?" Eva wrinkles up her nose.

"Not really." Mary Jane takes off her boots and makes for the washstand, filling it with a few inches of water poured from the ewer. "He likes a bit of red as much as he likes a bit of brown, though he's got himself a wife for that. I only take care of certain peculiar letches that she won't accommodate." She loads her toothbrush up with pasty, wetted tooth powder. "But you can wipe that rotten look off your mug in any case. Who's to judge what another does in their bed? Some would say what we want to do with each other ain't right, but you don't believe any of that nonsense, do you?"

Eva shakes her head.

"Good. It ain't no different for men, but they're the flavor of the day with the law-makers. Who knows, the peelers could be sent after us next."

Mulling that over in silence while Mary Jane cleans her teeth, Eva takes her turn with the brush, doing a thoroughly halfhearted job of it.

"Don't look so forlorn." Mary Jane finishes up and swills her mouth out, washing off her crimson lip paste and eye paint at the same time. "It might not happen." She nudges Eva toward the washstand, urging her to clean her teeth as well.

Not a minute later, the fighting starts up again next door. This time, it's swiftly concluded with the door

banging on its hinges as Billy storms out of the room and thunders down the stairs. In the lull following his departure, Missus Sullivan starts to wail.

Conscious of Eva's concern for her mother, Mary Jane rubs her back and strokes her shoulders, offering her some small amount of comfort. "You all right, my love?"

Eva nods unconvincingly, putting only minimal effort into her teeth cleaning.

"You sure?" Mary Jane prompts her, dragging a chair over to the washstand in preparation for the next part of her nightly cleansing. "Ought you check on her?"

Eva spits and rinses. "There ain't no point. She'll be passed out soon enough."

Not sure how she can help make things better, Mary Jane lets it go. Forging ahead, she pours the used water from the basin into the nearby chamber pot, refills it from the ewer, and empties her pockets, dumping three used hankies onto the washstand.

Keen to be near her, Eva perches on the repositioned chair. "Have you taken many up you tonight?"

"None." Mary Jane props her foot on the edge of the seat, flicks her skirts over her knee, and penetrates herself, fishing out her diaphragm. "But I like to wash. It makes me feel clean."

"Eww, whatever's that?" Eva grimaces at the slimy rubber contraceptive device. "You've had that up there this whole time?"

"It's called a diaphragm." Mary Jane chuckles, finding Eva's disgust comical. "It's some newfangled thing meant to prevent women from getting in the family way." She rinses off the squishy vulcanized rubber disc. "It seems to do the job, and I like it much better than that damned sponge." She points to the shelf beneath the basin where, among other contraceptive devices, soluble pessaries, ingredients for various cleansing douches, and a strange glass phallus, there's a walnut-sized, cream-colored shapeless blob attached to a piece of silk string.

Eva picks up the sponge, inspecting it at length. "How does it work?"

"You douse it in vinegar and push it up to the mouth of your womb," Mary Jane explains, dunking one end of a washcloth into the basin and wiping her outer sex. "Its purpose is to stop a man's spermatic fluid from getting inside and causing trouble."

"Yuck," Eva concludes, plopping the sponge back in its place. "I dunno how you puts up with it all."

"You get used to it." Mary Jane rinses off the washcloth. "That's the thing of it really: once you've done it, doing it again is far too easy."

"Have you always been a wh—" Eva stops herself from using such an indelicate term, for fear of causing offense. "I mean, have you always been someone what ..."

"Been gay?" Mary Jane spares her from having to say it. "I weren't much older than you when I first went wrong. My cousin led me into the bad life before I came to London, and I soon had the idea that, if I was going to be a harlot, I may as well get myself set up in the West End and earn a decent living at it."

"Did you not enjoy the West End?" Eva doesn't think that at all probable, but she asks anyway. "Is that why you come here instead?"

"Heavens, no. I loved it." Mary Jane beams. "I wore knit silk stockings, had the finest corsetry and nicest dresses. The madam of my house was French, and I was always wearing the very latest French fashions. She kept me in good health—made sure I saw the doctor twice a month to prove as much—and had me fitted for this." She shows Eva the diaphragm again. "I had the nicest gents calling on me, showering me with gifts. Every day I was riding around in carriages, being treated like a proper lady."

"So what happened?" Eva's thoroughly intrigued. "Why'd you come to leave such luxuries?"

"Well, that's a right tale to tell." Mary Jane turns solemn, saying nothing more on the subject, and proceeds to dry herself off with the other end of the washcloth before draping it over a small towel rail attached to the washstand.

Sensing she's not going to be hearing that tale any time soon, Eva turns her focus to other things. Namely, the continued exploration of Mary Jane's body.

While Mary Jane soaks the used hankies in the basin, adding a little soap to scrub them clean, Eva caresses her leg. Starting at her ankle, she slides both hands up, over a stocking-covered calf, above the knee and beyond the garter, stopping at her inner thigh.

"Can I see your grummit?" she asks boldly, her eyes pinned to the apex of Mary Jane's thighs.

Wringing out the last hanky, Mary Jane dries her hands and takes hold of her skirts, but doesn't immediately lift them. "You got thruppence?"

Eva's jaw slackens, mortified and astounded that she should be asked such a thing.

"Oh, your face!" Mary Jane cracks up, not having the heart to tease her. "I'm only pulling your leg." She adjusts her stance and bares herself. "You can peep at me all you want."

Eva's gaze drops south and her breath catches in her throat. Entranced by the view, she leans closer for a better look, gawping without fear of reproach, her cheek pressed to Mary Jane's alabaster thigh.

"More?" Mary Jane offers, spreading the petals of her sex with her fingers, simultaneously pulling back the protective hood covering her clit.

Trembling, the muscles in the core of her body clenching spontaneously, pulsing with longing, Eva ducks forward and drops a kiss on Mary Jane's hairless motte, then closes her eyes and turns her head, quashing the desperate urge to grab Mary Jane by the hips and bury her tongue between the folds of the older woman's satiny pink flesh.

In her sixteen years, she's seen her fair share of males. Growing up with her whole family occupying just one or two rooms, it was hard not to. On numerous occasions, she got to see her older brothers bathing in the their rusty tin tub, soaping their doodles in the lukewarm water. She saw them with cock-stands, and watched them frig themselves late at night, yet the workings of the male

body sparked not a bit of curiosity. She hadn't felt that until her first peep at their naughty French postcards.

From then on, the delicious curves and crevices of the female form tantalized her imagination. She sought to explore that fascination by soliciting closeness with any woman who drew her interest, but quickly found that, while her friendship was readily accepted, none were quite so accepting of her romantic overtures. She's been chided, mocked, and slapped, and one who first seemed flattered by her advances proceeded to beat her violently.

After that, she vowed she'd not cause any more grief. They left Bethnal Green, and she kept to herself, convinced that she was alone in her hidden desires. Then she met Mary Jane.

"Darling ..." Mary Jane lowers her skirts. "Shall we go to bed?"

Eva opens her mouth to reply, but all that comes out is a muted squeak. This might not be the first time she's been invited into Mary Jane's bed, but the repetition of the event does nothing to quell her nerves. Indeed, their encounters are becoming progressively more stimulating, and she finds herself becoming progressively more flustered.

Upon feeling a tremor in the quaking teen's hands, Mary Jane captures them in her own and pulls Eva to her feet, delivering a few quick kisses to her lips.

"May I unrig you?" she asks, groping for the bow keeping the cotton sash tied around Eva's waist.

Receiving no objection to that proposition, she undoes the sash and whisks it off, tossing it onto the table before starting work on the buttons of Eva's dress, unfastening the loose, ill-fitting bodice all the way.

Swiftly peeling the fabric back, she bares Eva's neck and upper chest, slipping the patchwork garment off her shoulders. As if kneeling in worship, she then drops to her knees and tugs the skirt all the way to Eva's ankles, pulling the teen's serge underskirt and flannel petticoat with it.

Sending them all the way of the sash, creating a billowing heap of crumpled clothing on the tabletop, she then rises back up and lifts Eva's camisole off over her

head, exposing her simple, cream-colored, corded and boned corset.

Though plain compared to Mary Jane's corsetry, it does its job. The woven coutil cloth is steam-molded and cane-boned, permanently holding its rigid shape. Like Mary Jane's, the steel busk at the center front has loops and posts for easy dressing and undressing, but the bust gores are much less prominent and decorative, having only a little patterned stitching, the top of the corset trimmed with a thin strip of white lace.

Mary Jane makes fast work of it. She strips it off and drops it onto the seat of the chair behind, Eva's breasts barely falling, held up naturally by youth.

"You're very beautiful." She sneaks her hands under Eva's chemise, blindly locating the fastening on her drawers and untying them. "And I'm very lucky." She slips her hands inside the waistband and over Eva's buttocks. "So lucky," she murmurs, caressing both firm cheeks before easing the drawers over Eva's hips and to the floor.

Crouching to retrieve them, she nuzzles her face into Eva's chemise-covered crotch, breathing her in through the fabric, kissing her there. She's tempted to lift the worn white cotton and bring her lips to Eva's mound, but restrains herself when Eva teeters precariously, on the verge of another swoon.

"Careful." Mary Jane steadies her.

She tosses the drawers aside and takes off her apron, preparing to disrobe, but Eva stops her at the first button of her bodice and takes over, attacking the garment with undisciplined urgency, going at it much too rapidly for Mary Jane's liking.

"Take your time," she coaches the overeager teen, momentarily staying her hands, not wanting the experience rushed. "Enjoy unveiling me."

Heeding that advice, Eva slows. She concentrates on one button at a time until she has the bodice and the under-bodice undone, then she lifts them both off Mary Jane's shoulders, exposing the corset beneath.

Immediately, she reaches for the bust gores, but curling her fingers around the cups, she feels nothing of

Mary Jane's body. The corset is too much like an armor plate: stiff and unyielding. Her impatience returning, she fumbles with the top clasps, struggling to get the first one undone, her hands shaking.

"Relax." Mary Jane snatches both of Eva's mitts up, kissing each finger before placing them back on her breasts. "Deep breath."

Sucking in a lungful of air and beginning again, Eva gets the clasp on her second try.

"That's it," Mary Jane encourages her. "Keep going."

The next clasp yields easily.

And the third.

The fourth.

Below the bust, where there's less tension in the garment, the clasps cooperate without much resistance, tightening briefly again at the narrowest part of Mary Jane's waist before easing out, allowing her body to flare naturally into her hips.

Feeling the last clasp release, Mary Jane takes a deep breath, expanding her lungs to their full capacity for the first time since dressing. As she does, Eva pulls the corset away, watching her weighty breasts fall and bounce and jiggle, both nipples stiffening directly.

Frozen, having never before been so close to a woman's naked breasts, Eva stands in silent admiration, the corset clutched in one hand, her other hand held in mid-air between them, not daring to touch.

"Here, let me." Mary Jane deposits the corset, bodice, and under bodice on the increasingly cluttered table and wriggles out of her skirts, shedding all but her silk petticoat.

By the time she turns back around, Eva's broken out of her paralysis. Standing there with Mary Jane's chemise in her hands, she fondles the lush fabric, eyeing it longingly.

"I wish I had silk."

"And so, one day, you shall." Mary Jane puts on the expensive shift, covering herself up. "For I'll buy it you." She moves over to the bed and sits.

Ready to be stripped further, she lifts her petticoat above her garters and extends a leg, presenting it to Eva for denuding.

Following her lead, Eva kneels in front of her and removes the elastic garter holding the stocking in place, then rolls the woolen garment down inch by inch, dropping kisses from thigh to ankle. When she's done, Mary Jane presents her other leg for the same treatment, and Eva repeats her ministrations, not letting go until she's kissed each one of Mary Jane's toes.

While she still kneels, folding the stockings in her lap, Mary Jane stands and drops her petticoat. Her sex bared in front of Eva's face, she sweeps her hands around the back of the teen's neck, drawing her forward and upward, onto her feet.

"We're a queer pair, ain't we?" She steps out of her petticoat and spins them around, pushing Eva onto the bed. "A woman of vice and a sweet, untouched flower girl." Their positions reversed, she gets on her knees and starts work on Eva's boot laces.

"Not untouched for very much longer, or so I hope." Eva makes herself blush.

Cracking a voluptuous smile, Mary Jane pulls off Eva's tattered boots, then bends forward and removes her makeshift garters: a pair of frayed silk ribbons. She does so with her teeth, emitting a deep growl, her playful antics making Eva giggle.

The white stockings come last, and as Mary Jane gets to the bottom of the second leg, she realizes next door's fallen silent. "Listen." She flings the laddered cotton hose away and crawls onto the bed. "It's gone quiet."

Easing herself forward, she maneuvers Eva into a supine position and lies beside her, stealing one lip-lock after another, igniting Eva's passions.

"Do you want to fuck?" She moves Eva's dark locks away from her neck, peppering her bare skin with kisses. "Tell me, darling." She trails her fingers over Eva's body, leaving goose bumps in their wake. "Is this what you want?"

"Oh, yes, do it to me." Eva mewls, her thighs opening readily. "I want it so."

Keen for the first taste of her, Mary Jane sinks between Eva's spread legs, ready to put her tongue to work, but her operations are abruptly stymied by a series of astonished ejaculations from Missus Sullivan, Billy having unexpectedly returned home for another poke.

"For heaven's sake." Mary Jane flops onto her back. "I give up."

Eva snuggles onto her chest. "It's all right, they'll be done soon enough. He never lasts more than a few minutes when he's in one of his ruts."

To pass the time—and partially to drown out the noise—Mary Jane croons an old Irish song, expecting her musical interlude to outlast the poking, but before she gets to the third verse, it no longer matters: Eva is snoring.

CHAPTER 11

Friday, March 4, 1887

MARY JANE WAKES ALONE, REACHING OUT TO CARESS A warm body that isn't there, disappointed when her hand makes contact with nothing but cool, empty sheets. Assuming Eva's already left for work, she rolls onto her back and dips a hand beneath the covers.

She's preparing to remedy the lingering frustration of spending an infuriatingly fuckless night in her young lover's arms when the door creaks open and Eva comes in fully dressed, carrying a selection of food stuffs on two filled plates.

"You're awake." She beams. "I was hoping you would be."

"Whatchu got there?" Mary Jane withdraws her hand and rubs her eyes, squinting to see.

"Breakfast." Eva sets the plates on the table. "Bacon, sausages, bread, and eggs."

"You didn't have to do that," Mary Jane mumbles through a yawn.

"I wanted to." Eva picks up her skirts and clambers onto the bed, stealing a peck from Mary Jane's lips. "You've been so good to me."

"Well, that's because I seem to have developed a great weakness for you." Mary Jane slides a hand around Eva's waist, yanking her down to the palliasse. "Have you noticed?"

"Aye." Eva grins. "And I reckon I have one for you n'all."

Still feeling spreeish, Mary Jane lets some of her lusts escape unchecked. "Take off your clothes and come back to bed awhile. I should like to hold you."

Eva does so directly, stripping to her white stockings and chemise and diving back into bed without question or hesitation, promptly tumbling into Mary Jane's outstretched arms and welcoming a rapid peppering of kisses on her lips.

"You know how I feel about you, don't you?" Mary Jane runs the tip of her thumb over Eva's mouth. "How desperately I want to have you." She moves closer, taking Eva's chemise-covered breast in her hand for the first time.

Eva offers a faint murmur of appreciation for Mary Jane's sudden bawdiness, her passions stirred by her first dose of such lewd talk accompanied by the touch of a warm hand.

"That don't scare you?" Mary Jane wants to make sure, teasing Eva's nipple between her fingers, making it stiff. "If it does, I'll restrain myself."

Eva groans, shaking her head and arching her back, pressing her breast into Mary Jane's palm. "Why ought it scare me when I want it just the same?"

"Let's take this old thing off, then." Mary Jane fingers the shoulder strap of Eva's chemise. "Show me your charms."

"You first." Eva blushes.

In a second, Mary Jane's chemise is cast off, flung onto the washstand, and she's helping Eva off with hers. As she pulls the cotton up and over Eva's head, whisking it away, Eva brings an arm across her chest, clutching one breast and squishing the other behind her forearm, suddenly bashful. Lying back down, she flings her other arm over her petite bosom for good measure, grasping a breast in each hand and keeping them hidden.

"Them's only small," she mumbles apologetically. "Not at all like yours."

"Don't be shy." Mary Jane eases her hands away. "Let me look at you."

Concerned that she won't be enough of a woman for Mary Jane's tastes, Eva closes her eyes and lets her arms go limp, allowing Mary Jane to manipulate her as she wishes, moving her arms and legs this way and that, posing her so as to admire her nudity from all angles.

Awaiting an appraisal, she grows forlorn, expecting the worst. "Do I look all right?"

No sooner have the words left her lips than she feels heat engulfing one of her plump nipples, the other encased in a soft palm. Peering down, she finds Mary Jane's mouth to her breast, a hot tongue swirling around the rubbery protuberance.

"You're perfect," Mary Jane assures her, breaking away temporarily. "And delicious."

As she returns her mouth to Eva's breast, sucking, tugging, and biting, Eva's legs open freely, signaling her renewed want.

Responding swiftly, Mary Jane lifts herself up and repositions between Eva's inviting thighs, working her kisses from breast to ribcage to stomach and below, stopping just short of Eva's motte before trailing back up to her chest.

It's not enough. Instinctively, Eva jerks her hips, attempting to close the gap. Bucking up toward Mary Jane's pelvis, she seeks genital contact, grunting with frustration when her repeated efforts achieve nothing but the fruitless humping of air.

Keenly aware of her young lover's restlessness, Mary Jane disengages her lips and shifts upright. Remaining on her knees, she tucks herself up to Eva's crotch, their bodies coming neatly together, her peachy skin meeting Eva's thatch of dark curls.

With a whimper of satisfaction, Eva peeks down at their joined articles, analyzing their differences. "Your grummit looks so different from mine." She waggles her bum, rubbing their contrasting mounds together. "So smooth."

"I like yours better." Mary Jane runs her fingers through Eva's pubic hair. "I have to shave mine nearly every day."

"Why?"

"Men like to see that I'm clean."

Eva digests that, but doesn't dwell on it. "My mam shaved all mine off once," she muses. "She said it was best I keep it that way if I didn't want no livestock, but I come out all in a rash and it weren't half itchy after. I said I weren't gonna do that again in a hurry, so she made me promise to keep it trimmed instead."

"You didn't care for that, neither?"

"I done it for a while, but there ain't no point so far as I can see. I washes it every other day, when I does my feet, and ain't never suffered on account of it."

"Well, I think it's delightful, just like the rest of you." Mary Jane takes Eva by the hips and thrusts forward, angling her body to ensure that clit bumps against clit.

On the second thrust, Eva gasps, her eyes opening wide in shock and realization.

"What's wrong, love?" Mary Jane stops, thinking her to be displeased.

"This is just how it was in my dream." Eva runs her hands up Mary Jane's arms and over her strong shoulders. "You was on top of me, shoving and shoving."

"With my doodle in you?" Mary Jane smirks.

"Don't tease." Eva retracts her hands and covers her burning cheeks. "I'm sure I dunno why I ever dreamed up such a wicked thing."

"I ain't teasing." Mary Jane grinds against Eva's crotch. "Was it big? Did it fill you up?"

Eva closes her eyes, recalling the dream and reliving it in vivid detail, the sympathetic movements of her hips coming naturally to her. "That would be tellings."

"Don't be coy with me, Miss Sullivan." Mary Jane leans over her, pressing their bodies together. "I think it was a beautiful dream, and if I did have a doodle, I reckon you'd give me stiff-standers night and day." She rocks her hips in rhythm, simulating phallic penetration. "I'd be up you at every available opportunity, poking you until you'd drawn every last drop of my spendings from me."

"Lor'!" Eva slides her hands around Mary Jane's back and over her rump, feeling the fucking motion of her buttocks. "I ain't never heard such words."

"Tell me everything, darling," Mary Jane urges, her voice husky and low. "Tell me how it felt when I was up you."

Eva keeps her eyes closed, relishing the friction between her thighs. "It was long and fat, and I felt it all the way inside. Like you was in my belly."

"I bet I didn't last a minute." Mary Jane fucks harder. "Did I wet inside you?"

"Yes." Eva whines, gripping Mary Jane's rear. "You put your stuff all up in me."

Mary Jane encourages Eva to wrap both legs around her waist, heels pressed to her lower back, maximizing their contact, ensuring that they come together in all the right places every time she drives forward, and it's not long before her continued exertions are rewarded with the first signs of Eva's impending peak.

"Em ..." Eva groans, feeling a tightening in her abdomen.

"What is it, my love?" Mary Jane slips one hand under Eva's bum to keep her pelvis tilted upwards. "Do you feel your pleasure coming?"

"Coming ..." is all Eva manages to rasp, bobbing her head up and down.

"Me, too." Mary Jane moves a little faster, increasing the friction. "Let it come. Oh, my darling, let it come." Her own pleasure begins to crest. "I want to spend with you."

Eva begins to shake. "Oh, I'm doing it!"

She moans loudly at the ceiling, her orgasm crashing over her, the intensity of it quite taking her by surprise. Clutching at Mary Jane's waist, she savors every cuntal spasm, wailing at a pitch that could rival her mother's.

Brought over by Eva's unrestrained cries of sexual delight, Mary Jane's climax comes upon her hard and fast. She keeps moving, but her rhythm breaks. Her legs trembling and her breathing staggered, she has difficulty holding herself up. Dropping her head into the pillow, she twitches and jerks against Eva's pulsing sex, their flesh gliding smoothly together, well lubricated by their combined lusts.

Her paroxysm over, she slows to a stop, vital parts of her anatomy too sensitive to continue. In this moment of respite, she takes time to delight in this new intimacy, their naked bodies tight against each other, breasts crushed together.

"Did that feel good, darling?" she manages to ask at length, her faculties returning to her.

Eva nods vigorously, words eluding her as she peers down to find her pubic hair matted and glistening with moisture, Mary Jane's article equally slathered in their mutual spendings. "We're all slippery." She wiggles her bum, smearing more fluid between them.

"Mm-hmm." Mary Jane kisses her lips. "We spent together."

Beaming with pride for having given Mary Jane as much pleasure as she received, even though Mary Jane was responsible for doing much of the work to achieve it, Eva writhes happily on the bed, her first full sexual experience far exceeding anything her under-educated mind could've possibly conceived.

"Did we just ... ? Was it ... ?"

Mary Jane nods, interpreting her question. "We fucked."

Eva breaks into a grin. "When can we do it again? I like the rubbing."

Barely recovered, Mary Jane dismounts and pulls Eva onto her side, rolling her into an embrace. "We can do it like that whenever you want." She runs a hand over Eva's bum. "We could even do it like we did in your dream."

"How?" Eva jabs a finger to Mary Jane's wetted mount. "You ain't got the right bits and bobs for that lark."

"Not God given," Mary Jane grants her. "But there's ways around that."

Eva thinks back to the night she saw Mary Jane possess Maria on the bed, the point of connection concealed from view. Both were nude, excepting a pink ribbon tied around Mary Jane's waist and thighs, and now she fancies that pink ribbon might be a harness of

some description. But harnessing what precisely, she still can't fathom.

"Is that how you done it with Maria?" she asks then, keen to learn. "You was doing it to her dog fashion the other night. I knows what that is."

"You saw?" Mary Jane arches an eyebrow.

"I peeped through a crack in the door," Eva admits, coloring up. "I seen your bum."

"You naughty little thing." Mary Jane bops her nose, not in the least bit angered or shocked by her voyeurism. "Do you want me to show you?"

"Show me what?"

Mary Jane leans close and whispers, "My cock."

Sadly, she never gets to find out what Eva's answer might be. A fist beats on the door to her room and a male voice booms out, "Rent's due."

Mary Jane rolls her eyes, cursing under her breath. "Just a minute." She clambers out of bed, pulls on her chemise, and delves through the pockets of her dress, digging out the key for the lockbox under her bed. "How much do you want?"

"You know how much, you cheeky mare," the voice retorts.

Mary Jane counts out a small portion of what she has in the box, puts the box back in its place, winks at Eva, then opens the door a crack, handing over the money to the deputy's grown son. "I'm a shilling short. It'll have to do."

"Again?" He ruffles a hand through his greasy mop of dandruff-flecked dark hair. "You was short a fortnight ago n'all."

Mary Jane shrugs. "So? I have to eat."

"Aye, and drink." He shakes his head and moves on to the next door.

Hoping to steal a few more minutes of nude cuddling before Eva has to get ready for work, Mary Jane locks the door and heads back to the sheets. Unfortunately, Eva's already out, stockinged, and covered up by her chemise.

"You ain't running away from me again, are you?" Mary Jane pouts, returning to the lingering warmth of the recently vacated bed.

"Not likely." Eva snorts, fastening her corset. "Not after what you just done to me." She walks over to Mary Jane's cupboard and helps herself to the lemon juice for her underarms. "Why'd you do that with the rent? You lied." She pulls on her camisole and searches for the hairbrush. "You've got plenty coin. I seen it."

"It builds trust." Mary Jane props her head up on her hand and watches Eva get dressed. "See, if I make a habit of coming up short here and there, but always pay off what I owe, then he'll come to know I mean what I say when I tell him he'll have it in a day or two. That way, heaven forbid I should ever be really stuck for coin, I'll be more likely to get a bit of extra leeway on account of my good record."

"That's clever," Eva mumbles through a mouthful of toothbrush and powder, then spits and rinses. "I wish I thought of things like that."

She hurries into the rest of her clothes and sits at the table to scoff down some food, but can't stop looking over at Mary Jane. There's a deliciously sticky mess between her thighs and she doesn't want to wash. It gives her a thrill to think of passing the whole day with the residue of Mary Jane's climax smeared on her hitherto untouched nethers, and she wants more.

"Whatchu looking at?" Mary Jane flashes her a knowing smile.

Not so many years ago, she was in Eva's shoes. Having experienced the sensual delights of female coupling for the first time—after failing to find her pleasure in the company of a man—she was in a permanent state of arousal. She yearned for the soft caresses of a woman's hands on her flesh, and wet kisses on her lips or elsewhere. Not long after, she brought a hand to herself, replicating the sensations as best she could until finding some modicum of relief, and she has no doubt that Eva will do the same before the day is out.

Indeed, already struggling to contain her burgeoning passions, Eva bites on her lower lip, abandons the food, and dives for the bed. "I still feel so randy." She straddles Mary Jane's crotch. "Is that normal?"

Mary Jane flips her onto her back, eliciting a squeal. "Have I made you hot cunted?"

"P'raps." Eva rucks her dress up around her middle, showing off her naked sex, still bedewed with their spendings. "I ain't put my drawers on yet."

What a difference a fuck makes! Mary Jane admires Eva's new found lasciviousness and the evaporation of her modesty, trailing a hand up her leg to caress her inner thigh.

"I want you so much," she coos, nuzzling her face into Eva's tresses, slipping her fingers through the teen's damp pubic curls. "Let me have you again."

"We oughtn't. I must get me-self off to work." Eva looks apologetic and conflicted, neither pushing Mary Jane away nor encouraging her to continue. "I wish I didn't, though. I'd much rather stay in this bed with you."

Ignoring that weak cautioning, Mary Jane glides her fingers beyond the firm nub of Eva's clit and curls them inward, touching her for the first time, finding the flesh of her core slick with their spendings and fresh arousal. Probing a little deeper, she feels the entrance to Eva's body, the small slit partially obstructed by a thin barrier of skin.

"Oh, my God." She stifles a groan, a small orgasm catching her off-guard.

"What's wrong?" Eva cringes. "Do it not feel right?"

"Darling, you feel incredible." Mary Jane strokes her virginity, worshipping her innocence. "Such a treasure." She gropes every inch, touching the tip of her index finger to Eva's slippery opening, tempted to push inside. "So precious." She withdraws, retreating to Eva's clit. "Let me give you another pleasure."

"Ooh, heavens, don't." Eva squirms at her touch. "I'm gonna be so late."

"Just a quick tickle," Mary Jane insists, putting her fingers to work.

Despite her initial protests, Eva succumbs to Mary Jane's skilled titillation. She opens her legs wider, rolling her hips in time with Mary Jane's caresses, and within a few short minutes, her fist is clenched around the hem of her dress as a tightness builds in her southern regions.

"I'm doing it again ... oho!" She throws her head back and quivers, her orgasm announcing itself with an involuntary jerk of her belly and several rapid contractions followed by a soft sigh and a release of tension, her limbs flopping limply to the palliasse.

A few seconds later, she smiles up at Mary Jane. "You fetched me so quickly."

"I told you I would." Mary Jane seeks out her lips for kisses.

"No, no more. Mercy!" Eva giggles, wriggling away from her. "You have to let me go." She slides off the bed and puts on her drawers. "I very much hope to see you later, though."

"Dinner? Supper? Or both?" Mary Jane snuggles back into the sheets.

Contemplating what answer to give, Eva suddenly realizes she has no money left to buy herself dinner while she's working. As she brings a hand to her empty pocket, there being nothing in it but crumbs and lint, a crease of panic spreads across her brow.

"What's that face for?" Mary Jane indicates her frown.

"I spent all my money on breakfast," Eva admits, feeling foolish. "I didn't think ..." She glances at her offering of bacon, sausages, bread, and eggs. "I just wanted to do summink nice for you, and now I ain't got nuthin' left to buy stock." She turns her gaze back to Mary Jane. "What am I gonna do?"

Mary Jane can't help it; she laughs. She tries to suppress it by pressing her face into the pillow and feigning a cough, but the earnestness of Eva's distress is so disproportionate to the triviality of her dilemma that she finds it impossible not to find humor in the matter. Then a sausage hits her in the back of the head.

"Ow!"

"Well, don't be mean." Tears well in Eva's eyes. "It ain't funny."

"Oh, darling, sshhh." Mary Jane straightens her face and pats the bed. "Come here." She snatches up the sausage missile and takes a bite out of it as Eva settles beside her.

"Can I borrow from you?" Eva loathes having to ask, the furrows in her brow deepening. "I'll give it you right back, I swear. I ain't never owed nuthin' to no-one in my life."

"Listen here." Mary Jane munches on the cold sausage. "You can have the money—of course you can, it goes without saying—but it comes with two conditions."

"Name 'em."

"First"—Mary Jane waggles the sausage stump at her—"you shan't be borrowing it, you'll be taking it."

Eva opens her mouth to object, but Mary Jane shoves the remainder of the sausage into her gaping yap before she can get a word out.

"Second," she goes on, "you let me do the taking care from now on, eh? You just worry about staying straight and coming home safe. Leave the rest for me to sort out, all right?"

Eva gulps down the sausage. "I don't wanna be a burden to you."

"You ain't." Mary Jane dries her weepy eyes. "I wanna be sweet with you, so let me." She rubs Eva's arm soothingly. "I ain't good at much, but I know how to care for a woman."

Eva forces a small smile. "I'm sure as I dunno what I've done to deserve someone as good as you doting on me. I can't even buy you breakfast without making a muck of it."

"Don't fret it, love." Mary Jane points to her clothing on the table. "There's coin in my pocket. How much do you need?"

Eva shrugs, not wanting to take advantage of her generosity. "Two bob?"

"Is that all?" Mary Jane strokes her back, knowing that two shillings won't leave her much for food and incidentals after buying the flowers she needs from Covent Garden market. "Take a half-crown to be sure."

Somewhat forlornly, Eva picks herself up, crosses the room, and fishes a half-crown out of Mary Jane's pocket, holding it to her chest like gold.

"Why's you so good to me? Tell me honest." She returns to the bed. "Why me and not some other girl? There's prettier ones about, I'm sure."

"No, there ain't."

Unaccustomed to receiving compliments, Eva's bashfulness returns, her gaze dropping to her lap. "There's more experienced girls, I knows that."

"But your innocence is part of what I love." Mary Jane runs her fingers through Eva's mane. "I don't even remember a time when I was as pure as you." She lays a kiss on Eva's pinkened cheek. "And I would do anything to keep you from falling into my bad ways."

Eva intercepts another kiss aimed for her cheek and takes it on her lips instead, then breaks away. "I'd best go."

"Do." Mary Jane relinquishes her. "Before I drag you back into this bed with me."

Still clutching the half-crown, Eva retrieves her grimy, third-hand boots off the floor, the soles more padded with horse dung than they are rubber. Two new holes have appeared in the worn leather since she started working as a flower girl, and they don't have much life left. Nor do her laces. Constructed from various bits of twine knotted together, they must be tied with extreme care and caution, lest they should snap.

Sitting at the table, easing the twine through the eyelets, she takes one last look at the crispy bacon on the laden breakfast plate, burning the image of the fried rashers into her mind. No longer feeling as though she has any claim on the enticing victuals, given that Mary Jane effectively paid for every morsel, she limits herself to a quick sniff.

"Take it." Mary Jane gives up her acquired rights to the meat. "You'll be on your trotters all day. You need it more than I do."

That's all Eva needs to hear. In a second, her hungry hands are on the bacon, stuffing it into her pocket along with the half-crown. "I'll make it up to you," she mumbles, also pilfering a chunk of the bread. "I swear I will."

As she hurries off, Mary Jane rolls onto her back and rubs sleep out of her eyes, trying to summon the energy to get up and eat. Realizing her fingers still smell like Eva, she runs the tip of her middle digit through her lips, sucking the faint taste of Eva's sex onto her tongue.

That's better than a breakfast of cold eggs and bread any day.

CHAPTER 12

HAVING CLEARED UP THE REMAINS OF BREAKFAST AND gone back to bed, Mary Jane sleeps for several more hours, roused at last by the angry barking of a stray dog that's competing with some local children for scraps of discarded food in the gutter.

A gurgle in her stomach tells her it's dinnertime, so she rises and heads out, grabbing a quick bite to eat before checking in at the post office on Whitechapel High Street.

There's just one piece of correspondence for her.

A short note in a plain envelope.

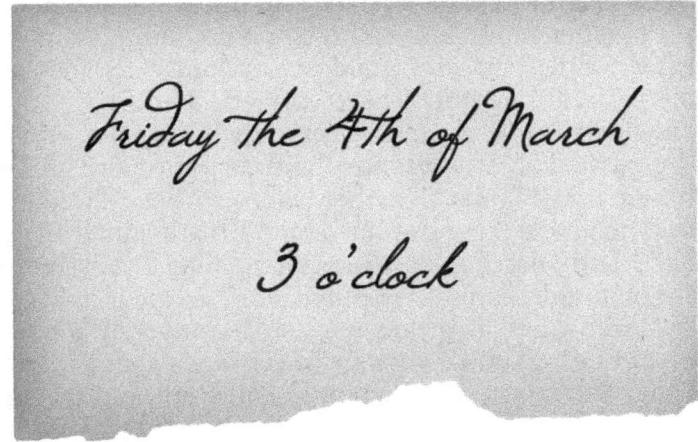

Friday the 4th of March

3 o'clock

Friday, March 4, at three o'clock.

That's today.

The note's not signed, but she knows who it's from. She has only one amour who so fears the exposure of their doings that all correspondence is written under a feigned hand, never daring to leave even the faintest trace left of who might've penned it: Missus B——. A West End amour whose name she's sworn never to utter. A female amour. A married woman of title, who would be badly injured if word of their clandestine assignations ever spilled.

For her discretion, Mary Jane is rewarded handsomely. Over time, she's received a silk chemise, two new corsets, some silk stockings, a dress or two, and many other things besides. This woman is the wealthiest customer on her list of specials, and also bears the distinction of being the only one she looks forward to seeing. The only one who doesn't make her cringe. The only one who ever makes her spend.

The latter gives her some cause for concern now, on account of her blossoming relationship with Eva, but she puts that out of her mind. As long as she has no pleasure with her from hereon out, then their arrangement is no different from that of any other paid liaison.

Convincing herself of that, she hurries back to Thrawl Street, destroys the note on the fire in the kitchen, and returns to her room. To prepare for this meeting, she drags a leather steamer trunk out from under her bed and dons her finest attire, the trunk containing two silk dresses with perfectly modest necklines, some silk hosiery, and another new corset. For this more sophisticated look, she abandons her white apron, applies no lip paste, and even spends the time to properly pin up her hair. Lastly, she fixes her violet to her new outfit, checks to make sure she has some breath mints in her pocket, and snatches up the glass phallus she keeps on the shelf underneath her washbasin.

At almost eight inches long, with a tapered, bulbous knob at one end and a very slight curve, its shape mimics the male member. At the root, it flares out and has one hole on either side of its slightly concave base. Through

these holes, silk ribbon is to be fed, and Mary Jane unties two silk bows from the headboard of her bed for this purpose.

Packing all into a small box padded with linen rags to protect the delicate glass, she leaves Thrawl Street and makes for Commercial Street, shortly passing the familiar face of Edmund Reid: a detective inspector with the Metropolitan Police's J Division in Bethnal Green.

He's lurking pensively in the doorway of the Princess Alice public house opposite the Victoria Home: an imposing four-storey lodging house exclusively for working men. His dark eyes are fixed on the main entrance, as if waiting for someone to emerge, his lips taut, almost completely concealed by his full beard and mustache.

There's tension in the forty-one-year-old's jaw, the muscles bulging behind his thick salt-and-pepper sideburns, the rest of his short locks hidden beneath a pristine bowler hat. Deep, permanent furrows in his brow are the marks of a man with heavy thoughts, his fists clenched in the pockets of his gray tweed suit.

Spotting Mary Jane immediately, he tips his hat to her. "Miss Kelly."

"Inspector." She acknowledges him with a nod and a warm smile as she walks past, not intending to strike up a conversation, but he follows her, matching her pace.

"May I walk with you a way?" Coming up shoulder to shoulder with her, he's an inch shorter, but his hat makes up for it.

"Could I stop you?" Mary Jane doesn't break stride.

As she steps off the curb, she lifts her skirts so they don't drag in the accumulated pile of manure, straw, and other debris that litters the gutters, and Reid holds his hand out for hers, offering to aid and escort her across the busy street.

Not used to such chivalry, she laughs, accepting the proffered hand. "Heavens, Inspector. You must be mistaking me for a proper lady."

"You look lady enough to me," he flatters her, looping her arm through his.

"Magic what a bit of purple silk can do, eh?"

"It's not just the silk, Miss Kelly. A whore in silk is still a whore when the money's on the table, but you have not the temperament of a gay woman, nor a liking for the work. I confess, your insistence that you should belong to such a class quite confuses me. You're an educated woman, and you can't hide that, as much as you do try."

"I fear you're imbuing me with altogether too much grace, Inspector. And I must warn you, if you continue to build up that pedestal you're placing me on, I shall have a frightful tumble down to Earth when you finally see the truth of me."

"Truth? I daresay there's not a soul in London who knows the truth of you, Miss Kelly. The tale of the prepossessing Irish girl who was married and widowed young, became destitute, and fell into a bad life is a good one for your customers, I'm sure, but I wouldn't go nearly so far as to call it the truth. What was the tragic accident that took your dear husband's life again? An oil lamp explosion?"

Mary Jane stops in her tracks, turning to face him. "A mining disaster." She looks him dead in the eyes, a smile tickling at her lips. "Are you trying to catch me out, Inspector?"

"Are you admitting there's something to be caught?"

Mary Jane lets the smile free. "Nice game." She turns her back on him. "I have to go."

He grabs her elbow and holds her back.

"Oi!" She smacks at his hand, still smiling. "I've got an appointment to keep."

"He's here." Reid holds onto her, forcing her to listen, all levity gone. "He's been hanging around Whitechapel."

Mary Jane's smile falls. "Aye, I know."

"You've seen him?"

"He spotted me on the street last night." Her stomach turns over, unsettled by the brief sighting of Fleming. "Didn't say aught to me, mind."

"Well, if he does—if he gives you any bother—you be sure to let me know."

"Why would I?" Mary Jane shakes her head. "I'm grateful for your concern, and all that you've done for me,

but I'm no longer under the purview of your division, Inspector. What goes on in this quarter should be of no concern to a Bethnal Green copper." She tries to walk away, but Reid won't let go.

"I'm being transferred to Whitechapel," he informs her. "Before the year is out."

"You poor bastard." Mary Jane flashes him a look of pity. "Whatever did you do to deserve that?"

"Nothing of any importance."

She eyes him curiously, not sure if she believes him. "Certainly nothing at all on my account, I hope."

He ignores that.

"I found you in the street," he reminds her. "You were lying prone in the Gosset Street gutter, beaten within an inch of your life by the man you thought was your protector. If he was a threat to you then, he's a threat to you now, and in all good conscience, I cannot look away."

Mary Jane's memories of that night are splintered and foggy. Of the initial beating, she can only recollect the first punch. It blindsided her, knocked her clean off her feet, and sent her to the filthy floor of their two-room Bethnal Green lodgings.

When she was down, she was kicked repeatedly, the brutal assault leaving deep purple boot-print-shaped bruises all over her chest and mid-region. At some point, that wasn't good enough and he straddled her, choking her until she passed out. She knew that when she saw the finger-shaped bruises on her neck.

Believing her dead, drunken Fleming then took all the money she had in her pockets and quit their rooms, returning to the pub he hadn't long left. He was still gone when she regained consciousness twenty minutes later, and she didn't hesitate. Though groggy and in agonizing pain, she gathered up her few belongings in her steamer trunk—the very same one she had when she first came to London—and bolted, having not a farthing to her name.

Dizzy and weak, she staggered and stumbled through Bethnal Green, sticking to the back alleys and side streets so as to remain out of sight. Unable to catch her breath, her progress was slow. She wheezed and

gasped, struggling to keep going despite the pain shooting through her chest with every draw of breath, but it was too much.

Exhausted, she slumped against a wall at the end of a row of tenements, where she was promptly set upon by a gang of roughs from the nearby Old Nichol rookery. Surrounding her, taunting and jeering at her, they shoved her off the pavement and into the gutter, the fall into the debris strewn street twisting her ankle and jarring her wrist.

Collapsing there, clutching her trunk, defending her worldly goods from theft, she anticipated another assault and braced herself for it, but the next hands she felt upon her person were lifting her up out of the street and the roughs were scattering like startled pigeons.

It was Inspector Reid.

He wanted to take her straight to the infirmary, but she wouldn't hear of it. From there, having no place of residence and no employment, she'd have taken a short trip to the local workhouse, and she'd rather have died than be locked up there.

Ignoring her pleadings to be left as she was, hurt and alone, Reid took her home. Out of his own pocket, he paid for a doctor to assess her injuries, and his wife, Emily, settled her in the guest bedroom of their modest lodgings.

She slept for twelve hours straight. Upon waking in crippling pain, her entire body feeling as though she'd gone fifteen rounds in a boxing ring, she had no idea where she was. After a panicked shriek came confusion, tears, and finally, recollection. According to the doctor, the sum of the damage was a sprained ankle and wrist, two black eyes, a few broken ribs, a bad head, and a whole lot of welts and bruises.

Though she tried to get up and leave—wearing only a borrowed nightgown—her ankle gave out in the hall and she had to be carried back to the bed by the kindly inspector, whose wife then spent much time by her bedside, tending to her as she needed.

Little by little, she regained her strength, her fractures healed, and during this time, she found herself

incorporated into Reid family life. She ate their food, drank their brandy, and played with their two children. When she was completely laid up, she read books and sketched. When she could walk a few steps, she helped Emily in the kitchen.

At mealtimes, she found Reid surprisingly open to the opinions of women. They conversed at depth on such topics as local politics, the moral degradation of London, women's emancipation, and the right to vote. In return, he was surprised to find her so articulate and well-spoken, though she stuck rigidly to the tale of her provenance: born in Ireland, moved to Wales as a young child, married a Welshman, was widowed, became destitute, and went wrong.

Her father? The gaffer at an ironworks.

Any siblings? Plenty.

How old when married? Sixteen.

To every question, an answer. Each one entirely believable in its mundanity.

Weeks passed this way and all went well, excepting one embarrassing incident when Reid knocked upon her bedroom door to offer her a cup of tea, and she, knowing they were alone in the house, mistook his solicitation of her company for something else entirely.

Thinking the inevitable time had come, she sat further back on the bed and pulled up her skirts, whereupon Reid shielded his eyes with his hand and turned his back, his astonishment quite genuine—and hers equally so.

"Not all men are animals, Miss Kelly," he assured her, cutting her off in the midst of a profuse and rambling apology.

Utterly perplexed, and disconcerted by his altruism, Mary Jane then tried to pack up her things, intent on making herself scarce after disgracing herself in such a manner, but Reid stopped her.

"You'll remain till you're well," he insisted. "And we'll speak no more of this."

Then he made the tea.

In time, she did get well, and she did leave. Reid sent her on her way with a half-sovereign: enough to pay for a week's rent and buy herself some food.

She wouldn't make a police report. It was a singular act of violence, she said. A fit of rage or madness. Fleming had never done such a thing before, and wouldn't have the chance to do it again. To protect herself from him, she went to the most over-crowded place in the East End: Whitechapel. Here, she could disappear among the slums and lodging houses, living anonymously and quietly while saving enough money to buy herself a one-way train ticket to somewhere far, far away. She thought she'd be difficult to find. Apparently not difficult enough, she reflects, glancing up the street in the direction of the Queen's Head, half expecting to see Fleming standing there.

"You should've let me make a report," Reid grumbles at her for the umpteenth time.

"What good that?" Mary Jane rolls her eyes. "It'd be the word of a common harlot against a good, honest working man. You know as well as I that the magistrates would've acquitted him, and then what? He comes after me again and does worse."

"He ill-used you. You were afraid."

"I haven't forgotten, and I shall keep well clear, I promise you." She takes a half step away. "But now I really must be going."

"Before you do, let me help." He reaches out to her. "You appear to have something shiny caught in your hair."

In the midst of Mary Jane's momentary confusion, he flutters his fingertips behind her ear, using well-practiced sleight of hand trickery to magic a polished half-crown out of thin air, having it drop into the palm of his hand with a gentle tug on her earlobe.

"There you are." He shows it to her. "All yours."

Enchanted by the trick, though it's not the first time she's seen it, her lips curl into a fresh smile, yet she hesitates to take the coin, regarding it suspiciously. "What do you want for it?"

"Only the satisfaction of knowing you'll take one less risk today."

"You're a sweet man, Inspector Reid." She accepts the monetary offering with a sigh. "A rare commodity indeed, so I've found."

Parting from him, she walks to the junction of Whitechapel High Street and Leman Street—a stone's throw from H Division police headquarters—where she's picked up by a brougham: a private, single-horse-drawn, two-door carriage.

Black, with a golden trim around the door, it's sleek and elegant and kept in perfect order, being regularly cleaned of the splattered dirt and horse muck kicked up from the street by its four large, slender wheels.

Seeing Mary Jane approach, the driver hops down from his perch and opens the door for her, helping her inside. It smells like clean leather. The walls have been recently polished, the mirror buffed, and Mary Jane checks her appearance once more as she slides onto the padded blue velvet seat. It's a comfortable ride. Much more agreeable than the cheap, overcrowded omnibuses which all too often stink of sweat and feet, or the single-horse, two-wheeled hansom carriages available for public hire. There's also less chance of picking up ticks, mites, or some other vile infestation.

After a short ride, traffic being in their favor, the brougham drops Mary Jane off at Seven Dials: a large circular street junction at the southern tip of Camden borough, not far from what remains of the notorious St. Giles rookery. From here, she heads south, passing a clumsy hodge-podge of shops, public houses, tenements, and lodging houses, all crammed into irregular triangular configurations. She stops for nothing and talks to no-one, wishing she had a veil to conceal her identity.

When the street she's on reaches its terminus, she turns onto Lichfield Street, the angular division of the streets creating yet another triangular parcel of land, this one comprised mostly of private dwellings. Along it, the large, imposing houses are split into several different residences, single rooms or entire floors being let out to young families or wedded couples.

On this street, however, there is one building that's licensed as a lodging house. At least, that's what it says in the city records. In reality, it is—and has for quite some time been, under varying ownership and control—a first-rate house of accommodation. That is to say, it's a type of brothel where the rooms are let out by the hour or night, no questions asked.

No girls work in the house, although a good number who frequent it are regulars. This is just one house of many in this locality where *les grandes horizontales* of Leicester Square and the surrounding area can bring their customers, should they not desire to take them home to their private lodgings. Known to be a discreet house, it's favored by those who require an extra degree of secrecy surrounding their furtive assignations. It's the only house Missus B—— will consent to patronize, and moreover, it's the only house Mary Jane feels comfortable frequenting. Any further west and she'd risk running into the people known to her from her early days in London, the outcome of which would surely not be pleasant.

Shuddering to think of it, Mary Jane raps her fist on the street door, her knock responded to promptly and without fuss by a plump woman in her early thirties. This woman, the landlady—well fed on the profits of the house—recognizes her at a glance and lets her in, asking nothing of her.

"Is my friend already here?" Mary Jane inquires, her skirts rustling as she moves through the narrow, carpeted hallway.

"Aye." The landlady nods, pointing to the staircase. "Front room, first floor."

CHAPTER 13

ALL THE ROOMS IN THIS HOUSE OF ACCOMMODATION ARE impeccably clean and richly decorated, giving the place an air of sophistication, despite its purpose. It's a first-rate house, with first-rate prices.

Skipping up the staircase, Mary Jane makes her way across the landing, passing several closed doors behind which an endless stream of girlish giggles, voluptuous sighs, and bawdy ejaculations can be heard. At the front room, she knocks twice sharply and opens the door on a lavishly bedecked bedroom lit by three oil lamps, the heavy velvet curtains drawn for privacy, and to keep out the stench of horse sweat that hangs perpetually on the London air.

A four-poster bed takes up much of the available space, the rest occupied by a plush sofa by the fire, a mahogany vanity, and a small bedside table upon which sits a bottle of brandy and two glasses.

The carpeted floor absorbs sound, as do the tapestries hanging on the walls, and for added discretion, the bed and sofa have been pulled several inches away from the walls so as to eliminate the risk of any telltale thudding.

On the vanity, a bowl of water sits in a cradle above a candle, the flame keeping the water hot. Beside the vanity, an elaborately carved washstand is prepared for

use, the basin clean and the ewer full of fresh water. Plenty of towels are in ready supply on a nearby rack.

For the convenience of guests, there's a chamber pot tucked beneath the bed, and an abundant array of cushions and pillows in varying shapes and sizes have been placed throughout the room, along with a variety of mirrors. Small and large, these mirrors can be positioned anywhere, upright or lengthways, however it suits the couple's pleasure. Today, though, they're pushed off to the side; this lady has no interest in watching herself fuck.

Though nearing forty, Missus B—— is a beautiful woman in every degree. She's well-built, from her dainty ankles to her full bosom, her exquisite curves and narrow waist epitomizing the fashionable figure of the day. From top to bottom, her skin is soft, unblemished, and pale as the moon. Her long yellow tresses, curled and pinned high on her head, shimmer in the warm glow of the room's oil lamps. She's always groomed to perfection, draped in silk and lace, her neck adorned with diamonds, though her beauty needs no ornament.

From sitting primly on the bed, she rises and steps forward to greet her cyprian lover. "I had such difficulty getting away"—she extends her arms for a hug, a pair of white kid gloves gripped in one hand—"but I had to see you."

Mary Jane places the dildo package on the nearby sofa—upon which Missus B——'s pristine drawers have already been folded—and accepts the embrace. "Did you miss me?"

"I always do."

"Have you been frigging yourself?"

"Oh, hish!" Missus B—— draws back and bats the kid gloves at her, feigning shock. "What cheek of you to ask a lady such a thing."

Though she plays the part of the innocent and virtuous, her smile gives her away: she enjoys the taunting. She likes to hear Mary Jane use bawdy language—it gets her steam up—and Mary Jane has no objection to this manner of foreplay.

158

"I know you give yourself a tickle," she goes on, walking Missus B—— backwards toward the bed. "Does it bring you pleasure?" She slides her hands over the lady's rump, giving her a squeeze and a light tap. "Do you think of me when you spend?"

Missus B—— nods, whimpering, stumbling over her own feet, the kid gloves slipping from her grasp and becoming trodden underfoot. "Every time."

Her ego boosted by that admission, Mary Jane gets bolder. "Is your cunt longing for me now?" She lets her breath kiss the older woman's neck. "Wait." She puts two fingers to her lips. "Don't answer. Let me see for myself." She drives a hand up Missus B——'s skirts and feels her core, finding that anticipation alone has already suitably roused her lusts. "Oh, you're so randy." She pushes two fingers inside, paddling in her lubricity. "You must want a fuck dreadfully."

Missus B—— mewls, clutching the bedpost.

"Tell me," Mary Jane insists. "Tell me you want a fuck."

"Do let me down," Missus B—— pleads, her legs threatening to give out beneath her. "I shall go into a faint if you don't."

"Say it." Mary Jane grips her tighter, probing deep into her moist channel.

"Oh, I shan't," Missus B—— protests with little feeling, the way a woman always does when she knows she's being asked to do something unbecoming of a lady. "Don't be so lewd."

"I want to hear you say it." Mary Jane gives her no respite, groping her all the harder for her refusal to comply. "Tell me what you want, else I shan't do it."

Weakening to desire, Missus B—— moans softly, her head lolling onto Mary Jane's shoulder. "I want you to fuck me."

With that, Mary Jane shoves her onto the bed and throws up her silk skirts and petticoats, kneeling between her flailing legs to inspect the state of her loins, baring the untamed thatch of flaxen hair on her motte and the delicate pink flesh beneath.

"Does this pretty little cunt need to be kissed?" she asks, flicking her tongue over a largish, well-formed clit. "I know it does."

"Yes, yes, yes." Missus B—— drapes one leg over Mary Jane's shoulder, the other flung over the footboard. "Kiss it." She wriggles her bum to the edge of the bed. "Lick it, please. I'm thrilling for a spend."

As always in their meetings, it's not long before Missus B—— loses herself in the spirit of fucking, her true bawdy colors showing through her prim and proper façade.

Deprived of such delights at home, she's as randy and lewd as they come. Her husband, a degenerate gambler and whoremonger, caught a clap from a cheap French paphian four years ago and very kindly brought it home and shared it with her. Ever since then, she's refused to tend to her wifely duties for fear of contracting something far worse—heaven forbid, something incurable—and thus has rendered herself chaste and miserable, with nothing but her right hand for comfort. That is, until she met Mary Jane.

Their secret assignations are her only solace, and as Mary Jane puts mouth to cunt—something which her husband, considering it vulgar and beastly, has never once attempted—she begins to shiver, her first pleasure arriving in under a minute.

"I'll never know how you do that so well," she exclaims, pausing to catch her breath for a few seconds before tearing off her clothes, stripping down to her diaphanous chemise, stockings, and boots.

Doing the same, Mary Jane opens the package she brought with her and pulls out the dildo, placing it carefully in the bowl of hot water above the flame to let it warm while she discards everything but her decadent blue satin corset, silk stockings, and boots.

When it's sufficiently heated, she plucks it out of its bath and passes the silk ribbon through the holes at the root, fastening the top ribbon securely around her waist before passing the lower ribbons between her legs and tying them at her hips.

"Do get it in me," Missus B—— begs, ogling the phallus with greedy, lust-filled eyes as she lies back on the bed and tugs her chemise up to her navel. "I so need it."

For all that she's a lady, Mary Jane's never seen anyone so desirous of a fuck. Buttocks wiggling and chest heaving, Missus B—— waits impatiently to be lanced, closing her eyes so as to relish the sensation as Mary Jane clambers over her, cock in hand, and rubs the bulbous head along the furrow of her glistening sex, letting it tease her enlarged clit before directing it lower and pushing it through her puffy labia.

As the hot shaft pierces her, she cries out, jerking her pelvis up to embed the cock deeper, accepting every inch into her neglected body in a single thrust, all the while proclaiming her love of a big prick and shaming her husband for being outdone by a woman.

Undeniably, she likes to be fucked, and to be fucked hard. Never has Mary Jane come away from one of their sessions having administered anything less than five pokes and several lickings, during which the fine lady spends frequently and copiously.

It's always a licking first, followed by a deep, firm fuck that brings her off twice more before she demands to feel the gentle sucking of Mary Jane's mouth accompanied by three groping fingers. By then abundantly wet, she'll often roll onto her belly and present her white, round bum, liking Mary Jane to plug her dog fashion as she screams into the pillow.

It's her letch to feel the cock ramming into her fast and deep, and to feel the pain of it as it relentlessly batters the gateway to her womb, safe in the knowledge that no ill can come of their connection. This is pure fucking for the sheer pleasure of it, and it's at this juncture of their union that she usually begins to gush.

Such is her delight at receiving Mary Jane's prick in this attitude, with great force and violence, that her whole body shakes quite tremendously. Barely breathing, she'll tuck her head down and whine through her pleasure as a steady stream of her salt effusion flows from her and wets the counterpane.

Temporarily sated, she'll then collapse on the bed, requiring several minutes of respite before flopping languidly onto her back and urging Mary Jane to lick her once more.

If she's feeling particularly lewd or lickerish, and craving the male article, she'll roll onto her side and suck her own spendings off Mary Jane's cock while Mary Jane laps up her quim, but this is a rare game, and when over, she never fails to minimize her part in it.

"You make me so lewd," she grumbles, as if it's only at Mary Jane's insistence that she should be coerced into doing such a filthy thing.

In any case, whatever the order or variance of her fancies, this routine of licking and sucking and fucking continues until both women are exhausted, the pair stopping only for a glass of brandy here and there, or to tend to the call of nature.

At the finish of it, her sex burning and throbbing, Missus B—— finally, begrudgingly, relinquishes Mary Jane's ever-ready prick and declares herself to be all fucked out before she slips into a comfortable doze.

Mary Jane, on the other hand, never sleeps, but rests quietly, taking a few sips of brandy and watching the fire burn, remembering a time when all her days were spent like this: in a decorated bedroom with the finest sheets, tending to the sexual needs of lords and ladies, Colonels and Commandants, and even the occasional prince.

Lounging there, she keeps an eye on the clock, being sure to rouse Missus B—— before their time in the room expires so that she might have the opportunity for one more fucking of her choice before they part ways.

"Do you want to make use of me again?" she asks, reaching down to fondle the amorous housewife's hot, sticky nethers.

"I'm exhausted." Missus B—— turns onto her back, yawning. "But do me once more before you leave. Just a quick poke."

Mary Jane grins. How much she enjoys having a prick up her! Even if it is made of glass. Getting into position, she mounts Missus B—— for the last time, the cock gliding into her well-fucked hole without resistance.

162

"Oh, I'm so sore." Missus B—— winces. "But I want you up me."

Her own body aching, her muscles fatigued from so much strenuous action, her thighs like jelly, Mary Jane holds Missus B—— in a close embrace and fucks into her with slow, deep plunges so as to cause the least amount of friction, stirring the cock inside her on every upstroke.

In this intimate position, Missus B—— reaches around Mary Jane's back and clasps both hands over her tensed buttocks, pulling her deeper.

"Fuck me, fuck me, fuck me," she murmurs breathlessly, all sham modesty lost in the in the heat of the operation. "I love the way you fuck. Your prick ... my cunt ..."

When she reaches her final orgasm of the session, she shivers, gasps, and spends, and in the grip of it, Mary Jane can resist her own pleasure no longer.

Through it all, she's been able to restrain herself, but in this position, with their bodies nestled so snugly together, her clit is receiving altogether too much stimulation. That, combined with the erotic thrill of delivering Missus B—— another spend, fetches her immediately.

Yielding to it, she grunts and bears down harder, her jaw clenching as the first unwanted contraction ripples through her, her body rejecting all mental efforts to suppress her enjoyment, though it is dulled somewhat.

As her peak hits, she'll quite often envisage her cock erupting inside the woman beneath her, spilling her imaginary seminal libation into the fertile womb of her lover, but not today. When the business is over with—indeed, even before the involuntary spasms cease—she wants nothing more than to leap off the bed and wash away all trace of arousal, but as is recently her habit, Missus B—— has her trapped.

Liking to lie with the prick buried in her for a long as possible, squeezing her love-trap around it, delighting in the feeling of being stretched open by the thick rod—there being no immediate reason to rush to the washbasin for the purpose of performing any post-coital

ablutions—she has her shapely legs wrapped around Mary Jane's back, preventing her from withdrawing.

"That was beautiful," she whispers at last, releasing her hold. "I'm sated."

Seething with anger at herself, Mary Jane uncunts directly she's released and heads straight for the washstand, stripping off the dildo along the way.

In the years since she first took to whoring, she's felt plenty dirty. The first time she accepted a prick in her mouth, she was so revolted by the deed that she spat out his stiffened pipe, tumbled off the bed, and threw up in the chamber pot. Of course, the gentleman—if you could call him that—in a state of equal repulsion on account of the sound of her retching and the foul stink of her regurgitated stomach contents, upped and left in a huff, declaring quite sternly that he should never call upon the house again. That, of course, resulted an irate bawd and the prompt dispensing of what she considered to be a fitting punishment.

For the rest of the night, Mary Jane was forced to kneel on the floor, her arms and legs bound behind her as prick after prick was directed into the room to receive oral pleasure from her while she sobbed her way through one miserable minette after another, receiving not a penny for her troubles.

When the first prick spat its salty emission in her mouth, she felt she might choke. It hit the back of her throat and started to trickle down her gullet before she was able to pull away and dispense of it in the chamber pot beside her. After the second, she *wanted* to choke and be done with it. Let them toss her body in the Thames. Let the rats eat her. After the fifth, she threw up again. There being nothing left in her stomach, she brought up bile. It burned her throat, but did at least leave a better aftertaste than that of male spendings.

By the time she'd serviced the last, she was, if nothing else, fully in control of her gag reflex and fairly expert at the art of oral sperm-drawing. The harshly enacted reprimand did not succeed in breaking her distaste of the operation, though. Every time she parts

her lips to receive another cock, her stomach churns. In those moments, she feels most like the harlot that she is.

Whore.

Tart.

Pinchcock.

Slut.

Yet never was she more a slut than today. She could take a thousand pricks in her mouth, or her commodity, and still she'd not be half the loose bitch she is for fucking another woman—and having the audacity to like it—mere hours after claiming Eva.

Intent on concluding her business here as swiftly as possible, she submerges her dildo in the glass bowl above the flame and swills off Missus B——'s secretions, the frosty shift in her mood noted immediately.

"You were holding back." Missus B—— watches her intently. "Whatever for, I wonder?"

Mary Jane dries the dildo on a towel, refraining from making eye contact. "I was afraid it might bring my poorliness on, that's all. It's due today."

"Don't tell me lies," Missus B—— admonishes her. "You didn't want to spend with me. Why? What's happened to make you dull?"

Mary Jane replaces the dildo in its box, nestled in the folds of the soft linen. "I met someone," she admits slowly. "I'm not sure how she'd feel about me tending to your needs."

"She doesn't approve of your being gay?"

"This is different." Mary Jane bundles the dildo up, banishing it from view.

"Is it?" Missus B—— sits upright, resting her back on the headboard, reaching in her clutch purse for a cigarette, the luxury of smoking being one other unbefitting habit she's grown to occasionally enjoy on the sly. "There's no love here. You fuck me for money, not pleasure."

"I fuck you for both," Mary Jane corrects her. "You know I do." She pulls on her petticoats and skirts, hyperaware of her partial nudity. "I never spend with any of my other customers, but with you ..." She sighs,

annoyed by her own weakness. "I can't take a beautiful woman to bed and feel nothing."

Missus B—— lights her cigarette, tossing the spent match into her abandoned brandy glass. "Well, I'm glad. Although I confess I don't truly understand your predilections, I'm happy to know that I've been capable of pleasing you all these years. Even a little."

More than a little, Mary Jane thinks, keeping the extent of her enjoyment to herself.

"Sadly, I suppose this means you'll be terminating our arrangement?" Missus B—— reaches again for her clutch purse, removing a crisp five pound bank note and laying it on the bedside table. "Though I sincerely hope not."

Staring at the money, allowing herself to be seduced by it, Mary Jane thinks hard before she answers. "No, it doesn't."

CHAPTER 14

THE BROUGHAM LETS MARY JANE OFF AT THE SAME TOWER Hamlets junction where it picked her up, returning her to the slum where she belongs. She'd be on her way home now, except that she stops in at the first public house in her path: the Princess Alice.

It's one of her more regular Commercial Street haunts—especially when she's working. On those nights, she traipses between it and the Golden Heart on the corner of Hanbury Street, only venturing further afield when the right customer proves elusive to find, which isn't often.

Keeping the dildo package tucked under her arm, she pulls a hanky from her pocket and dabs at her damp eyes, taking care not to smudge her powder. She spent much of the return journey sobbing pitifully and sucking on the mints from her pocket, trying to get the taste of Missus B—— out of her mouth, and now she feels sordid and cheap, unworthy of Eva's affection.

Miserable and alone, she drinks away a few pence in gin, sinks deeper into self-pity, and hones in on the attentions of a potential customer at the other end of the bar. He's staring at her, and has the look of a man who's unsure whether or not the creature he's admiring is gay, and daren't risk insulting her by asking. No doubt her fine clothing has him confused, but he ought to know that

no respectable lady would walk into a pub so brazenly. In any case, to allay his uncertainty, she lets down her hair.

It has no effect. Whether he's too elevated on ale to think coherently, or simply doesn't have the courage to pick her up, he says nothing, and she's growing tired of his lecherous gaze. Knocking back the last of her drink, she leaves, turning right onto Wentworth Street and heading for home, but the man totters out behind her, trailing after her.

"Do you want something?" She turns to face him, performing a swift mental assessment.

He's short, but broad shouldered, and his hands look rough and calloused. He could probably hold his own in a fight, but not in his current state. Very nearly insensible with drink, it takes a mighty effort to plant one foot in front of the other, and Mary Jane, herself only half-screwed, sees an opportunity to take advantage of his condition.

"Are you looking for company?" she asks, softening her voice.

In response, he merely grunts and scratches at his cods, his gaze lodged at her breast, mentally divesting her of all the silk and lace.

"Does it stand?" Mary Jane points a finger at his groin, wondering if he might be too inebriated to achieve an erection. "Let me see." She palms his crotch, finding his average-sized prick half-fattened with lust and rousing it to full rigidity.

"Prick ... cunt ... fuck," he mutters, closing his eyes, humping her hand.

"Where's your lodgings?" Mary Jane terminates her manipulations.

Preoccupied with his stiff-stander, he doesn't answer.

"Oi." She taps his cheek several times quick, jolting him out of his mental fog. "Have you, or have you not, got a bed to fuck me on? Answer now."

He nods, waving his hand in a vaguely easterly direction, and it occurs to her that he may not have been following her, but simply going home. Nevertheless, she's

made her mind up to the job and won't be dissuaded from it. Besides, she deserves the punishment.

Spotting a peeler walking his beat along Commercial Street, she grabs her fuddled customer by his shirt and drags him into a service passage beside the Princess Alice, not wanting to be caught conducting her business out in the open. Here, where it reeks of piss and detritus, she throws him against the wall, half to stabilize him and stop him from tripping over his own shoelaces, and half to get him under her control.

"You got four bob?" She holds her hand out expectantly, leaving no room for negotiation.

Not that he's in a fit state to haggle, which is precisely why she prefers to find her customers in the public houses. Drunk men are freer with their coin. Quite up to fun and ready for a spree, no matter what the cost, they'll quite happily drain their pockets on a pretty face or a warm cunt, and this man is no exception.

He fumbles in his pocket, coins jangling, but he's not doing it fast enough for Mary Jane's liking. Growing impatient, she thrusts her own hand in his pocket and delves for the money, blindly calculating the value of the coins contained therein and selecting five shillings, confident that she's only taking tomorrow's drinking money and not his rent.

Upon pulling the coins out, she captures one in her palm, holds it there with her thumb, and upturns the rest into her other hand, showing the four remaining shillings to him while she pockets the concealed fifth, thereby ensuring herself a shilling regardless of whether or not a bargain can be struck for her flesh.

"Are we agreed?" she prompts him.

Bleary-eyed, he looks down at the coins, prodding a fat, clumsy finger at each one in turn, counting out loud.

Not hearing him utter anything that resembles an objection, Mary Jane pockets her fee and urges him onward, keeping on his heels as he bumbles and staggers a short way down Wentworth Street, then into the littered alleyway leading to George Yard Buildings.

She's been this way before. It's usual for her to take customers in the covered passage at the southern mouth

of the alley off Whitechapel High Street, or in the beveled archway leading into the model lodging house itself, but today she's shown straight through the arched, tunnel-like entrance and onto the concrete galleries beyond, the piss-stained and vomit-splattered steps leading up to the first-floor landing, where her customer roots in his pockets for a key.

Clothing, pegged to bits of wire or twine and crudely strung up by iron nails bashed into the brickwork, or wound around pipes and railings, zigzags across the narrow walkway, left to dry in the crisp spring air. They flutter and whip and twist in the breeze, some garments so worn through that they look as though they might disintegrate on the wind. Others are so stained they'll never come clean, even with the benefit of soap.

A girl's rat-chewed ragdoll sits propped on a window ledge, its lidless stare fixed on the stark concrete courtyard below, as if on watch over the young children playing there. The boys kick around a makeshift ball constructed of strips of rag cloth knotted together into a rough spheroid shape and bound inside the remains of an old stocking, while the girls—sisters and neighbors—sit on the sidelines, darning their fathers' socks and sewing patches into their tattered petticoats.

Eventually, Mary Jane's customer locates his key, finding it attached to a string fastened to his drawers, where it was no doubt affixed by a frustrated wife who's grown tired of forking out her hard-earned money to have the locks replaced on account of his losing the key in a drunken stupor.

Inside, the small rooms are cheaply and minimally furnished. The living room consists of a second hand sofa, a table, one shelf above the fireplace, and a threadbare rug. The table looks homemade, it being little more than a few pieces of wood slapped together, and the sofa is covered with beer stains, the cushions sagging, the horsehair stuffing poking out through holes made by wayward springs.

Her man heads for a closed door which presumably leads to the bedroom, but she grabs the collar of his jacket and redirects him.

"Never mind that. We'll do the business here." She pulls him toward the ugly sofa.

In her experience, letting customers get her into bed gives them the impression she's going to unrig and let them take their time, and she certainly has no intention of that.

As he kicks off his boots and sheds his jacket, she gets to work on his trousers, yanking them down to his ankles. After performing her routine check for a love ailment, she slips a French letter out of her pocket and promptly sheathes him in it. Not having planned on taking any men thus far today, she left her diaphragm at home and won't risk receiving his seminal injection unprotected.

As for most in her trade, the French letter is a last resort. Men generally don't carry them, and they're expensive to keep on hand. On top of that, the vast majority of customers, unless particularly concerned about disease, refuse to use them, claiming that it reduces their pleasure to an unreasonable degree. Of course, there are the few rare ones—often the young ones—who won't fuck without the rubber barrier. Not because it protects them from the pox, but because it dulls the sensation around their overly sensitive glandes, thus ensuring that they get their money's worth. These men, Mary Jane notes, like to draw out the fucking until their spunk is positively bursting for ejection. Quite often, they'll stop and start their pokings in fits and spurts, shoving until they feel their pleasure coming before easing off, waiting for the threat to pass, then resuming at the same pace.

For some women, this delay in final emission affords them the opportunity for at least one spend. For Mary Jane, it's an annoyance. She wants the cock in and out in the fastest attitude possible, often anticipating the moment of ejaculation and giving her hips such a wiggle so as to ensure the deposit erupts near the entrance to her channel instead of far up it, and she uncunts immediately. There's never any pleasure.

Getting straight down to the task, as always, she lies on the sofa and pulls up her skirts, bunching them

around her lower back and belly to lessen the chance that they might get messed.

"Fuck me," she demands urgently. "Get on and fuck me."

Grunting and huffing like an enraged bear, he scrambles between her legs, plunges his sheathed prick into her, and ruts vigorously for a good minute, the sofa springs digging into her bum every time the force of his weight pushes her onto them.

"Fuck harder," she spurs him on, inciting brutality. "Hurt me, and tell me I'm a bitch."

He's not listening.

"Tell me!" She reaches up and slaps him hard across the face, sobering him and disrupting the rhythm of his fucking. "Do as I say!"

"Damned bitch," he rasps, his brain chugging along at half speed, his response time delayed. "You struck me." He gets his dander up, realizing his cheek's stinging. "Fucking whore bitch!" he snarls, and means it, pinning her to the sofa as he looms over her, getting his prick deeper up her. "Is this what you want?" He clamps his hand around her throat, half choking her, doing his best to murder her with his cunt-rammer.

Mary Jane cries out, the friction hurting her as much as the repeated battering against her unprotected cervix. This is just what she deserves. Unfortunately, he lacks stamina. Finishing without warning, howling at the ceiling as his priapus expels its muck, he promptly passes out on top of her, his dead weight falling square on her chest.

"Arsehole," she mutters, shoving on his shoulders until he rolls off her and onto the floor, landing there with a thud, his softening prick still encased in the French letter, the trapped sediment sloshing down the shaft and puddling around the root.

Getting up to leave, she spits on his crotch, the ball of her saliva landing in his sweaty pubic thatch. He disgusts her. She disgusts herself. This was meant to be her penance, but sadly, she feels no better for the abuse.

She returns to Thrawl Street in a sulk, pulls the five pound note out of her corset, and locks it away in her tin

box, wanting to be rid of it. Next, she restores herself to her usual likeness—old clothes, gaudy lip paste, pristine white apron, and the ever-present violet—and banishes her silk finery to the steamer trunk beneath her bed. She's no lady.

Realizing her hands still smell like Missus B——, she almost breaks down again. Thoroughly repulsed by the reminder of her infidelity, she fills her washbasin with a pint of water and mixes up an astringent blend of alum and zinc sulphate, then scrubs herself clean, douching and cleansing her sex with the same caustic solution, thereby stripping herself of the filth of her actions.

Ready to subject herself to more punishment, she inserts her diaphragm and returns to Commercial Street, hoping to snare a customer in the Ten Bells, but her plan is thwarted by Eva before she ever gets through the door.

Hailing her on the street, the grinning teen dashes up to her, handing her a single, thornless red rose from the empty wicker basket hooked on her arm. "For you, Miss Kelly."

Every bit of anger dissolving, unable to hold even a single negative thought in Eva's presence, Mary Jane greets her with a fond smile.

"To what do I owe this gesture?" She takes the rose, knowing it to be symbolic of love at first sight. "Might you be courting me, Miss Sullivan?" She brings the flower to her lips, the petals matching the color of her lip paste.

"Aye." Eva flings her free arm around Mary Jane's neck. "Where's you been?"

"I had one of my regular appointments in another quarter." Mary Jane pulls her into a hug. "Whatchu doing back in these parts so early?"

"I only took a light basket today." Eva stays close, feeling Mary Jane's hands settle on her lower back. "I didn't want to be gone too long, but I daren't return to Thrawl Street in case Billy sees me and gives me a basting."

"How are you fixed for coin?" Mary Jane pulls a hand back, reaching for her pocket.

"I ain't worried about that." Eva stops her, returning hand to bum. "I just wanted to see you." She wriggles into

another hug, mashing herself to Mary Jane's breasts. "I can't stop thinking about this morning."

She steals a peck on the lips, but isn't satisfied with that. In full view of the street—in front of the costers, shoppers, and hawkers—she helps herself to another, refusing to let Mary Jane's lips go, determined to harness intimacy.

"Don't, love." Mary Jane disengages and puts the rose between their lips, holding Eva off. "You oughtn't be so free with me on the street." She bops Eva's nose with the soft red petals. "People will think we're of the same sort."

"We *are* the same sort."

"Not in the way they'll think."

"Just one more," Eva barters. "I'm dying for your lips."

Mary Jane relents without shamming objection and presses a chaste but lingering kiss on Eva's mouth, only forcing herself to break it when she realizes her lusts are up. After first having a desire to be thoroughly sullied, she now has a desire to reacquaint herself with true pleasure, and to affirm her newly established bond with Eva.

"Come with me."

She takes Eva firmly by the hand and pulls her into a covered passage beside the Ringers' Buildings on Commercial Street, dragging her through to a small enclosed courtyard. Bounded on all sides by brick warehouses and storage spaces used by the surrounding businesses, the relatively secluded courtyard is cramped and claustrophobic. Access to the first- and second-floor dwellings above the warehouses is provided by a single set of steps leading to rickety wooden galleries overlooking the court, and there's a small outhouse nestled into the near left corner, partially propping up the gallery above it.

Nothing is leveled. The shoddily constructed upper storeys tilt precariously into the court, as if peering down on it. Ramshackle gutter pipes catch rainwater from the roof and direct it to the ground, but there's nowhere for it to go; there aren't any drains. When the heavens open,

the water simply floods into the court, picking up the trampled horse dung and straw, making a manure paste. Thankfully, today is dry.

Mary Jane leads Eva beneath the gallery at the far end and tucks her under the sloping overhang, depositing her basket on the ground and pushing her against a warehouse wall, their presence obscured by a stack of old crates. There, she kisses her.

It starts like any other kiss they've exchanged before, but then Mary Jane flicks her tongue against Eva's lips, seeking entry into her mouth.

Assuming it a mistake, Eva jerks her lips away with a giggle. "I felt your tongue."

"It's a different kind of kiss," Mary Jane enlightens her, unrepentant. "A wet one." She nuzzles Eva's nose. "Might you like to kiss me that way?"

"I've never ..." Eva touches her fingers to her moistened mouth, feeling where Mary Jane's tongue grazed her lips. "Ever ..."

"Do you want to?"

Eva bobs her head rapidly, eager to learn any and all of Mary Jane's erotic fancies.

"Part your lips," Mary Jane instructs her. "Do as I do."

She pinches Eva's lower lip between her teeth and sucks on it, slithering her tongue over it before pulling back, tugging on it a little, then letting it go. Reengaging almost immediately, she crushes their lips together, then darts her tongue forward, meeting nothing but Eva's teeth on the first assault. On the second assault, however, she petitions for entry into Eva's mouth and is met by the teen's own advancing tongue.

At the first caress, Eva sinks deeper into Mary Jane's embrace. Yearning for more, her blissful sighs increase in frequency and intensity when Mary Jane's tongue finds its way into her mouth, and she brings a hand to the nape of Mary Jane's neck, under her hair, cradling the back of her head.

Upon finally breaking for air, Eva moons up at her, seduced by this new intimacy. "I like your wet kisses."

She licks her lips, tasting Mary Jane's lip paste. "I didn't know a kiss could ever be so lewd."

"I've been longing to kiss you that way." Mary Jane admires the flush of excitement on her cheeks. "So deeply."

All atingle, Eva's modesty goes to the winds. "P'raps you oughta do it again." She coaxes Mary Jane's hands onto her bum. "It's making me feel ever so wicked."

Groping the teen's tight rump, Mary Jane gives her what she wants, only breaking from her for need of air.

"I missed you today," Eva mumbles, grinding her southern parts against Mary Jane, subconsciously humping her. "I couldn't concentrate on nuthin', and I kept giving out the wrong change."

"What was distracting you?" Mary Jane fishes for a sexual confession. "Were you feeling lickerish? Did you put a hand to yourself? Tell me, darling. Tell me."

"Yes," Eva mewls, tossing her head back, accepting Mary Jane's kisses all over her neck. "I was so sodden in my drawers that I feared my courses had come on all a sudden. I ain't a full woman yet, see. My mam says they'll come soon. Anyway, I didn't know what to do, so I locked me-self in a public privy and had a feel to see how much of a mess I were in, and I weren't half drenched, only ..."

"You wanted a fuck."

"I done it with my hand, right there in the bogging place." Eva grasps Mary Jane's breasts over her clothing. "I ain't never done nuthin' like that afore in my life."

Imagining Eva hiding in a privy, one foot propped on the bench, her back to the wall and a hand to her treasure, Mary Jane's ever-simmering lusts are stoked higher.

"My beautiful girl." She drives a hand up Eva's skirts. "I need to feel you again."

"Oi!" Eva yelps, trying to keep her skirts down. "I can't let you have me here," she whispers earnestly, a touch of fear in her voice. "What if someone comes?"

"No-one will," Mary Jane answers assuredly, making the declaration with such unflinching certainty that it leaves no doubt as to how she came upon that knowledge.

She's been fucked here before. Probably in this very spot, and against this very wall, Eva thinks, the thought fluttering briefly through her mind, swiftly ejected.

Determined to tickle her into delirium, Mary Jane aims her hand straight for Eva's core, the action promptly impeded by Eva's undergarments.

"To hell and buggery with these damn drawers," she grumbles, forcing her hand through the overlapping split in the cotton, her desperate fingers seeking out Eva's lubricious furrow.

"Oh, pray don't," Eva pleads feebly, demonstrating no inclination to stop her. "Not here ... oh ... no ... not here."

Weak to Mary Jane's whim, she relaxes her thighs and quits her hollow objections. In the blacked out glass of a warehouse window, she gawks at their reflection as Mary Jane scoops a hand around the back of her knee and lifts up her leg, making the work easier—just as she did with Maria on the lodging house staircase.

It excites her. Keeping her eyes pinned to the glass, she anchors her arms around Mary Jane's neck and admires the display, her leg hooked over Mary Jane's hip, her calf pressed to a soft rump. To her shuddering delight, one of Mary Jane's hands is gripping her thigh, her drawers bunched up, exposing her pale flesh, her stocking and garter bared. The other hand is rubbing vigorously between her legs, frigging her violently, giving her the most intense pleasure.

"Oh, lummy," she sobs out, the vision of their lewdness tipping her over the edge, her orgasm engulfing her, her voluptuous cries smothered with the fabric of Mary Jane's bodice as she slumps forward, wilting into her lover's arms like an unmanned marionette.

As her weight drops, enervated by her crisis, Mary Jane lets down her leg and wraps one arm around her buttocks, the other around her waist, holding her upright until the crest of her paroxysm passes and she suitably recovers.

"Mary ... oh, Em ... you ..." Eva murmurs, clinging to Mary Jane's neck. "You make me ... oh ..." Another small shudder ripples through her.

"You spend beautifully." Mary Jane delivers a flurry of tender kisses all about her mouth, cheeks, and neck, then separates from her, patting down her skirts. "Now, shall we get some supper in you?"

CHAPTER 15

MARY JANE SIPS A CUP OF TEA, WATCHING EVA DEMOLISH A piece of sponge cake following her supper of stewed lamb and peas, astounded by the amount of food she can put away in one sitting.

This little coffeehouse on Commercial Street is a quiet one, frequented by older clientele. It's filled with odd chairs and odd tables, nothing matching. One table is little more than two damaged wooden steamer trunks, one on top of the other, strapped together. Like most other places, the floor is sprinkled with sawdust to mop up any spillages, but this sawdust is speckled with crumbs and what looks to be black grains of wild rice. A second glance reveals it to be mouse feces.

A sign in the window advertises cheap beds, and the rooms above are let by the hour, no questions asked. As Mary Jane and Eva enjoy their supper, Mary Jane notices a steady stream of men and women coming and going from the upstairs rooms. In the space of forty-five minutes, one woman—appearing not much over sixteen— entertains three different gentlemen, and upon peering outside, it becomes clear that a small queue has formed for her services.

The men, who all seem to know one another, congregate on the other side of the street, smoking and chatting, waiting for their turn, and Mary Jane can't help but wonder how much money they're dropping, and

whether or not the woman washes after each, or if they're just going up into one another's spendings.

"What's out there?" Eva follows her gaze.

Mary Jane snaps her eyes back to the table. "Nothing, darling. Are you full?"

When they first walked in, Eva set her hungry eyes on a meat pie, but Mary Jane warned her off it. Though it's meant to be steak and kidney, it could just as easily be cat. Unadulterated food is often hard to come by, and there are plenty of strays around if you can catch one. Or you could pick up one of the many dead ones lying in the gutter, having been knocked down by the wheels of a hansom carriage, or trampled by a horse. The lamb and peas seemed to suffice instead, but it didn't fill her. Hence the cake.

Though Eva remains oblivious to the suspicious goings on in the rooms upstairs, she does notice that the coffeehouse's other customers are flocking to the far side of the room, clustering together, some women on the laps of others rather than taking any of the available seating beside Mary Jane.

"Why ain't they sitting here?" she wonders. "There's plenty chairs."

"Because they know what I am." Mary Jane ignores the sly, judgmental looks thrown her way. "Don't dwell on it." She rubs her ankle on Eva's leg under the table, making her color up. "Do you want more food?"

Not wanting to appear greedy, or to exploit Mary Jane's kindness, Eva shakes her head, dabbing up the crumbs on the plate. "Nah."

"Tell me the truth," Mary Jane urges her. "What do you *want*? I'll get it for you."

What she wants is bacon, and within minutes, she has a few crispy rashers on a plate and Mary Jane's pocket is another thruppence lighter.

"You're gonna make me fat," Eva mumbles, her mouth full of pig.

"I don't think there's much chance of that." Mary Jane laughs at her spindly companion. "But it couldn't hurt to put a bit more meat on you."

Eva thinks that over, struck by a sudden bout of insecurity, knowing that she far from embodies the figure of the ideal woman. "Would you prefer it if I looked more like Maria?"

Mary Jane snorts into her fresh cup of tea. "Where did that come from all a sudden?" She dabs at her lips with a napkin. "Why ever would you ask me such a thing?"

Eva shrugs, licking grease off her fingers. "She's got more to her than I have."

"But she's not you." Mary Jane reaches for Eva's hand across the table. "You're the only woman I want." She weaves their fingers together. "I already told you there won't be no-one else in my bed from now on. I'm all yours."

As those words leave her lips, a twinge of guilt for her earlier activities resurfaces. There's a chemist across the street, and in a moment of spontaneity—determined to commit herself to Eva in every way—she excuses herself and dashes over there, returning five minutes later with a small brown paper bag.

"What'd you get?" Eva pokes at it.

"Take a look." Mary Jane nudges the bag toward her.

Eva has a quick peep inside, finding two brand new toothbrushes.

"Mine's past its best," Mary Jane volunteers, seeing the questions form on her face.

"And the other?" The teen dare not presume.

"I think it's about time you had your own." Mary Jane finishes her tea, pausing for dramatic effect. "Because I want you to live with me."

Eva breaks into a grin. "Do you really mean it?"

"Would I say it if I didn't?" Mary Jane pushes her teacup aside and rests her elbows on the table. "Just so you know, I work five days a week, for up to eight hours. I won't do more. All being well, I bring in about thirty shillings a week. That's six bob a day, give or take, and that don't include my specials, like the one I spoke of the other night. If I'm lucky, I have one or two of those a month, and whatever money I get from them—be it ten bob or a sovereign—I save directly. I need that put by,

just as I said. It's the only way I can see to crawl out of this wretched bloody mess I got myself in."

Perplexed by the financial lesson, Eva frowns. "Why's you telling me this?"

"I want to be frank with you about what I can offer you." Mary Jane clasps one of Eva's hands between her own, holding it tightly. "I can't keep you quite as well as I might like, but I *can* keep you. There won't be no silk dresses presently—nothing quite so lavish—but I can put food in your belly, ensure a good wash at the public baths once a week, make sure there's a solid roof over your head, and I can most certainly keep you warm at nights."

"I don't give a fig for silk dresses," Eva lies.

"All girls care about silk dresses," Mary Jane teases her, inspecting her fingernails. "I've known many fine young women give themselves up for a nice new frock."

"Not me." Eva smiles bashfully. "You're all I want."

"Nevertheless, I hope one day I'll be better off and able to give you the best." Mary Jane picks dirt and grime out from under Eva's nails. "For now, I can give you my love, my bed, and I reckon I can even manage the odd night out at the Paragon, or the Royal Cambridge."

Eva's eyes light up. She knows all about London's music halls, but she's never been in one. "You'll take me out? Ain't no-one ever took me out afore."

"I'll take you out and show you off." Mary Jane finds a broken nail and tears the raggedy end off with her teeth, spitting it on the floor. "When was the last time you cleaned these mitts?"

Eva shrugs. "Yesterday."

"Well, I think someone needs a wash," Mary Jane declares. "Shall we go back to our lodgings and get you in the tub?"

Under normal circumstances, Eva would find the thought of getting completely unrigged and sitting in a few inches of tepid water for a mediocre scrub down to be thoroughly unappealing. In fact, it would be downright unpleasant. As the youngest member of the family, she's always the last one in, by which point, the water generally resembles that of the Thames: gray and full of sediment. And nowadays, there's Billy to contend with. He's

invariably present when she bathes, and she struggles to keep her charms covered from his lecherous eyes. The thought of having a bath in the presence of Mary Jane, however, has her filled with erotic excitement.

She imagines sitting in the oval tin bucket as Mary Jane, kneeling beside the bath with a washcloth in hand, soaps and rinses her back, neck, and behind her ears, first doing all the bits she can't reach, but not stopping there.

Mary Jane would go on to lather up her breasts, making her skin slippery and wet, then she'd squeeze the washcloth out above her chest, the water cascading over her small, firm diddeys, her nipples swollen and hard. When the soap was washed away, she'd bring her mouth to those nipples, sucking and biting on them as her hand dropped below the surface of the water ...

"I think someone likes that idea." Mary Jane smirks, getting to her feet and pulling Eva up from the table. "I ain't never seen you with so much pink in your cheeks."

On the short walk back to Thrawl Street, arm in arm—Eva holding on tight, proud to be seen as hers— they pass Spitalfields church and its disused cemetery. Strolling by the wrought iron railing enclosing the unlit former burial area known as Itchy Park, Eva stops in her tracks, arrested by a woman's frantic voice.

"Unnggghhhh!" The woman grunts loudly, not seeming to care if anyone hears. "Do it!" There's a rustle of skirts and petticoats. "Get your prick up me!"

Her demands are followed by swift compliance, and after a moment's fumbling, the rhythmic sounds of human coupling filter through the air.

Squinting to see, Eva peers through the railings and trees. "Is that ... ?"

Mary Jane presses two fingers to her lips, hushing her, and points to a gaudily-dressed tart who has her skirts rucked up around her waist and her legs spread around the hips of a well-rigged customer. They're having a poke up against an obelisk-style burial monument, apparently unaware that they're on view.

Eva grimaces. "That ain't very godly."

183

The woman starts cursing like a sailor, spewing an endless stream of bawdy words, a few oaths, and praise for the man's "fine fucking" and the size of his "tooleywag."

At that, Eva's jaw drops. "I ain't never heard such bawdiness come from a woman's lips." She gawps at the clandestine doings, repulsed by the mere thought of accepting the male reproductive appendage into her body. "Not even in the kitchen at Thrawl Street."

Mary Jane chuckles, urging her from the railing and down Commercial Street. "Come away before they catch us peeping."

"Is that how you are with your fellas?" Eva asks then, intrigued. "All bawdy like."

"Don't ever ask me such things, darling." Mary Jane shuts the topic down, injecting a little sternness into her voice. "You need not know anything of that life."

"Well, what do it feel like? Will you tell me that?" Eva persists, her curiosity inflamed. "I know a fella stuffs his doodle up a woman and that gives him pleasure, but ..." She chews on her lower lip, not knowing if she should continue. "It looks violent."

"Some women enjoy having a prick up them, others don't," Mary Jane answers succinctly, willing to give Eva the facts as long as they don't pertain directly to her own business practices. "There ain't no right or wrong to it."

Satisfied with that, Eva remains silent the rest of the way home. Inside Mary Jane's room, she sets down her flower basket and drags the tin bath out from under the bed, doing so at Mary Jane's instruction. Meanwhile, Mary Jane lights a pair of candles and digs out an empty ginger beer bottle from her growing stash of recyclables, filling it with a few inches of water before standing Eva's rose in it and giving the makeshift vase pride of place on the tabletop.

"You're keeping it?" Eva smiles.

"Course I'm keeping it." Mary Jane tosses her shawl over the back of a chair. "It ain't every day a pretty girl gives me flowers."

Eva hangs her head, knowing that her single rose can't even begin to compete with all the money Mary

Jane's lavished on her thus far. "I wish I could buy you more tokens."

"But I already have the gift of your company." Mary Jane sweeps the willowy teen into a bear hug. "What more could be better?"

"Am I really to live with you?" Eva gazes up at her, eyes wide and almost fearful, as if afraid that Mary Jane might change her mind about the proposition.

"Only if you think I can make you happy." Mary Jane casts a glance around her simple room. "I know I don't have much, but—"

"Ain't no-one ever missed a thing they never had. I don't care for fancy bits and bobs in any case, and you *do* make me happy." Eva initiates a kiss. "I ain't never been so happy as when I'm with you." Another kiss. "I wanna be yours."

"Good." Mary Jane backs her toward the bed. "Now let's consummate."

"Wait." Eva breaks away from her, grinning. "Don't get me started yet. Let me go tell my mam. She'll be dead pleased."

"Don't be too long." Mary Jane plants more kisses on her. "And fetch your belongings over. I'll stoke up a fire."

Giddy, Eva skips next door. Mary Jane turns her attention to the hearth, but doesn't get more than a peek into the coal scuttle before Eva lets out a heart-wrenching scream. Feeling her heart drop into the pit of her stomach, she rushes next door, finding Eva backed up against a chair, her eyes fixed on the bedstead.

Missus Sullivan is lying prone, fully clothed, one arm dangling limply off the edge of the soiled palliasse. Her head is turned sideways, facing the wall, her other arm crooked beside her chest, a bottle of laudanum clutched in her hand.

"She ain't moved." Eva sniffles, shaking uncontrollably. "I seen her sleeping this morning and I come in all quiet. I didn't wanna wake her." She drags her eyes away from the vacant shell of her mother, turning them to Mary Jane. "She's cold."

Swallowing hard, Mary Jane steps into the dank room and approaches the bed. She can see that blood has

pooled in the lower parts of Missus Sullivan's body. The hand clutching the laudanum bottle is blotchy and blanched, the plum-colored fingertips slightly swollen. The hand hanging off the bed is entirely purple, the discoloration continuing some way up the wrist. Though she doesn't need any further proof of the haggard woman's condition, she reaches a shaky hand toward Missus Sullivan's neck to feel for a pulse, recoiling from the task when her fingertips make contact with unnervingly icy flesh.

Drawn to the room by Eva's earlier scream, the deputy's son barges in, catching himself in the doorway and shrinking back. "What in the Lord's name?" He points at the bed. "Is she ... ?"

"Fetch the police." Mary Jane retreats to Eva's side. "Ask for Detective Constable Dew at the Commercial Street station. Go now."

Missus Sullivan's body is removed to the mortuary in a shoddily constructed shell: a temporary coffin used and reused for this purpose, scratched and dented from careless handling and stained with the blood of those who've been carried in it before.

Mary Jane sits on her bed with Eva, comforting the distraught teen as best she can, watching as two uniformed policemen carry the battered shell past her open door and down the staircase. Following their departure, Detective Constable Dew—a clean shaven man in his mid-twenties—appears in the doorway, ready to wrap things up for the night.

"How is she?" he asks softly as Mary Jane meets him at the threshold of the room.

"Not good." Mary Jane sighs. "As one might expect."

"She gave me the names of her siblings, so we'll set about contacting them first thing." Dew consults his notes. "And she says she's got an aunt living in Camden."

"There might've been a falling out between her and the mother. I ain't sure." Mary Jane recalls Missus Sullivan's comment about Bessie's attitude toward Eva. "And then there's her fella, Billy. He's a lush with a penchant for thumping women."

Dew nods. "I'll make inquiries." He peers over Mary Jane's shoulder at Eva. "You'll be keeping an eye on her?"

"Aye, she'll be in my care."

Just then, a ruckus kicks off downstairs. A drunken Billy barges his way into the hall and gets into it with the uniformed constables, causing the shell containing Missus Sullivan's body to crash onto the floor. Two officers try to restrain him, but he succeeds in kicking the lid off the shell, directing a slew of insults at his deceased lover.

"Whatchu gone and done, you stupid bloody woman?!"

"Has he had a bladder full?" Dew yells over the banister. "Take him down the station and shut him up." He turns back to Mary Jane only to bid her a goodnight and let her know he'll be in touch, then he and his men are gone.

In the wake of their departure, Eva cries herself to sleep. Mentally exhausted, but unable to doze off with her, Mary Jane retrieves a piece of unfinished crochet work off the mantel and settles herself at the table. At the moment, it's only a few square inches of wool, but she's determined to transform it into a scarf. When it's finished, she'll get a bit of money for it, and every little helps.

Working by the light of two farthing dips, she passes a few hours this way, stopping only when she hears some clattering noises in the neighboring room. Setting the soon-to-be scarf down, she rises and unlatches the door quietly, so as not to wake Eva, then tiptoes down the hall, thinking she might catch looters in the act of plundering what few possessions Missus Sullivan had. But it's not looters, it's Billy. Like a scavenging rat, he's rummaging

through the cupboard for food, the door flung open, half hanging off its hinges following last night's bout of fighting, the lock broken.

Mary Jane leans on the doorjamb, regarding him with disdain. "They let you out, then?"

Her voice startles him and he smacks his head on the cupboard shelf as he attempts to get vertical. "I didn't have aught to do with it, that's why." He rubs his crown.

She doesn't argue with him. She already knows near enough what happened. Missus Sullivan had a nice fish supper, saw her littlin partnered off, had one last poke, and then ...

"Shame they can't lock you up for being an arsehole," she cracks. "I'd testify against you."

"Brazen little bitch, aintcha?" Billy strides toward her. "Someone needs to put you back in your place, I reckon."

"Oh, aye? Wanna try your luck?" She stares him down.

Perturbed by her lack of deference to his masculinity, he diverts his attention to the smaller target who appears behind her. "Come on, girl." He hooks his thumbs suggestively over his belt. "Get in 'ere where you belong."

Mary Jane feels Eva huddle against her back, seeking protection.

"Whatchu doing up, love?" She reaches behind her, giving Eva's hip a squeeze, then locks her eyes back on Billy. "You ain't got no claim on her." She stands up straight, ready to defend Eva if need be. "She'll be keeping with me from now on."

"You gonna teach her your trade?" Billy sneers.

"I'm gonna keep her away from blokes like you what'd fuck her soon as look at her."

"Is that right?" Billy laughs. "Who'd want her now, though? She's used goods, ain't she?" He gets closer, leering at her. "I heard you flat-cocking her, you filthy doggess." He spits on the floor at her feet. "So take her. Let her be a drain on you."

Mary Jane opens her mouth to bark something back at him, but Eva grabs her hand and pulls her toward their room.

"Please don't," she mouths silently, hoarse from crying. "He ain't worth it."

Acquiescing without fuss, Mary Jane retreats, refocusing her attention on the grieving teen. With a little coaxing, she's able to get Eva stripped to her chemise, her teeth brushed and her face washed. Ready for sleep—and to bring on the end of this wretched day—she turns down the blankets, fluffs the pillows, and clambers into bed, leaving the candles to gutter.

Eva slides in after her, but knowing what intimate delights they had planned for tonight, she hesitates to curl into Mary Jane's open arms.

"I don't feel ..."

"Sshhh." Mary Jane drags her closer. "Of course not, love. We'll just lie here together, warm and safe." She drops a gentle kiss on Eva's lips, keeping it tentative and brief, then rubs their noses together. "We have all the time in the world for other pleasures."

CHAPTER 16

Saturday, March 5, 1887

MARY JANE WAKES UP WITH A SHUDDER, FEELING A COLD chill ripple through her. On opening her eyes, she finds Eva sitting up, exploring her charms. The blankets have been pulled down to her knees and her chemise tugged up to her belly, the frigid morning air giving her gooseflesh.

"Whatchu doing awake?"

"I woke up in a panic thinking I were late for work." Eva drags a finger along Mary Jane's stubbly motte. "Then I remembered ..."

Her eyes look vacant, bloodshot from last night's crying, dark rings under them. With no particular aim, she trails her finger over Mary Jane's abdomen, feeling her soft belly and comparing their navels, giving each a poke to see whose is deepest. Mary Jane wins.

That done, she resumes her digital exploration, twice circling a beauty mark on Mary Jane's hip before bending to kiss it. In doing so, her hand slips around Mary Jane's body and grazes her lower back, discovering a ticklish spot just above her bum.

Trying not to flinch, or swipe Eva's hand away, Mary Jane bites on her lower lip and buries her face in the pillow, twitching and mewling. Eva then rolls her completely over, bum up, and investigates her rear, even pulling her cheeks apart for a quick peek of the pink orifice.

At that, Mary Jane looks over her shoulder. "What *are* you doing?"

Eva doesn't immediately answer, but turns her over again, putting her on her back. "I'm just looking." She carries on. "I wanna know every inch of you." She returns her finger to Mary Jane's pubic mound. "You're all prickly today."

"Aye, I need to—" Mary Jane stops short.

Without warning, Eva pushes on her inner thighs, spreads her legs, and dives for her core. Astonished and a little thrilled, Mary Jane gasps, emitting a surprised groan-like squeal as Eva drops a series of kisses on her sex, starting at the motte and working her way along the cleft.

"Oh, my darling." Mary Jane whines, feeling Eva's hot lips close around her plump labia.

Then it's over.

Eva surfaces, licking her lips, and flops down on the bed. "I do want to, you know."

"Want to what?" Mary Jane asks, bewildered.

"Do to you what you does to me." Eva plays with the tip of Mary Jane's loose braid, breaking off split ends. "The tickles and the rubbing and that. I ain't gonna be neglectful."

"I know, love." Mary Jane kisses her forehead. "I ain't worried."

Resuming her explorations on a whim, Eva pushes Mary Jane back into a supine position and straddles her, yanking up her chemise to expose her breasts in order that she might have access to higher grounds.

"My mam gave my backside a right smack when I told her I ran off from you," she reflects, teasing one of Mary Jane's nipples with her finger. "She said I were a fool for making you displeased." As the nipple stiffens, she dips forward and kisses it, sucking it into her mouth and releasing it with a pop. "I was only telling her 'cause I were in a right muddle about the queerness that come over me," she goes on. "But she thought I done a runner 'cause I was scared to let you have the first of me." She grabs both of Mary Jane's breasts, pushes them up and

together, then releases them, watching them bounce. "That weren't even a bit true."

The mention of her mother dulls her mood again and she dismounts. "I dunno what I'm feeling from one minute to the next." She slumps against the headboard. "I'm all in a muddle."

Thump! A heavy fist falls against the door to Mary Jane's room.

"Oi!" The deputy's son gives the door several more whacks. "Where is he?!"

"Where's who?" Mary Jane sighs, fixing her chemise.

"That lushy arsehole from next door."

Mary Jane rolls her eyes theatrically. "How the flaming hell would I know?"

"'Cause you's got the girl in there. I knows you do." He raps his foot impatiently on the floor. "Now he's only gone and done a bloody runner without paying up the rent, and he's ransacked the room n'all."

Curious to see what damage Billy's done, Mary Jane—wearing only her chemise—opens the door to the beleaguered rent collector and wanders over to the neighboring room, followed closely by Eva.

At first glance, she can see no discernible difference in the overall quality of the squalid hovel. The bed's unmade, the soiled palliasse sticking out from the frame, an additional urine stain marking the spot where Missus Sullivan's bladder released postmortem. The table's cluttered with dirty plates and molding bread, a collection of flies already gathering on the greasy paper leftover from the fish and chip supper bought by Mary Jane.

Some dirty linens are strewn about the floor, along with Eva's pilot coat and a raggedy old doll with choppy hair, threadbare clothes, a worn-out nose, and a missing eye. The fetid chamber pot has been tipped over, its contents oozing through gaps in the floorboards. Apart from the lack of a man's coat that was hung on a hook by the door, not much has changed.

Eva scans the room, looking for any sign of her mother's existence but finding none. "I'm all alone."

"Don't talk nonsense." Mary Jane rubs her back. "You're my girl now, aintcha? You won't never be alone. I'll take care of you."

Eva picks the doll off the floor, brushing a woodlouse off its face.

"She looks like she's seen a few better days." Mary Jane rubs one of the doll's ears, the misshapen flap hanging on by a thread. "What's her name?"

"Mollie." Eva musses with the snipped hair on the doll's head. "I gave her a haircut once 'cause I thought it would grow back like mine does." She holds Mollie to her chest. "My mam was well cross with me when she saw the state of her, and I cried for a week."

"Anything else in here yours?"

Eva fetches her pilot coat, the gray fabric covered with dirty boot prints, then hesitates, looking about the floor.

"Is that it?" Mary Jane prompts her.

Sheepishly, Eva picks up one of the scattered rags. It's gray, once white, now more holes than it is cotton, the hem brown where the chamber pot spilled on it. Judging by the shape of it, Mary Jane suspects that it's meant to be a nightgown.

"I don't think so, darling." She shakes her head. "If you really want one, I shall buy you another." She plucks the tattered garment out of Eva's hand, using only her fingertips. "I'll not have you wearing this in my bed." She flings it onto the table. "Where's your Sunday best?"

Eva shrugs. "Pawned? My mam used to pawn everything on a Monday, buy it back on the Saturday, wear it Sunday, then pawn it again."

Resigning herself to a premature dip into her modest savings, Mary Jane sighs. "We're done here by the looks of it, then. Let's be off." She steers Eva out of the room, her elbow snagged by the rent collector in the hall.

"You got the rest of your rent yet?"

"You can have it later, I promise you." She jerks her arm free. "I've got bigger things just now, all right? You know my word is good."

No sooner are they back in Mary Jane's room than Eva is back in bed, sobbing. She has one-eyed Mollie on

the pillow beside her, her pilot coat draped carelessly over a chair back, half of it crumpled on the floor.

"I feel so queer in my head." She snivels. "It's all swimming."

Mary Jane climbs into bed with her, holding her. "Is there aught I can do to help?"

There isn't. Eva cries herself to sleep for the second time, and Mary Jane falls asleep with her. When she wakes, Eva is sitting at the table, picking halfheartedly at yesterday's bread, reminding her that most of the day has been slept away and she's yet to earn a penny.

"Oh, darling, you should've woken me." She rubs her eyes. "If you're hungry, I'll get off my arse and fetch us some proper food. How about that?"

Eva says nothing, just keeps nibbling at the bread.

Deciding on that course of action anyway, Mary Jane gets up, takes care of her ablutions, and dresses, turning her back to Eva as she props her foot on a chair and inserts her diaphragm, not wanting to draw any more attention to it than necessary. That dealt with, she takes a moment to dust some rouge on her cheeks, applying it with an ostrich feather puff.

"You paint yourself up so pretty." Eva ogles her from the table.

"I'm vain." Mary Jane smudges a little black powder on her eyelids, blending it with a cotton ball until it forms a subtle, smoky shade of gray. "I need these tricks to conceal the encroachment of age." She powders away the dark circles beneath her eyes. "You don't need to paint yourself in order to be pretty. You are so naturally."

"You reckon so?" Eva pulls a broken piece of mirror out of her pocket and gazes at her distorted reflection, her cheeks puffy and streaked red from crying.

"I bloody well do." Mary Jane flashes her a smile. "Now, I'll only be gone for a few hours." She picks up her shawl. "You'll be all right by yourself for a bit?"

Eva nods.

"Keep the bed nice and warm for us." Mary Jane kisses the top of her head, stroking her shoulders. "I shan't be too long."

As she reaches the door, Eva leaps out of her chair and seizes her, flinging both arms around her middle. "Be careful."

"I always am, love."

Though less experienced in the street trade than much of her competition, Mary Jane considers herself a fairly savvy judge of the male sex. During her time in the brothels, she became acquainted with many a different breed of man, from sailor to gent, and takes care with her selections. Some days, the coin comes easy. Other days, not so much.

Today, her first stop is the Ten Bells, where one small glass of gin keeps her in the pub long enough to secure her first customer. She takes his coin happily enough and leads him away to one of her usual spots, but upon his failing of her routine prick tip examination—a quantity of greenish, foul-smelling gunk oozing from the hole—she promptly refunds him and sends him on his way.

The next man, snared on Commercial Street, is a loss for a different reason. He passes the test, but fails to achieve connection. Preparing for a standard upright in the nearest alley, Mary Jane lifts up her skirts and places her back to the wall, ready to accept him, but she's too tall. Bending her knees, she drops to a half crouch and he tries again, but after several rough thrusts and a faint jabbing sensation in her nethers, she's still not convinced that it's in.

Pushing her skirts out of the way, she peers down, trying to ascertain the problem, but she can't see his tool. "Where's your prick?" she asks, thinking he must've tucked it away, then she spots his pink cockhead poking out through the front of his trousers. Confused, she reaches for it, grabbing and tugging on it, but it refuses to grow. When she'd performed her inspection, he was soft, and she assumed he'd gain length. Alas not.

"Is it always like that?" She bends to study it further, genuinely fascinated by the lack of growth, despite now being fully hard. He's got no more than two inches, topped with a modest, mushroom-shaped cap. "I ain't never seen one like it."

196

Sadly, under her inquisitive gaze, he deflates, and all attempts to revive the tiny poker fail. She gets to keep fourpence for her trouble, but he leaves with the rest, and from this point on, her day takes a turn for the worse.

The next customer she hooks in the Britannia. Now three gins down and barely a farthing in profit, she's fast losing her patience. In the same courtyard where she frigged Eva, she readies herself against the wall, holds up her skirts, and beckons him in.

"Go on, have your poke."

The burly man, tall and muscular, shows off his pipe. "See how fine it stands for you?" He lets go of it, flexing his muscles to make it bounce.

"Ooh, what a big one!" Mary Jane enthuses, with perhaps a touch too much sarcasm.

"Let me look well at your cock-trap." He drops to a crouch.

Thinking he wants to inspect her for cleanliness, she obliges, though many women—even those in her game— would not allow it. Moreover, they would be offended by the request. To show one's commodity is considered vulgar and unnecessary, and it's quite the usual course of business for a man to feel and fuck a woman's parts— even his wife's—without ever having cast his eyes upon those sacred grounds. Mary Jane reasons that's how she gets away with charging thruppence for a good peep. For her, the exhibition of her various charms has proved rather lucrative.

But this customer has other ideas. He extends a hand toward her and she slaps him away.

"That's not on offer."

"Let me feel your cunt." He tries again, undaunted. "When were you last fucked?"

"I said no." She shoves him away harder.

At that point, he stands up, pinning her to the wall with one hand while he forces the other between her legs and tries to kiss her. "I *will* have you as I like. Did I not pay you?"

"Hands and mouth to yourself," she insists, evading his kisses and clamping her thighs together. "Otherwise, you can find yourself another doxy to stick it in."

He gets his middle finger to her core, burrowing between her labia.

"Don't!" She struggles fruitlessly. "I won't do it that way!"

Afraid that she can't stop him, she closes her eyes, refusing to look at his ugly mug. She's been fairly lucky with customers till now. When she first took to the streets only a handful of months ago, she heard stories of rough men taking more than what they paid for, or throwing the odd punch, but thought all could be prevented by sticking to the upper end of the market and choosing her clientele wisely. Already, she's made a name for herself as a bawdy fucktress who's well worth any price, her services being a downright bargain for the relative pittance she's forced to accept in the East End. But none of that's helping her now.

She winces, expecting to feel his rough fingers probing into her tender flesh, but then ... release! He's flung away from her, his head cracking against the brick wall of the warehouse. One thump sends him to the ground, discombobulated, with no chance to fight back. A few kicks soon render him virtually unconscious, and the beating continues until Mary Jane snaps out of her trance and calls off her dog. Her unlikely protector, Fleming.

"That's enough!" She grapples to get hold of his coat, tearing him away. "If you don't lay off, you'll kill the man."

"So be it." Fleming tries to resume his attack, but Mary Jane gets in front of him and pushes him back, both hands pressed to his chest.

"Have you gone quite mad?" she snarls at him, boldly clouting him around the ear. "You're a loon, and no mistake. Why are you here? Where did you spring from?" She narrows her eyes, glaring at him accusingly. "Have you been watching me?"

"I worry for you." Fleming tries to get his arms around her. "This is a bad life."

"Gerroff me!" She wrests herself free. "You've got some nerve showing you face to me, Joseph Fleming." She huffs, straightening her clothes. "After all you've

done. What do you want with me? I ain't got no business with you."

"You were fond of me once."

Mary Jane laughs. "Aye, I was. More fool me, eh?"

She tries to leave the courtyard, but Fleming blocks her way.

"I thought you was doing me wrong," he offers by way of explanation. "Some strange impulse came upon me, and I was made insensible with a jealous rage." He drops to his knees. "Forgive me."

He looks like a forlorn puppy, his eyes desperate and pleading. He doesn't look cruel. Not that he ever was, excepting that one incident, and when it comes to that, she *was* doing him wrong. Not with another man, mind you, but with Maria. So although he was mistaken as to the nature of her infidelity, his instincts were otherwise correct: while he was at work, she had someone else in their bed. But that doesn't excuse the degree of his wrath.

On account of that, despite how much she likes to see a man suppliant, and as much as it gives her a perverse thrill to be the subject of his adoration and worship, she turns her back on him. "You don't deserve a minute more of my time."

She tries again to walk away, dodging around him, aiming for the narrow entrance to the courtyard, but he grabs one of her ankles and holds onto her boot, trapping her.

"What in God's good name are you doing, Joe?" Hopping to retain her balance, only one foot on the ground, she swivels around and swipes his hat off, sending it tumbling and rolling toward the overflowing privy. "Get your grubby mitts off me!"

"So lovely," he coos, roving his hands reverently over her calf, rubbing his face on her shin. "What a leg! And such charms!"

He pushes his face up her skirts, aiming for the apex of her thighs, but she jerks her foot out of his grasp and plants it firmly on his chest, pushing him backwards, causing him to topple off his feet and onto his posterior, landing in a pile of horse dung.

"If you want my company"—she pins him to the privy wall—"then you can pay for the pleasure of it, like everyone else."

"How much?" He dives into his pockets, drawing out coins left and right, collecting them in his palms. "I have money." He shows her the growing pile of silver and coppers. "How much will take you off the street tonight?"

Mary Jane's resolve wavers. Seduced by the thought of some easy coin and not having to take anyone else for the remainder of the day, she considers his offer. Plus, the sooner she's done, the sooner she can get back to Eva.

With that thought foremost in her mind, she gauges how much she ought to ask for. Knowing how much he earns as a mason's plasterer, and how much he's likely to be carrying in his pocket, she arrives at the figure of, "Ten bob."

"Christ almighty." Fleming looks incredulous.

"Well, I ain't had no-one yet today, apart from that arsehole." Mary Jane jabs her thumb at the groaning bundle of man flesh on the cobbled ground. "And I got bills to pay."

"Where you been staying?"

"Why do you wanna know?" She increases the pressure on his chest, digging her heel into his sternum. "So you can harass me there n'all?"

Fleming fishes a half-sovereign out of a pocket in his waistcoat, triumphantly showing her the gold. "Ten shillings! I'll give it you if you'll have a drink with me."

"Aye?" Mary Jane cocks her eyebrow. "A drink, and then what?"

CHAPTER 17

MARY JANE LIES NAKED ON THE SAGGING MATTRESS OF A cheap double bed in one of the best rooms in the Ringers' Buildings, her expression vacant. Fleming is sprawled beside her, snoring, his flaccid prick coated from root to tip with their combined secretions.

When she's certain he won't wake, she slips off the bed and digs through a pile of their clothes, searching for her own. He'd insisted on having her nude. He likes to look at her.

Crouched at the edge of the bed, she feels his sediment slopping southward and dripping onto the floorboards. After helping it along and squeezing much of it out, she snatches the red silk handkerchief from the pocket of his coat and plugs her hole. Minutes later, she's fully dressed, rooting through his pockets for some of the silver and coppers, taking as much as she dares before tiptoeing from the room.

Ill-gotten gains in hand, she hurries from one shop to another, making all the essential purchases: cheese, soap, lemons, tea leaves, some smoked sausage, candles, and so on. It's enough to keep them going for a few days at least. With the remainder, she picks up a few bottles of ginger beer from a street seller, then buys them a hearty supper of baked potatoes and bacon.

Returning to Thrawl Street with a large paper bag of supplies, she sees she's not the only one who's been busy.

Eva, freshly washed and cleaned, is sitting on the bed in her chemise, waiting patiently. A fire's been lit, the room's been tidied, and the table's been laid out for supper, the rose still the temporary centerpiece.

Awed, Mary Jane looks around, admiring Eva's efforts, noting that the floor's been swept and scrubbed, the bed made, and everything put in its place.

"You did all this?" She dumps the bag on the table.

"Sorry." Eva fidgets with her thumbs, prepared to receive a chastisement for meddling with Mary Jane's belongings. "I wanted to keep me-self busy."

"Don't apologize." Mary Jane tugs Eva off the bed and into a hug. "It was nice of you to do, but you didn't have to."

"I honest wanted to." Eva sinks into Mary's arms. "I wanted to surprise you."

"How're you feeling?"

Eva half shrugs one shoulder. "She's still dead." Breaking away and changing the subject, she retrieves something from the floor by the cupboard. "I found this under your bed, and I'm sure I dunno what to make of it."

She holds up a thick bunch of woven silk strings, braided together at one end, forming a short handle. At the other end, the long strings are unbound, hefty knots tied at the tips. Looking at it, Mary Jane's buttocks twitch involuntarily, her muscles clenching.

"Whatever is it?" Eva fingers the knots, pondering what application they might have. "The end of a mop maybe?"

"Not exactly." Mary Jane runs a hand over her rear, remembering a time when she hadn't been able to sit properly for three days.

"I was also having a think about these birch rods," Eva goes on unawares. "Whatever do you use them things for? My mam kept one years ago, but she only ever used it to smack my arse when I were small and naughty."

Realization hits her as the words leave her lips, and she throws Mary Jane a questioning glance, hoping for an alternative explanation. Instead, the apologetic, slightly embarrassed look on Mary Jane's face confirms all.

"I told you some of my special customers have peculiar letches." Mary Jane plucks the flogger out of Eva's hands. "And flagellation's the commonest letch of them all."

"Does you do it to them?" Eva grimaces. "Or does they do it to you?"

Mary Jane tosses the flogger into the corner of the room, where the birch rods are leaning up against the wall. "Depends how much they're paying."

"You like it?" Eva visualizes Mary Jane on all fours, in stockings and corset, receiving repeated lashes from one of the birch rods, not sure if that arouses or terrifies her.

"I can't say as I much care for having my bare arse thwacked with a big stick"—Mary Jane sees a sigh of relief ripple through Eva's body—"but there is something oddly pleasurable about having a man on his knees, bent over, imploring me to flog him. I suppose there's a cruel streak in me that rather likes causing a man pain."

"Even though he's asking for it?"

"He ain't asking, he's begging." Mary Jane's voice is laced with venom. "To see a man beg at the feet of a woman is an intoxicating sight. One could get drunk on it." Snapping herself out of a burgeoning daydream before she gets caught up in it, she slaps on a smile and moves to the table, lifting items from the grocery bag. "Anyway, come see! We're all stocked up. I've got plenty of the basics to keep us going for a while, and I paid my arrears on the way up."

"You got well poked, then." Eva doesn't mean that to sound callous, but it does.

Mary Jane's smile falls from her lips, the apologetic look returning. "I don't know how to do this, Eva." She turns her back on the food, resting her bum on the edge of the table. "What can I do to make this easier for you? You knew what I was when we met, and I've kept nothing from you in that regard. I know it's ugly."

Regretful for her sharp tone, Eva turns her gaze to the floor. "I wish you didn't have to earn for us that way, that's all."

"I've mucked my life up right and proper, but I'm trying to fix it." Mary Jane hooks her finger under Eva's chin, tilting her head up. "In the meantime, it's a living, ain't it?"

"You don't have to keep me," Eva volunteers to lessen her burden. "I don't mind working. I'll go on selling flowers and—"

Mary Jane puts a finger to her lips, hushing her. "I *want* to keep you. Let me do that for you. It would please me a great deal." She sweeps her hands around Eva's waist, reeling her in. "I only want the best for you. You know that, don't you?"

"You *are* the best for me." Eva presents her lips for kisses, but upon receiving one, smells the gin on Mary Jane's breath and withdraws. "You been drinking?"

"Only one or two." Mary Jane plays it down. "I use the pubs to find customers."

"How?"

"I go in, order a glass, and wait for someone to flash me a look. If I don't find no-one suitable, I move on to the next, walking the streets a little in between and after."

"You drink every night?"

Knowing how Eva lost her father, Mary Jane keeps her obstinance in check, even though she feels like she's being upbraided. "It's the nature of the work," she explains truthfully, unable to put the teen's mind at ease about the matter. "I get most of my earnings that way."

After a short silence, Eva's eyes flit to the washstand. It's half-filled with water, heated from the kettle, a clean washcloth draped over the side. Mary Jane follows her sightline.

"It's still warm." Eva slides into a chair at the table, unable to make eye contact. "And there's enough left in the kettle if you wants a cup of tea."

Wishing she was a better woman, Mary Jane plants a kiss on top of Eva's head and takes the hint. "Thank you."

While Eva pulls their supper out of the bag and divvies it up, she empties her pockets of hankies—one used to wipe off her hand after her pox-struck customer, another used to clean gunk off the petite customer's grub

worm—and retrieves Fleming's sodden red silk hanky from her sex, his viscid mucilage trickling into the basin.

Eva counts them. "Does that mean you've had three up you?"

"No, darling." Mary Jane retrieves her douching syringe from the shelf beneath the basin. "But please don't ask." She prepares the syringe with the usual mixture of water and vinegar. "I don't want to tell you."

"It won't change how I feels about you." Eva watches her squat above the chamber pot.

"You don't know that." Mary Jane cleanses her vaginal canal. "I don't want our intimacy tainted by what I have to do for coin, so the less you know about that side of my life, the better."

Waiting politely for Mary Jane to join her at the table, Eva keeps eyes on her as she removes her diaphragm and douches again, then piddles.

"What's all that other stuff?" Eva points to the washstand shelf, where Mary Jane keeps her contraceptives and douching products. "I can't make out half them big words."

"All sorts." Mary Jane gives her outer sex a quick wash, then wipes herself with a towel hanging on a hook by the fireplace. "Soluble pessaries for neutralizing a fella's muck, alum and zinc sulphate for giving myself a more thorough swilling out." She washes her hankies, wondering whether there's an element of concern behind Eva's questions. "I'm clean, darling. I promise you." She wrings the hankies out, draping them over the mantel to dry by the fire.

Offering nothing in the way of a response, Eva stares at her plate, taking her first bite only when Mary Jane sits with her, and they eat in a strained silence, Eva alternating between fork and fingers, Mary Jane sticking to the cutlery. As soon as they're done, Eva makes a move to clear away the plates, mumbling something about washing them outside at the water pump, but Mary Jane puts a hand on her shoulder, keeping her seated.

"Did you see what else I brought home?"

Eva shakes her head.

"I got you something." Mary Jane puts on a smile and reaches into the bag, digging out a small bundle wrapped in one of her silk hankies. "It's a little surprise for you." She moves the plates aside and sets the modest gift in front of Eva. "I hope you like them."

Not quite sure what she's done to deserve a present of any kind, Eva peels back the corners of the folded hanky, unveiling a small bunch of green grapes.

"Oh!" She lowers her head to the table, resting her cheek on the dry wood, looking at the fruit sideways. "I ain't never seen grapes up close afore." She touches one with the tip of her finger, feeling the cool, smooth skin. "However did you afford 'em?"

Mary Jane doesn't answer, her smile waning.

"I'm sorry." Eva retracts the question. "That was daft of me to ask."

Dragging her chair closer, Mary Jane plucks one of the grapes. "Close your eyes."

She waits until Eva picks her head up and complies, then leans forward and delivers the teen a kiss, their mouths meeting ever so briefly. It ends almost as soon as it begins, and Eva wants more. Her lips remain parted expectantly, but instead of feeling the return of Mary Jane's warm mouth, she feels a grape bumping on her lower lip.

She captures it, closing her lips around it, as if in a kiss, sinking her front teeth into the fruit's moist flesh and biting it in two. Immediately, her eyes spring open, startled by the sugary sweetness of it, its juices coating her tongue.

"Good?" Mary Jane offers her the other half.

Together, they make short work of the bunch. When it comes to the last one, Eva is happy to relinquish it, but Mary Jane insists on sharing. She holds it in her teeth, wraps her hand around the back of Eva's neck, and moves in, getting Eva to bite down on the exposed portion, their lips grazing, pressing together to trap the escaping juice, finishing with a kiss.

"I'm sorry I'm not everything you want me to be," Mary Jane says then, gazing fondly at her. "You deserve so much more."

Not trusting her mouth to come up with the right words to convey how she feels, Eva pulls Mary Jane out of her chair and leads her across the room. "Can we lie down together?" She flings back the blankets and gets onto the bed, remaining on the nearside.

Lying on her back with her bare legs apart, she gives Mary Jane no room to lie beside her, only on top of her. Yet when Mary Jane tries to crawl over her, she's held off.

"Wait." Eva places a hand on her chest, preventing her from getting any closer. "Unrig first." She hands Mary Jane her chemise off the pillow. "I want to touch you."

Strangely full of nerves, Mary Jane undresses in front of Eva, showing her everything, then puts on her chemise. She makes a second advance onto the bed, but is met once again with a halting hand, this time accompanied by a fretful look.

"What happened?" Eva traces her fingers over a fresh purple bruise on Mary Jane's shoulder. "You're hurt."

Mary Jane glances at it, having forgotten all about her minor encounter with the touchy-feely man in the courtyard. "I had an over exuberant customer, that's all."

"Does that happen often?"

Tiring of the third degree, Mary Jane maneuvers over her, dropping onto the bed next to her. "Why so many questions tonight, love? Is there something troubling you?"

"If aught ever happened to you, I dunno what I'd do." Eva pulls Mary Jane over her, half onto her. "You're all I have." She wraps a leg around Mary Jane's middle, anchoring her there. "I love you, Em."

Mary Jane scoops her up and kisses her. "I love you, my darling," she whispers against Eva's lips, knowing she needs to hear it. "And I know you're feeling insecure." She pulls Eva against her chest. "What can I do to help you feel safe?"

"I just need to be close to you." Eva grabs a handful of Mary Jane's boob, massaging it with her palm. "I want you all over me, holding me and kissing me. Please." She attacks Mary Jane's lips with her own. "Kiss me like you did yesterday. I do like 'em that way."

207

Cautious of Eva's sudden exuberance—well aware that it's not a symptom of genuine lust, but that of grief-fueled anxiety—Mary Jane tenders her an endless series of wet kisses, refraining from initiating anything further. She slips her hand up Eva's chemise, caressing her bare back, drawing her into a tighter embrace, loving her as deeply as she dares, but it's not long before even that becomes too much for the hormonal teen.

Eva pulls away, severing their kisses. "My body's betraying me." She tugs the hem of her chemise down between her legs, rubbing her motte with the heel of her palm. "I can feel it." Ashamed, she rolls over, turning her bum to Mary Jane. "I do enjoy them wet kisses of yours such an awful lot."

"My lips are forever at your service." Mary Jane snuggles behind her, kissing her head and neck, only stopping when she feels Eva tense up.

"Is it wrong?" Eva asks at last, looking over her shoulder at Mary Jane. "Is it wrong that I can't stop wanting your tickles?"

"No, darling. It ain't wrong," Mary Jane puts her mind at ease. "You're cut up about your mam. You want to feel loved and protected, and all of this is so new to you. It's never easy to suppress the passion of a new love, least of all when it's your first. That's why so many girls get themselves into trouble so young. Once you start exploring these feelings, it's difficult to stop."

Eva chews that over. "What would my mam think of me? Lying here with you, wanting a rub when I oughta be grieving."

"Honest?" Mary Jane nibbles lovingly on her earlobe. "I think she'd have a right laugh about it. Your good old mam was thoroughly hot cunted."

She expects that to generate a giggle, but it doesn't.

"Do you think I'm gonna be like her?" Eva frets, biting on a nail. "I don't wanna be, but I can't seem to help the way you makes me feel, and if that's what it means to be hot cunted—to be how she was—then I'm afeared I'll turn out the same. But it's only you I want, I swear it is. I won't never give me-self to no-one else."

Guessing Eva might have developed some suspicions about the way her mother used to earn extra coin, Mary Jane reins in her ardor. "What do you mean, darling?"

Eva hesitates before answering. "I think my mam was ... after my dadda died, I think she ... when we had no money, she might've ... found money in company, the way you do."

Equipped with the knowledge she has about the sailor and the French letter, Mary Jane isn't surprised. Still, she keeps her voice neutral. "What makes you think that?"

Eva turns her mind to childhood, viewing certain events in a new and much less flattering light since meeting Mary Jane. "She and my dadda were always having a poke. After he was gone, she seemed lonely, and there was always plenty fellas around. Some we only saw once. Some kept coming back regular, but none stuck. She called 'em her friends, and they was always mighty generous. Every one we saw left money for us to buy food and that. I just thought we was fortunate that she had so many openhanded friends." Eva peers up at Mary Jane. "I never thought nuthin' of it. Not until I heard you calling your fellas 'friends' n'all." Eva drops her head. "My mam turned gay, didn't she?"

"I dunno one way or the other about that." Mary Jane tries to pacify her. "But even if she did, then so what? There's no shame in it, love. What else is a widow with a gaggle of young children to do? She had to put food in your mouths somehow."

"I s'pose." Eva reflects solemnly on her past, recalling a few of the hardest months in the dead of winter, when money was particularly scarce.

By that time, they were living in a single room on the ground floor of a ramshackle house in the heart of the Old Nichol rookery in Bethnal Green. Virtually every street in the rookery was filled with houses of this kind: overcrowded, decrepit, and unmaintained, with utterly inadequate sanitation.

They had a fire, but could only afford to light it on the very coldest nights, so when Missus Sullivan didn't have company, they'd all cram into her bed, bundling

together for warmth, each of the five children taking it in turns to occupy the middle.

Being the baby of the bunch, eight-year-old Eva always got more than her fair share, the elder children taking pity on her, but the middle position was not always an enviable one. It often meant ending up wedged between her older sister, Kate, and one of her brothers, and as time went on, she got mighty sick of feeling their errant erections jabbing at her body.

"Mammy," she'd whine, "John's poking me with his thing!"

After a grumble from Missus Sullivan and a slight shuffle around, everything was taken care of. The offending brother would be relocated next to his mother, who would then proceed to resolve the problem with her hand, frigging him quickly and quietly, taking his deposit on her thighs and belly so as to save the bed sheets.

Whatever else they did, Eva never knew, though she suspected that the boys sometimes repaid the favor, using their mother's freely available body to learn all they needed to know of female anatomy. Certainly, her strangled moans suggested as much.

Still, sharing a bed was moderately preferable to the sleeping arrangements they had to endure on the nights when Missus Sullivan *did* have company. Eva remembers being nine years old and lying awake in the middle of the night, sharing a flea-infested palliasse on the floor with Kate. Her three older brothers shared another palliasse on the other side of the room, while her mother and an unknown male occupied the main bed.

Exhausted from their earlier pokings, the man, naked from the waist down, wearing only his shirt, lay sleeping—or trying to—as Eva's chemise-clad mother stroked his worn out tool, trying to work up an erection.

"It won't stand again, woman," the man grumbled, half asleep. "You've had the best of it for tonight. Its starch has gone."

Eva's mother—who was then a much finer example of a woman, full-fleshed with a soft, round face—was relentless in her desire. Elevated on gin, she applied her mouth to his wilted pego, determined that it should rise

for her. In the light cast by the fire, Eva could see her head bobbing up and down on the soft, fleshy stick protruding from his groin, then saw the stick swell, gaining length and thickness.

"See, there!" Missus Sullivan tugged on it a few times for good measure, demonstrating its stiffness. "You've a fine poker."

The man grunted. His lusts were up, but he was hesitant to perform. During their earlier doings, the children had all been sent from the room, but now they were back, all tucked up for the night, and their presence unnerved him.

"Your littlins ain't yet asleep," he griped. "They'll see."

Regardless, Missus Sullivan flopped onto her back and lifted up her chemise. "No worry. Get on and show 'em how it's done. They all has to learn somehow."

Too randy to put up much fuss, the man rolled on top of her and rammed his prick inside her, but soon found he had nothing left to give. After fifteen minutes of strenuous rutting, he began to tire.

"I can't do no more." He withdrew from her, breathing hard. "I'm fucked out."

"Oh, get back on." Missus Sullivan jerked her hips agitatedly. "I was just coming."

Not up to the task, the man was about to gather up his things and leave when he noticed Eva's oldest brother watching them from his spot on the floor. The sixteen-year-old had the blanket thrown off him and his prick out, his fist working the shaft.

The man chortled. "I bet you'd rather be up your old mam, wouldn't ya?"

"You rotten sod." Missus Sullivan slapped his chest.

Undeterred, thinking it a lark, the man invited the boy on. "Go on, son. Get it wet."

Incensed, Missus Sullivan sat up and closed her fleshy thighs. "You're a monster, you are. That's my boy you're talking to."

"Aye, and he's got a big stiff one. Look at it." He turned her head, making her look at her son's youthful erection.

The sight lessened Missus Sullivan's protests, but didn't silence them. Full submission to the idea came later, when the man said: "I'll give you five bob if you let him."

Grumbling under her breath, Missus Sullivan turned to the man. "The boy ain't never done it afore. He won't last in me."

"Then you can let him do it twice." The man opened up Missus Sullivan's legs and patted the mattress. "Come on, boy. She wants ya."

"It's all right," Missus Sullivan encouraged the tentative teen. "Just this once."

Hormones won out and the boy crept into position, lining himself up with her hair-covered hole, his cock already wet with pre-fuck.

"That's it." Missus Sullivan grabbed it, lodging the tip inside herself. "Now push."

He did, and went up in her one stroke, making them both cry out, then remained still, afraid to move until she wiggled her hips impatiently.

"Shove, boy. Whatchu waiting for? Gimme a good shove."

He tried his best, and managed twelve hard thrusts before erupting into her depths. The second time, he lasted longer, and Missus Sullivan kept at him all through the night, long after the strange man left. At some point, Eva fell asleep. When she awoke, all three boys were sleeping in the bed with their mother, and it didn't take too much imagination to figure out why.

A short time later, Missus Sullivan rose to piddle, and to fish a semen-soaked, folded-up handkerchief out of her polluted depths. Lacking the funds to purchase any proper birth control, she relied on the wadded up fabric to trap a man's fluid, preventing it from traveling up into her womb, and since she hadn't been caught with child in a fair long while, she assumed it worked.

She had no way of knowing that she was already infertile, on account of the various diseases slowly wreaking havoc on her insides. She thought the infrequent bouts of pelvic pain were the natural workings of the female body, related to the coming and going of her

irregular monthlies. The painful urination, she concluded, was simply due to the repeated friction of numerous lovers.

As she squatted over the chamber pot, thick globulous strings of her sons' spunk dripping from her abused sex, she looked down at her youngest daughter. "A bit o'stiff is nice," she said, presumably by way of explanation for her actions. "You'll know how it is when you get older."

But Eva never did. Recollecting many more sordid tales from her childhood, she bursts into tears, seeking solace in Mary Jane's breast, her emotions tumbling into freefall.

"I don't wanna be like she was."

"Oh, darling. You're not." Mary Jane comforts her.

"It's not the same."

"But I thinks about doing it with you all the time," Eva sobs, her voice muffled in Mary Jane's cleavage. "More and more every day."

"You're in love." Mary Jane rocks her, trying to calm her. "It's different when you're in love." She lifts Eva's head up, wiping away her tears. "It's perfectly natural."

"You're sure it don't mean I'm going bad?"

"Craving intimacy with the person you love won't ever make you go bad, darling." Mary Jane kisses her damp cheeks. "I promise you."

Her panic dissipating, Eva settles back down in Mary Jane's arms. "I forgot to say that detective bloke come round while you was gone." She sniffles. "He said my aunt Bessie wants me to visit her, and I'm to go there tomorra. Will you come with me? I ain't seen her for years."

"Course I will, darling. If you don't think I'll be in the way."

Eva shakes her head. "I want her to meet you." She tucks herself against Mary Jane's body. "Then she'll see that I'm cared for and she won't fuss."

Mary Jane's not so sure about that, but keeps her reservations to herself. All Eva needs now is a soothing hand and a warm embrace. The troubles will wait till tomorrow.

CHAPTER 18

Sunday, March 6, 1887

MARY JANE RETURNS TO THRAWL STREET FEELING A GOOD deal worse than she has in a long time. Despite her Roman Catholic upbringing, she's let the formalities of her religion fall by the wayside. For her, church means confession, and confession means facing her guilt. She'd sworn she wouldn't go back until she was ready to leave this rotten life behind, but Eva had never missed a Sunday service and didn't want to go alone.

After much begging and pleading, she'd acquiesced, accompanying Eva on her quest for religious comfort, the trip culminating in a flood of tears from both of them. Eva crying for her mother, who, according to Detective Dew's medical man, took her own life and is therefore quite probably condemned to hell. Mary Jane crying for her sins, which are many and varied, and will most likely send her there in the end.

Now back in the safety of her room, she'd rather have a nap and forget all about heaven and hell and eternal damnation—some gin would help with that—but there's barely time for a bite to eat before heading out to visit Eva's aunt.

"Where does she live exactly?" Mary Jane inspects her appearance in the mirror, hoping she'll pass muster. "We should get going if we want to make it there in good time." She rubs at her cheeks, smudging away some of her rouge, fearing that she's applied too much.

215

"Regent Square," Eva answers, her mouth full of the last bit of Mary Jane's cheese, scavenged from the cupboard. "But we don't need to go nowhere. She's sending her brougham."

Mary Jane stops fussing with her perfectly plucked eyebrows. "You what?"

"She's sending her brougham," Eva repeats casually, not understanding the implications of the fact. "Why?" She looks up, perplexed to see Mary Jane pulling a steamer trunk out from under the bed. "Whatchu doing?"

"I can't wear this." Mary Jane points to her bodice, indicating her décolletage. "Whatever would your aunt think of me?"

Having not thought of this problem till now, Eva suddenly feels a little less confident. "Should we not tell her what you are?"

"No." Mary Jane shakes her head, tossing away her white apron. "We bloody well should not. No woman who has her own brougham is the kind of woman who wants to hear that her niece plans to spend her life knocking about with an old pinchcock."

"Then what's we to say? She'll ask how you plan to keep me, I know she will."

"Seamstress," Mary Jane suggests, stripping off her clothes. "A woman skilled with her fingers and swift with the work can make a few bob. Not enough to get her own brougham, but certainly enough to keep her lovely young companion in food and rent."

No longer embarrassed by Mary Jane's nudity, Eva pores over her exposed body, noticing how she responds to the attention by drawing out her movements, slowly and elegantly rolling on a pair of a woven silk stockings.

"You enjoy being admired," she concludes.

"What woman don't?" Mary Jane puts her boots back on, then slips into the silk shift she normally reserves for sleeping.

"I dunno." Eva shrugs. "I'm much too shy."

"Well, I had the last of that knocked out of me when I was new to London." Mary Jane lays her best clothes out on the bed. "Among everything else I did for coin in

the West End, I was a posture girl. You know what one of them is?"

Eva shakes her head.

"When I had my courses on, I wouldn't take customers the usual way. A lot of others just shove a bit of sponge up there and carry on, but I weren't up for that. Instead, to keep me earning, the madam who ran my house had me take my togs off and make a show of it." Mary Jane turns around, putting on the same blue satin corset she wore to her assignation with Missus B——. "I sang a little, I danced, struck a few poses, and"—she doubles over, peering at Eva upside down through her legs—"showed off my bits and bobs." She flips her chemise up and gives her naked bum a shake, making Eva giggle.

When she rights herself, Eva gets a proper look at the custom-made corset. "Oh, that's just the prettiest thing I've ever seen." She wanders nearer, her eyes glued to Mary Jane's bust. "So lovely." She reaches out to touch it, then thinks better of it, lifting her skirts and wiping her hands off on her petticoat before she goes for it a second time.

Still adjusting to the novelty of having a woman's body readily available to her, she whimpers as she runs her hands over Mary Jane's waist, all the way up to those prominent bust gores, cupping them. Then, she notices the dress.

"Oh, lummy." She steps back, giving Mary Jane enough space to finish donning the exquisite outfit, the deep purple silk contrasting with the white lace trims.

"Silk ..." Eva picks up the hem of Mary Jane's skirts, admiring the rich fabric.

"I knew you wanted a silk dress," Mary Jane teases, pinning up her mane.

"You look so different. So nice." Eva looks down at her own raggedy dress, feeling distinctly sub-par. "I dunno how I shall dare to be seen with you."

In an attempt to cheer her, Mary Jane grabs her around the waist and bum, picks her up, and carries her to the table, making her squeal.

"I think we ought to go shopping tomorrow. Do you agree?" Mary Jane sits her on the tabletop, sweeping her skirts above her knees and parting her legs. "I shall buy you a new dress." She budges between the teen's bared thighs. "Would you like that?"

Catching movement over Eva's shoulder, she looks out of the window, watching as a dark green brougham pulls up on the street outside the lodging house.

"Our carriage awaits."

After making a few finishing touches to her outfit, and giving Eva a quick kiss for courage, Mary Jane leads the way to the brougham and helps Eva into it, reassuring her several times that there's no need to remove her shoes.

"If your aunt can afford a brougham, I'm sure she can afford someone to clean it."

"I feels all fancy." Eva strokes the padded velvet seat, giving the carriage a thorough look over, committing this experience to memory. "My mam woulda piddled herself to see me riding around in one of these." Imagining that, her excitement sinks beneath a swell of grief, remembering why she's in this carriage in the first place.

Seeing the tears come, Mary Jane wraps her arm around Eva's shoulders. "It'll get better. I promise you it will."

"Did my mam ..." Eva swallows hard and clears her throat so as not to choke on the words as she forces them out. "Did my mam really do away with herself?"

"It appears so," Mary Jane replies after a while. "She was in a lot of pain. She didn't want to keep hurting, I suppose, and I'm not sure I blame her. Did she and your aunt have a falling out? Is that why you ain't seen her in so long?"

"I dunno all the stuff of it." Eva wipes her nose on her sleeve, rolling up her cuff to hide the snot trail. "What she said to me was that Aunt Bessie couldn't wrap her head around me, and I were best away from her. Not much afore that, there was some quarrel to do with my sister."

"What do you mean? What happened to your sister?" Given what Missus Sullivan did to Eva's brothers, Mary Jane almost dare not ask.

"When she were fourteen, Kate started seeing a boy." Eva messes with a new hole forming in her dress. "He wanted to put his thing in her, but she was scared of doing it 'cause another girl told her it hurt real bad and made her bleed for a solid week." She picks at the fraying fabric, making the hole bigger. "Kate tried putting her fingers up one night, but couldn't get more than her little one in." Eva pokes her finger through the hole, wiggling it around. "She asked me to try, but I wouldn't, so then she asked our mam what she oughta do."

Mary Jane feels a pang of dread. "What did your mother do to her, Eva?"

"Nuthin' directly." Eva adjusts her sash, covering the hole. "But she brung a fella over one night, and said he was to teach Kate the way of things. She said he were a doctor."

Now thinking that to be a lie, Eva relates the tale of Kate's initiation into the carnal world when she was just fourteen—which was then a year over the age of consent. The man, doctor or otherwise, was brought to their room to perform the examination, and to advise her on when she might expect her monthlies to start.

Sensing something afoot, twelve-year-old Eva peeped through the door as her mother stripped Kate to her chemise, got her on the bed, and spread her legs for the man, drawing a candle near to let him see the unbroken flesh. When Kate started crying, Missus Sullivan slapped her till she was quiet, repeatedly calling her names and cursing.

"Don't be such a fool. Ain't he a nice young man? A doctor, no less. Ain't I always told you to trust what a doctor says? He'll show you what it's all about, then you needn't be afeared no more."

"Here"—the man took out his rigid tool—"feel me, won't you? See, this is how a man's organ gets when he wants to have connection with a woman. You know this, yes? You've seen a few pricks before, no doubt. Don't sham. I'll give you a shilling if you will."

Kate started to shake her head, but Missus Sullivan clipped her ear and took the shilling.

"Hurry and toss the gent off, you ungrateful little wretch. You've done that afore, I knows you have. And ain't got nuthin' for it, neither."

Trapped, Kate did as she was told and wrapped her hand around the stiff shaft, stroking it up and down. His lusts rising, the man—who called himself Walter—felt her commodity as she frigged him, and she must've been affected by it, for she soon opened her legs wider and her head sank onto his shoulder.

"Your quim's weeping, darling." He kept stroking. "You've been felt before, haven't you?"

Kate nodded through her tears.

"Doesn't it feel nice?" he went on.

Kate nodded again. "It do, but I'm so afeared."

"Have you ever spent?"

Kate shook her head, declaring that she wasn't even sure what a girl's spending was, never mind what it felt like. Upon being quizzed about a man's crisis, all she knew was: "His thing spits out white stuff."

She said the first time her lad's thing spat at her, he got it all over her dress. Terrified to come home, she'd washed her frock at the water pump. Better to come home all wet than to come home with a man's muck all over her, she reasoned.

Laughing, the man told her it would be better to let the poor boy put his libation in the proper receptacle, then there'd be no need for panic. He then withdrew his hand.

"Lie back on the bed, my dear."

Obediently, Kate released his priapus and lay down, letting him lift her skirts to inspect her bits and pieces once more before resuming his manual stimulation.

Moments later, Kate started to squirm. "Ooh, whatchu doing down there? I feel ever so queer."

"You're ready for a prick, my love." He dropped his trousers and clambered over her. "Your cunt is hungry for it, and look how stiff you've made me." He wrapped his fist around his cock-stand, presenting it to her. "It wants to be up you."

Kate looked for her mother, ready to spring from the bed. "I ain't sure ..."

"Trust the doctor," Missus Sullivan barked. "He knows what's best."

Not wanting to anger her mother, Kate let herself go limp and closed her eyes as the man went belly to belly over her. Eva turned away, but she heard the creaking of the bed and a few primal grunts, followed by Kate's distressed wail.

"You hurt! Oh, do stop, sir! It hurts me!"

But he didn't stop. He impaled her, crying out victoriously, "I'm up her!"

That first fuck didn't last long. He was too full and too impatient, and spent inside her within a minute. Throughout, he gave her a running commentary. "I'm fucking you, darling! You're being fucked! Don't you want to be fucked? Cunt loves prick!"

When it was over, he supped gin with Missus Sullivan—his mixed with water, hers neat—and they passed the minutes with idle chitchat until he could be ready again. Both of them ignored poor Kate, who lay sobbing on the bed, a pinkish mixture of blood and spermatic fluid soaking into her chemise, but as soon as his prick was able to rise to the task, more coin exchanged hands and he mounted her a second time.

"I shall have her again!" he declared triumphantly, getting over her on the bed and dipping his fingers in her to admire his handiwork before driving his tool up the ravaged, semenalized cock-channel.

Seizing the opportunity for some carnal gratification of her own, Missus Sullivan assumed the spot beside them, close enough to see the ins and outs of the operation, and urged the man on, feeling his heavy cods.

The business lasted longer than the first connection, Eva noted, now peeping again, and Kate didn't sob even once. She winced as he went up her, then lay quiet, then whined, but in a different manner from before.

"Oh, mama!" she sobbed out. "What's happening?"

Curious, Eva could just make out her mother twiddling Kate's southern parts as the man rutted on her, determined that she should get a pleasure with her

second fuck. Then, the room was filled with voluptuous moans.

Kate spent for the first time, all resistance gone, and as she did so, the man was fetched by the tightening of her love-trap and came inside her. All the while, Missus Sullivan frigged herself beside them.

"Do me next," she then demanded, as the man pulled his prick from her daughter.

"I can't," he argued breathlessly. "I've no more money."

"Never mind that, just do it to me." She yanked him to her, for he was still stiff. "Put your prick up me. I need it badly."

And so he did. Without washing, he drove his spendings and Kate's right up into her, fucking her as Kate lay in a stupor, her battered sex leaking onto the bed sheets.

"I ain't seen her since," Eva laments, remembering how Kate went out to buy a loaf of bread one day and never returned. "I think she must've gone to Aunt Bessie and told her of the man who had her firsts, 'cause Aunt come visit soon after, threatening to take me away."

"Take you away?"

"She said I'd be better off with her. Said she'd set me straight, whatever that means. I reckon she prob'ly thought I'd go wrong like my mam if I stayed put, but I ain't never."

Concerned that Aunt Bessie's interests extend beyond protecting Eva's innocence and into suppressing her natural passions, Mary Jane lets the topic dissolve, not wanting to fill Eva's head with any more negative thoughts.

Minutes later, they disembark in front of a four-storey, stock brickwork house in Regent Square, opposite the disused St. George's Burial Grounds in St. Pancras, Camden. It's an area of middling wealth, with clean streets and respectable families, just a stone's throw away from the foundling hospital.

Fraught with nerves, Eva hangs on Mary Jane's arm, clutching tightly. "Gimme a kiss afore we go in?"

If Mary Jane knew Aunt Bessie was watching them from an upstairs window, she'd be more restrained. As it is, she glances up and down the street, sees no-one coming, and welcomes Eva in for a lingering smooch.

When it breaks, "Are you ready now?" she asks, pulling back to a respectable distance.

Eva isn't at all sure about that, but she walks up to Bessie's front door with determination, giving the brass knocker a few good taps.

In a short time, the door is opened by a young, plain-faced maid with a crooked smile. She welcomes them, invites them into the hall, and divests them of their outdoor clothing as the mistress of the house surveys them from the staircase.

In her early thirties, Bessie is a brunette with stern but pleasing features. She's much alike to Eva's mother in height, but not in weight. Good eating and childbirth have put meat on her, fleshing out her thighs, rump, and breasts, and despite her lower half being masked by full skirts and ruffles, Mary Jane can tell she's sturdily built.

Her silk dress rustles with every step as she descends to greet them, her movements lacking some of the grace and refinement that a truly well-bred lady would've honed long before her ascent into adulthood. It gives her away. She's nothing more than a common working class girl who's done well for herself, enhancing her station in life by virtue of a good marriage.

"Eva, my dear girl." She puts her hands on Eva's shoulders, straightening her posture and patting her as one might a dog, offering no further signal of familial affection. "I see you've brought a friend."

Proud to show off her companion, Eva wraps her arm around Mary Jane's. "This is Mary Jane." Remembering her manners, she rethinks her words. "This is Miss Mary Jane Kelly, I mean to say. She's my dearest friend."

"It's a great pleasure to meet you." Mary Jane smiles politely, suddenly realizing she doesn't know Bessie's married name, or how to properly address her.

Bessie has bigger concerns, though. After a moment's thought, giving her guest a brief look over from

head to toe and not much liking what she sees, she offers her hand for shaking. "Did you forget your hat in the carriage?"

And so it begins, Mary Jane thinks, answering honestly. "I'm afraid I don't possess one."

"Oh." Bessie forms an immediate—and wholly unflattering—impression of her guest's character. "What a pity." She ushers them into the parlor, offering them the sofa. "Do sit. I'll pour you some tea." Her eyes meet Mary Jane's, her lips taut and thin. "I saw you arrive and had the maid bring it in directly."

Mary Jane reads Bessie's mind perfectly: keep your hands and mouth off my niece. Nevertheless, she doesn't push Eva away when she sits too close. Nor does she object when Eva seeks out her hand, clasping it tightly.

During the course of pleasant conversation over tea, she learns much. Bessie's husband is a solicitor, which accounts for the comfortable living. He's away on business, and the children—all boys, all under ten—are with their grandparents in Bermondsey, getting some country air in their lungs, while Bessie enjoys the respite of a quiet house. Eva's never met her cousins.

Happy to take a lesser role in the exchange of personal tales, Mary Jane remains quiet, letting aunt and niece reacquaint themselves. Momentarily forgetting where she is, she becomes too relaxed and crosses her legs at the knee, the action resulting in a startled intake of breath from Bessie and an immediate cessation of dialogue. When Mary Jane corrects herself and the conversation resumes, it veers off in another direction altogether.

"It's a shame to see you in such dreadful rags." Bessie turns her displeasure on Eva, picking faults with her dress. "Could your mother do no better? Stand up now and lift your skirts." She snaps her fingers. "Let me see the state of your drawers."

Eva blushes fiercely, flashing Mary Jane a bashful smile. "I ain't wearing any."

That sets Bessie off on a rant about the appalling state of affairs in which Eva was forced to live, while Mary Jane feels a glorious shiver run through her. She

knows the only reason modest young Eva wouldn't have put on her drawers is so that she'd be ready should the opportunity for coupling happen to present itself, and her cunt pulses.

As Bessie ushers Eva and the maid out of the room, instructing the maid on where to find some alternative attire, Mary Jane looks down at her crotch.

"Stop that," she chastises her greedy sex. "You're not getting anything."

When Bessie returns, Mary Jane does her best to keep the small talk flowing, complimenting the stern-looking woman on her home, her tea, and anything else she can think of, but the conversation soon takes a dive.

"How long have you known Eva?" Bessie asks, steering them onto dangerous ground.

"Not long."

"You met the mother?"

"On several occasions." Mary Jane latches onto an opportunity to legitimize her relationship with Eva. "She was pleasant to me, and glad that Eva had found companionship."

"Hmm." Bessie raises an eyebrow, ruminating on all the different connotations of 'companionship.' "Do you know what sort of life she led?"

Anticipating a moral lecture on the wrongs of prostitution, Mary Jane mentally prepares herself and answers diplomatically. "I know she suffered difficulties after she lost Eva's father, and those difficulties led her into a bad way of life."

Bessie guffaws. "Ha! That woman didn't need an excuse to go bad, she was never any good to begin with. You know, she was only twelve when she first had it. The little harlot couldn't even wait till she was thirteen. She gave herself up to the first man who offered her a piece of gold for it and came home with her shemmy all bloodied, her thighs covered in his muck." Bessie snorts scornfully. "Our mother and father tried to keep her in after that, but she wouldn't have it. Once that girl had a cock up her, she'd go to any lengths to have one again."

"Some girls lose their way easy," Mary Jane responds with a sharp edge to her voice, her defenses triggered.

"But it's not always as straightforward as it seems. There could be mitigating factors which—"

"Mitigating factors?" Bessie huffs disbelievingly, cutting her off. "If she couldn't have a poke, she'd let men get their hands up her skirts for a tanner. Walking me home from school, she'd do it with them right there on the street, whilst I kept watch for the peelers. She was practically begging for it. It was vulgar."

"Girls of that age don't know any better." Mary Jane continues to give Missus Sullivan the benefit of the doubt, projecting events in her own past onto the deceased woman. "That's why the law was changed to protect them. They're too easily led."

"I wasn't." Bessie refuses to soften her judgment. "I would not be corrupted by such wickedness, no matter how she tried."

Rippling with anger, she recounts how her older sister, Sarah, came home one evening and woke her in the bed they shared. She flopped onto the mattress and lifted her skirts, showing off her hairless mound, dripping sex, and semen-splattered thighs.

"I'm a woman now," she said, oozing pride. "I have pricks up there every night." She pointed to her slopping hole, unwashed between each paying guest. "They fill me with their stuff." She reached for her sister's hand. "Here, have a feel of it."

Not knowing any better, seven-year-old Bessie let Sarah take her hand.

"Feel all their spunk in me." Sarah placed Bessie's tiny mitt on her saturated commodity. "Rub it, Bess. Rub it for me. Rub all over."

Sobbing, Bessie did as she asked, watching in bewilderment as her sister writhed on the bed until, finally, she appeared to have a fit. All went quiet then. Sarah turned over and went to sleep, just like that.

As they got older, Sarah's desperation grew. On more than one occasion, she clambered on top of Bessie in the middle of the night, driven by a letch to show her how a man ruts on a woman in fucking. Though Bessie fought and kicked, Sarah was bigger and stronger and pinned her to the bed.

He'd never seen such sexual force in a young girl. Four fucks later, when he was temporarily drained, he called three of his friends over and they all had at her, one after the other. By the time Bessie went up to sleep, Sarah was lying naked on their bed, barely conscious and utterly incapable of coordinated movement. The sheets were soaked with sweat and spendings. White, gooey residue was oozing out of Sarah's body, completely obscuring her privy parts, and the same was smeared all over her abdomen, stomach, and chest, her under-developed breast buds glistening in the candlelight.

Bessie cried then, and she dabs at her eyes with a hanky now, the memory bringing with it a whole host of unpleasant emotions, including pity. Not pity for Sarah, mind you, but pity for her own ruined childhood.

"Stupid wretch got herself in the family way when she was fifteen." She sniffs, tucking the hanky back up her sleeve. "She'd only been a full woman two months, and didn't know a speck of anything about how it all worked. She was crafty, though. To spare herself the indignity, she went out and found some gullible bloke with a kind heart, got him up her, then told him the babe in her belly was his."

"Eva's father?" Mary Jane guesses, listening to these tales with a heavy heart.

"He married her, of course, but he was never enough for her," Bessie openly criticizes her late sister. "I daresay any man this side of the Thames could well be Eva's true blood. The same goes for her siblings."

"Where are they all?" Mary Jane inquires, saddened by Eva's circumstances.

"Only God knows that." Bessie sighs, sipping the last of her tea. "They all did the wise thing and got well away from her as soon as they could. I tried to take Eva into my care, but she wouldn't hear of it. Do you know what happened to the older girl?"

Mary Jane nods. "Some."

"She lived with me for a time afterward, but was heartily sickened on this city. Now she's vanished like the others." Bessie stares at the dregs of tea leaves left behind in the bottom of her cup, as though she might find

answers there. "I feared for Eva, though Sarah swore to me she'd never do anything to harm her. Eva was different, she told me. Not built for the love of a man." She locks her eyes onto Mary Jane, waiting for a reaction that doesn't come. "Perhaps the girl's simple. I'll be damned if I know what to make of her."

"Eva's not simple," Mary Jane defends her young lover without hesitation. "She knows well what she wants."

"But not what's good for her." Bessie glares at Mary Jane, full of disdain. "Clearly."

Before the verbal exchange has a chance to escalate, the maid brings Eva back into the room. Transformed from a young girl to a proper woman, her hair's been pinned up and she's wearing a new, ankle-length frock: yellow cotton-backed satin with white lace trims, ruched at the rear to create a cascade of ruffles and flounces. Though the skirt portion has a drawstring waist and is tightened to fit, the bodice is loose around her chest and middle.

"It needs taking in a bit," the maid addresses Bessie. "But don't she look lovely?"

"Divine." Mary Jane stands to greet her, unable—or unwilling—to conceal the affection in her eyes, her arms held open, inviting a hug. "Simply divine."

Eva dashes into her embrace. "I'm glad it pleases you."

Scowling, Bessie watches Eva press herself to Mary Jane's bosom, Mary Jane's arms wrapped around her hips and lower back, lightly caressing her, their intimacy plain to see. The scowl sticks when they return to the sofa, Eva practically sitting in Mary Jane's lap, their thighs touching from knee to hip, hands entwined.

Keen to wedge some distance between them, Bessie extends an invitation to her niece. "I do hope you won't be hurrying off later. I have the guest bedroom all made up."

Before answering, Eva checks with Mary Jane, it not occurring to her even for a second that the invitation wouldn't include both of them. "Do you mind if we spend a night?"

Mary Jane shakes her head. "Course not, darling. Whatever you want."

Bessie clenches and unclenches her jaw. "I'm afraid we've taken in a couple of lodgers, so there's only one bedroom. Unless one of you wants to sleep in the maid's quarters."

Snickering at that ludicrous notion, Eva pulls Mary Jane's hand into her lap, blissfully unaware of her aunt's disapproval. "One bed suits us fine. We always sleeps together."

CHAPTER 19

MARY JANE LIES IN BED IN HER SILK CHEMISE, HER NIGHTLY ablutions tended to, waiting for Eva to do the same. The bedroom, like every other part of Bessie's house, is modest but comfortable. The bed is soft and warm, the linens clean, and the pillows are soft and plump, not lumpy and malformed like her own. Everything is just as it should be. The window closes all the way and the panes aren't loose, keeping in the heat from the fire that's dancing in the hearth.

"Everything here is so fancy," Eva states for the fiftieth time, still awed by their surroundings as she tiptoes back into the bedroom from the shared bathroom at the end of the hall. "I'm afeared to touch aught in case I leaves a dirty mark."

She pads across the hardwood floor and leaps onto the bed, tripping over herself when the ankle-length nightgown Bessie put her in limits the spread of her legs, hampers her ability to jump, and she tumbles face first onto the mattress.

"So graceful." Mary Jane gives her rump a playful tap.

"Stupid nightclothes," Eva grumbles, rolling onto her back. "I'm wearing too much. I shall get hot." She pulls the nightgown up over her knees, revealing a clean pair of drawers. "And these don't even have no split in 'em. See?" She gives the seamed crotch a tug.

231

"Gosh, a proper nightgown *and* closed drawers." Mary Jane chuckles, running her fingers up Eva's bared calf. "Your aunt really don't want me getting any ideas in my head, does she? I'm surprised she hasn't sent you to bed wearing a chastity belt."

Eva responds by lifting her nightgown higher, showing Mary Jane the drawstring waistband of her undergarments. "She done it up in a such a tight knot I can't get it out." She fumbles with the string, trying to unpick it, her fingertips already pink from struggling with it in the bathroom. "I think the blasted thing needs scissors brung to it."

Still laughing, scoffing at Bessie's vain attempt to prohibit the expression of affection between them, Mary Jane dips her head and pinches the knot between her teeth, gradually working it free. She's close enough to Eva's core that she can smell the musk of her sex, and if Eva weren't so emotionally fragile, she'd ditch the knot, rip open the buttons running down the hip of the drawers—so designed to allow for quicker access when tending to certain privy needs—and put her mouth to much better use.

Similarly affected by the proximity of Mary Jane's face to her crotch, a flush spreads over Eva's cheeks. She can feel Mary Jane's hot breath penetrating the thin cotton, stirring her up, and this time, she doesn't want to stop.

"Ta-da!" Mary Jane gets the knot loosened with her teeth, then finishes the work with her hands, tearing the drawers off Eva's hips. "Freedom, my love."

Eva does the rest herself and kicks the unwanted garment to the floor, immediately presenting herself for cuddles. "Give me kisses." She rolls into Mary Jane. "Wet kisses," she insists. "I likes them the best."

Wrapping her arms around Eva's lathy body, Mary Jane initiates a series of deep, passionate kisses, sliding one hand down to grip Eva's bum and pulling her close. Of her own accord, Eva then hooks her leg over Mary Jane's hip, getting closer still, thrusting her pelvis forward in the hope of achieving genital connection.

Her efforts result only in the uncoordinated bumping and grinding of their pubic mounds, but Mary Jane gets the hint. She crooks her knee through Eva's parted legs and rocks her hips, causing Eva's crotch to rub against her thigh, generating a delightful friction.

In minutes, Eva recognizes the sensation of wetness in her southern regions. It's the same feeling she had when she panicked and locked herself in the public privy, only to discover that the deluge wasn't the onset of her menarche, but a symptom of her newly awakened hunger for physical pleasure.

Severing their kisses, "I want it," she whispers urgently. "I want fucking."

A bolt of arousal shoots through Mary Jane to hear Eva ask so plainly for a touch. If she were possessed of a cock, it would've sprung to full hardness in that moment and been driving up Eva the next, their bodies joined in passion until the precious moment of mutual satisfaction was reached, Eva's immature womb flooded with the consequence of their lusts.

Overcome with desire at the mere thought of it, Mary Jane has to restrain herself. "Are you sure?" she forces herself to ask, wary of Eva's fragile mental state.

By way of assurance, Eva places Mary Jane's hand on her throbbing sex. "Don't I want it?"

Mary Jane feels the measure of her lust, her clitoris prominent and hard, her cleft drenched. "You do." She groans. "You're so wet."

"I want a pleasure." Eva shuffles onto her back and opens her thighs, encouraging Mary Jane on top of her. "Fetch me, please. I need it so."

"Will you promise to be quiet?" Mary Jane gives her a light tickle.

Eva nods.

"All right, then." Mary Jane pulls her hand away, rucks Eva's nightgown up to her hips, and wriggles into position, preparing to gamahuche her.

"Whatchu doing down there?" Eva frowns. "You wanna look at me?"

"I'm going to kiss you."

Mary Jane dips her face to Eva's motte, kissing there, and Eva giggles, thinking she's going to drop a few tender kisses, then withdraw. Instead, she feels Mary Jane spread open the folds of her sex, kissing her slit.

"Oh!" She gasps. "You're never ... ?"

"I am," Mary Jane answers, her voice muffled against Eva's flesh.

Astonished by the sensation of Mary Jane's hot tongue pressed firmly between her labia, probing the entrance to her body, Eva cries out with a squeal. "What are you about!"

Every hot lash feels like a tendril of fire kissing her flesh. It's too much and it's not enough. When Mary Jane sucks directly on her clit, she feels as though she might have a fit, her entire body racked with jolts of electric sensation emanating from her womanhood. Yet when Mary Jane moves lower, kissing and licking the flushed slit, she finds herself straining to open her legs wider, yearning to accept Mary Jane's slithering tongue deeper into her body, wishing it could plunge up her, caressing her insides.

Forgetting her promise to be quiet, she lets out a mighty yowl, causing Mary Jane to desist immediately, frightened that she'll wake the house.

"Do try to hush, love." Mary Jane hates having to remind her. "We're not alone."

Eva nods hurriedly. "Uh-huh, sshhh." She pushes on the top of Mary Jane's head, forcing her back down. "Like a mouse in a cheese."

Doubting her ability to harness such restraint, Mary Jane tentatively reengages, resulting in the escape of another loud moan. She tries to leave off again, but Eva won't let her get free.

"Don't stop doing me," the enraptured teen begs, holding Mary Jane's face to her crotch. "I ain't never felt such a delicious tingle."

Overwhelmed by her own desire for Eva's flesh, Mary Jane nestles her face into Eva's mound of dark pubic curls, inhaling the heady aroma of her arousal.

"Oh, fuck it," she mumbles, diving in and devouring Eva's sweet sex.

All the while, Eva paws at her head, tugging and gripping her hair, clutching frantically at her tresses. When Mary Jane tries to pull back to get some air, Eva bucks and writhes, jerking her bum upwards, determined not to break contact, even for a second.

Though Mary Jane can barely breathe, she tongues Eva with fury, ignoring the pain as the teen's flailing feet repeatedly strike her shoulders and back.

Trying to retain some semblance of control, she finally grabs the back of Eva's thighs and pushes her skinny legs up and apart, keeping her feet out of trouble. In this position, Eva looks down at herself, the obscenely lewd posture triggering the first tremor of her orgasm.

"I'm nearly coming," she warns, not sure if Mary Jane ought to take her face away before the moment of crisis, but then ... "Oho! Arhhhh!" She lets out one guttural cry and convulses into Mary Jane's mouth, watching Mary Jane lap up every drop of her spendings.

Panting and barely conscious, she whimpers softly, relishing the powerful contractions of her climax—her most intense yet.

"That was ... oh, lummy ..." She takes a deep breath and closes her eyes, incapable of articulating the degree of her pleasure.

"You taste heavenly." Mary Jane releases Eva's limp limbs. "I knew you would."

Too delirious to respond, Eva lies in a swoon, her legs still spread and her nightgown still crumpled around her middle, not a care for modesty.

Pleased that her ministrations were received so rapturously, Mary Jane rearranges Eva's legs, straightens her nightgown, and pulls the covers over her, tucking her up. By the time she's done, Eva is sound asleep.

Mary Jane wakes up as a beam of early morning sunlight strikes her face, the heavy drapes flung open by Bessie's young maid. As usual, Eva is sprawled over her, one leg flung over her hips, one hand on her breast. She doesn't stir.

"Good morning, Miss." The maid smiles bashfully, glancing at the position of Eva's hand. "I do hope you slept well."

Mary Jane places her hand over Eva's. "Very."

As the maid gets to work laying out some fresh towels, folding and arranging them on the vanity, Eva rouses. Not realizing there's anyone else in the room, she kneads Mary Jane's breast, rubbing herself on her bedmate.

"Good morning, sleepyhead." Mary Jane kisses her forehead.

"How long's I been asleep?" Eva murmurs groggily. "I can't remember the last time I ever slept so good." She rolls onto her back, pulling Mary Jane's arms around her. "I dunno if it's this bed, or what you done to me in it."

"I'm happy to take the praise." Mary Jane leans over her, locking their lips together.

She intends for only a brief display of affection, but Eva instigates more.

"Do it to me again." She tugs up her nightgown, struggling to get the cumbersome garment above her bum, her feet getting tangled in the bed sheets. "Put your mouth to me." She kicks off the blankets. "Lick me. It did give me such a pleasure."

Stepping near the bed to empty the chamber pot, the maid stifles a giggle. "Lor'! Wait till I'm out of here first. I don't think my poor heart could take it!"

Startled to see her there, Eva shrieks, twisting out of Mary Jane's arms and yanking her nightgown down, covering her nethers.

"It's all right." Mary Jane coaxes Eva back into an embrace, making a bid for another kiss. "She don't mind. She knows what we're about."

"Aye, and so will everyone else if you don't watch out." The maid dumps the contents of the chamber pot into a bucket by the door. "The missus is already up, so if

you're planning on any more doings such as the likes of what went on last night, she'll surely know of it."

Eva gasps, mortified. "You heard us?"

"I couldn't much help it." The maid laughs, amused by the look of horror on her face. "I was coming up to bed right as you was having your pleasure." She fixes Mary Jane with a cheeky grin. "Whatever you was doing to her last night, I bloody well wish someone would do it to me." She picks up her slop bucket, preparing to leave. "Now, there's fresh water in the ewer and clean towels on the vanity. If you need aught else, just call for me."

Once she's gone, Eva smacks Mary Jane's shoulder. "Why'd you let me say all that bawdy stuff in front of her? She must think I'm proper hot cunted."

"You are." Mary Jane helps Eva off with her nightgown, flinging it onto the vanity. "You're so wonderfully voluptuous."

"Only with you," Eva reminds her, pouting. "I love doing it with you."

"Do you still want it now?" Mary Jane fondles Eva's breasts, kissing her way down the teen's stomach. "If you do, you must really be quiet this time. Your aunt doesn't approve."

"She said so?"

"Not in as many words, but I can tell." Mary Jane tongues Eva's bellybutton. "She looks at me queerly, as though she suspects me of forcing my way with you."

"Why ever would she think such daftness?"

"Something must've happened to set her against the kind of love two women can have for one another," Mary Jane answers vaguely, keeping Bessie's confidence. "Some people's like that anyway. Not everyone will understand the way we feel for each other."

Her kisses reach Eva's core, and for the second time, she brings Eva to an exquisite climax with her mouth, this one culminating with a delightful trickle of honey.

"Oh, darling." Mary Jane sucks Eva's copious spendings into her mouth. "I can't get enough of you. I'll drink everything you can give me."

"Do I really taste nice?" Eva twitches and squirms

"You have the sweetest cunt I've ever licked." Mary Jane clambers up Eva's body. "But don't take my word for it." She leans in for a wet kiss. "Taste for yourself."

They share a sex-flavored kiss, Eva's nostrils filled with the scent of her own womanhood, her lips smeared with the residue of her amatory juices.

"I wish I could stay in this bed with you forever." She grabs Mary Jane's buttocks, pulling her into position for a rubbing. "Can we skip breakfast?"

Mary Jane smirks, knowing that idea won't last long. "What if there's bacon?"

Immediately, Eva's grip slackens, her eyes widening. "Do you honest think there is?"

Not waiting for an answer, she wriggles out from beneath Mary Jane and starts dressing, doing it with such clumsy haste that she has to fix her corset three times before she manages to get all the hooks fastened in their proper places.

"Do come on," she hurries Mary Jane out of bed. "There might be bacon!"

Having no patience to deal with her hair, she leaves it in a loose braid and rushes through the rest of her morning hygiene rituals, Mary Jane not far behind her. Fifteen minutes later, they join Bessie in the dining room, finding there a delicious spread of toast with butter and jam, freshly steeped tea, a pot of scrambled eggs, and a plate of bacon.

"I trust you had a good night." Bessie targets her comment at Mary Jane, accompanying it with a fierce glare. "And morning."

"Indeed." Mary Jane puts on an amiable smile. "You've been most hospitable."

Beyond the obligatories, breakfast is conducted in relative silence. Mary Jane enjoys a slice of toast while Eva concentrates on the bacon, taking as much as she thinks she can get away with before she risks being called a glutton.

"Worked up an appetite, have we?" Bessie picks at the scrambled eggs on her own plate.

"She's a fiend for bacon," Mary Jane answers on Eva's behalf, wiping a dribble of grease from the corner of

the teen's mouth. "Didn't have much meat growing up, I suspect."

"Just as well that's all behind her, then." Bessie continues to eat, averting her eyes. "Now it's time we spoke of the necessary arrangements for her future."

"My future?" Eva halts with an over-sized forkful of bacon en route to her mouth. "What arrangements? My future is with Mary Jane."

Bessie huffs. "It most certainly is not." She finishes her eggs and dabs at her mouth with her napkin. "You'll be living here with me from now on."

"No I won't."

"I'm afraid you will."

Eva shares a look with Mary Jane. "How long for?"

"Permanently."

Eva drops her fork onto her plate. "No!"

"Don't argue, child, and don't be petulant," Bessie chastises her. "I'm not above drawing you over my lap."

"Em." Eva turns to Mary Jane, pleading. "Tell her I'm to be with you." She clamps her hand over Mary Jane's on the table. "Tell her how you plan to keep me."

"Keep you?" Bessie snorts. "How does she reckon on doing that? What's the going rate for a Whitechapel whore these days?"

Mary Jane's jaw tightens.

"Yes, that's right," Bessie sneers at her. "I've made some inquiries into your character."

"And that's why you don't want me near Eva? Because of how I earn my wages?" Mary Jane suppresses tears. "Why don't you just say what you mean?"

"Very well." Bessie dishes herself up some more eggs. "I'd sooner see her follow her dear mother into the ground than be with the likes of you."

Eva weeps silently onto her bacon, her tears puddling in her plate.

"Is it necessary for you to be so cruel?" Mary Jane pulls her chair closer to Eva, rubbing the teen's back. "She *wants* to be with me. Does that not matter to you?"

"When she was five, she wanted to join the Royal Ballet." Bessie carries on eating, unconcerned. "A child's fancies pass quickly."

"She's *not* a child."

"She's under twenty-one, and I'm her next of kin," Bessie imparts with a smug smile. "If you try to remove her from this house without my consent, I shall notify the police that you're attempting to procure my sixteen-year-old niece for immoral purposes. I believe the penalty for that is two months' hard labor, is it not?"

"You think I'm grooming her for the street?"

"You don't want to know what I think," Bessie growls, snatching another slice of toast from the rack. "She won't spend another night in your company. In fact, you'll not set eyes on her again. You're no good for her. She's already her mother's daughter. The poor girl has enough to contend with."

"I would never let her make the same mistakes as I have." Mary Jane abandons the thought of breakfast, tossing her napkin onto her plate. "I love her, and she loves me."

"It's unnatural." Bessie reaches for the butter knife.

"Unnatural?" Mary Jane keeps her sharp tongue locked behind her teeth. Well aware this is all a symptom of the abuse Bessie received at Sarah's hands, her indignation is laced with sympathy. "I understand why you might feel that way, and I'm sorry for what happened to you, I truly am, but not all love between women is wrong. I would never do anything to hurt Eva."

"That's good, because if I find out you've ruined her, I shall put an end to you, Miss Kelly." Bessie clutches the butter knife in her hand, her knuckles as white as the bone handle. "A doctor will be sent for this afternoon, and if she is not verified *virgo intacta*, I will come after you. Mark my words. I know where you live."

At the end of her tether, Eva leaps to her feet, her chair toppling over, crashing to the floor. "Stop!" she screeches at her aunt. "Why's you doing this? Meeting Mary Jane was the first good thing that ever happened to me. I ain't never been loved by anyone the way she loves me."

Bessie spears the knife into the heart of the butter. "She's using you."

"For what?" Eva upturns both palms. "I ain't got nuthin' to give her."

"Don't you see, girl? Are you so blind?" Seething with anger, Bessie shakes her head, despairing of her unworldly niece. "What she's making you do to her is pure wickedness."

Blissfully ignorant of her aunt's childhood trauma, Eva rants. "Ain't it my choice who I love? Ain't it my choice who I shares a bed with? And ain't it my choice who I fuck in it?"

"Enough!" Bessie slaps her hands on the table. "You will not use such revolting language in this house." She turns her venom on Mary Jane. "That's your influence, I presume?"

Ignoring her, Mary Jane stands to comfort Eva. "Darling ..."

"Don't you dare touch her!" Bessie snarls, punctuating her ire with another smack on the tabletop, but her warning goes unheeded.

Eva falls into Mary Jane's arms, sobbing, and Bessie calls for her maid.

"Annie! Get in here this instant!" She grabs Eva by the tail of her braid and yanks her away from Mary Jane, forcibly restraining her. "Escort Miss Kelly out."

"I'm not leaving Eva." Mary Jane stays put. "I'm all that she has."

"No," Bessie corrects her, shoving Eva at the maid. "*I'm* all that she has. You're nothing more than a three bob whore with a vile predilection for young girls." She delves in her pockets. "Here"—she slaps three shillings on the table—"that's your rate, isn't it? Take it and leave."

Mary Jane swipes the coins off the table, scattering them to the floor. "I don't want your money. No amount will change how I feel about Eva."

"That's as may be, but if you don't leave right this minute, I shall send for the police." Bessie directs her toward the door. "The brougham is waiting for you."

Making no further argument, Mary Jane heads out.

"No!" Eva howls, held back by the maid. "Mary Jane! Don't go! Don't leave me here!"

"Ridiculous," Bessie mutters, reclaiming her seat at the table, dismissing the maid and her wailing niece. "Take her upstairs."

The maid heaves Eva into the hallway, toward the staircase, but as soon as they're out of Bessie's sight, she lets go, giving Eva a shove toward the front door.

"Say goodbye," she whispers. "And be quick about it."

Half-blinded by tears, Eva dashes out into the street, catching Mary Jane before she steps into the brougham. "Em!"

They collide, locking themselves in an embrace.

"I love you, Eva." Mary Jane's tears wet Eva's chestnut locks. "We *will* be together, I promise you." She clutches Eva's head, pulling back to look at her. "That's all I want."

"But how?" Eva mewls piteously, clinging to Mary Jane's jacket.

"I'll think of something." Mary Jane presses her forehead to Eva's, their tears mingling on Eva's cheeks. "Do you trust me?"

Eva nods, brushing her salty lips against Mary Jane's.

"Write to me when you can." Mary Jane speeds up their parting, spying Bessie and the upbraided maid in her periphery. "I will *not* abandon you."

She crushes her lips to Eva's, not caring who sees, and Eva kisses back with equal fervor, slipping her tongue into Mary Jane's mouth, the affectionate display broken all too soon by Bessie's dutiful maid.

"Come away now, Miss," the maid urges, tugging on Eva's shoulder. "Before your aunt has a fit and gives us both a birching."

She hooks her arm around Eva's waist, dragging her away as Mary Jane pulls a hanky from her pocket and boards the brougham, the lovers parted.

CHAPTER 20

Wednesday, March 16, 1887

A WEEK AND A HALF AFTER BEING EJECTED FROM BESSIE'S Regent Square home and Eva's life, Mary Jane lies naked in bed, half-screwed and wholly fed-up. She wants to cry, but she can't do that here: it's not her bed, and she's not alone.

Flinging back the covers, she eases herself out of the well-used double bed in one of the Ringers' Buildings cheap rooms, mindful of not waking her newest regular customer: her former lover, Joseph Fleming. He thinks he's earning his way back into her life with an endless supply of booze, the odd compliment, and plenty of coin, but as far as she's concerned, he's no different from any other man with well-lined pockets and a standing prick. He's a convenient source of income, no more.

While he sleeps, she gets dressed and raids his pockets, relieving him of a little over seven shillings before plugging her dripping sex with another of his red silk hankies. Though she'll loathe herself for it when the elevating effects of the liquor wear off, there's a reason why she sought him out tonight: she was in need of some quick and easy coin.

This morning, while sitting at her table, performing some minor surgery on Mollie the one-eyed doll—namely, stitching her deformed ear back on and giving her a new nose—the deputy's son pushed a letter under her door. It was from Eva, addressed to 'Fair Emma' and

delivered to the lodging house with the landlord's daily post.

She tore it open with her thumb and pulled out a small wad of mismatched writing paper, some watermarked pages stolen from Bessie's bureau, some plainer notepaper given to her by Bessie's maid, and some taken from her new employer, for as the letter explains, Bessie sent her into domestic service without delay.

Written over the span of several days, in several different pens and inks, paragraphs scribbled down in disorganized chunks whenever she had a moment to herself, Eva's first attempt at a letter is a disjointed collection of thoughts, littered with crossed out words, ink splotches, and the odd fingerprint.

For the past week, she's been working as a general servant at a private house in Cavendish Square. Her aunt insisted upon that placement in particular because the house is within walking distance, and that means she's able to remain living at Regent Square for the foreseeable future. In other words, she can remain under her aunt's careful watch.

She'll be leaving work in an hour, and Mary Jane wants to be there to meet her—hence the need for Fleming's silver. Foregoing an early supper, she returns to Thrawl Street at sunset, washes her love avenue, hurries into her finest clothes, and pays for a hansom cab to take her to Cavendish Square. Along the way, she re-reads Eva's letter, poring over her words.

Firstly, Missus Sullivan's funeral—held at Bessie's local Roman Catholic church—went well, but was a dismally quiet affair, what with her parents already deceased, only one of her five living children attending, and her sister only doing so begrudgingly.

There were tears aplenty. Bessie forced a glass of brandy down Eva's throat in an attempt to calm her, but it only made her vomit on the floor of the brougham— much to Bessie's displeasure. Eva wished Mary Jane could've been there, but her aunt expressly forbid her from extending the invitation. No surprise.

Speaking briefly of her new situation in service, she tells of how the family has indoor plumbing and electricity, and hot water that comes straight from the tap—what a thing! Sometimes, she runs her hand under the stream, just to feel the heat, marveling at it.

In the main bathroom, they have a luxurious cast iron claw-foot bathtub with a porcelain interior and Eva's jealous. The servants aren't allowed to use it, of course, but Eva has to draw a bath for the lady of the house on a weekly basis and often has to fight the urge to jump in it, clothes and all. Some nights, she fantasizes about taking a bath like that with Mary Jane, their bodies submerged in the hot, soapy water, skin gliding over skin.

Here, the writing leaves off for a while, and Mary Jane imagines Eva tending to herself in bed, affected by her own words as she wrote them. Returning to the missive some time later—perhaps with a clearer head—the heavy-hearted teen delves into another topic without segue, complaining of her aunt's strict rules and repeated moral lectures.

Though Bessie generally treats her well—excepting the occasional slapped buttock for blurting out an oath—she's cold and unfeeling. Eva writes that she longs for cuddles, and to feel Mary Jane lying close to her in bed, for she has the cozy double all to herself and can't pass but a minute in it without thinking of her 'vorayshus tung' and the intense pleasure it gave.

Even though Eva's language skills aren't in the least bit sophisticated, and the letter is, in some places, completely indecipherable, the many romantic sentiments Eva successfully manages to convey in her own phonetic way have Mary Jane's loins weeping. Primarily, she focuses on a portion of the letter that rather graphically describes a 'delishus spending dreem' that had Eva waking up with a 'speshul sqeezing' between her thighs.

In the dream, Mary Jane's anomalous appendage was back and at full strength. Having spent an evening at the theater together, they were riding home in a brougham, exchanging kisses aplenty, when Eva felt the hard protrusion in Mary Jane's lap.

Curiosity getting the better of her, she got a hand up Mary Jane's skirts and felt it for the first time, wrapping her small fist around it. Keen for the pleasure, Mary Jane showed her how to hold it, how to grasp and stroke it, and soon they were frigging each other with abandon.

When it became too much to bear, burning lust compelling them to incorporate their bodies, Eva hoisted her skirts and sat on Mary Jane's lap, bum to crotch, and lowered herself onto Mary Jane's waiting prick.

It slid in easily, without pain, and they fucked in that attitude till the journey's end. As in her previous dream, Eva woke at the moment of Mary Jane's climax, her own spending triggered by the thought of Mary Jane filling her womb.

Reading that section of the letter over and over again, adding more imaginary details to it each time, Mary Jane slips a hand up her skirts. In desperate need of her own relief, her thighs part and she works her fingers at her needy sex, achieving one bosom-quivering—and somewhat loud—pleasure before the carriage stops at Cavendish Square.

Here, she pays the driver through a small hatch in the roof of the carriage, and he releases the spring-loaded, folding wooden doors designed to prevent dirt and horse muck from getting kicked up into the open-fronted carriage by the horses' hooves. It doesn't offer much protection from the elements—and certainly not much privacy—but it does prevent one's skirts and stockings from getting dirty, and conveniently conceals the goings on in one's lap.

Still relishing the contractions of her orgasm, her movements sluggish and her head a little foggy, she barely has time to close her legs and restore her dignity ahead of the overeager young footboy leaping down from his perch at the rear of the carriage next to the driver and offering his assistance to help her disembark. The eight-year-old's grubby palm is upturned for a farthing tip before her feet are even on the ground.

"Cheeky." She ruffles his hair, giving him a generous ha'penny before departing in to the cool evening, certain that she's leaving the tiny carriage reeking of femininity.

And now the waiting begins.

Not wanting to be seen lurking for fear of appearing suspicious, she confines herself to the shadows, keeping away from the gaslights, her breath misting on the air. In particular, she doesn't want to appear as though she's soliciting for business, since Cavendish Square is but a few hundred yards away from Great Portland Street, on which lies one of the most decadent brothels she used to frequent in her West End days. Though she was owned by another madam at another gay house in Knightsbridge, she was frequently hired out to perform specialist services for choosy customers, including one who liked to be treated like a dog, right down to the collar and leash and being thwacked on the nose with a rolled up newspaper.

He only ever barked, growled, and whined. She never heard him speak. If he was well behaved, he'd get to roll over onto his back, stark naked, while she straddled him and rubbed his belly, telling him over and over again what a good little boy he was.

Without a doubt, he was one of the queerest individuals she ever serviced, closely followed by a man who liked to dress her up in boots, stockings, and a double-breasted jacket belonging to a fancy woolen riding habit, then have her climb on his back and ride him around the room like a small pony until he collapsed from exhaustion.

Some other men have slightly darker fancies, though. For a time, Mary Jane tended to the needs of a well-born young man who never showed his face for fear of recognition. He always awaited her in an ominously darkened room, his identity obscured by a venetian mask. The bed was lit so that he, lying naked and supine, was cast in shadow, but she, instructed to get on top of him, was illuminated perfectly.

His particular letch was that he was only ever able to reach his crisis when she was bouncing up and down on his cock, wearing a blonde wig and calling herself 'mama.'

Mama loves you, darling.

Mama wants your prick.

He always dressed her in a silk robe with a gaudy floral print. She was to open the robe as she approached the bed, asking him if he wanted one of mama's special cuddles, and that's how it would invariably begin. When he was finished, he'd cry, and she'd sing to him and pet his hair as he curled up with his head in her lap.

She soon lost his business, though. He found another tart who not only had a figure that compared well to his mother's, but was also lactating, and she heard later that he liked to conclude their sessions by suckling from her like a little baby.

He was strange, but harmless. Most of them are. She was never quite sure about the one who used to make her wear his wife's clothes, though. She only saw him a handful of times, at her madam's insistence, and he was rough. He pinned her to the bed and forbid her to utter a sound, stabbing her with his cunt-rammer as he spewed his hatred for her.

I could kill you, you bitch.

You worthless whore.

He was the first man who ever gave her real pain, forcing himself upon her so hard and deep that she felt he might rip her open, tearing her commodity to shreds. It felt like punishment, and she supposed it was in a way.

Punishment for living that life.

Punishment for her sin.

She deserved it.

In the midst of this morbid reminiscence over the highs and lows of her short-lived West End life, Mary Jane finally sees Eva leaving work with three other young domestics. Watching her from the edge of a circular public garden in the center of Cavendish Square, she debates approaching.

Eva looks so different in her maid's uniform: a black blouse with a high white collar, a long black skirt, a plain white apron, and a white lace headpiece, her tresses neatly done up in a bun. She's laughing and chatting with the other girls, all alike in age, and Mary Jane wonders if her desire to see Eva is little more than a selfish whim. But before she's entirely made up her mind one way or the other about that, Eva clocks her.

Even from a distance, the teen recognizes the statuesque figure of Mary Jane standing under a gaslight.

Her purple silk dress.

Her distinctive coppery mane.

Making an excuse to her coworkers, she parts from them and darts across the street, following Mary Jane into Cavendish Square Gardens, away from the street lights, and straight into her waiting arms.

"Em!" She flings herself into an embrace, both feet leaving the ground. "I've missed you so! Whatchu doing here?" She hangs on, spun in circles by Mary Jane, her skirts twirling.

"I had to see you." Mary Jane sets her back on the ground, but doesn't terminate the embrace. "God, I'm such a misery without you."

"Are you taking me away?" Eva hopes, ready to pick up her skirts and leave without a moment's notice. "I shall run away with you this minute. Say the word."

"We can't, love. Not yet. I haven't the money." Mary Jane puts the brakes on before she gets carried away. "Besides, you know your aunt's right about me. I'm not good for you. You should remain with her and never look back on Whitechapel. Opportunities to make a clean break from the East End don't come often, and when they do, they ought to be seized without delay."

Eva shakes her head. "That ain't what I want." She strengthens her grip around Mary Jane's neck. "I want *you*. I ain't never gonna stop wanting you." She initiates a volley of kisses. "I wanna be with you more than anything. Did you get my letter?"

Mary Jane backs her against a tree. "You wrote me such bawdy words. How could I not come see you right away? And how could I resist giving myself a tickle in the carriage on the way over?"

"Did you honest? You liked it?" Eva pinches her lower lip between her teeth. "I know I ain't so good with my words and that, 'specially the big ones, but I've been practicing, and—"

Mary Jane silences her with another kiss, at the same time working a hand up under her skirts, hoping for flesh but finding cotton.

"Damn drawers," she grumbles, fumbling for a non-existent split, prepared to tear open the garment's seam if necessary.

"Oh, do be careful of my clothes," Eva frets. "If my aunt sees me all messed, she'll know I've been up to no good."

Conceding that she's right to be concerned, Mary Jane suspends her advance and cups Eva's sex over her drawers, rubbing her through the fabric. "I'm sorry." She rests her forehead on Eva's shoulder. "I want you so much, but we shouldn't. Not here." Under her ministrations, the cotton dampens, heightening her passions. "When do you get a holiday?"

"I only gets a full day once a month, and I ain't due one till after Easter," Eva laments. "I gets an evening to me-self once a week, but Aunt expects me to spend those evenings with her. I wouldn't be able to get away until after supper."

"That'll have to do." Mary Jane withdraws her hand. "When's your next?"

"Day after tomorra."

"All right." Mary Jane thinks fast. "Meet me."

"Where?"

"The south side of Seven Dials. Shall we say eight o'clock? In the meantime, may I walk with you, Miss Sullivan? You're heading home, yes?"

Eva nods. "I should like that very much, Miss Kelly."

Playing the role of gentleman, Mary Jane walks Eva back to Regent Square, instructing her to pick a local post office on her regular route to and from work so that she might receive letters there *poste restante*, since any correspondence sent to Bessie's house would surely be withheld and burned. Along the way, lust gets the better of them both, and they stop for a quick tickle in a covered walkway. Here, Eva receives a swift, much needed climax and a few more kisses, the pair parting with declarations of love and devotion.

CHAPTER 21

Friday, March 18, 1887

HATING TO LINGER ON THE STREET CORNER, WHERE SHE could be so easily observed, Mary Jane waits anxiously at the southern end of Seven Dials in her best West End clothes, anticipating Eva's imminent arrival. It's past eight o'clock, and just as she's starting to wonder whether Bessie's prohibited her from leaving, the harried teen—her new yellow dress now tailored to fit—scurries from a side street, her cheeks flushed from walking so briskly.

"I'm so sorry I'm late." She greets Mary Jane with the usual reserved peck on the lips. "I thought she was never gonna let me leave."

"Come with me, darling." Mary Jane takes her by the hand. "I've got us a room."

Allowing no time for questions, she hurries Eva to the bawdyhouse in Lichfield Street, where she routinely entertains Missus B——. To spare her from having to witness the seedy transaction, she arrived early and paid for the first-floor front room, making sure it would be available for their tryst, and upon her return, all she has to do is lead Eva up the staircase. No words need be exchanged, though the lewd noises emanating from the other bedrooms don't escape Eva's notice, and suitably rouse her suspicions about the house's respectability.

Once inside the bedroom, she looks around the lavish room, admiring the fire burning in the hearth, the four-poster bed, rich carpeting, cheval mirrors, expensive

bed linens, and other decorations, hoping for the best. "Have you brung me to a hotel?"

"No, darling." Mary Jane removes her jacket, draping the black velvet garment over the arm of the sofa. "Not exactly."

Exploring her surroundings, Eva finds a recently opened tub of pomatum on the vanity. "Is it a brothel, then?" she asks, inspecting the greasy substance, knowing from her mother's antics that such a thing can be used as an anal lubricant.

In reply, Mary Jane chooses her words carefully. "It's a place where they aren't quite so fussy about who comes and goes, that's all."

"Oh, Em." Eva drops down on the sofa. "It's a brothel." She buries her face in her hands. "You've gone and brung me to a bad house." She peeks out through her fingers, eyeing the bed, wondering if Mary Jane's ever received someone on it. "Have you been here afore?"

Opting to tell the truth, Mary Jane nods. "Yes."

"With customers?"

"Just one." Mary Jane settles on the edge of the bed and removes her boots.

"Why did we have to meet here?" Eva gripes. "Couldn't we go somewhere else?"

Mary Jane shakes her head. "I have to be careful. I oughtn't show myself about this far west, but this is a quiet house and I trust the landlady."

"Why can't you?"

"I fear I might come upon my old employer." Mary Jane unpins her hair, shaking it loose. "Some people from that life ain't so nice, and I have debts. Let's just say it would be much to my detriment if I should ever meet them again."

Eva's stomach turns over. "Would they hurt you?"

"They would do the very worst." Mary Jane scoots back on the bed and reclines, leaving an inviting space next to her. "Will you join me?"

Unsettled by the nature of the house, Eva stays put.

"If you're not comfortable here, we needn't do anything." Mary Jane tries to put her at ease. "But please, darling, do come to bed and let me hold you."

Eva marvels at Mary Jane's elegant figure, from her slender feet, stockinged in silk, to her form-fitting bodice, thinking she looks every bit like a lady. Albeit an immodest one.

Exercising her mastery of seduction, Mary Jane responds to the attention of Eva's eyes by trailing a hand up her body, from hip to breast, letting her fingertips direct the path of Eva's gaze. When she reaches the neckline of her bodice, she begins work on the buttons, eventually peeling the fabric back to bare her chest and corset.

"Come to bed," she repeats, adopting a sultry tone. "Let me hold you."

Affected despite her apprehension, Eva succumbs. She sheds her hat, boots, and jacket and clambers onto the four-poster, struck by the feel of it. "Ooh, ain't this bed soft!" She wiggles her bum on the counterpane.

"It's the finest in the house," Mary Jane brags, hoping that might sell her on testing out the feather-stuffed mattress, but it has the opposite effect and puts another worry in her head instead.

"How much is this costing?"

"Don't worry on that, love." Mary Jane fawns over her. "This is more important."

"But your savings—"

"Sshhh," Mary Jane cuts her off. "I have to be near you." She places a hand on Eva's ankle, surprised to find not a thread of wool or cotton, only woven white silk. "Your stockings ..."

Eva blushes. "My aunt bought 'em for me. She made me swear I'd only wear 'em on Sundays, but I wanted to look nice for you."

Mary Jane keeps her hand on Eva's ankle, stroking and caressing the rich fabric. "You always look nice."

"Do you like 'em?" Eva tugs her skirts up to her knees, revealing more.

"They're lovely." Mary Jane slides her hand up Eva's calf. "How high do they go?"

"A little higher." Eva draws her skirts up to her thighs, Mary Jane's hand following.

"Such fine legs." Mary Jane's hand comes upon Eva's garter a few inches above the knee, finding nothing but bare skin beyond the stocking top. "No drawers?"

Eva shakes her head. "I took 'em off afore I come out." She leans back, resting on her hands, keeping her knees together, but letting Mary Jane feel where she may.

"It's been so long since I've had a housemaid." Mary Jane repositions, dropping kisses along Eva's stocking-clad shin. "If I recall, they're a randy bunch. Isn't that true, Miss Sullivan?"

Eva's heat rises. "I should say not, Miss Kelly. We're all very good girls, so we are."

"Really?" Mary Jane places her hands on Eva's knees. "Are you sure about that?" She pries them apart. "You don't want fucking?"

Eva closes her eyes, struggling to play along. "I wouldn't dream of it, Miss."

"I bet every bloke in that house is after you." Mary Jane drops a kiss on Eva's knee and steals a peek up her skirts, relieved to catch a glimpse of her unharmed virginity. "I know I would be."

"They pinches my bum a lot," Eva confesses. "I told 'em I've got a sweetheart, and that I'm true as the day is long, but that don't seem to stop 'em. They's always asking if I've had it done to me." She watches Mary Jane advance further up her thighs.

"And what do you say?" Mary Jane works her kisses higher.

"I weren't sure what to say for the best." Eva hikes her skirts up to her belly, giving Mary Jane better access to her. "Tell 'em I'm untouched, and they'll want to have the first of me. Tell 'em I've already had it done to me, and they don't see the harm in making me do it again."

Mary Jane picks her head up, sensing real stress in Eva's voice. "Are they giving you a hard time, love? Are you unhappy there?"

All jesting aside, she knows much too well how young housemaids very often become the unwilling sexual targets of the men they work for. It's become something of a fetish for men of wealth and authority to break in virgin servant girls, giving no thought to how the

careless obliteration of their maidenheads might ruin them for their future prospects.

It begins lightheartedly enough, with a bit of flattery and some bawdy language, but escalates until the poor girls are being hounded relentlessly, their resistance worn down. If the men succeed in their game, they fuck the poor girls till the novelty expires, or until they get a belly full, then turn them out without reference. It's a particularly harsh and cruel way to learn the wiles of men, and Mary Jane would do anything to keep Eva protected from such abuse.

"Tell me, darling," she prompts her young lover. "How is it there?"

Eva shrugs. "It's fine enough, but the missus don't care for my name. She says I'm to be called Ethel from now on." A pout takes over Eva's plump lips. "I hates being called Ethel, but she reckons Eva's too grand for the likes of me."

Having once worked for a bawd who insisted upon changing the names of all the girls in her house for no other reason than to suit a peculiar whim, that's no surprise to Mary Jane.

"She's probably jealous. What's her name? Lady Cuntingdon?"

That turns Eva's pout into a grin. "You will take me away, won't you? You won't leave me there? We *are* gonna live together?"

Mary Jane grabs Eva's hips and yanks her down the bed, putting her on her back. "I want you. I *love* you." She settles herself over her young lover, breast to breast. "I ain't no smooth talking gent making you hollow promises just so as I can get in you." She gives Eva's flat belly a poke, her finger jabbing into nothing but taut abdominal muscles, no fat.

"You've already had in me." Eva giggles.

Mary Jane shakes her head. "I've never yet been up you, darling. I've kissed you, licked you, and felt you, but never breached you."

Eva's brow creases with confusion. "Don't you want to?"

"Very much."

"Then why ain't you?"

In the back of her mind, Mary Jane harbors a lingering concern that Eva's aunt might continue to perform random checks on her innocence.

"After I left your aunt's house that day, did she send a doctor for you?"

"Aye." Eva snorts. "The dirty old bald-head wanted a peep up my skirts, but I wouldn't let him. I knows that trick." She scowls, annoyed by the experience. "I screamed the place down and he soon left. Aunt sent the maid in to have a gander at me then, but she only pretended to do it. I dunno what she were meant to be looking for, though."

"It doesn't matter." Mary Jane brings her hand to Eva's sex. "Are you ready?" She pushes the tip of her middle finger to Eva's opening.

Eva nods, parting her legs as wide as she can. "I want you up me."

Taking care not to tear her hymen, just in case, Mary Jane pushes through Eva's tiny slit, sinking her long finger into the tight channel as Eva's eyes widen, her mouth agape.

"Is this all right?" Mary Jane checks, sliding her single digit in and out, not daring to try to add a second for fear of causing her discomfort.

Eva nods and Mary Jane delves deeper, swirling her finger around the teen's pulpy insides, familiarizing herself with every ridge and groove before seeking out a deep, spongy button and concentrating her efforts there. When she finds it, Eva lets out a surprised squeal.

"Oh, my good Lord!" She grabs fistfuls of the quilted counterpane. "I feel so odd ... oh, you must stop." She clutches at Mary Jane's shoulder. "I think I have to piddle."

Mary Jane keeps going.

"Do leave off, or I'll ... unghh!" Eva begins to shake from head to toe, her nails digging into Mary Jane's flesh. Feeling pressure building deep inside her body, she lets out a continuous moan, her belly jerking and her legs shaking, her toes curling. "I think I'm coming!" She cries out, finding herself held on the cusp of pleasure for so

long she feels she might die of spending. "Oh, it's here! Oh, lummy! Oh-oho!" Her orgasm crests and she gushes all over Mary Jane's hand, her abundant effusion drenching her chemise.

"That's it, darling." Mary Jane probes harder and deeper. "Come for me."

Eva's climax lasts for a full thirty seconds, during which time Mary Jane keeps paddling in her pulsing, throbbing sex, drawing out her pleasure. When her peak finally wanes, she lets out a contented sigh and promptly passes out.

Coming back to her senses a minute later, she finds Mary Jane—now stripped down to corset and stockings—lavishing oral attentions on her, her legs akimbo, pushed wide apart.

"Did I die?" she murmurs, thoroughly out of herself.

Mary Jane lifts her head, licking her lips. "No, you daft apeth. You were overcome by your spend, that's all." She directs her kisses to Eva's inner thighs, working back up to her sopping treasure. "And I'm very glad to have been the cause."

"Why ain't you ever done that afore?" Eva props herself up on her elbows, peering down at Mary Jane, seeing nothing of her but a bobbing mass of auburn hair. "I should not at all mind if you felt inclined to touch me that way again." She presses a hand to her spinning head, her own hair now in a state of dishevelment. "This is all fucking?"

"Mm-hmm." Mary Jane hums her reply against Eva's flooded core.

"So much pleasure," Eva muses in wonderment. "The rubbing, the tickles, the licking, and the jiggering. Whoever needs a prick?"

Mary Jane laughs, sitting up. "My thoughts exactly."

Feeling distinctly damp around her crotch and bum, Eva puts a hand between her legs, investigating her seepage, shocked to find her chemise soaked through.

"Oh, lummy!" She ducks her head forward, looking up at her grummit. "My shemmy! I'm in such a mess. Why's it so wet? I've gone and piddled me-self, ain't I?"

"No, you ain't," Mary Jane assures her. "It's just your spendings."

Eva takes another look, rubbing some on her fingers to smell it, satisfying herself that it's not piddle. "Why ever's there so much of it?"

"Some women spend buckets when they're touched inside." Mary Jane gives her room to move. "P'raps you ought to unrig and put your underclothes by the fire to dry."

Concurring with that suggestion, Eva slides off the bed and divests herself of her pretty yellow dress, taking the utmost care with it, making sure to lay it in such a way that it should not crease. She then spreads her saturated chemise neatly over a footstool in front of the hearth and wipes her sticky crotch with a towel before returning to the four-poster, finding Mary Jane's corset and stockings in a small heap at the bedside, a naked Mary Jane awaiting her under the covers.

"I can't believe I let you do it to me in a bad house." She crawls onto the bed, looking around the room again. "Did you really work in a fancy place like this?"

"For a little while." Mary Jane sighs, reminiscing. "Then a charming French toff took me for his courtesan, and off I went to Paris."

Eva gawps at her, mouth open. "You've been to France?"

"*Oui*." Mary Jane smirks. "But the life didn't suit me." She pulls Eva into a cuddle. "And I'm so glad for that, else we might not have met."

"I'd pick France over London any day." Eva snuggles up to her. "And I'd love to go somewhere exotic. Maybe somewhere there's lions and tigers and such." She paws at Mary Jane's face. "Rawr!"

"I'd pick *you* over anything." Mary Jane snaps playfully at her fingers, trying to bite her. "I could eat you." She growls, pouncing on her, tickling and kissing her neck. "You're yummy." She scrapes her teeth over Eva's alabaster skin, sucking and biting and licking on her shoulder, leaving a deep purple love bite behind.

Eva admires her marked flesh. "When my sister went to visit her boy, she'd come home with these bruises on her neck. Had to hide 'em from our mam."

"Make sure your aunt don't see." Mary Jane kisses it. "She'll think you're getting poked by one of the other domestics."

"They's always saying such bawdy things." Eva sulks, her mood turning at the thought of work. "They likes to tease me 'cause they think I don't know nuthin' about anything, but I reckon they don't even know half of what I does about a woman's spending. They says two women can't ... well, that we can't do it together. Not prop'ly."

"A woman don't need a prick up her to bring on her pleasure." Mary Jane fondles Eva's chest. "You know that well enough by now."

"Aye, I do." Eva grins. "Sometimes, I feels like telling 'em all about the pleasures you gives me, but I don't want no-one thinking I'm up for fun."

"Are you really all right there?" Mary Jane fusses, caressing Eva's midriff.

"It's long hours, but I ain't sure as I mind that so much most days 'cause it keeps me busy." Eva nestles against her. "Whenever I gets a minute to me-self, I'm always thinking of you, then I gets all weepy." She massages one of Mary Jane's breasts. "I wish they wouldn't keep me so late of an evening, though. I have to sleep over sometimes, and then I must share a bed with the cook. I ain't so fond of that."

"Need I be jealous?" Mary Jane strokes Eva's pubic thatch.

"I should think not." Eva pulls a face. "She's old and flabby and always frigging herself. Her doings keeps me up at night."

"Maybe she's lonely."

"That's all very well, but why does she have to be so vigorous about the business? It don't half jiggle the bed, and she ain't quiet in the operation, neither."

Mary Jane's fingers stray into Eva's pink valley. "Do you ever give yourself a tickle?"

"Now and then," Eva admits freely. "But it's so much better when we does it together." She pushes Mary Jane onto her back and clambers on top. "I want a rub."

Pleasantly surprised by Eva's heightened confidence, Mary Jane breaks into a wry smile, running her hands over Eva's body. "Is that so?"

"I want it like we did the first time." Eva positions herself between Mary Jane's legs and looks down, lining up their girl parts. "How does I do it?"

"Lie over me," Mary Jane instructs, shifting beneath her, shivering when everything meets as it should. "Now move your hips." She lays her hands on Eva's bum, helping her along. "Fuck me." She directs Eva into a few firm thrusts. "Do fuck me."

Determined to give her a pleasure, Eva wriggles and jerks and grinds, adjusting her movements according to Mary Jane's responses, trying to ignore her own impending crisis in order that she might satisfy her bedmate first.

"Am I doing it right?" she rasps, breathing heavily. "Will you spend with me?"

Mary Jane grips her bum tighter, moving her more vigorously. "Yes, my darling." She pulls Eva onto her over and over again. "Keep fucking me. We'll come together."

After a while, Mary Jane's doing all the work. Eva's a shuddering bundle above her, utterly incapable of coordinated movement, leaving her to buck her hips and drive their bodies together, taking complete charge of their mutual pleasure ... until there's a knock at the door.

"Are you almost done?" the landlady harps.

"Fuck off!" Mary Jane snaps, her rhythm disrupted.

"I need the room," the landlady retorts.

"I'll pay for another hour."

Fading footsteps signal the landlady's agreement, and Mary Jane attempts to resume their coupling, but Eva's gone quiet, the interruption having reminded her that she's in a house of ill repute.

"Oh, fucking Christ." Mary Jane gives up. "That impatient bitch."

"It's all right." Eva sits up, preparing to dismount. "You done me once."

"And I'm doing you again." Determined to get her money's worth for the room, Mary Jane flips them both over and dives for Eva's sex, commencing another enthusiastic oral assault.

In the midst of it, Eva—still moderately subdued—realizes she can see their reflection in one of the cheval mirrors, its placement giving her a prime view of Mary Jane's operations.

"Heavens!" She pulls her knees back as Mary Jane had done the first time they enjoyed each other this way. It enhances her visual delight, and all previously extinguished voluptuous sensations return to her a hundred fold, the strength of her orgasm quite taking her by surprise.

Wailing through her crisis, she sobs out her love for Mary Jane, making all sorts of bawdy promises, then pulls Mary Jane up beside her. "I want to touch you," she declares, recovering from her paroxysm. "You haven't had a pleasure yet."

Before she loses her nerve, she brings a hand to Mary Jane's sex and dips in the tip of one exploratory finger, surprised by the wet heat engulfing her. "Oh!" She pushes in all the way. "It's so tight inside!" She swirls her finger around. "And wet!"

Groaning, Mary Jane crooks her leg over Eva's hip. "Use two fingers, darling." She holds up her hand, showing Eva which two digits to plunge into her.

Eva complies with the request, but then falters, not at all sure what to do next. "How do I bring your pleasure on?"

"Take your time." Mary Jane rolls her hips, impaling herself deeper. "Enjoy."

Eva does just that, discovering all the ridges and grooves, the smooth and rough flesh. In curling her fingers to the anterior wall, she finds a spongy mass and Mary Jane moans. Testing the sensation, she prods the fleshy button and gets the same reaction.

"Oh, that's it," Mary Jane cheers her on. "You almost have me. Can you feel it? Just a little more."

Eva nods, focusing her ministrations on that most sensitive spot, her fingers hugged by Mary Jane's body. "You're squeezing me so."

A minute later, she notices the first tremors of climax in Mary Jane's thighs and the contractions begin.

"Oh, yes, you're coming!" Elated by her success, she probes harder, not stopping until the very last spasm has subsided. Then, she collapses into Mary Jane's arms. "That was extraordinary."

"It most certainly was." Mary Jane helps herself to Eva's lips. "It was perfect."

The bedmates lie in an embrace, sharing soft, deep kisses till a disquieting thought leaps into Eva's head and refuses to be ignored.

"Is we doing summink bad?" she asks abruptly, not really wanting to know the answer.

"Why?" Mary Jane frowns. "What's your bloody aunt said now?"

"Only that a girl ain't s'posed to give herself up to no-one till she's wedded. I didn't think of it afore, but we've done it loads now, ain't we? And we ain't wedded."

Cursing Bessie's strict moral code, Mary Jane does her best to put Eva's mind at ease. "Marriage isn't an option for us, love. Not a legal one anyway. But once we're free of your aunt, I should like to buy you a ring. Would you wear it?"

Eva's eyes sparkle. "Course I would. I'd wear any ornament you buy me, and not be ashamed to tell people who gived it me, neither."

"I know I can't marry you properly, but once we're living together, you'll be as good as my common-law wife, and I shan't think of you as anything less." Mary Jane coaxes more kisses from her. "I'll make you mine in every way I can. Even if it's only symbolic."

Indeed, throughout the many different tiers of English society, the definition of marriage varies a great deal. For the wealthy, it has but one meaning: the legal binding of a man and a woman under the eyes of God. For those on the lower rungs of society, however, the practice of marriage is somewhat more organic. Any symbiotic partnership between two cohabiting

individuals may well be called a marriage if so desired. In such cases, the act of first coupling often marks the unofficial marriage night, taking the place of a formal binding ceremony.

Rings may be exchanged, if finances permit the gesture, and Mary Jane wants Eva to have that at least, if only as a token to commemorate their commitment to one another. But they have to deal with Bessie first, and that's never far from Eva's mind.

"I shall have to go soon, else my aunt will fret." She stares at a clock on the mantel, willing time to turn backwards. "It ain't fair that I'm being kept from you."

"I know, love." Mary Jane registers the time. "But it won't be forever." She puts on a brave face. "And when we leave here, you must let me pay for a hansom. A single woman can't be seen alone on these streets at this time of night. I shan't allow it."

"When will I see you again?"

"Soon." Mary Jane tries to sound positive. "We'll meet on your night off next week, and every one thereafter. When you get a holiday, we'll spend the whole day together if we can, and we must write."

Eva accepts that, but isn't satisfied by it. "How much time do we have left in this room?"

"Long enough." Mary Jane kisses her way down Eva's body.

CHAPTER 22

Friday, April 8, 1887
Good Friday

MARY JANE CRACKS A SMILE, HEARING FOOTSTEPS IN THE hall and a letter slipped under her door. She knows it's from Eva and gets out of bed in high spirits, eager to read her words. It's been three weeks since they first met in the Lichfield Street house, and since then, they've seen each other at every available opportunity.

One night a week, they get an evening in a warm bed next to a hot fire, but a few stolen hours simply isn't enough. When the need proves too great to ignore, Mary Jane surprises Eva as she finishes work, and they make do with a quick fuck in the disused St. George's Burial Ground near Regent Square. It's five or ten minutes of pleasure against a tree, or over an altar tomb, followed by hastily whispered declarations of love and a few kisses.

Twice, Eva's snuck out of the house on an errand and met Mary Jane on the street, submitting to a frantic grope in the nearest alleyway. On another occasion, Bessie was but a few yards away, waiting for her in café, none the wiser.

In addition to the time spent in the brothel, it's routine now for them to share a hansom cab from there to Regent Square. Or at least, as near to Regent Square as they dare come, lest Bessie should catch Eva returning home in a carriage and become suspicious. On the relatively short ride, Eva's taken to sprawling on the seat

265

in some contorted fashion, clinging on as Mary Jane tickles or jiggers her to climax, the bumping and vibration of the carriage serving to drive Mary Jane's finger in deeper, or to increase the friction of her ministrations.

Much to Mary Jane's delight, she's developed a letch for it, and watching her passions blossom is not only a true pleasure, but also a beautiful thing to nurture. And she's a fast learner. With increasing frequency, Mary Jane meets her with the intention of giving her a swift knee-trembler, only to end up the recipient of her eager attentions instead. Each beautiful orgasm is then recounted and relived in graphic detail in their frequent correspondence, combined with the sharing of fantasies and erotic promises.

Keen to see what new bawdy surprises await inside Eva's latest letter, Mary Jane retrieves it from the floor and tears it open, tucking herself back up in bed to read it.

Already, Eva's language skills are improving. Using Mary Jane's responses as templates for her own efforts, she's started to construct better sentences, her thoughts flowing smoothly from one paragraph to the next. Her spelling is improving, too, which makes it easier for Mary Jane to lose herself in the narrative.

After giving the letter due appreciation and penning an equally bawdy letter back, she spends the early part of her day crocheting in her room, singing softly to herself and passing the time until she's set to meet one of her specials at his residence. To prepare for him, she inserts her diaphragm and reads Eva's letter again, giving herself another quick pleasure.

The man she's meeting rents the top floor of a modest house at the north end of Whitechapel, close to the Commercial Street Police Station. The street door is always open during the daytime, and she lets herself in, making her way up the sturdy, freshly-scrubbed wooden staircase to the top floor, trying not to alert the neighbors to her presence. Here, as always, the door to his rooms has been left on the latch for her, so she pushes it open and walks through without knocking.

All is quiet.

His living quarters consist of two rooms—a bedroom and a living-dining area—and both are furnished well. Though his possessions are by no means extravagant, they're in fine order and everything is well kept. He has a maid who works here a few hours per week, cleaning things up and doing his laundry, and it's one of her old uniforms that's waiting for Mary Jane on the table, laid out there with a gold half-sovereign and a few coppers, next to a glass of brandy and a small brass bell.

Pocketing the money, she strips to her chemise, stockings, and petticoats, and dresses herself in the maid's black blouse and skirt, finishing the outfit off with the standard white apron. When she's ready, she rings the bell.

The bell gives her customer—who's waiting for her in the bedroom—a two minute warning, affording him some time to make any final preparations for her visit while she sups the complimentary glass of brandy in front of the fireplace.

He's an eccentric sort of fellow, she muses, spotting one or two newcomers added to the collection of ceramic frogs he keeps on the mantel. His letch is to take her virginity somewhat against her will. As per his instruction, she's to begin each session in opposition and protest, gradually yielding to his advances. Sometimes, they do it on the table, playing the scene through as if he's come home from work to find a new young maid there. On other occasions, they do it in the bedroom, with her in the role of his visiting niece.

In fact, he now has so many different fantasies that he's taken to writing them down in a notebook, listing how many times they've engaged in each one, and the variances they've tried. Of them all, the maid character is her least favorite, and now, with Eva in service, her prior uneasiness is distinctly amplified.

Today's particular scenario is that of a virginal maid lured into a house of accommodation by her master—which happens all too often—and as she finishes the brandy and enters the bedroom, she assumes an appropriately apprehensive demeanor.

"Whatever sort of place have you brought me to, sir?" She looks around, taking in every detail of the room, as if doing so for the first time, noting the clean sheets on the double bed and the ottoman stuffed full of the clothes he couldn't be bothered to fold away.

The vanity is still covered in his late wife's perfumes, hairbrush, and a solid silver mourning brooch containing a lock of woven hair from their deceased child. A grief from which neither of them ever truly recovered.

Her customer is sitting on the foot of the bed, a broad smile fixed on his face. He's an older man, his hair and whiskers gray. In his youth, one might've described him as dimber. Widowed some years before and not inclined to remarry, he spends every penny of his expendable income on various local paphians, of which Mary Jane is his clear favorite. The others, he says, are good enough spunk-emptiers when his ballocks are full to bursting and his prick is in a furious rut, caring not where it goes, but none have her flare.

"Come sit with me, my dear girl." He pats the mattress, inviting her near.

Wringing her hands in a nervous manner, doing her best to appear ill-at-ease, she sits primly on the foot of the bed, leaving enough of a gap between them that their bodies aren't touching. He closes it immediately.

Getting straight down to business, skipping some of the preliminaries he usually indulges in, his gaze trails downward, admiring her ankles. "What pretty ankles." He extends a hand toward her, shaking not from anxiety, but encroaching infirmity. "Let me feel them."

"Oh, sir! Don't!" Mary Jane puts on a matchless rendition of aghast and swats his hand off her person, angling her body away. "It ain't proper."

"Don't be silly." He chuckles, reaching a heavy hand out for her again. "They're just ankles. What's the harm? Let me."

This time, following his preferred script to a tee, Mary Jane lets him touch her, but no sooner does he get a hand on her ankle than he thrusts it up her skirts.

"Oh! How dare you!" She pushes her skirts down, making some weak effort to push his greedy mitt off her lap. "You're taking such advantage!"

"Nonsense." He keeps his hand where it is, at the top of her stocking, dangerously close to bare skin. "You have such lovely thighs."

"Stop now, sir." Mary Jane puts on a pout. "Pray do."

"Just a little higher ..." He makes a brash drive for her guarded commodity, but she clamps her thighs together, trapping him en route.

"No!" She slaps his hand inside her skirts. "You shan't!"

"Don't be such a little fool." He forces her legs apart. "Let me feel your cunt."

"You blackguard!" Mary Jane sobs, an undercurrent of her distress genuine.

"Such a beautiful little cunt." He strokes her freshly-shaved motte, its hairlessness heightening his thrill, enhancing the fancy that she's young and untouched. "Now let me feel the slit." He twiddles her clit, moving lower.

"Oh ..." She lets some of the tension in her legs dissipate, feigning confusion, as though acclimating to the first pangs of sexual want. "Whatever are you doing?"

"Feels nice, yes?" He finds her opening. "Tell me, have you ever frigged yourself?"

"No, sir."

"Never spent?"

"Certainly not, sir!"

"Then you shall." He pushes inside her. "I shall fetch you."

Whimpering like a frightened kitten, Mary Jane leans back and closes her eyes, ignoring the clumsy prodding of his fat fingers and pretending to succumb, confident that she's still thoroughly sodden from her earlier pleasures.

"There," he encourages her. "That's it now." Responding to her perceived enjoyment, he works his fingers deeper and harder. "I'm feeling you, darling. I'm feeling your cunt."

"You oughtn't ..." She squirms on the bed.

"But I am, and it does feel good, doesn't it?" He lets out a soft groan, believing the moisture coating his fingers is entirely attributable to his digital attentions. "You wouldn't like me to stop now, would you? You're getting so randy."

"You'll ruin me!" Mary Jane sits up in imaginary fright. "I'm being so dreadfully bad."

"Nonsense." He shoves her back down. "It's just a feel. What harm in this?"

"You promise I'll be all right?"

"You'll be fine, my love." He lifts her skirts up to her belly, unveiling her charms, muttering the obligatory hollow promises concerning his respect for the sanctity of her virtue.

Playing along, Mary Jane's protests momentarily subside and she changes the pattern of her breathing, drawing air into her lungs in short, sharp gasps, shamming pleasure. In reality, he's hurting her. His doings are much too rough.

"I do feel so queer, sir." She opens her legs wider.

"You want a fuck, I daresay."

"Oh, no!" She clamps her legs together again. "What a shame it is for you to say such a thing to me!" She scoots away from him, retreating deeper onto the bed.

"Do let me fuck you." He scrambles after her. "It's nice to be fucked, and you've made me so stiff." He unbuttons his trousers, pulling out his engorged prick. "See my cock-stand?"

"Oh! Your thing is out!" Mary Jane grimaces at his swollen tool, the base surrounded by a thick gray pubic bush. "How awful! Put it away!"

"I shan't." He looms over her. "I shall put it up you. I shall fuck you!"

"Such words! I ain't never ... never!" Mary Jane shakes her head vehemently. "I won't let you ruin me!" She tries to crawl away from him, but he grabs her by the legs and drags her toward him, flipping her onto her back like a ragdoll.

"You want a fuck, I know you do." He yanks up her skirts again, getting between her thighs. "All women want a prick up them." He rubs the fat head of his cock along

her slit, lubricating it. "All women are whores for the prick."

"Oh, you monster!" She beats her fists on his chest, thrashing violently.

Genuine tears well in her eyes at the thought of Eva being ensnared against her will, but their sham struggle comes to an abrupt end when he forces his priapus up her channel.

"Ahhh!" she wails in imitation pain. "You beastly man!" She tenses her thighs around him, her non-existent hymen breaking. "You lewd animal! You've hurt me so."

"But we're fucking now, and isn't it delightful?" He plunges himself inside her. "Your cunt feels so tight around my prick, darling. I shall spend in you in a minute."

"Please don't, sir!" Mary Jane pleads. "You'll get me in the family way."

"You'll be quite all right," he declares emphatically, as all men in his position do. "And I shall give you your first pleasure."

Timing the climax of her performance to coincide with his release, Mary Jane pays special attention to his labored breathing and the increasing note of desperation in his rhythmic grunts. When she senses him on the cusp, she starts moaning.

"There you are!" he exclaims triumphantly. "Your pleasure's coming. Tell me it is."

"I feel so wrong, sir." She bucks up into him, meeting his thrusts.

"All cunt wants is prick," he mumbles to himself, lost in the ecstasy of his own impending crisis. "All cunt hungers for a man's spendings."

"Oh, sir," Mary Jane whines. "I think it's happening in me ... oh, Gawd!" She squeezes her cock-trap around him several times in quick succession, adding a little shiver to her thighs by rapidly flexing her buttocks and twitching her hips, feigning a spend.

That does the job.

"I'm coming, my darling!" Hilting himself, he wets inside her, making sure to give her every drop, wasting

nothing and refusing to uncunt until his prick withers and flops out of its own accord. Then, he opens her up with his fingers, watching the thick white cream dribble out like hot icing. "Look how gloriously wet you are! You did want it ever so much."

She says nothing.

She fears for Eva, petrified that her naivety will make her vulnerable to the lecherous whims of the men around her. The only way to secure her safety is to remove her from service and whisk her away from London, and for that, she needs money.

Though she makes good coin from her specials, she's been spending much of it on visits to the Lichfield Street house. Compounding the problem, any time spent visiting Eva is time taken away from her normal working hours, which is already resulting in the need to dip into her savings to cover her everyday expenses. At this rate, her small reserve fund will be depleted in no time, and she'll be no closer to saving Eva. Something must be done.

As evening descends, Mary Jane promenades along bustling Commercial Street in the company of three other harlots, the jovial trio regaling one another with comical stories from their most memorable nights on the street. Though her friends—their spirits elevated on rum—remain oblivious, Mary Jane notices a youngish man in shabby clothes gawking at her, keeping his distance.

He appears to be following them. When they stop to peruse the goods on the stalls of the street-side barrow sellers, he stops also, removes his bobbin—the distinctive wood and tarred, flat-topped leather hat identifying him as a Billingsgate Market fish porter—and twirls it in his hands.

Too shy to approach, he worries the wide, upturned brim with his thumbs, scanning her from head to toe. Still damp from a day's work, the deep well in the brim of the hat—so designed to prevent unwanted liquids from dripping in his face while lugging cases of fish on his head—is smeared with piscine juices, his grubby hands equally imbrued.

He looks thoroughly cunt-struck, and growing tired of his dithering, Mary Jane spins to face him. "Are you gonna stare at me all night, man?" She slips her shawl off her shoulders, baring her décolletage. "Or I have I got something you want?"

Prompted to do so, he steps forward. On his way to her, he passes a hand through his ruffled blonde hair and straightens his mustache, hoping to make a decent first impression, and Mary Jane has him pegged in a second.

He's in his late twenties, she guesses, and a novice at engaging a woman in this manner. Either stepping out on his wife for the first time, or tired of waiting to procure one, he's in great need of companionship, and that's just how she likes her men: low risk and easy to please. While a seasoned whoremonger who knows how to get the most for his money will haggle with you, care naught for your comfort, and always try to take more than he's offered, timid men are often kindhearted, grateful, and generous with their coin. For that reason alone, she wants him.

"What's your name?" she asks of him as her friends respectfully depart, wishing her well for the rest of the night.

"Joe," he mumbles, his pasty cheeks flaring red. "Joe Barnett." He flits his eyes up and down the street, afraid to be spotted securing her services. "D'you have a room?"

Ten minutes later, the full price for her flesh being swiftly agreed upon, they're in a room in the Ringers' Buildings, and she's stripped down to her corset and stockings. She's about to get on the bed as she is, but spots a hint of disappointment in Joe's eyes, mingled with the desire she's excited in him. Guessing the nature of his disenchantment, she fingers the top clasp of her corset, toying with it.

"Do you want me quite naked?"

He nods, the disappointment fading.

She seldom strips completely nude for her customers, unless they're paying a premium for it, or have earned the occasional perk and deserve to be rewarded for their generosity, but she fancies Joe as a potential regular and so obliges him, hoping to snare him with her charms.

It works.

He's transfixed.

Sitting on the edge of the bed, she motions him closer. "Let me look at your prick."

As he casts off his jacket, she drops his trousers to his ankles, his proud stiff-stander flopping forward. Though it's nothing special in length or girth, it's clean, oozing nothing but pre-fuck, and it passes her inspection.

"Come on and do me." She positions herself for mounting, laying a towel under her bum ready to soak up any seepage. "My cunt's all wet for you. See?" She opens herself up to him. "I'm clean as a pin and ready for a fuck."

His cock pulsing, Joe kicks off his trousers and scrambles onto the bed.

"Go on, love," Mary Jane encourages him. "Get it in."

He pushes forward, nudging the head of his priapus through her labia, but as the sensitive tip becomes enveloped in her slick folds, he loses all control. With a groan, he erupts, his deposit spurting on her motte, thighs, and belly, only the last few droplets making it inside her as he wedges himself in her entrance, bathing himself up the crown in her warmth.

Somewhat astonished by his premature emission, Mary Jane laughs. "You really did want it badly, didn't you? Ain't you having your needs met at home?"

He shakes his head, turning from her to conceal the color of embarrassment on his cheeks. "She won't give way to me till I gives her a ring, and I've been true to her all the while."

"Do you frig yourself?"

More head shaking. "I ain't had my pipe proper emptied for weeks."

"No wonder you went off so bloody quick." She reaches for his cods, feeling how full they still are. "You must've been bursting."

"You gived me such a stiff one directly I saw you." He peers down at the shrunken, flaccid doodle between his legs. "And now I ain't got enough coin on me to have you again."

Taking pity on him, she offers him a do-over. "Well, we've got the room for a full hour, and it's a shame to waste it." She fondles his tool. "Why don't we relax here for a while, and when you're ready to go again, I'll let you have a proper shove in me. How about that?"

He perks up.

To occupy him in the meantime, she poses for him on the bed, giggling as he kisses and feels his way around her body, over her arse, back, thighs, and belly. He's getting spoony on her already, and she's not about to discourage him from it, even though his bushy mustache prickles her sensitive flesh, and his hands—laborer's hands—are coarse and calloused, like sandpaper grating against her smooth skin. She lets him do what he pleases to a point, but when he assumes one liberty too much and puts a hand to her sex, she smacks him away.

"Not that," she scolds him, pitying his circumstance but feeling as though she's already being generous enough. "I don't care to have a fella's mitts on me there."

Before he works up a protest, she feels his fattening cock brush against her thigh and snatches it up, diverting his attention. "You're almost ready for a poke." She wraps her hand around it, tugging and squeezing and stroking, feeling the blood rush in. "Let me frig it up."

He stiffens immediately. Seconds later, he's plunging up her, their bodies slamming together, his heavy ballocks slapping against her rear.

"You're such a fine fucker," she mewls. "Wherever did you learn to fuck so well?"

She has a stock of these compliments, and throws out the odd one here and there, punctuating her praise with various moans and groans. Trained well, she puts on a first class show of it, her performance rivaling any you could find in a West End gay house, but despite her

valiant efforts to fetch him—using all the tricks any experienced cyprian knows well to exploit—he shows no sign of nearing his crisis.

Twenty minutes later, she's starting to get sore, and he's tiring. Not used to such vigorous fucking, his brow is beading with sweat, his shirt sticking to his damp body, his thrusts weakening. Seeing him struggle, and snatching up the opportunity to assume control, she places her hands on his chest.

"Whoa, boy. You'll cause yourself a strain." She halts him, uncunting him with a jerk of her pelvis. "Let me do some of the work." She urges him onto his back.

Though it's unconventional for a woman—harlot or otherwise—to do so, she straddles him, lowering herself onto his wet pego. Trying to hurry on his pleasure, she grinds her hips, bearing down on him and clenching her muscles around him. When she senses that he's getting close, she grips his shaft inside her, massaging his length.

"Do it now." She feigns her own spend, quivering above him. "Let it come in me."

Responding to her command like an obedient dog, he floods her with his abundant libation, his release accompanied by several grunts of satisfaction, his hips twitching beneath her, nudging his prick up to the rubber barrier protecting the entrance to her womb. Finally, it's over.

"I think you've filled me right up." She lifts herself off his softening tool and brings a towel to her sex, catching his seed as it slops out of her. "Goodness! You've put such a lot in!" She wipes herself at the edge of the bed. "Do you always spend in bucket loads?"

"I reckon so," Joe reflects. "Women's always afeared I'm gonna give 'em a swelling with it."

"Well, I hope you feel better for getting all that lot out." She cleans his piercer off.

"That was the best fuck I've ever had." He marvels at her. "I ain't never had a woman squeeze my prick so. Nor had one on me, neither."

Mary Jane accepts the compliment with a warm smile. "I know how to please a man."

"That you do." Joe muses on their protracted coupling, loath to let her go. "You're a fine-looking woman, and the most talented fucktress any man ever had, I'm sure of that." He keeps his eyes pinned to her chest. "Will you have a drink with me?"

Getting the impression he'd rather like to occupy her for the rest of the evening, Mary Jane agrees. "Go on, then. I wouldn't say no to a glass or two." She picks her clothes off the floor. "Get us one in at the Britannia, and I'll be down in a jiffy, after I wash myself up."

She helps him into his clothes and shoos him away, then gives herself a cursory swill at the ewer. Using her fingers, she scoops out his sediment before wetting one of her silk hankies and pushing it up into her body, swirling it around, wiping her vaginal walls. It's not as good as a proper douche, but it'll suffice for now.

Once finished, she joins him in the pub. Finding him agreeable enough in character, if a little dull, she remains engaged in easy conversation with him for a good while, laughing at his jokes and accepting the drinks as they come, exploiting his company until his pockets run dry. As soon as that happens, she makes her excuses and prepares to leave, disappointed that he hasn't yet made any proposition to her, but the threat of her departure spurs him into action before her bum rises from the seat.

"I should like to keep you." He holds onto her like a precious gem, refusing to let her slip through his grasp. "Would you consider such a thing?"

Having only expected him to profess a desire to become her regular friend, Mary Jane reins in both her surprise and her enthusiasm. "Keep me?" She raises an eyebrow, suspecting he misspoke. "You mean you wish to procure me for your convenient?"

"Aye," he confirms his proposal. "That is, until I marry."

Intrigued by the potential of the situation, Mary Jane thinks on it, considering its benefits. Though it comes at the cost of her newly-attained independence, securing someone to keep her—even if only for a few months—would alleviate much of her burden in

balancing her visits with Eva and the accumulation of savings.

"I can get us a fair rate on a room in a house in George Street," Joe continues, stroking her thigh. "I'm known there."

"That's all very well, but I don't come cheap," Mary Jane warns him, picking his hand off her lap. "If you want me to yourself, you'll need to keep me in a fair amount of coin as well as food and rent. Is that agreeable to you?"

Willing to consent to anything if it means having exclusive access to her, Joe makes no complaint. He arranges to meet her the following day—at the same time, in the same place—whereupon he helps move her few personal belongings into a furnished room in a common lodging house on George Street, their new living arrangement consummated with a few celebratory drinks, a quick fuck, and a bite to eat.

CHAPTER 23

Tuesday, April 19, 1887

MARY JANE STANDS ON THE NORTHEASTERN CORNER OF
Leicester Square, watching the entrance to the Empire
Theatre, her sentiments mixed. Existing as a theater of
burlesque, opera, and musical extravaganza since 1884,
its opening—three years ago, almost to the day—
coincided with her arrival in London, and was her first
experience of theater in any of its forms.

She was treated to the occasion by a well-to-do
Frenchwoman whom she met in the square a day or two
previous. The woman, exuding what for all the world
appeared to be genuine concern and compassion for the
young Irish beauty who had no permanent lodgings and
no money yet to obtain any, pegged her inexperience
immediately. Though Mary Jane was no fresh turn-out,
and entered London under no illusion about how she
intended to earn her wages, she was, as yet, naive in the
workings of the street. But that soon changed.

The Frenchwoman, upon declaring that Mary Jane
was too fine a woman to promenade herself like a
common harlot, extended an invitation into her
Knightsbridge home. There, she met four other girls,
alike in age and personal attractions. One was tall, one
short, one plump, and one so slight in all respects that
she could, without much of a strain on the imagination,
pass for a girl of thirteen. Indeed, there was a woman to
suit every taste. The set was comprised of two blondes, a

279

brunette, and one with silky raven locks, and Mary Jane soon saw her place: she was to fill in the busty redhead quotient.

Plied with good food and good booze, she was divested of her old clothes and thrust into a silk dress of the finest quality—perfectly appropriate attire for the theater. That evening, they were to see *Chilpéric*, an appropriately French *opéra bouffe*, which the kindly Frenchwoman—now revealed to be little more than a procuress and bawd, not worthy of naming—first saw in Paris in the late sixties.

It was an evening of delights for Mary Jane, who was then introduced to an array of wealthy gentlemen. They spoke in accented English, all fluent in the French language, and broke away at intervals to converse with the bawd in their native tongue. Mary Jane never knew what matters they discussed, though she suspects now that they were engaging in financial negotiations, coming to terms on a price for her flesh.

The enchantment didn't last, however. Arriving back at the Knightsbridge house, she realized all her dresses and underclothes had been discarded. She was stripped of everything but a few sentimental possessions and cried herself to sleep in her new silk frock, for which she now owed the house a considerable sum. Without knowing it, she had unwittingly become a dress lodger.

She needed to remain there and work to pay off the dress, and although it was said that she was free to leave once she was straight with the house, the debts kept accruing. Like the other girls, she was sent out every night to work, frequenting the clubs and theaters in and around the Haymarket, and dining at the Hotel De l'Europe in Leicester Square, followed at every turn by a servant of the house to make sure she didn't skim, for the house took most of her nightly earnings.

It shocks her still how many impressionable young women fall for the same trick, and she wonders if the girl in the black silk dress, appearing no older than Eva and on her way to the Empire in search of money, knows that the exquisite clothing isn't hers to keep. She's a harlot, no doubt. She lifts her skirts too high as she crosses the

street, exposing an indecent amount of calf, and a matronly woman—her minder—follows closely in her wake, struggling to keep up.

Mary Jane didn't discover the full truth about her fine attire until her return from France, whereupon she went to the Knightsbridge house to reclaim what she thought was hers, only to be told by one of the other girls that she didn't own a stitch of it. Not only that, but she still owed money to the house for the gown she was wearing when she left—one of purple silk, that she wears still—and had amassed even greater debts besides by absconding and failing to remain on the continent.

Mourning the loss of her expensive silk frocks, and her dignity—the last of which was literally beaten out of her with a broom when she was swept off the porch like yesterday's rubbish and told she ought never to show her face in the West End again—she slinked back to her new bawdyhouse near the notorious Ratcliffe Highway, where, instead of entertaining lords and princes, she sold herself to sailors and dockworkers for considerably less than half the price.

As she's contemplating her rather drastic plummet from west to east, a pair of hands slips around her waist. Terrified that she's been spotted by one of her old customers, she spins on her heels, ready to throw a punch and bolt, but her diminutive mystery hugger captures her again, crushing their bosoms together. It's Eva.

"Oh, my darling." Mary Jane reciprocates the embrace, trying to keep the brim of Eva's straw hat from jabbing her in the face. "I've missed you."

"Why's we meeting here?" Eva looks around the square, seeing the gardens and the theaters and the hotels all for the first time.

"I'm taking you someplace different." Mary Jane leads her southward, cutting diagonally through the manicured gardens. "Just this once."

"Whatever for?" Eva holds her hat to her head, afraid that all her delicately placed pins will come loose and she'll lose it beneath the wheels of a passing brougham.

"You'll see!"

This is Eva's first holiday—her first full day off work—and thus this is the first chance they've had to spend more than an hour or two in each other's company since that fateful trip to Bessie's house. Determined that this meeting should be something worth remembering, Mary Jane's made special plans. She pulls Eva to the southwestern corner of Leicester Square, hurrying her towards a small street in the Haymarket. Here, they stop in front of a building with the word BATHS written in large white lettering on the window, and Eva digs in her heels, refusing to move.

"This is for gentlemen, ain't it?"

"Aye, but I've already made inquiries." Mary Jane lowers her voice, lest anyone passing should hear. "They have a private room in the back. It's for couples."

Trusting that Mary Jane knows what she's doing, Eva allows herself to be led inside, but dips her head so as to conceal her blushing face from the men they pass in the halls. She doesn't even raise her gaze when they're safely confined in the pre-arranged room, fearful of what she might see, although the potent floral aroma hanging on the air is intoxicating. It reminds her of Covent Garden Flower Market at dawn, but without the underlying stench of stale urine and vomit in the gutter.

"Do you like it?" Mary Jane nudges her further into the room, urging her to explore the romantic effort. "It's all for you."

Daring a peek, the first thing Eva sees is a large cast iron claw-foot bathtub—just like the one at the house in Cavendish Square. It's big enough for two, complete with hot and cold running water, and surrounded by tilted mirrors suspended from the wall. Scattered beside it, for use in it, there's an assortment of soft leather cushions. Differing in shape and size, they're perfect for sitting on, kneeling on, or for supporting various limbs in any position one might be able to contort.

"A proper tub!" She squeals. "I'm to go in it?"

"Of course." Mary Jane turns the hot tap on full, adds a generous splash of lavender and chamomile bath oil, then starts undressing. "We both are."

"Together?" Eva whispers, as if someone might hear.

"Aye, together." Mary Jane flings her bodice onto a velvet sofa at the foot of a queen size bed, shedding one layer after another until she's completely unrigged. "It'll be just like it was in your dream."

Unpinning her hat but keeping her mane up, not wishing to get it wet, Eva admires the rest of the lamp-lit room: a fire burning in the hearth, warm brandy and water on the vanity, and a warmer tucked in the bed, heating the counterpane. On one of the pillows sits a raggedy, threadbare doll with mismatched eyes, the hair on her head patchy and uneven.

"Mollie!" Eva snatches up her only surviving childhood toy and holds it to her bosom, a wide grin etched on her face. "You fixed her up."

"I performed a little surgery on her." Mary Jane swishes the bath water, making sure it's neither too hot nor too cold. "She was rather in need of it."

"Thank you." Eva inspects Mollie's mended ear, her new eye, and the reconstructive work done on her nose, her grin slowly fading. "I wish I could take her with me."

"You can't?"

She shakes her head. "My aunt would notice. She'd want to know how I came upon her again, then she'd chuck her in the bin." She sets Mollie back on the pillow. "Will you keep her safe for me? Until we're together prop'ly."

"I'd be honored to foster her in your absence." Mary Jane shuts off the taps. "Is everything else in the room to your liking?"

"It's perfect." Eva spins in a circle, her concerns dissolving.

"So are you." Mary Jane steps into the tub, lowering herself into the steaming water and spreading her legs. "Now come on, love." She splashes water in Eva's direction. "Get your firm little arse in here with me."

Her grin returning, Eva strips and takes her place between Mary Jane's thighs, gasping with appreciation for the first hot water she's ever been immersed in. "Is it really all right for us to be in here like this?" She scoots her bum up to Mary Jane's crotch. "It feels naughty."

"It *is* naughty." Mary Jane kisses her neck, fondling her breasts. "But I paid for it, so it can be as naughty as we like."

"You're bringing my randiness on." Eva groans.

"Good." Mary Jane drives a hand to her sex. "I want a fuck."

Eva lolls her head on Mary Jane's shoulder and reaches behind her. "Let's do it to each other, then," she murmurs, finding Mary Jane's submerged article. "It's nice when we come together, ain't it? And this is so much better than a quick tickle in the park."

Realizing the angle of the mirrors gives her a perfect view of their doings, she arches her back, making her small breasts jut out, and increases the intensity of her rubbing.

"You like to watch?" Mary Jane presumes, whispering her thumb over Eva's swollen clit.

On the cusp of a spend, Eva nods, quivering from head to toe, her head flopped over Mary Jane's shoulder. Overcome with her own pleasure, her hand moves frantically between Mary Jane's legs, missing the mark by some considerable margin, clipping Mary Jane's clit with the edge of her nail at intervals.

The pain is electric, but rather than break Eva out of the rapture she's swathed in by offering her direction, Mary Jane repositions. Shifting slightly to Eva's side, she steals back her hands and lifts one of Eva's legs out of the water, draping it over the side of the tub and resting it on one of the leather cushions for comfort.

"Whatever are you doing with me?" Eva scowls, momentarily dissatisfied by the abrupt cessation of their mutual operations. "I was just coming."

"Patience, my darling." Mary Jane slides a firm cushion under her rump, raising her several inches up. "You'll have your pleasure."

Supporting Eva's neck with another cushion on the lip of the ceramic tub, she frees up her arm to wrap around the teen's back, holding her upper body so that it remains above the surface of the water, her nipples stiffening when they make contact with the air. For Eva's visual delight, she then sucks a wet, soapy nipple into her

mouth, ignoring the bitter perfume of the bath oils, and returns her other hand to work.

"Ooh, no jiggering." Eva peers down through the rippling water, the furrows of a concerned frown creasing her brow as she feels Mary Jane's probing finger seeking entry into her body. "You'll get water up my grummit."

"It won't hurt you," Mary Jane assures her, temporarily relinquishing the nipple. "I put water up mine every day." She pushes through Eva's slit. "Now watch me fuck you."

Alternating between thrusts, taps, and strokes, Mary Jane tries to maximize Eva's pleasure, but her young body has already become accustomed to the sensation of a single digit. In this attitude, the jiggering alone no longer provides an adequate level of stimulation, so Mary Jane eases in a second finger, the intrusion quite taking Eva by surprise.

"Lummy!" She gasps and tenses, gripping Mary Jane's shoulder.

Fortunately, the initial discomfort doesn't last long. Her well-lubricated body stretches to accommodate Mary Jane's manipulations, and as two fingers sink all the way up her, she throws her head back and closes her eyes, wailing at the ceiling.

"Do you like that, darling?" Mary Jane strokes the rough, spongy walls of her tight channel, remaining hilted. "It doesn't hurt you?"

Eva gives no answer, but wriggles her hips, encouraging Mary Jane to move. The sensations radiating from her core remind her of the few spending dreams she's had in which Mary Jane penetrates her with something more than fingers, and her peak builds as she relives those fantasies, her erotic imaginings bringing her over in under a minute.

"Here it is." She jerks her hips up to meet Mary Jane's thrusts. "Oh, your prick!"

Caught up in her climax, she has no idea of herself. Words leave her lips without a thought, sobbing out the bawdiest ejaculations as she shivers and convulses, cradled in Mary Jane's arm.

When she's recovered the use of her legs, they clamber out of the tub, dry each other, and move to the bed, relaxing naked in front of the roaring fire. Enjoying the rarity of being unhurried, they lie in silent appreciation of one another, kissing and caressing, lavishing attention on each other's bodies ... until Eva puts her foot in it.

"Have you had a baby?" she asks suddenly, studying Mary Jane's soft belly, thinking nothing much of it until she feels a distinct chill descend upon the room.

"Why would you ask me that?" Mary Jane demands coldly.

"My mam had lines like these on her belly, and she said it was having all of us what gived 'em to her." Eva traces her fingers along raggedy faint pink marks visible on Mary Jane's abdomen, proceeding with caution. "But I knows that ain't always the case," she backtracks. "I got some here, see?" She shows Mary Jane her inner thighs, pointing to a few darker pink streaks. "I think them's from growing, 'cause I ain't never had a baby in me."

Mary Jane says nothing.

"I'm sorry." Eva curls up facing the fire, sensing she's taken a wrong step. "I meant nuthin' by it. It's no matter to me if you have or you ain't, and it ain't none of my business neither when it comes to that. I was curious is all."

Softening, Mary Jane tucks up behind her, kissing her hair. "You've got nothing to be sorry for, my love. It ain't your fault I'm so guarded."

Eva stays quiet.

After a while, "Whatchu thinking about?" Mary Jane squeezes her. "Don't be upset."

"It ain't that." Eva looks pensive, her insides still throbbing from their earlier poking, the thought of babies rebounding her mind back to Mary Jane's non-existent appendage. "You know them dreams I keeps having?"

"The ones where I have a doodle?"

Eva nods. "A real big fat one, sticking straight out from your girl parts."

"What about them?"

"Is it queer that I should fancy such a thing?" She fusses with a loose stitch on the counterpane. "I think of it often, and I ain't got a clue why."

"There ain't no rhyme nor reason to our letches so far as I can see." Mary Jane resumes her kissing and caressing, trying to restore the mood. "Don't worry on it." She pulls Eva backwards onto her chest, forcing her into a hug. "Were you thinking of my doodle when we were in the bath?"

Eva rolls over, pressing her face to Mary Jane's sternum and squishing both breasts to her cheeks, concealing her blush. "How'd you know that?"

"You cried out for my prick as you were spending." Mary Jane laughs, her breasts jiggling around Eva's buried face.

"I did not!"

"You did, my love, and it's perfectly all right." Mary Jane pries Eva's face free, lifting her chin up. "Now do tell me more about your dreams. What was it like the first time?"

Eva settles back on Mary Jane's chest, but doesn't hide. "You was on top of me, atween my legs, then all a sudden you gived your thing a right push and it went all the way in me."

"Mmm." Mary Jane strokes her dark tresses. "Was I gentle with you?"

"At first." Eva licks her finger and swirls it around Mary Jane's nipple. "You done me nice and slow for a bit, then you started banging it up me like you was hammering in a nail."

"I must've been enjoying it."

"You were." Eva kisses her way down Mary Jane's body, pausing for a good long while at her breasts. "And I hopes you enjoy this n'all." She dives south.

"You don't have to." Mary Jane groans, feeling Eva's hot breath on her core.

"I want to. Desperately." Eva drops a kiss on her smooth motte, then dips lower, inhaling deeply, filling her lungs with that intoxicating scent of womanhood that she's been longing for since their first meeting. "How do I do it good?"

Happy to be her educator, Mary Jane conjures up a quick and playful analogy. "You ever had one of them penny ices?"

Eva smirks, nodding. Though her mother repeatedly warned her away from the sugary ice-cream treats sold by the Italian ice-men from barrows on the street, she's been known to sneak one on occasion. Served in a penny lick— a small, thick fluted glass designed to magnify the contents inside—they're almost impossible to pass up on a hot day, despite being frequently contaminated with human hair, fleas, dust, straw, and other questionable debris, and the fact that the many-times-reused glasses are merely given a perfunctory wipe with a dirty rag from one customer to the next.

"I'm a terror for 'em," she confesses her guilty pleasure. "Why?"

"Well, you know how you wrap your lips around it and suck it into your mouth like a big, sloppy kiss?" Mary Jane snatches up Eva's hand and demonstrates on the back of it. "And then you make your tongue stiff, swirling it around the flute?" She pokes her tongue out, waggling it up and down. "You gamahuche me just like that. Eat me out like I'm a penny lick."

As she parts her legs wider, spreading the lips of her glistening sex, a small droplet of arousal glides between the folds of her labia and Eva extends her tongue, dabbing it up. Taking her time, she explores the apex of Mary Jane's cleft, finding there the dainty, protruding nub of engorged flesh she's been learning so much about.

Flicking her tongue over it, she elicits a gasp. Pleased with that, she tests for confirmation that oral stimulation of the tiny bump might produce other pleasant vocalizations and closes her mouth around it, sucking on it. Better than a gasp, this generates a lustful moan, Mary Jane's long fingers clutching at the bed sheets.

Her confidence increasing, Eva slithers her tongue north from Mary Jane's perineum, traversing the full length of her valley before targeting her clit once again. On the fifth repetition of this rhythmic alternation, Mary Jane's thighs begin to tremble, her breath caught in her lungs.

Recognizing that she has her lover on the cusp of that elusive pinnacle, Eva concentrates her efforts on that swollen, hardened nub, swirling her tongue around it until Mary Jane lets out the most exquisite whimper, her legs quivering uncontrollably, her cunt in spasms.

Then come the tears.

"Why's you crying?" Eva frets, wiping her lips. "Did I not do it proper?"

Mary Jane draws her into a sweet kiss. "You're magnificent. It's been such a long time since I've been licked, that's all."

"Maria didn't ... ?"

Mary Jane shakes her head. "Not often. The intimacy in our friendship was very one-sided, which suited me fine up to a point. I do love to give a woman pleasure."

"Have you had many?" Eva pries cautiously, gun-shy from her earlier misstep beyond the heavy veil covering Mary Jane's past. "Women, that is."

"Not too many." Mary Jane soothes the insecurity in her. "My last proper companion was a young woman called Lizzie. We met while I was working at the Ratcliffe house."

"Was she gay?"

"Not often." Mary Jane hates to paint her with that brush. "She was a laundress, but she worked the streets now and again, as so many single women do. In any case, we were only friends for a year or so, and that was that."

"You had a falling out?" Eva guesses.

"Of a fashion." Mary Jane gives up a few meager details. "I received an offer from a fella who saw me regular at the house. He wanted to keep me, I wanted out of the life, and she didn't approve."

"Was this the Bethnal Green bloke?" Eva dislikes him on principle.

"He made a proposition of marriage, and I thought for a while that I should go through with the business, but never did." Mary Jane speeds through her recent life history, bringing Eva up-to-date. "I put him off for as long as I could, then he got it stuck in his head that I'd taken a fancy to another man, and I ended up ill-used for my trouble."

She hopes that's it for the inquisition, but Eva's curiosity abounds.

"Was Lizzie your first taste of a woman?"

"No." Mary Jane sticks to her honest streak. "There were a few others in London, but nothing particularly meaningful. Most of them were harlots. Men like to watch, and will pay handsomely for it. Before that, there was only one of any true importance. She was the one who broke me in."

Making the most of this rare opportunity to learn more about her mate, Eva bombards Mary Jane with questions. "How old was you? Did you love her? Was she pretty?"

"Lor'! So nosey!" Mary Jane leans over her, blowing a raspberry on her stomach. "If you must know, I was sixteen. The first of me had already been claimed by a fella, but I'd never yet spent. She told me a man don't always excite the passions the way a woman can, and she taught me well in that regard. I spent with her almost directly she touched me."

"She taught you, like you're teaching me." Eva grins. "But you haven't yet taught me everything." Her gaze drops to Mary Jane's article, glistening with spittle, her puffy labia still inflamed with desire. "How did you do it with Maria? You did have a doodle in her, didn't you?"

Nodding, not trusting herself to speak for fear of blurting out something aggressively lewd, Mary Jane concentrates all her efforts on suppressing an immediate and intense lust for strapping on her sturdy glass cock and showing it off, if only to have Eva touch it and gawp at it in the first instance, arousing her interest.

Several years ago, she discovered an immense pleasure in watching a woman fondle it. Though it began as a joke, it soon became an erotic fascination. Indeed, by the time she met Lizzie, she'd developed a true letch for having it stroked and fellated prior to coupling, and when Lizzie wasn't in the mood to oblige, she'd seek out a willing tart: a young harlot she knew from her days in the Frenchwoman's brothel.

At that earlier time in her life, she once serviced an entire group of married women from Chelsea with it. The

bored, neglected housewives, dissatisfied with their inattentive husbands, banded together and responded to an advertisement in the paper. The delicately-worded ad, placed monthly by Mary Jane's French bawd, promised to teach married women of class how to improve their physical health and prevent the onset of hysteria, and for a time, these discreet sessions proved popular.

The women, all masked and fanning themselves furiously, sat in a half-moon arc around a table draped with a thick quilt in a quiet stock room above a large shop in the Burlington Arcade, in Piccadilly. Here, in this well-known paphian paradise, the women were educated by a beautiful French cyprian with a luxurious accent—the old bawd's niece, Mary Jane suspected—while in identical rooms above other shops in the arcade, men with coin-laden pockets enjoyed the company of the area's finest harlots, and the occasional shopgirl in need of a few bob.

Lesson one began with the women listening intently as the French cyprian placed a naked young tart—an experienced toffer of the highest degree—on the tabletop and instructed her to spread her legs, using her perfectly-formed body to teach the women about their own. At the conclusion of this introductory tutorial, after the tart brought herself to orgasm with the aid of only her hand, thus demonstrating how such was to be achieved, the room not only reeked of fine perfume—layered on to drown the nervous sweat—but was also permeated by the unmistakable musk of so many weeping cunts.

Lesson two aimed to show the women some of the many different ways in which they ought to coax their unimaginative husbands to ignite their passions before the commencement of marital congress, so as to ensure their pleasure. It opened with Mary Jane gamahuching the hot-cunted toffer, and ended with full penetration.

While locked together, they posed like a *tableau vivant*, assuming various positions as and when commanded by the French cyprian, who matter-of-factly went about explaining how the housewives might angle their bodies to enhance their enjoyment of their husbands' operations. For the licentious young woman on the receiving end of Mary Jane's cock, this was a sweet

agony. On her back or on her knees, forbidden yet from moving, save for a few demonstrative thrusts, she'd pant and mewl, her body shaking with anticipation.

"Oh, let her do it to me now," she'd finally plead. "I do so want a fuck."

Upon being released to do so, they'd complete their union in whichever attitude was most desired by their audience. Sometimes, it was a deep, hard fuck from behind. Dog fashion was always a favorite. Other times, it was a gentle, tender embrace. Rarely, if left to their own devices and rampant imaginations, it was something much more creative and energetic.

When all was over, the housewives were given the opportunity—for an extra fee, of course—to experience Mary Jane's tongue and cock for themselves. Made so lickerish by the display, most accepted. In fact, only one ever refused. The striking blonde twirled a gold wedding band around her finger, too flustered to make eye contact, and eventually fled, concealing her face with a veil.

For the rest, gender was rendered irrelevant in their quest for a spend, seeing only the potential pleasure of the impressive phallus and thinking not of the woman wearing it. Even the shy ones, and those who claimed only to come for the novelty of it, gave way in the end, and these assignations took place on a small bed in a candlelit area set up behind a heavy velvet curtain. It was so designed that while one woman was receiving her pleasure, the others could hear every strangled gasp, thus keeping them all well primed for their own turns.

Gamahuching, Mary Jane learned then, never fails to adequately prepare a woman for penetration. Scarcely any woman will turn down the opportunity for further pleasures after she's been sufficiently licked, the moment of full surrender coming in the euphoria of her climax when her thighs relax and part readily, inviting full connection without ever saying a word.

Thanks to these clandestine gatherings, Mary Jane became very much in demand. The greedy French bawd even went so far as to declare that one session with Mary Jane could cure all manner of marital malady, from

genital congestion, and other symptoms of hysteria, to painful coitus. The latter of which was simply alleviated, in most cases, by the complete obliteration of a stubborn hymen, Mary Jane's perfect cock successfully accomplishing what their husbands' inferior equipment could not.

Trouble only came when one former attendee discovered a closer relationship with God and denounced the sessions for promoting sinful behavior among well-bred women, claiming that it was tantamount to seduction by the Devil himself, and if the practice was not nipped in the bud immediately, there was likely to be an epidemic of women becoming addicted to carnal delights. As a result of her outburst, the newspaper refused to run any more advertisements, and so ended the short-lived heyday of Mary Jane's career in harlotry.

Caught in forlorn reflection of the highlights of her West End life while idly caressing Eva's southern parts, Mary Jane is brought back to the present by a snappish voice and a rough shake.

"Mary Jane, is you listening to me?" Eva pouts, tempted to cross her legs in protest, withdrawing her charms. "You wanna do it with me that way, I knows you do. I sees it in your face when I talk of it."

"I love being in control of a woman's pleasure." Mary Jane burrows her fingers between Eva's labia. "However the method and whatever the attitude." She tickles the thin pink membrane obstructing the entrance to Eva's body, entertaining a fancy of driving her priapus through it, causing it to split. "But I only want what you want."

"How does it work? Will you show me one day?"

Mary Jane showers her with kisses. "Darling, I will show you anything you want to see, and please you however you want to be pleased. I want you to have nothing but pleasure, and to be happy always."

Cognizant of the fact that Mary Jane's promising a romantic ideal she never got to have in her own life, Eva's thoughts are sobered. "How's things with Joe?" A twinge of jealousy escapes into her voice. "Does he love you?"

"All's well enough in order, and you know it ain't like that." Mary Jane ceases her ministrations, licking her

fingers clean. "He's already got himself a wife, or is soon to. What he wants in me is a wife's convenience without the *in*convenience, and I might as well give it a go, don't you think? Regardless of the particulars, I can't stand the life of the street."

"How many customers have you kept?"

"Not many. Only my most generous gentlemen." Mary Jane considers pouring herself a glass of brandy, wondering if Eva would object. "Joe keeps me in lodgings and food, and I've been saving every spare farthing."

"Really?"

"Of course," Mary Jane assures her. "This is all for us, my darling. You believe that, don't you? As soon as I have enough saved, I'll be taking you away from here."

"You promise?"

"I promise." Mary Jane punctuates her words with a kiss, assuaging Eva's concerns. "There's nothing I want more in this world."

CHAPTER 24

Wednesday, May 11, 1887

DEEPLY CONFLICTED, MARY JANE STANDS IN THE HALL outside the first-floor front room of the Lichfield Street house, late for an appointment with Missus B——. Tonight was meant to be her weekly evening with Eva, but she begged off for the opportunity to earn an easy bank note. It seemed like the sensible choice at the time, for five pounds is no paltry sum and would help her dearly, but now she can't shake the unsettling feeling that she's betraying Eva's love.

Steadying her breathing, she knocks and enters, fussing with the dildo package under her arm. Inside, Missus B—— is posed alluringly on the bed, wearing only her chemise and knit silk stockings, her unpinned golden mane cascading over her shoulders.

"It's about time." She sits up, beckoning Mary Jane closer. "What kept you?"

Determined to see this through to its ultimate conclusion and claim her fee, Mary Jane lunges into her work. Flinging her package onto the sofa, she dives for the bed and pins Missus B—— on her back, both arms above her head.

"Oh, God, yes!" The lustful socialite submits readily, thrilled by such aggressiveness. "Take me as you will. All this waiting's left me hot."

Keeping both of Missus B——'s dainty wrists trapped, Mary Jane plunges two fingers up her lubricious

295

slit, working them in her as she would a dildo, synchronizing each thrust with a shove of her hips, hoping it will suffice.

It doesn't.

"Use your mouth," Missus B—— demands huskily. "Give me your wicked tongue."

Obediently, and after only an imperceptibly brief hesitation, Mary Jane wriggles into position and trails kisses all over Missus B——'s thighs, working her way north. Eyes closed, she tries to sum up a desire for the work by visualizing Eva's bared flesh before her, but the fantasy doesn't hold. The dissimilarities in her subjects prove much too jarring.

For one thing, Eva smells natural. Whenever Mary Jane lifts up her skirts, she's greeted with the unadulterated aroma of a woman, the hot, pungent musk of her impatient sex mingled only with the salty sweat of her skin, unabashed in its femininity.

In contrast, Missus B—— smells like a summer day. Her natural scent is masked by a thick blanket of sweet honeysuckle, its intense fragrance harnessed in a perfumed douche intended to combat the perceived unseemliness of womanly odor, and as she parts her legs, so the honeysuckle blooms, releasing its inviting bouquet.

Like the hummingbird lured in by the splendor of the blossom, Mary Jane probes into the silky petals, ready to lap up every drop of the sweet nectar within, but as she explores the saccharine dew seeping from the central well, her appetite dissolves. Defeated by her own distaste for the operation, she stops, hanging her head between Missus B——'s creamy thighs.

She says nothing.

Diagnosing the problem instantly, Missus B—— nudges her away and covers herself, reacting coolly and with great restraint, as befitting a woman of her class.

"Go to her." She waves Mary Jane off the bed. "Our business is concluded." Dipping into her clutch purse on the bedside table, she fishes out the usual five pound fee.

"I've not earned it." Mary Jane refuses the crisp note.

"Nonsense." Missus B—— forces it on her. "Consider it a parting gift, and a token of my sincere thanks. You've opened my eyes to so much, and I shall be forever grateful."

"What will you do now?" Mary Jane pockets the bank note, feeling guilty for doing so.

"Who knows." Missus B—— shrugs. "Perhaps I shall entice my new maid to the lark. She seems the type, and she does look at me queerly."

"Well, it oughtn't take much convincing." Mary Jane flashes her a warm smile. "You're a delicious woman in every regard. She'd be mad to refuse you."

"You flatter me." Missus B—— lights a cigarette. "Indeed, I do believe that's how you got me to give way to you in the first place."

Mary Jane has a slightly different, if a little foggy, recollection of their first intimate encounter, but doesn't disabuse her of the notion that she was skillfully seduced.

By her account, the serendipitous event occurred while she was still under employ at the Frenchwoman's Knightsbridge house. She'd been paid to escort one of her regular gentlemen to a social function at a Mayfair hotel, and during the course of the evening, was introduced to a familiar-looking blonde: the only woman ever to decline her services at the Burlington Arcade group sessions.

Of course, neither of them said anything to give away their prior acquaintance—much to Missus B——'s quite obvious relief—and as soon as they had a moment alone, Mary Jane received the most profuse thanks for her discretion. That thanks was accompanied by a glass of champagne, and as the men amused themselves in the smoking room, they drank late into the night.

From the onset, Mary Jane suspected that a woman of great sexual force lurked behind the lady's prim exterior, and once Missus B—— was sufficiently inebriated, she was proved right. The conversation turned bawdy, and after having Mary Jane reiterate all she knew about the pleasures of oral stimulation, Missus B—— surrendered to her desires and they retired to her room. A minute later, Mary Jane's head was up her skirts.

Remembering that night with great fondness, Missus B—— reins in her sentimentality. "I daresay we shan't see each other again." She brushes a stray tear from her eye. "But if you ever become available, do write to me." She reaches out for Mary Jane's hand, giving it a squeeze. "I shan't forget you."

On her way home from work, passing the covered walkway in which she and Mary Jane have once or twice, in the heat of lust, conducted their illicit fondlings, Eva is seized by the waist and yanked from the pavement. Her distressed shriek is smothered with a hand over her mouth, and she's pulled tight to a warm body.

"I had to see you," Mary Jane whispers, announcing herself before she releases her grip. "Forgive me for being impulsive."

"You gave me a damned fright," Eva gripes, turning to face her. "I thought you said I wouldn't be seeing you tonight. What happened to your other commitment?"

"I couldn't bear to be away from you a minute longer." Mary Jane backs her against the wall. "Let me have you here."

"I can't." Eva battles temptation. "I don't wanna be late. My aunt's expecting me."

"Just something quick," Mary Jane haggles, ready to get down on her knees and beg, not caring how desperate she appears. "Anything you please."

Eva flits her eyes to the street, making sure there's no-one in eyeshot. "I'll permit you a kiss, but that's all." She tries to stand firm. "I mustn't be waylaid. I don't want to get in trouble."

Mary Jane pounces on Eva's lips, her hands soon wandering.

"Oh, stop." Eva pushes her away. "You're making me want it."

"Darling, we haven't had each other in days." Mary Jane gets her hands under Eva's skirts, groping her bum and thighs. "Let's make the most of whatever precious time we have." She palms Eva's cotton-clad sex. "Please."

Rebuffing her immediate bid for intimacy, but with little conviction, Eva comes up with a compromise. Since her aunt has a social engagement after supper, she daringly invites Mary Jane to the house, telling her to wait by the back gate until the coast is clear. In that moment, she's overcome with desire, but by the time she's facing Mary Jane in the parlor, having embraced a moment of clarity since their fumble in the alleyway, anxieties have taken hold.

"I dunno if we oughta ..."

Regardless, Mary Jane pushes her onto the plush velvet cushions of the sofa and follows her down, landing above her, primed for fucking.

"I ain't never seen you in the grip of such a letch." Eva giggles, enjoying the playful tumble.

"I want you," Mary Jane declares feverishly, setting her dildo package on the floor and reaching up Eva's skirts. "It's been too long. I want to bury my face in your quim." She flips Eva's skirts up and ducks down.

Startled by her fervor, Eva howls, holding Mary Jane's face to her crotch. "Lor'! This is so indecent. We're being such beasts." She catches the maid lingering in the doorway with a silly grin plastered on her face. "Oh, heavens!" Coming to her senses and rediscovering her modesty, she bats at Mary Jane's head with a throw pillow. "Get off it. Take me upstairs and do me proper."

Growling, Mary Jane backs off the sofa, retrieves her package—afraid to let it out of her sight—and grabs Eva by the hand, dragging her out of the parlor and up the stairs.

"Keep a lookout," Eva calls over her shoulder to the maid. "If you see Aunt's brougham, run and fetch us. Or shout out. Or ring a bell!"

Slam!

Mary Jane kicks the bedroom door closed behind them, tosses her package on the floor, and seizes Eva's

waist. "Such a lovely dress." She roves her hands over the satin. "It seems a shame to tear it off you."

"None of that." Eva wags a finger at her. "We ain't got time to—"

Not interested in hearing the rest of that thought, Mary Jane sweeps her up, carries her across the room, and throws her onto the bed, eliciting a surprised yelp.

"Mary Jane!" Eva lies in a heap of ruffles and lace. "Why's you so ... oh!"

She's silenced by the hot lashes of Mary Jane's tongue and the sudden intrusion of two fingers. The unexpected combination—despite stretching her to the point of causing flashes of discomfort—brings her to a counterpane-wetting orgasm in under five minutes, but Mary Jane doesn't stop. She stays put, kissing, licking, and probing, the tremors long passed.

"I'm done." Eva winces, her hypersensitive flesh stinging with every lap around her clit. "Enough now. Leave off." She flips her skirts over Mary Jane's head. "If you don't come up from there, you'll suffocate."

"I don't care," is the mumbled reply.

"It's too much." Eva clamps her thighs around Mary Jane's face. "Do me the other way if you must."

"Which other way?" Mary Jane surfaces, licking her lips, raring for whatever form of intimacy Eva has a hankering for. "How do you want it? Tell me. God, I'll do anything."

Scanning the room, contemplating whether or not they should advance to something more adventurous—like doing it on the sofa, as they were about to downstairs—Eva notices Mary Jane's box lying on the floor. "Whatchu got there?"

Tired of waiting for an answer to her own question, Mary Jane dives back down, dropping kisses all over Eva's motte. "It's my cock. My prick, my doodle, my pego, my tooleywag, my priapus, my piercer, my cunt stretcher."

Assuming that Mary Jane must've brought the toy especially for her, Eva draws a most logical conclusion. "That's why you're so ruttish tonight?"

Mary Jane has no decent answer for her—certainly not a truthful one—but it's of no consequence. Her failure to provide confirmation goes unnoticed.

"Show it me." Eva sits up. "Do."

Her stomach turning over, Mary Jane retrieves the box from the floor and unveils the extension of her anatomy, placing it in Eva's waiting hands.

"Oh, Lordy." Eva gawps at it. "It's so big!" She wraps a fist around it. "Whatever do you call such a thing?"

"A dildo." Mary Jane dare not hope how this evening might conclude. "Liberated women use it to please themselves. Women like us use it to please each other. Some's made from leather, carved wood, ivory, or horn, but mine's of the finest quality glass made anywhere in the world. It's French."

"This goes inside?" Eva runs her fingers over the shaft.

"It does if you want it to."

The weighty toy inspires Eva's curiosity, but also brings to mind a disheartening evening spent among the domestics at Cavendish Square, when hours of unremitting teasing culminated in a humiliating experience with the cook.

"They don't believe me," she mumbles, tears pricking her eyes.

"Who?" Mary Jane frowns, her passions quieted. "Who don't believe you about what?"

"The other domestics." Eva sets the phallus aside. "They won't believe I've done it. They said they could tell just by looking at me, and that it would be easy enough to prove, so I let the cook look up my skirts." She tucks her knees up to her chin, self-comforting. "I only wanted 'em to stop having a go at me, so I shown her my grummit."

"And?" Mary Jane asks, though she already knows.

"She laughed and called me a liar." Eva's lower lip quivers. "She says I've still got my innocence, but how can that be? You've done it to me so many times."

Mary Jane shakes her head. "I've been careful. I haven't breached you."

"How come?" Eva sniffles. "You've been up me plenty."

301

"Young girls have a barrier at the entrance to their womanhood," Mary Jane enlightens her. "That's why my fingers sometimes cause you pain." She fetches a hand mirror from the vanity and passes it to her. "Here, look."

She bends Eva's legs at the knees and pushes them apart, showing her precisely how to angle the mirror for optimum viewing. Once settled, she uses her fingers to open up the folds of Eva's sex, pointing out her hymen, the skin stretched but not broken by their fuckings.

"When a girl has a prick up her for the first time, this tears." She runs her index finger over the tender pink membrane. "Then she's a girl no more."

"It hurts." Eva makes a face. "I've seen it."

"It's not so terribly bad." Mary Jane gives her a kiss of encouragement. "For most girls, it's a sharp twinge and some mild discomfort. That's the whole of it."

Eva doesn't look convinced. "I cleaned the sheets after my sister." She turns glum. "There was blood in the muck of the fella."

"On occasion, yes." Mary Jane strokes Eva's locks. "But it very much depends upon the girl. It's by no means a certainty, and often times, if the girl's been adequately prepared—that is to say, received her pleasure—the injury may be greatly reduced."

Downhearted, it being apparent that Mary Jane has some particular expertise in the matter of defloration, Eva's heart plummets. "You've done this afore?"

"Several times," Mary Jane confesses. "Why? Does that disappoint you?"

No answer.

"You thought you were the only one," Mary Jane infers from her downturned face and forlorn expression. "You wanted to be." She moves away, retreating to the cold side of the bed. "I told you I don't deserve you."

"Have there been many?"

Mary Jane doesn't want to lie, but she isn't sure of the truth. While the French bawd was still booking her for sessions at the Burlington Arcade with the unhappily married ladies of the West End, she's sure she had one or two younger women with incomplete disseverance of their maidenheads. Beyond that, following the

disbandment of those educational gatherings, she was sent out for private sessions. Such work was rare, but she became something of a specialist.

Her clients ranged from teenage newlyweds to lonely spinsters who, having given up on the hope of marriage, wanted to experience the pleasures of amorous connection without the sin of giving themselves to a man. Of all these encounters, the most memorable was Adel.

She was a nineteen-year-old bride who'd yet to enjoy true and proper connection with her clumsy, inexperienced husband because each infrequent and unpleasant coupling was accompanied by searing pain and she wouldn't see a doctor. The thought of baring herself to any man other than her husband was simply intolerable, but she did—upon the recommendation of her aunt—eventually consent to a discreet visit with a woman. Of course, in her mind, that woman was a nurse, not a local prostitute, but needs must.

When Mary Jane met her, she was sitting on the edge of her quilted bed in her gas-lit bedroom, racked with nerves. Her breathing was fast and shallow, her hand shaking as she sipped from a glass of diluted brandy. Every few seconds, her hazel eyes flitted to a bottle of smelling salts on the bedside table, anticipating the need.

Her lady's maid, at the direction of her aunt, had prepared the room precisely as Mary Jane requested, though she knew not what for. Some towels were warming by the open fire, there was a deep bowl of hot water on the vanity, and a tub of cold cream by the bed.

"How do we begin?" Adel asked, finishing her drink.

"I must look at you." Mary Jane approached the bed, her dildo package in hand. "Are your drawers removed?"

Adel glanced at an ottoman set against the far wall, upon which was folded a clean pair of white drawers, then again at the smelling salts.

"Very well." Mary Jane knelt before her. "Would you lift your skirts for me?"

Taking a break from worrying her lace sleeve cuffs, Adel inched her floral-patterned skirts up, visibly trembling. Unable to look, she squeezed her eyes shut,

gasping when she felt Mary Jane's hands on her stockinged knees, moving her legs apart.

"Is it ... all right?" Her voice cracked. "Will you be able to help me?"

Though diagnosis of the problem was easy, and achieved with a single glance, Mary Jane took her time. The honey-colored hair on Adel's motte matched perfectly the hair on her head, and her alabaster skin smelled like fresh peaches. She was beautiful. Diminutive and deliciously formed, she was soft, curvaceous, and ... aroused.

Mary Jane took a second look at her weeping flesh, finding the scent of her exhilarating. "I know the cause of your discomfort, and it can be remedied," she concluded at last, admiring Adel's partially intact hymen. "We can proceed now if you wish."

"Must the lights be on?" Adel fretted, casting her eyes around the richly decorated room, not a shadow or a darkened corner in sight.

"I'd prefer it."

Adel nodded, subdued. "What does this business entail in any case? I'm not sure I quite understand what we're—" She stopped abruptly, her thought stalled.

Mary Jane unwrapped the dildo and placed it in her hands.

"Golly! It's a ... a ... oh, heavens, it's ..." Flustered, Adel tossed the toy onto the bed, wiping her hands of it. "Are they meant to be so big? That monstrosity shall cause me an injury."

"Any pain will be brief." Mary Jane took the phallus and set it in the bowl of water, letting it warm. "But unfortunately necessary."

"Oh, my head is spinning." Adel pressed the back of her hand to her brow.

"Lie down and close your eyes." Mary Jane removed her boots and hiked up her skirts, climbing onto the bed in preparation for the preliminaries. "This part will not hurt, I promise you." She helped Adel into position. "It will give you the greatest pleasure."

Since her eyes were closed, Adel didn't see what was coming. Mary Jane's oral ministrations took her by

surprise, and judging by the force of her climax—in addition to the astonishment and confusion present in her ejaculations at the onset of her paroxysm—Mary Jane was left entirely convinced that it was her first spend.

"Whatever did you just do to me?" Adel whimpered, recovering on the bed. "I've never felt anything so queer." Lust ignited in her, she peeked at Mary Jane, watching her strip to corset and stockings and strap the heated dildo to her crotch.

"I needed to make sure you were ready." Mary Jane clambered back onto the bed, sliding one of the warm towels under Adel's rump. "Did you enjoy it?"

Flushed with awakened desire, Adel eyed the large cock bobbing in Mary Jane's lap. "I should very much like to feel that way again." She opened her legs freely, inviting Mary Jane to mount her. "Will you do it to me?"

"I'll make certain of it." Mary Jane lined herself up. "Now take a deep breath."

Dealing with the unpleasantness swiftly, she gave a sharp thrust forward and Adel cried out. There were tears, she sobbed, and her nails dug into the soft flesh of Mary Jane's rear, then there was silence.

"It's done," Mary Jane informed her, remaining hilted but resisting the urge to commence fucking. "Do you wish me to stop?"

"No." Adel shook her head, not ready for this experience to end. "You're in now. Keep on." She encouraged Mary Jane to move. "Make me shiver."

Dutifully, Mary Jane wrapped one arm around Adel's neck, holding her snugly, and gripped her bum with the other, raising her to meet every shove, helping to synchronize their movements.

Unlike the other women she'd helped in this way, Adel didn't close her eyes again. She didn't try to pretend she was somewhere else, with a man above her. Rather, she gazed up, transfixed on Mary Jane's face, both hands roving over the curves of her body, their lips inches apart.

Mary Jane could feel Adel's labored breath on her mouth, arms around her neck, pulling her closer ...

"Oh, God." Her rhythm faltered, their lips brushing together. "I want you." She crushed her mouth to Adel's, relieved and emboldened when Adel kissed her back.

From that moment on, their coupling was enhanced far beyond that of the mechanical thrusts she was used to providing to these women in need. It was passionate. It was frenzied. As they held each other in a tight embrace, they locked lips, fucking together until Adel reached her second peak, her voluptuous moans tipping Mary Jane over the precipice with her.

In the wake of it, Mary Jane eased herself out and retrieved another of the clean warm towels, wetting it with the hot water before kneeling at the side of the bed and dabbing at Adel's sex.

"You have a beautiful cunt."

"Do I?" Adel looked at herself. "I suppose you ought to know." She blushed, touching her flushed slit. "What makes one beautiful and not another? Do they not all look the same?"

"Yours is perfection." Mary Jane bent forward and dropped a kiss on it, one kiss turning to several when she felt Adel's hands slip around the back of her neck.

"You excite me," the young socialite confessed, her passions not yet sated. "Will it hurt to have you up me again?"

Smirking, Mary Jane rose from her knees, helped herself to Adel's brandy-flavored lips, and they fucked twice more. Not for money, mind you. No coin was exchanged beyond what was agreed upon for that first poke. They fucked only for pleasure—and what pleasure it was! Their affair lasted almost three seasons, coming to an abrupt end when Adel, then heavy with child, went into her confinement and took leave of the city. The move away from London was facilitated and encouraged by her kindly aunt, who felt that a spot of peace and tranquility and the hearty country air would do her good. They haven't seen each other since.

CHAPTER 25

RECEIVING NO ANSWER TO HER QUESTION, EVA WATCHES the emotions of a memory play out on Mary Jane's face, catching a fleeting glimpse of something that might be love.

"Who was she?" she asks at last, her chest tight with envy.

"Who was who?" Mary Jane snaps back to the present.

"You went away somewhere in your head when I asked how many maidenhoods you've claimed." Eva closes her legs, feeling vulnerable and exposed. "So who was she? Did you love each other? Where is she now?"

"She's nobody," Mary Jane plays it down, fibbing only slightly for the sake of alleviating Eva's concern. "Just another paying customer."

Eva swallows hard, the thought of Mary Jane taking female customers having never occurred to her. "You see to the needs of women?"

Thinking of Missus B——, Mary Jane keeps her voice neutral. "Does that make a difference? Them being men or women?"

Eva scowls. "Course it does. I knows you don't enjoy doing it with men, but if you was touching another woman's bits and pieces, how could you not enjoy that? Even a little bit." She chatters on, oblivious to the look of concern on Mary Jane's face. "To think of you putting

your mouth on another woman the way you do me ..."
She shakes her head, expelling the unwanted thought.
"What we do is just for us. It's special."

When Mary Jane doesn't immediately volunteer
anything reassuring, Eva's stomach churns, a ripple of
nausea swelling up in her gut.

"There ain't no women, are there? Not no more?"

Her relationship with Missus B—— now severed and
Adel long gone, Mary Jane shakes her head. "No, not
now." She kisses Eva's forehead. "You're my only
woman."

"But there's been many?" Eva continues to fret.

Rather than tell an untruth to spare her feelings,
Mary Jane tells her only what matters, hoping that will
suffice. "I've loved before you, but none so much as you."

In the contemplative silence that follows, Eva
resumes the mirror inspection of her core, poking at her
hymen and examining the size of her cavity, comparing it
to the girth of the dildo. One finger slides in easily, but
she gives up at two.

"That ain't never gonna fit in me," she concludes at
last, shaking her head. "It's too big."

"Your body's designed for it, darling. Of course it'll
fit." Mary Jane rolls onto her back and lifts her skirts,
offering up her own body for further investigation. "Do
you want to put it up me and see? I don't mind." She
holds herself open, showing Eva her unobstructed slit
and the raggedy edges of her long-torn, barely visible
hymen. "Explore me as you please."

"You're all wet." Eva giggles, scrutinizing Mary
Jane's womanhood, poking her fingers in one at a time
and seeing how many it can accommodate.

At three fingers, Mary Jane lets out a muted peep,
signaling the extent of her comfortable capacity, so Eva
switches up her fingers for the phallus, pressing the
bulbous head to Mary Jane's opening.

"Push," Mary Jane encourages her. "Don't be
frightened. You won't hurt me."

Not sure how much force to apply, Eva eases the
cock forward, watching it sink into the cavernous pink,
the fat crown stretching the elastic opening then popping

through, sliding smoothly down the channel. Fascinated by how Mary Jane's flesh expands to suck the phallus inside, conforming around it like a velvet glove, she slides the tip in and out.

Then, "How far does it go?" She pushes it in all the way, applying steady pressure until she feels the tip meet resistance at the entrance to Mary Jane's womb. "Oh, it's so deep." She marvels at it, wiggling it around. "Will it make you spend?"

"It's difficult for me to get a pleasure this way—my work has ruined me for it—but if you poke me in just the right way, touching all the right places inside, it can sometimes be brought on despite myself." Mary Jane tickles her fingers over her clit. "Do you want to try?"

Eva nods, pushing and jiggling the phallus in Mary Jane's carmine furrow, coating it in her fluids.

"Move it faster." Mary Jane groans, rubbing the swollen protuberance at the apex of her cleft. "Fuck me with it."

Eva tries but becomes distracted. Lacking rhythm, she stabs the cock at a staccato pace with no particular aim, her attention focused on Mary Jane's clitoral titillation, seeing how she circles the nub, applying pressure above and below it, reserving direct contact for featherlight flickers with her fingertip. Enthralled, she forgets to move.

"Don't you dare stop." Mary Jane grabs Eva's limp wrist and tilts the head of the cock toward the anterior wall of her canal. "I'm so close." She shows Eva precisely how to coax her pleasure on. "Keep working it there and you'll fetch me in a minute."

Once Eva's able to maintain the tempo on her own, Mary Jane returns her fingers to her clit. She moves her hips in synchrony with Eva's upstrokes, her orgasm erupting with a series of bawdy ejaculations.

In the midst of it, Eva loses her grip on the slick dildo. Before she gets it back in her grasp, she sees it twitching inside Mary Jane's body, the exposed portion wagging in response to her contractions. Afraid that it might get completely sucked up, she snatches the base

and jerks it out mid-spasm, a trickle of salt effusion cascading down Mary Jane's cleft.

"Unghh!" Mary Jane clasps a hand over her pulsing sex, shocked by the sudden evacuation. "That was a thoroughly unpleasant way to finish," she chastises Eva lightly. "Be gentle with me next time, yes? No need to whip it out so soon."

"I thought it was gonna get stuck." Eva looks apologetic. "Your grummit was trying to eat it, I think." She runs her finger along the shaft, smearing it through Mary Jane's spendings. "What's them holes for anyway?"

"That's how I wear it." Mary Jane clambers off the bed, taking the dildo with her. "Let me show you." She rinses it at the washstand, affixes the ribbons, and strips down before tying it around her waist, returning to the bed with the large phallus projecting from her groin. "Do you think you might like to try it?"

"Oh, lummy!" Eva gawps at it. "I'm afeared I won't never have the nerve, but I wanna know what it feels like to have you inside." She reclines, spreading her legs.

Water dripping from the bulbous cockhead reminds her of the first spending dream she ever had, and just like in the dream, Mary Jane takes hold of the cock and rubs the tip along her cleft, smearing it in her amatory juices, letting it bump against the underside of her clit.

Retaining Mary Jane's body heat, the phallus feels hot like flesh, its warmth radiating against Eva's sensitive skin as Mary Jane pushes it between her labia, lodging it at her entrance.

"Are you ready, my love?" Mary Jane applies just enough pressure to keep it in place, the resistance of Eva's hymen barring her way. "There's no going back from this."

"Do it." Eva nods feverishly, her breathing ragged. "I do want it."

Familiarity with the process tells Mary Jane that a short, sharp thrust is best, thereby lacerating Eva's maidenhead in one fell swoop instead of working her way in inch by inch and tearing it in increments. So violent though it appears, she places both hands on Eva's hips and jerks her pelvis forward. In that instant, the barrier

gives way and Eva yelps, a sharp stab of pain shooting through her core.

"Are you all right, my darling?" Mary Jane embeds herself, the obstruction obliterated. "I'm in you," she whispers. "I'm all the way up you. How does it feel?"

"So full," Eva mewls, peering over her bunched up skirts and watching the cock disappear inside her, creases of pain intermittently crossing her brow. "What a sight!"

"I told you it would fit." Mary Jane pulls back till only the head is embedded—experience letting her know precisely when to stop—then she drives forward, keeping to a gentle pace and moving in long, slow strokes.

Groaning, Eva flops her head back onto the pillow and turns to ogle their reflection in the cheval mirror, her stockinged legs wrapped around Mary Jane's undulating rump, her skirts thrown up over her belly, a bundle of silk ruffles and white lace.

"We're fucking," she murmurs. "Oh, look at us fucking. We're so lewd."

Mary Jane has a peek, then adjusts. Increasing the lewdness of it all, she sits upright and tears off her corset, freeing her constricted breasts.

"Touch me," she commands, resuming movement. "Give me your hands."

"Diddeys ..." Eva clutches at her swaying breasts, grabbing and squeezing them, making the most of this rare opportunity.

For a disappointing majority of their assignations, full nudity isn't an option. Breasts are usually off-limits, confined as they are beneath layer upon layer of cotton, satin, silk, and lace, and imprisoned behind steam-molded corsetry, and as a result of this prolonged deprivation, Eva's fascination with her bosom has been amplified.

Taking her by the hips, Mary Jane lifts Eva's bum, positioning her for deeper penetration, and plunges rhythmically inside her, wishing it were real. She wants to feel Eva's body clenching around her, milking her, urging her to spill, and that very thought drives her much too soon toward her own crisis, necessitating another change of position.

"You must have a pleasure." She drops forward, holding Eva as she once held Adel, grinding into her, clit to clit. "I want you to feel good."

After a few minutes, Mary Jane feels Eva's buttocks clench, her thighs trembling.

"It's coming soon." Eva gasps. "Coming, coming, coming ... oho, coming!"

Mary Jane bites her lip, holding in a yelp of pain as Eva's fingernails claw into her back, tearing through her skin, starting between her shoulder blades and scraping down to the base of her spine. It stings, her flesh grated, Eva's hands moving lower and groping at her rump, pulling her deeper, moaning and wailing through her orgasm.

Close to her own peak, Mary Jane shoves a few times more, then hilts herself, rubbing their articles together and spending as Eva shivers and spasms around her, their combined cries echoing throughout the house.

When it's over, they remain locked together, delaying the inevitable uncunting until Mary Jane's legs start to cramp, the onset of pins and needles in her lower extremities forcing her to move. As she does, she withdraws little by little, getting Eva to take a lungful of air and exhale slowly, hoping that will minimize her discomfort.

Still, Eva winces as the fat cockhead pops out. Afraid to see the damage, she turns her head and covers her eyes with her hands. "Am I bleeding?"

Mary Jane dips down to check, finding the telltale pink stain of defloration seeped into her chemise, and the tiniest amount of crimson mingled in with her spendings, the jagged edges of her shredded hymen raw, but not gushing.

"Only a little," she diagnoses, fetching a washcloth and soaking it in the washbasin. "I'll clean you up and kiss it better, then you ought to have the maid wash your shemmy before your aunt sees it, else she'll know what's been done."

Eva lies quiet as Mary Jane dabs at her tender sex, soothing her ravaged flesh, the loving act capped off with a few soft kisses on her throbbing slit. Once all's done,

Eva reaches for the hand mirror and looks at herself again, her lips curling into a smile at the sight of her freshly-pierced maidenhead.

Seeing that and the enraptured glint in her eye, Mary Jane is flooded with relief. "You're smiling. Does that mean you like it?"

"I don't half." Eva grins, proud of her broken hymen. "I'm gonna show the cook! She'll see that I've had my sweetheart up me well and truly, then they'll not have nuthin' to tease me for." She tosses the mirror onto the counterpane and lunges at Mary Jane, hugging her. "I was scared at first, but I'm so glad now that we've done it. You've had all there is to have of me."

"I'm honored to have received it." Mary Jane welcomes the embrace, capturing her lips for a wet kiss. "You've given me the greatest gift, and I shan't waste it."

"Whatever does that mean?"

"It means I take this as seriously as a vow before God, Eva." Mary Jane sheds the priapus and lies down beside her. "I won't ever betray your love."

Eva's smile broadens. "You're mine for always?"

"I most certainly am."

With that, they fold into a bundle of entwined limbs, kissing, groping, and fondling until Eva grows wary of the time, fearing that her aunt will soon return. Separating from Mary Jane with great reluctance, she changes into a clean chemise, re-dresses, and dashes off to hand the maid her dirtied undergarments for a discreet washing.

While she's gone, Mary Jane packages up her phallus, slips back into full attire—prepared to leave at a second's notice—and has a peep around the room, admiring the many new possessions Eva's acquired since leaving Whitechapel. Among the various knick-knacks on the vanity, she finds a copy of an evening paper, open to a page describing a grisly discovery made by a lighter-man in Rainham, Essex.

A canvas bundle was found floating in the Thames.

A canvas bundle containing the torso of a young woman. No head. No limbs.

"Gruesome, ain't it?"

Eva's voice makes Mary Jane jump.

313

"Can you even imagine it? To go out like that," Eva goes on, oblivious to Mary Jane's unease. "Butchered, and all hacked up to bits. They don't even know who the poor woman was, and I daresay they shan't. Not without the rest."

Struggling to control a tremor in her hand, Mary Jane drops the newspaper back on the vanity, disturbing a single sheet of watermarked paper that was once tucked beneath it.

A crisp sheet of watermarked paper, headed by the British coat of arms.

A passport.

Eva's passport.

Miss Eva Louise Sullivan ...
Traveling on the continent ...
To pass freely without let or hindrance ...
Given at the foreign office ...
London, the 6 day of May, 1887 ...

Distracted from the Rainham torso, Mary Jane picks the travel document up for a closer look. "Eva, why on Earth do you have a passport?" She scans the date on the paper twice, just to be sure she's not mistaken. "It was only issued this past week."

"Oh, heck." Eva hovers in the doorway, not knowing where to begin, the healthy glow of sexual satisfaction draining from her cheeks. "The missus is going to Italy with her husband."

"And?" Mary Jane lays the document down, preparing herself for the worst.

"Her lady's maid got in the family way by the first footman and was dismissed," Eva blabbers, skirting around the crux of the matter. "It caused quite a to-do."

"So?" Mary Jane compels her to reach the point. "Go ahead and spit it out."

Adopting a preemptively apologetic expression, her eyes wide and forlorn, like a shamed puppy, Eva wrings her hands. "She asked me to go along in her place."

Feeling faint, Mary Jane drops onto the sofa, flicks her skirts up, and props her elbows on her parted knees,

her forehead resting on her hands. "Were you not going to tell me?"

"Of course I were." Eva rushes up to her. "I was gonna say of it tonight, but in the jumble of things—what with you saying we wasn't meeting as we planned, then showing up as you did—I s'pose I forgot."

"You forgot?" Mary Jane looks incredulous, anger seeping into her voice. "How could such a thing ever slip from your mind?" She hangs her head, staring at the hardwood floor, trying to keep a level head. "When is it that your missus plans to leave? Not until after the Queen's Golden Jubilee, surely." She hopes for at least another month, but she's denied.

"Next week."

"So this could very well be the last time we'll see each other." Mary Jane sighs, coming to terms. "How long will you be gone?"

"A year or so, but I ain't yet agreed."

"Why ever not?" Mary Jane pushes her own feelings aside, knowing this is a prime opportunity for Eva to better her circumstance. "You don't want to see the continent?"

"Not half as much as I want to be with you." Eva presses her cheek to Mary Jane's shoulder, snuggling against her. "But p'raps it might be for the best," she adds hesitantly. "You've been spending so much money of late."

"Oh, Eva." Mary Jane rolls her eyes. "Don't you worry about that."

"Mary Jane, please," Eva begs her. "I wanna live with you—I want a *life* with you—but if I remain in London, we won't never get away. You'll spend every last penny of your earnings visiting me, and I won't never stop you. It ain't helping us."

Mary Jane doesn't argue. She can't.

"I'll be true and come back to you," Eva swears, creeping a hand onto Mary Jane's thigh, giving her a squeeze for emphasis. "Honest, I will."

Mary Jane shakes her head. "Why ought you? There's so much better out there in the world." She smiles wanly at her young companion. "I wouldn't blame

you for putting me out of your mind, and you'd do well to forget all of this life. You could have a finer woman than me. Someone more deserving of your love."

"How could I forget about you when you've made a true woman of me in this bed tonight?" Eva cups Mary Jane's cheeks, bringing her into a kiss. "I'm gonna write to you every chance I get."

"I hope so." Mary Jane plants kisses all over Eva's face, on her forehead, eyelids, cheeks, nose, and mouth, committing every inch of her to memory, little relieved by her promises, heartfelt though they are.

Deep down, she knows it's a dangerous thing to initiate a girl into fucking, then let her loose on the world. Once a girl's been so thoroughly acquainted with amorous pleasures, she becomes weak to the temptation of it, and Mary Jane fears that Eva will succumb to her natural desires long before the year is up. She leaves that night feeling hollow and empty, struck with an unshakable fear that she may never see her young love again.

CHAPTER 26

A THAMES MYSTERY

"Don't run away with the idea that this Jubilee month of June is to be free from those horrors of which London has of late plentifully supped. On Sunday last, the thigh of a woman was found in the Thames off the Temple Stairs, which is supposed to be part of the body of which the lower half of the trunk was found on May 11, off Rainham, in Essex. This portion was wrapped in coarse sacking, and tied with a thick cord, and had evidently been divided by someone expert in surgery. After a postmortem, Dr. Calloway came to the conclusion that a murder had been committed."

-- Penny Illustrated News (London), June 11, 1887

Saturday, June 11, 1887

MARY JANE PINCHES THE TIP OF HER INDEX FINGER, drawing a tiny bubble of blood to the surface. In the course of sewing together the fabric for a new bodice she hopes to wear to the Queen's Golden Jubilee celebrations, she's pricked herself countless times. Her finger pads are sore, and wrapping small strips of fabric around them is doing little to help.

Giving up on it for the time being, her eyes aching from the strain of attempting such fine needlework with no natural daylight and only a single paraffin lamp, she

317

sucks her bleeding finger into her mouth and drapes the incomplete garment over the arm of her tatty armchair in the rented room she shares with Joseph Barnett.

Rescued from the gutter, the armchair has a faint odor of rot about it, but it's still marginally better than sitting on the wooden floor. Of course, the cushioning had to be ripped out and replaced on account of it being contaminated with the bowel contents of the elderly man who died sitting in it, but apart from some residual staining on the underside, there's no trace of that left, and the repair work was easy. It took her only a few minutes to stitch some pieces of old cloth into a makeshift pouch, which she then stuffed with horsehair, straw, and rags, providing both padding, and a convenient hiding place for her letters from Eva.

It's been a month now since Eva left for the continent, and the days have started blending together, every new one coming and going much like the last, the routine of life becoming dull and repetitive. Since meeting Joe, she's been living here, at Satchell's Lodging House on the east side of George Street, and she loathes the place.

Narrower than her old room at Cooney's in Thrawl Street, these dreary, windowless lodgings can accommodate no more than a small bed, a table, a washstand, and the cumbersome armchair. She misses her old fireplace, but fortunately, since spring is now giving way to summer, she has no need of the extra heat. In fact, some ventilation would be nice.

Most days, she leaves the door open when at home, relishing the infrequent breeze that drifts up the lodging house staircase. It helps to air out the stale, musty room, dissipating the stench of male sweat which seems to linger in the bed sheets, and on everything else Joe touches.

He's not a dirty man, but he works hard for his wages and bears the odor of his labors, the oils from his pores blackening the bed sheets between washes. Looking over at the bed, the ruffled linens still displaced from this morning's fuckings, she can see the outline of

his body on the discolored cotton, and a large gray smear where his filthy, greasy hair rubs on his pillow.

Before bed, she'll have to turn her pillowcase inside out. She didn't notice it earlier, but there are several streaks of dried semen splattered up one side of it, a few stray droplets even managing to hit the headboard. She can see it glistening in the lamplight.

Reaching over the edge of the armchair, she swipes a sticky washcloth off the floor, spits on a corner of it, and rubs Joe's muck off the bedstead, getting remnants of cold cream all over her hand in the process. The washcloth was last used that very morning to mop dollops of cold cream and spermatic fluid off her chest and neck after Joe satisfied his recently acquired letch for her bosom by slathering a copious amount of the cream over the shaft of his erect cock and thrusting it through the valley between her naked breasts.

Though messy, he developed a peculiar fascination with her bubbies soon after they moved in together and her courses came on. Unable to make use of her in the usual manner, he sought other ways to achieve his pleasure, and found that his lusts were suitably inflamed by the thought of exploiting her other womanly assets.

By the time her poorliness was over, the letch was fixed in his mind. With increasing regularity, he'll now forego a proper fuck for the strange pleasure of straddling her upper body, squashing her ample breasts around his cream-coated prick, and humping on her till he spends all over her nude body. She'd think the business quite weird if she hadn't already been subjected to such doings many times over.

Several years ago, while working in the Frenchwoman's house, she learned that her breasts were quite suitable for the purpose, and once she realized men were willing to pay a steep premium for the novelty, she added it to her repertoire of services offered. She even had one man request that she let him use her armpit.

In broken English, he insisted that she disrobe completely and kneel on a low chair in front of a cheval mirror. Once she was positioned to his satisfaction, he got behind her and drove his erection under her arm,

having her press down tightly, gripping him as hard as she could while he worked his little pego back and forth in the most furious manner, watching her breasts jiggle.

Throughout the operation, she bit her tongue and struggled not to laugh. For her, the sensation was a rather ticklish one, culminating in much hilarity when he finished without warning, spraying his deposit on the reflection of her face in the mirror.

She never saw him again, and later found out that he complained about her hairlessness, the stubble on her underarm having given him a frightful friction burn. He was a foreigner, used to the more natural ways of some European women, and not at all accustomed to the relatively modern—and still uncommon—notion of removing body hair for sake of personal hygiene.

Nevertheless, that's how she began to forge a reputation for herself in the market of peculiarities. On another occasion, she had a gent instruct her to kneel on the bed and piddle into a chamber pot while he frigged himself. That in itself was tolerable, but halfway through, he lost control of himself, dived for the bed, and let her urine flow over his fingers, catching the golden stream in the palm of his hand and lapping it up.

The whole business rather revolted her, but he paid well so she kept seeing him. Once, he filled her up with brandy and made her relieve herself all over his face and chest, but even that was by no means the foulest thing she was ever asked to do. She drew the line when he wanted to piddle on her and up her, though she heard some months after that one of the other girls in the house had allowed him to urinate all over her commodity.

Sickened to think of it, Mary Jane banishes the memory and sprawls on the armchair, flinging her legs over one arm, not caring that her stockinged legs are on display all the way up to her knees. She has an hour or so until she's arranged to meet one of her specials in the Ringers' Buildings, and is about to curl up for a quick nap when a young blonde raps on the doorjamb of her open room.

"Emma?"

Mary Jane looks up and smiles, motioning for the spindly scrap of a girl to come inside. "Hello, Rosie, my dear." She remains slumped in the chair, swinging her legs from side to side, thinking nothing of being so exposed. "You need something?"

"I had a rough one." Rosie plops onto the squeaky bed. "Can I sleeps here for a bit? I'm awful tired, and if I goes back to my lodgings, I might have to take another."

This isn't the first time Rosie's sought shelter in her room. The gaunt eighteen-year-old lodges next door in a disreputable house that only takes in *filles de joie*. The women—mostly young girls under twenty—pay nightly for their beds, and give up a small portion of their fees whenever they bring men back. There's no bawd to manage them, only a heartless lodging house deputy who cares little for their wellbeing and encourages men into the house night and day.

"Course you can rest up here awhile." Mary Jane heaves herself out of the sagging armchair and moves over to the bed. "May I see?"

Rosie lies down and pulls up her skirts, letting Mary Jane take a good look at her battered sex. Her labia are inflamed, a little blood matted in the small quantity of flaxen curls around her opening, the dregs of some man's mucilage seeping through the folds of her flesh, her own bodily discharge unusually thick and accompanied by an unpleasant odor.

Reaching a diagnosis, Mary Jane presses the back of her hand to the girl's forehead, gauging whether or not she has a fever. "You've been clapped, love."

"Oh, I ain't, have I?" Rosie itches at her grummit. "That's the second time this year," she grumbles. "I reckon I know who it is what's mucking me up n'all. Filthy bastard he is."

"Ain't you been checking your men like I taught you?"

Rosie looks sheepish. "I forgets." She keeps scratching at herself. "I thought I's been itchy these past days, but I reckoned it was just my reds coming on."

"You've got to be more careful," Mary Jane chides her. "You can't rely on a fella's word."

321

"It's all right for you." Rosie sulks. "You're a lucky tart, you am."

"How's that?"

"You're out of the life." She flaps her hand around the room, indicating Mary Jane's success in the world. "You got ye-self a good man what takes care of ya."

Mary Jane wouldn't exactly consider herself completely out of the life, but teetering on the fringes of it. Still, she hasn't the energy to set Rosie right.

"My Joe's a good man, I'll give him that." She knows she could do much worse. "It's a shame about the smell, though."

Rosie snickers. "Fish porters do have a certain whiff about 'em, don't they? I had one the other day what stunk like a great big whelk. I hadn't got no dinner in me yet, and in the midst of his doings, my belly let out such a mighty growl it gave him a fright."

"You need to get yourself down to the infirmary before you see any other fellas." Mary Jane wags a disciplinary finger at her. "Get your bits seen to before you end up in a worse state."

"I will, I promise." Rosie yawns. "Just after I has a snooze."

"However you like." Mary Jane gets up, flattening creases out of her apron. "I'm gonna hop off and run a few errands. You make sure the door locks behind you when you leave, my pretty, and be gone before my Joe comes home, else he'll have a bloody fit."

Rosie mumbles something vaguely affirmative, and Mary Jane heads out. Hoping to receive something from Eva, as she does nearly every day, the first stop she makes is at the post office on Whitechapel High Street. There, she collects any correspondence being held for her—which today consists of only one letter delivered with this morning's post—and buys a copy of the Penny Illustrated News.

Too impatient to wait until she gets home, she tears the letter open on the street and pores over Eva's words, delighted to read about all of her new adventures. This missive's highlights include her first close encounter with a Sicilian donkey—a cross-eyed jack called Pogo—and a

billy goat that urinated on its own head, then ran off with her hanky.

Folded into the letter is a pressed flower: a violet orchid native to Italy. The paper smells like the perfume Eva's taken to wearing, and there's a lock of her hair bound in silk ribbon. Smiling, her spirits cheered by the token, Mary Jane twirls the brunette curl under her nose, inhaling the sweet scent of Eva's chestnut mane. She sent a lock of her own hair to Eva just last week, so that she might have it woven into a brooch, and now she can do the same. In that way, a little piece of Eva will be with her always, no matter the vast distance between them.

The good feeling doesn't last, though. On her way to get a bite to eat, she flicks through the Penny Illustrated News, shortly falling upon the headline: A Thames Mystery. Much to her revolt, she reads all about the dismembered thigh of a young woman that was found on the Thames embankment a week previous. The police suspect that it belongs to the same nameless, faceless woman in her late twenties whose torso was found in Rainham a month ago, but there's not yet any clue as to who the unfortunate creature might be.

Mary Jane hadn't thought too much of it all at first, but the more she reads ...

This new sad case reminds her of the Thames torso murder of 1873, which she learned of while living at the Frenchwoman's house in Knightsbridge. The house bully—a gruff, burly man with tanned skin and a ponytail of long, dark hair—liked to use such tales of murder and menace to scare any new girl who came to work in the house. He had newspaper clippings pasted into a scrapbook, and took much joy in reading the most ghastly details of the crime and showing them his knives, telling them they would meet the same ugly fate should any of them dare to disrespect the house. In particular, some snippets from an article in the Lancet are permanently scarred into Mary Jane's memory:

"It would appear that after the victim had thus been stunned, the body was immediately deprived of all its blood by a section of the carotid arteries in the neck ..."

"The scalp and skin of the face were removed by making a longitudinal incision through the scalp at the top of the head and a horizontal incision behind. The skin and peri-cranial tissues were then forcibly drawn forward and the skull thus laid bare ..."

"Contrary to popular opinion, the body has not been hacked, but dexterously cut up ..."

Throat slashed.

Skinned.

Dismembered.

Pieces of the poor woman were found up and down the Thames. Her trunk and left forearm were washed up near Battersea, one of her breasts at Nine Elms, pieces of her decapitated head at Limehouse, and pelvis at Woolwich. There was no skull, so in the hopes that she might be identified by photograph, the skin of her face was stitched back together and draped over a butcher's block. It didn't help.

The killer was never caught, and the whole thing gave Mary Jane nightmares. On the evening she returned to the Knightsbridge house from the theater and discovered that her belongings were gone, leaving her with nothing to her name but the dress on her back, she was treated to this threatening tale and sent directly to her room.

There, in her gas-lit *chambre*—where she was also expected to conduct her business—she sobbed into her goose down pillows, surrounded by Egyptian cotton sheets and the softest satin cushions. Though she'd long dreamed of having a bedroom just like this one, decorated in deep purples and reds, the walls covered with the most expensive silk wallpaper, the ceiling painted black and adorned with stars, none of that decadence provided her any comfort. She was a prisoner, and she knew it.

An hour later, while she was still blubbering, a servant of the house—a young girl born and raised in Canning Town—knocked and entered, bearing a tall glass of brandy. Her name was Cherry. Or at least, that's what

everyone knew her as. It was a butchering of the endearment *chérie*, which was all the French bawd ever called her. Her real name—a traditional West African name—was never known, for she was forbidden from speaking it.

Wiping her puffy eyes on the corner of a pillowcase, Mary Jane glanced up to find the generously proportioned eighteen-year-old hovering near the door. She was barefoot, wearing only a plain white nightgown, no robe, the bleached cotton contrasting sharply with the rich tones of her skin.

"I was just getting off to bed, but the missus said to bring you some warm brandy," Cherry explained, approaching the bed. "She reckons it'll help you sleep."

Mary Jane snatched the glass out of her hand and downed it all in a few gulps, knocking it back like water— much to Cherry's astonishment. Throughout the house, the air was thick with the concentrated aroma of jasmine perfume and the commingled scents of a dozen different skin lotions, every room alive with the sounds of pleasure, and Mary Jane felt desperately alone. As Cherry took a step to leave, she lunged for her hand and held her back.

"Will you lie with me awhile?"

Cherry hesitated, eyeing the bed with caution. "I ain't really allowed to stay upstairs."

"Where do you sleep?"

"In the cellar." Cherry messed with her tightly-bunned black tresses, keeping her dark eyes averted. "The missus says that's the best place for me."

"Well, I strongly disagree." Mary Jane scooted over, inviting her onto the bed. "Won't you remain with me tonight?"

Despite her initial reservations, Cherry lay down, laughing as she sank into the warm bedding, her belly wibbling. "Ooh, I shall never get up from here!"

She was no stranger to bed company—Mary Jane already knew that. The story she'd been told by one of the bawd's gossipy tarts was that Cherry had left her Canning Town home at the age of sixteen and run off with the first boy who promised her marriage. She thought it love, but

he only saw in her an opportunity to expand the variety of his triumphs, for when the novelty of her wore away, he left without word. Her only bit of good fortune was that he hadn't filled her belly before he did so.

Too ashamed to return home, she tried to keep in good employment, but soon discovered that decent work was hard to come by. A month later, she met the Frenchwoman.

She was procured in order to satisfy the more exotic needs of the house's clientele, but the old bawd soon found her to be unsuitable for the work. A childhood factory accident had left her with an ugly scar across her midsection, spoiling the appearance of the goods, and so she was relegated to domestic servitude instead. Not that she minded.

Curious, Mary Jane asked to see the scar and she willingly obliged. Eyes closed, Cherry hoisted up her nightgown and bared the lower half of her body, flinching when she felt Mary Jane's lips graze her skin.

"What doing?" She gasped, recoiling from Mary Jane's advance. "We ain't meant to—"

Elevated by the brandy, Mary Jane went for her lips, melting her objections. The following morning, when the Frenchwoman strode in to rouse Mary Jane for work, she found the pair in bed, naked, and had only one comment to make.

"*Bravo. C'est bien,*" she praised Mary Jane in her native tongue. "You have special skills."

CHAPTER 27

DISCOVERY IN THE REGENT'S CANAL

"The police, in dragging the waters of the Regent's Canal near the Midland Railway Station on Friday morning, came across another bundle. The police authorities, being of opinion that a murder has been committed, and that after death the body of the victim has been divided into parts, are now engaged in having the waters of the Regent's Canal, from the Midland Goods Station to Primrose Hill, dragged. The sacking in which the limbs were found was found to be sacking of the same kind as that in which the trunk and other portions of the body found in the Thames off Rainham Creek, Waterloo, and Battersea bridges were wrapped."

-- Reynold's Newspaper (London), July 3, 1887

Monday, July 3, 1887

THUNK, THUNK, THUNK, THUNK ...

"Oh, shove harder!"

Thunk, thunk, thunk ...

"Oh, you naughty boy! Hell and buggery!"

Mary Jane lies in bed, listening to her upstairs neighbor receive a stallion of a man who is most definitely not her husband. For one thing, he's about twenty years too young to claim that dubious privilege. She'd have better luck passing him off as her son.

By Mary Jane's count, the lucky old tart's had her amatory delight five times over already and is now on her way to a sixth. How the fella has anything at all left in his cods, she can't rightly fathom. He must be spitting air.

Every time the headboard beats against the wall, the vibrations dislodge plumes of fine plaster dust from the cracks in Mary Jane's ceiling. The gray flurries drift downward, accumulating on the greasy, blackened floor and gathering in tiny mounds on the dilapidated furniture.

This place—a rented room in a sprawling lodging house opposite a row of tenements in Little Paternoster Row, off Dorset Street—is even worse than the room in George Street. It's one of several common lodging houses in this area owned by the same slumlord: William Crossingham. It won't do. In fact, it's enough to swear Mary Jane off lodging houses altogether, even before another piece of plasterwork breaks off and comes crashing down on her head.

That does it. Getting out of bed to hunt down better lodgings elsewhere, she brushes plaster dust out of her hair and gets dressed.

No longer working the streets, her décolletage revealing bodice has been relegated to her steamer trunk. In its place, she wears the new satin bodice she made for the Queen's Golden Jubilee. It's finer than anything she would usually wear from day to day, but she likes the way it makes her look. It's trimmed with lace around the cuffs and neck, the high collar keeping her decently covered, not a bit of flesh showing. She still can't bring herself to wear a hat, but every little helps. She's even getting used to putting her nearly waist-length hair up on a somewhat regular basis, gradually acclimating herself to the notion of someday being a respectable woman.

Adding the finishing touches to her outfit, she pulls a brooch from the pocket of her dress. The gold-filled frame is decorated with finely detailed acorns and oak leaves at each end, the adornment symbolizing steadfastness and honor. Behind the crystal casing at the center of the brooch, the lock of Eva's hair she received last month is woven together with a lock snipped from

her own auburn mane, the entwinement of their curls commemorating their love and commitment to one another.

As she does each morning, she polishes it up on her apron, kisses it, and pins it on her bodice, wearing it directly over her heart, just below her artificial violet. She wishes she were able to afford a custom piece, but with such limited funds on hand, the best she could do was purchase an older piece she found in a Whitechapel pawnbroker's shop.

Of course, she had to lie to Joe about the provenance of the hair. Put on the spot when he first saw her wearing it, she invented an absent sister who travelled from city to city, hawking goods at various markets. They were very fond of one another—as close as two sisters could be—and they missed each other dreadfully.

Content enough with that response, he never questioned her on it again. Once, while discussing his own siblings, he inquired about her brothers—supposedly six in number and living in London—but she distracted him with the offer of minette.

He never refuses her mouth. In fact, it thoroughly excites him. Kneeling at the bedside, reaching for her lockbox tucked away beneath, she grimaces at the remains of his last oral delight in the chamber pot, left floating on the surface of this morning's urine, where she spat it. It stinks.

Gagging, she counts up a few pence from her lockbox, tucks the coppers away in her pocket, and carries the chamber pot over to the window. Though not strictly allowed to toss dirty pot water into the street, she does so anyway. Most of the panes have been broken out, or fallen away with age and disrepair, the holes patched with brown paper and rags, so she eases up the sash window with care, then tips the pot forward, letting the contents trickle down the side of the building, not caring if she gets in trouble.

That done, she wipes off her hands and gets going, planning to be gone for the remainder of the day. Upon leaving, she finds a notice to quit tacked on her door. If

she doesn't pay her rent arrears in ten days, she'll be evicted from the room.

"What a crying shame that would be." She tears down the notice, scrunches it up, and kicks it across the hall.

She exits the lodging house at the main entrance on the corner of Dorset Street and Little Paternoster Row, the latter of which is no more than a narrow alleyway.

Across the alley, a bushel-bubbied woman with a scruffy up-do and a weary face leans out of the window of her one-room tenement, her weighty breasts exposed to the summer air, hoping to catch the attention of passing men.

Mary Jane's seen her there before, lazily plying her trade. Sometimes, she's joined by one or two of her neighbors, the ragged, bare-breasted women all lolling from their windows, sometimes smoking, sometimes drinking, their shameless exhibition of the female form turning the litter-strewn alleyway into a scene more familiar in a certain area south of the Thames.

In Granby Street, off Waterloo Road, it's a common sight. Women line the windows of their dingy rooms day and night, displaying their fading charms to the cunt-hungry men routinely perusing the street in search of cheap company.

Of course, the window women of Little Paternoster Row have no choice but to advertise their services in this manner. They can't walk the streets for they'd have no-one to care for their littlins, and so pick up whatever trade they can. When the bushel-bubbied woman's baby begins to cry, she disappears from view, cursing its existence.

Walking down Dorset Street, Mary Jane passes two more lodging houses, the Blue Coat Boy public house, a chandler's shop, and the covered entranceway to Miller's Court: a small, dead-end courtyard lined with tenements. On Commercial Street, she stops at the nearest newsagent to pick up one of the daily papers, then goes to a coffeehouse for a slice of toast and a cup of tea, adding one rasher of bacon to her order in Eva's honor.

She intends to pass an hour here, idly catching up on the news before heading down to the post office, expecting, as always, to receive something from her love, but when she stumbles upon an article about the latest body parts fished out of the Regent's Canal, everything goes sideways. Though she tries not to dwell on it, one night she spent in the Frenchwoman's Knightsbridge house stands out in her memory, refusing to be pushed away.

It was early on in her tenure there. Despite the open mockery of the other girls, she'd taken to sleeping with Cherry, and was in the habit of fucking her. Though she knew Cherry preferred a man's touch, the touch of a woman proved to be infinitely better than no touch at all, and they were mutually satisfied by the arrangement. Of course, when the rest of the house found out about their dalliance, the other tarts bombarded her with questions of the most ignorant variety. What does it look like? What does it feel like? Does a negress taste different? Can she spend? Mary Jane paid them no mind.

One night, while the rest of the house was sleeping, she had Cherry naked in her bed. Her face was between Cherry's thighs, licking her toward pleasure, when their amorous engagement was brought to an abrupt halt by a most disturbing occurrence.

"Marie ..." Cherry whimpered, trying to get her attention. "Marie Jeanette, please!" She wrenched Mary Jane's face away from her crotch.

"What?" Mary Jane scowled, loathing the new moniker dumped on her by the French bawd. "Ain't I said not to call me that?"

"The missus goes crackers when I don't," Cherry grumbled, drawing Mary Jane's attention to a few droplets of something dark and sticky collecting on her midsection. "Here, what's this mess? It's coming from up there." She pointed to the ceiling.

Peering up, Mary Jane saw a steady stream of the stuff coming through from the floor above, seeping around the base of an ornate light fixture and trickling down the fancy metalwork. Fearing what it might be, she dabbed her finger in the puddle accumulating on Cherry's

belly, the crimson color of the fluid showing plainly on her ivory skin.

"Is that blood?" Cherry scooted up the bed, moving herself away from the drip. "Gerrit off me!" She grabbed the nearest pillow and rubbed it over her stomach, wiping the fresh red goop off her body. "Where's it coming from?"

In pursuit of an answer, Mary Jane clambered off the bed and got dressed. Thinking one of the other girls might've been ill-used by a late customer, she crept up the stairs and down the hall, Cherry sticking to her heels. The door to the room above Mary Jane's was open a crack, and they peeked through, finding one of the other tarts on the bed, supine and naked. Her head and shoulders were hanging limply off the mattress, drooping toward the floor, while her feet were planted flat on the counterpane, her knees bent and pointed to the ceiling, spread apart as if she were positioned for mounting. But something was wrong.

Her vibrant green eyes looked like dulled marbles: glassy, cloudy, and devoid of life. She was pale. All the color was gone from her, except in a line around her neck where the flesh was pink and flushed, the skin slit from left to right, the gash cutting so deeply that her head was partially severed. Gravity was drawing her blood down, pouring from the wound in her neck, saturating her tresses and collecting in a chamber pot on the floor, but the pot was full.

Her blood spilled out, trickling down the sides of the white porcelain and disappearing between the floorboards. Nearby, a bloodstained Ghurka knife lay on a dirty rag, torn slivers of skin and flesh clinging to the blade.

In the hall, Mary Jane covered her mouth with her hand, stifling a scream before it could escape, and Cherry tugged on her arm, trying to pull her away.

"We didn't see," Cherry whispered. "We go to bed now."

Mary Jane took a step back, the floorboards creaking beneath her feet.

She froze.

Heavy footsteps stomped across the bedroom floor, then the house bully appeared at the bedside carrying an empty metal bucket. Grunting at them, he replaced the chamber pot with the bucket and kicked the door closed, slamming it in their faces. Later on that night, unable to sleep, Mary Jane witnessed the old bawd carrying a bundle of rags and rope up to the room, soon re-emerging with several tightly bound packages in her arms.

Though it happened three years ago, Mary Jane relives the unpleasantness like it was yesterday. She tries to lift her teacup to her lips, but an insuppressible tremor in her hands renders the task impossible, her struggle making the old lady beside her cackle.

"A wee drop o'rum will fix you right up, my lovey." The wrinkled hag pats her shoulder, mistaking her unsteadiness for a bad case of delirium tremens. "Get ye-self down the pub."

"Excuse me?" Mary Jane lowers her cup to the saucer, not trusting herself to get a single drop in her mouth without dribbling it all over the front of her dress.

"I'm saying the tea won't do nuthin' for ya." The old lady grips one of Mary Jane's hands in her own clammy mitts, her nails yellow and brittle. "You need summink stronger." She thieves a crust of toast from Mary Jane's plate. "Go and get it down ya."

Entertaining no more of this conversation, Mary Jane snatches up her newspaper and leaves, the old lady immediately claiming her leftovers. For once in her life, she feels quite confident that the pub is not what she needs. In fact, there's only one thing she needs, and that's to do what she ought to have done three years ago: tell the police.

To that end, she seeks out the only man she trusts.

Inspector Edmund Reid.

It's a twenty-five minute walk from Commercial Street to Bethnal Green Police Station, but Mary Jane makes it there in under twenty. She strides in, her step confident and determined, her cheeks rosy from the brisk walk in the summer heat. She can feel beads of moisture trickling between her breasts, soaking into the fabric of the light cotton chemise she's taken to wearing beneath her corset now that she no longer has to routinely bare herself for coin, her skin weeping under four layers of tight clothing.

Presenting herself to the front desk, she butts in on a heated conversation two junior constables are having regarding the use of rectal dilators for the purpose of promoting regular bowel movements, and whether or not this is likely to lead to the development of homosexual desires.

"I need to see Inspector Reid." She skips straight past the preliminaries and issues her uncompromising demand.

"What concerning?" One of the uniformed constables eyes her with contempt.

"Fetch Inspector Reid," she insists. "I'll speak only with him."

Disregarding her, the fiery-haired constable nods towards a row of wooden chairs near the entrance. "Take a seat, love."

Mary Jane does no such thing. Staying put, she glowers at the constable, her temper rising when he turns back to his colleague and mutters the word 'whore,' making a snide comment about the state of her hair, and how it gives her the appearance of just having rolled out of bed.

"Arsehole." She plants her hands on her hips. "I'm standing right here, you know. I ain't deaf, nor invisible."

"I said for you to take a seat, darlin'."

"And I said for you to fetch Inspector Reid," she snaps back. "I need to speak with him."

"You've got a proper mouth on you, aintcha?" The ginger copper locks eyes with her. "P'raps I oughta wash it out with soap."

"Wash your bloody ears out, more like." Mary huffs at him, her dander up. "I want to talk to Inspector Reid. Now."

For her insolence alone she'd probably have been booted out onto the street, but when she punctuates her demand by leaning over the front desk and knocking his helmet clean off, she's treated to a short spell in one of the station's grimy cells instead. Not that the confinement is much of a punishment, for the chilled air of the stone-walled cell is something of a relief from the sweltering heat outside.

Left alone—save for the young constable guarding the cells—she settles on a worn wooden bench bolted to the wall and unbuttons the top of her dress, easing the lace collar away from her neck, her skin glistening with a fine sheen of sweat. Seeking more relief, she parts her legs and bunches her skirts over her knees, letting a soft breeze cool her clammy thighs and the perspiring flesh above, not caring that the baby-faced constable is exploiting his peripheral vision to peep at her.

"Wanna take a picture?" she sneers, folding her crinkled newspaper into a makeshift fan, the black ink rubbing off on her fingertips. "I can't say as it would be the first time." She slouches forward, fanning herself. "You men are all the same."

To pass the minutes, she begins to sing, crooning old songs. Some Irish. Some English. Some of unknown provenance. She's stuck in the cell for so long that her entire range is almost exhausted by the time she hears Reid's thundering footsteps approach.

"I thought I recognized that voice, Miss Kelly."

Indeed, he's heard her sing many times. When she was a guest in his home, recuperating from the injuries given to her by Fleming, she was prone to bursting out in song. The heavy drugs she was taking to combat the pain of her broken ribs and sprained ankle frequently upset the fragile balance of her moods, and her more maudlin turns of mind were often accompanied by short spells of impromptu singing.

"It's about bloody time." Mary Jane gets up, dusting her skirts off and brushing stray wisps of hair from her

forehead. "Where in God's name were you? Timbuk-fucking-tu?"

Ignoring her coarse tongue, which she is apt to employ when on a short tether, or drunk—the pair usually going hand in hand—Reid instructs the constable to unlock the cell.

He knows her fierce temper is prone to rearing its ugly head without even the slightest provocation when she gives way to the lure of drink. In fact, he's never known such a quiet woman to turn so thoroughly abusive. Her antagonistic and self-destructive behavior betrays a deep-seated despondency that seems to lurk in the recesses of her mind, gnawing at her all the while and surfacing in moments of weakness. The intoxicants meant to suppress it only feed it, and on more than one occasion, he's had the misfortune of seeing her in the state of bitter repentance that often follows a bout of overindulgence.

At one of her lowest points, when her episodic tristimania was at its worst, he picked her off his kitchen floor in the small hours of the morning. She'd stumbled home from the pub and promptly collapsed, an empty flask of gin still clutched in her hand, and he feared her dead. She was taking many opiates for the pain of her injuries and oughtn't to have been drinking at all, never mind to excess. Fortunately, she roused as he lifted her limp body from the cold tile, and he sat with her there on the floor, comforting her until she cried herself to sleep in his arms.

They've never spoken of that night since, but it forever changed her in his mind. He saw the anguish that tormented her. She cried of past love, the pain of loss, and of loathing herself for what she had become. Why did he help her? Didn't he know that she was ruined beyond all repair? She thought herself little more than a body to be fucked and beaten on the whim of a man, and he wanted her to see that she was wrong.

"All lives matter," he told her, as he held her head to his chest. "Including yours."

Some months have passed since then, and he's relieved now, as she steps out of the cell, to see a woman who appears to be entirely in control of herself.

"I've heard a frightful rumor that a mouthy, red-headed woman of questionable character assaulted one of my men." He tries not to crack a smile. "That wouldn't have been you by any chance, would it?"

"Assaulted?" Mary Jane rolls her eyes. "I never laid a finger on the twerpy little shite. You East End coppers are all so tetchy."

In certain parts of the West End—the Haymarket in particular—it's thought a jolly game to run up behind a constable on his beat, knock off his helmet, kick it down the street, and do a runner. All in good fun. Do the same in the East End, though, and you'll wind up in front of the Magistrates for causing injury to a person of the law.

"Having a bad day, are we, Miss Kelly?" Reid upturns one of her hands, inspecting her blackened fingertips. "You've brought me something?"

"Nothing good." Mary Jane hands him the newspaper, folded to the article about the body parts discovered in the Regent's Canal. "May we speak in private?"

With a hand resting on her lower back, Reid shows Mary Jane into his small, cramped office, many of his files and personal effects packed up in boxes, preparing for his imminent move to H Division in Whitechapel.

"Does anyone know who the woman is?" Mary Jane asks directly they're alone. "Is there any chance she's ... of a certain immoral profession?"

Reid narrows his eyes, studying her. "What makes you ask?"

"There's a house in Knightsbridge." Mary Jane swallows hard. "A bad house."

"A brothel?" Reid invites her to use a small washbasin below the window so that she might wash the paper ink off her hands.

Mary Jane nods, pouring water from a ewer into the porcelain bowl. "The house bully took perverse pleasure in threatening the girls who worked there." She dunks her hands, rubbing away the ink. "He said if they

disobeyed the bawd, or stole from the house, or tried to flee, they'd be ... dealt with."

"In what way?" He hands her a towel.

"Like the woman in seventy-three." Mary Jane dries her hands. "You might remember. She was found in the Thames. A case very much the same as this one."

"You connect the two?" Reid withdraws a white silk hanky from his pocket and moves a lock of her hair aside, dabbing at a smudge of ink on her forehead.

"I don't honestly know." Mary Jane falters, questioning why she came.

"But you have reason to believe this latest girl worked at the house?"

"Not really." She catches her reflection in a mirror, realizing her dress is still unbuttoned to her bust. "But I did witness another woman meet her end in that vile place."

"You worked there?" Reid infers, pouring a glass of brandy from a decanter on his desk.

"Briefly." Mary Jane buttons herself up and dips her head, feeling no small amount of shame for the sins of her past. "In eighty-four."

"There's no need to be embarrassed, Miss Kelly." Reid lays a hand on her shoulder. "It's long done." He passes her the glass. "What was the girl's name?"

"I'm afraid I don't know." Mary Jane sips the brandy, glad of the comfort its heat brings. "The old bawd gave us all French *noms de guerre*. Our true names were never uttered."

"But you saw this man take her life?" Reid pulls out a chair for her at his desk.

"Well ... no." Mary Jane hesitates, accepting the proffered seat. "She was already dead."

"By what cause?" The lines on Reid's brow deepen.

"Her throat." Mary Jane messes with her lace collar, feeling choked by the fabric. "It was cut." She recalls the scene in vivid and impeccable detail. "With a large blade. A kukri, I think."

"A Gurkha knife?" Reid frowns. "You the know the type?"

"I've seen them before." Remaining tight on the facts, Mary Jane brings the brandy to her lips. "They're used by the British Indian Army."

Opting to leave that little snippet of information unexplored for the time being, Reid keeps to the topic at hand. "Why did you not seek out the police?"

"Oh, please." Mary Jane's eyes perform a little tumble. "The bawd has the police in her pocket, and I was in fear for my life." She finishes her drink, draining every last drop from the glass. "I suppose I still am." She wishes more brandy would materialize. "It could just as easily have been me in that canal, hacked to pieces, my shame bared to all the world."

"Are you in some danger?"

Mary Jane shakes her head. "They don't know where I am." She stares into the bottom of the empty glass. "But this isn't about me, it's about these other girls."

"I disagree." Reid crouches beside her, plucking the glass out of her hands. "You must know there is nothing I can do for the Knightsbridge girl. You're speaking of a three-year-old unreported murder with no witnesses, no body, and a victim with no name. What did you imagine?"

"You think I'm being foolish?"

"I think you're a good woman caught in a bad life." He sets the glass on his desk, rising to his feet. "And I think perhaps it's best if you look upon events of the past as a nightmare. One that's over, and never to be revisited. You understand?"

"You wish me to stay silent." Mary Jane holds back tears, her façade cracking.

"If anonymity keeps you safe, then anonymous you must remain."

"But what of the woman in the canal?" She protests. "Does she not deserve justice?"

Reid upturns his palms, unable to offer her any solution. "What would you have me do for her? I've no idea who she was, but I can ease your mind of one thing: she was no harlot."

"How do you know?" Mary Jane's voice is softer than a whisper.

339

"The coroner was able to verify that she was ... intact." Reid phrases it as delicately as he can. "She never had connection with a man."

Mary Jane is silenced.

Seeking to steer the conversation in a different direction altogether, Reid spots the new brooch pinned on her bodice. "That's a lovely ornament." He admires the woven hair-work. "You wear it over your heart. An absent friend?"

Mary Jane clasps a hand over her brooch. "An absent love, Inspector."

"Where is he?"

Mary Jane fishes a hanky from her pocket and dabs at her eyes, mopping up the tears before they escape. "Believe me, my happiness does not lie in the arms of a man. I might let men between my legs, but never in my heart. That, I save for a woman."

"Forgive me. I've been presumptuous." Reid accepts this new fact without fuss, or any hint of distaste. "She is to return to you soon, I hope."

A stray tear tumbles down Mary Jane's cheek. "So do I, Inspector. So do I."

CHAPTER 28

1888

Tuesday, February 14, 1888

MARY JANE STANDS IN THE MIDDLE OF A DANK ROOM NO more than twelve feet square, having just struck a bargain for the rent. A patch of black mold is creeping across the ceiling, fed by the damp emanating from a leak in the roof which puddles on the floor of the room above and seeps through the crumbling plasterwork.

Unlike some of her former residences, this room has windows. Two of them, both with old muslin curtains strung up on thin wire. Nearest the door, there's a small, four-paned window that's in relatively good repair. Beside it, there's a larger window that ought to open but doesn't. It's jammed shut, a yellowy splurge of crustose lichen growing in the gap where the putty securing the window frame to the wall has dried up and fallen away.

In an effort to liven the place up, the previous tenant attempted to paint the walls blue, but the color didn't stick. Due to the prevailing damp, it's bubbling and flaking off, leaving powdery traces of colored dust along the edges of the warped wooden floor, the loose boards creaking and shifting as she walks on them.

Once a parlor, this room has the benefit of having its own fireplace—a necessity in the cold months. Where there once was a doorway connecting the old parlor to the

rest of the house, there's now a crudely rigged partition wedged between the walls, blocking the hole. It looks sturdy enough, but it fits poorly. Along one side, there's a crack big enough for a cold draft to whistle through, disturbing the thin, over-washed, cheap linens on the three-quarter size bed that's jammed into the corner.

Everything is so crooked that the bed doesn't fit flush against the wall, though an attempt has been made to compensate for the sloping floor by propping one leg up on a brick. By way of other furniture, there's a large table by the windows, and a smaller one at the bedside. There are two plain wooden chairs, a couple of shelves, a cupboard that's missing one door, and a small pedestal washstand. The mirror above the washstand is cracked, distorting her reflection, the edges of it speckled with black spots.

Behind her, the landlord of this property—a square-jawed man with slicked, side-parted hair and a bushy mustache—stands in the doorway, waiting for her appraisal of the room. "It ain't much," he reads her thoughts. "But with a nice fire going, it'll soon warm up."

"It's fine enough." Mary Jane rolls the room key in her hand, watching an intrepid woodlouse scurry along the dusty fireplace mantel, leaving a trail of displaced dirt in its wake. "It suits a purpose anyway, and the rate is reasonable."

"Your husband ..." The landlord, John McCarthy, flits his eyes to her bare ring finger. "Will he be joining you shortly?"

"More's the pity," Mary Jane mutters under her breath, fussing with the sun-bleached muslin curtain covering the larger window.

"What's that?" McCarthy strains to hear.

"Yes." Mary Jane turns to face him, speaking up and forcing a smile. "He shall." She casts her eyes over the exposed oak support beams running along the ceiling, each one dotted with hooks for stringing up washing wire, or hanging a lamp. "He's at work presently."

She wonders on the time, for she must get a move on. Lately, Joe's taken to having her meet him in a pub on Fish Street Hill, near Billingsgate Fish Market, either

for dinner, or at the finish of his day's labors. Proud of his claim on her, he likes showing her off to his friends, parading her in front of them as his most treasured possession.

"He's a Billingsgate porter you said?" McCarthy is skeptical of the truth.

"Aye." Mary Jane peeks under the bed, pleased to find a tin bath tucked away there. "Joseph Kelly's the name. We've been at lodgings in Brick Lane these past few weeks, but I don't much care for the place. It's infested with rats."

Of the firm belief that a landlord ought only to know the bare essentials in order to conduct his business, she's economical with the truth and sprinkles it with a light dusting of lies.

"McCarthy's my maiden name, you know." She tests out the bed, finding the saggy palliasse lumpy and cold on her buttocks. "P'raps we're related."

Taking that with a pinch of salt, McCarthy checks his pocket watch and excuses himself to other business, leaving Mary Jane alone in her new room. Not a second later, the woman renting the room above lets out a pitiful groan, her wail of discomfort accompanied by a thunderous rumbling emanating from her bowels and the slopping of loose stool into a urine-filled chamber pot, the foul stench of festering intestinal juices and rotten fish filtering down through the cracks in the ceiling.

This place is definitely not the Langham Hotel.

Reflecting silently upon her choice of abode, Mary Jane knows that the weekly rent of four shillings and sixpence makes sound financial sense, despite the rather dismal state of the place. It's tuppence cheaper than paying for a double bed at a lodging house seven nights a week, and it provides a good deal more privacy. Not to mention the fact that it has a fireplace, which she can use to boil her own water and cook her own meals. Really, this filthy hovel is a step up.

Keen to examine the other meager amenities available to her—namely the water pump, the dustbins, and the privies—she leaves the door propped open to

vent the musty room and steps out into the whitewashed courtyard, which is lined with single-room tenements.

The water pump and dustbins are located just outside her room; she can see them from her windows. At the end of the court, on the left side, three privies are housed in a lopsided shed with a dirt floor. The grand tour takes all of thirty seconds. From there, she ventures out of the court through a narrow, covered walkway and emerges onto Dorset Street.

According to some, this is the worst street in London. They say it's home to the most vicious class, full of thieves and drunkards, but she sees nothing so different from any other street in this locale. Children playing barefoot in the gutter. Women with blackened eyes and bloodied noses, their aprons stained with the dirt of hard living. Mostly Emerald.

In any case, this is her home now.

Number 13, Miller's Court.

CHAPTER 29

ALLEGED FATAL STABBING CASE IN WHITECHAPEL

"On Tuesday, information was forwarded to Mr. Wynne E. Baxter, the East Middlesex coroner, of the death of Annie Millwood, aged 38, a single woman, who is alleged to have been the victim of a most violent and brutal attack. The deceased was admitted to the Whitechapel Infirmary suffering from numerous stabs in the legs and lower part of the body. She stated that she had been attacked by a man she did not know, and who stabbed her with a clasp knife which he took from his pocket."

-- Eastern Post & City Chronicle (London), April 7, 1888

Sunday, April 8, 1888

ALONE IN HER MILLER'S COURT ROOM, MARY JANE CUTS AN article out of the Eastern Post and City Chronicle, working by candlelight. She started following all manner of gruesome goings on in the East End when female body parts started washing up in the Thames, and now she finds herself hoarding anything concerning the ills that so often come to Tower Hamlets' most vulnerable women.

This case in particular is one she remembers from earlier in the year. The woman, Annie Millwood, was stabbed on Saturday, February 25. Mary Jane remembers that night precisely, for she and Fleming had a falling

out. He was irate that she'd moved into new lodgings with Joe, and they had a frightful row outside the Ten Bells.

While swearing he was done with her for good, he drew a knife on her and accused her of leading him on a merry dance, having made a string of hollow promises. Firstly, that she'd return to his company after Joe got married ... then it was after Christmas ... then after this, that, and the other thing. Of course, he was right: she hadn't meant a word of it.

At the time she was stabbed, Annie Millwood was living at a lodging house on White's Row, a single block from Dorset Street. She was admitted to the Whitechapel Workhouse Infirmary and survived, but died scarcely a month later, apparently from natural causes. It was a sad affair, and her attacker was never caught.

Writing it off as one more Whitechapel misery, Mary Jane lifts one of the loose floorboards beside the bed and pulls out from that hiding place a collection of newspaper clippings wrapped in a raggedy piece of muslin. Here, she keeps all the articles she's saved over the past year, starting with the Rainham torso, and adds this newest one to the pile.

Also in the hole is the desiccated rose Eva gave her during their early courtship, and all of Eva's letters, the bundle tied up with ribbon and steadily growing, taking up much of the available space. She slips the latest one from the bunch and re-reads it, reigniting the emotions evoked by it, tracing her fingers over the words and losing herself in a reverie until she's interrupted by a knock at the door.

"Just a minute." She tucks the letter away and quietly replaces the floorboard, dragging the bedside table over it.

She doesn't need to ask who it is calling upon her at this late hour. She knows it's Joe. Her situation with him was meant to be temporary, ending when he married, but when push came to shove, he couldn't quit her. Though he no longer sleeps with her every night—relief!—he visits often. When he wants her for conversation, he comes straight from work and brings her supper, doling out

whatever coin he can afford to spare before getting his fuck. When he wants a drinking companion, he comes empty-handed and spends all his money on booze, hoping for a quick, drunken fuck before he goes home to his frigid common-law wife, their union cemented with a ring, not a holy vow. When he wants her purely for other amusements, as he does tonight, he arrives late in the evening and stays till morning.

On these nights, few words are exchanged. He slaps some money on the table and urges her onto the bed, face down, rump up, no patience for disrobing her. Clambering on behind her, he hoists up her hips, flips her skirts over her back, and unbuttons himself, dropping his trousers before spitting on his hand and smearing a glob of saliva over her dry, unprepared sex.

This is less than ideal. If he gives her warning of his arrival, she readies her flesh with the aid of Eva's letters or a lewd book, indulging in some private cuntal delights prior to his making use of her, but when he shows up on a whim, he has to take her as she is, slathering on whatever substance is most readily available, whether that be cold cream, olive oil, or spit.

Every thrust up her tight, resisting channel sets her labia on fire, the friction akin to being rubbed with a sheet of glass paper while being poked with a small stick. Resting her elbows on the pillow and gritting her teeth, she measures the passing of time in grunts.

Ten ... eleven ... fifteen ...

At nineteen, he spills.

Five minutes later, he's asleep.

Waiting until he's in deep slumber, snoring like a flat-faced dog, she gets up. Even though she no longer works the streets, she finds it difficult to sleep at night, her body still wired like an owl. Wide awake, she pours some leftover water from the kettle into the washbasin and prepares to douche, having all the necessary accoutrements bar one: vinegar.

"Damnit." She tosses the empty bottle back into her basket of bits and bobs.

Forced to rinse with plain water for the time being, she slips on a gray pilot coat, takes some more money from Joe's pockets, and sneaks out to replenish her stock.

Exiting Miller's Court, she sees a man lingering in the doorway of Crossingham's lodging house on the other side of the street. He appears to be watching her, his hat pulled down low on his brow, his hands stuffed in his pockets. As she turns toward Commercial Street, he comes forward, stepping into the lamplight, his features and the red hanky in his pocket immediately recognizable.

It's Fleming.

He's been hanging about like a bad cold of late, and his obsessive behavior is rather starting to remind her of an incident that happened in Miller's Court some seven years ago. A George Street man—a resident of Cooney's Lodging House, so the rumors say—took a fancy to a prostitute living in the court and began following her about like a lovesick puppy. He wanted her to live with him, though she repeatedly refused, and what began as a mildly irritating infatuation soon escalated into a dangerous obsession. Enraged by her rejections, he at last barged into her room and brutally attacked her, receiving two months' hard labor for his crime.

Hoping Fleming's obsession doesn't escalate to that, Mary Jane dodges him. "What do you want?" she grumbles.

"Has he had you tonight?" Fleming keeps pace with her, like a dog yapping at her heels, pleading for attention. "I saw him go in."

"You're spying on me now?" She flashes him a sour look, thoroughly unimpressed.

"I'm keeping an eye out, that's all."

"What for? What's it to you?" Mary Jane faces him defiantly. "You said you didn't want nothing more to do with me. Remember that?"

"I worry about you."

"Oh, that's rich." She snorts. "This Joe's good to me, and he ain't never beaten me within an inch of my life, so he's already an improvement on you."

"I was in a fit. I don't even remember what I done." Fleming darts in front of her, cutting her off and grabbing her by the arm. "Get a room with me tonight."

"Fuck off!" She wrenches herself free and beats his chest with her fist. "I ain't going nowhere with you, you nasty shite!"

In response to that, Fleming pulls a clasp knife from his pocket, the six-inch blade glinting in the yellow light cast from Crossingham's lodging house across the narrow street.

"Whatchu gonna do with that?" Mary Jane glares indignantly at him. "Cut me?"

Enraged, his bloodshot eyes fixed on her, he lunges toward her, shoving her against the wall and bringing the blade to her throat, pressing the tip to her carotid artery.

"Go on, then!" she dares him. "Would it make you feel better?"

His jaw clenched, he looms over her, breathing hard, his hand crushing her sternum, pinning her in place. For a moment, she fears he might do it, but she won't look away. She won't back down. She won't beg. Masking her fear behind hatred, she keeps her eyes locked on his until he breaks, snarling like a rabid dog before punching the wall, bloodying his knuckles.

Ducking from his fist—though she doubts her face was the target—she spots a pile of construction debris on the ground: broken bricks, moldy plaster, and rotten flooring. As he storms off, she reaches for a weapon.

"Arsehole!" she shouts after him, picking up a piece of brick and hurling it in his direction, missing him by only a small margin. "Stay the fuck away from me!"

The brick hits the ground, startling a mangy cat in the gutter and exploding into a thousand powdery shards, rebounding into the street like shrapnel.

"For God's sake, shut up!" a disembodied male voice yells out of an open top floor window across the street, his whiskery face then appearing from the darkness beyond and leaning out. "If you don't quit your yelling, I'll come down there and cut you me-self!"

"Fuck you!" Mary Jane picks up another chunk of brick and hurls it at the stranger's window as he's closing it, shattering out the glass.

"Fucking Christ!" The stranger recoils, shielding his face.

"Serves you right, you cheeky bastard!" Mary Jane bellows at the top of her lungs. "Next time, mind your own fucking business!" Tucking her shawl over her head, she disappears back inside Miller's Court, retreating into the darkness.

For the remainder of the night, she sits at the table, reading by candlelight. Hearing one of her neighbors return home in the small hours, she steps out to borrow some vinegar and finally gets herself clean, then turns in for bed, laying down to sleep as Joe's getting up for work. With no engagements until late afternoon, she intends to sleep for a good eight hours, but is woken by a pounding on her door just a short while later.

"Who is it?" she mumbles groggily.

"It's me, darlin'," Maria's voice booms back. "Get your idle arse out of bed and let me in."

Mary Jane flings back the covers, wearing only her chemise, and opens the door, immediately returning to the sheets. Behind her, Maria—a copy of today's Morning Advertiser tucked under her arm—strips to her undergarments.

"This place is a dump." She follows Mary Jane into the bed without being invited. "Why ever did you pick it? Are you hard up, or what? I thought that fella of yours had good earnings."

"It's four walls and a roof. It'll do." Mary Jane yawns. "'Sides, it's cheap, and the more money I save on rent, the more money I get in my pocket at the end of the month."

"Whatever you say, Old Mare." Maria unfurls her newspaper. "Here, have you seen this?" She thrusts the paper at Mary Jane's face, jabbing her finger at an article with the headline The Horrible Murder in Whitechapel.

"What is it?" Mary Jane squints at the paper, her vision blurry.

"Emma's dead."

Mary Jane rubs her eyes. "Emma who?"

"Wake up." Maria swats her face with the newspaper. "It's Emma Smith from George Street. Your old neighbor, remember?"

Mary Jane snatches the paper off her, reading the article aloud. "Mister Wynne Baxter held, on Saturday morning, at the London Hospital, an inquiry into the circumstances attending the death of an unfortunate named Emma Elizabeth Smith, who was assaulted in the most brutal manner." She digests the words as they hit the air. "Oh, my good Lord." She slaps a hand to her chest. "How did I not know of this?"

"Because you've been absent."

"You what?"

"Ever since that girl of yours left." Maria snuggles up to her, slipping a hand onto her waist. "You've been all sulky and no fun."

Mary Jane brushes her hand away. "I'm waiting."

"How dull." Maria shifts closer, chancing a peck on the lips.

That accepted, she tries another, this one lingering, but after the third ...

"Stop," Mary Jane whispers, preventing a fourth. "Don't make me kick you out of this bed." She rolls over, shoving her rump at Maria. "I ain't breaking my vow."

Rejected, Maria pouts. "She's gonna come back and you'll be all rusted up."

"Shut up and go to sleep." Mary Jane turns her attention back to the paper, reading all about the cruel assault that led to Emma's death, knowing it's going to give her nightmares.

Emma was accosted by a gang near Whitechapel church. In the middle of the night, she was robbed, beaten, and violently raped with a blunt object, the thing being rammed into her with such force that it tore her peritoneum. She died a day later, having slipped into a coma.

Mary Jane wakes up alone, and in a hurry to make the first of her afternoon appointments on time. Maria is long gone, the newspaper she brought left open on the bedside table, and before doing anything else, Mary Jane cuts out the article about Emma Smith. Not that she needs the reminder. The mental imagery is unshakable.

Though still fatigued, she brushes her teeth, combs orris root powder through her mane to dry out the oils, and washes her privy parts in the leaky tin bathtub, making sure everything's adequately groomed and ready for business. Once all's done, she dresses in the cleanest clothes she currently possesses and walks the short distance east to Brick Lane, claiming a small table on the top floor of a quiet teahouse overlooking the busy market below.

Nearby, there's a selection of complimentary newspapers for customers to peruse, and after ordering a pot of tea for the table, she picks up a copy of the Eastern Post and City Chronicle from March 31. It was a day she missed entirely, on account of being solidly inebriated for nearly a week.

In it, there's an article about Ada Wilson, an East End woman who survived being stabbed in the throat, and as she engrosses herself in a statement made by another lodger residing at the address where the attack took place, a man creeps up behind her.

"You're late." She lowers the newspaper, having heard him approach. "Were you trying to sneak up on me? If so, I regret to inform you that you couldn't sneak up on a deaf man in a dark room. For a smaller fellow, you have surprisingly loud feet."

Inspector Reid steps into her field of vision. "A smaller fellow?" He looks down at himself. "Perhaps it is not I who is small, but you who is unusually gigantesque."

"I meant no offense." Mary Jane chuckles, folding the newspaper in her lap. "But I am rather tall for a woman, I'll admit."

Since their Bethnal Green meeting last summer, they've been keeping regular appointments with one another. Sometimes, they meet up for a game of

backgammon. If the weather's fine, they might enjoy a quiet chat on a park bench, watching the world go by. Other times, like today, when the elements are not quite so favorable, it's a cup of tea. Occasionally, she receives an invite to his home for dinner or supper.

"I couldn't help but see you were reading about that poor woman who was attacked the other week." Reid indicates to the newspaper. "Terrible business that."

"Aye, but I see nothing in it worthy of my sympathy." Mary Jane pauses to thank the young girl who brings their tea. "If you ask me, she brought it all upon herself."

"How so?" Reid pours Mary Jane a cup of tea, then himself. "I must say, that harsh stance seems particularly cruel coming from a kindhearted woman like yourself."

"Well, let's see, shall we? Perhaps I ought to educate you in the complexities of female-kind." Mary Jane flips open the newspaper, reading from the article. "Ada Wilson, the injured woman, is the occupier of the house, but at the time of the outrage, she was under notice to quit." Mary Jane quirks a smile at that. "Aren't we all? That's how things are done in these parts, by and large. Never pay a penny of anything until you absolutely have to." She resumes reading. "I knew Missus Wilson as a married woman, although I had never seen her husband." She looks up again. "Isn't that terribly convenient?"

"You think it a lie?"

"Of course. Just listen." Mary Jane reads on. "Last evening, she came into the house accompanied by a male companion, but whether he was her husband or not, I could not say." She peers at Reid over the top of the paper. "It's the perfect situation, don't you think? Any man seen walking through her door could be passed off as her legitimate doodle, and it need not look in the least bit unrespectable."

"You're a cynical woman, Miss Kelly."

"Oh, hish." Mary Jane reads more. "She has often had visitors to see her, but I have rarely seen them myself as Missus Wilson lives in the front room, her bedroom being just at the back, adjoining the parlor."

"The significance?" Reid has no clue.

"Women in a certain line of employment prefer to rent ground floor rooms, for the ease of their many comings and goings."

Reid nods, accepting the logic of it. "Go on."

"About midnight, I heard the most terrible screams one can imagine." Mary Jane reaches the conclusion of the article. "Running downstairs, I saw Missus Wilson, partially dressed, wringing her hands and crying 'Stop that man for cutting my throat! He has stabbed me!' She then fell fainting in the passage."

"And?" Reid waits for her analysis.

"Partially dressed?" Mary Jane raises an eyebrow. "She invites a man back to her room late at night and undresses in his company. What sort of women do you know who do that?"

"She claims to be a dressmaker."

"And I'm a seamstress, I'm sure." Mary Jane folds the paper away. "A bit of work on the side does not an occupation make."

"I concede to your expertise, Miss Kelly." Reid stirs a little sugar into his tea, adding a splash of milk. "She does appear to be a *grande horizontale.*"

"Aye, and not a very good one." Mary Jane sweetens her own tea. "I reckon she tried to do him over. That is to say, I believe she fucked him out and tried to rob him as he slept. He likely awoke during the attempt and lashed out with whatever he had to hand, which is the very reason why those who rob the prick that feeds them run a risky game." She nurses her teacup, warming her hands on it. "Mind you, she's young. The young ones are apt to try their luck, ill-advised though it is."

"You've never done it?"

"I shan't lie." Mary Jane answers coyly, as if deciding how much truth she ought to impart. "But you must be very sure that you won't see the man again, nor he you. Either that, or you need to be certain that you know him so well he might be counted upon to overlook it."

Reid nods, knowing better than to pry any deeper. "Since you seem to be so well apprised of recent events in this quarter, did you hear of the other woman, Emma Smith? I've been put in charge of that investigation."

"Well, that one's no mystery." Mary Jane sighs.

"Is it not?" Reid raises a bushy eyebrow. "We have no suspects."

"It's the gangs," Mary Jane enlightens him. "There's two of them that I know of. They cover a patch from Whitechapel High Street to the Old Nichol, extorting money from those who ply their trade on the streets. If you pay up, they leave you alone. If you refuse ..."

Mary Jane's mind drifts, thinking of Emma picking herself up off the street, battered and bruised and bleeding profusely, her shawl tucked between her legs in a vain effort to stem her vaginal bleeding. The pain she must've been in staggering back to her lodgings. The fear she must've felt when the blood kept gushing.

"Miss Kelly?" Reid prompts her to finish her thought.

"Sorry. Where was I?" Mary Jane returns to the present. "I daresay the intention of the gang was not to kill Emma, but to put her out of work for a while by way of punishment for refusing their demands. I've seen it done before."

"When?"

"You don't recall?" Mary Jane isn't surprised. "There was a woman named Emily Horsnell. She was residing at Satchell's Lodging House in George Street at the same time I was, which is how we met, although she'd been living there considerably longer. She was separated from her husband and having some difficulty making her rent, which is why she had to earn a bit extra the way she did. It wasn't for the love of it, you understand, but for the necessity—as is the case for most."

"I'm aware of the hardships women face alone." Reid focuses on his tea, conscious of the fact that he was, until recently, largely ignorant of the many difficulties and indignities Mary Jane and countless other women are forced to endure for their survival. "It's a cruel, hard world."

"Crueler and harder than you yet know." Mary Jane thinks back to her time at Satchell's, warmed by her fond memories of Emily, a petite brunette with odd-colored eyes.

They were of similar age and got on well, though they hadn't long been friends. One particularly memorable evening was spent drinking in the cramped lodging house bedroom Emily shared with two other women. It was barely big enough to accommodate the three beds, and one of those was little more than a single palliasse on the floor, pushed into a corner. All they had in the way of furniture was a washstand, no chairs, so Mary Jane and Emily were sitting together on one of the beds, passing a bottle back and forth between them.

They were alone, half-screwed and spreeish, and Mary Jane got ahead of herself. Emboldened by the liquor, and desperately missing Eva, she leaned in for a kiss. Only a kiss. Nothing more. She just wanted to feel another woman's lips on her own, but her brazen attempt to foster intimacy was met with immediate rejection. She tried to pick up and leave after that, amid a flurry of apologies, but Emily wouldn't hear of it.

"There ain't no need for you to go. It's all right." She rubbed Mary Jane's arm. "I ain't that way, but I knows you are." She giggled. "I'm sorry if I gived you the wrong notion about me-self, but I do like you for a friend."

They spoke then of past loves lost—and those currently absent—and Emily confided much. Glad of someone to share her sorrows with, she related how she came to break with her husband some four years since, following the death of their infant child—a bereavement from which she never truly recovered.

"He wanted another babe, but I just couldn't bear it," she sobbed, her tears dripping into the half empty bottle of booze in her lap.

"I don't blame you, my pretty." Mary Jane hooked an arm around Emily's shoulders, comforting her. "It's a terrible thing to carry a child in you for so long, only to watch it wilt and fade in your arms from the minute it enters the world."

As Mary Jane relives the memory, she lays a hand over her corseted abdomen, not aware of having done so until Reid's voice cuts in on her reminiscence.

"Are you unwell?" he asks, concerned that she might be feeling ill. "What happened to Emily?"

Returning her hand to her lap, Mary Jane resumes Emily's story. "She was beaten by a group of men on Guy Fawkes' night, November last. I imagine something was rammed up her, in much the same manner as this most recent attack, although she never said so. Had she confessed the true extent of her injuries, I've no doubt that someone at the lodging house would've sent her to the hospital."

"And rightfully so." Reid gets his dander up. "Why the bloody hell would she not go of her own accord?"

"You have to understand, Inspector, that admitting yourself for medical care when you haven't a farthing to your name is tantamount to getting a one way ticket into the workhouse. Most would rather die, and plenty do." Mary Jane tests the temperature of her tea, finding it cooled to her taste. "Emily suffered for five days before she finally succumbed. As with Emma, peritonitis was the cause of death. I read it in the inquest report they printed in the papers."

"What became of the investigation?"

"They didn't even conduct a postmortem. That's how little anyone cared about the death of an unfortunate in Whitechapel." Mary Jane doesn't bother to restrain her bitterness. "I know of another woman—a resident of the lodging house next door, as it so happens—who was attacked a month later, and by the same bunch of roughs I don't doubt. She was beaten about the face, but survived."

"Have you ever been troubled by them?" Reid's tone softens.

"Only once, so far. They mostly pick on the older women—the vulnerable ones. They're more often caught alone on a dark night and are less likely to defend themselves. When the bastards tried having a go at me, I sent one of them off with a broken nose."

"Any names?" Reid's right hand is primed to reach for his notebook.

"Course not." Mary Jane shakes her head. "If I knew, I'd surely tell you. Emily didn't deserve to go out the way she did, and neither did Emma. They were both good women."

"You knew Emma as well?"

"We used to be neighbors." Mary Jane reflects on the past, sipping her tea. "I was living at Satchell's Lodging House, as I said. She was a lodger in the neighboring house, number eighteen, which is, as you might know, one of notorious reputation."

"Is that how the two of you were acquainted?"

"No, although I was aware of her profession." Mary Jane hesitates, choosing her next words carefully. "We were alike in other affairs, if you understand me."

"She preferred the company of women," Reid infers, mentally logging the information and moving on. "Do you know anything of her family?"

"Only that they couldn't bear to know her for what she was."

Reid can see that she's holding back tears and settles his hand over hers on the table, offering her some silent comfort. Wondering if familial rejection is something she and Emma shared, he dares to ask, "What of yours?"

"Not quite the same." Her guard down, a little bit of truth slips from Mary Jane's lips unchecked. "They just couldn't bear to know me."

Reid rubs his thumb along the back of her hand. "You have someone who cares for you now? You're not alone?"

Thinking of Eva, Mary Jane retracts her hand and pulls out her hanky, soaking up the excess moisture pooling in her lower lids. "There is someone." She presses a hand over her brooch. "A truly delightful creature, and a much better woman than I."

"Ah, the absent love," Reid guesses.

"Not absent for too much longer." Mary Jane blows her nose. "She's due to return from the continent this summer." Before any more questions can be asked, she composes herself and gets to her feet, making her excuses. "I'm very sorry, Inspector, but I must go. I have another appointment to keep."

Reid stands with her, concerned that he's frightened the emotionally enigmatic turtle back inside its shell. "May I escort you?"

"I think not." Mary Jane manages a weak smile. "I fear it would make you blush."

Forty minutes after departing from the teahouse, Mary Jane is inside the peephole room in the Ringers' Buildings, cursing herself for not having requested a room in advance. This was the only one available, and now she's on her back, her head lolled off the foot of the bed, her legs straight up in the air, and her customer— one of her specials—on his knees between them, holding onto her thighs as he hammers into her like a demented woodpecker.

On the plus side, she doesn't have to do much. Lying still and taking it are the only real requirements of this position. Unfortunately, she's staring upside down at the spot in the wall where the peephole is located, and she's fairly certain they're being watched.

She wonders who might be gawping at her right now, getting a kick out of seeing her in corset and stockings, stuck in one of the most undignified positions she's ever found herself in, but before she can ruminate on it for too long, her customer finishes. He reaches his pleasure with one mighty thrust, promptly loses his balance and his grip of her, and shoves her completely off the bed, his spurting prick unsheathed and spraying all over her bare bum cheeks as she topples downward, hitting the floor headfirst.

Flopping arse over face, Mary Jane's semenalized backside slaps onto the floor with a squelch, and she looks up to find his wilting cock dribbling on the counterpane, his cheeks a deep shade of red.

"Please leave." She glowers at him, her head throbbing where she cracked it on the hardwood. "I never want to see you again."

Shamefaced, he gathers up his clothes, leaves her sixpence extra, and shuffles out of the room before he even has his trousers buttoned up. As soon as the door's closed behind him, Mary Jane clutches her head and curls up on the floor, waiting until most of the pain has subsided before heaving herself up, cleaning off her rear end, and getting dressed.

Upon making her exit, she creeps by the adjoining room, listening to see if there's anyone inside. All seeming quiet, she tries the handle and peeks in, finding the room empty, but the air heavy with the lingering scent of a male in rut. More telling than that, there's a red silk hanky crumpled on the floor by the peephole, filled with a fresh seminal deposit.

CHAPTER 30

Tuesday, July 31, 1888

MARY JANE HAS NOT THE ENERGY NOR THE INCLINATION TO rise from her musty, dilapidated bed. It's been a week since she last received a letter from Eva, and this absence of word is so irregular that she's rather shaken by it. Fearing the worst, she's been scouring the daily newspapers for reports of shipping accidents in the English Channel, or indeed, for any news from the continent that might account for Eva's sudden lapse in communication.

She's found nothing.

Over a dozen discarded newspapers are heaped on the floor beside the fireplace, one torn up in frustration, another wetted with her tears, the pages wrinkled and the ink smudged. Her chest aching with worry, she stares up at the ceiling, listening to the sounds in the court.

Women's hurried footsteps.

Laughter.

Men.

Someone knocks for her, but she can't be bothered to answer. Tenement-lined Miller's Court consists of twelve other rented rooms, most residents being women, and Mary Jane's made a few good friends of her neighbors. But none of them know about Eva.

Unable to sleep, her thoughts unsettled, she tries giving herself a pleasure, hoping that it might bring her some relief, but it only compounds her sorrow. When

hunger finally compels her to get up, she putters about aimlessly. At length, she manages to brush her teeth and take care of her other hygiene needs, but she still can't bear to face the world. Rather than go out, she pays a young girl—one of the few who regularly hang about the court, running errands for anyone who asks—to fetch her some essentials: bread, cheese, milk, and gin.

Filling her belly and dulling her pain, she sings to herself, crocheting idly at the table. She used to be a faster hand at it, but the last few years of doing the work in the half-light of darkened rooms is playing havoc with her eyesight.

When the gin runs dry, she wipes her watering eyes and goes out, taking with her a birch rod wrapped up in her maroon crossover shawl. As usual, the first stop she makes is the post office, but there's nothing for her. She checks the papers, but there's nothing to report. No ship wrecks. No outbreaks of cholera. Nothing.

Losing track of time, she wanders the streets in a sulk for an hour before arriving late for one of her standing appointments at a house in Aldgate. When she gets there, the door is opened to her by a plump, gray-haired woman smoking a pipe.

"You're bloody late." She grabs Mary Jane by the shoulder and drags her in. "Hurry on up. Them's waiting for you."

Built on uneven ground with a poor foundation, everything in his house leans slightly to the left, giving the impression that it's stuck in the hull of a listing ship. In fact, its construction is so precarious that it sways in the wind, creaking and groaning as wood grates against wood. One good gust would surely cause the entire structure to come tumbling down.

Though not technically a brothel, this ramshackle house is most certainly disorderly. Rather than a bawd, the woman who runs it calls herself a sin broker. She employs no harlots directly, and nor do any of the harlots who visit the house receive payment from her. She merely arranges the assignation—matching each customer to the local tart who best fits their requirements—and provides the room in which it takes

place. In exchange, she takes a small commission—her so-called introduction fee—from the amount paid to the attending paphian.

No fancy is too perverse for this house. In fact, the woman prides herself in accommodating every letch of man or beast. Or indeed, of man and beast combined. Four-legged guests are not an uncommon sight here, and as Mary Jane ascends the sloping staircase, a goat tethered to the banister rail on the first-floor landing tries to get a mouthful of her skirts.

Some letches do truly defy explanation. She was once asked to allow a Shetland pony to lap a dollop of strawberry jam out of her quim, but she refused. Unlike the sin broker, her moral compass is not quite so bent, and she has no desire to be hauled in front of the magistrates. Not that coming to this house to conduct business of a tamer nature is any less of a risk. The police raid this property so often that it's a wonder the place stays in profit.

Once, two men were caught buggering in the front room. On no less than four occasions, underage girls have been found on the property, being used for immoral means. During one raid, H Division police walked in on a woman who was bound and gagged on a bed. Her ankles were fixed to either end of a metal pipe, keeping her legs a fixed degree apart, and the pipe was hoisted upward by a length of rope connected to a small pulley system rigged onto the ceiling beams. Both wrists were fixed to the headboard, and a silk scarf was tied around her mouth. She was stark naked. On her breasts and belly were trails of wax, a hot candle having been held over her, its drippings drizzled onto her skin.

When one of the constables attempted to rescue her, she slapped his face and spat at him. As it turned out, she'd paid good money for the services she was receiving, and he'd burst in at the critical moment, severely curtailing her pleasure.

It's in that very room now that Mary Jane is awaited by a masked husband and wife. They've been amusing themselves with another doxy in her absence, but she's the main attraction. The fill-in will only submit to being

spanked, but Mary Jane—so they've been promised by the sin broker—is much more permissive.

As agreed upon, she hands over the birch rod, strips to her corset, stockings, and boots, and allows herself to be bound to the footboard of the bed. This is a first for her. Kneeling on the bed, bent over and ready to receive a lashing, she tenses as the wife moves onto the bed behind her, kissing and caressing her bare buttocks before picking up the birch rod and cracking it against her ivory flesh.

Once.

Twice.

Three times.

She wouldn't normally take customers of this sort. All times previous, when she's consented to being birched, it's been at the hands of a single woman or another tart. In the latter instance—done purely for the titillation of their audience—they take it in turns, and know just how to handle the rod so that it makes the loudest thwack with the least amount of pain.

She's never been trussed up. She's never put herself at the mercy of her customers, and were it not for her want of pain now, she probably wouldn't take the risk.

"Oh, mama, you're hurting me." She adopts a childlike voice, assuming the role of a penitent, yet oddly compliant daughter, as per her instructions. "Do it again."

The woman strikes her a fourth time, making her yelp.

"Harder, mama. Harder!" Mary Jane wiggles her rump at the enthusiastic flagellant. "You're making it so delightfully hot."

Taking her punishment as she always does—with determination and a twisted sense of deserving—Mary Jane bears the thrashes until her rear is thoroughly abused, blemished by pink welts streaking across her white flesh.

"Such a lovely round bum-be-doo." The wife giggles, giving Mary Jane's buttocks a hard slap with her open palm. "Like a juicy red apple." She grabs both cheeks in her hands, pinching and squeezing them. "I could eat it

all up." She drags her fingernails over the broken skin. "And you know what? I think that's just what I'll do."

Bending forward, she bites down on Mary Jane's backside, leaving behind the impression of her teeth. Then, she does something Mary Jane's never felt before. Spreading Mary Jane's cheeks, she nestles her tongue in the crack, circling the fundamental orifice.

"Oi!" Mary Jane breaks character and jerks her bum out of the wife's grasp, declaring that she's not being paid nearly enough to suffer such an indignity, her protest cut short by footsteps stampeding up the stairs, followed by the slamming of doors.

It's a raid.

While the husband and wife scramble into their clothes, Mary Jane struggles in her binds, the friction rubbing her skin raw.

"Hey!" She yells at her fleeing customers. "Untie me!"

Ignoring her pleas, they bolt, leaving the door flung wide open. In the same instant, a terrified and disoriented goat runs into the room at full tilt, circles the room three times, then leaps onto the bed and onto her back, bleating, its panicked cries soon drawing the attention of the copper in charge: Inspector Reid.

"What in God's name ... ?" He gawks at her from the doorway.

"Well, this is moderately embarrassing." Mary Jane shakes the goat off her back, angling her body to conceal her partial nudity. "Sadly, it's not the most outrageous situation I've ever been caught in, but I can assure you, on this occasion, it isn't entirely what it looks like."

Reid stands motionless and speechless, taking it all in.

"I have to say, I'm beginning to feel rather like a spectacle." Mary Jane looks away, shame creeping in. "Must you stare so?" She pulls her bound wrists taut, showing him her predicament. "I'd be ever so grateful if you'd lend a hand."

Shooing the goat out and closing the door behind him, Reid releases her from her tethers, unable to

overlook the marks of flagellation plainly visible on her buttocks.

"What do you think you're playing at?"

Her hands freed, Mary Jane snatches up a pillow and hugs it over her crotch. "Earning a living, same as anyone." She eases her bum to the mattress, gently settling her weight on it. "Would you mind fetching me my clothes? I'm afraid you've found me quite lacking my modesty."

Happy to turn his back on her indecency, Reid gathers her skirts, bodice, and under bodice off the floor, looking around for more. "I can't seem to find your drawers."

Mary Jane stifles a laugh. "Nor will you."

Keeping his eyes averted, Reid edges toward the bed and hands over the garments, immediately retreating to the edge of the room to root through the contents of a sideboard.

"Shocking, isn't it?" Mary Jane discards the pillow and slips into her skirts, assuming his rose-tinted view of her is now irreparably tarnished. "To see me as others see me." She covers her corset with the under bodice. "Like the whore that I am."

He makes no comment.

"I told you I'd fall off that pedestal someday." She fastens her bodice and lowers herself back onto the bed, lying on her side so as to keep her weight off her abused backside.

In amongst tubs of greasy pomatum and cold cream, Reid finds a tin of arnica salve and brings it over to the bed. "Roll over."

Mary Jane glances at the tin. "You're not serious?"

His face says that he is, so she shifts onto her belly and turns her head away, unable to look at him for fear that'd she'd see pity in his eyes. A second later, she feels a dip in the mattress as he perches beside her, then he raises her skirts up to her hips, exposing her rear.

"This will numb the pain." He smears a dab of the salve onto his fingertips and rubs it onto her maltreated buttocks, his coarse hand never once straying beyond the

damaged flesh, taking not a single liberty. "Why do you put yourself through this?"

Struck by his tenderness, her eyes prick with tears. "I'm a glutton for punishment."

"Is that what all this is? Atonement?" Reid puts her skirts back in place, noting how high she garters. "Atonement for what?" He wipes his fingers off on a nearby rag. "You're a good woman."

"So you say." Mary Jane remains as she is, keeping her face hidden. "You've always defended me fiercely, but I do wonder if I deserve it." Her silent tears soak into the pillow. "Whatever do you see in me?"

"More than you see in yourself, so it appears." Reid lays a comforting hand on one of her stockinged ankles. "You missed an appointment with me this afternoon."

"I did?" Mary Jane twists around. "What day is it?"

"Tuesday." Reid reaches into the inside pocket of his jacket. "I brought something for you." He pulls out a photo card. "I thought you might like to have it back."

He passes her the five-by-seven card which shows a woman lounging on a velvet sofa. She's clad only in corset and silk stockings, one hand shielding her sex, the other flung above her head, her thick mane of auburn hair spilling over the arm of the sofa.

There's no denying her identity.

"Oh, my." Mary Jane raises an eyebrow, scrutinizing the image of her younger self. "It's been a good long while since I've seen this. Might I ask where you procured it?"

"I arrested a couple of young lads selling indecent photographs from barrows on Whitechapel Road two months ago. We recovered over two hundred pornographic images that day, and this was among them," Reid recounts. "The rest were destroyed, but it seemed only proper to return this one to its rightful owner. Unless you'd prefer that I dispose of it?"

Mary Jane shakes her head, gazing fondly at it. "I shall keep it. When I'm old and past my best, I'll look at it to remind myself of the attractions I once possessed." She holds the picture to her chest. "This was one of my display cards at the Frenchwoman's gay house in Knightsbridge."

"Display cards?" Reid shows his ignorance of the paphian world.

"The bawd had a book with all our pictures in it," Mary Jane explains. "When gentlemen came to the house unsure of their taste, she'd show them this book so that they might be enticed by our charms and select the flesh that pleased them most." She steals another peek. "When I left, she must've sold mine on."

"There were others?"

"Oh, aye." Mary Jane feels her cheeks grow hot. "More provocative ones, if you can imagine that."

"I dare not." Reid presses a hand to his chest. "It wouldn't be good for my heart."

Before Mary Jane can accuse him of being a charmer, the door swings open and a uniformed constable barges in.

"Sorry, sir." He takes a step back when he sees Reid on the bed. "We're clearing out."

"Very good." Reid stands, straightening his waistcoat. "I'll be right with you."

"And I must go." Mary Jane pockets the photograph and wriggles off the bed, searching the floor for the remainder of her things. "I've taken up enough of your time." She locates her apron and shawl, scooping both up from the floor and shaking the goat fuzz off them.

As she turns to leave, Reid captures her by the elbow and makes two shillings appear from behind her ears, the trick still making her smile.

"You soft bastard," she teases him, sneaking out of the house between the goat and a young woman dressed as a nun.

By the time she gets back to Miller's Court, her bum's already starting to ache again, but before she has a chance to tend to it, there's a knock at the door. Assuming it's the neighbor who tried to rouse her this morning, she answers it with a smile.

But it's not a neighbor.

It's Fleming.

"Bleeding hell." She rolls her eyes, trying to shut the door on him. "Whatchu doing here? I thought I'd got shot of you."

"I've been gone." He jams his foot in the door.

"Should've stayed there." She tries to kick his foot out of the way. "Look, you can't be coming round here. What if my other Joe sees you? You'll get me in a fix."

As she pushes on his chest, trying to make him move, one of her neighbors—forty-seven-year-old Julia Venturney, a charwoman in a shabby dress and a dirty white apron—emerges from her room on the other side of the court. On passing them, she looks Fleming up and down, her dark eyes narrowed in thought.

"He's different," she concludes at length.

Not wanting to be thought churlish, Mary Jane introduces them with more than a pinch of reluctance. "This is my friend Joe." She eases up her grip on the door. "Joe, this is Julia."

"Another Joe?" Julia scratches at her bunned graying locks.

"Aye." Mary Jane rolls her eyes. "I attract 'em like flies, and they're just about as annoying."

"Pay no notice." Fleming grins. "She's very fond of me." Exploiting Mary Jane's distraction with Julia, he forces his way into the room.

"Oi!" Mary Jane swings round after him. "Who invited you in?" Apologizing to Julia, she gets in front of Fleming and tries to shove him back out into the court. "Fuck off now, for God's sake. You're being a nuisance."

Resisting, Fleming looks around the room. "Why's you still with this prick?" He picks at some of Joe's belongings, fiddling with a clay pipe on the table. "I could keep you in a place a damn sight better than this rat hole."

"Keep me?" Mary Jane snorts. "You can't keep a bloody job, never mind a woman."

Undeterred, Fleming digs around in his pockets, slapping three bob down on the table. "How's you fixed for coin these days?"

Mary Jane's heart leaps, but she eyes it warily. "Whatchu want for that?"

"Not a solitary sausage." He smiles broadly. "It's my peace offering to you, Mary Jane. The start of a new friendship, so I hope."

"Friends?" Mary Jane pulls a face. "You had a knife to me in the street. What makes you think I wanna be any friend of yours?"

"My mind was off then," Fleming dismisses the event. "But I'm all right now, and I should like to take you out. The theater, if you will. This coming Monday."

Mary Jane continues to regard him with some suspicion. "You're a queer bastard, you are. I'm quite sure I dunno what to make of you."

"Is that a yes?"

"Aye," Mary Jane relents. "If it'll shut you up and get you to hook it."

"I shall, but I must visit the facilities afore I go." Leaving his jacket on the back of a chair, he heads for the privy.

While he's gone, Mary Jane decides to have a sneaky peep through his pockets, hoping to find a few odd coins that won't be missed. Instead, in the front left pocket, she finds a bottle of Chlorodyne—a tincture of alcohol, opium, and cannabis—and a prescription of cannabis seeds, along with a doctor's note written on Whitechapel Infirmary stationery instructing him how to consume the seeds in tea in order to 'alleviate' his 'manic episodes' and help him sleep at night.

Perplexed by the find, she stuffs all three items back into his pocket and sits down at the table, waiting for his return as if she hadn't seen a thing. Thankfully, when he does get back—some twenty minutes later—he's in a hurry to leave.

"I'd best get off home." He rubs a hand over his gurgling belly. "There's a rumpus going on in my bowels today."

"How delightful." Mary Jane grimaces. "Go and soil up your own privy, then." She waves him off, making a mental note not to visit the outhouse for at least an hour.

Thinking she might now get a few minutes to herself to take a nap, she gathers his donation off the table and is about to secrete it in the cluttered lockbox under her bed when Maria appears in the doorway, having just crossed paths with him in the passage.

"Hello, Mare." She points in Fleming's direction. "The bloke with the red hanky. He's your old fella, ain't he? What's he doing here? I thought he was a goner."

"So did I." Mary Jane pockets the money instead. "Seems there's no getting rid of him."

"Well, don't look so bloody miserable about it." Maria helps herself to the bed. "He's paying you, I bet. And he always was generous with it."

"He's not the cause of my misery." Mary Jane kicks at the growing pile of newspapers on the floor. "I ain't heard from Eva in a week."

"Uh-oh, I know that look well." Maria rolls off the bed and takes her by the hand. "That's the look of a woman what needs a drink or three."

"I dunno about that." Mary Jane hesitates. "I'm knackered."

"Aww, c'mon." Maria pouts. "It's been an age since we've had any fun, and I know you's got a pocket full o'coin."

Despite all her good sense, Mary Jane lacks the willpower to resist.

Late Wednesday morning, Mary Jane wakes up to a soft but persistent knocking on her door. Groggy, she opens her eyes, but doesn't get up. "I think it's open." She talks through a yawn. "Just give it a shove.'

The door opens with a creak, the warped wood scraping along the top of the stone step leading into the darkened room, and in strides a young woman wearing a pale cotton dress with a floral print, her head topped with a straw hat covered in light blue fabric, ornamented with a small plume of feathers, tulle netting, and ivory lace. Her entrance is accompanied by a gust of warm summer air, the fluttering of her flounced skirts displacing the dust on the floor, causing it to scatter and swirl, a

weightless bundle of cobweb-covered fluff tumbling across the room and disappearing under the bed.

Temporarily blinded by the blast of sunlight cast into the room, Mary Jane squints at her unexpected visitor, seeing nothing familiar in the rounded hips, elegantly tapered waist, and generous bosom. Nothing familiar at all until she reaches the woman's head.

Long chestnut hair piled up at the back.

Hazel eyes.

A soft face.

A warm, hopeful smile.

"Eva!" Mary Jane sits up, their eyes meeting for the briefest moment before Eva's gaze drifts, drawn to something over Mary Jane's shoulder instead.

"Who is it?" Maria grumbles from the other side of the bed. "What's going on?"

Eva's smile fades. Moisture floods her eyes, and she flees from the room without speaking so much as a word.

"Eva, no!" Mary Jane leaps out of bed in her chemise and hurries into her clothes, but it takes so long to work through all the layers that Eva's long gone by the time she gets outside.

In an attempt to chase her, she darts out into the street, calling her name. From Dorset Street, she runs into Commercial Street, the crowded thoroughfare lined with street sellers and bustling with people. Again, she screams out Eva's name.

Again.

And again.

Spinning in circles, looking from one woman to the next, she stumbles off the pavement and into the road, an oncoming—and furiously driven—hansom clipping her and knocking her into the gutter.

Her shoulder throbbing from the impact with the powerful chest of the horse leading the carriage, she huddles into a ball, crying hysterically. As she tries to lift herself onto the pavement, a passing pedestrian smacks her with his walking stick, striking her in the ribs and knocking her back into the gutter muck.

No-one bats an eye.

CHAPTER 31

Saturday, August 4, 1888

NOT FOR THE FIRST TIME IN HER LIFE, MARY JANE WAKES UP in a strange room, on a strange bed, wearing nothing more than her chemise and corset, with no recollection of how she got there. She's been lushing for several days, she knows that. The more she looked for Eva, the more she drank, and the days started to merge together.

Her head spinning and gut churning, she jerks upright, trying to make sense of her surroundings, the sudden movement causing a swell of nausea.

"Oh, God." She clutches her stomach and leans over the bed, vomiting onto the floor.

When she's done, she keeps her head down and groans, feeling someone's muck dribbling out of her aching cunt and onto the bed sheets.

In trying to remember the events of last night, she has a vague recollection of drinking in a pub and being challenged to put coins up her love-trap. As much as she could hold up there, she could keep. According to one man, there was an Oxford Street cyprian who could fit eighty-seven shillings in hers. Not that these men had eighty-seven shillings between them, mind you. They did a whip around, collecting anything from farthings to tanners, and Mary Jane clambered up on one of the tables, ready to test her body's elasticity.

At one point, already intoxicated beyond the ability to stand, she was offered a drink of brandy. The glass was

put to her lips, the contents tipped into her mouth, and she was forced to take every drop, even though it tasted oddly bitter.

She coughed and sputtered as it went down her throat, and from thereon out, everything became a blur. Incapable of sound or movement—never mind objection—she was stripped to her undergarments and tossed onto a bed. Voices in the room were muffled and distant, one becoming indistinguishable from another. There was laughter. The door opened and closed and another man entered. He was tall, and she could smell his cologne. Hands were on her, all over her, flipping her onto her front. How many people were in the room? Three? Four? Was that a donkey? Where did the monkey come from?

Then, there was silence.

Then, darkness.

Now, in her sober state, she guesses the brandy was tainted with chloral hydrate.

Heaving herself out of the bed, a torrent of thick seminal fluid slops down her inner thighs. Not just one man's libation, but many. In a panic, she drives two fingers up her filthy channel, relieved to find her diaphragm in place.

Her vision clearing, she looks around the room. Or rather, the barn. It looks like an old stable, with a corrugated iron roof, dirt floors, and feeding troughs at one end. As it turns out, the bed isn't even a bed at all, but rather a rat-eaten palliasse dumped on top of some old crates, and it smells like dung.

Finding a relatively clean hanky beside her on the palliasse, she tiptoes over the soft floor, sidestepping piles of manure, and dips the worn silk in a bucket of water by the feeding troughs, using it to clean her battered sex as much as she can, wiping dregs of drying semen off her labia, her sensitive pink skin flushed from the repetitive friction of multiple bedmates.

On a mountain of straw, flung will-nilly over the heap, she locates her clothes. Curious to find out whether or not she got paid, the first thing she does is check her pockets, her heart sinking when she discovers that they're

all completely devoid of coin. Every farthing she had on her is gone, meaning that not only did she receive no payment from the men, but she's also been robbed. Or maybe she drank it all. There's no telling.

Dizzy, and sore all over, she struggles into her clothes and leaves the stable, wincing as she staggers out into a cobblestone yard, the midday sun hitting her face. Heading for the nearest main street, she tries to get her bearings, not having the faintest notion of where she might be until she stumbles out onto Commercial Road, south of Whitechapel High Street.

Feeling altogether rotten, and hoping some hair of the dog will improve her condition, she solicits company. Any company. Whatever man will take her before she throws up again.

She must look a pretty mess. The first two men she approaches pass her by without even casting her a glance. Fortunately, strolling not too far—her expectations suitably lowered—she runs into a grimy laborer on his way home for dinner and selects him for the operation, flaunting herself to him like the cheap sailors' whores on the Ratcliffe Highway.

"Want a fuck, love?"

He stops, looking her over. "How much?"

Thoroughly repulsing herself, she asks, "How much have you got?"

They settle on sixpence, and she leads him back the way she came, taking him down Berner Street and into the quiet yard—Dutfield's Yard, she now knows—where she emerged not ten minutes before.

"Do it here." She presses her back to the wall next to the stable door and lifts her skirts. "No-one will come."

Keen to get his unexpected afternoon treat, he unbuttons himself and shoves up her, sliding into her sopping hole without resistance. Still, despite the overly lubricious state of her parts, the burning friction on every upstroke causes her to moan, giving him the unintentional impression that her passions are heated beyond measure.

"You're a hot-cunted little bitch, aintcha?" He grips her bum, thrusting harder and faster, spurred on by her

apparent enjoyment of it. "You need a good hard fucking."

"Oh, God, finish in me," she begs, squeezing his shoulders, not in a hurry to be semenalized, but for it to be over and the pain to stop.

"Soon," he grunts, keeping pace. "You'll get it soon."

Hearing that she'll have to wait even another second for completion, she wails, her eyes watering. "Won't you come?" She sobs. "I need you to—"

There it is.

Her whole body tenses, her mouth held open in a silent scream, her breath caught in her lungs as a jet of liquid fire bathes her insides. The pain is excruciating, her broken flesh doused with his salty effusion. When she finally lets the trapped air out of her lungs, it comes out as a startled groan, ending with an execration.

"Fucking Christ-all-Goddamn-mighty!"

His pleasure over, the laborer breaks into a hearty chuckle. "You didn't half need that, eh?" He puts his wilted rod away. "I ain't never had a woman so up for it."

As he strides off whistling a merry tune, more than pleased with himself, Mary Jane leans against the wall, feeling weak and faint. Lowering herself into a squat, keeping her skirts hoisted, she squeezes his injection out of her depths, listening to it slap onto the cobblestones beneath her.

Sixpence.

She did this for sixpence.

Searching her pockets for a hanky to plug herself with, all she finds is one that looks like it might've once been used to blow her nose. At least, she hopes it was her nose.

Since it's all that she has, she uses it anyway. Upon attempting to get vertical, she feels bile rise in her throat and vomits again. Her stomach empty, the sludge that she throws up is so acidic that it burns her esophagus. She can't remember when she last ate.

Rubbing tears from her cheeks, she makes her way back to Commercial Road and straight into the nearest pub, ordering two large glasses of rum. Once she has that down her, she feels steady enough to be able to make it

home, and so begins the walk to Dorset Street, stopping only to swill herself out at a public water pump along the way, for the cool water soothes her raw skin.

At the home stretch, her energy begins to wane. Approaching Thrawl Street, she catches a face in the mass of people. A pale, beautiful, heartbroken face.

"Eva ..." she whispers, their eyes meeting.

In that moment, she watches a ripple of disgust and disappointment sweep across Eva's features. Knowing she must look a wreck, she sinks to her knees, weeping into her hands. Unable to take a decent breath, she begins to hyperventilate, the world turning gray, then black ...

For the second time in a row, Mary Jane wakes up in confusion, and with a bad head. She's lying in bed, facing an unfamiliar wall covered with bubbled and peeling wallpaper, the print faded and smoke-stained, the edges torn and raggedy. In one spot almost directly in front of her face, a blunt penknife has been used to carve a crude heart shape into the molding plaster. Inside the heart are the initials MJ. Mary Jane? Did she do that? She has no recollection.

There's warmth behind her. Exploring it, she brings a hand to her waist, feeling an arm draped over her. A slender arm with soft skin and a smooth, delicate hand. Not that of Joe, or any other man. It's a woman's arm.

Fearing the worst and hating herself for it, she pushes her face into the pillow, smothering a whimper of distress. Has she gone to bed with a woman? Who? Maria? What day is it? How did she get here? Where *is* 'here'? What did she do? Who was she with? Checking herself for clues, she finds that she's mostly clothed. Her boots are off, but her stockings are on. She's wearing a petticoat, but no other skirts, and her apron is missing.

On top, she's almost fully dressed. She's been divested of her corset, but her bodice and under-bodice are still on, albeit completely unbuttoned, her chemise intact beneath.

Still perplexed, she dips a hand to her core, feeling for any signs of recent connection but finding none. No salty libation. No arousal. Nothing of that sort. Instead, her pubic region—everything from her clit, all the way along her cleft—is slathered with cream. Curious to know what kind of cream, she lifts her fingers to her nose and gives it a sniff, concluding it to be some sort of healing balm.

All the more confused by this, she wriggles around to face her bedmate, exploring the woman's nicely rounded hips, narrow waist, and full bust, all trapped inside a cotton nightgown. Peeking beneath the blankets, she catches the nightgown bunched up, exposing a thick bush of dark brown curls covering the sleeping woman's motte.

Turning her attention to the woman's face, she lifts away locks of a chestnut mane, revealing what she already knows to be true: it's Eva. Greedy for re-acquaintance of the most intimate kind, she slips her hand between Eva's thighs, nestling her middle finger in the moist valley of her sex, but retracts it in a flash when Eva stirs from slumber.

"Eva," she coos, shedding a tear of bliss.

She moves in for a kiss, but Eva smells stale alcohol on her breath and recoils.

"Don't." She holds Mary Jane off. "You reek." Realizing she's indecent, she tugs down her nightgown and clambers out of bed. "I must get on my way to church anyhow."

"Church?" Mary Jane frowns, her headache aggravated by a screaming child on the other side of the thin walls. "It's never Sunday already?"

"Aye, it is." Eva moves as much as she can out of Mary Jane's sightline to put on her Sunday best—a simple blue satin dress—privacy being difficult to achieve in a room only eight feet wide and ten feet long.

"Oh, good God in heaven." Mary Jane flops onto her back, covering her face with her hands. "How long have I been asleep?"

Eva shrugs. "Sixteen hours or there'bouts." She laces her boots at a small table on the other side of the tiny room, close enough that she's within arm's length of the bed. "I had to pay a coster to wheel you over here on his barrow."

Teary-eyed, Mary Jane imagines the sight: an inebriated whore flung onto the back of a filthy costermonger's barrow and pulled through the streets like a decaying heap of rags flung haphazardly over a ragman's dray.

In silence, Eva continues with her morning routine: brushing her teeth at the washbasin and fixing her tresses. As she opens the patchwork muslin curtains on the room's only window, Mary Jane shields her face from the glare of daylight and groans, her retinas stinging.

"Serves you right," Eva remarks coldly, watching her droop her head over the edge of the bed. "Are you gonna need a bucket?"

"Not presently."

"Good, 'cause I don't possess one." Eva grabs a gray woolen pilot coat off a row of hooks behind the door and puts it on. "You'd have to chuck your guts up out the bloody window and hope for the best."

The pain subsiding, Mary Jane looks up, spotting a hair-work brooch pinned over Eva's heart, their woven locks combined.

In a fright, she clasps a hand to her own breast, searching for the brooch she always pins there, but it's gone. Only the violet remains. Thinking it stolen, she's about to burst into hysterics when Eva retrieves it from the cupboard.

"It was pinned to the inside of your corset." She hands it over. "I found it when I undressed you for bed."

"I've worn it every day." Mary Jane clutches it to her chest. "You believe that, don't you? I've thought about you every waking minute."

Eva offers no response.

"Eva, darling, we need to talk."

"I dunno that I have aught to say." Eva pins her straw hat on her head, preparing to go out. "Get yourself cleaned up and lock the door behind you when you leave."

With that, she's gone.

Alone in Eva's bed, Mary Jane sobs till her tears run dry and she starts to wheeze. Only then does she rise, wash, and dress, taken aback to find a large douching syringe propped in a chamber pot containing some murky water and a dirty hanky, a brand new bottle of vinegar set on the floor nearby. Did Eva clean her? Did she clean herself? She has a hazy memory of taking a man on the street and plugging herself with a crumpled hanky she found in her pocket.

Getting ready to go on her way, she takes a minute to make the narrow bed. It barely fits two people. When she's done with that, she straightens up the table—brushing off some crumbs and giving it a quick scrub—then sweeps the floor. In fact, she works her way around the whole room—still not sure precisely in what building it's located—pausing now and again to admire the odd knick-knack Eva must've brought home from the continent.

Once all's been cleaned, she stops to survey things. The cramped but agreeable room is so precise in its basic construction—a perfect rectangle with just enough room for a small bed, a table, a washstand, two chairs, and a dinky fireplace—that she concludes it must be part of a model housing development. Confirming that, the sash window—with its grubby panes of spider-cracked glass—looks out over the west end of Thrawl Street. The Charlotte de Rothschild model housing building looms opposite, making this large tenement block the newly-constructed Lolesworth Buildings: some of the cheapest housing available in this quarter. Mystery solved.

Struck by a maternal impulse, she then gives Eva's cupboard a once over, looking for food, but aside from a small tin of tea leaves, the shelves are bare. There's not even any stale bread. Intending to rectify that, she delves in her pockets for coin, hoping she might be able to scrape together enough for a cheap meal, temporarily

forgetting that she drank away every farthing of the few measly pence she earned yesterday.

This feeling is alien to her. She's not used to having empty pockets, and doesn't need to check her lockbox at Miller's Court to know there's nothing of any use left in that, either. Seeing only one avenue to remedy this miserable situation, she bucks herself up and goes out.

Eva's room opens into an interior hallway with blue painted walls: two doors on the left, two doors on the right. Leaving Eva's door on the latch so that she can let herself back in, she makes her way down the narrow hall, the scratched and dented floor speckled with spilt beer and a darker spatter that looks like it could be dried blood.

The crying baby is still wailing inside the room next to Eva's, and a dog is scratching at one of the doors opposite, trying to get out. It's succeeded in gnawing away a small corner of the wood, making a hole just big enough for the tip of its snout, and between bouts of frantic clawing and growling, it sticks its wet nose up to the hole, nostrils flaring as it sniffs and snorts at the passing stranger.

Exiting through the unlocked door at the end of the hall, Mary Jane finds herself on a narrow walkway overlooking a concrete courtyard, the design of which is similar to that of George Yard Buildings, but larger, and with a washhouse at the far side.

Protected by a metal railing and strung up with washing wire, the walkway leads to a covered stone stairwell, the dark passage cluttered with shoeless, rag-clad children who sought shelter there for the night. Huddled together, they extend their frail arms, clutching at Mary Jane's skirts as she descends, begging for spare coins or a bite to eat.

The littlest one, no more than five years old, cries in her older brother's arms, her puffy cheeks streaked with dirt, her hair matted with dung and straw from the barn they slept in the night before, her scalp crawling with livestock. The oldest isn't yet twelve.

All the way down, Mary Jane holds her breath. The acrid air inside the stairwell is a nauseating blend of

human excrement, urine, and vomit. Someone's attempt to sweeten it by fixing a tiny bundle of fragrant flowers to the handrail failed, the desiccated remains of the bunch now blackened and crumbling, and it's a relief to be spat out of the passage into the comparatively fresh air of the Lolesworth courtyard.

From there, Thrawl Street is accessible via an arched brick walkway—not unlike the one leading out of Miller's Court—and once she's back on familiar territory, Mary Jane takes a moment to steel herself for the punishment ahead. Given yesterday's unpleasantness, she's not prepared to offer anything more than her mouth, even though that means entertaining four men in the place of one. Luckily, she stumbles across those four men in the same group, and so saves herself some valuable time.

For some while now, it's been a lark for the well-to-do to dress in rags, rub dirt under their fingernails, and spend a night or two in the East End slums. This pastime, known as slumming, often brings in small gaggles of young men, easily identifiable by their good teeth and impeccably soft hands.

It's four of these such men that Mary Jane encounters in the Ten Bells—her arrival there prompting a small exodus of harlots—and she has no difficulty negotiating her one shilling fee for each of them, all of them being virgins in the delights of oral pleasure. In fact, when she first offered them minette, they guffawed, thinking it a joke. Only when she demonstrated the act upon a cold sausage did they come to realize she was serious, but appeared hesitant to conduct such an operation in the street.

In a patient and amiable mood, and not wanting to lose out on a few easy shillings, she didn't hesitate to dress up the proposition. "If you want somewhere private, I know a place." She placed a hand on the oldest one's thigh. "I'll do you all for four bob, plus the cost of the room." She ran her hand toward his crotch. "What say you to that?"

CHAPTER 32

EXPECTING TO COME BACK TO AN EMPTY ROOM, EVA returns to her eight-by-ten feet of space in the expansive Lolesworth tenement building, staggered to find that Mary Jane's been busy. Though it's still daylight, the curtains are drawn over the grimy window, as if barricading the tiny room off from the rest of the world, inspiring a more intimate atmosphere, and two farthing dips have been lit, bathing the room in a warm glow. The first candle is set on the cupboard by the fireplace, illuminating the bed and its crinkled sheets, one corner of the woolen blankets folded down invitingly, a sprig of lavender placed on the pillows. The other is set at the center of the table, upon which a steaming hot dinner is waiting to be devoured.

Eva can't help but wonder if one is meant to lead into the other, lavender being commonly symbolic of love and devotion. Stepping closer, she inspects the partially home-cooked meal, finding it to consist of fresh fish—filleted by Mary Jane's own hand and fried in a cheap pan on the grate above the fire—accompanied by two large baked potatoes, purchased from the tater man on the street, and a generous heaping of boiled peas.

"You cooked," she states blankly, giving up nothing encouraging.

"I ain't too good, but it's edible at least." Mary Jane stands by, waiting anxiously to see how her offering is to be appraised. "How was church?"

No answer.

Eva gazes at the spotless room, looking anywhere and everywhere but at Mary Jane, who she can see has scrubbed herself up as well as the room. "Why did you do all this?"

"I thought you might be hungry." Mary Jane sidles into her line of sight. "Darling, won't you look at me?"

"I can't." Eva flinches from her, knowing that if she casts so much as a glance at Mary Jane's smoky sapphire eyes with her long, soot-darkened lashes, she'll prematurely soften and forgiveness will follow. "Not yet."

"It's all right." Mary Jane nods, understanding. "You don't have to eat dinner with me. I'll go" She picks up her shawl and turns to leave, pausing at the door. "Thank you for all that you did." She hovers there. "Whatever coin you've spent, I'll see you right."

Hearing the door open, Eva panics. "Don't." She spins around and catches Mary Jane's arm, unable to let her walk out. "You went to all this trouble. You should eat."

Emboldened by the tactile advance, Mary Jane reaches for Eva's hand, but as their fingers brush together, Eva withdraws, afraid that she might be too easily melted by the possibility of physical intimacy. Indeed, she can already feel the thaw beginning.

At the table, Mary Jane sits in her usual manner, with her skirts flicked over her knees and her legs apart, one foot propped on the crossbar of her chair. It's quite a sight.

Sitting primly beside her, back straight and knees together, Eva giggles. "I ain't never met another woman what sits like you." She glances at Mary Jane's upper thighs.

"I'm obscene."

"You're liberated." Eva picks at her fish. "I thought that when we met, what with your dress, your red-painted lips, your rouge, your eyes, and your hair. You

were everything what a woman ain't s'posed to be, and I reckon I caught feelings for you right there and then."

Mary Jane remembers that evening in the Cooney's Lodging House kitchen vividly. There'd been not an ounce of judgment, only intrigue and sexual curiosity, both of which blossomed.

"I saw the way you looked at me. Ain't nobody ever looked at me the way you did when we first shared a bed, and I liked it. I *wanted* you to look."

"I was so happy there for that little while, despite what happened." Eva skirts past the issue of her mother's death, still refraining from eye contact. "I would've got a room there again, only I couldn't afford it. I nearly got one down the Peabody Buildings instead. Them's nicer than this, and you can rent three whole rooms for only six bob." She digs into her potato. "I thought we could live there together, 'cept I weren't sure how you were fixed, and they don't let in ... I mean, they don't allow ..."

"Whores, I know." Mary Jane spares her from having to say the word. "This place don't neither, but they ain't quite so strict on enforcing it."

They finish their meal in silence. Throughout, Mary Jane admires Eva's altered form. Her skin has a healthy glow, her hair looks vibrant, almost silken, and her figure ... oh, such a figure! She's stouter now than she was. Not plump by any means, but robust. How soft her thighs must feel. How padded her bum.

The attention starts to make Eva feel uncomfortable.

Sensing that, Mary Jane forces herself to look away. "I don't mean to stare, but the continent's agreed with you, darling."

Eva fidgets with her bust. "I've filled out."

"You most certainly have." Mary Jane gazes at her bodice, admiring the steep rise from ribcage to breast. "You're so beautiful."

"Does it please you?" Eva raises her eyes, meeting Mary Jane's for the first time since the street. "I had to get all new under-things."

"Seeing you again is a pleasure greater than any other on Earth." Mary Jane lays her hand over Eva's on the table. "How long have you been back?"

"I come to Whitechapel the day afore I went to you." Eva hesitates, letting Mary Jane entwine their fingers. "I wanted to surprise you."

On that note, "Darling, what you saw—"

"Don't," Eva cuts her off. "I can't bear to hear it."

"But it wasn't—"

"I don't want no lies." Eva whisks away her hand and retreats to the other side of the room. "You slept with Maria."

"Slept with her, yes." Mary Jane swivels to face her. "But that was all."

Eva plonks herself down on the bed, staring at the floor. "I think my heart is broken."

"Oh, Eva." Mary Jane dives off her chair and drops to her knees at Eva's feet. "I was true to you, I swear I was." She scoops up Eva's hands, clutching them in her own. "I didn't lay a finger on her, nor she me."

"I wouldn't blame you," Eva laments, having harbored a latent fear that Mary Jane would stray during the course of their separation. "It's been so long."

"But I didn't," Mary Jane insists, pressing her face into Eva's lap and kissing her fingers. "Maria was company, that's all. I was miserable and lonely and we slept together, but not a thing more." She looks up, pleading. "I'm so sorry. You're the only thing what matters to me—please believe that."

Eva's never seen Mary Jane look so vulnerable. The sight breaks her. "I've missed you so much." She sobs. "You was all I could think about. I ain't had no-one else."

"What happened to you?" Mary Jane dare not imagine what might've kept Eva from the pen. "Why'd you stop writing? I was so worried."

"Oh, I were in such a muddle." Eva bawls. "I didn't know the journey would take so long, and I was afeared to spend a penny more than I had to after I left my position."

"You left them in Italy? Why?" Mary Jane feels a pang of dread. "What happened? Did someone in that wretched house hurt you? Did they try to take—"

Eva puts two tear-dampened fingers to Mary Jane's lips, silencing her. "The missus extended her trip. When

she told me we'd be gone another season, I burst into a fit of tears. She asked what the matter was, and I tells her I couldn't stand to be away from home a minute longer. I says I had a love waiting for me." Eva's lip trembles, tears pooling in her eyes. "I says I only went away so as you could save enough for us to get our own place somewhere, and I s'pose she took pity on me 'cause she give me a tenner, put me on boat, and told me to get my arse back to you as soon as I could. I ain't never seen a bank note afore." She pulls a wrinkled five pound note out of her pocket. "I spent a few bob here and there, but I've still got this fiver. It don't look like much, though. Hard to see as it's worth more than gold."

Mary Jane covers the note with her hands. "Don't go flashing that about. Some folks round here could work for a month and not see five pounds." She stuffs the money back into Eva's pocket. "Does your aunt know you've returned?"

Eva shakes her head. "The missus wrote and told her I met a fella in Italy and run off. She won't be looking for me, and even if she does, she'll be poking around in the wrong place."

"So we're in the clear?" Mary Jane dares to sound hopeful.

"If you still want me." Eva sniffles, pulling a hanky from her sleeve.

"Of course I still want you." Mary Jane strokes her thighs. "Didn't I say so in all my letters?"

"I lived for your letters." Eva blows her nose. "The passion in your words left me in a fervor most nights." She tosses her saturated hanky in the direction of the washstand. "I had such fevered dreams of you."

"Spending dreams?" Mary Jane wonders, fishing for an erotic confession.

"Sometimes," Eva whispers, her already pinkened cheeks turning a darker shade at the thought of their lengthy correspondence, the content of which at once evolved from expressions of tenderness and affection to writings so bawdy and salacious that each letter may well be called a work of pornography, and would no doubt

make seasoned whores blush. "I needed only to see the word 'cunt' and mine pulsed with such a wicked lust."

"Mine, too." Mary Jane chances a peck on the lips.

"I've missed that." Eva remains poised for another. "And I've missed our other kisses, too." She pulls Mary Jane closer. "You know the ones I like so much? The wet ones."

Mary Jane knows very well. Initiating a kiss of that variety, she pushes Eva onto her back and leans over her, cradling the teen's neck in the crook of her arm, their lips locked together and not once breaking until Mary Jane runs her free hand up Eva's dress, coming to a halt at the pinched knee-band of a pair of lace-trimmed drawers.

"Bloody things," she grumbles playfully. "Bane of my existence."

"I didn't know we was gonna get reacquainted so quick, else I wouldn't have bothered with 'em." Eva wipes away the last of her tears, drying her cheeks on her sleeves. "I was gonna make you wait for it."

"Such cruelty," Mary Jane teases, untying the drawstring bow.

"Hold up, though." Eva stops her, denying her entry. "Afore I let you have me, I need you to know summink." She eases Mary Jane's hand away. "It hurt me to see you the way you was."

"I know." Mary Jane kisses her forehead. "But you needn't worry. I shan't see Maria again. Not if you don't want me to."

Eva shakes her head. "I ain't talking about Maria. That was bad enough, but I'm meaning when I seen you on the street." Her mood dulls. "That was so much worse."

She thinks back to the moment when she spotted Mary Jane coming up Commercial Street, hunched over, staggering left and right, plainly inebriated. She was utterly disheveled, her mane knotted and disarranged, her shawl hanging limply off one shoulder.

"When I got you home, I brushed your hair." She fingers Mary Jane's thick locks. "And when I was undressing you for bed, I saw you was in a vile, mucky

state down there"—she points to Mary Jane's private region—"so I cleaned you up."

"Oh, God." Mary Jane winces.

"I pulled out that dirty old snot rag you had stuffed up there, and all this white sticky stuff come trickling down." Eva wrinkles up her nose. "I knows that's what spits out of a fella's pipe when he spends, and I seen you swill it out that one time, using vinegar and such, so I went to the druggist and got the stuff for it. I hopes I done it right."

"I was such a mess." Mary Jane rolls onto her back, the mood lost, her heat subdued. "My head was all wrong." She closes her eyes, pinching the bridge of her nose between her thumb and forefinger, wishing she could erase the past week. "I drank so much I forgot myself."

"Why?" Eva asks, reckoning she already knows the answer.

"Because I thought you'd left me," Mary Jane replies bluntly. "Eva, without you in my life, there ain't no point to anything. And I know it ain't fair of me to tell you that," she goes on. "My intemperance is not of your doing. Indeed, I fear it's rooted in a far deeper misery."

Even so, Eva feels guilty. "I wanted to see you." She looks apologetic. "I hated not being near you them few days, but I needed time to settle things in my mind."

"I understand, love. I truly do." Mary Jane turns on her side, facing Eva. "Believe me, you ain't the one at fault." She drops a kiss on Eva's peachy cheeks. "I'm the one who's let you down. I'm the one who's disappointed you." She nuzzles the teen's dainty nose. "You could do so much better than me, and I well know it."

Eva shakes her head, toying with the bust of Mary Jane's bodice. "I don't want no-one else." She tiptoes her fingers up to the high lace collar and eases the buttons undone. "I want to do all that we promised each other in our letters."

"Darling, are you sure?" Touched by Eva's capacity for forgiveness, Mary Jane's heart swells to bursting.

"More than." Eva unfastens the bodice and under-bodice all the way and peels them back, exposing corset

and chemise. "Oh, heaven help me." She gawps at Mary Jane's chest.

The old lilac-colored corset, heavily worn, darned, and patched, is now losing its battle to confine her. The stitching, already twice reinforced at the bust where the tension in the fabric caused the seams to split at the busk, is fraying again. It looks ready to burst, as if, with one deep breath, the fastenings would wrench from the stitching, her painfully constricted breasts bulging forward, breaking free of their restraints.

"You're too much for it." She fingers Mary Jane's expert repair work. "Take it off."

"As you wish." Mary Jane sits up, running her hands over her bosom to emphasize the large swell of her bust before releasing herself from the corset and stripping to her chemise.

She can't help but make a show of it. Trained in the art of seduction, she moves with ease and fluidity, holding her audience in thrall from beginning to end. When all she has left is her chemise, she kneels before Eva, grips the hem, and inches it up.

At every increment, Eva's interest intensifies, a short, delighted gasp escaping her lips at the sight of Mary Jane's pubic mound, as though seeing it for the first time. No longer shaved completely bare, it's adorned with a small blanket of dark blonde curls that she hadn't previously been in the right frame of mind to appreciate.

"You have moss now."

"A little." Mary Jane drags her fingers through it. "You like it?"

Eva nods, leaning closer. "But it's different." She compares it to the richer auburn hair on Mary Jane's head. "It don't match."

Seeing her confusion, Mary Jane giggles. "I color this with henna." She buries her fingers in her lush, thick tresses. "Just like Madame Patti."

Eva's never been to the opera, but she's heard of Madame Adelina Patti, the famous opera singer who was born poor and rose into high society. By eight years old, she was singing in New York's music halls. By twenty-five, she was married to a marquis.

"You're far prettier than Madame Patti," Eva declares dismissively, delivering her proclamation with a kiss. "Lovelier in every regard." She messes with the lace trim on Mary Jane's chemise. "Will you pose for me? Like you did when you was a posture girl."

Whisking her chemise off over her head, Mary Jane frees her unfettered breasts, full and firm, her small pink nipples stiff, the areolae puffy and swollen. Now divested of every strip of clothing, she reclines on the bed. Ornamented with nothing but her silver earrings, she arches her back so as to make her breasts jut out, tendrils of reddish-brown hair cascading over her chest.

Propped on one arm, she then crooks her knees, drawing her thighs up perpendicular to her torso, the heels of her feet tucked to her bum. In this position, she clamps a hand over her sex, concealing it from view, then parts her fingers and spreads her folds, flashing Eva a mere glimpse of her pink slit before closing her fingers and withdrawing the delight.

"You tease." Eva slumps into a theatrical sulk.

"That's the point, silly." Mary Jane gives her another peep. "The sweet agony is that you may look, but not touch, and are always left wanting more." She sits up, hoping for a reciprocal display. "May I look at you now? I'm dying to see."

Attempting to unveil herself with the same grace and finesse that Mary Jane employed with such apparent ease, Eva begins removing layers. First, she gets the buttons of her bodice caught up in her hair. Then, she gets her arm stuck in her camisole. The laces of her boots get in a knot, one hook on her corset refuses to budge, and her skirts get twisted around her ankles. When it comes to her white patterned woolen stockings, Mary Jane stops her.

"Leave those." She lays a hand on Eva's thigh. "They look good on you."

The drawers come off next. Mary Jane helps tear them down Eva's legs, then hurls them across the room, her distaste for them making Eva laugh.

That leaves only her chemise, which she manages to get off without too much of a hitch, revealing her new form in its full glory.

"Oh, Eva ... you've become such a woman." Mary Jane scans her nude body, from her shapely thighs and padded hips to the small swell of her soft belly, then upwards to the two nicely rounded hillocks ornamenting her chest.

Gone are the spindly legs, bony hips, and prominent ribcage of an under-fed girl living below the poverty line, and gone are the small, firm breast buds that held high without the aid of a corset, unaffected by gravity. Now, she has the body of a true woman. A pair of well-formed thighs meet around the pouty flesh of her secret parts, the hidden treasure topped by her dark thicket of unkempt curls. A few inches have been added to her hips and waist, and her bosom ...

Eva follows the direction of Mary Jane's gaze. "They growed big. Not as big as yours, mind, but they jiggles now." She shakes her upper body, making her breasts sway and bounce. "See? They never did that afore." She cups one in her palm, squeezing it and lifting it. "And them's heavy n'all. Do you want a feel?"

Words escaping her, Mary Jane takes Eva's breast in her hand, fondling it, caressing the warm, soft flesh, feeling the nipple stiffen at her touch. It's a perfect handful.

Peering down, watching Mary Jane encase it in her palm, Eva grins. "Look how it fits!" She thrusts her chest outward. "Don't you like 'em better this way?"

With a growl, Mary Jane shoves Eva onto her back, sucking on one nipple as she massages the other, moaning into Eva's alabaster flesh. "I need you." She fumbles her free hand between their naked bodies, seeking Eva's core. "Oh, how I need you, love."

"Take me." Eva draws her knees up and wraps her legs around Mary Jane's back, writhing impatiently. "Give me a rub."

Before complying with that request, Mary Jane roves her hand over Eva's lust-saturated sex and slips two fingers inside her, relearning every inch of her. By the

time she lowers herself into position, their impassioned articles slipping and sliding together, both are already on the verge of a spend. In under a minute, their bums jerking and wiggling amidst a harmony of voluptuous sighs, they find pleasure together.

"I love you, Eva." Mary Jane lays a kiss on her. "More than you can imagine." She slithers her tongue down Eva's body, kissing her way through Eva's dense bush of pubic hair. "Oh, I've missed this." She buries her face in Eva's hot, wet flesh.

CHAPTER 33

TWO HOURS LATER, AS EVA RELISHES HER FOURTH ORGASM brought on by the combined titillation of Mary Jane's tongue and fingers, Mary Jane surfaces from beneath the bed covers, stretching her jaw and wiping her sex-slathered lips.

"I think I need a break, darling." She flops down beside her lover. "I'm only human."

"Wherever did you learn such delicious tricks?" Eva rolls onto Mary Jane's chest. "I ain't never felt a pleasure like it." She reaches between her legs, twirling her fingers through the matted curls on her motte, finding her inner treasure sopping with her spend and Mary Jane's saliva. "You've wetted it so. Ought I trim my moss down like yours?"

"Don't you dare." Mary Jane smirks, enjoying Eva's pet names for her various anatomical landmarks. "I love your moss just the way it is."

"But don't it tickle your nose?"

If anything, Mary Jane would argue that getting the odd hair caught in the back of her throat is the worst hazard of the work, but she laughs off the notion that there's anything objectionable in it. "Femininity, in all its forms, is divine," she insists. "You're a woman, and I love the feel of a woman in full bloom."

"I *am* a full woman now, you know." Eva beams, immeasurably pleased with herself. "My courses came on

last winter." She clasps both hands over her abdomen. "Someone should've warned me it was so awful, though. Feels like someone's stabbing my belly, pulling all my gubbins out."

Mary Jane grimaces. "What a frightfully unpleasant comparison."

"Ain't it like that for you?"

"Aye, but a drop of laudanum does wonders for it."

She speaks without thinking, Eva's mood sinking at the mention of the drug that brought about her mother's end. Realizing her mistake, she wraps Eva up in a hug.

"Do you miss your mam?"

Eva nods "I thinks of her every day." She tucks herself tight to Mary Jane's body. "Do you reckon she'd be proud? She'd never believe I spent a whole year on the continent."

"She'd be *so* proud, darling." Mary Jane kisses her forehead. "You know she'd want to hear all about it."

"Not all." Eva giggles. "Some stuff I only tells you, like how the cook broke her bed. She got too vigorous with her dilly one night and the whole thing collapsed. Caused a mighty bang."

"Her dilly?"

"That's what I calls the thingamabob she gives herself a poke with. It's like your doodle, but wooden, and it don't fix on." Eva rakes her fingers over Mary Jane's motte, trying to picture how the glass phallus looked protruding from her mound. "She tried rigging it up to the bedpost when we was in Paris, and that's what caused the trouble. The bed just weren't built for it."

"The bedpost?" Mary Jane frowns, having some difficulty conjuring the mental imagery. "How was that to work?"

"She tied it on with some ribbon, so that it stuck straight out, then she got down on her hands and knees, backed her grummit onto it, and started thrashing about like a wild beast." Eva gets on all fours and performs an exaggerated reenactment, jerking her bum on the imaginary shaft while tossing her head this way and that. "It was the queerest thing I've ever seen a woman do, and that's a fact." She collapses into Mary Jane's arms.

396

"I wholeheartedly concur." Mary Jane applauds her performance. "Anyway, apart from that, did you enjoy your time in Paris?" She leaves off the 's', pronouncing it as the French would. "It's been so long since I was there."

"That's where your French toff took you?" Eva infers. "Why'd you ever leave? I liked Paris the best of it all." She palms one of her breasts. "I think it's where I got these, on account of all them pastries I wrote you about."

"Then I shall have to keep you in a constant supply." Mary Jane pecks her nose. "It's a good job the baker's son thinks I'm sweet on him. He gives me all sorts without charging me a farthing."

"Why's he think that?"

Mary Jane opens her mouth to answer, but thinks better of it. Eva doesn't need to know about his mammoth-sized cock, or what she uses it for. Instead, she simply says, "Long story."

"And France?" Eva won't let her dodge the original question.

"It didn't suit." Mary Jane glosses over the facts. "I s'pose you can take the tart off the street, but you can't make her a lady." She shrugs. "The life just didn't stick."

"How long was you there?"

"A fortnight."

Eva snorts. "You gave it a good go, then."

"It was much too hoity for me. All airs and graces, and I ain't got neither of them." Mary Jane spouts the oft told lie, but puts no effort into it. She can't even keep on a smile, and without furnishing the tale with all the usual embellishments, it comes off hollow.

"What really happened to you, Em?" Eva suspects a sad truth lurking beneath the surface. "Will you tell me?"

After a brief hesitation, Mary Jane starts to talk. "I was working at a gay house in Knightsbridge—that part's true. A French procuress took me in, bought me all new dresses and the like, and put me straight to work. The enterprising old hag sold my innocence three times over, and I didn't even have it to give once. Anyhow, I told you I used to have this regular gent, a Frenchman, who'd pay me nice visits. He was generous with his coin and his compliments, and he took me to Paris under the promise

that I'd be a kept lady—a *demimondaine,* if you will. Which is to say that I expected to be a courtesan, treated to all the fineries of a lady's life." She shakes her head. "But that was all a load of rubbish."

"He lied?"

"He bought me from the procuress, as he and others like him bought many girls before me and since. I was shipped off to the French capital believing I was to be put to work in *Le Chabanais,* which is the most luxurious *maison de tolérance* in Paris, run by the Irishwoman Madame Kelly."

"I know of it." Eva hangs her head. "The missus flew into a rage one night on account of her bloke paying a visit to the place."

"I spent a night there." Mary Jane's gaze is vacant, numb to the pain. "The chap I was with wanted to lure me into a security, I s'pose. Then I was taken to an unlicensed *lupanar* in which I was confined as an inmate, obliged to accept any man who came to my room, no matter if they were vile or diseased. I was nothing more than a common *fille soumise*: a cheap whore."

"Oh, Em." Eva's stomach turns. "Did you ... ?"

Mary Jane shakes her head. "I was lucky. I never got clapped, or worse—I've always been clean, I swear to you—but if I'd been there longer ..."

"How'd you get out?"

"On the kindness of a British gent who frequented my room. He took pity on my circumstance and secured me passage home, but I could never go back to the West End. If any of those people should find me ..." She shakes the thought away. "Well, it don't bear thinking of. I was a bought and paid for commodity, and I absconded."

"How old was you?"

"Four and twenty, which is plenty old enough to know better."

Despite being thoroughly lousy with numbers, Eva locks onto a glaring discrepancy in the facts: Mary Jane declared herself to be only twenty-two when they met a year ago.

"Wait." She screws her face into a thoughtful frown. "How old is you now?"

"There's eleven years between us," Mary Jane confesses with an apologetic smile and a sigh. "I'm almost thirty now." She plods on with the truth. "I started knocking years off directly I came to London. I was already three and twenty by then, but paraded myself as nineteen."

"Why'd you lie?"

"Because I'm past my prime for the work and I know it." Mary Jane gives one of her breasts a squeeze, testing its firmness. "As I've always said: it's all downhill after a woman's twenty-fifth year, and I can ill afford to take any less compensation for my time."

"That's all very well, but why'd you fib to me?" Eva props herself up, looking down on her mate. "You can't think I gives two figs how old you are?"

Mary Jane shrugs. "Habit." She caresses Eva's face, admiring her youth. "Though if I'm being frank, I do reckon I'm a shade too old for you. I'll be a wrinkly old maid in next to no time, but you'll still be young and beautiful."

Eva sees it now, though she never saw it before: the first cracks of age threatening to tarnish Mary Jane's youthful complexion. From the faint lines appearing at the corners of her mouth when she smiles, to the permanent shallow furrows on her brow, visible even when she's not frowning, and the creases that form beside her eyes when she laughs. Eva sees it all, but none of it matters. They don't diminish her beauty, but enhance it. They're the marks of experience, symbolic of her fortitude, and an ever-present reminder that she's no unripe chit of a girl, but a full-fledged woman who knows herself, mind and heart. Her age is no obstacle to Eva's attraction, but a catalyst for its amplification.

Acting on that sudden realization, Eva dives on her, kissing and squeezing her. "Oh, I do love you so much." She wraps her arms around Mary Jane's body. "You're every bit a woman!"

"So far as I know." Mary Jane giggles, her girlish amusement soon cut short with a kiss, her lips engulfed by Eva's hungry mouth.

"You'll never be anything but beautiful to me," Eva assures her. "And if you'd been my own age, I daresay I'd not have been so seduced by you."

"Is that so?" Mary Jane arches an eyebrow, curious to hear more.

"I wanted to learn the ways of love from someone with an experienced hand." Eva lays her head on Mary Jane's breast, listening to the rhythm of her heart. "And after seeing you with Maria, I knew how lucky I would be to find my place in your arms."

"What opposites we are." Mary Jane scoops her into an embrace. "Before we met, I dreamt of finding a beautiful, innocent young girl who had all her charms to give. I swore if I was ever lucky enough to win the heart of such a creature, I'd treasure her till my dying day, honoring the sanctity of her love, making certain that it should never be sullied."

"Sullied?"

"I believe in the purity of love, Eva. Don't you? To my thinking, giving everything of yourself to the one person you want to spend the rest of your life with is exactly as it should be." Mary Jane picks Eva's head up. "Darling, p'raps it's selfish, but I love that you've had no-one else. I wish I could give the same to you in return, but I'm tainted by the affections and meddlings of others."

"You ain't tainted." Eva rejects her self-deprecation. "I reckon it's a testament to your good character that you've come through all what you have and remained such a decent woman, and you deserve so much better than what this rotten life's dealt to you." She tightens her grip, raising Mary Jane's chest to meet her lips, sucking on one nipple, then the other.

"Do I?" Mary Jane groans, feeling Eva's teeth scrape the delicate pink skin of her areola.

"You're the most kindhearted person I ever met." Eva kisses her way north and bites down on Mary Jane's neck, leaving a mark of love behind on her skin. "I wish you didn't have to ... do what you do."

"I ain't doing that no more," Mary Jane corrects her. "Not like I was."

"No?" Eva halts her ministrations. "Then how'd you pay for dinner? You hadn't a farthing on your person, and I knows that for a fact."

Mary Jane doesn't answer. Lying in Eva's arms, caught in her embrace, she feels a shift. She, now vulnerable and weak. Eva, confident and in control.

"Will you spend the night with me?" Eva moves the conversation on before it has a chance to fester, twirling her fingers in the triangle of trimmed curls on Mary Jane's motte. "Unless your fella's expecting you back, of course. I weren't even sure if I ought to show up the way I did in case he were there. I didn't know if that'd be right for me to do, but—"

Mary Jane puts a finger to her lips. "Joe knows about me. That is, he understands I have a certain partiality for the company of a woman, though he ain't yet caught on to the degree of my fondness."

"So will you stay?"

"He's with his other skirt tonight." Mary Jane pulls Eva to her breast. "But even if he weren't, I'd still sleep with you if you desired to have me. There ain't no-one else I'd rather be with."

CHAPTER 34

Monday, August 6, 1888

EVA'S VOLUPTUOUS WAILS RING OUT THROUGH HER SMALL section of the Lolesworth Buildings, her thighs shivering around Mary Jane's bobbing head. Fifteen minutes earlier, she was lying on her back, sound asleep, when she felt her legs being maneuvered this way and that, and Mary Jane's hot breath tickled her quim. In no time, her sex was pulsing and aching, yearning for another spend, and she had her fingers twisted through Mary Jane's hair, encouraging her in the oral operation.

When her cries subside, Mary Jane emerges, trailing kisses up her body. "Was that a nice way to wake up?"

"It's surely the best," Eva mewls. "But I can't take no more, Em. You'll do me in with pleasure if you keep at me this way."

Throughout the night, Mary Jane was overly attentive. Determined to make up for her transgression with Maria—innocent though it was—and her later ill behavior, she availed herself to Eva whenever the opportunity for intimacy presented itself. Every time Eva stirred, even if it was only to roll over, Mary Jane was ready with fingers or tongue, tickling or licking her to one pleasure after another until at last, exhausted and groggy, the teen begged mercy.

"Just a quick rub." Mary Jane assumes the position above her. "Then I'll leave off."

"You're voracious." Eva accepts her kisses. "But we haven't the time for more."

"Why not?" Mary Jane grinds against her.

"I needs to get to work." Eva grips her bum, moving with her. "You're gonna make me frightful late, and if I ain't there on time—that's eight-fifteen on the dot—they fines me sevenpence."

"Work?" Mary Jane halts.

"Aye." Eva smiles triumphantly, feeling smug about her self-sufficiency. "I've got me-self a job."

"Where?"

Some of Eva's pride dissolves. "Well, I tried getting a situation in a little shop, but my numbers ain't so good and they wouldn't look twice at me. I spent one day sorting rags in the rag factory, but I got bit by a horde of fleas and was soon put off it." She scratches at an itchy red bump on her wrist. "I nearly tried my luck at the match factory after that, but I've heard some terrible stories about what them places does to a woman's physical condition, so now I works at the cocoa factory on Brick Lane."

Mary Jane's glad of that, for there's not much in the world more injurious to a woman's health than the match factories. The white phosphorous used in the making of the matches has been the painful and miserable end of many a decent young girl, the progression of its effects causing intense pain and gross disfigurement.

What starts as toothache and swollen gums develops into abscesses as the phosphorous eats away at the jawbone, causing a foul-smelling discharge. Without medical help, one can look forward to brain damage and organ failure, then death, but the only treatment for so-called phossy jaw is the surgical removal of the affected jawbone, which in itself can be fatal. Mary Jane shudders to think of it.

"The cocoa factory is good, honest work." She approves of Eva's much safer choice. "How does it pay?"

Eva shrugs. "Same as anything. Shite."

"But you can afford this room by yourself?"

The fretful look on Eva's face says it all: she hasn't thought this through.

"I was so keen to get back in with you, I didn't really give it enough of a think," she confesses. "And as I said afore, I ain't never been that good with my numbers."

"But you're managing it?"

"I paid this week's rent with the money gived me by my old missus, and I reckon I can keep going on with that a short while, though I wants some for saving." She bites on her lower lip, not knowing how realistic that hope is. "I gets seven shillings a week at the factory, plus sixpence for good conduct."

"Your rent?"

"That's three bob, which don't leave much for food and incidentals, I know." Eva looks forlorn. "I don't want you to worry on it, though," she's quick to add. "I'll sort it somehow or another. Don't go taking no extra work just 'cause I'm lousy at my sums and got me-self in a muddle with my lodgings. I can always move someplace cheaper if I so needs, I just really wanted to be in a private room. Is that daft? I wanted somewhere we could sleep together."

"No, it ain't at all daft." Mary Jane appreciates the sentiment. "I don't always have my place to myself, so we need this. And I *will* see that you're all right, whatever it takes." She runs her hand over Eva's rump and hip, gripping her soft flesh. "After all, we've got to keep this delicious new figure on you, ain't we? I can't have you wasting away."

Eva manages a smile. She doesn't want Mary Jane to feel obliged to care for her, but loves the proclamations of protection and security nonetheless. "I'm glad you likes me this way. I feels more like a proper woman now."

"God bless them pastries." Mary Jane grins, dipping down to lavish kisses on Eva's breasts. "I think a small celebration is in order, don't you? We didn't do anything to commemorate your return, and I'd like to. What time are you let out of work?"

Excited by the prospect of being taken out and treated to something, Eva relates her entire work schedule, giving Mary Jane plenty of options. "I gets off at six all days 'cept Saturdays. Them's half days, and I gets off at half-one, or maybe two. That's how come I was

on Commercial Street when ... well, when I seen you there. I'm off altogether on Sundays."

"I can't wait that long. I'm too impatient." Mary Jane nibbles on the tip of her nose. "One of my friends is taking me to the theater tonight. Not some mucky old music hall, but a proper theater: the Lyceum. Would you like to come? I'll pay, so it won't cost you aught. It'll just be the cheap seats, mind. Nothing too fancy. I wish I could afford more, but—"

"I'd love it," Eva declares emphatically. "I truly would. I'd sit in the dirt and it wouldn't matter so long as I was there with you. You're sure I won't be a bother?"

Mary Jane's heart is warmed to see her so jubilant. As a girl who has nothing, is used to nothing, and expects even less from the world, she's delighted to get *something*, no matter how trivial it might be. Her only care is that it's given with love.

"It's *The Strange Case of Dr. Jekyll and Mr. Hyde.* I've read the book, I wanna go, and I'd much rather have you with me for it." Mary Jane brushes aside her concern. "We don't even have to pay for the hansom there and back. My friend will be taking care of that."

Assuming this friend is male, and fearing this night out might be a gift in contemplation of something immoral, Eva's excitement wavers. "What do you have to give him for it?"

"Nothing," Mary Jane assures her. "It ain't like that. Not anymore. He's just a friend."

The sparkle returns to Eva's eyes. "I ain't never been to the theater afore."

"Then this is long overdue." Mary Jane rolls off her. "Now you go on and get yourself ready for work. Don't be late on my account. May I remain here awhile?"

"Course you may." Eva wriggles out of bed, pausing to kiss her. "It ain't easy to leave this bed whilst you're still in it, though."

"It ain't easy to let you." Mary Jane savors the last few moments of contact. "Last night was so wonderful, Eva. Every minute with you makes me feel lucky to be alive, and even luckier that you found it in your heart to forgive me for my atrocious behavior. I know you wanted

to punish me, and that's no less than what I deserve for any hurt I've caused you."

"Why do you always say such things?" Eva lingers in the bed a moment longer, fingering the tousled locks of auburn hair framing Mary Jane's face. "I don't like what this place is doing to you. Nuthin' good stays here. It's like a poison."

She frees herself from the sheets, slipping into her chemise and drawers on her way to the mantel above the fireplace. There, she flips over a cheap ceramic figurine and pulls her crumpled five pound note from a hole in the base.

"You take this." She hands the money to Mary Jane. "Add it to your savings."

"No, Eva." Mary Jane pushes it back to her. "It's yours. Buy yourself something nice with it, or keep it for a rainy day."

"I have all that I want." Eva picks Mary Jane's skirt off the floor and stuffs the note inside the pocket. "When we're set up away together, if there's any to spare, then I might let you buy me a new shemmy, or a pair of boots. Until then, I'll wear a sack and eat nuthin' but bread as long as it means I get to be with you in the end. You do still want that?"

"Course I bloody well do, you daft little thing."

"No argument, then." Eva plumps herself on the edge of the bed and rolls on her stockings.

"I love you, Eva." Mary Jane stops her, securing her full attention. "With all my heart."

"I love you n'all." Eva smiles. "I don't never want no-one else."

Following the exchange of one more sweet kiss, Eva tears herself away. In a rush to keep on time, she's out of the room in under ten minutes, promising Mary Jane that she'll pick up something to eat on her way to the factory. Meanwhile, Mary Jane plans her day.

Dutifully, the first thing she takes care of when she rises from Eva's bed is to secure the five pounds, putting it out of sight and out of mind. In need of some money of her own ahead of tonight's outing, she then seeks out one

of her specials, enticing him to engage her well in advance of their next scheduled appointment.

Her spending money is something that would normally be taken care of by Joe, but his visits have been irregular of late. He's been taking care of his most basic obligations to her—that of food and rent—but leaving her with very little else besides, and she wonders if he's tiring of her. At the commencement of their acquaintance, he was generous with his compliments. Quite often, he'd see to it that she had a few spare shillings above and beyond what she needed for the necessities of living, but such bonuses have been steadily dwindling.

Not relying on him to put in an appearance before she's due to meet Eva, she only stops off at Miller's Court for a few minutes to wash up before dragging her steamer trunk out from under the bed and lugging the whole thing over to the Lolesworth Buildings. There, she plants herself on the narrow walkway outside the door to Eva's room and waits for her to return, the role reversal striking her when Eva comes home bearing two large portions of fish and chips.

"This is backwards," Eva muses, the turnabout not lost on her, either. "Me coming home with supper and you sitting outside my door."

"I've brought over some of my things." Mary Jane gets up and dusts herself off, revealing that she was sitting on her steamer trunk. "I hope that's all right. I thought we could change into our good clothes together."

"Course it's all right." Eva ushers her into the hall. "I wanna live with you, don't I?" She unlocks the door to her room, plopping dinner on the table. "I was hoping you'd be here anyway. I bought two penn'orth of fish, and I can't eat it all." Her belly rumbles in anticipation. "Well, I prob'ly could, to tell you the truth. I'm bloody hungry."

"I've no doubt of it." Mary Jane sets her trunk on the bed and wraps her arms around Eva's waist. "You've a hearty appetite."

"I'm gonna get so flabby one day." Eva unwraps the fish and chips, licking grease off her fingers. "I hopes you realize that."

"S'all right." Mary Jane kisses her neck. "If you can put up with me getting older, I can put up with you getting wider." She pats Eva's bum. "Let's eat. We ain't got much time."

Supper being an unceremonious and informal affair, the fish and chips is consumed in a matter of minutes, leaving them just enough time to dress for the theater. To that end, Mary Jane opens her trunk and fishes out her silk.

"What else you got in there?" Eva peeks inside.

"Nearly all my worldly goods." Mary Jane lays out the dress. "I don't mind you looking. You might even find something in there what's yours."

Eva has a quick rummage, discovering her virtually hairless doll tucked inside a roll of blue and white fabric. "Oh, it's my Mollie!" She pulls the doll free. "I'd almost forgot her!"

"She used to smell like you." Mary Jane tickles Mollie's repaired ear. "I slept with her so many nights, I'm afraid she smells rather like me now."

Eva gives her a sniff, smiling. "Your perfume."

Returning her attention to the trunk, she inspects the blue and white material, finding it to be a high-collared blue dress with a starched white apron and a frilly white cap.

"A nurse's uniform?" She picks it up, unraveling it. "Why ever do you have such a thing? Are you Florence bloody Nightingale?"

"Only upon request." Mary Jane winks.

Eva starts to laugh, but stifles herself at the sight of Mary Jane's perfectly serious expression. "You ain't joking?" She folds the uniform away, baffled by the many letches of men. "What other dirty secrets is in here?"

She has another delve through Mary Jane's trunk, digging up a small ribbon-bound bundle of books tucked in with a few items of decent clothing and a plain but practical linsey-woolsey winter dress. The bundle is topped with a copy of an informative book written specifically for women. It's entitled: *Guide to the Unprotected in Every-day Matters relating to Property and Income.*

Flicking through it, she finds it to cover such topics as shares, loans, mortgages, marriage settlements, keeping accounts, taxes and deeds, and a glossary of technical terms often used in business.

"I believe a woman ought to be independent of a man in such matters," Mary Jane answers Eva's puzzled look. "I ain't no expert, but I reckon I know enough to manage my way in the world."

The rest of the bundle, Eva then discovers, includes *Memoirs of a Woman of Pleasure* by John Cleland, all four volumes of *The Romance of Lust*, and a few tatty old copies of the long-defunct erotic magazine *The Pearl*, printed for the Society of Vice in 1880. Before she can be warned, she opens up to a random page in the first volume of *The Romance of Lust*.

"I could see his shirt bulging out. He leant forward, and with his arms under my legs, lifted them well up, and I felt a stiff, thick thing pressing against my cunt. His left hand opened the lips, his right hand guided it between them, and a cruel push lodged its great head completely within."

Getting no further than that, Eva snaps the book closed. "What devilish things *are* these?!"

"My small collection of bawdy literature." Mary Jane plucks *Memoirs of a Woman of Pleasure* out of the trunk, opening it to one of several dog-eared pages marked by the folding down of corners. "You might prefer this." She hands it to Eva, then retreats to the washstand to pin up her mane. "There are a few passages in this one more suited to our particular taste, if you understand me."

Eva dares a paragraph.

"Here was no room either to sit or lie, but making me stand with my back towards the door, she lifted up my petticoats, and with her busy fingers fell to visit and explore that part of me where now the heat and irritations were so violent that I was perfectly sick and ready to die with desire; that the bare touch of her

finger, in that critical place, had the effect of a fire to a train, and her hand instantly made her sensible to what a pitch I was wound up ..."

"Oh!" Eva's jaw drops. "How's a woman to read such things without losing her rational mind?" She tosses the book back in the trunk. "I dare not cast my eyes over a single word more, else I fear we might not make it to the theater."

"I have others of a more humorous nature." Mary Jane strips to her chemise, re-dressing in the purple silk she always wears to the West End. "P'raps *The Pearl* will entertain you." She flips to a page in volume three and recites a short rhyme. "There was a young lady of Harrow, who complained that her cunt was too narrow. For times without number she would use a cucumber, but could not accomplish a marrow."

Giggling, Eva undresses to her underclothes, her progress then impeded by Mary Jane, who thrusts both hands up her petticoats, targeting her drawers.

"You don't need these."

"Oi!" Eva tries to evade her, but the tiny room doesn't provide enough room for escape. "I can't go out in the company of a fella and not be wearing my drawers!"

"But they get in my way." Mary Jane pouts. "'Sides, who's gonna know? Only us two, and it'll stir my passions all night to know you're bare beneath your skirts."

Rather liking the sound of that, Eva caves. "Unrig me as you will, but if there happens to be a mighty gust of wind and I ends up showing my grummit to half of London, you'll be to blame." She lets Mary Jane divest her of the cotton barrier, then slips on her best petticoats and skirts. "What's this show about anyway?"

"The duality of man." Mary Jane flings Eva's drawers onto the bed, victorious. "The beast in all of us. Good and evil. Murder."

"Sounds perfectly gruesome." Eva buttons up the blue satin bodice she usually reserves for church, then stops to inspect herself, smoothing out invisible creases in her dress. "Do I look all right? I always feels like such a ragamuffin compared to you."

411

"You look divine, love. As ever." Mary Jane checks her appearance in the mirror, dabbing a little tinted beeswax on her lips and freshening the faint rouge on her cheeks. "I'll be delighted to have such a beautiful young woman on my arm tonight."

Watching her apply the rouge, an idea sparks in Eva's mind, excitement budding in its wake. "Will you paint me up? It makes you such a woman."

Mary Jane hesitates, the tin of rouge still open in her hands. "You must be careful. It's not considered proper for a woman to paint her face." She dips the tip of the ostrich feather brush into the powder. "Any application must be so subtle that you're able to flatly deny the color on your face is anything more than your own natural blush." She flutters the feather over one of Eva's cheekbones. "You merely kiss the cheeks with the plume, like so." She does the other cheek, then stands Eva in front of the mirror. "See?"

Eva beams at her reflection. "What about my eyes?"

"We could darken your lashes a little." Mary Jane sets the rouge aside and plucks a jar of uncolored beeswax from a pouch in her trunk, rubbing a pinch onto the tips of her forefinger and thumb. "First, we prepare them for the color." She smoothes the beeswax onto Eva's eyelashes. "Then, we apply the black powder." She cleans her fingers of the wax and fetches a lump of coal from the fireplace, smearing its soot onto her fingertips before applying it to Eva's lashes in the same manner as the wax. "See how it makes your eyes stand out?"

Eva nods. "And the lips?"

"Now here you really must be cautious," Mary Jane warns. "I don't want you touching my red lip paste. Not ever. You understand? That draws the wrong attention." She fetches the jar of beeswax used moments ago on her own lips. "This is tinted with carmine. It's a pale pink, meant to enhance the color of a woman's lips without appearing garish. All the finest women use it, though they may well pretend otherwise." She dabs it onto Eva's lips with her finger, then steps back to admire her handiwork. "There. *Tu es très belle, Mademoiselle Sullivan*."

Hearing those foreign words spill off her tongue as if it were her native language, Eva squeals delightedly. "Is you speaking French to me? What's it mean? Will you teach it me?"

"I only know a few words." Mary Jane suitably lowers the teen's expectations, her entire experience of the language stemming from her work. "I weren't in France long, and I seldom heard anything polite."

"I'm sure you knows more than me." Eva plucks her outing hat from the coat rack. "I have trouble with the 'nunciation."

"Well, maybe later." Mary Jane takes her by the hand, leading her to the door.

"Wait." Eva keeps her back. "You wear this tonight." She passes Mary Jane the hat—a simple black straw affair, adorned with plum-colored feathers, artificial flowers, and tulle netting—and sets her in front of a crooked mirror. "It goes with your pretty dress."

True enough, the plum-coloring is a nice compliment to her gown, though she would never usually give it much thought. She hasn't possessed a hat in years.

"What will you wear?"

"My usual one." Eva retrieves her everyday blue hat. "It's no matter."

Entirely to please her, Mary Jane dons the decorative hat, wearing it slightly off to the side, as is fashionable to do in France.

From the Lolesworth Buildings, it's just a short walk to the pre-arranged meeting spot on Commercial Street, where Fleming is waiting next to a two-person hansom carriage. Expecting only Mary Jane, an obvious streak of annoyance flickers across his brow to see her approaching arm in arm with another female.

Though a hansom will—and frequently does—accommodate three at a squash, it's a tight and less than comfortable fit. Not that a hansom is particularly cozy at the best of times. The leather seats are hard and lumpy, often covered with crumbs and other debris, and the floor is usually splattered with horse muck and dirt. You might even pick up a flea.

"You don't mind if my friend Eva joins us this evening, do you, Joe?" Mary Jane preempts any objection that might be forthcoming. "Only she's just come back from the continent and I've missed her dreadfully."

Given that Eva's standing right in front of him, and any protestation made in her presence would be unconscionably impolite, Fleming has no choice but to grudgingly comply. Mumbling some greeting to her, he whisks off his hat—lest the rear-seated driver's overhanging reins should knock it off—and gets into the hansom, convention dictating that the gentleman always enters the carriage first so that he might help the lady up.

Mary Jane gets in next, and as she turns to aid Eva, Fleming issues her a private warning, snarled in her ear like a curmudgeonly dog.

"I ain't paying for her."

"No, you ain't," she hisses back. "I shall take care of my woman."

Leaving the exchange at that, Mary Jane helps Eva inside the cab, then slides over on the padded leather seat, squishing in next to Fleming and making just enough room for Eva to fit snugly beside her, hips and thighs all touching, shoulders rubbing.

Throughout the journey, conversation comes in fits and starts, with a fidgety Fleming constantly leaning one way then another, shifting forwards and back, paying particular attention to the way Eva clings on Mary Jane's arm, as though scared to let her go.

"She ain't gonna drift away, girl," he calls her on it. "You can loose your hold."

Eva squeezes all the tighter for his words.

Ten minutes later, at Fleming's instruction, the hansom drops them off at a cab rank behind the Lyceum, conveniently near a public house. Paying the driver through the hatch, Fleming steps out of the cab first, practically leaping off the seat, and offers no assistance to Mary Jane as she alights next, ahead of Eva.

"Who's for a drink?" He claps his hands together.

The question's rhetorical. He's already on his way to the pub, leaving Mary Jane to play the chivalrous

gentleman for Eva, helping her out of the carriage by offering a hand so that she might steady herself on it.

"Step careful, love."

As Eva jumps down, Mary Jane is standing by to support her, then escorts her to the pub, their arms looped together. Fleming's waiting for them at the entrance, but approaching it, Eva hesitates, coming a dead stop in the middle of the pavement.

"What's the problem?" Fleming checks the time on his pocket watch. "Hurry in."

Like a stubborn horse, Eva refuses to budge. "I ain't never been inside a pub afore." She eyes the façade with trepidation, the windows filled with hand-painted signs advertizing cheap rooms above, rented by the hour. "My mam said they's dens of iniquity."

"For God's sake," Fleming grumbles, striding in without them, having no patience for Eva's childish insecurities.

"You'll be safe with me, love, I promise." Mary Jane coaxes her forward. "Stick close by me and no-one will bother you."

Eva peers in through the greasy windows, spying Fleming at the bar. "That's him, ain't it? That's the fella what wanted to marry you."

"How'd you come to think that?" Mary Jane responds evasively.

"He's all green-eyed over you. Can't you see it?" Eva turns away from the window. "I thought he roughed you up and you split from him?"

"I did."

"But you're seeing him again?"

"I was, for a short while." Mary Jane isn't proud of it, but it's the truth. "He paid well, and I needed the extra coin."

Eva grows more concerned by the second. "What if he hurts you?"

"He won't." Mary Jane takes her by the shoulders, making sure she's paying absolute attention to the assurances being issued to her. "I've got him under control, and in any case, I ain't even seeing him as a customer no more."

"Then why's he taking you out?"

Rather than recount the whole story and run the risk of needlessly heightening her concerns, Mary Jane condenses the facts into a much simplified overview. "We had a falling out some weeks ago. This is his way of coming to terms with me, I s'pose."

"So there ain't nuthin' going on atween you?"

"Not at all, darling." Mary Jane scoops up her hands. "If this was aught to do with work, I wouldn't have asked you along." She edges toward the entrance. "Now shall we go inside?"

Receiving no resistance, she opens the heavy oak door and guides Eva through, steering her toward a corner table in the smoke-filled room and settling her in it, sandwiching her there against the wall, making sure she's protected from both sides. As they sit, Fleming leaves the bar to join them, bringing over a pint of ale for himself and a large glass of unrequested gin for Mary Jane. Nothing for Eva.

For the sake of politeness—though she knows what the answer will be—Mary Jane rectifies the deliberate oversight. "Do you want anything, darling?"

Eva shakes her head, staring at the sawdust-coated floor beneath the table, making patterns in it with her feet.

"What's wrong with her?" Fleming asks, not caring how gruff he seems.

"She don't drink." Mary Jane places a supportive hand on Eva's lap, far above where she garters, her fully extended arm acting as a shield across Eva's body.

"Bloody teetotaler," he mutters. "Christian temperance horseshit."

He might not care, but Mary Jane does. Well aware that Eva wishes her to remain sober—and well aware, too, that if she finishes this drink then another one is likely to materialize—she nurses her gin, taking small sips at intervals. Given that such restraint is jarringly out of character for her, Fleming soon adopts a scowl.

"Drink up," he encourages her. "You know you like to have a drop in you."

Rather than give way, she waits until he gets up to use the facilities, then dumps a quantity of the gin out onto the floor, kicking a pile of sawdust over it.

"Whatchu do that for?" Eva eyes the puddle of wasted pennies.

"I need to be a better woman for you." Mary Jane licks a drop of gin off the rim before it dribbles. "You want me to lay off the drink, and so I will."

The gesture sweetens Eva's mood, and by the time they're lining up for entry to the cheap seats in the pit— relegated as they are to a side entrance, on account of being inferior persons in this quarter—she's giddy with excitement.

CHAPTER 35

DURING HER SHORT TIME AS A FLOWER GIRL, EVA WALKED past the Lyceum every day. Covent Garden Flower Market isn't far off, and every morning, she'd stop along Wellington Street and stare at the theater's massive Greco-Roman portico, six colossal stone columns invading—and almost completely engulfing—the pavement. Flower basket in one arm, she'd weave in and out of them, feeling dwarfed by the enormity of it all, never believing she'd ever get to step inside.

Her hands are clammy. Mary Jane can feel the excessive heat from her palms as she worries the silk sleeve of her dress, rubbing and squeezing, gripping and hugging, determined not to be separated from her, despite the jostle of people around them.

Since the cheap seats aren't numbered or reserved, it's every man for himself, and everyone is striving to claim the best ones. Or rather, the best spots on the best benches, as what passes for seating in the pit and the galleries is nothing more than a few rows of cloth-draped benches with no backboards, where people are crammed in shoulder to shoulder.

As they pile through, Eva gawps at the more respectable classes filling up the stalls and the dress circle above, all the ladies wearing their finest evening gowns. She's as taken with them in all their finery as she is with the decoration of the theater itself. The ornate plaster

419

reliefs adorning the private boxes. The red velvet curtains. The exquisite gilding. Not to mention its sheer size, the scale of the place reducing men to mice on the vast stage.

Hip-checking people out of the way, and showing no mercy about it, Mary Jane—aided by Fleming—manages to secure them a place in the front row of the pit and assumes the position in the middle, with Eva to her left and Fleming to her right.

Not so many years ago, the pit was located directly behind—and level with—the orchestra, but with the increasing popularity of the stalls, it's now been relocated to the far back of the room, separated from the richer classes by a small wooden divider. Bar the upper galleries, they're the worst seats in the house, but while Mary Jane laments her position—wishing she were able to afford better, and yearning for those sumptuously padded seats in the stalls—Eva, wide-eyed and agog, is perfectly thrilled with everything just as it is.

"You always said you was gonna bring me to the theater one day." She beams.

"I did, and I have, and I shall again." Mary Jane plants a kiss on her forehead.

"How much did this cost you, though?"

Mary Jane rubs her fingers over Eva's brow, smoothing out the emerging frown before it can take hold. "That's not important, love."

Dissatisfied with that response, Eva flips through her copy of the playbill, finding the theater's pricing on the back page. Much to her horror, private boxes range from two pounds and two shillings, to a staggering four pounds and four shillings, which is almost three months of her wages. The stalls—the second best seats in the house—are ten and six. Seats in the dress circle go for seven shillings, while the upper circle is set at four. The pit is only a half-crown in comparison, but even that's dear enough in Eva's eyes.

Her jaw hangs open. "Oh, Mary Jane." She points at the number. "It's too much."

"Not for you it ain't."

"But, Em," she protests. "It's almost half of what I earns in a week. Seats in the gallery would've been fine enough for me, and them's only a shilling."

"It's a small luxury, darling." Mary Jane pats her thigh. "Barely fifteen minutes work for me. Now let's hear no more about it."

That hits Eva right in the chest. The sudden thought that her presence here was funded by Mary Jane's acceptance of a prick between her thighs causes an instant flood of tears. A moment later, Mary Jane is alerted to the deluge by a small heave of her shoulders, a strangled sob, and the faint slap of tears falling on the playbill in her lap.

"Oh, darling. I'm sorry. I shouldn't have said that." She pulls a hanky from her pocket and turns Eva's head, dabbing at her eyes. "That was thoughtless of me." She kisses away another salty droplet as it emerges. "There's no need for tears. I didn't mean to upset you."

"I knows what you have to do for us—for our savings—but you said there'd be no more of the street." Eva feels a sniffle coming on. "You said you was done with that."

"And I am, love. Honest." Mary Jane keeps her voice down, hoping no-one else can hear. Especially not Fleming, who's currently far too preoccupied with a new scuff mark on his boots to notice much of anything going on around him.

"Joe hasn't been coming around as often of late, that's all, so things have been tight." She downplays her recent cash-flow troubles. "But what if I promised you we'll be a new place together by Christmas? Would that help to put your mind at rest?"

Eva's eyes brighten again. "Do you really mean it?"

Mary Jane nods. "I'll make that happen for us. I truly will."

As the large gas-lit chandelier hanging above the stalls dims and the proceedings start, Eva keeps her eyes on Mary Jane, hungering for a kiss.

She inches forward.

Mary Jane's lips part in expectation, her heart pounding. "You ain't never gonna dare to kiss me in this room full of people?"

"What if I am?" Eva moves in.

Their lips meet. Oh, the audacity of it! Though it's chaste—their tongues kept locked behind their teeth—it's so daring. Mary Jane's never been kissed in such a public arena, and she's in no hurry for it to end ... but it does. A gentleman seated in the row behind them clears his throat and gives Mary Jane's back a sharp prod with his walking stick, breaking them up.

Were they elsewhere, Mary Jane would bark some vulgarity at him and tell him to mind his own, but given that they're in polite company, she keeps her mouth shut, turns her head forward, and slips her arm around Eva's shoulders, flipping him a rude hand gesture as she does so. That causes him to utter a startled execration of his own, which swiftly results in a smack to the chest from his blissfully unaware wife.

And so the show begins. The tale of upright gentleman Doctor Jekyll and his sinister—and murderous—alter ego unfolds for a packed-out audience, but Mary Jane spends more time watching Eva than she does the performance.

Like a small child seeing the inside of a sweet shop for the first time, Eva is enthralled. Every minute it seems her bum edges forward on the bench, and she leans closer and closer to the proscenium arch, as if she plans to jump right over the stalls, and the orchestra, and join the actors on the stage. Every now and again, she looks over her shoulder at Mary Jane, beaming a smile that says: "Can you believe we're here?!"

All the while, Mary Jane rests her hand on Eva's lower back, softly rubbing, unable to sit beside her without making some small demonstration of affection, completely oblivious to the fact that Fleming has his keen eyes trained on her.

In the periphery of his vision, he sees her hand make repeated passes over Eva's back, detecting an amorous spark he's never before seen in her. Undoubtedly, she's a woman of heated passions this evening, but her

tenderness for the girl confuses him. During the intermission, he goes outside to smoke—and to puzzle over Mary Jane's behavior—leaving them together in the darkened pit, saving his spot on the bench.

"Are you having fun, my darling?" Mary Jane twists sideways on the bench, facing Eva. "I want this night to be memorable for you."

"This is the best night of my life," Eva proclaims. "I'm so lucky."

She means that wholeheartedly, but Mary Jane's feeling devilishly spreeish.

"The best? You're sure?" She quirks a lopsided smile. "Better than the first night you spent in my bed?"

"All right, second best," Eva concedes, giggling.

"Better than the night I first put my mouth to you?" Mary Jane goes on, whispering in her ear. "Better than the night I pierced your maidenhead?"

Eva whimpers, shifting uncomfortably on the bench. "You're teasing me deliberate."

"What's the matter? Are my words having an effect?" Mary Jane tickles her fingers over Eva's outer thigh. "What effect might that possibly be?"

"You know well." Eva clamps her thighs together, trying to quell the burning restlessness between them. "And I ain't listening to you no more." She covers her ears with her hands. "You're trying to make me bad."

Mary Jane snatches up one of her hands, laughing. "There ain't nothing bad in a little anticipatory heat."

If this were the Empire in Leicester Square, Mary Jane would lead Eva into a quiet little alcove and give her a swift pleasure, but she's not familiar enough with the Lyceum to know of a place where they won't be found out. It's a much more respectable establishment than any in Leicester Square, and she doesn't want to be responsible for getting Eva booted out of her first West End show, so she stables her passions.

As the second act begins, she can see Eva struggling to keep upright, her back tiring of being so rigid and her bum aching. Halfway through, she whispers for the teen's attention, urging her to take off her hat and shuffle closer.

"Here, love." She pulls hatless Eva against her. "Lean on me."

Murmuring appreciatively, Eva snuggles up to her, cheek to breast, both arms wrapped around her waist. As it happens, Mary Jane's bust provides a convenient padded shelf on which to rest a weary head, and the warmth radiating from her body in the drafty auditorium is welcomed, too.

Virtually hip to hip with Mary Jane, Fleming sees Eva's pale hands appear around Mary Jane's middle. Leaning forward, resting his elbows on his knees, he glances over at the pair, getting a clear view of Eva's face pressed to Mary Jane's breast. Not only that, but Mary Jane's arm is around her shoulders, languidly caressing her. If Eva were very much younger, or Mary Jane very much older, one could be forgiven for thinking them to be mother and child.

Indeed, Fleming attempts that arithmetic in his head, but not being sure precisely how old either of them is, he fails to draw a definitive conclusion. Though rare, he's known girls as young as twelve or thirteen to become mothers, and he can think of no other explanation for such uncensored intimacy.

Catching him staring, Mary Jane raises an eyebrow, challenging him to voice an objection. When he doesn't, she returns her attention to the stage, and the rest of the performance passes without incident. On the way home, however, while crammed together in another hansom, there's yet more perplexing intimacy.

Eva, exhausted from the evening's excitements, falls asleep with her head slumped on Mary Jane's shoulder, both legs tucked up and flung over her lap. Fleming's never known Mary Jane to be so tolerant of such needy behavior, and yet she seems not only to abide it in this instance, but to be outright desirous of it. One of her hands is resting in Eva's lap—clasped tight by Eva—and the other is hugging her knees.

Though ultimately confused by it, their closeness intrigues him. Wondering whether or not Mary Jane's ever suckled Eva on her breast, he develops a certain swelling, the thought of her being a mother having an

unexpectedly rigoring effect, which he can neither suppress nor contain. Struck by this sudden letch, he unbuttons himself, letting his bare cock stand stiff in his lap.

Seeing it, Mary Jane huffs disapprovingly, unable to vent the true extent of her revulsion for fear of waking Eva. "Who's done anything whatsoever to cause that? Have you no self-control, you dirty beast?" She gives the fleshy rod a sharp slap. "Put the damned ugly thing away."

"Frig it off." Fleming seizes her hand, forcing it around the shaft.

"I will not!" Outraged by the demand, she's about to wrest herself free when Eva stirs and shifts, disturbed by the noise and movement.

"If you cause a fuss, you'll rouse the girl." Fleming holds her still, trapping her on his erection. "Is that what you want?" He moves her hand up and down.

Terrified that Eva might open her eyes, Mary Jane grits her teeth and makes no further objection to Fleming's manipulations. She dare not risk it. After all, Eva's already been so forgiving. If she were to revive and see such vulgarity being conducted in her presence, that would surely be more than she could withstand.

Barely breathing—ready to whisk her hand away at the first sign of Eva's fluttering eyelashes—she glides her fist over the length of Fleming's engorged prick, applying a firm but gentle pressure, the sordid operation making her nauseous. It reminds her altogether too clearly of the first time she was coerced into performing manual stimulation in such a manner.

She was just fourteen at the time. Walking home from work in the pouring rain, she was hailed by a well-rigged gentleman riding in a brougham. He took pity on her, she presumed, for she must've looked like a drowned wretch. Her cotton dress was clinging to her body like a second skin, her blonde hair drenched and plastered to her neck.

When his carriage drew up, he flung open the door and beckoned her in, offering to take her home. Of course, she accepted. Innocent to all things, and not yet

acquainted with the quirks and quillets of men—especially those with a letch for piercing novel cunt—she saw nothing untoward in it. She simply didn't know any better.

He asked what she was doing out in such dreadful weather, and when she told him that she hadn't enough money for the omnibus, he mocked her. He said he knew all about girls her age, and reckoned she'd spent all her money going to visit some boy she liked.

"No, sir, I ain't." She shook her head. "I ain't got no boy."

That, he declared, must be a lie, for she was such a comely young girl and all comely young girls soon attract the interest of boys. He reckoned she'd already had plenty pricks up her—an accusation which made her cry, for she hadn't had any.

Drying her eyes, he apologized and offered her a shilling.

"What for?" she asked, admiring the coin.

He said she could have it for nothing, but that if she wanted a half-crown more, then she must do him a simple favor. Thinking he probably needed an errand to be run and didn't have an umbrella on his person, she readily agreed. Then, he unbuttoned his prick.

"Oh!" She shielded her eyes. "Your tooleywag is out! Why's it so frightful big?!"

Until that moment, she'd only ever seen her brothers' things in the bath, and they were not nearly so monstrous.

"It's mightily swollen," he stated matter-of-factly. "And it aches so dreadfully."

"You need me to fetch a doctor?" young Mary Jane asked, at once thinking that must surely be the errand for which she's about to be paid.

"There's no need," he assured her. "Your assistance is all I require, my dear." He reached out to her. "Give me your hand now. I'll show you just what to do."

Presently, he explained that the soft stroke of a woman's hand—and only a woman's hand—would, after a fashion, release the pressure in the thing that was causing it to swell so enormously, and that once the operation

was done, the swelling would reduce almost immediately, thus restoring him to perfect health.

Certain she was being misled in some manner, but not at all sure how, Mary Jane took hold of the man's fattened priapus and did as he requested.

"There you are now." He watched her little hand do the work. "Keep going."

She refused to look, but kept her fist in motion, soon feeling a trickle of something hot and sticky seeping over her fingers.

"Oh, you're doing it, my darling!" he exclaimed, appearing to near some sort of crisis. "Quick! Let me feel your thighs!"

Before she could shield herself, he had his hand up her dress and on her bare sex, cupping her smooth mount in his large palm, his fat fingers prying between her silken labia, upon which the dense curls of a woman hadn't yet begun to sprout.

"What a beautiful, hairless little cunt you have!"

She was wailing then, her desperate tears soaking into the velvet upholstery. Mercifully, he was too near his spend to achieve any significant damage. Not a second after his emphatic praise of her treasure, she felt his prick erupt. Opening her eyes, she was horrified to see the vile thing spurting globs of some thick white muck all over the carriage floor as he groaned and bucked into her clenched hand, his hips jerking and wiggling.

"You've done something nasty with your thing!" She withdrew her hand—now covered in his repulsive sediment—and shot over to the other side of the seat, escaping from his trespassing fingers. "You're a truly rotten man! I want to go home!"

As he'd promised, the swelling in his thing subsided then and he was once again calm. Ten minutes later, she left the carriage with three and six in her pocket and a very confused head, the whole encounter having quite upset her. Before letting her go, he told her that if she should be walking along the same road at the same time tomorrow, he would have another few shillings for her. On account of that assurance, she never took the road again.

She didn't have the same sexual curiosity of other girls her age. If she had, she feels sure she would've met the carriage the very next day, and no doubt lost herself to him, whoever he was, for he wasn't so bad looking. But the sight of his organ stirred no lust in her, only revulsion, and over the years, that feeling never changed. She waited for it to, but it didn't. In fact, the more men took from her, the worse it got. Even now, she wants to retch.

Fleming's cock is leaking all over her hand and he's starting to pant. A moment later, his body stiffens, his hips twitch, and he comes. Milking the thing like a cow's udder, she directs the contents of his ballocks downward toward the wooden doors, hearing it splat against the lacquered wood. When he's done, his prick shriveling up, she snatches the red silk hanky from his jacket pocket and wipes her hand on it.

"You disgust me," she growls, scraping traces of his mucilage out from under her fingernails. "I am *not* your whore. Not anymore." Seeing that they're at the corner of Whitechapel High Street and Commercial Street, she then taps on the roof and opens the hatch. "Stop here, driver. Two of us are getting out."

"Whatchu doing?" Fleming buttons himself up.

"We'll walk the rest of the way." Mary Jane drops the dirty hanky into his lap and nudges Eva awake. "Darling, we're here." She puts on a smile. "Ups-a-daisy now."

Getting out first, she helps a groggy and disoriented Eva safely onto the ground and leads her along Whitechapel High Street, never looking back.

"Why's we have to walk?" Eva grumbles, yawning.

"He was going a different way," Mary Jane lies, knowing full well that Fleming's been staying in the Victoria Home for Working Men on Commercial Street, and that the route back to his lodgings would take them almost directly to the Lolesworth Buildings.

Distracting the sleepy teen from a potential sulk, she stops suddenly and picks her up, lifting her a few inches off the ground and spinning her in a full circle before setting her back on her feet, eliciting a surprised shriek and delighted laughter.

"I love you, Miss Sullivan." She slips her hands onto Eva's hips, keeping her close. "You make me an exceedingly happy woman."

She wants a kiss, but they're not alone. Among many other characters of dubious nature, women of a certain sort routinely promenade up and down Whitechapel High Street looking for work at this time of night, and two are within eyeshot at this moment. They're standing on the pavement, talking to two men in full military uniform, the pair dressed up as they are—bayonets and all—on account of it being a Bank Holiday.

For privacy, Mary Jane tugs Eva past the nearby White Hart public house and pulls her under the arch of the covered walkway at the entrance to George Yard: the narrow, unlit alley leading from Whitechapel High Street to Wentworth Street, in which many a nefarious business transaction is conducted on a nightly basis.

Here, in this darkened passage, she pushes Eva's back against the cold brick wall and kisses her, the lip-lock immediately broken when one of the women from the street enters the alley behind them, accompanied by her man.

"Naughty, naughty." The bonneted woman cackles, flashing a set of yellowed teeth and wagging a finger of mock disapproval. "I sees you."

Despite smelling like a brewery, she doesn't appear drunk. She walks on northward, toward Wentworth Street, quite capable of putting one foot in front of the other and pulling the soldier along behind her, the frayed hem of her tattered green skirt scraping along the ground. It's not even fit for the ragman, and her long black jacket is in a similar state of disrepair.

"C'mon, let's go home." Eva urges Mary Jane in the same direction. "I wanna go to bed." She scratches at her right buttock. "I think I got bit by summink in the hansom."

Further up the alley, the woman and her soldier turn into George Yard Buildings—a place Mary Jane knows well. Having taken many customers there herself, she can guess as to their purpose. It's pitch black in these parts,

the lamps having already been extinguished for the night, and there's little risk of being disturbed.

With Eva leading the way, they turn into the Lolesworth Buildings off George Street, through a covered passage and into the concrete courtyard, illuminated only by the soft glow of candlelight emanating from the surrounding rooms, the pale, waning crescent of the moon being entirely obscured by clouds.

"Can you sleep with me again tonight?" Eva stops suddenly to ask.

"I want to." Mary Jane steals a kiss. "I will."

"What about your other Joe?"

"Fuck him."

Pleased with that answer, Eva breaks into a grin, hitches up her skirts, and dashes across the courtyard. "Catch me!"

Up for the game, Mary Jane grabs a fistful of her skirts, hikes them above her ankles, and makes chase. Every time she comes close to seizing Eva by the waist, Eva darts out of her grasp, the two twirling around each other, barely touching.

Eva's a tease, lingering in one spot just long enough, waiting for Mary Jane to pounce, then evading her lunge at the last moment. Feeling brave, she inches her skirts a little higher, almost to her knees.

"Oh, you coquette!" Mary Jane begins to tire, her lungs impeded too severely by her corset to achieve anything even remotely resembling strenuous exertion.

At the stone stairwell, she finally captures her prey. Startled by a scavenging rat, Eva stumbles backwards, drops her skirts, and falls into Mary Jane's waiting arms.

"Gotcha!" Mary Jane holds her in a tight embrace, directing her up the steps.

As they ascend, she can't quite shake the feeling that they were being watched in the courtyard, but surrounded by so many naked tenement windows, that's hardly surprising. Once they get up to Eva's lodgings, their passions inflamed by the game, they spill into the darkened room, a clumsy, tangled bundle of groping hands and rustling skirts. First, they knock into the washstand, almost tipping it. Then, they hit the bed, Eva

getting the carved wooden knob atop the bedpost jabbed into her buttocks.

"Ow! Wait!" She separates herself from Mary Jane and the knob. "Let's light some candles first. I wants to look at you while we're doing it."

Having just purchased the candles and matches yesterday, Mary Jane finds them by memory and gets them both lit, placing them on the mantel to concentrate the light at the head of the bed. She divests herself of Eva's loaned hat next—lest she should forget that she's wearing it and crush it in some activity upon the bed— then resumes more playful pursuits.

As Eva plants her bum on the edge of the table to unlace her boots, Mary Jane steps in, taking charge of removing her boots, garters, and woolen stockings.

"Such lovely legs." She kisses her way from thigh to ankle and back again, peeking up at Eva's bare sex. "Oh, how I want you."

"You can have me." Eva leans back on her hands.

"Right here on the tabletop?"

"If you fancy." She props her feet up on the edge of the table and parts her thighs, unashamedly presenting herself for fucking. "I'd give me-self to you anywhere."

"Oh, Miss Sullivan." Mary Jane feigns shock. "You're so terribly wicked." She moves between Eva's legs and plants a kiss on her, oblivious to the fact that the curtains are open and they can be seen by anyone looking up at the window from Thrawl Street. "If I had my doodle ..."

"Ain't it in your trunk?"

Mary Jane shakes her head. "My lockbox at Miller's Court."

"But I wanted it." Eva goes into a slump.

"Well, you'll have to make do with this." Mary Jane wraps one arm around Eva's lower back, holding her in place, and drives two fingers into her sex.

At first, Eva surrenders to the jiggering. Then, realizing their lewd display could be witnessed by all and sundry through the window, she regains some of her modesty.

"Cripes, the curtains." She grabs Mary Jane's wrist and forces her out, afraid that someone in the Charlotte

de Rothschild Building across the street might see. "There's some right nosey bastards across the way, and I don't wanna be giving 'em a free peep."

"Fair enough." Mary Jane scoops her off the table and carries her to the bed, straining only a little as she throws her onto the palliasse. "Heaving you around ain't as easy as it used to be."

"Careful of my hat!" Eva squeals.

As she unpins it, Mary Jane returns to the table and pulls the curtains closed, catching sight of a man down below. He's standing under a gaslight, staring up at the room, his face clearly illuminated. It's Fleming.

"Arsehole," she mutters, shutting him out.

"What's wrong?" Eva sits up, flicking her hat onto the table. "Was someone having a look? I told you: nosey bastards, the lot of 'em."

Not wanting to worry her, Mary Jane says nothing of their peeper's identity. Instead, she flicks her skirt over her knees and clambers onto the bed.

"Now, where were we?"

CHAPTER 36

MYSTERIOUS TRAGEDY IN WHITECHAPEL
A WOMAN BRUTALLY MURDERED

"About ten minutes to five o'clock this morning, John Reeves, who lives at 37 George Yard Buildings, Whitechapel, was coming downstairs to go to work when he discovered the body of a woman lying in a pool of blood on the first-floor landing. Dr. Keeling of Brick Lane was communicated with, and promptly arrived. He immediately made an examination of the woman, and pronounced life extinct, and gave it as his opinion that she had been brutally murdered, there being knife wounds on her breast, stomach, and abdomen. The woman is unknown to any of the occupants of the tenements, and no disturbance of any kind was heard during the night. The circumstances of the tragedy are, therefore, mysterious, and the body, which up to the time of writing has not been identified, has been removed to Whitechapel Mortuary, and Inspector Elliston, of the Commercial Street Police Station, has placed the case in the hands of Inspector Reid, of the Criminal Investigation Department."

-- Echo (London), August 7, 1888

Tuesday, August 7, 1888

MARY JANE STIRS AWAKE, BECOMING AWARE THAT HER nude body is on display, the bedclothes pulled away and her legs positioned a frog-like manner, knees bent and

akimbo. Peering down, she finds Eva half-dressed and poking at her commodity.

"You look confused, love." She yawns, pondering what time it is, the dim light outside suggesting dawn. "Ain't you figured out how it works yet?"

"It feels different." Eva puzzles over it, wiggling her finger along the dry slit and dipping inside, taking an internal measure of the supposed problem. "I ain't never known it to be like this." She retreats to the exterior, twiddling her fingers around Mary Jane's hidden clitoris, trying to coax it out, troubled by its apparent reluctance to emerge. "Are you unwell?"

Amused that Eva should think it the natural state of the thing to be primed for pleasure, Mary Jane chuckles. Since she's generally the one to initiate their fuckings, and often tends to Eva's needs and wants before considering her own, her body is usually in a condition of full arousal long before the first tickle, lick, or rub. It must be a startling contrast.

"You need to get my passions up." She beckons Eva closer. "Keep touching me as you are, and kiss me."

Eva does as she's told, locking their lips together while fondling the curiously dormant article until a profusion of moisture seeps between Mary Jane's labia, coating her fingertips. In that moment, she moans, breaking their kisses.

"The wetness just come flooding in." She increases the frenzy of her touches, encouraged by its sudden lubricity. "What a difference in it! It feels proper now."

"You stoke me up like no other." Mary Jane swings one leg up, hooking it over Eva's shoulder and pushing her southward. "Lick me, my darling. Gamahuche me." She closes her eyes, basking in Eva's ministrations. "You're making me ache so delightfully."

Before the words are even out of her mouth, Eva is kissing a trail down her soft body, from her breasts to the golden curls on her motte. She's yearning for a taste of Mary Jane's womanhood—as she has been since she allowed Mary Jane back into her bed the night before last—but Saturday's unpleasantness proves still too fresh in her mind.

She hesitates at the apex of Mary Jane's slit, recalling the warm tackiness of the saturated silk on her fingers as she parted Mary Jane's thighs and pulled the wadded hanky out, a pale white ooze then issuing forth from the unplugged hole. The odor of it lingers in her nostrils even now. The pungent, unmistakable stench of a man's spermatic muck.

Aware that her passions have dulled, though unsure why, Mary Jane releases her from the obligation to continue. "It's all right." She slips her leg off Eva's shoulder. "You don't have to put your mouth on me. Use your fingers instead."

"No, I want to." Eva prevents her from closing her legs. "I do."

With that, she wrenches Mary Jane's thighs apart and dips her head to the task.

Though she'd be lying if she said that the thought of countless men using Mary Jane's body for their pleasure didn't sully the treasure that ought to be hers and hers alone, as soon as her tongue presses into the soft flesh of those parts, all other thoughts are forgotten. Oh, the taste of her! The heady aroma of her weeping sex drowns Eva's apprehension, rendering abstinence inconceivable. No more dithering.

Her tongue moves fast and hard, sweeping upwards from perineum to clit before plunging into Mary Jane's flushed opening, forcing its way through. Using her thumbs to hold open the lust-swollen petals of Mary Jane's core, she gets deeper, her aggressive mouth devouring all that she can reach, her tongue working all the more furiously when she feels the first trembles of impending orgasm rippling through Mary Jane's body.

And then it comes.

Not used to being on the receiving end of such unreserved fervor, Mary Jane is reduced to a panting, whimpering mess, unable to form the words to articulate her rapture. As Eva's mouth closes around her engorged clit, she's brought over, locked in the grip of her spend until Eva disengages from her, letting the spasms subside.

In the wake of her crisis, she regains the ability to speak, albeit softly, as though the very breath of life were being exhaled through her lips. "I can die a happy woman."

"No dying." Eva wipes her mouth on the back of her hand, getting out of bed. "I expressly forbid it."

Taken aback by her abrupt departure from the sheets, Mary Jane snags her arm. "Where are you going? I haven't had you yet."

"I mustn't dally." Eva resists all efforts to reel her back in. "I need to get a wriggle on if I'm to have breakfast afore work."

Submitting to good sense, Mary Jane releases her. She's about to curl back up under the covers and attempt a few more hours of sleep, but last night's unsettling discovery of Fleming watching them through the window keeps gnawing at her brain. What must he have thought? What if he gets in one of his fits? What if he takes it out on Eva? Frightened that he might just be mad enough to lie in wait and lash out at her in some way, Mary Jane swings her legs out of bed, making herself vertical.

"Hold your horses." She scrambles for her clothes. "I'll go with you."

"Whatever for?"

Not wanting to worry her unduly, Mary Jane veils the act as a romantic one. "I want to walk my love to work. What's wrong in that?" She starts pulling on her clothes. "Plenty girls have their young lads drop them off of a morning. You don't mind, do you?"

"Why would I? I ain't ashamed." Eva laces her boots. "You can meet me after I'm done n'all if you want, and I gets an hour for dinner at one."

"Is that a hint?" Mary Jane whisks her hair up into a scruffy bun, putting off the need to brush it. "I'll see what I can manage."

Rushing through their ablutions, they manage to leave the room by seven thirty, allowing just enough time for Eva to visit the facilities before taking care of breakfast.

"Ain't it grand?" She shows off the flushing toilet in the small communal water closet that serves several rooms on her floor. "It's a flusher!"

'Grand' might not be the word Mary Jane would use. The crooked seat has a suspicious ruddy stain on it, the toilet bowl is streaked with feces, and the floor is splashed with urine. To combat the smell, the tiny window set high in the wall has to be kept open at all times, and one of the tenants has taken to sprinkling bicarbonate of soda on the tiled floor. It's not helping.

On a small ledge beside the vile, disgraceful example of a modern convenience, lies the toilet's one redeeming feature: a healthy supply of thin square sheets of paper, the tidy pile weighted down with a lump of broken brick. But that's Eva's least favorite part.

"I hates that wretched paper." She grimaces at the stack. "It makes my bum itch." Urged on by the call of nature, she then nudges Mary Jane out the door, shooing her away. "Go on now. Don't listen to me doing my bogging business."

For someone who grew up in such close quarters with her family, Eva's frightfully modest about her bodily functions. She won't uncork her scent bottle—not if she can at all help it—and she still can't piddle in the chamber pot without humming a tune to herself so as to cloak the sound of her water tinkling in the porcelain. Her natural diffidence never fails to make Mary Jane smile.

Upon retreating to the concrete walkway outside— glad to be ushered way from the water closet—Mary Jane takes the opportunity to look around for Fleming. Even though she doesn't see hide nor hair of him anywhere in the courtyard, she feels no relief. Nor will she until she's delivered Eva safely to the factory. First things first, though: breakfast.

At Eva's direction, they grab bacon sandwiches from a little coffeehouse on Commercial Street and eat them as they walk. Slathered in butter—or at least, something that very closely resembles the consistency of butter, but which may in fact be some other form of yellow grease— the thick cut bread is loaded with salted rashers of bacon.

437

It isn't at all what you'd call healthy, but it is hearty—and tasty.

Along the way, Mary Jane keeps an eye out, half expecting Fleming to accost them. In these busy streets, he could leap out from anywhere and catch them unawares. Paranoid, and hearing footsteps behind them, she twists around, making sure they're not being followed.

"Who you looking for?" Eva mumbles, her mouth full of pig. "That busybody who was peeping on us last night?"

"P'raps." Mary Jane remains deliberately vague.

"I wouldn't worry on it." Eva gulps down the last bite of her sandwich and sinks her head onto Mary Jane's arm. "It was prob'ly just some nosey Jew from the Rothschild buildings."

"Men are men, Jew or otherwise. What's the difference?" Mary Jane's tone is laced with contempt. "Men are defined by what they do, not by their beliefs or their blood." She pulls a hanky from her pocket, wiping off her greasy fingers. "And I know all about what men do."

"You speak as though all men's bad, but that can't be right, can it?" Eva looks to her older, wiser companion for the truth on the matter. "My dadda was a good man. Or so my mam always said anyway. Ain't some men good?"

Turning onto Wentworth Street, Mary Jane spots Inspector Reid standing at the entrance to George Yard, talking to a small gaggle of women.

"Aye, I s'pose." She sighs, watching him pull a ha'penny from behind a small child's ear. "But good men are rare creatures indeed."

Eva follows her gaze. Across the breadth of the street, cutting off foot and carriage traffic, people are milling around, their attentions focused on George Yard. Amidst the hullabaloo, several women are crying, and three uniformed police constables are barricading the alleyway, preventing people from exploiting the shortcut to Whitechapel High Street.

"What's the to-do?" Eva takes hold of Mary Jane's arm, guarding against being separated on the jam-packed street.

"Nothing good." Mary Jane catches Reid's eye.

"You reckon someone died?" Eva tightens her grip. "It looks like a right kerfluffle."

"A what now?"

"A kerfluffle," Eva repeats her mistake.

"A kerfuffle," Mary Jane corrects her.

"That's what I said." Eva frowns. "A kerfluffle. Ain't that right?"

"Perfectly."

Reid approaches, removing his hat to greet them. "Good morning, Miss Kelly."

"Is it?" Mary Jane tips her head to the ruckus behind him. "Trouble at mill?"

Reid logs the casual use of that uniquely northern expression, but says nothing. The idiom first sprang up around the country's cotton mills, particularly in and around Manchester, and he's only ever heard it roll off the tongues of Lancashire natives.

"There's always trouble somewhere, Miss Kelly."

"Don't I know it." Mary Jane directs his attention to Eva. "Mister Reid, this is my companion Miss Eva Sullivan. You'll remember I've spoken of her to you."

"Of course." Reid acknowledges Eva's presence with a nod and a smile. "You must be the dear young woman Miss Kelly's been pining for all these months."

"How do, sir?" Eva dips her head politely. "How do you know my Mary Jane?"

"We go back a short way," he answers carefully, not sure how much information Mary Jane wants him to give up. "I helped her out of a small spot of bother when she was leaving her former residence in Bethnal Green."

Knowing that whenever her mother was in 'a spot of bother' it was to do with being run in by the police for some minor offense or another, Eva looks up at Mary Jane, horrified. "You ain't on the run from the coppers?"

Mary Jane laughs. "Hish, no! When I got into difficulties with my old fella, Mister Reid very kindly helped me out of my situation. That's all."

Distracting her from asking any further questions, should she be inclined to do so, Reid employs his faithful sleight of hand magic, telling Eva she has something caught in her hair before making a penny appear from behind her ear.

The never-before-seen trick genuinely thrills her, and sets her giggling like a schoolgirl, admiring her shiny new penny, utterly preoccupied with it.

"Congratulations, you've won her over." Mary Jane chuckles. "But we really must be getting on, else I fear she'll be late for work."

Reid catches Mary Jane's elbow, preventing her departure. "I should like to speak with you, if I may." He keeps his voice low so that Eva won't hear. "And soon."

Mary Jane nods. "I'm just dropping her off. I shall walk back this way."

Reid stays put, keeping an eye on them as they walk to the factory at the end of the street, parting ways with a peck on the lips and a quick hug, the affection between them unconcealed. Mary Jane seems happier than he's ever seen her, and he remarks as much when she returns to him.

"It's good to see you smiling again, Miss Kelly."

"Isn't she beautiful?" Mary Jane brags. "I think I've done rather well for myself, given that I'm nothing but a common harlot who hasn't got a scrap of anything to offer her."

"You are many things, indeed, Miss Kelly, but common certainly is not one of them."

"You're flattering me again, Mister Reid." Mary Jane blames a southerly breeze for the pink in her cheeks. "What's gone on here?" She cocks her head to George Yard. "I presume that to be the reason you desire my company this morning."

Reid nods, skipping past any further pleasantries. "A woman met her end here last night, and in a most violent manner. We don't yet know her name."

Thinking of her late night encounter with the woman in the black bonnet, Mary Jane feels a sharp twinge in her chest. "What sort of woman?"

"I daresay you might guess the sort." Reid lays his hand on Mary Jane's back, guiding her to a quieter edge of the street. "Although it should be said that I've yet to have that supposition confirmed, and indeed, may have found reason to challenge it."

"Is that what you require me for?"

"In part, perhaps."

"What was she wearing?" Mary Jane scarcely dares to ask. "Black bonnet, green skirt, long black jacket?" she guesses. "Generally disheveled in appearance. Plump, with a round face. Of middling years, I'd say. Shorter than myself. Maybe a smidge over five feet. Is that the one?"

Reid's expression turns grave. "You know her?"

"No, but I might've seen her."

"When? Where?"

Mary Jane turns her head, presenting her ear to him.

"Is that all you think a man's good for?" Reid digs in his pockets for another coin.

"Such has been my experience."

"Well, as I've told you often enough before, I believe your experience has been with the wrong men." He hands her a tanner.

"I don't doubt it." Mary Jane inspects the coin in her palm, expecting to receive only a penny. "Ooh, careful now, Mister Reid, or I might start to think you like me."

"It's not without a caveat," Reid reminds her. "I'll need you to come to the mortuary and confirm that she's the woman you saw. You must tell me everything."

"If I do, and she is, will I be called upon at the inquest?"

Reid shakes his head. "I wouldn't compromise your anonymity."

"My name must not be in the papers, nor in any official record," Mary Jane warns him. "There must be no mention of me at all. Not even that you know me."

Reid nods. "You'll be aiding me in a confidential capacity, I assure you."

"Very well, then." Mary Jane agrees. "How is this done?"

In a nondescript building of brick construction, situated to the right of a large yard used by the Board of Works as a storage dump behind the Pavilion Theatre, rests the unidentified body of a woman, stabbed thirty-nine times and left dead in a stairwell, lying in a pool of blood.

Escorted into the yard by Reid, the first thing Mary Jane sees is a bucket of rags deposited on the flagstones. At least, they look like rags at a glance. A closer inspection reveals that the bucket contains the green skirt, black bonnet, and jacket Mary Jane saw on the woman in George Yard, along with a brown petticoat, a pair of striped woolen stockings, and a pair of old spring-sided boots, long past their best. The coat is saturated with blood, as are portions of the skirt, petticoat, and stockings.

"You recognize those?" Reid follows her gaze.

Mary Jane nods. "I think so."

Reid places a steady hand on her lower back, directing her inside the coffin-lined dead-house. Not proper burial coffins, that is, but the unfinished shells of coffins, used and reused for the transport of bodies from one location to another. They're no more than cheap wooden boxes, stained with blood and any other bodily fluids that might've oozed from the many corpses placed inside them.

The sole mortuary attendant, at a nod from Reid, opens up a shell on a table running parallel to the wall. Inside it, a woman lies naked under a thick, dark mortuary blanket, only her head and neck visible above the coarse woolen fabric.

"Leave us." Reid ushers the attendant out, closing the door behind him.

In the ensuing silence, Mary Jane approaches the opened shell and peeks in at its contents, the heels of her boots clacking on the tiled floor.

"Is it her?" Reid's hand returns to her lower back.

Mary Jane nods, stepping away from the sight of the pallid woman with the rounded face, her eyes closed, but her mouth slightly open, her dark hair bunched behind her head, propping it up. "This is the woman I saw last night."

"You're certain?"

More nodding. "And it's very likely that I saw her in the company of the man who brought about her end."

"Go on."

Turning completely away from the shell, Mary Jane takes a deep breath and composes herself, feeling shaky and unsteady on her feet, overwhelmed by the acrid smell of wet pennies. "Eva and I were returning from the theater when we crossed paths with this woman and a gentleman—a soldier—entering George Yard from Whitechapel High Street."

"What time was this?" Reid's voice is deep and monotone, not an ounce of emotion in it.

"Shortly before midnight." Mary Jane swallows hard, her throat dry. "They went into the passage of George Yard Buildings together, and that's all I can say of it."

"For what purpose do you suspect they went that way?"

"An immoral one, I daresay." Knowing that this is the area in which she is of most use to Reid, she furnishes him with all the details she possesses. "The lights are extinguished at eleven o'clock there. After that, it becomes a place commonly used for such business."

"Did you exchange any words with her?"

Disinclined to discuss those particular details of her brief encounter with the dead woman, Mary Jane tries to dodge the question. "Nothing of any importance."

"Might I decide that for myself?"

Mary Jane clenches her jaw. "Might I remind you that I'm here as a friend to you, Mister Reid? Please do not speak to me so coldly." She finds a chair in the corner and sits on it, needing to get off her feet. "If you must know, this woman and her friend entered the alleyway behind myself and Eva. She caught us engaged in some private expression of our affection for one another, made some comment of it, and walked on. Is that explanation

443

satisfactory, Inspector?" She doesn't wait for an answer. "Now, what might be of some actual use to you, is the fact that I've seen her around George Street before. I believe she's been a resident at Satchell's Lodging House, so you might check there for a name."

Reid notes it down in a pocket notebook. "That'd be the house next door to the old lodgings of Emma Smith, is it not?"

One of Mary Jane's eyebrows goes up. "There's some link between the two?"

"I cannot say."

"Was it the gangs?" She presses on.

"I'm not certain."

"Well, what was done to her, Inspector?" Mary Jane folds her arms, annoyed. "I cannot be of any help to you unless you provide me with some further information. That is what you want me for, yes? *You* approached *me* on the street—I did not come to you. You sought me out, and the reason for it is because no other woman who knows what I do about vice in this quarter is going to speak to any copper as freely as I will speak to you."

Reid studies her for a moment, then nods. "You have insight that is valuable to me, Miss Kelly. I should appreciate your observations."

"So tell me."

Using the most sensitive language, he describes to her the condition of the body. "She was found supine, her clothing disarranged, bodice torn, hands clenched by her sides. Her legs were positioned as if for connection, but ..." He runs his fingers through his beard. "No trace of any such activity was found."

"That's why you doubt her profession?"

Reid shrugs. "Clearly, this soldier you saw her with did not engage her."

"I'm sorry, Inspector, but how did you arrive at that conclusion?" Mary Jane gets back on her feet, her wooziness subsiding. "Was there no seminal muck found in her cuntal orifice?"

Reid winces, unaccustomed to hearing such vulgar language from a woman's lips. "You are utterly indelicate, Miss Kelly, but you are correct."

444

"Well, what does that prove? Nothing." Mary Jane brushes it off. "He might've used a French letter, or perhaps he couldn't afford to give her a wetting."

"Excuse me?"

"You've never heard of a dry bob? The fella puts it in, has his wiggle, then withdraws before his crisis. It's cheaper than the full thing." Mary Jane holds up a finger, another thought occurring to her. "Of course, that's assuming she used her commodity for the business at all, which she may not have done."

"Meaning?"

"Other of a woman's parts can be used for the bringing of pleasure, Mister Reid." Mary Jane refrains from being more explicit. "I knew one woman who earned a very fine living as a *manuelle*—a harlot who only uses her hands. She had chronic inflammation in her wrists, but always paid her rent on time."

Reid tries not to let that mental imagery stick in his mind. "So you've no doubts that our victim was an unfortunate?"

"None whatsoever," Mary Jane answers, confident in her proclamation. "The fact that you found no trace of a fella inside her goes no way to proving otherwise, and I saw her with a gentleman. Whether he was her last or not, I surely cannot say, but I can guarantee that he had engaged her in some fashion or another." She takes the next logical step. "So now you're wondering if the gangs are responsible for her death." She pauses. "And how did she die exactly? You haven't yet said."

"She received thirty-nine stabs to the chest and abdomen." Reid raps his fingers on the rim of the open shell. "The thing of it is, two blades were used. Thirty-eight of the wounds were caused by something akin to the blade of a penknife, but the thirty-ninth wound—the fatal one—was made with something different. Possibly a surgical blade. It pierced her sternum with great force and penetrated her heart."

"So there were two men?"

"It appears that way."

"That's why you suspect the gangs," Mary Jane infers.

"Do you think it conceivable?"

Mary Jane sways her head, not quite committing to shake it. "Thirty-nine wounds seems far too extreme. It sounds ... frenzied. As I've said to you before, it's not the intention of the gangs to kill, but to punish. They punch and kick, often causing damage to a woman's critical parts in an effort to render her unable to work." She ruminates on it for a moment, then shakes her head more firmly. "I cannot account for the ferocity in this."

"So then we have two madmen on our hands." Reid closes the shell lid.

"Or one madman and an angel of mercy," Mary Jane posits. "Is it not possible that someone came upon her as she lay dying and delivered that fatal wound? Ended her misery and suffering, so to speak."

Reid says nothing.

Sensing his despondency, and wishing she had more to give him, Mary Jane questions the value of her assistance. "Have I been of any aid to you at all?"

"A great deal." Reid forces a smile of encouragement. "I may call upon you again." He heads for the door, ready to escort her home. "And fear not, Miss Kelly, we shall catch the man. Mark my words."

"I don't doubt it, Inspector." Mary Jane tries to sound more hopeful than she feels, masking a deep-rooted fear that this woman's death, like those of the other Whitechapel unfortunates—her friends among them—will be all too easily brushed aside.

CHAPTER 37

MARY JANE STANDS ON THE CORNER OF WENTWORTH Street and Brick Lane, bearing a single coral rose in full bloom. In declaration of love, Eva once gave her a single red rose. It was thornless, symbolic of love at first sight, and she still has it. She keeps it safe beneath the floorboards at Miller's Court, though it's now fragile and desiccated.

This coral rose is an advertisement of her desire, and when Eva emerges from the Taylor Brothers Chocolate and Mustard Factory at a few minutes past six, catching immediate sight of Mary Jane and the dusky orange flower, her cheeks flush with color.

"Whatever's this for?" She accepts the offering, burying her nose in the petals of the sweet-smelling bloom. "I'm sure I ain't done nuthin' to deserve such a gesture."

"Is it too much?" Mary Jane thumbs some factory dust off Eva's forehead. "Am I embarrassing you dreadfully?" She brushes her fingers over Eva's pink cheeks.

Eva shakes her head, standing on tiptoe to peck Mary Jane's lips. "I ain't embarrassed to be your girl. Not a bit." She holds the flower to her chest. "Where was you at dinnertime?"

Between the hours of noon and two o'clock, Mary Jane was taking one of her specials at his residence in

447

Shadwell. So while Eva was sitting on the front steps of a vacant warehouse lot, demolishing a hot meal of jellied eels and whelks bought from two of the various barrow sellers pitched along Brick Lane, she was wearing a pair of knee-high lace-up boots, a ruby-colored corset with black leather facing, and a felted beaver fur top hat. Her eyes were painted the darkest black, and she was wielding a wooden paddle. But Eva doesn't need to know any of that.

"I'm sorry." Mary Jane takes one of Eva's hands in hers. "The day rather got away from me, but I'd very much like to make it up to you. May I buy you supper?"

Eva pretends to give the matter some serious consideration before arriving at a decision. "You may take me out, Miss Kelly." She loops her arm through Mary Jane's. "I do believe I shall allow it."

Arm in arm, they head off down Wentworth Street, passing the mouth of George Yard alley on their way to Lolesworth. Though all is much quieter now—children playing the street as though nothing happened—the gossipmongers are still gathered around the sight of the tragedy, trading snippets of distorted facts passed from ear to ear.

"Did you find out what happened there?" Eva glances at the foreboding passageway. "Some other girls in the factory was whispering about a murder."

"They're right." Mary Jane keeps her eyes averted from the scene. "She was an unfortunate."

"Do they know who done it?"

Mary Jane shakes her head. "They don't even know who she is yet."

"Well, I'm glad you don't have to do none of that no more." Eva twirls the rose in her hand. "All that nasty business on the street, I mean." She grazes her lips with the soft petals. "I don't like to think of it."

"You used to envy me. Remember that?" Mary Jane accompanies the painful reminder with a soft jab of her elbow into Eva's ribs.

"My thinking was daft." Eva stops her in the middle of the street, clutching her cinched waist. "I don't feel that way no more, and you'd best know that." She flings

herself into Mary Jane's arms. "I love you too much, and I can't bear the thought."

"You're such a sweet girl." Mary Jane picks Eva up and turns her around, reversing their positions. "Let me take you somewhere special tonight instead." She pulls Eva along, taking her back toward the factory, retracing their steps. "Someplace I can show you off."

"What sort of place?" Eva drags her heels.

"Somewhere we can be around other women like us." Mary Jane leads them past the factory and onto Brick Lane. "Somewhere I can flaunt my love for you."

"Is it a pub?"

Mary Jane can hear the concern in Eva's voice. Stopping at the junction where Brick Lane dissolves into Osborn Street, she sandwiches the teen's anxious face between her palms. "I shan't drink. I know that's what troubles you." She kisses Eva's wrinkled brow. "I'll quench my thirst with ginger beer, and if you really don't like the place, we'll leave. How's that for fair?"

Her assurances do the trick. She's able to coax Eva down Osborn Street, past the spot where Emma Smith was attacked April last, and through an unmarked door beside a wine shop.

This nondescript entranceway leads down a flight of deep stone steps to an unlicensed cellar club, the heavy metal door of which is elegantly hand-painted with a motif of violets surrounding the words 'The Velvet Teacup,' and is guarded by a cigarette-smoking figure sitting on a bar stool. The slender doorman, wearing pressed trousers and a clean white shirt with a snugly fitted waistcoat—an artificial violet pinned to it—looks up as they descend, his face half cast in shadow, the only source of light being that of a flickering oil lamp hanging above the door.

"Mary Jane, *mon amie*," he purrs with a thick French accent, whisking off his bowler hat and holding it to his chest. "My old heart does beat again." He taps the hat against his breast, mimicking a heartbeat. "*Je n'arrête pas de penser à toi.*"

"Such a sweet tongue you have." Mary Jane greets him with a kiss on cheek, seeming to enjoy his words. "I do hope it's getting you into plenty of trouble."

Disliking Mary Jane's apparent fondness for this man, and the fact that he's speaking French to her, Eva scrutinizes his appearance, finding him strangely effeminate. His forearms are bared, his sleeves rolled up to the elbows, exposing lightly sun-kissed skin. One long-fingered hand clasps the rim of his bowler hat, while the other taps ash from the cigarette before putting it to his mouth. His delicate, soft mouth.

"This is *une nouvelle fille*," he remarks, giving Eva the same scrutiny.

"Ain't she pretty?" Mary Jane beams, sweeping her arm around Eva's waist. "She's every bit mine, and I'm hers. I wanna shout it out to the world, but failing that, I'll settle for flaunting it to every one of our kind in Whitechapel." She winks. "So let us in, *s'il te plaît*."

Grinning, the doorman pinches the cigarette between his lips and pulls open the door, revealing the lively room beyond and unleashing a cacophony of noise. To the left, people—mostly women, it appears—are playing cards, winning and losing farthings with each hand dealt. To the right, there's a full bar, staffed by two women—one older, one younger. Both are sans bodice and camisole—wearing only their corsets and shemmies from the waist up—but fully dressed below, and both have their hair loose.

All about, violet-ornamented women congregate around a cluttered, disorganized array of mismatched tables and chairs, smoking and drinking freely. Circulating throughout the room, a quartet of topless women take drink and food orders, clear away emptied glasses and filled ashtrays, and flirt with the patrons. All four—wearing only their petticoats, stockings, and boots—receive arse slaps, whistles, and tips aplenty. Available to service any and every need of whosoever wants them, one dazzling blonde, her tresses flowing nearly to her waist, makes no objection to being bent over a table and having her petticoats lifted over her rump, her

cunt swiftly plugged with the cock of the man standing behind her.

Eva averts her gaze, her eyes widened in horror. "Oh, lummy ..." She pulls Mary Jane aside. "Whatever sort of place have you brung me to now?"

"I told you." Mary Jane breaks into a broad smile. "It's a sort of sanctuary for women who share our particular lusts." She looks around, pleased to see so many familiar faces. "Before I met you, I used to come here regular. I'm sure as you can guess the reason why."

Flustered and agitated, Eva points first to the rutting couple, then to a dapper young man seated at the bar. "But them's men!"

"No, my darling." Mary Jane shakes her head. "Not a single one." She spins Eva around, forcing her to re-examine their surroundings. "Look harder."

Eva takes a second glance toward the man sitting at the bar. Like the doorman, he's dressed in trousers, shirt, and waistcoat, complete with a silver pocket watch. Unlike the doorman, however, his shirt is half open, exposing a pair of small, unfettered breasts beneath.

Women.

They're all women.

Seeing that Eva's overwhelmed by this sudden bombardment of new sensory information, Mary Jane tries to put her at ease. "I wanted to bring you somewhere we don't have to act quite so proper with one another." She plucks the coral rose from Eva's clammy, clenched hands before it gets crushed. "We can be as free as we like here, and you can meet my closest friends."

"Friends?" Eva scans the room, not recognizing anyone until she spots Maria sitting at a large rectangular table in the far corner, a dozen other women—several of them *filles de joie*—seated all around her.

"Come on now." Mary Jane breaks off the stem of the rose and discards it, tucking the delicate flower into the tulle netting on Eva's hat. "I shan't leave your side. Not even for a second." She wraps her arm around Eva's shoulders, guiding her toward the daunting cluster. "You'll be perfectly safe."

Planting herself at the head of the group, she introduces Eva with no small amount of pride, letting her friends get a good eyeful before sliding into a padded booth running along one side of the table, those already seated shuffling down to accommodate them.

"So this is the one." Maria leers drunkenly across the table. "Very lovely she is, too."

"Keep your distance, wench." Mary Jane holds Eva protectively. "She's vowed to me, as I am to her."

Swaying over a glass of rum, Maria narrows her eyes at Eva, trying to place a faint glimmer of prior acquaintance. "Have we met afore?"

"Not really." Eva finds it difficult to look at her.

She's uncomfortable with Maria's proximity to Mary Jane, hates the thought of having to make pleasant conversation her, and is noticeably relieved when one of the topless girls arrives to take their order, her interruption preventing further dialogue.

"Whatchu having?"

Sticking to her word, Mary Jane orders them each a bottle of ginger beer. Along with those drinks, she requests two baked potatoes and some fish cakes.

"I ain't got enough coin to spare for all this," Eva whispers urgently. "I only gets one shilling and thruppence a day, and I needs most of that for rent."

"Don't you worry, love." Mary Jane kisses her cheek. "I'm treating you."

"You're sure it won't leave you short?"

"Positive." Mary Jane counts out the coins from her pocket. "In any case, what's the point of having a bloke to pay for everything if you can't indulge every once in a while, eh?"

She leaves out the fact that it wasn't Joe who provided the money for tonight's adventures, but a man dressed in an oversized baby's bonnet, holding a rattle. A man who, by the time she left the Stepney brothel, was weeping into a pillow, his buttocks raw and bleeding, rivulets of crimson liquid trickling down his hairy thighs. Just the way he likes it.

Fascinated by all the different goings on in the room, Eva surreptitiously casts her eyes from left to right,

catching women with loosened bodices fondling each other's breasts, couples kissing, caressing, and doing all that couples do.

"Many of the women here have husbands," Mary Jane explains without waiting for Eva to pose the query as to why such deep affections are being exchanged without so much as a drop of modesty. "They can't go home where the men are, and can't afford a room elsewhere. This is the only opportunity they have to explore their passions."

"Ain't they afeared of being caught by the coppers?"

"Caught doing what? We're breaking no law, love." Mary Jane pauses to thank the topless girl who brings them their ginger beers. "Some might not understand it— they might even be angered by it—but that don't make it wrong."

"Angered?" Eva stares into her lap. "Like my aunt?"

"Or worse."

Not wanting to put a scare in her, Mary Jane keeps to herself the well-concealed fact that Emma Smith was leaving the Velvet Teacup with another woman on the night she was attacked. As Mary Jane later learned, that's why she was assaulted so savagely by the gang. It wasn't merely about extortion, it was about hatred and intolerance.

She couldn't confess this to the police, of course. That would not only have disgraced her and put her companion at risk, but also exposed the Velvet Teacup, and this place is a lifeline for those in need of a little feminine affection. It's one of the few clandestine establishments in London where two women bonded in intimate love can be accepted for who they are, without fear or shame. It's a haven, and Eva's getting used to the idea.

As one of the other topless women walks by, her full, round breasts bouncing with each step, her prominent nipples teased stiff by the experienced ministrations of the last customer she served, Eva gawps.

"Oh, diddeys ..." She likens them to Mary Jane's. "This ain't like no place I've ever been in. However did you find it?"

"The violets," Mary Jane lets her in on a secret. "Most of us wear them, and if you ever should see violets painted on the side of a building, or spot a small sprig of them tucked by the corner of a window, you can be sure those premises are accepting of our ways."

Clueing in, Eva touches a finger to the violet pinned on Mary Jane's bodice. "That's why you pin this on every day." She turns her eyes back to the room, finding violets everywhere now that she's attuned to look for them.

"Careful, Mary Jane," one of the other women at the table cackles, pointing at a mesmerized Eva. "Her eyes is straying."

"No, they ain't." Eva snaps her head back. "I won't look no more, I promise. I was only—"

"Sshhh," Mary Jane cuts off her apology. "She was teasing, my love. No fretting." She gives the topless waitress a quick once over, seeing the resemblance. "Do they look like mine?" She unbuttons the top of her bodice and under-bodice, peeling back both layers to flash Eva her old lilac corset, no chemise beneath. "Shall we compare?"

Eva's interest is sufficiently redirected. First and foremost, by the ocular exploration of Mary Jane's cleavage. Secondly, by the arrival of their food.

As they eat, a large jug of beer is brought to the table and shared around, Maria taking it upon herself to pour Mary Jane a glass—much to Eva's chagrin.

"May we live to be a hundred years, with one extra year to repent!" She clinks their glasses together.

Following that, pipes are lit, cigarettes are passed from one hand to another, and the conversation turns bawdy. One of the younger women kicks the lewdness off by complaining of her last customer: a man known amongst them as Ten Second Teddy. Standing, she lifts her skirts to show how her red and black striped woolen stockings are covered in white splotches.

"He didn't even get his thing in me this time." She picks at a crusty patch of dried spunk on her knee. "He's mucked me right up, and them's me only good pair."

Mary Jane has a chuckle at her expense. "You have to cover his eyes. If he gets even so much as a glimpse of

what's coming at him, the anticipation fetches him directly."

Among the other stories shared, Mary Jane is goaded into telling of the time a father brought his fifteen-year-old son to her. He was convinced the lad was old enough to begin his learning of women, but the poor boy was shaking from head to toe. Accepting the father's money for her time nonetheless, Mary Jane took the child to a room in the Ringers' Buildings, sat him down on the bed, and assured him they didn't have to do anything untoward. Then, she instigated a pillow fight. By the time they left the room, her mane was in a tangle, her clothes were in a state of disarray, and they were both out of breath. One glance at her had the father suitably convinced that the business had been seen to, and everyone went home happy.

Unfortunately, not all tales are quite so pleasant. Eva ends up learning a lot more than she ever wanted to know about the flesh trade, including how one woman has to stuff a hanky in her mouth to prevent herself from laughing every time she has to take a man for a dry bob.

"It tickles," Maria says in her defense, taking it upon herself to volunteer a tale from Mary Jane's stock of horror stories, the short but graphic narrative leaving Eva with a very clear picture of a fella panting with lust, his prick working feverishly between Mary Jane's labia, his eyes riveted to her jiggling bosom and his clammy hands groping at her waist.

As if that weren't bad enough, she then gets to hear all about the various vulgar special requests made of these women on a regular basis, and a disturbing number of them involve urine.

Horrified, hoping much of it is exaggeration or invention, Eva seeks the truth from Mary Jane. "Do them really do all these larks?"

Overhearing the question, an older woman with sagging jowls and limp gray hair volunteers an answer. "Men'll put their things anywhere, love. In yer cunt, up yer arse, atween yer bubbies, in yer gob, or under yer arm. They ain't fussy. I reckon them'd put it in our bloody ear holes n'all if they could. I had one fella who wanted to

piddle up my cock-trap whilst he was having his shove. Dirty beast, he was."

In short order, more cigarettes make their way around the table, one of them reaching Eva. Not wanting to be thought immature, she takes it and puts it to her lips, trying a small, tentative puff, but it makes her cough and sputter. Thoroughly revolted by it, and left with a foul taste in her mouth, she thrusts it off on Mary Jane, having no desire ever to repeat the experience.

As she expects, Mary Jane passes the cigarette along without giving it a thought—smoking isn't her vice—but shortly thereafter, Eva sees her whisper something to the woman beside her, slipping her a coin. This coin makes its way down to the end of the table, and another cigarette—this one slightly larger and hastily hand rolled—is swiftly passed back up. Receiving it with thanks, Mary Jane lights it using the flame of a candle on the table and takes a deep draw from it, holding the smoke in her lungs for as long as she can.

Taken aback by the strong odor to it—as well as by the sight of Mary Jane smoking it—Eva flashes her a curious look.

"This one ain't tobacco." Mary Jane blows smoke at the ceiling.

"Whatever is it, then?" Eva wrinkles her nose up. "It's proper whiffy."

"Something what makes me very spreeish." Mary Jane leans over to nuzzle and kiss Eva's neck, making her blush and shy away.

"Get them lusty advances under control, Mary Jane," the woman seated beside Maria squawks, chucking a cachou at her head. "You's embarrassing the poor girl."

"You're gonna make my supper come up," someone else jokes.

From another, "For Gawd's sake, Mary Jane. Get the girl a room for the night."

"I wouldn't mind if you necked on me like that," Maria chimes in.

The unwanted commentary from her fuels Eva's smoldering jealousy. Harnessing courage, she plants a

deep kiss on Mary Jane's lips, not caring that she tastes of beer and has a lungful of the whiffy smoke.

When it ends, Mary Jane begs for more. "Eva, my darling ... do that again."

Finding it exhilarating to kiss in public—especially in front of Maria—Eva has no trouble going for seconds. This time, the passionate display triggers a wave of whistles and bawdy praise from the rest of their group, glasses and tankards being drummed against the tabletop, the percussion continuing until they finally break apart for air.

"You surprise me." Mary Jane stays close, pecking her nose. "I love you."

Things quiet down then. Once Mary Jane's cigarette is burnt down to a stub, she flicks it into the nearest ashtray, exhales the last breath of smoke, and grabs Eva's waist. With one firm tug, she heaves Eva onto her lap, holding her securely by the hips.

"I think I'm ready for bed. Are you?" She rocks her pelvis against Eva's buttocks, simulating phallic penetration. "May I take you home with me? I'll show you my doodle."

CHAPTER 38

MARY JANE AND EVA TUMBLE INTO MILLER'S COURT, kissing and groping. Held tight by the waist, eyes closed and walking backwards, being pushed into the room by Mary Jane, Eva is completely helpless. She clings to Mary Jane's neck for support, staggering on the uneven floor, afraid of knocking into something and taking a fall.

"Do slow down," she pleads, tearing her lips away. "Let's not be in such a rush."

Mary Jane aims her toward the bed, accidentally shoving her into the bedside table.

"Ow!" Eva fights her off, giggling. "Be gentle." She looks around the room, suddenly realizing there somewhere dark and chilly, her smiling waning. "Where are we?"

"My room." Mary Jane kicks the door closed and searches for a candle. "I know it ain't much, but it serves its purpose." She lights a half spent farthing dip, illuminating the dilapidated old parlor. "If it displeases you, we can go back to yours."

Eva shrugs, getting her first proper look at the place. "It's nice enough." She rubs her hands over her arms, feeling the damp seeping in. "You've got a fireplace at least. Plenty others don't have that."

"It's not as nice as what I had at Thrawl Street, but it's cheaper." Mary Jane sets the candle on the bedside table. "And I can't say as I care much what sort of place I live in, so long as I have some spare coin to put by each month."

Seeing the state of the unmade bed—the sheets rumpled and displaced, a small patch of dried semen soaked in where it trickled out of her after her last evening with Joe—she quickly rearranges things, pulling the blankets over the dried muck and fluffing the pillows. But that's not the only shame exposed by the candlelight. Behind her, Eva unpins her hat and sets it on the table, inspecting an array of empty liquor bottles there.

"I should've cleaned up." Mary Jane finds another bottle on the floor by her feet and rolls it under the bed, banishing it from sight. "I'm sorry."

Making no comment, Eva turns her attention to the mantel, admiring a cheap print propped there against the wall. It depicts a woman kneeling on the floor of her small cottage, crying in her mother's lap. Food is laid out on the table, uneaten, and a candle is about to gutter and die, having burned all night. Outside the cottage window, the tide rolls in on a beach, the sea empty and desolate.

"It's called A Hopeless Dawn." Mary Jane sweeps in behind her, embracing her. "I bought it from the Royal Academy of the Arts at their summer exhibition."

"It looks sad." Eva studies it.

"That was how I felt when I saw it. It reflected me perfectly." Mary Jane rests her chin on Eva's shoulder. "The young woman in the picture just became a widow. Her husband was a sailor, and she was waiting for his return, but he never came. He died at sea."

Spotting Mary Jane's higgledy-piggledy stack of newspapers on the floor, all of them open to pages reporting on foreign events or ocean travel, it doesn't take much of a leap for Eva to make the connection.

"You ain't a widow." She spins to face Mary Jane, feeling rotten for having caused her to fear the worst. "I came back home to you." She presses her palms to Mary Jane's cheeks. "You never lost me, and you never will."

"Promise?"

"A thousand times over." Eva kisses her. "I'm yours always."

Her simmering passions returning to a boil, Mary Jane pulls Eva to her chest. "I want you." She tugs up Eva's skirts. "Let's fuck."

"Oi!" Startled by such force, Eva denies her access. "Get me on your bed first." She relegates Mary Jane's roaming hands to her waist. "Don't think you're gonna be giving me a tickle without laying me down and treating me proper."

Suitably reprimanded for her clumsy haste, Mary Jane drags Eva to the bed. She intends to lower herself gracefully and alluringly to the palliasse, enticing Eva to join her, but she trips on an old clay pipe dropped by Joe. Her reflexes dulled on account of the cigarette she smoked, she hasn't the coordination to regain her balance. Spilling onto the bed, she lands arse first and pulls Eva down on top of her, the pair colliding hard.

"I ain't never seen you like this," Eva exclaims, lifting herself off Mary Jane's chest and straddling her. "Whatever was you smoking? Is that what's done it?" Her face falls, concern seeping in. "It weren't nuthin' bad, were it?"

"Course not, darling." Mary Jane flips them both over, positioning herself between Eva's spread thighs. "It was a little herbal remedy, that's all." Too impatient to undress her, she throws up Eva's skirts, fumbling for the split in her drawers. "I need to taste you."

"Mary Jane!" Eva squeals, frightened that her undergarments will get torn. "Be careful."

"Blasted buggering things." Mary Jane finds the overlapping flaps and wiggles her fingers through them, yanking the hole open and diving for Eva's crotch, lavishing kisses on her motte before pressing the flat of her tongue to the pink flesh below.

Determined to watch her at work, Eva beats the puffiness out of her bunched up skirts, flattening them to her belly and craning her neck, trying to get a better view of Mary Jane's bobbing head. She wishes there was a cheval mirror in the room.

At the introduction of Mary Jane's fingers, she drops one leg off the edge of the bed, plants her foot on the floor for leverage, and grinds her hips up to Mary Jane's face.

The movement enhances the sensations pulsing through her core, but also makes it nearly impossible for Mary Jane's mouth to remain locked on her clit.

Remedying that, she clamps one hand to the back of Mary Jane's head, aiding her in the pursuit.

"Oh, Em!" She clutches the headboard with her free hand, anchoring herself there. "I'm gonna make such a mess of your sheets."

On the verge of a spend, she bucks and twists and writhes, her pleasure disrupted seconds before the onset of her paroxysm by the sudden opening of the door, a heavy-footed and mildly inebriated Joe striding into Mary Jane's room without announcing his arrival.

"What the flaming hell ... ?" He rubs his eyes, squinting at the bed.

At the sound of his voice, Mary Jane whips her head up and Eva lets out an unearthly shriek. Jerking herself away, Eva uncunts Mary Jane's fingers and retreats to the far side of the bed, curling into a fetal ball and pulling her skirts down to her ankles. Utterly horrified, and scared to witness Joe's reaction, she keeps her back to the room, waiting for Mary Jane to pacify him before she dare even breathe.

Surprisingly calm—having the 'herbal remedy' to thank for that as well as her slight lack of co-ordination—Mary Jane sits up and scowls at him, licking traces of Eva's dew off her lips. "Can't you knock, you great big arse? I have company."

"Are you tailing a whore in our bed?" Joe takes a step closer.

"It's *my* bed, so I can tail who I want in it." Mary Jane clambers to her feet, standing defensively—albeit unsteadily—between him and Eva. "And the only whore in this room is me."

Mere inches in front of her, he studies her for signs of intoxication. "You been drinking again?" He grabs her chin, tilting her face toward the light, examining her dilated pupils. "Or is it summink else this time?"

"That ain't none of your business." Mary Jane smacks his hand away and stares him down, not moving a muscle until the silent standoff is broken by Eva's plaintive cries.

"Mary Jane," she mewls from the bed. "I want to leave." She shuffles behind her protector, hiding from Joe.

"It's all right, my darling." Mary Jane keeps one eye on Joe and reaches for Eva's hand, pulling her to her feet. "I'll walk you home. There's no harm done."

Keeping between them, she guides Eva to the table to retrieve her hat, and from there to the door, Joe seizing her by the arm before she can get to it.

"She's got her own feet, ain't she?"

"I ain't letting her walk alone." Mary Jane wrests herself free. "You know how the streets are at this time of night, after all the pubs kick out. That is why you're here, ain't it? Like all the other men out there looking for a place to lay their head, you've had your drink and now you want your poke." She snatches her shawl off a hook on the back of the door. "Well, you can fucking wait for it." She flings the door open and ushers Eva through it. "I'll be back in a few."

She makes sure the door slams hard behind her and escorts a traumatized Eva out of Miller's Court. This is the worst time for a woman to be out on the street, and within a minute of leaving, some drunken rough is hurling vulgarities in Eva's direction.

"Lay a bloody finger on her, and you'll have me to answer to." Mary Jane, now on a short tether, clenches her fists, fully prepared to wallop him. "I'll beat you worse than your old mam did when she caught you peeking up her skirts, you nasty little turd."

"Please don't." Eva wrangles her, squeezing her arm, begging her to walk away. "He ain't worth a fight." She pulls Mary Jane to her. "Just get me home."

Biting her tongue, Mary Jane manages to do that without further incident, walking Eva down Thrawl Street and through the covered passageway into the Lolesworth courtyard. There, saying goodbye at the bottom of the stone stairwell, Eva stands on her tippy-toes, flinging her arms around Mary Jane's neck.

"Will I see you tomorra?"

"You might," Mary Jane teases. "I'll have to check my engagement book to see if I can fit you in between my weekly manicure and afternoon tea with the Queen."

That generates only a fleeting smile.

"I'm sorry about Joe." She holds Eva to her chest. "I never know when the fool might be by these days, and—"

"Thank you for taking me out tonight." Eva tries to put a positive spin on the evening. "I liked going to that place. It was nice to be seen with you that way, and I was mostly having fun right up until the end." She peers up at Mary Jane, racked with anxiety. "He won't hurt you, will he?"

Mary Jane shakes her head. "He ain't that kind of bloke, so don't waste another thought on it." She wipes a tear from Eva's cheek. "Are we all right, though? I feel as though I keep mucking things up."

"You ain't done nuthin' wrong." Eva sinks back into Mary Jane's arms, reluctant to part from her. "It weren't your fault."

Equally disinclined to end the night on such a flat note, Mary Jane tries to reignite the dampened spark with soft caresses and a few gentle words. "I don't want to let you go," she whispers, her hot breath kissing Eva's neck. "Invite me up."

Still concerned about Joe's temper, Eva hesitates. "Don't you have to be getting back?"

"Invite me up," Mary Jane insists, fondling her rump. "Let's finish what we started."

"But he's waiting for you." Eva sulks, separating herself. "And I ain't in the mood for it no more anyhow."

"Are you sure?" Not about to give up so easily, Mary Jane recaptures her, chancing a wet kiss. "Let me take you to bed. Let me make your cunt weep."

Though weakening, Eva still dithers.

Refusing to quit, and ready to deploy everything in her arsenal in order to garner an invite into the little sanctuary of Eva's charms, Mary Jane calls upon some of the few scraps of the bawdiest French she ever learnt.

"*J'ai envie de toi, ma chérie*," she whispers hotly. "*Je veux te baiser*."

At the first syllable, Eva melts in her arms. "What's it mean?"

"I want you, my darling," Mary Jane tenders a translation. "I want to fuck you."

The effect of those words is immediate.

Eva surrenders.

"How am I to resist when you say such perfectly sweet things?" She takes Mary Jane by the hand and leads her up the darkened steps, flashing her a coy smile. "You may have your way with me tonight, Miss Kelly. I shall permit you."

Inside her tiny room—which is far warmer, drier, and certainly a good deal cleaner than Mary Jane's—she strips to her corset and chemise and positions herself on the edge of the palliasse, letting Mary Jane see to the curtains and candles. When all's ready, Mary Jane kneels at the side of the bed.

"This is much better already." She kisses her way up Eva's bare thighs, glad that the dreaded cotton barricade has been cast off. "So much nicer."

"I dunno if I'll be able to do it," Eva cautions, watching Mary Jane's ascent toward her core. "It was nearly coming over me when ..."

Those words die on her lips as Mary Jane's mouth reaches its target. A minute later, when Mary Jane's fingers enter her again, all doubts are erased.

"Oh, Em, fetch me a towel. Quick!" Her orgasm builds rapidly, taking her by surprise. "I've got that piddling feeling." She grasps at Mary Jane's head, her thighs twitching uncontrollably. "I'm gonna gush, I know it, and I ain't got no cleaner sheets."

Ignoring the warning, Mary Jane brings on her peak. Fully prepared to receive whatever Eva is about to give her, she clamps her mouth over Eva's sex, drinking the salty, sweet amatory juice as it pours from her, swallowing almost every precious drop.

Overwhelmed by the sight—half worrying that she might drown Mary Jane in her spend—Eva forgets to breathe. In the grip of her climax, she slips into a swoon, first becoming dizzy, then faint, then passing out, her eyes rolling back till only the whites show.

"Mmm." Mary Jane rises from the floor, dabbing at her sex-coated lips. "That's better than gin. I could drink it in buckets."

Finding Eva unresponsive, she leans over the bed and taps her flushed cheeks, trying to revive her. It doesn't work. Checking to make sure she's still breathing, Mary Jane places her palm flat on Eva's chest, relieved to feel her ribcage rising and falling in rhythm, albeit slow and shallow.

Afraid that her clothing might be constricting her, she unfastens Eva's corset, relieving the pressure on her lungs. When that doesn't seem to help, she looks around for smelling salts—a corseted woman's staple—and eventually finds a small bottle in a basket containing other odds and ends of female importance, including a catamenial bandage and a razor.

"Darling." She wafts the harsh ammonia under Eva's nose. "Come back to me."

That does the trick and Eva wakes with a jolt, immediately sitting up to inspect the state of the bed, shocked to find only a small puddle between her legs.

"Lummy ..." She runs a hand over her saturated grummit. "Where'd it all go?"

Giggling, Mary Jane sticks out her tongue and licks the tip of Eva's nose. "I drank you."

"You never did?" Eva's eyes widen. "The whole lot?"

"You're delicious." Mary Jane lounges on the bed with her, making the most of every last second. "I wish I could stay."

Saddened by the prospect of her imminent departure, Eva tucks herself into a ball. "What must you give him tonight?"

"Oh, darling." Mary Jane strokes her hair. "Don't ask." She gets up, setting the smelling salts on the mantel. "Just know that it gives me no pleasure."

"I'm being daft, ain't I?" Eva tosses her corset to the foot of the bed and slumps against the headboard. "I knows it ain't your choice."

"It ain't daft." Mary Jane leans over the bed to give her a kiss. "I hate this. I hate leaving your bed for ..." She can't bring herself to say it. "But it puts money on the

table, and it's only for a few more months—don't forget that. I love you."

She takes one more kiss from Eva's lips, then forces herself to leave, returning to Miller's Court much sobered. Before going inside, she takes a moment to steel herself for the punishment ahead, drawing breath deep into her lungs through her nose and exhaling through her mouth. When she's ready to face him, she swings open the door, breezing into her room with a practiced aloofness, suppressing her irrational loathing for the man sitting on her bed.

"Still here, then." She flings her shawl over the back of a chair, her attention snagged by a few coins stacked on the table.

"What took you?" Joe asks, removing his waistcoat and shirt.

"I had to finish what you interrupted." Mary Jane counts the money, separating it into its various denominations. "I weren't gonna leave her hot."

"How long you been bedding that one?" Joe pulls off his boots, releasing a stench akin to aged cheese and rotten cabbage.

"Longer than I've been bedding you," Mary Jane replies, totting up his offering. "Three bob? Is that all?" She turns to him, scoffing at the pittance. "I don't see you for a week, then you show up unannounced with three lousy shillings?!"

"Better than nuthin', ain't it?" He tears down the blankets on the bed, inspecting the sheets for any sign that Mary Jane's been in the company of other men.

"You reckon so?" She snorts, scooping the tarnished coins—two shillings, nine pennies, three ha-pennies, and six farthings—into the palm of her hand and hurling them in his direction, sending them clattering all over the floor, losing at least one farthing under the warped boards. "It ain't even enough for my rent, you cheap bastard." She plants both hands on her hips. "Where you been anyway? You been sticking your pipe in another tart? Is that why you've got nothing left to give me? You spent it all on drink and some pox-ridden doxy."

KEIRA MICHELLE TELFORD

Joe fixes her with a glare. "You done ranting at me, woman? I ain't been seeing no-one else. You know me better than that, duntcha?"

"What is it, then?" Mary Jane demands to know, her cool façade evaporated. "Did I get a week older and go down in value? Is my cunt not as tight? That wife of yours giving you grief? Or are you just being a stingy arsehole all a sudden?"

"I lost my job," he mumbles, staring at the floor.

"You what?"

"I got the bloody sack," he snaps at her. "I ain't got no spare coin at the minute."

Silence.

Mary Jane glowers at him. "You'd best be pulling my leg."

"I've been doing casual work this past fortnight, and I shall keep doing so." He gets up, his hands pressed together as if in prayer, beseeching her to show compassion. "I'll find summink proper soon enough."

As he steps within arm's reach, she lashes out, slapping his face. "What did you do?"

"Nuthin'," he claims indignantly, his denial garnering him another sharp slap.

"Don't you lie to me, Joseph Barnett." Mary Jane wags a finger in his face. "What did you do?! They ain't just gone and given you a sacking for nothing."

"I took some fish to pay off a debt, that's all."

"You stole?!" She raises her hand to strike him again, but he grabs her wrist.

"Enough!" He holds her off. "I didn't come here to fight with ya."

"No, you came here thinking you could help yourself to me for a trifle, after you tossed God knows how much away in the pub."

"I paid you, didn't I?" He grips her harder, preventing her from struggling. "Or don't you want my money? You'd rather get your bubbies out and find your supper on the street?"

Mary Jane falls silent.

"Aye, that's what I thought." He maneuvers her toward the bed. "Now get on."

"Ease off, Joe." She twists out of his grasp. "I need my thing-bob."

Forcing him to give her some space, she fishes the concave rubber disk out of a basket on the floor, props her foot on the bed, and inserts it, her time with Eva having left her lubricated enough to accomplish the fiddly task with relative ease. By the time she's done, Joe's trousers are around his ankles, his erect cock jutting out from a dense mass of light brown curls.

Since he usually expects reciprocal nudity, she reaches for the top button of her bodice, preparing to unrig, but tonight he hurries her on.

"Don't bother with all that." He urges her onto the bed, pushing her down on all fours. "I'll be quick tonight." He climbs on behind her and throws up her skirts, his fat pego prodding her naked buttocks. "I ain't had my pipe emptied since I last seen ya."

She grits her teeth, waiting to be impaled, but instead feels his fingers invading her wetness.

"Whatchu doing?" She wriggles her backside, trying to uncunt him.

"Is that what your girl does to ya?" He probes her channel.

"Are you complaining?" she growls, glaring at him over her shoulder. "Hurry up and get it in me before I lose my patience with you."

With a grunt, he pulls his fingers out and replaces them with his prick, slamming into her hard and fast, showing no consideration for her comfort. All the while, she sobs quietly into her pillow, her immediate future now suddenly uncertain.

CHAPTER 39

CRIME IN EAST LONDON

"It has been our unpleasant duty, these last few weeks, to chronicle an exceptional amount of crime which has been committed in the East End. We readily admit that it is to the sensitive mind unpalatable reading, but the obligation is laid upon a newspaper to reveal in its social diagnosis the worst as well as the best features of human action. This week, the record of crime has been increased by another tragic murder, together with three cases of supposed infanticide. So quickly has one tragedy followed another that it would almost seem as if there was a reason for crime as well as a reason for everything else. But after all, reducible as most things are now to a spiritual or natural law, all these unhappy circumstances may only be a chain of singular coincidences, having not the remotest connection with each other. However, it is not our present intention to view the facts from a scientific or psychical standpoint, but to consider them in a social and general aspect.

Now a murder in Whitechapel or Bethnal Green is regarded by the public altogether differently from a similar occurrence in Belgravia or Mayfair. 'Crime clothed in greatness'—or in wealth, the two are identical—is always treated very tenderly by Mrs. Grundy, who has ever much sympathy for those 'rich in this world's goods.' But let a poor man sin in East London—that dreadful vile place to her way of

thinking—then 'virtue rears a high seat, and justice stern must fill it.' Perhaps she even goes so far as to suggest a moral top-boots and blanket society for the poor savages in the howling wilderness of the East End. Indeed, some fearful-minded persons think the inhabitants of particular parts of our district are all ruffians and viragos who acquired a taste for thieving and violence in their mother's arms.

The finger of scorn is only too frequently held up to us by those whose sense of justice, and even common honesty, should tell them how undeserved is this wholesale condemnation. Such opinions and sentiments are so ridiculous that were it not for the harm they do, it would not be worthwhile to notice them. What are the facts? The statistics or returns of criminal offenses show that, in proportion, there is really no more crime, either of a greater or lesser degree, in East London than in any other part of the metropolis, or, for the matter of that, in Great Britain. Taking into consideration its area, which is extensive, and its population, which is most varied, there is but an ordinary average of public offense, although the customary sensational headline, 'Another East-End Tragedy,' is frequently to be met with.

Now, it is very much easier to particularize loosely and condemn than to generalize logically and be just. Notwithstanding the unusual amount of recent crime in our district—crimes in which the worst human passions have been shown in all their fiendish ignominy—there is no cause for despair over the state of the people. Strike an average in this generation and in the last, and when they are compared together, there will be shown a happy improvement in our condition. East London is not on a moral and social 'down grade,' for the lower strata in our population, in which most of these evils arise, is slowly but surely being reached by the influences of a better age and a truer charity."

-- East London Advertiser, August 25, 1888

CHAPTER 40

Thursday, August 30, 1888

BECOMING INCREASINGLY DOWNHEARTED, MARY JANE adds together an updated list of the potential costs involved in getting Eva out of London. Over the course of the last year, she's made hundreds of these lists, each one simpler than the last, each one making more concessions for less available funds, and each one ending up burnt in the fireplace.

There are so many variables. Annual rent for a small coffeehouse could be as low as sixty pounds, or as much as a hundred and sixty, depending on the location and the number of rooms above. She rather fancies running a public house, but Eva would never tolerate it. What else could she do? She once received some training as a seamstress, but didn't complete her apprenticeship and has never worked on the machines. Though she's still fairly skilled with her fingers—enough to complete the odd bit of piecework here and there, and to make up her own dresses from the cut fabric—her eyes suffer in the work.

During the brief term of her instruction in the craft, she—and several other girls alike to her in age and circumstance—were set to work in the garret room of an old convent, the nuns being their teachers. It was all very well when the sun was up and beaming down through the skylight windows, but after sunset, they would all huddle around a single candle, the older, more experienced girls

473

always stealing the best light. Her eyesight was never as sharp after that.

As she's about to commence another set of calculations, factoring out the possibility of picking up more work in that occupation, her stomach grumbles, reminding her that it's dinnertime. Setting down her pen with a sigh, she reaches for the bottle of ginger beer she's been nursing since mid-morning and finishes it off, then counts up all the coins in her pockets, there being only two pennies and a farthing.

It's been several weeks since Joe lost his job, and his compliments—those of a monetary nature and otherwise—have been wildly irregular, just like his visits. Sometimes, he shows up with her full rent and spends the whole night. Other times, he brings her a piece of meat or fish—probably stolen—and has her use her mouth on him before he hurries home to his legitimate skirt.

Budgeting a penny for dinner, she makes a quick trip to Thrawl Street and buys herself a portion of fish and chips, consuming most of it in the short time it takes her to walk back to Miller's Court. Once home, she plans on taking a quick nap before tackling the numbers again, but gets a shock to find Joe sitting at her table, stuffing tobacco in his pipe.

"Jesus Christ." She slaps the remnants of her dinner on top of the arithmetic she left out, hoping he didn't peep at it. "How'd you get in here?"

"You left the door on the latch." He lays the pipe down. "Where's you been?" He glances at the food. "And where'd you get the money for that? You working again?"

"You would really ask me that?" Mary Jane's jaw tightens. "This body has to eat, and I do what I have to, as I've always done. Whatever that entails ain't none of your concern."

"I should say it bloody well is." He gets up, moving toward her. "You're my woman."

"Let's not have this conversation again, Joe." Mary Jane angles her back to him, picking at the scraps left of her food. "You've no right to tell me to keep my cunt in at night. I ain't your woman, or your wife, I'm your whore."

"Aye, *mine*." He lays his heavy hands on her waist, rubbing her with his thumbs. "I don't like you on the street."

Suppressing the impulse to punch him in the gut and run off, she instead leans over the table and juts out her rump, pushing it into his crotch. "I don't care for it that much, either, just so as you know." She softens her voice, wiggling her buttocks against a hard lump in his trousers. "I'd much rather be with you."

"I love you," he growls, gliding his hands up her bodice and grabbing her breasts.

Not in the mood to be molested in such a manner, she pivots in his arms. "Love ain't gonna pay my rent." She runs a hand over his chest, noting that his clothes are a shade dirtier than usual, his overall appearance a touch more ragged. "You got anything for me?" She drops her hand lower, squeezing the erection lurking in his trousers.

"Aye." He groans, digging in his pockets and pulling out three florins. "That's the rest of the rent I promised for this week, and then some." He flicks it onto the table, returning his hands to her waist. "What'll it get me?"

Underwhelmed by the donation, but willing to take whatever she can get from him, Mary Jane offers him her breasts, agreeing to full nudity as an added perk. That being settled upon, she removes her clothing and lies down on the bed, waiting for him to drop his trousers and slather his cock in cold cream.

Though at best this operation is uncomfortable—at worst, painful—she'd rather have him on her than in her, even if it is repulsive. As he straddles her chest, his sagging cods plop on her sternum, the lopsided balls swollen with lust.

"Look how big them are." He catches her looking and shows them off to her, mistakenly thinking she's impressed. "Full o'spunk." He fondles them. "I ain't had a come in days."

"How lucky am I?" she mumbles, wincing as his coarse hands envelop her breasts, squashing them around his lubricated prick.

Satisfied with the position, he begins to thrust, slowing to twiddle his thumbs over her nipples at intervals. All seems to be going well, but he wants more.

"I need to have in you," he declares, freeing her breasts and shuffling down to her crotch.

"No!" She clamps her thighs closed, panicked by the thought of accepting him inside her. "I ain't got my thing-bob in."

"Let me." He wrenches her legs open. "I shan't wet inside."

"Oh, aye?" she scoffs. "I've heard that before."

She tries to get her feet on his shoulders to push him off, but he's too strong for her. Pinning her knees to her chest, he forces his tumescent rod up her channel and commences rutting on her like a wild beast.

"You'd best not put your stuff in me, Joe Barnett." She writhes and bucks beneath him, trying desperately to uncunt him. "Or I swear you won't never get near me again."

"Oh, it's coming." He moves faster, her frantic squirming doing little but to drive him closer and closer toward his crisis.

"Don't you dare make a mess of me!" She beats a fist at him.

"Ha! I'll show you a mess." Triumphant, he withdraws at the last moment. Gripping his cock in his hand, he aims it at her body, his hot salty muck jetting out onto her stomach, breasts, and face.

"Ugh!" She shields her eyes. "You filthy bastard!"

Laughing, he gets up and hunts down a towel by the washstand. "That was a jolly lark." He wipes off his withering instrument, then tosses the towel at her. "I told you I weren't gonna give you a wetting, so don't whinge about it."

"Feel better now?" She sits up, mopping globs of his mucilage off her cheeks and neck. "Now that you've marked your territory."

Ignoring that, he pulls on his trousers, preparing to leave. "I'll come by again in a few days." He gathers up his pipe, hat, and jacket. "If you know what's good for ya, you'll be here."

Happy to see the back of him for the time being, Mary Jane clambers out of bed and gives herself a proper wash, swilling out her insides with alum and zinc sulphate as well as vinegar, even though he didn't finish in her. When she's done, she starts to get dressed, hesitating before she puts on her bodice.

The income she's receiving from Joe simply isn't enough, and it'll be days before her next appointment with a special. Everything she was just given must go on rent, which leaves her very little for supper and breakfast, and nothing at all for Eva. It won't do.

In the secluded courtyard beside the Ringers' Buildings, Mary Jane crouches on the straw and dung strewn ground, fighting the reflex to vomit as she works her mouth up and down the shaft of a stranger's prick, trying not to breathe.

The man is a tosher, and it's not his fault but he stinks. Such is the nature of his work that the stench of feces is permanently leeched into his clothes, his hair, and oozing from his pores. No wonder he's forty and unmarried. What woman could stand it? He spends his days scavenging the sewers for anything of value, poking around in the muck with an old hoe, looking for silver-plated cutlery, lost jewelry, and the occasional coin. It's revolting, but he regularly brings home two pound a week.

When he erupts without warning, she almost chokes. The first spurt of spermatic fluid hits her tonsils and drips down her throat, making her gag, and the only thing preventing her from pulling away and gasping for air is the man's hand on the back of her head. He holds her there till he's done, then she jerks away from him, spitting on the ground.

477

"All better, my dear?" She coughs and sputters, wiping her lips.

A shilling no longer seems enough compensation for the work. To get rid of the bad taste left in her mouth by the unsavory business—both literally and figuratively—and to shelter from a sudden thunderstorm, she stops in at the Britannia and orders herself a beer, catching sight of her reflection in a mirror as she sits down at the bar.

This is the first time in over a year that she's completely let down her auburn mane, dabbed on some red lip paste, and worn her old bodice with her décolletage on display, and she barely recognizes herself. Far from being proud to flaunt her womanly assets, as she once was, she now feels cheap and ashamed, the advertisement of her charms no longer representing a display of her beauty, but of her disgrace.

In need of some distraction from her heavy thoughts, she flicks through a copy of today's Echo left behind on the empty stool beside her, and gets caught up in a story about a married woman from Hahn Street, Whitechapel, who recently charged her husband with assault after he 'beat her with a broom, caught her by the hair of her head, and punched her in the face.' According to her testimony, he was 'in the habit of thrashing her.' His punishment for this? He was bound over to keep the peace. Even if he defaults, he'll only be sent to prison for seven days.

"Men are arseholes," Mary Jane mutters under her breath, lamenting her path in life, having taken her own fair share of beatings.

"Blimey, don't you look bloody miserable?" Maria appears beside her, shaking rain off her shawl and helping herself to the empty stool. "Who died?"

"Only my dignity." Mary Jane discards the paper, not caring for the news it brings.

"Why? What's gone on?" Maria glances at Mary Jane's dress, knowing what she's resorted to. "You short on funds? Ain't that Barnett fella taking care of you no more?"

"He lost his job." Mary Jane sips her drink, the taste of the tosher coming back to her. "I tried taking one

tonight, but it seems worse than I remember." She peeks again at her reflection, grimacing at the paphian staring back at her. "I can't do this no more."

"What else can you do, then? How about that other bloke of yours?" Maria suggests, ignorant of Fleming's abusive ways. "Any chance you can bilk summink out of him? He's still sweet on you, ain't he? It'd be better than taking some fat, bald bloke down a slimy alley."

Disinclined to relate the whole story, Mary Jane shrugs. "I haven't seen him in a while."

"Well, maybe you should." Maria gives her a nudge, encouraging her to buck up. "It won't do you no good to sit here moping."

That might be true, but Mary Jane has no intention of seeing Fleming. After a second glass of beer and the clearing of the storm, she takes to the streets again, determined to re-acclimate herself to the work, but finds herself rejecting one potential customer after another for a whole host of increasingly ludicrous reasons. One had some kind of foul-smelling weasel living in his trouser pocket, and she couldn't face another stinker. One had a metal hook prosthetic in place of his left hand, and she was scared of getting poked in the eye. Another was a pure collector, and so was in possession of a dirty shovel and a sack of animal feces, his job being to wander the streets scraping animal turds off the ground. The one after that was simply too ugly.

On her way back down Commercial Street, having refused the last man on account of him only being in possession of one shoe, his exposed foot ravaged with some vile fungal infection, she spots Fleming entering the Victoria Home for Working Men: the four-storey model lodging house on the southwestern corner of Wentworth Street.

This expansive property—a former warehouse—provides five hundred beds for working men, mostly in the form of long dormitories containing ten to twelve beds each, with some private 'cabins' available on the top floor.

Unlike so many other lodging houses in the area, this one is picky about its residents. Order and decorum

are insisted upon, and its rules must be observed at all times. Those with a reputation for being 'bad characters' will not be admitted. If you stumble home from the pub intoxicated, expect to be sent away. If you use coarse or obscene language, or cause problems with any of the other lodgers, you'll be ejected.

Submitting much too easily—convincing herself that it's the much lesser of two great evils—Mary Jane alters her course, turns down Wentworth Street, and slips along a small cul-de-sac providing rear access to the Victoria Home. Since women are excluded from the lodging house at all times, if she's to enter, then she must sneak in through the back.

Creeping up to the unguarded door, past a few ramshackle dwellings and an old shed, she tucks herself into a secluded corner and checks the state of her bone-dry commodity, her presence ignored by an elderly woman beating an old rug out of a window and some feral children playing in an open hay loft.

It's always been routine for her to indulge in some cuntal manipulations before going to work, as it not only leaves her well-lubricated and lessens the discomfort caused by so many unwanted male intrusions, but also serves well to delude even the savviest of customers into thinking she shares their need of a fuck. So, pressing her back to the wall, she gives herself a tickle, conjuring up a daydream of Eva for inspiration.

Suitably rosy-cheeked, she then eases open the unlocked back door, relying upon it being wedged ajar with a lump of brick or a stick for the benefit of those most daring residents who wish to welcome in a bit of entertainment on the sly.

In that event, the business is seen to swiftly and quietly in a back storage room filled with cleaning equipment and old pots, and Mary Jane knows that the lodging house deputy, if caught in the right mood, will happily look the other way. After all, a little light exercise before bed can be inordinately beneficial to the mental and physical wellbeing of the lodgers.

Sometimes, the men form a neat line in the back corridor, waiting their turn with whatever cyprian

happens to be available. On these nights, a trio of harlots have been known to work in rotation, taking up to ten men in a row before swapping out to have a quick wash.

It's all extremely well organized. A shilling gets you five minutes, which is more than enough for most men. At the door, the first harlot inspects each incoming prick for cleanliness and health, then passes him on to the next, who—perched on the edge of a table, ready to receive him—pockets his money and lets him go up her, while the third member of the trio times the business on a pocket watch, promptly cutting off the operation when his allotted session expires.

On the face of it, a shilling doesn't seem like much, but with five hundred beds in the lodging house and word spreading fast, there's plenty coin to be made with very little work. Once, Mary Jane took a total of twenty men here in under two hours. The first five went in a row, each one going up into the spendings of the one before, then she washed and the cycle was repeated. She walked away with a pound for her time, but fear of disease kept her from going back for more.

She's never known of any women being invited up to the bedrooms for private sessions, and at the risk of being forcibly removed from the premises, she makes for the nearest staircase, walking on tiptoe so that her heels don't clack on the floor.

It's almost suppertime, and the comforting smell of cooking meat drifts up from the communal kitchens in the basement, making her hungry again. A proper dinner can be had here for only fourpence, or you can get a bowl of soup for a penny, and Mary Jane knows a few women from the Velvet Teacup who are so convincing in their male attire that they frequently bed here, and brag of the decent hot meals available.

Indeed, for those who can get away with it, these are easily the best lodgings in Whitechapel. A bed in one of the dorms is just fourpence a night, or you can get a ticket for the whole week for two bob if you pay upfront. The private rooms are sixpence, or three bob for the week, which makes them comparable to the Peabody Buildings,

or to Lolesworth, but with the added benefit of the communal kitchens and the washing facilities.

What Mary Jane wouldn't give for the washing facilities! Not only are there flushing lavatories, but there are baths! A warm bath will set you back a penny, but that's a price Mary Jane would gladly pay if it meant not having to repeatedly heat small amounts of water in her tiny kettle, only to fill her tin bath with barely enough water to cover her ankles.

Pushing aside her envy, she begins her search for Fleming on the top floor, where the private cabins are located. He'd never settle for a dormitory bed. Each room here is numbered, the last name of the long-term occupant scrawled on a tiny blackboard hung there on a peg, and she keeps her eyes peeled.

Since silence must be observed on the sleeping floors at all times, no man who catches sight of her dares to cause a fuss for fear of commencing a ruckus and being pegged as a troublemaker. Lucky for her. When she eventually locates a room marked with Fleming's name, she flings open the door without knocking, finding the room empty. He's not there.

As she expected, these lodgings are simple but nice. The single bed—comprised of a well-stuffed mattress on a sturdy iron bedstead—has two sheets, two blankets, and a thick quilt. That's more than she has at Miller's Court. There's even a small writing desk, a chair, and a washbasin—everything a person needs. To top it off, a working sash window—one with all its panes of glass intact—lets in a reasonable amount of light and keeps the room well ventilated. There's not a trace of any mold.

Taking a closer look, she spots the handle of a small clasp knife sticking out from under a pillow, immediately recognizing it as the one he twice put to her throat. Besides that, Fleming has very few personal belongings. There's a small cloth bag of clothing stashed underneath the bed, a hat and his great coat on a hook on the wall, and some odds and ends on the writing desk. Amongst those odds and ends, she notices he has a small collection of newspaper clippings.

All of them are about the gruesome murder in George Yard, the first clipping being from the Echo on August 23:

"No further clue has, up to the present, been gained by the police as to the perpetrator of the murder of the woman whose body was found on the landing of George Yard Buildings, Whitechapel, on the morning of August 7. The Deputy Coroner resumed the inquest on the body of the murdered woman this afternoon, in the Library of the Working Lads' Institute, Whitechapel Road."

The next clipping is from the Star on August 24:

"The mystery surrounding the murder of Martha Tabram in George Yard, Whitechapel, has not been cleared up. The woman, it may be remembered, was found brutally murdered, no fewer than about thirty stabs having been inflicted on her body. The husband of the woman can only speak of her antecedents and her drunken habits. Inspector Reid is still hard at work following up probable clues, and made a statement of the efforts made by the police to trace the perpetrators of the murder. He said a large number of persons had volunteered statements, and in each case the statement had been thrashed out."

Next to that, there's a clipping from the East London Observer on August 25:

"The resumed inquiry into the death of the woman, Martha Tabram, who was found on the morning after Bank Holiday, lying on the first-floor landing at 37 George Yard, Whitechapel, wounded in thirty-nine places and dead, took place on Thursday afternoon ..."

"What d'you want?"

Fleming's voice startles her and she spins around, finding him standing in the doorway. Returning from a bath, his shirt is slung over one shoulder, a towel over the

other, his chest still glistening with moisture and his hair dripping down his back.

"Hello, lover." Mary Jane smiles sweetly.

"You can't be in here." He points to the door. "Get out now. I don't wanna see you."

"Since when?" Mary Jane sits on the bed, feigning nonchalance as she lifts her skirts to adjust a garter that's in no need of adjusting. "You don't want to fuck me no more?"

"You wanna know how I feel about you?" He strides over, grabs a fistful of her glossy auburn locks, and yanks her off the bed. "You sicken me."

"Ow, Joe!" Mary Jane elbows his chest. "Gerroff me!"

He clamps a hand over her mouth, quieting her. "You come here looking for money, is that it?" He scowls at her bodice. "You started whoring again?"

She bites down on his finger.

"Bitch!" he hisses, jerking away his hand and releasing her hair.

"Oh, come on, Joe. Don't be like that." Mary Jane swallows her hatred, willing to say whatever needs to be said if it means walking away with coin in her pocket. "I miss you."

"Miss me?" He backs her up against the wall, nursing his wounded hand. "You put an end to us when you started dipping your fingers in your own kind."

"That's what you're so sore about?" Mary Jane reins in her revulsion and palms his swelling priapus through his trousers. "I don't know my own mind, Joe. It's been so long since I've had a proper good fuck, that's all. Don't you wanna set me straight? Remind me what it's like to have a nice, fat prick up me."

He looms over her, his eyes hard and full of loathing. "I hate what you do to me."

Seizing her by the arm, he manhandles her onto the bed, shoving her down headfirst and demanding that she get on her knees.

"That's it." She complies willingly, presenting her arse to him, expecting to receive him dog fashion. "Fuck me, Joe. I know you want to."

"Shut up." He pushes her face into the pillow, stifling her, then unbuttons his cock and forces it up her well-prepared channel, driving it inside her as hard as he can, as if he means to do her some damage with it, grunting with the exertion of every firm thrust.

To get better leverage, he leans over her, putting his weight on her head and shoulders, suffocating her every time he hilts himself. At first, she struggles, her screams muffled by the fabric. Then, all resistance ceases.

"I could kill you," he snarls, bearing down on her, her face smothered in the pillow, her neck contorted so awkwardly it looks like it might snap.

Reaching his crisis, he rams himself up to the root, injecting his seed into her depths, his thighs trembling with the force of his ejaculation. Once every drop's been milked from him, he withdraws and buttons himself up, exhibiting not an ounce of concern as her limp body flops onto the mattress, her face still buried in the bed linens.

"Get up." He kicks her.

She doesn't move.

"I said get up." He furls her flowing mane around his hand and yanks her backwards off the bed, causing her to hit the hardwood floor with a heavy thud, the sudden jolt reviving her.

Gasping and sputtering, she rolls onto all fours, trying to draw air into her lungs. Her corset's so tight she can't catch her breath and her vision closes in. All she can see are the mottled floorboards directly in front of her face; everything in her periphery is gray. She has no idea where Fleming is until she feels his fingers wrap around her throat and he heaves her off the floor, throwing her against the wall.

"Joe," she rasps, beating at his wrist and prying at his fingers, her feet virtually lifted off the ground. "You're hurting me."

In response to that, he puts greater pressure on her carotid arteries, choking her, making her lightheaded. When she's on the verge of passing out again—her head slumped forward, her resistance fading—he slams her into the wall, her head snapping back and bashing a hole in the cheap plasterwork.

"Don't you ever call on me again," he growls, letting her go and watching her plummet onto the floor. "You filthy sapphic bitch."

Wheezing and coughing, she crawls toward the door, needing the support of the wall before she can drag herself back onto her feet.

"Here, let me help you." Fleming raids his pockets and tosses some coins into the hallway. "Fetch, doggess." He grips her by the arm and flings her back onto her knees, booting her out of the room before slamming the door behind her.

In the hall, shaking and practically in tears, but determined not to cry, Mary Jane scoops up the money under the jeering eyes of a dozen other lodgers. Standing in their doorways, laughing, some of them decide to join in, flicking farthings at her. A few of the coins hit her in the face, others get caught in her hair, and one tumbles down between her breasts.

The amusing diversion causes such a commotion that the lodging house deputy is drawn up to investigate, the lodgers rapidly dispersing into their rooms as he storms up the staircase. By the time he reaches the hallway, Mary Jane is alone on the floor, too weak to move.

"You've got a right bloody nerve, you have." He hauls her up.

Seeing that she's having difficulty maintaining her balance, he flings her over his shoulder, carrying her down the stairs in a fireman's lift. Not wanting to tarnish the house's good reputation by kicking her out of the front door, he tosses her out the back like trash, dumping her disoriented, barely conscious body on the ground next to a pile of putrid vegetables.

It's now well past sunset. Mary Jane isn't sure of the time, but she remains where she is until she feels strong enough to move, then staggers out of the alley and back to Dorset Street. After cleaning herself up at Miller's Court—and changing her semen-drenched petticoat—she intends to swill away her sorrows in the Ten Bells, but becomes distracted by an unnatural orange glow in the sky and talk of a fire at the docks.

Thinking a walk might do her some good, she follows a group of curious locals to the South Quay Warehouses, where a massive storehouse in the center of the docks—one filled with two of her most favorite things: brandy and gin—is violently ablaze.

Some people have been crowded around the gates, gawking at the fire's progress since it first broke out shortly before nine o'clock, and now the flames are tearing through the roof and raging behind the iron-barred windows. Every now and again, a tendril of bluish fire bursts up into the sky, exploding bottles of brandy and gin adding fuel to the enormous furnace.

In efforts to extinguish it, twelve steamers have been called in from all over London. Firemen, policemen, and dock officers are all aiding in the endeavor, the steamers pumping continuously—the cacophony of noise tremendous—the granite stones of the docks being deluged with torrents of water.

By eleven o'clock, the force of the fire is somewhat diminished, the top two floors of the warehouse all but completely destroyed and the roof partially collapsed. By one o'clock, Mary Jane tires of the show. Having lost the will to do anything—be it drink or work—she wipes off her lip paste and wanders in the direction of home, making one quick stop on Brick Lane for a bite of supper before turning down Thrawl Street.

Ahead of her, a heavily inebriated woman with salt-and-pepper hair is arguing with the deputy of Wilmott's Lodging House, demanding that he save her a bed. Found to be lacking the appropriate amount of doss money, she's been booted out into the street, but doesn't appear in the slightest bit fazed by the expulsion.

"Never mind!" she declares, wielding a velvet-trimmed black straw bonnet. "I'll soon get my money." She dusts off the little bonnet and shows it to him. "See what a lovely bonnet I've got now."

Not looking where she's going, she totters away from the house, swaying from side to side, and bumps straight into Mary Jane.

"Oi, watch it!" Mary Jane gives her a light shove, not wanting the dirt and grime on the woman's grubby

ruddy-brown Ulster coat to rub off, the back of it covered with street muck where it's been brushed up against various walls in the course of her evening's work.

"Hello, dear!" The woman smiles up at her, baring several gaping holes where teeth ought to be. "Fine night, ain't it?" She plops the bonnet on her head, smoothing loose curls of unkempt hair off her forehead, the skin blemished with an old scar.

Being all too familiar with the type of customers who remain to be unearthed at this time of night—the very dregs of mankind, lurking on the streets after the church clock strikes twelve—Mary Jane doesn't share her optimism. Not that she has a choice. No work, no bed.

Seeing a hideous flash of her future, Mary Jane hurries on. As she passes Lolesworth, the flicker of candlelight inside Eva's room, despite the late hour, inspires a change of course. Rather than return to Miller's Court and spend the night alone, she mounts the stone steps and knocks on Eva's door, weary and forlorn.

"Who is it?" comes the muffled, suspicious reply.

"It's me, darling." Mary Jane tries to force a smile into her voice. "May I come in?"

Before the words are even out of her mouth, she hears the hurried padding of bare feet across the hardwood floor, followed by the click of the lock.

"I weren't expecting you tonight." Eva beams, reeling her in. "But I'm very glad to have you." Her eyes drift southward, grinning at the sight of Mary Jane's full cleavage. "Golly, it's been a while since I've seen your diddeys like that."

A moment passes, then it hits her.

"Why? When?" Her grin dies away and she retreats to the bed. "How long have you ... ?"

"Joe lost his job." Mary Jane drapes her shawl over a chair. "I didn't want to worry you, and I've been trying to keep things going as they were, but ..." She hesitates. "Do you hate me?"

"I'd never hate you." Eva reaches for her hand.

"May I spend the night?"

Eva pulls her onto the bed. "I wouldn't want you anywhere else."

CHAPTER 41

HORRIBLE MURDER IN WHITECHAPEL
WOMAN SHOCKINGLY MUTILATED
HEAD NEARLY CUT OFF

"A tragedy even more revolting in its details than that of George Yard, and surrounded apparently with circumstances fully as mysterious, has just occurred at Buck's Row, a low-class neighborhood adjoining Whitechapel Road. Passing the Essex Wharf, in Buck's Row, at about 4:30 this morning, Constable Neale, 97J, found lying on the pavement there the dead body of a woman. On further examination, her head was found to have been very nearly severed from her body. A horrible gash, fully an inch in width, extending from one side of the neck to the other, completely severing the windpipe. The lower portion of the abdomen was also completely ripped open, causing the bowels to protrude. The woman was at once conveyed to the mortuary, where she now lies."

-- Echo (London), August 31, 1888

Friday, August 31, 1888

ARMED WITH TWO BACON SANDWICHES—EXTRA BACON ON the side—and a bottle of ginger beer, Eva bursts into her room at Lolesworth, dumps breakfast on the table, and leaps onto the bed, her thunderous entry waking Mary Jane out of a deep sleep.

"Em! There's been another one!" She shakes Mary Jane's shoulder, forcing her to pay attention. "Everyone's nattering about it."

"Hmm?" Mary Jane rolls onto her back, rubbing crusty gunk out of her eyes. "When did you get out of bed? Do I smell bacon?" She props herself up on her elbow, looking around for the food, but Eva blocks her view.

"They're saying them's connected." Eva shuffles closer, seeking contact. "One last night, the Tabram murder, and that poor woman what had a walking stick rammed up her grummit."

"Whatchu going on about?" Her vision clearing, Mary Jane can see the fright in Eva's face. "What happened last night? Who you been talking to?"

"Another woman got done in." Eva swallows hard. "Like the one what come to harm in George Yard a few weeks back." She glances at Mary Jane's bodice, dangling off the bedpost where it caught after a frantic disrobing. "You worked last night. The fella what's doing all these wicked things, he could've—"

"I didn't." Mary Jane doesn't let her get the words out. "I was going to, but I didn't." She strokes Eva's rosy cheeks. "I came home to you instead."

"Honest?" Eva suspects a fib.

"Honest, love."

Unconvinced, Eva flips Mary Jane's hair over her shoulder, baring her neck and exposing the light bruising now visible around her throat. "I worry about you." She trails her fingers over the marks of a man's fingertips.

"I'm careful, darling." Mary Jane has nothing but assurances of her experience to assuage Eva's fears. "One of my specials got a little over-exuberant. It ain't nothing for you to worry about." She lies without hesitation, peeling Eva's hand away. "And it's only temporary. Are you forgetting that I've promised you we'll be in a new place together by Christmas?"

"I ain't forgot." Eva leans over the edge of the bed, pulling a few scraps of paper out from their hiding place underneath. "I've been marking it all down. See?"

On four separate sheets, she produces hand-scrawled calendars for the months of August, September, November, and December, scratching out each day as it passes, counting down to Christmastime. Though she has all the days in order, some of her numbers are malformed. Errors are crossed out and re-attempted, usually without success, her threes have quite often ended up backwards, and each month has been given thirty-one days. Still, she admires her handiwork.

"What's we gonna do for money when we're set up together? I was thinking I could learn my numbers better, then I could do all sorts." She tears up August, discarding it to the fireplace. "Will you teach me? You know your numbers good, duntcha?"

"I know enough to get by." Mary Jane points to November 31. "This month only has thirty days, my darling."

"Do it?" Eva perks up, excited to be able to scrap another day.

"And this one." Mary Jane indicates September, noticing that the fourth day of the month is marked with a heart. "What's this for?"

Eva colors up. "That day, it'll be eighteen months since you first had me. I knows 'cause I counted it five times to be sure."

"Really?" Mary Jane pinches the calendars out of her hands and drops them to the floor. "The first time I gave you a rub." She rucks up Eva's skirts, swiftly unfastening her drawers and tearing them down to her ankles. "The first time you spent with me."

"You know I ain't got long afore work," Eva warns her to be mindful of the time. "If we're to have pleasure every morning, I reckon I ought to start waking earlier."

Mary Jane kicks away the blankets, tugs Eva horizontal, and mounts her. "If I had my way, we'd have our pleasure at every available opportunity." She parts the folds of her sex, ensuring that pink meets pink. "Night and day."

"Oh, Em." Eva clutches Mary Jane's rump. "Do others do it so much?"

"If passion moves them to it." Mary Jane finds a slow, steady rhythm. "What a joy for two people bound in love to spend their nights undivided, their limbs entwined in the most sacred embrace, sharing such divine pleasures."

Eva whimpers in agreement, nearing a spend. "Oho, that's it." She grips Mary Jane's backside harder, encouraging her to move faster. "My hiccups are coming on." All at once, her thighs quiver, her bum twitches, and she's engulfed by her orgasm, the sensations amplified when she feels Mary Jane shudder in her arms, following her into bliss.

"Hiccups?" Mary Jane questions her afterward, remaining locked in place by Eva's hands.

"Don't it feel like hiccups? The squeezes of a spend." Eva relishes her ebbing climax, not letting Mary Jane free until the very last of her contractions has passed. "Them's like hiccups in your girl parts."

"I suppose they rather are." Mary Jane rolls off, laughing. "You have quite the delightful way of saying things."

"Will you still be here when I gets off work?" Eva wriggles back into her drawers, immediately realizing how unlikely that sounds. "Or come by and have supper with me at least?"

"I should be delighted." Mary Jane watches her fasten the drawstring in a bow and slide out of bed. "Ain't you gonna wash?"

Eva shakes her head, straightening her skirts. "It might be dirty, but I likes knowing I'm covered in your spendings." She leans over the bed for a kiss, her lips noticeably sticky and moist.

"You've been at my beeswax again."

"It feels nice." Eva rubs her lips together. "Don't it make 'em soft?"

"Aye." Mary Jane slides a hand around the back of her neck. "And irresistible." She pulls her into another kiss. "You may help yourself to it."

"And you, Miss Kelly, may help yourself to my kisses."

"I should hope so." Mary Jane feigns offense. "For who else might you give them to?"

"I save every single one for you." Eva giggles, pulling away. "Stay safe today."

After voicing that thinly veiled plea for Mary Jane not to work, she grabs one of the sandwiches and some of the extra bacon—leaving one sandwich and the ginger beer for Mary Jane—and departs with words of love on her glossy lips.

Lacking any fixed plans for the day, Mary Jane sleeps a while longer and rises at her leisure, finding a new toothbrush awaiting her at the washstand, her heart warmed by Eva's unspoken consideration. After taking care of her ablutions—and spending a moment to inspect the shadowy blemishes on her neck—she dresses in yesterday's clothes and eats, her late breakfast cut short by a stern knock upon the door.

"Who is it?"

"Inspector Reid, Miss Kelly. Open up."

Given that he's never sought her out in this way, Mary Jane guesses this isn't a social call. "Good morning to you, Mister Reid." She opens the door to him, inviting him in. "How did you know where to find me?"

"I'm a copper, Miss Kelly. I have a knack for that sort of thing." He removes his hat, setting it on the table. "Is Miss Sullivan at work? There's a delicate matter I wish to discuss with you. It's not for her ears."

"Aye, she is." Mary Jane sits down to lace her boots, her suspicion about the nature of his visit confirmed by his grave tone and the lack of pleasantries. "What fresh hell is it that you've brought me today? You've come about the murder?"

"What do you know of it?"

"Not much." Mary Jane flicks her mane over her shoulders, covering her breasts. "Only what Eva told me this morning: that another woman was found dead, and that some connection's been made between this, the George Yard murder, and my dear friend Emma. Is that true?"

"This morning's tragedy was not the work of the gangs," he states decisively, ruling out any connection

493

with Emma Smith. "Death was intentional, and no mistake."

"The cause being?" Mary Jane hardly dare ask.

"Her throat was cut." Reid goes light on the details. "I shan't burden you with the grotesque nature of her injuries, but there were certain ... indignities caused to the body after death. Her abdomen was slashed deeply and with much violence."

"Are you in charge of the case?"

Reid shakes his head. "It occurred in my old patch— J Division—but I know the men put on it. I informed them I had access to someone who'd proved to be a great asset to me in the Tabram case, and said that I would ask some questions on their behalf. You shall remain anonymous, of course. I've told them that you'll only speak with me, and only under the strictest confidence." Having already imposed upon her once this month, he hesitates to ask, "That said, might you accompany me to the mortuary to view the body?"

"Why? You have reason to believe she might be known to me?" Forgetting her bruises, she flips back her hair and wraps her shawl around her shoulders, unwittingly baring herself.

"Miss Kelly." Reid stops her from covering up, his attention instantly funneled into concern for her wellbeing. "What harm has come to you?" He brings his hand to her neck, establishing that the marks match that of a man's hand.

"Please don't fuss." She sweeps his hand away. "It won't happen again."

"One of your men has done this to you?"

"What of it?" Mary Jane roots through a basket of bits and bobs on top of Eva's cupboard. "It's not the first time."

"What's the man's name?"

"Why? What use a complaint?" Mary Jane plucks a length of silk ribbon from the basket and ties it around her neck like a choker, concealing the bruising. "What would the law do? Bind him over to keep the peace? Imprison him for seven days?" She scoffs at the notion. "There's no recourse for a battered woman in this world,

Mister Reid. If no-one cares for the wife beaten by her husband, why ought they care for the harlot beaten by her customer?"

"You misunderstand me." Reid fixes his eyes on her. "I didn't tell you to report the beast, I asked you only to tell me his name."

Taken aback by his unflinching and unconditional desire to protect her, and scared of how far he might go to do so, Mary Jane shakes her head, rejecting his help. "So that you can do what on my behalf? You aren't my bully, Mister Reid, you're a copper. A Local Inspector can't go about threatening to bash the head of any man who ill-uses his pet whore. I shan't have it." She turns from him, trying to appear unmoved by the gesture. "You're the only decent man I've ever met. Don't compromise your integrity on my account." She hides her cleavage with her shawl, obscuring the most blatant advertisement of her profession so as to lessen any embarrassment he might feel at being seen with her on the street. "Shall we go?"

For the second time in a month, Reid leads Mary Jane into the tiny brick dead-house in the Board of Works storage yard. As before, the poor woman's clothing has been dumped outside the door, this time slopped all over the flagstones rather than contained in a bucket.

Glancing at them, Mary Jane distinguishes a dull red Ulster coat, a dark-colored bodice of no particular design, and a shabby brown skirt, all of which are remarkably clean in comparison to a flannel petticoat bearing the mark of Lambeth Workhouse. The petticoat is saturated with blood, as are a pair of ribbed woolen stockings lying at the bottom of the pile, seeping crimson fluid, their original color indeterminate.

Atop the oozing mound are a pair of men's spring-sided boots and a battered black straw bonnet with a velvet trim, and of all the items, it's this oddly familiar-looking bonnet that snares Mary Jane's attention, causing her to come to an abrupt stop in the doorway.

"Is there something you recognize?" Reid prompts her.

Writing it off as a coincidence—after all, black straw bonnets are hardly a rarity—Mary Jane shakes her head and moves on, entering the mortuary to find the woman's body occupying a shell in the same spot where Martha Tabram had been laid.

After ushering the mortuary attendant out for privacy—thus assuring Mary Jane that anything she might feel inclined to say shall remain entirely between them—Reid places his hands on the shell.

"Are you ready?"

Mary Jane nods, thinking herself prepared, but as Reid lifts the lid, exposing the face of the victim therein, her stomach churns. Though the woman's body is covered with a mortuary sheet and a blanket, concealing the grotesque horrors of her mutilation, her head has slipped off the padding it was propped on, causing it to tilt back, revealing a deep, eight-inch-long gash over her throat. Worse still, the weight of the unsupported head has opened up the wound, exposing a valley of flesh over an inch wide, her severed trachea and esophagus plainly visible, her neck cut down to the vertebrae.

"God almighty." Mary Jane covers her mouth, staggering back from the shell.

"Damn it." Reid reaches in and hastily adjusts the woman's head, lifting it back onto the padding and closing the wound, tucking the mortuary blanket around it. "You have my apologies, Miss Kelly." He closes the shell. "Are you quite all right?"

Doubled over, Mary Jane breathes shallow and fast, afraid of passing out or throwing up. She can't manage words, but Reid aids her into a chair and fans her with his hat until she's steady enough to grasp his wrist, standing him down.

"Do you mind?" She brings a hand to her bodice, unfastening both it and a little of her corset, enabling her to get more oxygen into her lungs. "You've seen a good deal more of me than this, and I'm a little beyond upholding any sham modesty at this moment."

Despite not wearing a chemise beneath it, she unhooks her corset to the bottom of her sternum, releasing much of the tension in the tightly-laced garment, leaving her breasts loosely cupped in the bust gores.

Reid appropriately averts his gaze. "Do pardon my observance, but it seems you might be in need of a new *corsetière*, Miss Kelly."

Mary Jane isn't sure if that's a comment aimed at the overall state of her well-worn corset, or the fact that her breasts barely fit in it, but she opts to take it as a compliment on her physique rather than as a critique of her rather worse-for-wear undergarments.

"Point me in the direction of some spare money first, won't you, Mister Reid?" She leans back, regulating her breathing, keeping a hand clasped across her chest so as not to expose herself any more than necessary. "Failing that, I could always stop eating. That ought to rectify both problems fairly swiftly."

"May I fetch you something?" Reid rises to his feet, looking around for anything that might be of help to her. "A glass of water perhaps? Smelling salts?"

"I shall be fine, thank you." Recovering somewhat, she restores her decency, conveying her gratitude with a smile. "I had a fright, that's all."

"Please forgive me." Reid helps her up. "You were not meant to see all that you saw."

"It's not only that." Mary Jane composes herself, the horrific injury to the woman's throat being but one contributing factor in her near-collapse. "Her face ..."

"You know her?"

"May I look again to be sure?" Mary Jane approaches the shell, steeling herself for another glimpse of its sickening contents.

When Reid opens it, she focuses on the woman's pallid features. Her face appears to be caught in an

expression of pain, her parted lips revealing wide gaps where several of her discolored teeth ought to be. Her half-lidded eyes are so pale they might almost be gray, though the whites are turning ruddy-brown from exposure to the air. Her hair is dark but losing its pigment, and she has a small scar on her forehead.

Nodding, Mary Jane signals for Reid to close up the shell. "I do not know her, but—odd as this sounds—I did see her last night."

"Tell me what happened."

"There's nothing much to it." Mary Jane hugs her shawl around her shoulders. "I had a fairly disheartening evening"—she indicates the concealed bruising on her neck—"and went down to the Shadwell docks to watch the fire. I was returning home—home to Eva, that is, not to my own lodgings—when I saw this woman in Thrawl Street. I'd say it was approximately one-thirty, and she was being given her marching orders from Wilmott's on account of being short on her doss money. I daresay she's a regular there, and someone may well be able to identify her."

"What sort of house is this?"

"Not a good one." Mary Jane lets herself out into the yard, in need of some fresh air. "They rent almost exclusively to unfortunates, and the deputy is a sort of bully."

"Did you exchange any words with her?"

"Nothing beyond a comment on the weather." Mary Jane presses her back to the dead-house wall, letting a cool breeze tickle her face. "She seemed rather inebriated. She bumped into me, I gave her a shove, and she staggered off."

"And two hours later, she was dead," Reid muses. "Same with Martha Tabram."

"I hope you're not implying that these foul crimes are in some way *my* doing, Inspector?" Mary Jane glares incredulously at him. "We all live in close quarters here, and the nature of our work puts us in contact with many people. Ask around and I'm sure you could find a dozen people who'd all swear to seeing me, speaking with me,

drinking with me, or fucking me on any given day of the week. We are not solitary creatures."

"I meant no offense." Reid adjusts his hat, shielding his eyes from the autumn sun. "But do you not find it a curious coincidence that you encountered both women mere hours before they met their ends?"

"I suppose I do." Mary Jane shrugs it off. "But what links the two in any case? Martha Tabram was stabbed, yes? Yet when you spoke of this woman's injuries, you said she was slashed. So upon what evidence are you making the connection?"

Reid appears disinclined to answer. "I fear we're venturing into territory best kept from a woman's ears, Miss Kelly."

"Please, Mister Reid." Mary Jane rolls her eyes. "Since coming to this city, I've seen my share of things that would make your toes curl. Do not think me so delicate."

Regarding her carefully, not sure that he believes her to be quite as tough as she proclaims, Reid divulges all. "It's my thinking now that our first victim was positioned in a particularly undignified manner so as to facilitate horrors akin to those inflicted upon this poor woman. Being disturbed in the process, he fled, having made only one cut in her southern regions and leaving her not quite dead." He pauses to let that information sink in. "As regards our second victim, she received two stabs to her external organs of generation, and I surmise that these stabs were the first of the postmortem injuries committed—thus concluding our madman's earlier attempt at the work. But the fascination for this now being dulled, he proceeded to perform the other atrocities upon her—for what thoroughly revolting purpose I dare not speculate—at which point, he was again interrupted."

Mary Jane infers the logical conclusion. "You think there'll be another?"

"I fear it."

Parting from Reid with the promise that she'll keep off the streets tonight, Mary Jane spends the rest of the day lost in her thoughts. She has dinner, though she

doesn't feel like eating, and in the course of her aimless wanderings, she ends up in Buck's Row.

Illuminated only by a single gaslight at the end of the street, the pathway is cast in shadow, providing the perfect place to broker a little sin. Or to die.

The weather's been clear thus far, and the patch of ground upon which the woman was slaughtered outside the gateway to Brown's stable yard is still covered with blood. No-one's yet thought to wash it off.

As Mary Jane stands there, a woman passes by, pausing briefly to lay a single dark crimson rose of mourning at the heart of the critical spot before moving on, no words exchanged.

"Morbid, ain't it?"

Maria's voice startles her.

"I come just to have a peep me-self," she carries on, approaching the crusted blood and poking the toe of her boot in it. "Fancy a drink?"

Mary Jane does, and she accompanies Maria to the Ten Bells, there finding Joe drinking with a group of friends, some of whom she's had occasion to meet in the course of her work. They're drunk and rowdy, entertaining a trio of tittering young harlots.

"Drinking your hard-earned money?" she sneers, turning her back to them, reaching the bar before she realizes the hypocrisy in her words.

"Ain't that your woman?" One of Joe's impudent pals points a tremulous finger at her. "I've been meaning to give her a go. Heard she's a right little fucktress."

"Aye, I've been up her," another remarks. "Tight as a clam, she is."

"Fuckadilla!" one more yells. "Show us yer madge!"

"I ain't showing you lot of soakers nothing." She pockets her money, changing her mind about placing an order at the bar. "Vile, stinking pigs, all of you."

With that, she bids Maria an abrupt goodnight and starts to leave, taking only a few steps before Joe gets the unwise notion to defend what's his. Made brash by drink, he captures her by the arm, reeling her in.

"My turn tonight, Fuckadilla."

"Don't you bloody well call me that, and gerroff me!" Mary Jane jerks free, kicking his shin. "I ain't your property."

Witnessing this act of insolence, one of Joe's friends chortles. "Duntcha know, Joe? There's three things in this world without rule: a mule, a pig, and a woman."

Enraged by her defiance, and spurred on by his friends, Joe tries to bring Mary Jane under his control, but she resists. In frustration, he backhands her, but she strikes back, slapping his cheek hard enough to leave behind the imprint of her hand.

"You want me, you pay down." She squares up to him, showing no fear. "You'd best have another three florins, though."

The resulting derision from his peers causes Joe to lash out. He grapples with her, knocking against a table and spilling someone's beer, their tussle concluding with a single punch, his fist colliding with her cheekbone and sending her to the floor.

In an instant, harlots swoop in from all angles, gathering to guard their fallen comrade, helping her off the floor while Maria forces Joe back, the ensuing uproar culminating with the disgruntled proprietor ordering all the disruptive parties out.

Happy to get away, Mary Jane snatches up her shawl and storms into the street. Maria tries to stop her—doubtless to entice her into the Britannia instead—but she won't be halted.

"I can't bear that man!" She keeps walking, heading straight for Lolesworth.

Walking briskly so as to deter Maria from following, she darts into the Lolesworth passage and up the stone stairwell, rushing to Eva's door.

"Who is it?" Eva calls out warily, responding to an impatient knock.

"It's me, darling. Am I late for supper?"

Eva answers in a flash, opening the door with a wide grin that fades the instant she catches sight of a nasty purple bruise already forming on Mary Jane's cheek.

"Oh, my God. Em ..." She pulls Mary Jane inside, leading her to the bed and sitting her on it. "Who's done this to you now?"

"There was a bit of a kerfluffle in the Ten Bells."

Eva's concern deepens. "You been drinking?"

"I was going to, but no." Mary Jane lunges for Eva's lips, stealing a kiss and letting her taste for herself. "See? Not a drop of booze on my breath, nor my tongue."

Comforted by that, Eva returns the full measure of her attentiveness to Mary Jane's brand new shiner. "Does it hurt dreadful?"

"It ain't so bad." Mary Jane flops onto her back. "I've had worse."

Not caring for the casual manner in which she says that, Eva retrieves a copy of this evening's Star newspaper off the table. "How can you say I needn't worry when you're having the daylights beat out of you and other women's dying?" She reads the headline. "A revolting murder. Another woman found horribly mutilated in Whitechapel." She reads every word slowly, concentrating on her enunciation. "Ghastly crimes by a maniac."

Mary Jane snatches the paper away from her. "Stop reading that." She shoves it in the gap between the bed and the wall. "You don't need them thoughts in your head."

Not in the mood to have her fears unjustly minimized, Eva gives up for the time being and leaves her be. "I have to fetch up some water." She collects the empty ewer from the washstand and makes for the door. "Help yourself to some food if you're hungry."

Tempted, Mary Jane eyes a fresh half loaf of bread, a blob of butter, and a crumbly block of cheese on the table, but first, she fishes the crumpled up newspaper out of the crack and gives the article a thorough read.

"Her throat was cut from ear to ear. The wound was about two inches wide and blood was flowing profusely. She was immediately conveyed to the Whitechapel mortuary, when it was found that besides the wound in the throat, the lower part of the abdomen was

completely ripped open and the bowels were protruding. The wound extends nearly to her breast, and must have been effected with a large knife. As the corpse lies in the mortuary, it presents a ghastly sight.

The ghastliness of this cut, however, pales into insignificance alongside the other. No murder was ever more ferociously and more brutally done. The knife, which must have been a large and sharp one, was jabbed into the deceased at the lower part of the abdomen, and then drawn upward, not once but twice. The first cut veered to the right, slitting up the groin and passing over the left hip, but the second cut went straight upward, along the centre of the body and reaching to the breast bone. Such horrible work could only be the deed of a maniac.

The other murder, in which the woman received thirty-nine stabs, must also have been the work of a maniac. This murder occurred on the Bank Holiday. On the Bank Holiday preceding, another woman was murdered in an equally brutal but even more barbarous fashion by being stabbed with a stick. She died without being able to tell anything of her murderer. All this leads to the conclusion that the police have now formed, that there is a maniac haunting Whitechapel, and that the three woman were all victims of his murderous frenzy."

Before Eva gets back, Mary Jane stuffs the newspaper in a small scuttle full of coke, firewood, and scrap paper, and sits down to eat. She'll have to work tomorrow. Eva's been spending extra to feed them both, and she'll never have enough for rent.

She's been deliberately shorting a little every week as it is—following the example set for her by Mary Jane at Thrawl Street—and although she believes she's been managing her affairs well, Mary Jane's been slyly making up the remainder on her behalf, preventing her from slipping continually further behind.

Still subdued upon her return from the water pump, the huffy teen has little to say. Exhausted as she always is

by the time Friday night rolls around, she brushes her teeth, changes into her nightdress, and clambers into bed early. Usually, Mary Jane would respect her need for sleep and occupy herself reading or crocheting until too weary to continue, but tonight, she has other ideas. After putting away the leftovers, she undresses, slips under the covers behind Eva, and sets about stirring her up, kissing her neck and caressing her back.

"Em," Eva groans, annoyed. "Leave off."

Though she juts out her bum, trying to nudge Mary Jane away, Mary Jane is bigger and stronger and easily turns her over, raising her onto her knees and propping her on all fours.

"I shan't leave off." Mary Jane tugs up her nightdress, kissing her bare bum. "You're in a grump with me, and I don't want us to go to bed in a grump."

Eva hangs her head, peering beneath herself as Mary Jane gets between her thighs. "What are you about tonight? I ain't randy."

"Are you sure?" Mary Jane gets a hand on her sex, finding her wet and burying two fingers inside her without warning or preparation.

"Oh, stop!" Eva makes a weak attempt to uncunt her. "Give me your mouth, then," she pleads, unaccustomed to this attitude. "That'll fetch me the quickest."

Instead of relenting, Mary Jane adds a third finger, stretching her open.

"Ahh!" Eva wails, gripping the iron headboard for support, her shuddering body responding to Mary Jane's ministrations despite her protests, her ensuing orgasm accompanied by a slight twinge of pain.

When it's over, Mary Jane relinquishes her hold and Eva sinks back to the sheets, nursing her abused treasure. "You ain't half made it sore." She pouts, clamping her thighs together. "Why ever was you so rough with it?"

"I'm sorry, love. I got carried away." Mary Jane scoops her into an embrace, pulling the covers over them both. "Did you not enjoy it?"

Eva shrugs, content to roll over and go to sleep, never speaking of this experience again, but Mary Jane surprises her by tearing the covers away.

"Oi!" She attempts to snatch them back. "Whatchu doing now?"

"Kissing it better." Mary Jane wriggles into position, making Eva melt in her mouth.

CHAPTER 42

Friday, September 7, 1888

MARY JANE LIES AWAKE IN HER MILLER'S COURT BED, JOE snoring beside her. As she's come to expect, he fell asleep minutes after their business was concluded. He simply rolled off, closed his eyes, and conked out, not even bothering to tuck his wet prick away, never mind unrig.

Tonight was especially taxing for him, since he insisted on taking her twice. The first poke—conducted dog fashion, as is frequently his letch—was declared unsatisfactory on account of his being fetched much too quickly, so he forked over an extra sixpence and had her perform minette on him until he was back to full standing. Once that was achieved, he went up her again, driving straight into his own muck.

That time, he did her belly to belly, insisting that she remain as quiet and still as possible, thus preventing her from utilizing any of her paphian spunk-drawing tricks. He wanted her limp and unresponsive, so for all intents and purposes, she played dead—and not for the first time.

One of her old specials preferred to receive her that way. Perhaps disturbingly, he liked her to await him on the bed, fully naked and exposed, sprawled there as if discarded. In his fantasy, she was La Païva: a once beautiful, now dead courtesan who, some decades ago, sold her charms in the various cyprian haunts around Covent Garden.

507

Whether he hated her or loved her, it was impossible to distinguish. At times, it seemed like both. When he was ready—when her flesh had been suitably chilled to a dead-like frigidity by the deliberately cooled air in the room—he'd approach her with nervous excitement, pretending to come upon her fresh corpse quite by accident.

On each occasion, he'd explore her for some time, caressing her lifeless limbs, posing her as he pleased. Quite often, he'd enhance the fantasy by paying extra to have her receive a man before him, making her promise to leave every drop of the man's sediment inside her. This, so he said, made it appear as though she'd been slain by her last customer, and he liked listening to the squelching of his instrument as it glided in and out, the sliminess of it all bolstering the illusion that he was fucking a loose, unresponsive hole.

Once, she accidentally sneezed and he lost his stiffening. Any sign of life and all urge to have her would depart from him completely. Not a whimper. Not a wiggle. Not a twitch. She stopped seeing him after he grew bored of their usual doings and took it upon himself to increase the realism of the experience by knocking her out with chloroform. Several hours after their engagement, she woke up naked, cold, and alone, with his seminal deposit dribbling onto the counterpane and a bite mark on her inner thigh.

The pity of their parting was that it was easy work. Most men—Joe especially, since he feels he's paying a premium for it—believe they deserve a full performance every time, and it gets tiresome. Tonight was a rare relief, and a well-earned one at that.

In an attempt to make up for his drunken behavior in the Ten Bells, he's been trying harder to please her this past week. Much to her chagrin, his visits have been almost daily, and he's starting to get spoony again. She wouldn't go quite so far as to call him generous, but her rent's paid up and he's been complimenting her well. Not well enough to make her feel guilty about deserting him in her bed, though.

Lying there just long enough to ensure he won't be easily woken, she bides her time and eases herself off the bed, douching quickly before collecting the money he brought—a meager half-crown, with the promise of more tomorrow—and sneaking out to see Eva.

Due to the late hour, she expects Eva to be getting ready for bed. Instead, when she arrives at Lolesworth, she interrupts a verbal confrontation between Eva and a boisterous young man in charge of the collection of rents. It appears he caught her by the stone steps in the courtyard—either on her way in or out, hoping to slip by unnoticed—and now he's puffing out his chest, making demands while she sobs helplessly into a hanky.

She owes him money, as per usual, but is pleading poverty. At the mention of eviction, Mary Jane steps in.

"What's the trouble here?"

"This little piece of rotten mischief owes me three shillings," the man is quick to state, recognizing Mary Jane as Eva's guarantor, having received small amounts of money from her in dribs and drabs throughout the course of Eva's short tenancy. "That's a full week's rent, and if I don't get it, she'll be out on her ear." He casts his eyes over Eva's form. "Unless there's summink else she wants to give me for it."

In her naivety, Eva thinks he's asking for a simple barter of goods. "Like what?" she asks, willing to darn his socks for a month if he should so request it.

"That's enough." Mary Jane puts herself in front of Eva, reading his intentions better. "I don't care how you conduct your business with others, but you shan't muck this one about." She pulls Eva aside, asking her quietly, "Do you really not have it?"

Eva shakes her head, sniffling. "I needed a new pair of boots. I'm sorry, I—"

"No apologies. Go up to your room, love." Mary Jane ushers her in the direction of the steps, not needing to hear another word from her. "I'll sort it."

Afraid of what that might entail, Eva shakes her head and refuses to budge. "No ... don't." She grabs a fistful of Mary Jane's apron, holding onto her skirts like a fearful child.

"Please." Mary Jane strokes her damp cheeks. "I'll be up in a bit." She moves closer, dropping a kiss on Eva's neck, whispering, "Keep the bed warm."

"But it's not fair." Eva begins to sob again.

"Just do as I say. No arguments now." Mary Jane turns her in the direction of the stairwell and pats her bum. "I shan't be long."

Not brave enough to defy her—and not knowing what good that would do in any event—Eva slinks away, looking over her shoulder every few steps. When she's finally out of sight, Mary Jane pulls the half-crown she received from Joe out of her pocket.

"Easy come, easy go." She hands it to the rent man. "Will that suffice till Monday?"

Since it's late on a Friday night and he's in want of a woman, no, it won't.

"There's still sixpence owing." He scratches at his crotch, drawing her attention to the bulge restrained therein. "I'll let her off it if we can come to some arrangement."

Five minutes later, Mary Jane's on her knees in a humble ground floor room accessed directly from the courtyard. The cheap furnishings are not so unlike those found in the other rents in the Lolesworth Buildings, except that his fireplace has a better range and he's crammed a padded armchair in front of it. There's only one bed, and his seven-year-old daughter is in it, watching the proceedings as he lights a candle on the mantel and sits himself in the saggy chair, his engorged prick sticking out through his unbuttoned trousers.

"She's but a child," Mary Jane protests from her position on the scrubbed and polished hardwood floor, her knees resting on the man's rolled up tweed jacket. "Let us conduct our business elsewhere."

Those words are barely out before he yanks her head into his lap and forces the full length of his pipe inside her open mouth, stifling a cry of disgruntlement. Once in her, he proceeds to fuck hard, pinching her nose to ensure that she doesn't bite down on him, his other hand on the back of her neck, thwarting any attempt she might make to pull away.

He's done this before, she can tell. Her desperate need to breathe keeps her mouth wide open for his use, despite the fact that he's choking her with every thrust, the head of his leaking priapus scraping her palate and battering her tonsils. Were she in control, she would limit his depth, taking only what was comfortable for her, and at the moment of crisis, she'd direct his spurting pipe to one of her cheeks, collecting his spunk there to avoid having it splash on her tongue, lessening the taste. But she's not in control tonight.

To finish, he rams deep into her mouth, jetting his mucilage down her throat, and as soon as his cods have emptied, he ejects his softening tool with a jerk of his hips and clamps her mouth closed, preventing her from being able to spit.

When she refuses to swallow, struggling in his grasp, he pinches her nose again, cutting off her air until she has no choice but to drink his deposit—something she's never before done.

Directly it's over, he releases her and she bolts from the room, his hearty guffaws echoing through the courtyard. Sickened by the act, she staggers to the washhouse and throws up over a sewer grate, not only expelling his salty muck, but also the supper Joe bought for her.

Tears running down her face, her body shaking with anger, she heaves until she has nothing else left, then wipes her mouth with the hanky she had prepped in her hand during the assault. Determined to return to erase all trace of this vile encounter before returning to Eva, she swills her mouth out at the water pump, cleans her face, and roots through her pockets until she finds a fluff-covered, broken piece of mint. It's better than nothing.

Once she's assured that she neither smells of vomit nor masculine spend, she heads up to Eva's room, pitying the young girl who must grow up with such a repugnant father. Like so many others in her position, she'll learn the worst ways of men and women from his actions, receiving her education in dissolution from the home hearth and growing up to expect nothing more from her own wretched life.

It's no wonder people think depravity breeds in the East End. They think it festers here like a grotesque wound refusing to heal, resisting all attempts to subdue it, the infection spreading. As moss flourishes in the dark, damp recesses of the forest, so the twisted and the perverse are drawn here, to a place so cast off from good society that it's become a veritable playground for the most wicked and degenerate specimens of mankind, and they thrive, corrupting all they touch.

From Bethnal Green to Limehouse, this place is thought a plague upon London, to be avoided at all costs. But public perception is skewed. Dissoluteness isn't conceived here, it merely convenes on these overcrowded streets, where good, hardworking people are denigrated and neglected, abandoned to the cruelties of poverty. It's not an East End problem, but a human one.

Trying not to dwell on it, Mary Jane knocks on Eva's door. "Darling, let me in."

"It's on the latch," is the muffled reply, and Mary Jane enters, her heart aching to see Eva weeping on the bed, her back to the wall, her knees tucked to her chin, and tatty old Mollie the doll crushed to her chest.

"Hush, love." Mary Jane kneels at the side of the bed. "I've settled it with the rent man. You're all paid up for this week."

"What did he make you do?" Eva peers over her knees, her eyes puffy and red.

"Not the worst thing." Mary Jane reaches for the teen's feet, pulling her legs out and dragging her across the bedspread. "Have you eaten?"

"I ain't saying." Eva blows her nose on her already saturated hanky, smearing the snot around her face more than she is cleaning it. "You do too much for me as it is."

"Ain't no such thing as too much. Not for you." Mary Jane fishes a clean hanky out of her pocket and trades Eva for it, depositing the sodden one in the nearby empty chamber pot.

Assuming she hasn't had a bite to eat since they parted company at breakfast, Mary Jane plans to fetch her a decent supper, but first, a little cheering up is in order—for both of them. To start, she takes one of Eva's

feet in her hands and begins unlacing her new footwear, which, it should be stated, is new only to her and not the market.

"I shouldn't have bought 'em." Eva laments, looking at the scuffed boots on her feet. "Only my old ones was letting in water and winter's on its way."

"You did right." Mary Jane pulls off one boot, then the other. "But you ought to have told me." She bunches up Eva's skirts, removing the elastic garters holding up her stockings. "I'd have seen to it that you got what you needed."

"Whatchu doing?" Eva sniffles, watching Mary Jane roll down her stockings.

"I'm taking your clothes off."

"I sees that." She giggles. "But why?"

"Because I want to have you." Mary Jane tugs her to the edge of the bed, pleased to find that she's not wearing her drawers. "You smell so good." She buries her face in Eva's mound, inhaling the inimitable scent of her arousal before snatching up one of her feet and planting kisses all over the sole.

"Oh, Em!" Eva clutches the bedpost, squealing. "That tickles!"

Mary Jane keeps hold of her foot, sucking the big toe into her mouth.

"Lor'!" Eva squirms, laughing and flinching. "Let go of it, or I shall have a fit."

Giving her some relief, Mary Jane releases the foot, placing it on her shoulder and kissing her way from ankle to shin to thigh, dragging her fingernails along Eva's milky skin, working all the way up one leg and down the other, bypassing her sex altogether.

"Don't tease," Eva whines, scooting forward, positioning her sex closer to Mary Jane's roving mouth. "Lick it."

"Is that what you want?" Mary Jane trails her tongue along Eva's calf.

"Please," Eva mewls, hooking both knees over Mary Jane's shoulders, locking her in. "Put your mouth to me."

Ready to devour her, Mary Jane glides her hands up Eva's inner thighs and spreads her open, admiring her

dripping flesh. "You have such a sweet cunt." She drops a kiss on Eva's motte. "The best I've ever tasted." Nuzzling her face in Eva's core, she slithers down to the pink, snaking her tongue along Eva's cleft and delivering hot lashes to her valley. "Like the most precious honey," she mumbles, her nose bumping Eva's swollen clit, making her twitch.

As Eva's wails and moans become more frantic, her toes curling and her legs trembling, Mary Jane concentrates on that plump bundle of nerves. She flicks the very tip of her tongue over it and around it, then takes it completely into her mouth, bringing on Eva's crisis.

When it's over, Eva grins, wiping a smear of her amatory fluids off the tip of Mary Jane's nose. "I do so much prefer it this way compared to the other."

"What other?" Mary Jane doesn't follow.

"The way you done me last week, when you was all rough with it." Eva gives her treasure a rub, remembering how it felt. "That was different from our usual fuckings, and it weren't quite so nice. I likes it best when you're gentle. I feels truly cherished when you does me like that."

"You *are* cherished. So much." Mary Jane hikes up her skirts and climbs onto the bed between Eva's legs, kissing her lips and pushing her down.

"I'm spoiled by you, ain't I?" Eva lets Mary Jane mount her. "When the other girls at the factory talks about what it's like with their fellas, it don't sound at all the same as it is with us. They speak of it as though it's a chore, and I don't say nuthin' 'cause I knows I'm getting more pleasure from you than the whole lot of 'em put together. Going to bed with you ain't a chore, it's the best part of my day." She peers down, Mary Jane's breasts in front of her face. "Oh, Lordy. I'll never get tired of looking at your diddeys."

"I hope you wanna do more than look." Mary Jane smirks, unbuttoning her bodice and instigating a particularly energetic romp involving several different attitudes and a variety of exquisite pleasures that leave Eva utterly worn out.

Once she falls sound asleep, Mary Jane works over a plan in her mind. She's hungry after vomiting everything up, and Eva needs sustenance, but she gave every bit of coin she had on her person to the rent man. Her lockbox at Miller's Court contains a few pence, but she doesn't want to go back there for fear of waking up Joe, so there's only one thing for it: she must work.

It's that prime time of night when all the drunkards are stumbling home from the pubs, so finding a willing man with loose pockets oughtn't be hard. Leaving Eva sleeping, she creeps out of bed, dresses, and preps one of her silk hankies. Though she doesn't often resort to the underhanded tricks common to some in her profession, she'd rather risk angering a customer than have to return to Eva's room with a semenalized commodity, so she lays the hanky out on the table and slathers one side of it with a generous quantity of cold cream. Once it's sufficiently daubed, she rolls it up and holds it in her palm, warming it, then thieves Eva's room key and slips out.

Being not in the least bit picky, she lurks outside the Ten Bells until a short man with a thinning head of white hair stumbles out alone. Under the guise of helping him across the street, she injects herself into his personal space, letting him drape his arm over her shoulders, using her for support. Meanwhile, she runs her hands over his pockets, feeling for the presence of coins within.

"Where you headed, love?" she asks, hoping he has a bed not far from here.

In answer, he mumbles something that sounds like Crossingham's and waves a finger in the direction of Dorset Street. To clarify further—since the slumlord William Crossingham owns two lodging houses in this street—he slurs out the number thirty-five, indicating that it's the lodging house on the north side of the street to which he refers.

Having once lived there, Mary Jane knows she'll have no trouble entering the building with him. The deputy cares little for what goes on inside, as long as everyone forks out their bed money and has the good grace not to die on the premises. The Crossingham's

lodging house on the south side has a similar reputation, and Mary Jane's no stranger there, either.

Women and men can come and go from it virtually unquestioned, as they can at most of the low lodging houses littered along either side of the street, garnering this short thoroughfare the dubious nickname Do-As-You-Please Street. No-one with any modicum of respectability would ever want to be seen walking down it, nor would they have the temerity to do so.

On the way to Crossingham's, Mary Jane offers the soaker her services, which he's much too fuddled to refuse. His gray whiskers tickle her face as he leans in, confessing that it's been a solid year since he's had a woman. The last one only cost him fourpence, which he thought was a jolly good bargain until he found out she'd clapped him.

"Does it stand?" he asks, sitting himself on the edge of a narrow cot in a shared room, his roommates not yet returned from liquoring.

"Oh, Aye." Mary Jane gets him unbuttoned and wraps her fist around his pego, giving it a few tugs. "You've a mighty fine stiff-stander."

"Let's have it up you, then." He fumbles for her waist, trying to get her onto the bed.

"Now, now, you lie down and close your eyes." Mary Jane maneuvers him onto his back. "I shall take care of the business." She straddles him, pulling the creamed hanky from her pocket. "You just relax now." She unfurls the tool of her deception, swiftly getting into position with his cock in front of her, concealed by her skirts. "We'll fuck well."

Sliding the slimy hanky over his prick, squeezing her fingers down the shaft, she feigns penetration, accompanying the motion of her hand with a sympathetic drop of her hips and a soft moan, hoping he's too drunk to notice anything amiss.

"Ain't that nice?" she encourages him, moving rhythmically. "We're having a nice fuck."

He mutters something affirmative, appears almost to doze off, then his body stiffens. Spewing a string of nonsensical gobbledygook, he announces the arrival of

his peak, and Mary Jane ensures that he spills into the hanky, catching most of it, with only a few stray droplets finding their way onto her mount.

"That's a good boy." She milks him. "Let it spill."

His spend rendering him insensible, he pays no notice when she rises off him and flings the revolting hanky into the corner of the room, letting his dirty prick flop onto his belly, remnants of cold cream caught in the wrinkles of his shrinking pipe. In a flash, she then takes what's hers—the few coins counted out and set on the bedside table prior to connection—and helps herself to a bit extra from his jacket pocket, hesitating when her fingers come into contact with the smooth, rounded surface of a pocket watch case.

Though she's made a nasty habit of pinching a few extra coins whenever the opportunity arises, she's never robbed a customer of his possessions before, and she frowns upon the devious wenches who do. Nevertheless, she wraps her fingers around the watch ...

Clasping the simple silver timepiece in her palm, she lifts it from his jacket and turns to leave, horrified to come face to face with Fleming in the doorway.

He's been standing there, observing the proceedings, privy to the deceit, the theft, and now her discomfiture at having being caught. Rumors can be damaging, and if he spreads the word that she's a dishonest harlot, she'll lose valuable trade. More imminently, he might alert her passed-out customer to the fact that he's just been robbed, and that could start a fight.

Afraid of that, she flees, pushing past him and down the stairs in a hurry to get away. In her haste, she runs headlong into a short, stout woman some twenty years her senior—a woman she knows only as Dark Annie. The pair crash into one another at the main entrance, spilling out onto Dorset Street.

"Lor'! What's the hurry, dearie?" Annie steadies herself against the wall of Crossingham's, her breathing shallow and labored. "I didn't know you was working again." She pulls a white neckerchief from her pocket and ties it around her neck, knotting it at the front. "It's been an age since I's seen you out and about, you old toffer."

Mary Jane's known Annie for nearly two years. Though faring less well since the death of her husband, Annie was once a respectable woman, living a respectable life in Windsor. Losses came, as they do, accompanied by a liking for rum, and now she dosses at common lodging houses, earning her money wherever she can and latching onto one man or another, hoping he can ease the financial burdens of living.

"It ain't a permanent thing," Mary Jane says of her own unfortunate circumstances, eyeing a bruise on Annie's temple. "That from one of your men?"

Annie snorts, dislodging some mucus in her nasal passages. "Eliza bloody Cooper, that's who done it." She buttons up her long black coat, covering her shabby black skirt and brown bodice. "Calls herself my friend, yet she set upon me for borrowing a piece of soap off her and not returning it quite so fast as she would like. I gived her a ha'penny for it and slapped her pretty face, then she flew into a mighty rage and we had fisticuffs." As she croaks the last words out, she succumbs to a hearty, fluid-filled coughing fit, doubling up and spitting a ball of discolored, slightly bloody phlegm onto the street.

"You all right?"

"I ain't feeling at all proper." Annie beats a hand on her chest, trying to dislodge some of the fluid. "But I've got me-self some pills for it now, and it's no use my giving way in any case." She looks up at Mary Jane, a thought occurring to her. "You ain't got tuppence I could borrow, have you? Only I'm short for my lodgings."

"You don't need no bed money from me." Mary Jane chuckles, pointing to three brass rings on Annie's ring finger. "You're wearing it."

"Ain't I allowed to have pretty things?" Annie huffs, wheezing.

"Hungry? I'll buy you a baked potato, how's that?"

That being agreeable, they leave Crossingham's together and head for Commercial Street, where Mary Jane hunts down a tater man set up outside the Queen's Head. This is his usual patch, and he's here most nights, staying out late to catch the last of the trade from the closing pubs, selling his hot potatoes from a portable

baking oven on a cart pulled by a rather miserable-looking donkey.

"Nice floury taters!" he yells, drawing customers in. "Come and get 'em. Tops only a penny. Middles a ha'penny, and you's robbing me."

Mary Jane purchases three tops: large potatoes dusted with salt and a yellowy, greasy substance that somewhat passes for butter. She then bids Annie goodnight, hopes her condition improves, and returns to Lolesworth, the smell of food rousing Eva in an instant.

"What's that you've got?" Eva yawns, wiping drool off her face.

"You need to eat." Mary Jane sets both potatoes on the table and cleans off two forks on her apron, wishing she'd had the opportunity for a sneaky wash. "As I've said before: we need to keep that figure on you."

Grinning, Eva wriggles out of bed and slips into her chemise. "Where'd you get the coin? You didn't ... ?"

"Don't you worry." Mary Jane sits her down and thrusts a fork in her hand. "Eat."

Hunger temporarily overriding all other thoughts and concerns, Eva devours her potato in under a minute, getting the imitation butter all over her lips. "You're so good to me." She waits for Mary Jane to finish eating, then dives onto her knees. "I love you bucket loads."

She reaches for the hem of Mary Jane's skirts, starting to lift them, but Mary Jane prevents her from getting them up.

"Don't." She keeps Eva at bay, tucking her skirts between her thighs and crossing her legs at the knee. "Please. You mustn't."

"Why not?" Suspicion creeps into Eva's voice.

Ashamed, Mary Jane refrains from making eye contact. "I need a wash first," she admits, loathing having spell it out.

Silence.

After a while, Eva dips her head into Mary Jane's lap and begins to sob. "I'm so afeared of it all, Em. If anything ever happened to you, I—"

"I'm sorry, my dear love." Mary Jane caresses her heaving shoulders. "I don't know how else to take care of

you." She holds back tears of her own. "Do you wish me to sleep with you tonight? Or shall I leave?"

"I want you with me," Eva mumbles, her voice muffled in Mary Jane's apron.

Wiping her eyes, she battles Mary Jane for access under her skirts, eventually succeeding in getting them up high enough to spread her thighs and take a peek. She expects to find the article in a similar state as it was on the last occasion she saw it freshly used: plugged with a hanky and oozing. Instead, it looks relatively unsoiled.

"I didn't take him inside," Mary Jane explains.

Glad of that at least, Eva crosses to the washstand, pours some water into the basin, and lathers up a wet washcloth with soap. Without saying a word, she washes Mary Jane's commodity, intrigued by her scent, despite it being tainted by the pungent and unappealing odor of male spendings. When it's all clean, she dries and kisses it, pressing her lips to Mary Jane's soft pink folds.

"Oh, Eva ..." Mary Jane eases her hips forward.

"I love you." Eva lays another kiss on her. "No matter what."

CHAPTER 43

HORROR UPON HORROR

"This morning, the district was thrown into a panic by a fourth murder committed in an exactly similar manner to the three mysterious and unpunished crimes which have preceded it. The scene of this latest horror is Hanbury Street, hardly a stone's throw from Osborn Street and Buck's Row, where the two other victims were butchered. Indeed, through Hanbury Street on Thursday Mary Ann Nichols' terribly mutilated body was carried on the way to its place of burial. The fourth victim to what must be a madman's insatiable thirst for blood is, like the other three, a poor defenseless walker of the streets. A companion identified her soon after she had been taken to the mortuary as 'Dark Annie,' and as she came from the mortuary gate bitterly crying, said between her tears, 'I knowed her; I kissed her poor cold face.'"

-- The Star (London), September 8, 1888

Saturday, September 8, 1888

AS IT APPROACHES NOON, MARY JANE SITS ALONE IN THE Brick Lane coffeehouse where she regularly meets Inspector Reid. Though he should be away on annual leave—enjoying the sterling British weather at the seaside with his family, so she'd been told—she was surprised to receive a letter in the second morning post, confirming their usual appointment.

The concise note was delivered to Lolesworth as she slept, and she found another in her room at Miller's Court when she returned there to change into her more respectable clothes. This second letter, pushed under the door by her landlord, John McCarthy, who receives all tenant mail at his chandler's shop, had another brief message scrawled on the envelope: arrears due.

As if she could forget. She told Eva they'd be away from this place by December, but that was before Joe lost his job. In consequence of his ill-timed sacking, much of the money she's been getting from her specials—in amounts ranging from six bob to a sovereign, and numbering only one or two per month—has been going directly on food and rent.

She ought to work more to cover the deficit and keep saving, but having heard whispers of yet another murder committed last night, the thought of trying her luck on the street makes her stomach churn. Luckily, Joe's reserved her for the evening.

Thanks to that, and the money she received not half an hour ago from pawning the stolen pocket watch, she'll be able to keep herself and Eva fed for a few more days. There won't be much to spare for savings or luxuries, but the bare necessities will be covered, and she hasn't yet lost hope of Joe regaining some form of steady employment.

He's always worked. Though no stranger to hard times, he's consistently paid his way and never once had occasion to be committed to the workhouse. For that reason, when he says he intends to see her right, she believes him. At least, she's willing to give him a few more weeks before cutting her losses and quitting Miller's Court.

Waiting for Reid to arrive, she reads through a copy of today's East London Observer, catching the headline: The East End Tragedies.

"Again does the East of London, to our regret, stand forth in unpleasant prominence by reason of the brutal crimes which have recently been committed. It is the reverse of encouraging to find that each unmitigated

ferocity is in existence, in spite of the efforts that are made on all sides to improve the lower class of citizens; and such fearful blots on civilization's record prove that it is not necessary to go far to find human nature at its worst. The two murders which have so startled London within the last month are singular for the reason that the victims have been of the poorest of the poor, and no adequate motive in the shape of plunder can be traced. The excess of effort that has been apparent in each murder suggests the idea that both crimes are the work of a demented being, as the extraordinary violence used is the peculiar feature in each instance."

"You're not meant to be here," she comments casually, sensing Reid standing behind her, reading the article over her shoulder. "Why ever are you not enjoying your leave elsewhere? Far away from London and its filth."

"I was." He helps himself to the paper before she discards it. "But duty called." He flicks through its pages, looking for anything written about the latest crime.

"Duty?" Mary Jane adds a little more milk to the tea in front of her, hastening its cooling. "In your absence, the case of this most recent horror has been assigned to someone else quite capable of the task, I'm sure. Do your superiors even know you're here?"

"I needed to see the body for myself." Reid justifies his actions without confirming their irregularity. "She'll be interred before I return from leave."

Mary Jane lifts her cup, ready to chance a small sip. "Has she been identified?"

"Minutes ago." Reid nods. "It's believed her name is Annie Chapman, though she may have been known to some as Annie Sivvey, or Dark Annie."

Mary Jane's teacup never makes it to her lips, her hand frozen mid-air.

"You know the name?" Reid is quick to leap on her apparent recognition of the moniker.

"I might," Mary Jane answers guardedly, giving nothing away. "But so many here use such *noms de guerre* that it would be impossible for me to say. Indeed,

there are several names by which I myself am known, including Dark Mary."

"What sense that?" Reid looks puzzled. "You're of fair complexion."

"I rather fear it's my mood to which the appellation refers, Inspector." Mary Jane takes her first sip of the tepid tea. "On these streets, a woman must learn to be sharp of tongue and quick of temper, lest she should be thought weak."

"You fight?"

"If I have to." Mary Jane recalls some hair pulling that ensued outside the Ten Bells when a young harlot hailing from Waterloo Road was in need of tearing down a peg or two. The matter was settled with fists, and that reminds her of the bruise she saw on Annie's temple. "The woman I know as Dark Annie is swift with her fists also." She hesitates. "May I see the body?"

Although this isn't Reid's investigation, and he has no authority to do so, he requires no persuasion to sneak Mary Jane into the Whitechapel mortuary. On this occasion, the body—washed and stripped of clothing—is not hidden away in a shell, but has been laid out on a table and covered from head to toe with a white sheet, prepared for the impending postmortem. Around the woman's midsection, the sheet dips between her hips, highlighting the unnatural concavity of her abdomen, the linen clinging to an open wound beneath and soaking up the seeping fluids.

On another table, the woman's clothes have been deposited in a semi-orderly manner, her minimal possessions collected in a small basket and placed next to her old, scuffed and filthy lace-up boots. Pitiably, the basket contains only a scrap of dirty muslin, two combs— one in a paper case—and two pills folded inside a torn corner of an envelope. This represents the entirety of her belongings. No brass rings.

Of the clothing, two bodices and a long black coat are stained with blood around the neck. Two petticoats and a black skirt have only a little crimson soaked into the back of the fabrics, and a pair of red and white striped woolen stockings have no mess on them whatsoever.

Draped over the edge of the basket, a large old-fashioned pocket—of the kind worn under the skirt and tied about the waist—is torn in two places.

There's no red and white neckerchief in sight, and Mary Jane feels a small measure of relief. Perhaps this is a different Annie.

As she approaches the table, a vile stench assaults her. Not merely the customary smell of blood and death— the pungent aroma of wet pennies—but feces, and something akin to putrefying eggs.

"What is that dreadful stink?" She bunches up part of her shawl and presses it to her nose, using the thick wool as a makeshift mask. "It's worse than pig muck."

"Some of her innards were ... displaced." Reid can't bring himself to be any more descriptive, even though the horrific nature of the wounds will be made public soon enough.

"How was she done?"

"She was found like the others: on her back, knees crooked and apart, splayed open in the most undignified manner for a woman, and her throat was most viciously cut." Reid relates facts gleaned from the police file, having not attended the scene himself. "It is the belief of our police surgeon, after only a cursory examination conducted at the scene, that our man took her by the chin and stifled her breath."

He demonstrates this by plucking a handkerchief from his pocket and stepping behind Mary Jane, pressing the heel of his palm under her chin and clamping his fingers around her mouth and nose, holding the handkerchief over her airways in such a way as he could easily apply enough pressure to cause suffocation.

"In this manner," he continues, the back of Mary Jane's head held tight to his shoulder, "the beast muted any cries for help the poor creature may have tried to make, then slit her." Reid swipes his free hand in front of Mary Jane's throat from left to right. "As she wilted from the injury, he laid her upon the ground and completed his gruesome work."

The reenactment over, he releases Mary Jane from his grasp, and she takes a bold step toward the head of the corpse.

"Show me."

At her request, Reid peels back the white sheet, revealing the face of the woman beneath. Her eyes are closed, her mouth agape, and there's a white neckerchief with a wide red border tied around her neck, knotted at the front and saturated with blood.

Recognizing her at once, Mary Jane backs away from the table. "It truly is," she croaks, unable to look away. "It's her. Annie, my dear friend."

In dire need of fresh air, she rushes from the mortuary, Reid keeping close behind her in case she should succumb to a faint and do herself some injury on the flagstones.

"Why is this happening?" She supports herself against the dead-house wall. "What did any of us ever do but try to keep ourselves fed?"

Seeing that she's unable to hold herself upright, Reid retrieves a chair from the mortuary and settles her into it. "These crimes are a reflection of some madness, Miss Kelly. Do not suppose it to be a moral judgment."

"Then why choose women of this profession?" Mary Jane counters. "If not to punish us for the lives we've come to lead."

"It is a matter of accessibility, I should say." Reid shields her from a small group of onlookers hovering by the entrance to the yard. "Is there a woman of any other sort who, quite of her own volition, will lead a man—a stranger, no less—into a darkened corner where there's no hope of disturbance, so affording him the perfect opportunity to do her harm?"

"I suppose that's true." Mary Jane scarcely dares to think of all the times she's been alone with unknown men, entirely at their mercy. "We offer ourselves up for slaughter."

Harnessing the conversation before it has a chance to stray too far into such ponderings, Reid commences his questioning. "How well did you know Annie?"

"We saw each other on the street from time to time." Mary Jane racks her brain for pertinent information. "Her husband's deceased gone two years, hence her resorting to this life, and I believe she was lodging at Crossingham's on Dorset Street. Number thirty-five, on the north side."

"Crossingham's?" Reid frowns. "Where you also once lived?"

"Don't be starting that up again, Inspector." Mary Jane glares at him, wary of adding fuel to his lingering suspicions. "If you're not careful, you shall make me disinclined to confess that we ran into each other at the lodging house last night."

"You did? When?" Reid hands her a hanky so that she might dab at her weeping eyes.

"It must've been one o'clock or thereabouts." Mary Jane mops away the teardrops clinging to her eyelashes. "I shan't say what my business was at the place, though you might well guess. I bought her a baked potato on Commercial Street and we parted ways." She clasps a hand to her bosom, trying to regulate her breathing. "God, I'm in chronic need of a drink."

In wholehearted agreement with that sentiment, Reid invites Mary Jane back to his home and sits her on the sofa in his living room with a cup of brandy-laced tea.

"Better?" He nurses his own cup.

"Infinitely." Mary Jane takes a gulp, hoping there'll be a second cup coming in due course. Maybe even a third. Maybe without the tea.

Reid's home—a small private residence in the vicinity of Leman Street Police Station—is full of family warmth. Pictures on the mantel. His wife's cross-stitching framed and hung on the walls. Some children's toys gathered beside a small oak chest. It's comforting. The furniture is clean, well-padded, and Mary Jane's only complaint of the place is that Reid seems to have acquired a fat orange cat that keeps staring at her, swishing its bushy tail.

"Have you had any trouble lately?" Reid asks at last, after giving the brandy some time to loosen her tongue and ease her defenses.

"Trouble?" Mary Jane raises an eyebrow. "Of what sort?"

"When I saw you last, you had marks of violence upon your neck." He broaches the subject tentatively. "Is there anything you wish to tell me of that?"

Mary Jane purses her lips, questioning the reason for his inquiry. "Are you asking me because you're concerned for my welfare? Or because you've developed some ludicrous notion that I might provide a connection to the man responsible for these crimes?"

"Three women have been murdered, Miss Kelly." Reid forges on, unapologetic. "All I can see that links them is the manner in which they were killed, and you." He slides his cup onto a side table beside his armchair and leans forward, resting his elbows on his knees. "So I shall ask you again: Is there any man in your current acquaintance who's caused you fright of late?"

Fleming's name is primed on the tip of Mary Jane's tongue, but she says nothing.

"Who hurt you, Miss Kelly?" Reid urges her to unburden herself. "Tell me now, for other women could well be—"

"It was Fleming," she admits shamefully, preparing to be lambasted for her continued involvement with him. "He and I have been on strained terms this past year."

"You're seeing him again?" Anger seeps into Reid's voice.

"Not anymore. We had a falling out the night ..." Mary Jane falters. "The night of Martha Tabram's death," she realizes. "The three of us went to the theater: Fleming, Eva, and myself. When we returned to Whitechapel, he followed us home. He saw us together in Eva's room and it enraged him. He wasn't aware of my liking for female affection until then."

"What of the night Polly Nichols was murdered? The night of the Shadwell dock fire. Did you see him then?"

"Yes." Tension creases Mary Jane's brow. "I visited him at his lodgings."

"What for?"

"Money." She hates it. "We fought."

"And last night?"

"He was there, at Crossingham's Lodging House. He saw me ... working." She leaves out the part about the theft. "You don't honestly think ... ?"

"Does he carry a knife?" Reid chugs on like a steam engine.

"Yes, a clasp knife." Mary Jane's mind flashes back to that night on Dorset Street. "But most men in this quarter are apt to carry them about their person. That's hardly—"

"Has he ever threatened you with it?"

"Only twice." Mary Jane swallows hard. "He put it to my throat."

"How long ago was this?"

"The first occasion was last February," Mary Jane recalls. "I remember it because I'd not long moved to Miller's Court. He was furious that I was still cohabiting with my other man, and we argued on the street." She hesitates. "It was the night Annie Millwood was stabbed in White's Row, but this cannot be as it seems." She shakes her head, rejecting the neatness of the aligned coincidences. "It cannot be him who's done these terrible things."

"Why not?"

"I have slept with this man, Mister Reid. I have lived with him. How is it possible that my judgment could be so poor? A man capable of such vile atrocities against women is surely not a man at all, but a monster."

"Could he not be both?" Reid lets that thought settle, then reaches for his tea. "In any case, this is all mere supposition." He sips carefully, trying not to get his mustache wet. "Upon my return from leave, I shall make some discreet inquiries. In the meantime, you keep from the streets and don't sleep alone at nights. It isn't safe."

Only when Mary Jane completes the last stitch of a shawl she's been crocheting at infrequent intervals over the last week does she realize how dark it's become outside. Her eyes aching from working in the light of a small paraffin lamp borrowed from one of her neighbors, she folds the shawl neatly on the table and puts down her hook for the night.

Joe was meant to turn up after work—bringing her supper as well as the usual monetary offering—but judging by the color of the sky, it must be gone eight o'clock already and he's yet to make an appearance.

Hungry, she scavenges some stale bread from the cupboard and breaks it up into bite-size pieces, submerging the lumps in a small bowl of milk leftover from dinner, making it mushy but edible. She's been spending so much time with Eva at Lolesworth that stocking her own cupboard hasn't been necessary. For the time being, it's either this or nothing, so she consumes every bite of the tasteless slop, hoping that Joe will turn up with a meat pie.

But he doesn't. Time ticks on and she grows weary. Fed up of sitting on the wooden chair, staring at the door like a dog awaiting its master, she lies down on the bed, soon drifting off to an unpleasant and fitful sleep filled with dark and morbid imaginings. One moment, she's witnessing Fleming kill Dark Annie in Hanbury Street. He's subduing her just as Reid had posited, shedding her blood without getting a single drop on him, and as he kneels between her lifeless legs, his knife ready for cutting, he turns his head, grinning at his audience. Crying out, Mary Jane runs for her life, locking herself in her Miller's Court room, breathing hard and fast.

A second later, he's in the room with her, bearing down on her, forcing her onto the bed. She tries to scream, but can't. She tries to fend him off, but he's much too strong. Feeling the tip of his glinting blade touch her throat ...

"Oh! Murder!" She wakes up in a fright, clutching at her neck.

She's alone.

Panicked by her nightmares and not caring what time it is, she leaps off the bed, snatches her shawl off the footboard, and leaves Miller's Court. She intends to visit Eva, but gets no further than Dorset Street. A shadowy figure is watching the entrance of Miller's Court from the lodging house across the way, huddled in the porch.

Such a sight is not unusual, for some of the working women in the court have been known to bring men back to their lodgings when the weather turns, and it has been drizzling tonight. While entertaining one, they might have another two or three waiting their go, keeping an eye on the court, ready to dart down it at a moment's notice, so to see a man standing there, lurking in the gloom, ought not to be a source of fright. And yet it is.

Disconcerted by his presence, Mary Jane is about to retreat to the safety of her room when she spots Maria exiting the lodging house, thrown out by the deputy.

"To hell with the bloody lot of you!" she screeches at the top of her lungs, kicking a pebble in the direction of the porch. "Ain't got no hearts, nor any care for a woman's safety on these wicked streets. I could be done in tonight, so I could, and it'd be on your heads!"

"Ain't you got no lodgings?" Mary Jane hails her.

"Not the coin for it," Maria responds, crossing the street to meet her friend.

"I'll give you a bed if you like," Mary Jane offers. "I don't want to be alone, and you can't be wandering about all night with that mad butcher on the loose." She leads Maria down the passage. "Keep your mitts to yourself, mind," she warns, knowing well how amorous Maria gets when horizontal.

Promising to behave, Maria starts shedding her clothes as soon as they're in the room. The door isn't even locked before she's down to her undergarments, and Joe bursts in as she's getting Mary Jane to help her unfasten a tricky clasp on her corset.

"This one again?!" Joe throws up his hands. "Half the bloody time you ain't even here, and when you are, you're always in the company of a wench. I hope she's paying you at least. You making a bit extra lapping up her madge?"

"Where the bleeding hell have you been?!" Mary Jane strides up to him, sniffing his breath. "Oh, of course. You've been drinking away my money. Why'd you bother coming?"

"Get her out of here," Joe snarls, pointing a finger at Maria. "Now."

"She don't have nowhere else to go, you callous prick." Mary Jane isn't in the mood to obey. "You'd see her turned out on the street with that slasher out there?! How could you? And why? I didn't hear you complaining when you was in the bed with us."

Joe clenches his jaw, resenting the reminder of his male weakness. On a handful of other occasions when Maria was lacking a place to sleep, the pair abated his complaints about her sharing the cramped bed by teasing him stiff. Their operations obscured by the bed sheets, which kept them covered from the waist down, a chemise-clad Maria would mount Mary Jane and simulate the undulations of flat-fucking, while Mary Jane feigned pleasure beneath her. Though they never had any genital contact, Joe believed they were engaged in the occupation and once spontaneously erupted into his undergarments.

He detested the frequency with which Mary Jane began inviting Maria to share the room, but had trouble being quite so staunch in his objections when he was receiving some benefit from the arrangement.

Determined not to let himself get caught in the same predicament again, he repeats his demand. "Get her out. I'm paying for this room, and I don't want her in it."

Mary Jane plants her hands on her hips, remaining defiant. "Give her fourpence for a bed of her own and she'll go gladly."

Fuming, Joe delves a hand into his pocket, pulls out four tarnished pennies, and thrusts them in Maria's direction. "Hook it."

Content to take his money and return to the lodging house from which she was just ejected, Maria dresses, pecks Mary Jane on the cheek, and leaves without a word of thanks.

"She's a bad 'un," Joe condemns her in the wake of her departure. "And she's turning you wrong. You didn't have such queer fancies afore she started mucking about with ya."

"Is that whatchu think?" Mary Jane laughs, taking great pleasure in correcting him. "As it so happens, I love the touch of a woman. I always have, and I don't care who knows it. Not once have I ever had pleasure with a man. Do you hear me? Not once. Not with you, nor any other fella." She snatches up her shawl and turns for the door. "I hate the bloody lot of you!"

"Where d'you think you're going now? You'd best not be walking out on me, woman."

"Damn right I am!" She slams the door behind her and heads for Lolesworth, stopping only once to punch a staggering drunk in the face as a result of him accosting her and trying to kiss her in the middle of the street.

Upon knocking on Eva's door, she hears the creak of the bed, followed by the striking of a match and the pitter patter of bare feet across the floor. There's a moment's silence, then:

"Mary Jane, is that you?" Eva calls out softly.

"Yes, my darling," Mary Jane coos back. "Let me in."

Wearing only her nightgown and a fretful frown, Eva opens the door just wide enough to pull Mary Jane through, then hurries to get it closed and locked, fumbling the latch twice.

"What's you doing out so late?"

"Joe and I had words." Mary Jane slips off her shawl. "I couldn't stand to spend another minute with the man." She regards Eva's face, troubled by the dark circles of fatigue under her eyes. "Did I wake you?"

Eva shakes her head. "I've been thinking of you all night." She hurls herself into Mary Jane's arms, stretching as tall as she can on tiptoe, tucking her head against Mary Jane's neck. "I couldn't sleep. Not knowing of what happened in the wee hours last night."

Mary Jane glances at the table, a farthing dip casting an orange glow over two evening newspapers, both carrying headlines about the most recent murder and mutilation.

"What've I said about you filling your mind with all these thoughts?" She rubs Eva's back. "It ain't good to have such fears weighing on you."

"Sleep with me tonight, Em." Eva squeezes her, frightened to let go. "Don't leave." She tightens her grip. "I knows you has to work, and I ain't got no right to say such things, but I don't want no-one else touching you. Not even Joe."

"My love, you have *every* right to say such things." Mary Jane feels Eva's tears soaking into her bodice. "I'm yours, and yours alone. You just have to be patient a little while longer. It'll all come good in the end, you'll see."

As she says those words, she hopes they're true.

CHAPTER 44

WHITECHAPEL IS PANIC-STRICKEN AT ANOTHER FIENDISH CRIME
A FOURTH VICTIM OF THE MANIAC

"London lies today under the spell of a great terror. A nameless reprobate—half beast, half man—is at large, who is daily gratifying his murderous instincts on the most miserable and defenseless classes of the community. There can be no shadow of a doubt now that our original theory was correct, and that the Whitechapel murderer, who has now four, if not five, victims to his knife, is one man, and that man is a murderous maniac.

Hideous malice, deadly cunning, insatiable thirst for blood—all these are the marks of the mad homicide. The ghoul-like creature who stalks through the streets of London is simply drunk with blood, and he will have more. The question is, what are the people of London to do? Whitechapel is garrisoned with police and stocked with plain-clothes men. Nothing comes of it. The police have not even a clue. They are in despair at their utter failure to get so much as a scent of the criminal.

Now we have a moral to draw and a proposal to make. We have carefully investigated the causes of the miserable and calamitous breakdown of the police system. They are chiefly two: (1) the inefficiency and

timidity of the detective service; (2) the inadequate local knowledge of the police.

Now there is only one thing to be done at this moment. The people of the East End must become their own police. They must form themselves at once into Vigilance Committees. There should be a central committee, which should map out the neighborhood into districts and appoint the smaller committees. These again should at once devote themselves to volunteer patrol work at night, as well as to general detective service. The unfortunates who are the objects of the man-monster's malignity should be shadowed by one or two of the amateur patrols. They should be cautioned to walk in couples. Whistles and a signaling system should be provided, and means of summoning a rescue force should be at hand. We are not sure that every London district should not make some effort of the kind, for the murderer may choose a fresh quarter now that Whitechapel is being made too hot to hold him.

We do not think that the police will put any obstacle in the way of this volunteer assistance. They will probably be only too glad to have their efforts supplemented by the spontaneous action of the inhabitants. But in any case, London must rouse itself. No woman is safe while this ghoul is abroad. Up, citizens, then, and do your own police work!"

-- The Star (London), September 8, 1888

CHAPTER 45

Saturday, September 29, 1888

COMMERCIAL STREET IS GLARINGLY DEVOID OF ITS USUAL vibrancy. As the sun sank in the sky, so women of all social groups departed from the streets like a silent migration of multicolored birds, fear having taken a stranglehold on Whitechapel.

Prior to the onset of the murders, Commercial Street was awash with color. Women promenaded from north to south and all around, their bonnets decorated with dyed feathers or artificial blooms, their outfits ornamented with dashes of pinks and reds. Now, only the unfortunate few who cannot afford to take measures to protect their safety are left behind.

These are the widowed mothers who must feed their children, the destitute women in need of their doss money, and the chronically intemperate, willing to sell anything for a glass of gin. Wherever possible, they keep in twos or threes, using the same trusted hideaways and never straying far from the gaslights, one always knowing where another is.

Intending to assist them in their efforts to remain safe, Mary Jane began her evening in such a group. She's been walking the street for several hours, watching others conduct their business and turning away fuck-hungry men as they approach her. The fact that she's wearing her respectable clothes, is lacking her red lip paste, and has

her hair pinned up, does nothing to dissuade them from trying their luck.

"No, love." She rejects yet another, refusing to be swayed by the production of two overly shiny gold coins, each supposedly being half-sovereigns. "I ain't taking no-one tonight, and even if I was, you'd have to try harder than that."

She plucks one of the gilded coins from his palm and tilts it toward a gaslight, a thorough look and a feel of the weight of it revealing it to be a sixpence, scrubbed up and gilded to imitate a coin of higher value. It's a sham she's seen before.

In dim light, or at a hurried glance, a gilded sixpence of the particular design minted last year, to commemorate the Queen's Golden Jubilee, is almost indistinguishable from a half-sovereign. They were soon withdrawn from circulation on account of how easily they could be counterfeited, but there's still a few making their way around. If that fails, a well-polished farthing can give the appearance of a sixpence in the right light, but it's a swindle best reserved for the pubs and the low beer shops during their busy hours. Women of vice in this quarter ought to be sharp enough to question the authenticity of any coin offered above thruppence.

"Cheap trick." She flicks the fakement into the street, making him chase after it. "Give it a go on someone less canny than me."

At that moment, without the slightest warning, the heavens open. Rain comes down hard, catching everyone unawares, and Mary Jane seeks shelter. Being closer to Miller's Court than to Lolesworth, she lifts her shawl over her head, hunches forward, and scurries in the direction of the Britannia, one hand clasping her shawl, the other in her pocket, gripping her room key.

Blinkered by the shawl, her peripheral vision severely compromised, she doesn't see a figure rushing at her from the street. Indeed, she knows nothing of his presence until she feels a hard blow to her left side, a punch to the kidney momentarily crippling her. A second later, she's dragged off her feet and down the passage beside the Ringers' Buildings, her mouth and nose

smothered by a red silk handkerchief, a man's strong arm around her waist, lifting her off the ground and manhandling her into the courtyard.

As they emerge on the other side of the covered passage—her shawl lost somewhere along the way—she manages to bite down on the hanky, pinching one of his fingers between her teeth and causing him to relinquish his grip, enabling her to wrench herself free.

Spinning to face him, she then retaliates without hesitation, striking his cheek with her fist, her room key clenched tightly in her palm, the rough metal edges of the bit gashing him below his eye.

It's Fleming.

"Gerroff me, you arsehole!" She wallops him. "What do you think you're playing at?!"

"You been talking to the coppers about me?" He advances on her, rain gathering in the brim of his bowler hat and spilling from it like a burst gutter pipe. "You been telling the p'leece I had summink to do with them murders?"

Mary Jane backs away, her bodice already soaked through and her auburn tresses sticking to her neck. "Let me by." She keeps her head down. "I ain't said nothing."

"Liar!" He grabs her by the chin. "But you'll be good from now on, I daresay. If you behave, I'll behave. How about that? I don't wanna see no harm come to you." He tilts her head back, raindrops splashing on her face and tumbling down her cheeks like tears.

Fear struck into her by the sight of a woman's brass ring on his pinky finger, Mary Jane struggles to speak. "Whatever you think I've done—"

On a short tether and in no mood for her denials, he winds her with a hard punch to her solar plexus before knocking her onto the flagstone ground. "How would you like it if such unsavory things was being said about you behind your back?" He flips her over, planting his foot on her chest. "P'raps we'll find out."

Unable to make any sound, Mary Jane lies still, gasping for air as he looms over her, concluding his reprimand with a few kicks to her ribs and stomach, his

assault continuing until she curls into a helpless ball, shivering and sobbing.

Not sure whether it lasts one minute or twenty, she stays put until she's certain he's gone, then heaves herself up. In agony, she staggers from the courtyard, collecting her shawl from the passage along the way, and hobbles back to Miller's Court.

Slumped against her door, the torrential rain still beating down, she searches her pockets for her key.

It isn't there.

"Goddamn it." She checks again.

Still nothing.

Wondering if she might be able to reach the latch from the window, she has a rummage through the dustbins by the water pump, looking for something heavy enough to smash glass, and eventually pulls out an old round bed knob the size of her palm.

Satisfied that it'll do the job, she totters to the four-paned window nearest the door and—with a look of concentration fixed upon her face—chucks the knob at the lower right pane of glass, shattering the top right corner. That done, she grips the nearby drainpipe with one hand, props her knee on the window ledge, and reaches through the broken window, fumbling to unlatch the door by feel alone.

It works.

Following the relenting click of the lock, she dodders inside and strips to her undergarments, discarding her sopping wet, dirt-smeared dress and apron in her tin bath. Since all her decent outfits are at Eva's, she has no choice but to change into her working clothes. At least they're dry and clean.

After brushing out her drenched auburn mane, she turns her mind to the shards of glass littered about her floor. Her broom being on loan to a neighbor, she opens the door, gets down on her hands and knees, and gathers the fragments by hand, flinging them outside into the court, some of them landing on the adjacent doorstep of number one.

"What's all this?" The room's past-middle-aged occupant, Julia, opens the door and looks out, assuming

Mary Jane's dropped an empty bottle of booze. "Been on the gin again, have we?"

"Not yet." Mary Jane sweeps the smaller slivers of glass out with a hanky. "One of my men just gave me a basting. I ain't feeling so good."

"You'll be needing a drink, then," Julia concludes, as if one is a logical accompaniment to the other. "C'mon, lovie. Get yer coat."

Mary Jane shouldn't, but she does. She dons her old black velvet jacket, raids her lockbox for some coins, and heads for the Ten Bells to indulge in some self-pity, spinning Julia the tale that her other Joe ill-used her in a jealous fit. She doesn't intend to stay out long.

One drink.

Two.

Just enough to dull the pain.

Not long to closing, an undeniably inebriated Mary Jane leads the loyal patrons of the Ten Bells public house in an off-key sing-song. Sitting on a tabletop, belting out an Irish folk ballad while wielding a large glass of gin, her legs unabashedly crossed at the knee, she's the center of the room's attention until the door opens and a young woman walks in unaccompanied, all male interest immediately diverted to new flesh.

Afraid to step any further than the doorway, aware of so many pairs of eyes upon her and the sudden cessation of drunken crooning, the new arrival clears her throat and announces the purpose of her visit, her voice quaking.

"I'm looking for someone." She fidgets with the hair-work brooch pinned to the neck of her bodice, worrying it with her fingertips. "A woman," she adds for clarity. "Her name's Mary Jane. Is she here?"

541

Hearing her name, but too intoxicated to recognize the sound of the person who spoke it, Mary Jane downs her gin, hops off the tabletop, and approaches the voice, assuming she's been sought out for a fight. "Who wants me?" she demands to know, abating her aggressive stance the instant she manages to focus her bleary eyes on the face of the timid teen hovering by the door.

"Eva!" She throws open her arms. "My love!"

To see her so obviously screwed, Eva's heart breaks. "I was waiting for you. When you didn't come home, I ..." Her lower lip trembles, her eyes wet with tears. "I've been looking everywhere. I didn't know if you was ..." She can't bring herself to say the words. "Why's you doing this to yourself? Ain't you had the fear of this life put in you yet? I hate seeing you in such a dreadful state, and you knows what liquoring does to a woman." She spies Maria sitting at the table Mary Jane just vacated. "How could you let her get like this?"

Not caring to wait for a response, she strides into the room and loops Mary Jane's arm over her shoulder, determined to extract her from this wicked place. As she does so, she's heckled from all angles.

"Look elsewhere," Mary Jane snaps at any man who dares to leer in her direction. "This flesh is *not* for sale. Not at any price."

When one man dares to pinch Eva's bottom, Mary Jane lurches toward his table and cracks him in the face with her elbow, snapping the cartilage in his nose and causing a bleed. As he reels from the hit, she slips her hand around the back of his head and slams him forward, smashing his nose and forehead into the table and knocking him out.

"Anyone else wanna try my patience?" she challenges the testosterone-filled room, alcohol fueling her impudence.

"Mary Jane, no!" Eva darts in front of her, pleading her to stand down. "Leave 'em be."

Preventing the outbreak of a messy brawl, she manages to get Mary Jane outside and back to Miller's Court, surprised that she's still capable of holding herself upright. With no small amount of effort, she then gets

Mary Jane to hush, holding a hand over her mouth to keep her from waking up everyone in the court with an impromptu musical number.

"Hold still now." She props her against the wall of number thirteen. "Where's your room key?" She runs her hands over Mary Jane's thighs, feeling her garters for any telltale lumps.

"I dunno." Mary Jane giggles. "But you're welcome to keep looking."

Moderately annoyed, Eva crouches on the ground to check Mary Jane's boots, being not in the least bit amused when Mary Jane lifts her skirts and flings them over her head.

"This ain't funny." Eva beats her way out. "How's we gonna get inside?" She delves her hands into Mary Jane's pockets and has a good rummage, finding nothing but a few farthings, three silk hankies, and a French letter, the latter giving her some confusion. "What thing is this?"

"A prick sheath." Mary Jane nabs it back. "They ain't cheap, so don't chuck it." She pockets the unwelcome reminder of her profession. "And don't fret about the key. It's lost."

Offering no explanation, she toddles around the corner and performs a repeat of her earlier trick, gripping the drainpipe with her right hand while she rests her knee on the ledge and reaches her left arm through the broken pane, unlatching the door with surprising ease.

"Whatever have you gone and done?!" Eva glares at the busted window. "For God's sake." She helps Mary Jane extract her arm from the jagged hole, scared that she might dismember herself. "Let's get you to bed afore aught worse happens."

Exhausted, she guides Mary Jane in and deposits her by the bedstead, turning from her for only a few moments to light a candle on the bedside table. By the time she's done, Mary Jane is swaying precariously, her apron strings twisted to the front and knotted up, all attempts to remove the garment—including jiggling and tugging on it—having failed.

"Steady on." Eva seizes her above the waist, clamping both hands around her.

A little sobered by the walk, Mary Jane shrieks. The pain in her ribs is fresh again, and she recoils from Eva's touch, wincing and gripping the bedpost. "Fucking arse shite and buggery," she spews a string of coarse execrations, gritting her teeth until the agony subsides.

Looking on, confused and concerned, Eva waits until the outburst is over before asking meekly, "Em? What's wrong?"

"It's nothing of concern." Mary Jane wipes her profusely watering eyes. "I had a small accident earlier this evening, that's all."

Unconvinced by the assurance that she oughtn't be worried, Eva forces Mary Jane onto the bed and unfastens her clothing, tearing back every layer until she reaches bare skin, horrified to discover that Mary Jane's ribcage, stomach, and abdomen are covered with deep purple splotches, one of which is distinctly shoe-shaped.

"Oh, my Lordy." Eva turns her around, getting a good look at her bruised and battered body, assessing the extent of the damage. "You need to get down to the infirmary."

Mary Jane shakes her head. "Don't be daft. This ain't the worst he's ever given me."

"Who?" Eva can barely speak, her voice choked in her throat. "Who's done this to you?"

"Joe." Mary Jane attempts to take a deep breath for the first time since her beating, only to be met with more searing pain shooting through her ribs. "Other Joe," she rasps. "Not the docile one what sometimes smells of fish."

"The one who used to knock you about in Bethnal Green?" Eva clenches her jaw, fetching Mary Jane's chemise from the washstand. "I knew that bastard was trouble. Have you reported him yet? If not, we'll go to Leman Street first thing in the morning and—"

"No, Eva." Mary Jane eases herself into the silk, groaning as she raises her arms above her head, stretching out her torso. "There won't be no peelers."

"Why not?" Outrage escapes into Eva's voice.

"It weren't without provocation." Mary Jane lets Eva help her out of her knotted apron, then her skirts and

petticoats. "I deserved his punishment this time—I truly did. It served me bloody well right."

Not believing even a shred of that, Eva kneels on the floor to remove Mary Jane's boots. "Whatchu always punishing yourself for? Whatever it is you think you've done, I'm sure as you don't deserve this." She yanks off one boot, then the other. "I dunno who you was afore you come to London—I ain't even sure I knows who you was in Whitechapel afore I met you—but I *am* sure I knows you now." She starts work on Mary Jane's stockings. "And the woman I love is too good to be treated like muck. She ain't meant for this life, and that's for no doubt."

Mary Jane looks earnestly into Eva's eyes, moved by her unconditional and unwavering affection. "Do you want to know?" she volunteers her truth. "Do you want to know who I am? If you do, I'll tell you everything."

Eva thinks carefully before answering, knowing this emotional, gin-induced offer may not be made again. "As I said, I already knows who you are," she concludes at last, feigning conviction. "Who you were afore don't matter a bit."

"Oh, you beautiful, perfect girl." Mary Jane dives for her, planting woodpecker kisses all over her head. "Will you stay here with me tonight? I don't want to be alone."

"Course I'll stay." Eva tugs back the covers and gets her tucked up. "I wouldn't even think of leaving you like this. Is there aught I can give you for the pain?"

Rolling onto her stomach, Mary Jane dangles her arm off the edge of the palliasse, pointing to the floor beneath the bedside table. Puzzled but compliant, Eva drags the table away from the bed and exposes the bare floor, Mary Jane's outstretched finger directing her to a scratched corner of one of the loose boards. Prying it up, she uncovers the hidey-hole beneath.

Mary Jane's lockbox is buried under a mound of newspaper clippings, the disorganized pile topped with a bundle of letters tied up with silk ribbon. They're her letters from the continent. Every single one. Sifting through it all, she lifts the lockbox out, gaining access to it using a key from the pocket of Mary Jane's dress.

545

Inside, the first thing to catch her eye is an empty coin pouch and her heart sinks. Momentarily fretting that this depleted leather purse might signify all there is to their savings, she's relieved—albeit confused—to then uncover a post office savings book in the name of Miss Mary Malone.

"Who's Mary Malone?" She picks it up, frowning at the name.

"I s'pose that's me." Mary Jane chortles.

Unable to determine precisely what she means by that, Eva flips through the book. Regular monthly deposits have been made since the beginning of 1887, the amounts varying from six to seven pounds when the account was first opened, to two or three soon after. Later in 1888, the amounts drop to one or two, right up until the banking of the five pounds she brought back from the continent.

"Is this all yours?" She pores over the figures.

"Ours," Mary Jane corrects her. "It's all *ours*."

Focusing on the more recent transactions, Eva spots a significant withdrawal made on August 3. That being in the midst of Mary Jane's four-day drinking binge, she's quick to assume the worst.

"What's this?" She points it out.

"I needed something," Mary Jane answers without looking, knowing precisely what it is that Eva's indicating, for there's only one such transaction in the whole book. "I can't say more than that, but it weren't frivolous, I promise you."

Less than satisfied with that response, but choosing not to dwell on it, Eva studies the various denominational breakdowns of the deposits, the last of the very large sums having been banked in April of last year. "You was putting in at least five pounds regular to start," she observes, noting that the decline roughly coincides with their meeting. "What changed?"

"I stopped seeing one of my specials."

Eva doesn't need many minutes to put two and two together, arriving at the most obvious explanation with a forlorn sigh. "It was a woman, weren't it? Why ever was

she paying you so much? What was you giving her for all that?"

"It's not what you think it to be." Mary Jane prepares to divulge all. "She didn't lay a finger on me; she had no inclination for that. She never even saw me completely unrigged. I touched her, I gamahuched her, I frigged her, and I fucked her. I did all that a man would, only better. She paid me handsomely for my services and my discretion, but I called off the engagement after you and I consummated our love. It felt wrong."

Eva is silent for a long while, then the questions come. "If she don't like to have a woman that way, why was she doing her business with you?"

"Life's complicated for her type," Mary Jane turns onto her back, trying to get comfortable. "Her husband's a beast of a man who drinks and gambles and whores. There ain't no affection between them, but she can't risk chasing pleasure with another man. If she were caught, she'd be disgraced and left penniless. If she were to get in the family way ... well, that would be the end of her. With me, the risk was greatly diminished. She felt quite safe in the arrangement."

"How long was you engaged by her?"

"Years, but our visits were infrequent. We met while I was working at the Frenchwoman's house." Mary Jane hopes to avoid having to relate how she was once in the business of educating gaggles of neglected West End women in the pleasures of onanism, and demonstrating how they might enhance the voluptuous sensations of marital union. "She told me of her unhappiness—particularly in matters of wedded love—and I told her I could please her every bit as much as a man could."

Silence.

It seems as though Eva's curiosity has been sated, but then, "Did you enjoy fucking her?"

Treading on shaky ground, Mary Jane sticks to the truth. "I'd be lying if I said that I did not."

"Did you spend with her?" The questions don't stop.

"Sometimes. Not always."

"Does she have a nice cunt?"

"Eva, I *love* you." Mary Jane flings an arm around Eva's neck, drawing her in for a kiss. "You make my heart ache. Ain't never in my life have I felt for anyone as I feel for you, and there's not a cunt on this Earth that compares to yours."

"You're drunk." Eva pushes her away.

"It's still true."

Moving on, leaving the past where it lies, Eva scoops a picture book out of the lockbox. Presuming it to contain family photographs, and thinking that dreadfully fancy, her imagination takes off. Before she's even opened it, she's concocted an elaborate fairytale in which Mary Jane was raised in a big country house with an array of servants. Her well-to-do parents had arranged her marriage to a handsome Spanish prince, but Mary Jane ran off on the eve of the wedding, forsaking home and riches for the chance to find true happiness in the arms of a woman.

Keen to see what truly lies inside, she flips to the first page, taken aback to find a picture of two naked women sat astride a taxidermied stallion, kissing and caressing each other's breasts.

"Whatever bawdiness is this ... ?" Her cheeks turn scarlet as she turns the pages, shocked to see image after image of undisguised love between women.

"It's a naughty picture book." Mary Jane breaks into a grin. "Do you like it?"

Eva keeps looking, fascinated by the range of creative poses, the models enjoying each other in an endless variety of attitudes, some using dildos. Just as she's becoming accustomed to the raunchiness of it all, a loose photograph slips out, dropping into her lap.

This pornographic card shows a woman sprawled over a velvet sofa, clad only in corset and silk stockings. One hand covers her sex, the other draped over the arm of the sofa, her long auburn hair cascading around her shoulders.

Eva gasps, transfixed on the woman's face. That familiar, dazzling face.

"You ..." She angles the image toward the light, just in case she's mistaken.

"If you like it"—Mary Jane leans over the edge of the bed to whisper in her ear—"turn to the next page."

Scarcely daring to do so, Eva flips up the corner and peeks, peeling it back an inch at a time until the full image is revealed. In this one, Mary Jane is lying on a velvet chaise, sans clothing, her legs spread while another woman licks her quim.

"More?" Mary Jane turns over another leaf ... and another ... and another ... "I s'pose I ought to be ashamed that the only pictures ever taken of me are vulgar, but I like them." She gazes at her twenty-four-year-old figure. "Is that dreadfully vain of me? I enjoyed being an artist's model, and it paid generously."

"You're so beautiful." Eva traces her fingers over the curves of Mary Jane's body. "Who's all these other women? Toffers, like what you was?"

"Aye." Mary Jane sighs. "Some of them worked with me at the Frenchwoman's house."

Braving another turn of the page, Eva comes upon a picture of Mary Jane wearing an open kimono, her lips locked with a fully nude Japanese woman. "You've had an Oriental." She makes no effort to conceal her shock. "Whatever does one of them taste like?"

"The same as any woman." Mary Jane dispels her ignorance. "Women are women, no matter the color of their skin, and you ought to know better than to think different."

On the next leaf, Eva is disturbed to look upon a picture of Mary Jane sprawled nude on a bearskin rug, smoking from a long wooden pipe. An opium pipe.

"Don't fret that." Mary Jane covers the image with her hand. "It ain't the woman I am." She fumbles for the corner of the page, keen to put it out of mind. "I haven't done such dreadful things in years." She directs Eva to another photograph. "Here, look. I like this one."

The subsequent image is much more pleasing. A blonde woman, wearing not a stitch of clothing but a top hat, is squatting over Mary Jane's face, receiving oral titillation while tipping her hat as if in greeting.

"Tipping the velvet." Eva giggles. "However do you breathe under there, though?"

"I manage." Mary Jane smirks, tickling her finger over Eva's neck. "And I'm ready for it whenever you are."

Still blushing, Eva closes the book. "P'raps another night."

Resuming her hunt for whatever pain medication Mary Jane has, the next item she pulls out is Mary Jane's glass dildo, wrapped in an old cotton chemise. Over the course of the last two months, it's been carted back and forth between their residences at least a dozen times.

Most recently, Eva brought it over after work. Though Joe was due home imminently, she wanted a fuck. Perhaps she even wanted them to be caught in the act, for when he walked in on them, she begged Mary Jane not to stop.

"Keep doing me," she said, loud enough for him to hear. "Make me come."

Of course, it was purely possessive. She wanted Joe to see that Mary Jane was hers—that her needs surpassed his in Mary Jane's thoughts—and that there wasn't a damn thing he could do about it. She wanted him to know that he'd been relegated to an afterthought, and he received the message loud and clear when corset-clad, cock-wearing Mary Jane barked at him to wait outside.

His interruption didn't even break her rhythm, and Eva was too far gone to care that he watched them through the window, biting on his fingernails. He couldn't see anything of value, for she was fully clothed beneath Mary Jane. The most skin she had on show was a splash of thigh above her white stockings, and most of that was obscured. Mary Jane's hand was on her bare rump, lifting her to meet every thrust, their bodies crushing together over and over again until she came with such force that she felt the bed might collapse.

The mere memory of it brings a noticeable heat back into her cheeks, and Mary Jane isn't so fuddled that she can't recognize the look of a hot-cunted woman when she sees one.

"Do you want it tonight?" she offers, ready to snatch her priapus out of Eva's hands and strap it on, if only Eva should say the word.

Instead, "I ain't sure." Eva runs her hand over Mary Jane's sore ribs. "I don't wanna hurt you."

At the faintest touch, Mary Jane flinches, her intense discomfort settling the issue.

"Another time." Eva wraps the phallus back up, and upon returning it to its hiding place, comes across a small bottle of laudanum. "Is this what you wanted?" She starts to uncork it.

"Wait." Mary Jane stops her. "It'll put me out for the night."

"That's the point, ain't it?"

"Aye, but let me have you first." Despite her injuries, Mary Jane tries to haul Eva onto the bed. "Do you fancy a tickle?"

"No, Em." Eva rebuffs her. "You're not in fit shape."

Having hurt her ribs in the attempt to facilitate intimacy, Mary Jane rolls onto her back, moaning and clutching her side.

"See? You ain't strong enough for it tonight." Eva consults the smudged label on the bottle of laudanum. "How much do I give you?"

Mary Jane shrugs. "A teaspoon."

"You're sure?"

"Give or take." Mary Jane reaches out for it. "I'll just have a swig."

"No, you won't." Eva holds the bottle away from her and gets up to find a spoon. "If it's a teaspoon, then it's a teaspoon, and not a drop more." She finds an abandoned spoon on the floor, spits on it, and wipes it off on Mary Jane's apron before pouring into it a fraction less laudanum than the directions on the bottle state, just to be safe.

"Don't be stingy with it." Mary Jane pouts.

"It ain't stingy, it's proper." Eva feeds it to her. "I wanna make you well, not send you the other way." She puts the bottle down far out of Mary Jane's reach, just in case, then returns to the bed, fussing over her like a nervous mother.

She expects Mary Jane to fall asleep, as her dear old mam had always done, but instead, once the laudanum's

been absorbed into her bloodstream, it appears to have some surprisingly restorative effects.

"Get in this bed with me." Mary Jane grabs her and pulls her down, elevated by the medicine. "And do let me have you. I'm bloody randy." She fumbles her hands under Eva's skirts.

"Em!" Eva tries to resist her. "Don't! You ain't well."

Knowing she hasn't the coordination for it, Mary Jane doesn't even attempt to remove Eva's drawers, she just holds open the split and buries her face in the general vicinity of Eva's privy parts, working by feel and taste alone.

Of course, directly her tongue makes contact, Eva ceases to object to the operation. Her passions inflamed, she's nearing that divine peak of pleasure when Mary Jane's ministrations begin to falter, soon ceasing completely. A moment later, Mary Jane begins to snore.

CHAPTER 46

MORE EAST END TRAGEDIES

"At an early hour this (Sunday) morning two women were found murdered in the East End of London. Both had their throats cut in a shocking manner, but in the case of one found in the back yard of a house in Berner Street, Commercial Road, it is thought that the murderer may probably have been disturbed, as there was no further injury to the body. In the second case, which was discovered about three-quarters of an hour later, many of the horrors of the recent Whitechapel murders were found to have been repeated. The poor woman's throat had been savagely cut, and there was a large wound on the face, cutting into the nose. Her legs were apart and the clothes thrown right up, revealing the mutilated abdomen. Parts of the entrails had been torn out. Blood had flowed freely both from the neck and body, saturating the pavement. Besides the fearful wound on the face, the tops of both of the thighs were cut across. The intestines, which had been torn from the body, were found twisted into the gaping wound on the right side of the murdered woman's neck."

-- Lloyd's Weekly, September 30, 1888

Sunday, September 30, 1888

MARY JANE WAKES TO KISSES, EVA'S SOFT LIPS EXPLORING her neck while a furtive hand sneaks up her chemise and fondles one of her breasts.

"Good morning," she murmurs groggily, reaching behind her to caress Eva's thigh. "I hope you slept as well as I did."

"Mm-hmm." Eva tugs and pinches Mary Jane's nipple between her fingers, hoping that a night's rest will have done wonders for her healing. "How's you feeling?"

In all honesty, Mary Jane feels as though she's been run over by a brougham, but she's not about to let that stop her from giving Eva pleasure, if that's what Eva wants.

To that end, "I'm much restored," she lies, steeling herself for the onset of more pain.

"Then do me." Eva flops onto her back, positioning herself for mounting. "Let's put our things together."

She's about to throw down the covers and spread her legs when she spies movement in the periphery of her vision: Joe's sitting at the table.

Alarmed, she squeals and dives for the sheets, all the audacity she once displayed in his presence now lost in her fright and surprise. "Mary Jane!"

Honing in on the source of her panic, Mary Jane eases herself into a sitting position. "What the bleeding hell do you think you're doing?" She glowers at him.

"I might ask you the same, Marie." He meets her glare, his use of the French variant of her name instantly souring her mood.

"Ain't I told you not to call me that?" she snaps, tucking the blankets around Eva's bared shoulders, protecting her modesty. "Now turn your back and let my woman get decent."

Joe doesn't budge.

"I said turn around!" She grabs the nearest weapon—a lump of stale bread off the bedside table—and launches it in his direction. "Let her get dressed in peace."

Under protest, Joe picks his chair up, reverses it, and plonks it down facing the window. "She didn't seem to mind so much the other day," he mutters, plopping himself back in the chair and opening up the newspaper he brought with him.

"She weren't so unrigged then." Mary Jane would chuck another piece of bread at him if she had one. "She

don't want you looking at her private bits and pieces, and neither do I. Her delights are for my eyes only."

Impassioned by Mary Jane's emphatic declaration of possession—and after a quick peek over her shoulder to make sure Joe's eyes are suitably averted—Eva sits bolt upright and plants a kiss on Mary Jane's lips, the covers falling away from her. "I love hearing you call me your woman," she whispers. "I can't hardly wait till you can call me your wife."

Yearning for that day, Mary Jane captures her lips in another kiss, then lets her up. "May I walk you home?"

Eva shakes her head, hurrying into her clothes. "I'll be getting off to church."

"Then I shall walk you there." Mary Jane plucks her corset off the floor, feeling a twinge of pain at the thought of squeezing herself into it.

"Nah, you're all right." Eva prevents her from getting out of bed. "You do what needs to be done here, but don't you dare work tonight." She lays a hand on Mary Jane's bruised ribs. "Say you'll spend the night with me."

Mary Jane nods vehemently. "There ain't nowhere else I want to be."

"I love you so much." Eva steals another kiss, not caring if Joe hears. "I'll pray for you."

As the door shuts behind her, Joe takes himself out of isolation. "I brung you breakfast." He indicates two smoked kippers wrapped in old paper. "What happened there?" He tips his head toward the broken window.

"I lost my key." Mary Jane fishes her clothes off the floor.

"No." Joe bats her bodice out of her hands. "Get back on the bed."

Mary Jane stands motionless. "If you ain't paying for it, you ain't getting it."

Unbuttoning his trousers with one hand, he digs two florins out of his pocket and slaps them on the table. "You want it or not?"

Without saying a word, Mary Jane inserts her diaphragm and lies down, ready to receive him belly to belly, only to be swiftly flipped onto her stomach.

"I'm gonna give you a good come, you'll see." He spits on his hand, rubs it on his erection, and lodges himself inside her with one vigorous push. "You've been turned wrong, but you like a prick up you, I knows you do." He takes hold of her waist and begins to thrust, the pressure on her ribs making her moan.

Mistaking her pain for pleasure, he fucks her all the harder.

"Oh, God!" she wails as his cock stabs into her. "Joe! Please!" She clutches at the bed linens, her knuckles turning as white as the sheets would be if they were clean.

Oblivious to her suffering, he keeps on until the eruption of his crisis, having no idea that the final, protracted sigh to leave her lips is not one of a woman who's just spent, but one of sheer relief that the excruciating assault is over. Unreasonably pleased with himself, he then releases her and clambers off the bed, leaving her in a whimpering heap.

"I knew it." He wipes his shriveling pipe off on an old washcloth and tucks it away, a victorious grin plastered on his face. "I knew you wasn't one of them sapphists." He returns to the table, resuming his reading of yesterday's Eastern Post and City Chronicle.

Since the inquests into the murders of Polly Nichols and Dark Annie have now been concluded, all the gruesome details have been released. The papers are saturated with it.

"Did you hear? They arrested someone for these murders." Joe flips to the relevant section. "He turned himself in."

"What's the name of the man?" Mary Jane asks cautiously, feeling Joe's sediment trickling between her thighs, but lacking the energy to rise and douche.

"Fitzgerald summink-or-other." He shrugs. "It says in here how the bloke does 'em."

"Read it to me."

Dutifully, Joe tilts the paper toward the window for light and proceeds to report the particulars of Dark Annie's demise, picking and choosing the points of most interest. "He seized her by the chin. He pressed her throat, and while thus preventing the slightest cry, at the

same time produced insensibility and suffocation. There is no evidence of any struggle." He reads slowly and carefully, taking his time with the words. "The deceased was then lowered to the ground and laid on her back. Her throat was cut in two places with savage determination, and the injuries to the abdomen commenced."

All that, Mary Jane knew.

"There are two things missing," Joe goes on. "The rings had been wrenched from her fingers, and have not been found, and the uterus had been taken from the abdomen. The conclusion that the desire was to possess the missing abdominal organ seems overwhelming."

Instinctively, Mary Jane lays a hand over her belly. "The essence of her femininity."

Joe grunts something incoherent and reads further. "It has been suggested that the criminal is a lunatic with morbid feelings. It seems beyond belief that such inhuman wickedness could enter into the mind of any man, but unfortunately, our criminal annals prove that every crime is possible." He puts the paper down. "I don't want you going out there tonight. It ain't safe." He affects an authoritative tone. "And I don't care for you having all these women in your bed. It ain't proper, and I'm putting an end to it."

"Excuse me?" Mary Jane snorts, bemused by the notion that he should fancy himself in control of her actions.

"I don't like to think of you being that way." Joe sticks to his decision. "I do love ya."

"You may love me, but you don't own me, Joseph Barnett." Mary Jane summons the will to get out of bed and prepares her glass syringe for douching. "I am *not* your wife," she reminds him for the umpteenth time. "And the women I take to my bed are none of your concern."

"You wouldn't like it," he mutters, irked by her dismissal of his feelings.

"I wouldn't like what?" She squats over the chamber pot, swilling out her vaginal cavity.

"If I had another woman."

"You *do* have another woman, you fool." Mary Jane laughs at him. "She's the one you call your wife."

"You know what I mean." He slaps down the newspaper. "I don't have to keep to you. I could get me-self a woman what's cheaper and more up for a lark."

"Go on, then." Mary Jane dries herself off with a towel, then shoos him away with it. "Fuck off and find yourself a new one. This one's heartily sick of you."

Rather than continue to fight with her, Joe leaves in a huff. While fairly confident that he'll be back in a day or two—with his tail between his legs and his pipe in need of draining—Mary Jane squeezes her bruised body into her corset, gets dressed, and sets out on a trip to the post office on Whitechapel High Street to collect any mail held for her *poste restante*, hoping that one of her specials might've written to her. But she never makes it that far.

The streets are filled with whispers, and she hasn't been gone from Miller's Court five minutes before she hears more than she wants to know about the murders of two more women that occurred last night, their bodies discovered a mere hour apart.

The first, she learns, was found in Dutfield's Yard, off Berner Street, south of Whitechapel High Street. Her throat was cut, but nothing more, the killer most likely being disturbed in the midst of his work. The second was found in Mitre Square in Aldgate, within the boundaries of the Square Mile. She was found as the others: on her back, her legs posed and spread, drawing all attention to the mutilations inflicted upon her groin and abdomen.

By all accounts, the violence of her death was an escalation of those crimes previous, and Mary Jane can't help but picture it in her mind. The woman was ripped open. Her organs were displaced, her uterus taken, her face gashed and disfigured.

Feeling nauseous and claustrophobic, she weaves her way through the hordes of people on Wentworth Street, her adrenalin spiking every time someone bumps her shoulder or brushes against her. Keen to get off the busy thoroughfare, away from the throngs of strangers, she cuts through George Yard without thinking. It's the

most direct route to the post office, and she's taken it a thousand times before, but today ...

As she passes George Yard Buildings—the place where Martha Tabram was stabbed thirty-nine times and left lying in a pool of blood—she has trouble drawing breath. Her airways constrict, and her heart hammers in her chest. In a panic, she ducks inside a small, uncovered passage leading to the back of a lodging house and leans against the wall, waiting for her heart to settle. In the same moment, a woman waddles out the back door of the lodging house carrying a bucket of dirty water, struggling with its weight.

Though she's wearing shabby clothes, her plain dark skirt covered by a dirty white apron, the sleeves of her bodice rolled up to the elbows, there's something about her that looks inauthentic. Perhaps it's the pale, unblemished skin of her forearms. Those aren't the arms of a seasonal hop-picker, nor a washerwoman. In fact, they aren't the arms of a laboring woman at all. Furthermore, her boots aren't worn through and her woolen shawl has not a frayed edge nor a pulled stitch. She's much too pristine.

Recalling that the Salvation Army holds regular prayer meetings at a lodging house somewhere in this vicinity, Mary Jane pegs her as a Slum Sister: a woman of middling class and superior moral fortitude who's devoted her existence to the saving of fallen women.

"You need some help, my lovely?" The woman rakes her eyes over Mary Jane's appearance, forming instant judgments about her character.

While Mary Jane's no stranger to the various forms of aid offered by the many charitable organizations focusing their good work in the East End slums, and will quite happily accept a free meal in exchange for a few prayers to protect against the demon of drink and the damnation of her soul, she shakes her head, concealing her cleavage with her shawl. "Not presently."

"Have you eaten?" The woman switches to a different approach, tipping the bucket out over a sewer grate. "You look ever so pale."

"I'm tired, that's all."

"Do come inside and rest your bones, then." The persistent woman ushers her toward the door, prepared to physically drag her in if necessary. "We're serving tea and breakfast."

If for no other reason than to get away from George Yard Buildings, Mary Jane accepts the invitation, soon finding herself thrust into the crowded kitchen of the lodging house, surrounded by other women of her class. Getting herself in the tea line, she peruses the variety of Christian literature scattered on the tabletops, ascertaining from it all that she is indeed at a Salvation Army prayer meeting.

Amidst the Slum Sisters, there are a few women of higher class. Dressed in their usual finery, their presence—doling out cups of tea and serving breakfast—is meant to signify female solidarity across all social divides. These women are bred into wealth, their marriages painstakingly strategized to benefit their family names, and their uteruses commandeered for the purpose of furthering their pedigree. They've never seen a day's work, and devote themselves to charitable causes of all varieties so that they might serve some function beyond the birthing of heirs.

One of these women, Mary Jane recognizes. Her honey-colored hair, braided and pinned with the help of her two maids, is topped with a delicate fawn hat, all velvet, feathers, and tulle, and worn to the side. Her silk dress is immaculate, not even a crease, almost every inch of her neck covered by the high lace collar, her pale skin never having seen a single drop of sunlight.

It's Adel, the teen bride she was once hired to fuck. The teen bride whose enthusiasm for female affection took her altogether by surprise. The teen bride she very nearly fell in love with.

Though she's wearing a Salvation Army apron, which does its best to obscure her figure, Mary Jane can see that she remains largely unchanged since their last meeting, but for a few more inches on her bust, an artificial violet pinned to the decorations on her hat, and the lack of a baby growing in her belly.

"Jesus Christ ..."

The uttering of such an oath prior to the commencement of a Christian prayer meeting brings breakfast to a standstill. Mortified, Mary Jane mutters an empty apology and cuts out of the line, bolting for the front door and exiting the lodging house into Angel Alley.

"Stop!" Adel whisks off her apron. "Mary Jane!" She makes chase. "Please don't run from me." In the alley, she stops dead, planting both hands on her hips. "I shan't pursue you," she shouts at Mary Jane's departing back. "It's unladylike."

Mary Jane comes to a halt, slumping against the weathered wall of a crumbling house. "I'm sorry." She keeps her back turned, listening to Adel walk up behind her. "You're not supposed to see me this way."

"What way is that?" Adel runs her hands over Mary Jane's back.

"At my worst." Mary Jane flinches from her touch. "It's unflattering."

"I'm delighted to see you, no matter what the circumstance." Adel steps in front of her, glancing up and down the litter-strewn alley. "This is where you live?"

"I hope time's been kinder to you." Mary Jane admires her figure. "You look exactly as I remember you, minus the delightful bump." She gives Adel a light poke in the belly. "What news of your child?"

"A son." Adel beams, pressing a hand to her abdomen. "He's almost four, and I've recently been blessed with a daughter. She's not quite six months old."

That accounts for the fullness of her bust.

"I've missed you, Mary Jane." Adel invades her personal space. "Upon my return to London, I did inquire of your whereabouts, but my aunt said she'd lost track of you."

"I've moved around." Mary Jane lets her get closer.

"Well, I'm certainly glad to have found you." Adel toys with the lacing on the bust of Mary Jane's bodice. "You will stay for the meeting, won't you? I shall introduce you to the Captain." She coaxes Mary Jane back toward the lodging house. "We'll pray together."

Not caring one way or the other for that, but willing to participate in it purely for the sake of remaining in

561

Adel's company a short while longer, Mary Jane allows herself to be led. At Adel's insistence, she meets Captain Walker, the officer leading the meeting, and even shares the good Captain's hymnbook, standing shoulder to shoulder with her as they sing and pray.

When all's done, she plans to slink off unnoticed, bidding Adel a silent farewell, but Adel has no intention of letting her disappear so easily.

"Shall we steal away?" She corners Mary Jane at the edge of the room, laying a furtive hand on her waist. "I'd so very much like for us to become reacquainted."

Uncomfortable with that proposition, whatever it might entail, Mary Jane peels Adel's hand from her waist. "I should tell you I'm no longer a free woman. I have someone. Someone very special."

Adel disguises her disappointment well. "I'm asking you to tea, not to bed."

"All the same." Mary Jane dithers, thinking it a tad improper for her to spend time alone with a former lover without Eva's consent, given the black mark already on her record with Maria. "I wouldn't know where to take you. This quarter isn't fit for a lady of your standing."

"Perhaps not alone." Undaunted, Adel loops her arm through Mary Jane's, more than happy to brave the Whitechapel streets. "But I shall feel quite safe with you."

Capitulating much too easily, Mary Jane escorts Adel from the lodging house and onto Wentworth Street, intending to take her to the coffeehouse on Brick Lane. It's a quiet establishment, where they're not likely to be disturbed, but their timing couldn't possibly be any worse. On her way back from church, Eva approaches from the opposite direction, justifiably peeved to catch Mary Jane in the company of another woman—a young and pretty woman at that.

"Eva, darling!" Mary Jane disentangles herself from Adel. "I must've lost track of the hour." She tries to greet Eva with a peck on the lips, but Eva thwarts her.

In demonstration of her displeasure, she turns her head, making sure the kiss lands on her cheek. "What's going on?"

"This is my old friend, Missus Adella Adkins." Mary Jane is quick to legitimize their closeness. "Adel, may I present my dear companion, Miss Eva Sullivan."

"It's such a great pleasure to meet you." Adel extends a hand to her.

"How do you come to know my Mary Jane?" Eva regards her with suspicion, noting the decorative violet on her hat and accepting the proffered hand only because it would be unconscionably churlish to refuse.

Keen to make their acquaintance appear wholesome, Adel and Mary Jane answer in unison with whatever immediately leaps to mind. Unfortunately, their minds work differently. While Adel thinks of Bible study, Mary Jane opts for a chance encounter at the theater, the glaring discrepancy leaving Eva rightly confused.

"Which is it?" She flits her eyes from one to the other, not sure that she believes either.

Deferring to Mary Jane, Adel remains silent.

"Both." Mary Jane puts on a confident smile. "We went to Bible study, then the theater."

Eva doubts that tall tale. Firstly, Adel is wearing a Salvation Army pin on her jacket, which leads her to conclude, "You ain't Catholic." Secondly, she's come to know Mary Jane's habits rather far too well. "And you don't even go to church."

Though she's right, technically, neither account is a complete lie. Since that first night in Adel's home, they met wherever and whenever they could. On one occasion, when Adel was having difficulty sneaking out of the house for their assignations, they arranged to meet at the theater. Adel was attending with her husband and mother-in-law, Mary Jane with Cherry, the maid from the Frenchwoman's house, and they stole a few moments of bliss together during the intermission. God bless the Empire in Leicester Square.

Another time, Mary Jane agreed to meet her at an Anglican church in Chelsea, where she was doing some volunteer work with her grandmother, and they gave way to lust in a small storage room filled with copies of the Bible and kneeling cushions.

Out of necessity, Mary Jane had worn her glass cock under her dress, the shaft strapped to her thigh with garter ribbon, and while seated to pray—while the eyes of all around them were closed—Adel slipped a hand onto her thigh. Expecting to find nothing but soft flesh, the young socialite gasped when she felt something long and hard and began to explore the shape of it, her nimble fingers navigating seven inches of rigid phallus topped with a bulbous head.

It was too much to resist. At every available opportunity from thereon out, Adel insisted that she arrive at their engagements so rigged. Indeed, it became her letch to know that Mary Jane was wearing the appendage beneath her clothes, no matter if they were in a house of God, a restaurant, or a filthy music hall. She wanted to touch it. In fact, she frequently stroked it with such vigorous enthusiasm that Mary Jane became quite convinced she was entirely deprived of the operation with her legitimate doodle, her husband most likely being set against the operation on the basis of some misguided moral principle. Perhaps he didn't think it befitting of a lady. Perhaps she was too ashamed to ask.

Whatever the case, by the time they got back to their private lodgings in Greek Street, Soho—a single-room rent paid for by Adel, but leased by Mary Jane, solely for the purpose of providing a safe place for them to conduct their affair—anticipation for Mary Jane's cock would have her in a frenzy. How she loved to kneel at the edge of the bed, lift Mary Jane's skirts, and release the proud phallus from its restraint, watching it bounce free in Mary Jane's lap. It even gave her pleasure to suck it, and she soon came to realize that a few minutes of minette would get Mary Jane's passions raging.

On those nights, Mary Jane would take her with an unparalleled ferocity that thrilled and excited her. She knew Mary Jane would spend with her always, but when she was in such a wild rut, her mouth would get away from her. She'd say the bawdiest things, speaking as though her prick were real, and as if it could really do all of a man's work.

"Come in me," Adel spurred the fantasy on. "Give me a child."

Of course, it was Adel's husband who ultimately succeeded in that particular operation, but her impending motherhood was no cause for their dalliance to end. Certainly, the opposite was true. As the husband's interest in her waned on account of her expanding belly, their visits grew both in frequency and intensity, her ripening body craving the erotic pleasures to which she'd become accustomed.

At first, however, she was shy with her charms. The social conditioning of her class predisposed her to find the increasingly noticeable—and utterly unavoidable— manifestations of her gravidity to be shockingly distasteful, making her reluctant to fully unrig for fear of putting Mary Jane off. Fortunately, she soon learned that her growing belly was not something to be hidden, but to be flaunted.

"It shows so," she protested the first time Mary Jane attempted to remove her tightly-laced maternity corset. "It'll dull you on me."

"Never." Mary Jane unhooked the flexible busk, the specially-designed corset having corded seams rather than rigid steel or whale boning, allowing for it to stretch with Adel's changing body. "There's nothing more delicious than a fine woman full with child."

Adel heard those words, but didn't believe them until she saw Mary Jane fawn over her belly for the first time. As the corset was unfastened, her rounded stomach—then just beginning to defy concealment altogether—bulged out like an inflating balloon.

"Oh, look at you." Mary Jane caressed the prominent bump, dropping kisses on Adel's taut skin. "Nurturing a darling babe inside you." Her kisses moved lower.

From then on, the removal of the maternity corset became a moment of sweet relief for Adel, her swollen breasts freed from their rigid confines, and her orb-like belly shamelessly let out to its fullest extent. She even came to brag about how much she had to loosen the side panels on the corset since their last meeting, thrilled to

show Mary Jane, inch by inch, how much her stomach was expanding to accommodate the growing life within it.

While others—namely her mother, mother-in-law, and maids—were busy trying to minimize the outward appearance of her parturiency with a combination of stricter lacing and ever flouncier skirts, Mary Jane encouraged her to embrace the natural beauty of the experience. Sometimes, they met at that secret rented room in Soho not for fucking, but for other affections. Adel would recline upon the bed, stripped down to her chemise, and relish being held in Mary Jane's comforting arms. Together, they'd feel the baby squirm and kick inside her. Mary Jane would massage her swollen feet, and they'd talk of running away.

It was all fantasy. Though Adel looked forward to being with Mary Jane right up until the end, when the time came for her confinement—when her beautifully large belly could no longer be hidden from polite society—her aunt sent her away. It was probably for the best.

Afraid that the lingering heat between them might be palpable to Eva, Mary Jane tries to minimize their relationship. "Until today, we hadn't seen one another in years," she volunteers. "We ran into each other quite by accident."

Mistrustful, Eva pries deeper. "Do you know each other well?"

"We'd have tea together when I was living in the West End," Mary Jane spouts another half-truth, recalling a few overnight stays in a Mayfair hotel prior to their acquisition of lodgings in Soho. There, with her posing as Adel's maid, they would share a room, a pot of tea inevitably growing cold on the vanity while they fucked each other into delirium on the bed.

"And the zoo," Adel reminds her. "Don't forget our visits to the zoo."

Mary Jane battles a smirk. How could she forget the zoo? Since Adel's parents are fellows of the Zoological Society of London, she was able to arrange a few afterhours excursions, and they gave each other pleasure in the aquarium.

"They used to have a quagga. Did you know that?" Mary Jane diverts the conversation into humorous territory. "A queer looking thing with the head of a zebra and the arse of a horse."

"It was from South Africa," Adel adds. "It's now quite extinct."

Eva looks blank, not knowing what to make of Adel, or this conversation. "I've always wanted to go to the zoo."

"Oh, you really must," Adel enthuses. "The animals are so majestic. Especially the lions. I'm sure Mary Jane will take you." She turns her smile on her former lover. "Of course, I still think it's terribly disappointing that you didn't have a pet tiger while you were living in India." She flashes Mary Jane a look of mock disapproval. "I'd have insisted upon it."

Silence.

India? Eva fixes a glare on Mary Jane, restraining her emotions only because she's in the presence of a proper lady. "Excuse me." She grits her teeth, determined not to make a scene. "I need to leave now." Close to tears, she pivots on her heels and walks away.

"Eva ..." Mary Jane attempts to catch her, but the livid teen slips through her grasp.

"Oh, dear." Adel frowns, confused. "Have I said something wrong?"

"It's not your fault. It's mine, as usual." Mary Jane takes a step in Eva's direction. "I must go after her."

"Wait." Adel raids her pockets. "Take these." She presses two gold coins into Mary Jane's palm. "Please."

"I don't want your pity." Mary Jane pushes them back to her.

"It isn't pity." Adel refuses to accept them. "It's bribery." She closes Mary Jane's hand around the shiny sovereigns. "I want to see you again."

Mary Jane opens her mouth to object, but Adel cuts her off before the first negative syllable has a chance to pass her lips.

"Not for anything untoward, I promise you." She keeps hold of Mary Jane's hand. "Eva seems like a delightful girl, and I'm very happy for you. Truly, I am. I

have no interest in compromising your fidelity, I simply want to talk. My one great regret is that we never got to say goodbye; I was sent away so suddenly." Sensing Mary Jane's lingering hesitation, she sweetens the deal. "If you'll consent to join me for tea at my home, I'll gladly compensate you for your time. And generously. Will you think it over at least?"

Agreeing to that, Mary Jane accepts a *carte de visite* Adel pulls from her pocket—her photograph on one side, her address on the reverse—and they part from each other with a tender hug and a gentle peck on the cheek.

CHAPTER 47

BEFORE HUNTING EVA DOWN AT THE LOLESWORTH Buildings, Mary Jane stops off at Miller's Court. Wasting no time, she lays her shawl out on the table and fills it with the contents of her hidden compartment under the floor: her lockbox, her bawdy picture book, their letters, and the desiccated rose. Once everything's gathered together—save for the dildo, which she straps on beneath her dress—she bundles it all up inside the shawl and turns to leave, bumping straight into Reid at her door.

"Oh, no." She shuts him down before he begins. "I know what you're here for, and I've got nothing to say about it." She hugs her belongings to her chest. "No more bodies, no more mortuary visits, and no more questions. I don't care who it is, or what happened. I'm not looking at it, and you have to leave from here right this minute."

"Why?" Reid stays put, blocking her exit. "It's important that I see you." He stops her from closing the door on him. "Two more women were done last night."

"So I heard, but it's got nothing whatever to do with me," she states flatly.

"Since when?" Reid refuses to budge.

Hearing footsteps in the court and not wanting to be seen in conversation with a copper, Mary Jane yanks him inside, slams the door closed, and lowers her voice. "Look, he knows you suspect him, he knows I've been

talking to you, and if he sees you in my room, it might just be me he does in next. You must keep your distance."

"Have you seen him? Has he threatened you?" Reid's posture stiffens, his defensive streak triggered. "Has he hurt you again? If he's done anything to—"

"Just leave off," Mary Jane snaps. "I can't help you. I wish I could, but I can't. Not that it makes a blind bit of difference anyway, since women are getting their blood shed left and right in this city and nothing's being done about it. First, there was the woman found in Regent's Canal last year, and now all this. You know they're fishing more limbs out of the Thames, don't you? It's starting again, just as I said it would."

"I thought your mind was settled on that business." Reid unwittingly glances at the bed, having deliberately tried to keep his eyes off the rumpled sheets. "She was not of that profession." He looks away, the sight of a small splotch of dried seminal muck causing an unpleasant tug below his diaphragm, as though his stomach were being wrung out.

"Perhaps not, but what of this one?" Mary Jane sets down her shawl and roots through a cluttered array of open newspapers on her table, digging out an article from the September 12 issue of the Daily Telegraph and paraphrasing from it. "Yet another outrage has to be added to the list of undiscovered crimes which have recently startled the inhabitants of the metropolis. Yesterday, soon after noon, a portion of a human body was found floating in the River Thames, near Grosvenor Railway Bridge." She stops to gauge his reaction. "That's awful close to Knightsbridge, wouldn't you say?"

The question is rhetorical, and she goes on without pause. "The theory which the police are forced to entertain is that the arm forms part of a woman who has met with a tragic end, and whose body is being disposed of in sections as opportunity offers." She shakes the article in Reid's face. "They say the arm was cut through by some big, sharp instrument."

"Like a Ghurka knife," he supposes her inference. "Or equally, many other things."

"Is it so absurd? If you ask me, he's done all of them. This one, the Rainham girl, and the one in seventy-three. Perhaps she was his first. Perhaps he has a penchant for it now." She flings the newspaper back onto the table. "No matter. It's only Whitechapel that concerns you."

"Whitechapel can go to hell," he barks savagely. "It's *you* who concerns me."

A moment passes.

Thrown by such an unexpectedly candid outburst, Mary Jane is slow to respond. "If that's true," she says at last, swallowing hard, "then call on me no more. We must put an end to this."

"An end?" Reid scoffs. "What end can there be whilst that ... that *man*"—he spits out the word, loath to use a vulgarity in the presence of a woman—"still walks free? Justice demands that he be punished for what he's done to y—" He stops himself a fraction of a second too late.

"To who, Inspector?" Mary Jane softens her tone, her brow creased with tension. "To the five women whose lives he's taken? Or to me?" She hangs her head, too afraid to see the truth in his eyes. "I know why you were transferred to Whitechapel. I've made inquiries, and I know the reason for the reprimand that saw you expelled to this foul pit of hell." She peers up at him. "You beat him."

"I acted out of turn." Reid downplays his momentary lapse of judgment.

"He was in the police station, sleeping off a drunk in one of your cells," Mary Jane relates what she was told. "You saw him there and proceeded to knock him so hard about the head that he was nearly put in the infirmary." She braves eye contact. "You could've killed him."

"I *should've* killed him."

For daring to say such a thing, Mary Jane strikes his cheek with her open palm, leaving the imprint of her hand behind on his skin. Anticipating retaliation, she instinctively flinches away, but he absorbs the hit silently, with a clenching and unclenching of his jaw, his hands never leaving his pockets.

Confidence returning, she then squares up to him. "Look at me."

571

He won't.

"Look at me!" She clamps her hands to his cheeks and forcibly turns his head. "Whatever you think I am, I'm not. I'm a whore—nothing more—and you cannot pursue this crusade in my name. I will not let you."

"You will not stop me." He tears her hands away, gripping her wrists. "You are a woman in need of protection, and I *shall* protect you."

"At what cost?" Mary Jane shakes her head, tears welling as she struggles to pull herself free. "Not at the expense of your career, and most certainly not at the expense of your life." She relinquishes herself to his hold. "Besides, if you had any evidence that he was responsible for these crimes, he would already be in your custody, would he not?"

"What are you implying?"

Mary Jane swallows hard before answering. "Is it not possible that you *want* it to be him?" She hesitates. "Is it not possible that you're allowing emotion to drive you?"

Displaying a glimmer of the hitherto unseen forcefulness that simmers beneath his restrained exterior, Reid backs her against the wall and bears down on her, her wrists pinned between them. He seems primed for something, his lips close to hers, his hard, muscled chest pressed to her bust, but then ... sense returns to him.

"If my actions have put you in the way of harm, then I am deeply sorry." He eases off and releases her wrists. "I will not impose upon you again, but nor shall I rest on this matter."

With that, he swings the door open and leaves.

For several moments thereafter, Mary Jane remains with her back to the wall, breathing deeply, collecting her thoughts and calming her nerves. Once sufficiently recovered, she picks up her laden shawl and hurries to Lolesworth, her heart aching to hear Eva sobbing behind the locked door to her room.

She knocks.

"Go away!" Eva wails, her voice muffled by a pillow. "I ain't letting you in!"

Rather than waste breath imploring her to unlock the door, Mary Jane dips inside her bodice and fumbles with a small square of fabric sewn onto the inside edge of one of the bust gores of her corset, unpicking the stitching with her fingernails until the patch comes adrift and she withdraws a woman's narrow gold wedding band.

"Let me in or don't, but I have something for you." She slides the ring through the large, uneven gap under the door, hoping to snare Eva's attention.

It works. Eva quiets down, her distressed sobs diminishing, and Mary Jane listens with bated breath as she rises from the bed and tiptoes across the floor to inspect the offering. A moment later, the door opens.

"Oh, Em ..." Eva gawps at the polished ring, clutching it with both hands in case it somehow slips away from her. "This looks like gold."

"It *is* gold." Mary Jane budges her way inside before Eva has a chance to overcome her surprise and remembers to be angry. "I told you the money taken from my savings weren't some frivolous expenditure."

"This ain't fair." Eva pouts, hypnotized by the precious metal. "I'm trying to be cross with you, and you're giving me gold. Ain't no-one ever gived me jewelry afore."

"Ain't no-one ever married you before." Mary Jane thinks that ought to make her smile, but instead, it sets her off on another wave of tears.

"How can I be your wife? I don't even know your name." She relinquishes the ring, shoving it back into Mary Jane's hands.

"Don't be like that." Mary Jane begrudgingly accepts the expression of her devotion back into her possession and dumps the rest of her things on the table. "I offered to tell you everything, but you said it weren't important."

"Because I thought *no-one* knew." Eva wipes her nose on a soggy hanky. "But you told *her*. Who is she? Does she know everything of you? Why? You've been with her, aintcha? You've fucked her." She jabs an accusatory finger at Mary Jane's chest. "I know she's that way inclined. I saw the violet pinned to her hat. Was she

your customer? The woman you was seeing when we met."

"No." Mary Jane captures that angry digit and kisses it. "It weren't never like that with Adel. She never paid me."

"You loved her, then." Eva jerks her hand away. "That's worse."

"Darling, it was four years ago. Whatever feelings I had for her are long dissipated." Mary Jane drops onto one knee at Eva's feet, holding her by the waist. "It's *you* I love, Eva. I want to spend the rest of my life with you, whether that be a week, a month, a year, or fifty. I'd spend eternity with you if I could, and whatever you want to know of me, I'll tell you. Ask me anything. Not a word shall leave my lips unless it's the truth."

Eva looks down at her earnest, pleading face. "You promise?"

"No lies, love. I swear it."

"Then get up and let me think." Eva sits at the table and dries her eyes on her sleeve, deciding where to start and ultimately arriving at the obvious. "You've been to India?"

"I was born there." Mary Jane pulls the other chair up beside her.

"But how can that be?" Eva frowns. "You're white as a snowdrop."

"Well, I ain't Indian. I'm Irish, and proud of it—that ain't no falsehood. My father was an army man, stationed in Delhi at the time of my birth, but I never knew him. He died when I was only three months old."

Eva's mind whirs. "How old was you when you came to England, then?"

"Nine." Mary Jane places the ring on the table in front of Eva, in case she wants to look at it again. "My stepfather was posted to Portsea in 1870, where we lived comfortably for the next five years until he was discharged and we moved to Manchester."

"So you ain't never been to Ireland?" Eva twirls the ring between her fingers.

"I'm afraid not," Mary Jane confesses, moving over to the bed. "My father's family are from Limerick, so I adopted that as my birthplace."

"Why don't you want people to know the truth?"

"My stepfather was not a pleasant man." At the mention of him, Mary Jane instinctively brings her arms across her chest, shielding her breasts. "At least, not to me he weren't. Not since the time I started looking less like a child and more like a woman."

"Like my mam's Billy always looked at me when I had my baths?" Eva twists to look at her, imagining her as an innocent fourteen-year-old, huddled naked in a large tin bucket, her stepfather's hand in his pocket, watching her soap the budding mounds on her chest.

"Aye, just like that." Mary Jane removes her boots. "When I left, I didn't want no-one to find me—especially not him—so I made myself as unremarkable as possible."

"So many fibs." Eva turns her eyes to the floor, not sure that it's even possible to unpick the intricately woven mistruths now becoming apparent in Mary Jane's personal history. "I dunno how you keep it straight. I'd get me-self all in a muddle."

"It's not too terrible," Mary Jane assures her. "There's a fragment of truth in much of it."

Eva waits for her to expound.

"The story goes that my family moved to Wales when I was young, and that my father was the gaffer in an ironworks." Mary Jane scoots back and makes herself comfortable. "Well, I did live in Wales for a time, albeit not as a child, and my stepfather was a puddler by trade. So you see, the truth is veiled, not dismissed. The only thing entirely a fabrication is the marriage tale, so if you've ever heard me speak of that, know that it's false."

"Marriage?" Eva leaves the ring on the table and joins her on the bed, having some faint recollection of a husband once being mentioned in the early days of their courtship.

"It was Lizzie's idea. You remember I told you of her?"

"The woman you was companions with down Ratcliffe?" Eva settles next to her.

"That's right. I'd just been kicked out of the first bad house on account of taking a leave to see my little brother married. By the time I returned to London, the wretched bawd had given my place in the house to another girl. I had to find a new situation sharpish, and Lizzie said I'd have better luck if I had a more pitiable history."

"Why?"

Mary Jane shrugs. "Sympathy. Everyone loves a good sob story, don't they? Lizzie was Welsh, and knew of a fella who died in a mining accident a few years back, so I adopted the tragedy for my own needs and became the young widow of a Welsh collier named Davies. I even got a bit carried away and said that I had a child."

"Do you?"

"Do I what?" Mary Jane feigns ignorance of the question, hoping it'll go away.

"Do you have a child?" Eva asks outright, leaving no room for evasion. Or so she thinks.

Remembering her promise not to lie, Mary Jane falls momentarily silent. In the end, she answers carefully, "I weren't never married."

"That ain't what I asked." Eva calls her on the dodge. "You wouldn't be the first woman to get one in her without being wedded, so why won't you say?"

Though tempted to prevaricate further, Mary Jane surrenders one of her most closely guarded secrets. "I was caught in the family way." She hesitates. "But the child died."

"Oh, Mary Jane ... I'm sorry." Eva nestles closer to her, ready to provide comfort if she needs it. "I feels rotten for asking now."

"It's all right." Mary Jane forces a smile. "God knows best, don't he? He took one look at me with that darling babe and knew I didn't deserve to be a mother."

"I'm sure that ain't true."

"No? What other reason is there to take away a helpless infant who ain't done nothing wrong a day in his short life?" Mary Jane bites back tears. "That handsome little boy paid for my sins, I'm sure of that."

Wishing she'd never brought the matter up, Eva changes the subject. "This morning, in your room, why did Joe call you Marie?"

Glad of the new topic, Mary Jane takes a deep, restorative breath. "That was the name assigned to me at the Frenchwoman's house. She gave us all French monikers. Mine was Marie Jeanette, and I hate to be reminded of it."

"Why'd you tell him?"

"It was a gross mistake. Liquor loosened my tongue, and now, whenever he wants to plunge the knife in, that's what he calls me."

"So your name's really Mary Jane?" Eva thinks on it. "Mary Jane ... Malone?"

"Malone was my father's name, but I ain't never gone by it. Not really." Mary Jane catches Eva staring at the ring. "Have you forgiven me now? Will you wear it?"

Eva shakes her head firmly. "Give it me when we're done of this place."

"It won't be very much longer." Mary Jane pecks her lips, drawing her into an embrace. "I shan't be paying any rent from hereon out, but I'll keep on at Miller's Court until I wear out my welcome—probably a good two months, given the current climate—and I'll keep earning. Just Joe and my specials. Nothing more. When I receive my notice to quit, we'll leave."

Eva perks up. "Do you really mean it?" She flings herself at Mary Jane, pressing up against something long and hard near her crotch. "Whatever's in your pocket?" She giggles, wiggling against it. "Feels like you've got a mighty stiff one."

"I do." Mary Jane takes Eva's hand and presses it over the concealed dildo beneath her clothes. "I thought you might want it tonight." She coaxes Eva to stroke it. "I know you did last night, and I'm sorry I weren't up to it."

Eva works her hand up and down the thick shaft. "Last night was a dreadful tease. You passed out with your face on my grummit and left me hot."

"I did not!" Mary Jane cringes. "Did I? Let's make up for it." She rucks up her skirts and unfastens the ribbon

keeping the phallus strapped to her thigh, causing it to spring skyward, then she yanks Eva into a kiss.

Presently, a rhythmic tugging at her groin alerts her to the continued work of Eva's hand on her priapus, the manual stimulation—entirely psychological though it is—reigniting her old letch for minette.

"Use your mouth on me," she whispers against Eva's lips. "Will you?"

"What? On your doodle? Why?" Eva glances down at the inanimate thing, perplexed by the request. "I wouldn't know how."

"That don't matter." Unable to put out of her mind how good it once felt to have Adel sucking on her, she urges Eva down. "If you don't like it, I'll never ask again."

Seeing no harm in the operation—in fact, finding the idea of it rather comical—Eva willingly dips her head and begins to fellate the glass cock, coating it with spittle as she slithers her tongue all around it, flicking, licking, and kissing it as if it were flesh. At intervals throughout, she peers up at Mary Jane, becoming increasingly intrigued by her obvious arousal, especially in those intermittent moments of eye contact. It spurs her on.

Curious to see how much she can fit in her mouth at once, she then sinks on the dildo, feeling its smooth shaft glide across her tongue, continuing to swallow it until the tip bulges out her cheek.

"Oh, Eva ..." Mary Jane watches the inches disappear. "If my prick were real ..." A small orgasm ripples through her.

Astonished to feel Mary Jane twitching beneath her, and now drooling profusely, her saliva dribbling down to the root of the cock and wetting Mary Jane's motte, Eva lifts up, easing her mouth off the toy and wiping her lips. "Did you just spend? How come?"

"It gets my passions up. I don't know why." Mary Jane flips Eva onto her back and throws up her skirts, wincing as she maneuvers into position. "Let's have a poke."

She lines herself up, but lacks the power to achieve full penetration in a single thrust. The pain in her ribs is so crippling that her first attempt only lodges the head in

Eva's opening, the widest part of the crown refusing to pop through.

"Stop." Eva holds her hips, preventing further effort. "You're hurting, and I shan't enjoy it if it causes you pain."

"I'm sorry." Mary Jane hangs her head, defeated. "We shall have to do it another way." She backs off and strips to her corset, sitting upright with her legs outstretched. "Unrig yourself and sit on my lap."

Unfamiliar with this attitude, Eva removes her clothes and clambers on, crossing her legs behind Mary Jane's back. "This is all a bit topsy-turvy, ain't it?"

"You'll be in control of your pleasure this time." Mary Jane instructs her to lift up, then guides her down over the phallus, lodging it securely inside her.

"But I want you to have a pleasure n'all." Eva grinds herself on Mary Jane's lap.

"I will," Mary Jane assures her, seizing her by the hips and rocking her back and forth, making sure she doesn't pull back too far and accidentally uncunt. "I love to watch."

Experimenting with different movements, Eva bobs up and down and wriggles around, fucking herself on Mary Jane's priapus. "Am I doing it right?" She jigs rapidly on the embedded pole, her unfettered breasts bouncing and swaying.

"If it feels good, you're doing it perfectly." Mary Jane wraps one arm around Eva's waist, anchoring her, and navigates the other between them, tickling her clit.

"Oh, Lordy," Eva groans, closing her eyes to concentrate on the sensations of the combined stimulation. "I shall make a precious mess of you if you keep on with that."

Receiving no objection to the prospect of being thoroughly wetted by her spend, Eva grips Mary Jane's shoulder and moves with frantic determination, jouncing ever harder and faster until a burst of hot fluid gushes from her, drenching Mary Jane's lap.

CHAPTER 48

THE QUEEN AND THE EAST-END MURDERS

"During the week following the Sunday on which the two murders were committed, the following petition to the Queen was freely circulated among the women of the laboring classes of East London through some of the religious agencies and educational centers:

'To our Most Gracious Sovereign Lady Queen Victoria.

Madam,—We, the women of East London, feel horror at the dreadful sins that have been lately committed in our midst, and grief because of the shame that has fallen on our neighborhood. By the facts which have come out in the inquests, we have learned much of the lives of those of our sisters who have lost a firm hold on goodness, and who are living sad and degraded lives. While each woman of us will do all she can to make men feel with horror the sins of impurity which cause such wicked lives to be led, we would also beg that your Majesty will call on your servants in authority, and bid them put the law which already exists in motion to close bad houses, within whose walls such wickedness is done, and men and women ruined in body and soul. We are, madam, your loyal and humble servants.'

The petition, which received between 4,000 and 5,000 signatures, was presented in due form, and the following reply has been received:

Whitehall.

'Madam,—I am directed by the Secretary of State to inform you that he has had the honor to lay before the Queen the petition of women inhabitants of Whitechapel praying that steps may be taken with a view to suppress the moral disorders in that neighborhood, and that her Majesty has been graciously pleased to receive the same. I am to add that the Secretary of State looks with hope to the influence for good that the petitioners can exercise, each in her own neighborhood, and he is in communication with the Commissioners of Police with a view to taking such action as may be desirable in order to assist the efforts of the petitioners and to mitigate the evils of which they complain.—I am, madam, your obedient servant.'

– Godfrey Lushington.

-- Evening News (London), October 25, 1888

CHAPTER 49

AN EXTRAORDINARY PARCEL

"Mr. Lusk, the president of the Whitechapel Vigilance Committee, has received by parcel post a cardboard box containing what has been pronounced by a competent medical authority to be half of the left kidney of an adult human being, and a letter, dated from 'Hell' stating, with illiterate brutality, that the half-kidney was a moiety of that taken from Catherine Eddowes, and that the other half had been fried and eaten by the writer. The box, with its contents, has been handed over to the detectives at the Leman Street Police Station."

-- Illustrated Police News, October 27, 1888

Tuesday, October 30, 1888

A MONTH HAS PASSED. MARY JANE'S RIBS HAVE HEALED, THE bruises have faded, and apart from her continued troubles with Joe—their fights escalating in frequency and intensity—things have been relatively quiet. Thirty days have gone by since the last brutal slaying of a woman, and she hasn't seen hide nor hair of Fleming. Not that he hasn't been meddling in her life.

Last week, she was paid an unpleasant visit by the white-haired man she took to Crossingham's, and there's no doubt in her mind who was responsible for telling him

where she lived. The man, demanding the return of his watch—or appropriate compensation for its worth—caused a scene in the court, bashing on her door and threatening violence.

"Open up, you thieving bitch whore!"

"I'll come in there and do for you!"

The landlord, McCarthy, was forced to eject him from the court, using his fists to ensure compliance, and Mary Jane hasn't seen him since. Still, she keeps an eye out, frightened she might run into him on the street and end up like Ada Wilson: stabbed in the throat.

At her table in Miller's Court, as the sun slowly sets, she reads by candlelight in her cave-like room, tilting the crinkled pages toward the flickering light, squinting at a transcription of the latest piece of correspondence to be received from the man now dubbed Jack the Ripper.

This poorly-spelled letter was sent 'From Hell' to Mister George Lusk—a local builder and founding chairman of the newly established Whitechapel Vigilance Committee—and arrived in an oozing package that also contained a portion of human kidney. It so reads:

Mr. Lusk,

Sir, I send you half the kidne I took from one woman, prasarved it for you; t'other piece I fried and ate, it was very nise. I may send you the bloody knif that took it out if you only wate a while longer.

Signed, Catch me when you can Mishter Lusk.

Catherine Eddowes' kidney.

Fried and eaten.

Picturing Fleming cooking the excised organ over the fire in the communal kitchens of the Victoria Home, Mary Jane shudders. She knew Catherine Eddowes as Kate Kelly, a woman who had a bed at one of Cooney's common lodging houses on Flower and Dean Street and sometimes earned her money through immoral means. They weren't friends, and hadn't crossed paths with each other for some time, but they did meet once or twice at

the London City Mission hall off Thrawl Street. Of the other woman, the one named Elizabeth Stride, she knew nothing.

Though she dared not see Reid to tell him as much, she wrote him a letter. It was unsigned, but she knew he'd recognize her hand. When he wrote back, he included with his letter a clipping from an article in the Daily Telegraph on October 3. It followed the discovery of a woman's dismembered torso in the foundations of the new police buildings being erected between Parliament Street and the Victoria Embankment, and so read:

"The corpse was a mere trunk, both head and limbs having been severed in an apparently brutal and unskillful manner. Evidently, the remains were those of a young and well-nourished woman, and there is every reason to fear that they form part of some person who has been murdered and made away with by an atrocious miscreant."

The torso matched the arm found in the Thames during the month of September, and a fortnight or so thereafter, the left leg and foot were uncovered by a journalist and his dog. From these parts, it was ascertained that the victim was a well-fed, statuesque woman with prominent breasts, fair skin, and dark hair, approximately twenty-five years of age, and on account of these rather familiar physical attributes, Mary Jane can see why the case caught Reid's eye. That, and the fact that her uterus was missing.

In their letters, Reid posited a link to the Whitechapel murders, but Mary Jane rejected the notion in favor of another possibility: a botched abortion. Not only would that account for the removal of such an organ—necessary to conceal the fatal deed—but also for the gruesome lengths taken to obscure the woman's identity. To bolster this assertion, she furnished Reid with more grisly details of her experience at the Frenchwoman's house on the night she and Cherry discovered a dead harlot in one of the bedrooms.

After the fact, she heard whispers that her unlucky coworker had found herself in the family way, and that the usual hickery-pickery—a potentially lethal purgative concoction composed of aloes, canella bark, and lead, mixed together with gin and honey—had no effect but to cause severe cramping, vomiting, and the rapid evacuation of her bowels. When she refused to take another dose, a midwife was sent for by cover of night, and it was this, Mary Jane informed Reid, that ultimately brought about her end.

Her uterus was perforated, there was a tremendous loss of blood, and as she lay dying upon the bed, the bully was instructed to fetch his knife. He hastened her passage into eternity by severing the major vessels in her neck, and so drained her of all her vital fluid before commencing the butchery that was to mask the true nature of her demise and enable him to dispose of her parts with little trouble.

Where those parts ended up, Mary Jane could not say, but the event left her in no doubt that all who lived in the Frenchwoman's house were at risk of meeting the same fate. As soon as she could, she saw to it that Cherry was offered a position in service elsewhere—in a good and decent house—and she left with the first man who wanted to take her for his own. Of course, that ended up being a disaster all unto itself. Au revoir, England. Bonjour, France.

Filled with regret for many of her life choices, she glances across the room at the one precious thing she has truly to be grateful for: Eva. Off work early due to the severe abdominal pains brought on by the imminent arrival of her poorliness, she's lounging on the bed, sketching on a piece of a paper with a charcoal stick. Her appetite sapped by the cramping of her womanly parts, she's been in a mope since half-two, lamenting the loss of four hours' pay after Mary Jane—upon seeing the intense discomfort she was in—flatly refused to allow her to return to the factory after her dinner break.

"Why do you insist on reading all that stuff? It's gruesome." The disapproving teen turns her nose up at Mary Jane's collection of newspaper clippings on the

table. "In any case, it's been quiet for weeks. It's all over now, ain't it?"

"I doubt that." Mary Jane brings scissors to the page, snipping the letter out and adding it to her pile. "How's your belly? I wish you'd let me give you something for it."

She means laudanum, and Eva remains adamant that she'll never touch a drop, her mother's addiction having left her fearful of its potency.

"Do you ever think of your family?" she asks then, her mind turning to thoughts of her early childhood, before her mother was so dissipated by the effects of poverty, drink, and the immoral life she was leading. "Your mam at least. Not that nasty old step-dadda."

"I try not to," Mary Jane answers absently, slinging the rest of the newspaper into a rusted bucket by the fireplace.

Ever since their heart to heart, Eva's been a fount of questions, some more mundane than others. When you was living in India, did you ever see a tiger? How about an elephant? Was the summers sweltering? Did you mingle with Sikhs?

She makes no mention of the Indian Rebellion that took place in those parts just three years before Mary Jane's birth. No mention of the massacres. No mention of the death toll, the fighting having claimed a vast number of lives on both sides, including those of many women and children belonging to the British soldiers in the East India Company. Indeed, Eva remains wholly ignorant of the horrors faced prior to the establishment of British Raj in 1858, and Mary Jane does nothing to disabuse her of the notion that India was some exotic paradise.

"What about your brothers?" Eva ponders next, keen to glean as much information as possible, finding it hard to imagine that Mary Jane never spares a thought for any of her relatives. "I heard you've got a whole gaggle of 'em living in London. Is that true?"

Mary Jane snorts. "How many have I said? Six? Seven? Joe's never known about me seeing my specials all this time," she explains. "He wanted me to keep to him exclusively, and had people watching me while he was at work, informing him any time they caught me in the

company of another man. When he confronted me with it, I laughed in his face and said I had half a dozen brothers living here, there, and all around, and if I should be seen talking to any man on the street, it was only gonna be one of them."

"He believed you?"

"Course he did, but then he's soft like that." She chuckles. "He still believes I was only twenty-two when we met, despite the age you can plainly see in me." She leaves the table, draws the curtains, and joins Eva on the bed, bringing the candle with her. "Just so as you know for your own mind, I only have two brothers. One older, one younger."

"Why do you never speak of 'em?" Eva discards her drawing on the bedside table, not caring for it so much once it's better illuminated by the candle. "Are they bad 'uns like your step-dadda?"

"There ain't much to say." Mary Jane drags the table closer and sets the candle on it. "The little one's a cabinet maker. He's just like our stepfather, and I don't have nothing to do. Not since eighty-four, when I made the mistake of attending his wedding with a woman on my arm. I should've known it would cause a fight." She peeks at Eva's sketch, not thinking too much of her attempt to draw a flying pig. "Our stepfather's named John, and we used to call him Johnto on account of him being so much like the old man. Course, he was only little when his real father died. Our stepfather as good as raised him."

"You all got different daddas?"

Mary Jane shakes her head. "Just him. My older brother and I are of the same blood." She picks up Eva's charcoal stick, flips the paper over, and starts her own impromptu artwork. "He was always my protector at home. Whenever our stepfather was having a go, he'd step in. It was only after he left that things went to the bad for me."

"Your step-dadda ..." Eva can barely bring herself to ask. "Did he ever ... ?"

"He tried." Mary Jane outlines the figure of a woman, stripped of clothing and recumbent on a bed, sprawled over the bed sheets. "He came home in drink

one night and gave it a good go, but didn't know then that my brother—before he enlisted in the army and got well out of the place—had taught me how to fight." She smirks at the memory. "I was only fifteen, smaller than I am now, and I cracked that wicked bastard in the nose."

"I wish I'd had the chops to do Billy like that." Eva scowls at the thought of him. "What did your mam say?"

"She took his side and chucked me out on my ear." Mary Jane adds a head of long dark hair to the figure in her drawing, glancing at Eva every now and again to match the likeness of her face. "She ain't a bad woman, but she's weak. She wouldn't never stand up to a man. Not even to protect her own daughter."

"Where's your brother now? Did you ever see him again?"

"Aye, just before the wedding, when he was posted back to England." Mary Jane adds two erect nipples to the woman on the page. "Upon learning what happened at home, he came looking for me, and we've kept up with each other ever since. Mostly through letters, though we've had a drink together on the odd occasion that he's come this way cunting. For those are the two things he loves most, besides me: drink and whores."

"How'd he find you?"

"He heard our cousin was in London and paid her a visit." She draws in a thick triangle of pubic curls. "Me and her came to London together, see, but ended up on different paths."

"Was hers better or worse?"

"Does it get any worse?" Mary Jane laughs at her own misfortune. "She fell in with a bloke who became her patron for the stage. Not the West End or nothing proper fancy like that, but the South London Palace: a music hall in the Elephant and Castle district. I go there quite often. She fancies herself as a bit of an Irish Marie Lloyd and goes by a stage name these days." Mary Jane pauses to smudge some of the charcoal with her finger, adding shadow to the woman's body. "Anyway"—she blows on the page, sending a plume of charcoal dust into the air— "she told him where to find me, and that was that. He said our stepfather was in ill-health and wanted to make

amends, but I wasn't having any of it. When the old man came looking, I kept away. Why ought I lessen his burden? Let him die in guilt."

"And did he?"

"Aye." Mary Jane spits on a corner of a hanky and wipes her mucky fingertips, her drawing finished. "After he was gone, our mam moved to Ireland and my brother went with her. She writes to me every once in a while."

"Do you ever write back?"

"Sometimes." Mary Jane sighs. "But I doubt as I'll ever see her again," she laments. "I know it ain't the Christian thing to bear a grudge, but I can't forgive her for what she did. I was not yet sixteen and had no way of getting on in the world."

Eva knows what it's like to be sixteen and motherless. "I'm lucky to have had you." She moves in for a kiss, catching a glimpse of Mary Jane's impromptu artwork on the table. "Lordy, is that me?" She picks it up, mentally comparing the image of the naked brunette with the landmarks of her own anatomy.

"It will be in a minute, if you let me have my way with you." Mary Jane scoops Eva's ankles out from under her, extending her legs. "How're you feeling?" She cradles Eva's neck in her hand and lowers her to the palliasse. "Shall we fuck?"

"It's only just gone half-five." Eva giggles. "We can't be going to bed. It ain't even suppertime yet."

"Not to sleep," Mary Jane concurs, dropping kisses on Eva's neck. "But who said anything about sleeping?" She slips a hand up Eva's dress.

"Ohh, do be gentle with it." Eva accepts a tickle. "No jiggering me about, else you'll make my reds come on, and you hasn't gived me back my drawers yet."

Mary Jane grins. Three days ago, she did away with Eva's drawers while the fucked-out teen was sleeping, and hasn't yet seen fit to return them.

"They're under your bed," she whispers, working delicately between Eva's thighs, coaxing moisture forth with her fingertips. "I tucked them inside the corner of the sheet."

She's about to disregard Eva's warning and dip her fingers inside when the door knob rattles. Someone on the other side twists it once and tries to push the door open, but upon finding it locked, appears to give up.

Silence.

Eva and Mary Jane watch and wait, frozen on the bed, barely breathing. For comfort and protection, Eva wraps her arms around Mary Jane's back, pulling her closer, unabashedly using her as a shield against whatever danger might be lurking outside. Then, the curtain covering the smaller window begins to shift. An arm pokes through—a man's arm—and fumbles for the latch on the inside of the door.

Her survival instinct triggered by the threat of his imminent entry, Mary Jane slides quietly off the bed to look for a weapon.

"No, no, no!" Eva mouths silently, pawing at Mary Jane's dress, desperately trying to prevent her from breaking away.

"Sshhh," Mary Jane mouths back, putting a finger to her lips. "I'll get him." She grabs her broom from its resting place beside the mantel and wields it like a big stick, standing ready for the intruder at the door, primed for a beating, while Eva cowers behind her, clinging to the hem of her skirts, terrified to let go.

When the disembodied—possibly drunken—arm finally catches the latch and gets the door unlocked, she takes a deep breath and raises the broom, and as the stranger breaches the threshold ...

Thwack!

She cracks the broom handle over his head.

Once.

Twice.

The first hit crushes his bowler hat and knocks it off. The second hit comes crashing down on his sandy hair. A third hit is deflected by his forearms as he hunches forward and folds his arms over his head, trying to defend himself. At that point, Mary Jane recognizes him.

It's Joe.

"What the fuck is wrong with you?!" She raises the broom again, beating him about the back and shoulders.

"Are you out of your small mind?! Creeping into a woman's home unannounced when there's a madman about." She gives him several more thwacks for good measure. "You scared the living daylights out of us, you ignorant little shite."

"Will you leave off me, woman?!" Joe yanks the broom out of her hands and throws it out of her reach. "You've knackered me bloody hat!" He swipes his damaged bowler off the floor, popping out the dent. "I've only got the one." He sways toward her.

"You stink." She pushes him back. "Where've you been? Drinking your money away with that new doxy you've been sticking it up?"

She sounds jealous, but she's not. The only emotion coursing through her is anger, for just over a fortnight ago—after he obtained more regular work as a fruit porter and felt a little freer with his coin—he showed up at Miller's Court with another woman on his arm.

They were both very much the worse for drink, and when Mary Jane opened the door to them, she felt like she was looking in a carnival mirror. The woman was buxom enough to fill out one of her corsets, but was several inches too short. She carried the same weight, but it was spread out wider. Her blue eyes were genuinely pretty, but her hair—still damp from its recent introduction to henna—was nothing like Mary Jane's plush mane, excepting in its new coloring.

Joe wanted Mary Jane to vacate the room so that he might make use of the bed with his older, cheaper imitation, but the request went over poorly and a fight ensued. Hair was pulled. Punches were thrown. If not weakened by her existing injuries at the time, Mary Jane would've laid the drabbish harlot out in a few seconds flat. As it was, the fight spilled into Dorset Street, they had to be separated by the police, and each side walked away from the tussle bruised, battered, and publicly humiliated.

Since then, things have been particularly strained between them, and when Joe notices Eva huddled behind Mary Jane on the bed, he blows up.

"Goddamn whores!" He screams at the ceiling. "I'm sick of it!"

Flinching at the sound of his voice, Eva clambers off the bed. "I'm gonna go."

"I wish you bloody well would," Joe snaps at her. "I can't be doing with this nonsense no more. If it ain't you, it's the other one."

"What other one?" Eva feels her stomach drop.

"Oh, you don't know about our Marie Jeanette's other bedmate?" Joe takes pleasure in ratting Mary Jane out, and using her French name to do it. "That old tart, Maria. They've been flat-cocking since afore you came along."

"You're still sleeping with Maria?" Eva backs away from the bed, shaking her head in disbelief. "After you promised me you was done with her?"

"Darling, please." Mary Jane tries to reel her back in. "It ain't how it seems."

Eva doesn't stick around for an explanation. She twists out of Mary grasp and runs for home, and rather than stop her, Mary Jane lets her get clear of the room, then lays into Joe.

"Happy now?" She gives him a thump in the chest. "Arsehole!"

"You need to be put right," he mumbles unapologetically. "We was good together afore Maria turned you wrong, and if you quit bringing all these wenches in here, we can be as we were."

"Put right?" Mary Jane glowers at him. "How many times need I repeat myself to you? Maria weren't my first woman, and as it happens, I ain't never fucked her in this bed. Not once! We was shamming, you fool. We was winding you up."

"Horseshit."

"Ha! As if you know aught about the love between two women." Mary Jane plants her hands on her hips. "Or even how to please a woman, for that matter. I can do more with seven inches of glass than you can with that repulsive thing you keep in your trousers."

The puzzled frown on Joe's face betrays his ignorance.

"Just get out." Mary Jane flaps her hand toward the door. "Leave me."

When he doesn't move, she picks up the nearest hard object—an empty ginger beer bottle—and lobs it at his head. "I said get the fuck out!"

He ducks just in time, the bottle flying past his head and toward the small window, ripping the curtain wire down and smashing out the top left pane of glass, shattering as it hits the ground on the other side.

"That's enough!" Joe clutches his bashed-in bowler hat and storms out. "You ain't getting a penny from me tonight!" He slams the door behind him and stomps off down the court.

"Good riddance!" she bellows after him.

Before darkness completely descends, she retrieves her broom from the floor and goes outside to sweep up the remains of her ginger beer bottle, the whitewashed court illuminated by the single gaslight opposite her room. She's not in the mood to discuss her business with her neighbors, but a snoopy Julia peeps her head out of number one.

"All clear now?" She looks around for Joe.

"Sorry for the racket." Mary Jane sweeps the debris up into a pile beside the dustbins. "He's being a right arsehole lately."

"So I heard." Julia sits on her stoop, beneath the gaslight. "Is you on a bust?"

"I reckon so." Mary Jane crouches on the ground, picking up the larger shards of glass and pottery. "I'll be sorry to leave him—he's been good to me overall—but I can't go on like this. It ain't no life for anyone."

"You working this evening?"

"Not likely." Mary Jane snorts. "I'm afraid to go out alone at night 'cause of a dream I had that a man was murdering me. Maybe I'll be next." She picks herself up, laughing. "They say Jack's been busy in this quarter, and wouldn't that be just my luck?"

Bidding Julia *bonne nuit*, she retreats to her room, flings the broken curtain wire onto the fireplace grate, and slumps into a chair at the table, contemplating her financial predicament. The money given to her by Adel is

long spent, she's not due a visit with one of her specials for a while, and she's low on funds—which seems to be a familiar state of late. Eva's rent was paid in full yesterday, while hers remained entirely in arrears, and they spent last Saturday night at the Paragon Theatre in Mile End. It was Eva's first experience of an East End music hall, and she'd been pleading to go for weeks.

"I'll let you have me in the gallery," she promised by way of enticement.

Not that any enticement was truly needed, and not that she actually did; she was far too engrossed in the performance. She saved her gratitude for when they returned home.

On top of all these expenditures, Mary Jane laments having given the boot to her main source of somewhat regular income, and questions her judgment in forcing Eva to miss half a day's work. In need of a way to replenish their coffers without resorting to the obvious, she finds herself considering Adel's generous proposition.

Tempted by the promise of monetary compensation for her time, she withdraws Adel's *carte de visite* from its hiding place—tucked inside the corner of the bed sheet—and stares at the image of her former lover for a few minutes before flipping the card over and contemplating the Knightsbridge address.

Knightsbridge.

Not a place she ever wanted to go again.

Nevertheless, she digs out some loose leaf paper from her cupboard and pens a quick letter, heartened to find some of the pages defaced with Eva's scribbles, including one that's filled with ink hearts of various sizes and flourishes, all containing the letters MJK, some adorned with wonky, misshapen flowers.

If she gets her letter in the pillar box before eight o'clock, it'll be picked up overnight and delivered to Adel with the first post ... but she vacillates. Lying on the bed, Adel's *carte de visite* in her pocket and the letter in her hand, she thinks back to the height of their illicit romance. Desperate to see each other at every conceivable opportunity, they'd taken many unnecessary

risks, not the least of which was a dinner party Mary Jane attended at Adel's home.

Rigged out in her finest clothes, she was introduced to the other guests—and Adel's husband—as a long-lost childhood friend. Throughout the evening, they flaunted an almost familial closeness, and Adel took great pleasure in duping her husband. After all, he saw whores while he was away on business, so why oughtn't she have her own amusements? The highlight of the evening came when she gave Mary Jane a grand tour of the house. Mary Jane bent her over the back of a chair in the library and fucked her to within an inch of her sanity.

The memory of that night has Mary Jane longing for company, and when she's woken from her doze by a harried knock at the door, her first thought is of Eva. Hoping it might be her—cooled off and ready to talk—she leaps off the bed and swings open the door without bothering to question the identity of her late visitor.

But it's not Eva, it's a woman she knows from the street. Though usually of neat appearance, she looks bedraggled and fatigued, her knitted shawl hanging limply off her shoulders and her up-do in disarray.

"Sorry to call on you so late, only my old man and I had a row and I'm a penny short for a doss." She digs in her pockets, pulling out thruppence. "Can I sleep here? I don't mind kipping on the chair, I just don't wanna be outside tonight. Not with the way things is."

"Go on, then." Mary Jane holds her hand out for the money, letting the woman in. "You can have the bed. I've got someone I need to see."

Armed with the thruppence, she leaves her guest to sleep in peace, drops her letter to Adel in the nearest pillar box, and heads straight for a pie shop on Commercial Street, getting there just before closing.

At any given time, there are a variety of pies on offer for only a penny: beef steak, eel, kidney, fruit, or mincemeat. Tonight, beef is the best of the pickings, and she arrives at Eva's door bearing two steaming pies upturned on a piece of paper, Eva answering her knock with a yawn and a pout.

"There's my beautiful girl." Mary Jane smiles warmly. "Did I wake you? I thought you might want some food." She holds up the pies. "I brought you supper." Seeing that Eva's reluctant to let her in, she wafts the pies under the teen's nose, appealing to her stomach. "Peace offering? You know there's no-one's company I'd rather be in."

"Do I?" Eva walks away from the door, letting her enter if she wishes.

"You have to know how much I love you." Mary Jane balances the pies in one hand and locks the door behind her. "I ain't sleeping with Maria, or anyone else."

"But Joe said—"

"Joe's a jealous bastard." Mary Jane cuts her off. "I was giving Maria my bed for the night, that's all. There weren't nothing to it. She had no lodgings, and I surely wasn't gonna leave her walking the streets with Jack about." She sets the pies on the table, pushing them in front of Eva.

"Where'd you get the money for these?" Eva stares at the food.

"I rented out my room for the rest of the night, so there's no need to get uppish." Mary Jane rummages in the cupboard for two forks. "It was honest money, and if you don't believe me, you can look for yourself." She sits down, props one foot on the edge of the table, parts her legs, and lifts her skirts. "I haven't had no-one but you."

"No-one?" Eva looks doubtful.

"You'd be able to tell if I had." Mary Jane opens herself up for inspection. "I gave Joe his marching orders. You're the only one I'm with."

Familiar with the scent of Mary Jane's soap, Eva kneels on the floor and dips her head, giving Mary Jane's article a good sniff, detecting no hint of male spendings, nor any trace of perfume to indicate that she's recently washed.

"Satisfied?" Mary Jane hopes.

"No." Eva drops kisses on Mary Jane's thighs. "Not until you are." She presses her lips to Mary Jane's motte, then over the nub of her clit.

597

Murmuring her approval for the attentions, Mary Jane leans back and relaxes, bringing her hand to the back of Eva's head. "No gentler mouth is there in all of London."

CHAPTER 50

THE WHITECHAPEL MURDERS

"The Central News is informed that Dr. Forbes Winslow and other leading authorities on mental disorders are still of opinion that the murders in Whitechapel were committed by a homicidal lunatic. Dr. Forbes Winslow believes that the murderer has lately been in a 'lucid interval.' In that condition he would be comparatively rational, and also forgetful of what he had done. As soon as this passes off, he will resume his terrible work."

-- Daily News, October 31, 1888

Thursday, November 1, 1888

A DAY HAS COME AND GONE, AND HALLOWEEN NIGHT passed relatively quietly. Eschewing theatrical séances and other morbid games, Mary Jane and Eva spent the evening at the Royal Cambridge Music Hall on Commercial Street. There, they were entertained with a number of wholesome variety acts, including several dancers, a juggler, a singer, and a comedienne.

Gallery seats were only tuppence, and since it was such a cheap night of fun, Mary Jane insisted that they indulge with a glass of champagne ... or two. Teetotal Eva got spoony, Mary Jane got spreeish, and by night's end they snuck out the back exit of the theater into an unlit,

dead-end alley and gave way to one another up against the wall of an old warehouse.

Neither could say whose digits wandered first, but by the time they were moved on by a patrolling bobby who shone his light in their direction and guffawed like an adolescent schoolboy, each had a hand up the other's skirts. By that point, Eva had completely forgotten all concerns for the onset of her monthlies. They hurried home and fucked vigorously—and in a number of imaginative attitudes—until Eva fell asleep in Mary Jane's arms.

Of course, all good fun must come to an end, and it does so abruptly when dawn comes and Eva wakes to the first trickles of a crimson deluge between her thighs, her head throbbing and her insides cramping.

"I knew all that jiggering would bring my courses on," she sobs, clamping a strip of linen to her crotch as she rummages through a basket of hygiene supplies in search of her catamenial bandage. "You made me so lewd I forgot me-self."

While Mary Jane prefers to use an internal absorbent contrivance for the mopping up of her reds—be it the trusty sea sponge, or a homemade contraption consisting of a tight wad of puffy cotton wool sewn into a linen tube—Eva sticks resolutely to the external catchment device she's used since her menarche. Much tidier than simply pinning rags beneath her clothes, the catamenial bandage is comprised of a slim belt and a linen pouch, the latter being attached to the former by loops at the front and back. These loops can be adjusted to make sure the pouch fits snugly against a woman's parts, and the pouch itself can be stuffed with all manner of absorbent materials: rags, cotton wool, hankies—whatever's to hand.

Once she has herself settled—washed, and dressed in bandage, drawers, and nightgown—Eva returns to bed, but thanks to her uncooperative uterus, rest proves impossible. Sympathizing with her, an exhausted Mary Jane—functioning on only an hour's sleep, having spent the better part of the night poring over Eva's sleeping body—wriggles out of bed.

"What doing?" Eva yawns.

"When I'm feeling bad, I like to treat myself to something nice." Mary Jane stokes up the smoldering fire, positions one of the chairs in front of it, and drapes two towels over the chair to warm, then fetches her nail buffering accoutrements. "Coloring my nails never fails to cheer me." She pulls the bed covers off Eva and sits cross-legged at her feet.

"I've never had this done afore." Eva lets Mary Jane scoop up one of her feet, and watches as she applies a colored paste to her toenails, rubbing it in with the corner of a washcloth. "It makes 'em look so pretty, don't it?"

"I've given you lots of firsts." Mary Jane works her way along Eva's toes, buffering each nail to a soft, pearly pink. "I do so like it." She finishes one foot and begins on the other. "And since you're unwell, you'll be keeping home today."

"You're sure?" Eva frets, chewing on her bottom lip. "It's only my monthlies." She rubs a hand over her abdomen. "Other women works when they's got theirs on."

"Aye, but other women ain't so stubborn. They take medicine for the pain." Mary Jane admires her handiwork. "You suffer rotten with your poorliness, and I pity you for that." She grabs one of the warmed towels off the chair, folds it, and lays it on Eva's belly beneath her chemise, pressing it to her abdomen, directing its heat there. "Feel better?"

Eva nods, her tense muscles unknotting. "You make everything better."

Doubting that, Mary Jane pecks her on the forehead and gets up. Though she'd rather be sleeping, she's anxious. It must be creeping up on eight o'clock—daylight's bleeding in through the patchwork curtains—and she's keen to find out whether Adel has sent a reply to her letter. She expected to receive something yesterday, but nothing came and the silence troubles her.

"Will you be all right if I leave you for a bit?" She warms her corset in front of the fire. "You can keep tucked up nice and cozy in bed, and I'll bring you back something to eat."

"You have money?" Eva asks, knowing that Mary Jane already spent the tuppence she got from letting out her room for the second night in a row.

"I can get some." Mary Jane squeezes herself into her corset. "What do you fancy? Bacon? Eggs? Sausage? Double the bacon?"

Receiving no reply, she turns back to the bed and finds Eva curled up in the sulks, having misinterpreted her casual certainty regarding the procurement of coin.

"My sweet darling." She kneels on the bed behind her balled-up lover. "I meant nothing immoral. As soon as the bank opens, I can—"

"Take my rent money," Eva volunteers, determined not to let Mary Jane leave with empty pockets, just in case. "Please do." Her stomach growls and she pleads urgency rather than distrust. "There's a little lion in my belly what wants feeding."

"Very well." Mary Jane peppers her head with kisses, agreeing purely for the sake of avoiding a fight. "I'll put it back before rent day." She eases herself off the bed and pulls the covers up around Eva's shoulders, making her as comfortable as possible. "And I'll color your fingernails when I get back. How about that?"

No answer.

Guessing that's the best she's going to get, Mary Jane completes her morning routine and steps out into thick fog. What she mistook for daylight seeping through the curtains was, in fact, artificial light from the various lamps on Thrawl Street, their glow reflecting on the heavy mist. Indeed, it's very much later in the morning than she first guessed, for trading is already in full force on Commercial Street, despite the uncooperative elements. Were it not for the hissing gaslights illuminating the streets, it would appear as night, the slate gray sky covered with a pendulous cloud of vapor, blocking out all appearance of the sun.

It's eerie and damp. Each step into the gloom feels startlingly unnerving, and Mary Jane draws what warmth she can from her black velvet jacket, tucking the fur collar around her neck. Soon, the weather will demand that she put away her nicer dresses in favor of the plain,

unflattering linsey-woolsey frock she reserves for the coldest winter days. Though rather unbecoming, the durable, ruddy brown outfit serves its purpose well.

Making her way onward, vision is limited to a few feet at best. Carriages come barreling out of nowhere, the sound of clopping hooves directly preceding the ghostly glow of the headlamps, and children dart about with impunity, committing all sorts of mischief.

Her first port of call is the post office on Whitechapel High Street. Any correspondence she dare not risk being seen by Joe still goes there, despite her Miller's Court landlord being willing to receive mail on his tenants' behalf, and this morning brings word from Adel. Finally. She wants to meet posthaste, apologizes for the lack of notice, and instructs Mary Jane to procure a cab at once, her travel costs to be fully reimbursed.

Hurrying on, Mary Jane makes one stop at a bakery on Commercial Street, appeals to the good nature of the baker's well-endowed son, and returns to Eva with a whole loaf of bread—hot, straight from the bake house—and a variety of fresh pastries, including brioche.

"This is what you call breakfast?" Eva grins, watching her set the assortment of iced buns and rolls out on a plate. "Them's all sweets."

"When feeling unwell, one should eat as one desires." Mary Jane delivers the plate to her in bed. "And one should *always* enjoy these treats in bed."

Happy to have any excuse to eat such goodies this early in the day, Eva digs in, expecting to be joined by Mary Jane at any moment. Instead, Mary Jane drags her steamer trunk out from under the bed and starts changing into her West End clothes, taking bites of food here and there and amusing Eva with verses of various Irish songs, as if that'll distract her from the irregularity of a wardrobe change. It doesn't.

"Where's you going?" Eva asks with her mouth full. "You ain't coming back to bed?"

"I've got some work to do today." Mary Jane buttons herself into the silk. "But I shan't be gone long, and my absence will give you a chance to rest."

Afraid of precisely what that 'work' might entail, Eva's appetite diminishes. "Please don't." She picks at the brioche, thinking of all the women who've lost their lives in recent months. "It ain't safe out there for women no more. What if—"

"Don't think such awful things." Mary Jane stops her from voicing any fear that she might be the next victim of the Whitechapel Fiend. "Besides," she adds cautiously, not sure how Eva will react to the truth, "that ain't what I'm doing. It ain't a fella I'm going to see." She prepares herself for chastisement. "It's Adel."

That's Eva's second worst nightmare.

"Why?" She pushes the pastries away. "What's she paying you for?"

"Only to talk." Mary Jane changes into her silk stockings and best boots. "We could use the money, darling, and it's just a harmless cup of tea." She hopes that's true.

Eva doesn't buy it. "Why would she pay you for that?"

"It's a gift."

"In contemplation of?"

"Nothing."

Rejecting that, Eva lunges for her, grabbing her around the middle and clutching on. "Don't do it! Please, Mary Jane." She wails. "Don't leave me!"

"You're being foolish now. I would *never* leave you." Mary Jane holds Eva to her breast. "Everything I do, I do for you. For *us*." She clamps Eva's ear over her heart, hoping she can hear it beating. "I love you more than life itself, and I would *never* behave untrue to you."

"Adel wants you." Eva sniffles.

"So what if she does? Listen here, love." Mary Jane pries Eva away from her bosom, forcing her to make eye contact. "What would you rather? I can continue to take money from our savings, which means we'll be stuck here in Whitechapel all the longer." She wipes the teen's cheeks. "Or I can go back on the streets and bring in a few pounds a week, taking my chances with the Ripper." She tries to put things in perspective. "Alternatively, I can drink a cup of tea with an old lover and bring home

604

enough to tide us over for a month." She pauses, letting that sink in. "What's it to be?"

Eva says nothing.

The fog appears worse in Knightsbridge, but Mary Jane is thankful for the cover. Adel's home isn't far from the Frenchwoman's house, and she doesn't want to be seen.

Though the cab drops her off directly in front of the Adkins family's impressive five-storey house along the southern side of Ennismore Gardens, on the prestigious Kingston House estate, she hesitates to mount the steps and ring the bell. The looming house—one of several in a row—has an impressive frontage. Two Corinthian columns support a wide portico, and the first floor has a balcony overlooking the private garden square in front of which its situated.

Needing some courage, she makes one brisk circuit of the square before retreating to the Ennismore Arms for a glass of brandy. Her nerves calmed by that, though the local crowd is somewhat taken aback to see a single woman enter a public house unaccompanied, she returns to the square and strides up to the door, exuding sham confidence.

To announce her arrival, she reaches for the brass bell pull set into the wall beside the door. One tug of this ornate knob applies tension to a wire concealed within the inner framework of the house. This wire, in turn, jerks a brass bell mounted on a coiled steel spring in the servants' quarters, causing it to chime out four times, thereby alerting the butler to the presence of a guest. But she never gets to ring it.

Presently, a curvaceous young maid of West African parentage throws open the door, bursts out onto the stoop, and flings herself into Mary Jane's arms, almost knocking her off the steps. It's Cherry.

"Ain't it been an age?" She squeezes Mary Jane tight. "I've missed your face."

"It's good to see you." Mary Jane wraps her arms around her former bedmate. "I'm glad to find you still with the Adkins family."

"I do like it here ever so much." Cherry releases her. "The missus said you was coming, and I been watching out for you." She leads Mary Jane inside and lowers her voice. "I'm under sp'ific instruction to take you upstairs directly, and we must be quiet."

"What? Why?" Mary Jane follows warily.

Cherry hurries her through the grand entrance hall— with its checkered marble floor and enormous oil paintings—and up the main staircase, their footsteps barely audible on the thick velvet runner cascading down the *escalier*. On the first floor, she goes straight for the master bedroom suite and Mary Jane panics, all confidence evaporated.

"No, Cherry. This is her bedroom."

"Uh-huh." Cherry giggles, knocking twice sharply on the door to Adel's private dressing room. "This is where she said to bring you."

Afraid that she might be about to walk in on Adel wearing only a silk chiffon peignoir, fresh from a bath and lounging on the double-wide blue damask chaise at the center of her lavish dressing room, ready for fucking, Mary Jane's stomach twists in a knot. Wishing now that she'd never embarked upon this foolish venture, she holds her breath as Cherry swings open the door, announces her, and shoves her in, promptly leaving them to their clandestine business.

But relief!

Exhale.

Adel, though reclining barefoot on her chaise, sprawled over the pelt of a polar bear, her waist-length golden hair brushed out and let down, her skirts gathered up so as to bare her slender ankles, is otherwise respectably dressed, amusing herself with a book.

"Mary Jane!" She puts her well-read copy of *The Wrongs of Woman* aside and beckons her guest closer,

standing with outstretched arms. "I wasn't sure if you'd come."

"Neither was I." Mary Jane greets her with a hug and a chaste kiss, taking a furtive look around the room, noting that the folding partition leading into the adjoining master bedroom has been left open, the four-poster bed in full view.

As befitting Adel's fortune and position, the whole suite is both elegant and comfortable. To preserve her privacy, the double curtains—one of silk, one of lace-edged tulle—are drawn across the windows, and the room is lit with a chandelier at its center and a roaring fire in the hearth. The bathing area is divided from the rest of the room by a heavy curtain, the scents of lavender, rosemary, and eucalyptus wafting in from the tiled alcove. She recently bathed.

Throughout the rest of the room, there's plush pearl-gray carpeting and silk wallpaper. Two tables stand at opposite ends of the room, a larger one for washing and a smaller one for hairdressing, both draped in silk. All dresses and other items of clothing are closeted away, the chamber pot is hidden beneath the flounces of the larger table, and satin-framed mirrors abound. This is a sanctuary of femininity indeed.

"Might I ask why you're receiving me here instead of the drawing room?" Mary Jane's eyes wander again to the nearby bed. "Isn't this rather irregular?"

"I suppose." Adel shrugs. "But I had to sneak you up here without the new nanny seeing. My mother-in-law hired her, and she's a dreadful spy. She tells the old witch everything."

"You're not allowed to receive visitors?" Mary Jane infers.

"Not presently." Adel invites her to the chaise. "That's why I wrote to you so urgently. The infuriating woman's taken my son on an outing and isn't due back for hours. Honestly, I do believe she'd lock me in this very room if she could. She thinks I need rest."

"Why?" Mary Jane sits, crossing her legs at the ankles. "Have you been ill?"

"Not in the least." Adel brushes off the concern. "The baby's still on my milk and I'm a little worn out, that's all. It's nothing to cause a fuss over."

"You feed her from your own breast?" Mary Jane is openly astonished. "No wet nurse?"

"My mother fed me from her breast, and so I shall do the same." Adel offers her a biscuit from a decorative platter on a coffee table in front of the chaise. "To tell you the truth, I rather like the solitude it affords. Nothing evacuates a house of this class faster than the threat of a woman exposing herself in another room. Would you like some tea?" She indicates a steaming teapot next to the platter. "I just had it brought up."

Mary Jane nods, encouraging normality. "Where's your husband?"

"Away." Adel pours Mary Jane a cup of the fresh brew, still remembering precisely how she likes it. "And before you ask, which I'm certain you will, all's functioning sufficiently, if a little infrequently, but what's a woman to do? I tend to myself, as you taught me, and have learned to be content with my lot, but it's hardly the same, and I do so miss the variety."

"You've had no other woman?"

Adel shakes her head. "I always hoped you'd return to me." She hands over the dainty cup. "Silly, I know, but I'd grown so comfortable with you. Commencing such a relationship with someone else just seemed like so much hard work, and I couldn't help but think that any attempt to replicate what we once had would end in miserable failure."

"Why?"

"It's not simply a matter of attraction." Adel pours her own tea, keeping her fingers busy. "You and I were ... perfect." Her hand shakes as she stirs in the sugar. "Compatible." She dare not pick up the cup for fear of spilling it. "If you'll permit me to be so blunt: you fucked me well." Coarse words sound even coarser coming from her genteel lips.

"We fucked each other well," Mary Jane corrects her, recalling how she'd been brought to tears the first time Adel put mouth to cunt. "The pleasure was mutual."

Losing interest in the tea, Adel slides deeper into the chaise. "My aunt knew I kept seeing you beyond that first night. That's why she sent me out of London." There's a trace of bitterness in her voice. "I almost think she was jealous. When she introduced us, I'm sure she never anticipated that we'd become so close." She touches a hand to Mary Jane's thigh. "I would've run away with you."

"I'd never have let you, but I loved the thought." Mary Jane sets down her cup and peels away Adel's hand, placing it on the cushion between them and keeping hers on top to hold it at bay. "Eva and I plan to leave London soon. I've promised her a new start."

"You're in love with her, I know." Adel slips her hand away. "I don't mean to behave improperly with you. I promised I wouldn't, and I shall keep my word." She folds her hands in her lap. "But I do miss you so frightfully much." Worried that her confession will make Mary Jane feel uncomfortable, she keeps talking, swiftly changing the subject. "I hope you don't mind, but I informed my aunt of your circumstance and she wishes to see you. Would you consent to it?"

"For what purpose?"

"I'm afraid it's not my place to say, but it would mean a great deal to her." Adel finally reaches for her cup. "She's been living here these past few months for her health's been in decline."

"It saddens me to hear that," Mary Jane sympathizes. "Will she recover?"

"Why don't you see for yourself?"

CHAPTER 51

Mary Jane knocks on the oversized lacquered wooden door of the main guest room, waits for the faint, barely recognizable command to enter, and twists the crystal doorknob, stepping into a lavish bedroom decorated in pastels and bursting with the fragrance of honeysuckle.

The curtains are half-drawn, casting shadow over the head of the bed, but leaving the rest of the gas-lit room in an eerie pale orange glow, its warmth diluted by the light spilling in from the street, the unusually heavy fog reflecting the golden hue of the gas lamps outside.

To the left of the room, in a queen size four-poster bed enveloped with a canopy of white netting and lace, a nightgown-clad woman sits with her back to the headboard, propped upright on cushions and pillows.

"Come to me," she coos, patting the mattress at her side before coughing so hard into a silk hanky that she almost retches.

"Are you dreadfully ill?" Mary Jane approaches and peels back the canopy, suppressing her shock to look upon the pallid, gaunt face of her former—and once beautiful—customer Missus B——, now ravaged with consumption.

"Congestion of the lungs." Missus B—— puts on a smile, her dry lips cracked and flaking.

Upon being invited to do so, Mary Jane perches on the edge of the bed, offering nothing but her sympathies for the progressive, wasting disease claiming the older woman's body, knowing that nothing can be done to relieve her of it.

"You oughtn't be in London." She eyes a lung tonic and three bottles of laudanum on the bedside table: one empty, one half-consumed, and one in waiting.

"I've only recently returned." Missus B—— breathes hard and shallow, wheezing with every rise and fall of her chest. "I want to spend the rest of my days at home. Among my family."

The brutal truth of her condition causes a lump to rise in Mary Jane's throat. "Where's your husband? He should be here, by your side."

"I'm now widowed."

Though Mary Jane's first thought is one of a much less compassionate nature, for lack of anything better to say, she volunteers an empty apology. "I'm sorry."

"So am I." Missus B—— smothers a cough. "I wish he'd died a good deal sooner."

Glad to see she hasn't lost her acerbic wit, Mary Jane chuckles. "The old fool was never worthy of you." She wipes a stray tear from her eye. "You deserved to be happy."

"I was." Missus B—— lays a hand over Mary Jane's on the counterpane. "For a few hours here and there." She caresses the back of Mary Jane's hand with her fingertips. "I want you to know that my sending Adel away from you had nothing to do with jealousy. That's not to say I wasn't out of my mind with envy, but it wasn't my motivation for breaking you apart, nor for keeping her from you when she returned from her confinement."

"You needn't explain."

"I want to." Missus B—— gives her hand a firm squeeze. "I knew she was seeing you. You awoke her spirit the night I brought you into this home. From then on out, every time I saw her, she was positively glowing with contentment." She pauses to cough into her hanky. "Over time, she couldn't keep it back. She began talking

to me of such pleasures I knew only too well—things I knew she could only have learned from you."

"Not from her husband?"

Missus B—— smirks. "You know as well as I that no man on this Earth could ever know so much about the intimate workings of the female body." She taps on her chest, dislodging some of the fluid pooling in her lungs. "Adel was so happy, but she was becoming far too attached. I feared she might soon act upon her feelings for you, and I simply couldn't allow that to happen. I hope you understand."

"I do." Mary Jane stares at the floor. "Is that why you wanted to see me?"

"In part." Missus B—— pulls out a drawer in the bedside table. "In part also because, when Adel told me of your situation, it spurred me into action." She withdraws a black leather folder. "I'm starting a business inspired by you."

"By me?" Mary Jane quirks an eyebrow. "How?"

"It's a small guesthouse." Missus B—— opens the folder, flipping it to the details of a property located on the outskirts of Ramsgate, in Kent. "It shall cater exclusively to women." She turns the folder to face Mary Jane. "In other words, it's to be a place for women to enjoy the company of other women—somewhere they can show their love for one another without resorting to the bad houses that populate this city—and I want it to be staffed entirely by women." She pauses. "Women like you. Women of a sympathetic nature. No men."

"It sounds delightful." Mary Jane runs her eyes over a photograph of a large stone-built building with a conservatory and a sprawling garden. "You purchased this?"

"I did." Missus B—— smiles broadly. "And I should like you to run it."

Mary Jane forgets to breathe. "Excuse me?"

"I can think of no-one more deserving, nor more qualified for the position," Missus B—— proclaims confidently. "If the guests are scared or confused, you can counsel them. If they're unaccustomed to the devices of pleasure, you can educate them."

"But I have no experience of—"

"Of course you do. You know how a guesthouse works, in principle at least, and I shall arrange for someone to teach you the ins and outs of it all. You have a grasp of mathematics, yes?"

"Yes, but—"

"Then there's nothing to discuss." Missus B—— won't hear a word of uncertainty. She manages a smile, her dry lips pulled taut. "My land agent will need to visit you to sort out the particulars, but I shall let Adel arrange that with you. It's hers to inherit in any case."

"I don't know what to say." Mary Jane stares at the photograph in her lap. "This is so very generous of you."

"Nonsense. It's a small gesture of my appreciation." Missus B—— fusses with the pillows behind her back, trying to get comfortable. "You've given so much of yourself to others, and I want to give you something in return." She wheezes, the strain of talking taxing her lungs. "I know it can't replace what's been taken from you. It certainly can't make up for the years of lost dignity you've endured—nothing can—but it does ensure a better future. For you, and for that dear young girl of yours."

"I care more for Eva than myself." Mary Jane devours the information in front of her: bedrooms, bathrooms, and grounds. "I want this for her."

In need of a dose of laudanum, and too weak to entertain further conversation, Missus B—— begs Mary Jane's pardon and sends for her maid.

Parting from her with more profuse thanks, Mary Jane returns to Adel's dressing room. There, she's taken aback to find Adel breastfeeding her infant on the chaise, her clothing unfastened down to her maternity corset, the buttons on one of the specially-designed bust gores released to bare one of her milk-laden breasts, the nipple and areola obscured by the baby's suckling mouth.

"Forgive me." Color rises into Adel's cheeks. "I wasn't sure how long you'd be with my aunt, and it was time for her feed."

Mary Jane struggles to know where to look. "Ought I leave?"

"I'd rather you remained." Adel smiles sweetly. "Nanny would have a fit if she thought I'd allow someone else in the room while I nurse, but I've nothing to hide from you." She makes no effort to conceal herself. "Did you have a nice visit with my aunt? She misses you."

"Still?" Mary Jane lingers at the edge of the room.

"Always, I shall think. She cares a good deal more for you than she'll ever let on." Adel scrutinizes Mary Jane's expression, trying to determine whether or not there's any cause for congratulations. "Did she discuss the business with you?"

"She did."

"And are you of a mind to accept?"

"I believe so." Mary Jane allows herself a peek at the wispy tuft of flaxen hair topping the blanket-covered bundle in Adel's arms.

"I'm ever so glad." Adel beams. "It sickens my heart to think of you putting yourself in danger day after day. I shall be much relieved to see you safe." Noting Mary Jane's interest in the bundle, Adel turns down the edge of the blanket that's partially concealing the baby's head. "Do you wish to see her? You're welcome sit with me if it doesn't offend you to do so."

"Offend me?" Mary Jane accepts the invitation a little too readily. "Motherhood is such a sacred, precious thing. I need only see an infant and my bosom aches." She hitches up her skirts and settles beside Adel, watching the baby suckle from her, forgetting all sense of propriety as she tucks one leg beneath herself, sitting as she would in her own room.

"I truly believe there's no other woman in the world quite like you." Adel leans into Mary Jane's shoulder, bringing the baby closer so that she might have a better look. "So unbound by convention. So honest with your feelings."

"Some call me boorish."

"But that's not the case at all," Adel defends her from such critique. "It's not that you aren't capable of conforming to the standards expected of you, but that you refuse to be defined by them. The same woman who slips seamlessly into a room full of her social betters and

converses with them about God and country as if she were their equal will then shamelessly and ardently fuck me out of my mind as soon as we're alone." She refers to that daring dinner party, throughout which she felt Mary Jane's cock at every possible moment. "You possess both good grace and animalistic passion. It's intoxicating, and I daresay that's part of your allure for women like myself. We're bred to be of one nature: demure. You make us fervid."

"I uncaged you."

"You enchanted me." Feeling the warmth of Mary Jane's arm resting on the back of the chaise, almost around her shoulders, Adel shuffles a few inches nearer. "I hope Eva appreciates how exceptional you are."

"She's never had another."

"Then she doesn't know how lucky she is." Adel tucks herself into the crook of Mary Jane's arm under the guise of facilitating her admiration of the baby, positioning herself so close that Mary Jane can smell the fragrance of her tresses.

"I'm still fond of you." Mary Jane nuzzles her face in Adel's flaxen locks, dropping a kiss there. "If circumstances had been different, I would've called you my wife."

"If I'd have met you sooner ..."

"If you'd have met me sooner"—Mary Jane injects reality into her blossoming daydream—"I'm afraid I'd have done damage equal to any man. I'd have ruined you."

Knowing that to be true, Adel recalls the night Mary Jane pierced her maidenhead with the dildo. "You gave me my first taste of pleasure. Did you know that?"

"I suspected." Mary Jane smirks. "There's a certain gratitude a woman exudes when she achieves her peak for the first time. It's a telltale mixture of startled disbelief and sheer delight, most often followed by the words"—she whispers in Adel's ear—"do it again."

Indeed, Mary Jane would wager that there's nothing else on Earth quite as delicious as the stunned gasp of a woman who's never before felt the lashings of a hot tongue upon her flesh. Such a gasp is invariably

accompanied by the slackening of her thighs and the astonished realization that there's more to intimacy than a few hasty shoves and a premature wetting.

"I daresay I'll forever miss that feeling," Mary Jane reflects frankly. "I shall never again get to feel the sweet surrender of a genteel woman begging for a fuck, her cunt inflamed with desire, despite all her breeding and refinement."

"Hearing you speak that way has a stirring effect on me." Adel squeezes her thighs together, suppressing her lusts. "I've never encountered another woman so free with her tongue, and my husband would never permit such language in our marriage bed." Having no-one else to discuss these matters with, she opens up. "May I confess something to you? When he's in the midst of his exertions, I sometimes find myself thinking of the letters I must write, the dinners I must arrange, and countless other mundanities. When I'm with you ..." She pauses to change tense. "When I *was* with you, there were no thoughts in my mind beyond the savoring of each moment of pleasure, for I was utterly incapable of them. My entire being was consumed by you."

Disrupting the course of the conversation, Adel's baby unlatches, releasing and exposing her full breast, a single droplet of milk clinging to the distended ruby tip. Her hands at work tending to the child, she can do nothing to cover herself.

"How undignified." She peers down at her leaking breast. "Now I see why this is kept a private business."

Thinking nothing of it, Mary Jane withdraws a folded hanky from her pocket and dabs at the lone drop, soaking it up, feeling Adel's swollen nipple behind the silk. Only when Adel lets out a soft mewl of appreciation does she question the appropriateness of the action.

"I should go." She withdraws in a flash.

"Of course." Adel lets her off the hook. "I've kept you far too long already. Your girl will be fretting." She tips her head toward the coffee table, directing Mary Jane's attention to a five pound note. "That's for you. Will it be enough to keep you well until I can arrange for the land agent to visit you with the papers?"

"It's really not necessary."

"Accept it for my sake." Adel saves Mary Jane's pride. "I shall only worry myself silly if you don't, and my mother-in-law's already convinced that I'm on the brink of collapse."

Mary Jane makes no further objection. Promising to see Adel the following Sunday for prayers at the Salvation Army meeting in Angel Alley, she creeps downstairs and lets Cherry see her out, the affectionate young maid sending her off with a giggle and two freshly baked scones she pilfered from the kitchen.

Still hot from the oven, Mary Jane warms her hands on them in her pocket, their heat radiating through the cloth napkin Cherry wrapped them in. She wishes she owned a pair of gloves. Having to keep her skirts pinched up, the hem lifted a few inches above the pavement to prevent the precious silk from trailing in the muck of the street, she can only warm one hand at a time, alternating them as and when her fingers turn numb from the biting winter chill.

The air is still thick with fog and she keeps her head down, moving as fast as she can without breaking into a trot, not realizing how perilously close she is to the Frenchwoman's house until she comes upon a large, tanned male loitering on the pavement near a hansom cab rank.

She recognizes him immediately.

It's the house bully, and as he locks eyes with her, she bolts like a rabbit from a fox, knocking into people left and right as she zigzags from one street to the next, darting down alleyways and cutting through storage yards. With the dense vapor cloud still hanging over Knightsbridge, she soon loses sight of him, yet she keeps running. She dare not stop.

Fueled by a sudden burst of adrenalin, she doesn't succumb to fatigue, but the more she runs, the harder it becomes to breathe. Not just from the exertion, but the panic. Her chest hurts. Rapid inhalation of the cold, dry November air irritates her airways, making it feel as though her breath is freezing in her throat, and her

corseting prevents the full expansion of her lungs, forcing her to take shallow, labored gasps.

Fearing that her heart might give out, she ducks into the nearest secluded yard and conceals herself behind a pile of debris at the back of a warehouse. Her head spinning, her vision reduced to a swirling mass of gray, her entire body trembling, she sinks to the ground between two overfilled dustbins, wheezing, panting, and clutching at her bodice, passing out as soon as her bum hits the damp, frigid ground.

The fog clears at dinnertime, but the day doesn't get any brighter. The heavy, gloomy mist is replaced with torrential rain, and Mary Jane regains consciousness when a gutter pipe bursts above her and a surge of water gushes down, splashing in her face.

Momentarily forgetting where she is, she jolts awake, shocked by the bitter cold, her shawl drenched and her silk dress wet up to her knees, the rainwater seeping ever higher. Her bones ache. She has no idea how long she's been sitting there on the wet ground, but her entire body is stiff and sore, her hands throbbing from clenching her fists so tightly that her nails dug into her sweaty palms, leaving behind half-moon-shaped purple bruises.

Thankful she wasn't robbed as she lay indisposed upon the ground, she picks herself up and takes a hansom back to Whitechapel. Weary, but knowing she can't return to Lolesworth empty-handed, having promised Eva dinner, she starts rounding up supplies, her hunt for a hot meal taking her past the Victoria Home, where Fleming is skulking in the main entranceway.

"You look like you've gone for a swim in the Thames!" He laughs at her, grinning. "You need to get ye-

self one of these beauties!" He brandishes a molding, much-repaired umbrella at her. "May I escort you somewhere, my darling?"

Finding his pleasantness discomfiting, Mary Jane scurries by, trying to give him a wide berth, but he persists. As she passes him, he releases the rider latch on the umbrella—which appears to be a lady's parasol, the thin material designed for protection against the sun, not the rain—and pops it open, one of the pointed metal arm ends nearly stabbing her in the eye.

With a squeal, she ducks from it and steps back, losing her balance on the curb and knocking into a coster's barrow, her bum dislodging a precariously piled pyramid of apples and sending the fruit tumbling to the gutter. Immediately, a swarm of children swoop in like carrion birds, clamoring for the fallen fruit—much to the coster's agitation. He fends them off, whipping their bony buttocks with a twisted up dishcloth, and in the ruckus that ensues, she slips away, gathering up a veritable feast of meat pies, baked potatoes, and jellied eels before returning to Lolesworth with her arms full and two soggy scones in her pocket.

She tries to creep in quietly, in case Eva's napping, but soon sees there's no need to be so light-footed: Eva is awake and sitting at the table, her attention fixed on something in front of her, a neglected fire smoldering in the hearth.

"Whatchu doing out of bed?" Mary Jane lays out their dinner, putting on her best motherly voice. "You're meant to be resting."

"Couldn't sleep knowing you was out there," Eva mumbles, not rising to greet her as she normally would. "Why do you carry Adel's picture in your pocket?"

Mary Jane sheds her shawl and looks around, finding her every day clothes folded in a neat pile on the washstand, Adel's *carte de visite* taken from the pocket and placed on the table.

"She's very pretty." Eva keeps staring at the photograph, her expression blank. "I thought so when I seen her with you."

"It ain't like that." Mary Jane scoops the card up and flips it over, showing Eva the reverse. "She wrote her address on it, see? I was gonna take it with me to be sure I went to the right place, but I forgot it in my other pocket." She pulls up the other chair, tossing the card in the direction of the fireplace, not caring where it lands. "Darling, if I want something beautiful to look at, all I need do is look at you."

She expects those words to have a reassuring effect, but Eva remains forlorn.

"What happened?" The downcast teen picks at a thread on her nightgown. "You've been gone hours." She eyes a small puddle forming at Mary Jane's feet, water dripping from her saturated skirts. "And why's you so wet?"

"It's raining, love." Mary Jane grabs Eva's chair by the legs and drags it sideways, turning it to put them face to face. "But I've returned with news: Adel's aunt offered me a job."

"Her aunt? Why?" Eva frowns, this unanticipated announcement bringing immediate suspicion rather than relief. "What's she got to do with aught?"

"She was my paying woman," Mary Jane confesses readily, keen to get it all out in the open. "I'd have told you of her, only I didn't know she'd be there. She's in ill health, and—"

"What's the job?" Eva interrupts the sob tale, reaching for the buttons on Mary Jane's bodice. "And where? And why you in any case?"

"A guesthouse in Kent." Mary Jane lets her peel off the sodden silk. "I reckon she may have feelings for me, but I don't want you to—"

"And you for her?" Eva strips her to her corset and chemise, not wanting her to catch a cold.

Mary Jane shakes her head. "Affection, certainly, but not love. I save all of that for you." She captures Eva's cheeks. "Darling, I said I'd take you out of this city, and I will. You'll be a kept woman, just as I promised you when we met. Isn't that what you want?"

Refusing to be seduced by the thought, Eva watches a droplet of water trickle off Mary Jane's saturated hair,

the tiny bead cascading down her glistening chest and disappearing between the upper swells of her confined breasts. "When?" she asks, snatching a towel off the floor and dabbing at Mary Jane's wet skin.

"I don't know." Mary Jane wrings her mane out over the chamber pot. "Soon, I hope. And in the meantime"—she pulls Adel's five pound note out of her corset, the thin paper protected by the sturdy material—"we have this to tide us over."

"She gived you this just for what? Nuthin'?" Eva inspects the money. "You think I believes that? Nobody ever gives up their coin for nuthin'."

"I did when I met you," Mary Jane reminds her. "It was unconditional."

Eva falls silent, mulling that over.

Taking the opportunity to distract her from her needless worries, Mary Jane puts the money aside and scoops up her hands. "I've not been untrue to you, and nor will I be." She kisses Eva's fingers, knowing just what to say to make her soften. "*Tu es la seule pour moi.*"

She regurgitates another snippet of French she heard a hundred times while working at the *lupanar* in Paris, though she edits it for Eva's ears. When it was said to her, it was always somewhat less flattering.

Tu es la seule pute pour moi.

You're the only whore for me.

Not that Eva knows or cares what it means. She swoons regardless, and Mary Jane follows it up with one more morsel:

"*Baise-moi.*"

Fuck me.

CHAPTER 52

THE EAST END MURDERS
A PROBABLE CLUE
KNIVES FOUND BY A POLICEMAN

"Considerable excitement has been created in Kensington owing to the discovery of two knives, one bearing stains of blood, in the front garden of a house in Harrington Gardens. The discovery has remained for some time a secret with the police, and has now only become known by mere accident. It appears that on the night of Sunday, October 21, a policeman on duty observed something bright close to some shrubs in the garden, and upon entering to satisfy his curiosity, discovered a sheath containing two large knives, which are stated to be Ghurka knives. An examination has been made, and it is asserted that bloodstains undoubtedly exist on one of the knives and upon the sheath. These stains are probably a month old, but certainly not more than six weeks or two months. The knives are as sharp as razors."

-- Evening News (London), November 2, 1888

Wednesday, November 7, 1888

MARY JANE WAKES UP TO A RHYTHMIC TUGGING AT HER groin, peering down to find Eva—fully dressed and ready for work—rubbing a damp washcloth up and down the shaft of her dildo, the ever-ready tool still strapped to her following the previous night's exuberant exploits.

"Mmm, good morning, my love." She rolls onto her back, causing the rigid pole to stand upright. "I love watching you play with my priapus."

"I ain't playing with it, I'm cleaning it." Eva grabs hold of it again. "You've had the thing on all night and it's covered in fluff."

That's an understatement. In fact, coated with a combination of crusted bodily fluids and lint, it looks thoroughly unappealing and could use a good scrubbing.

After celebrating the cessation of Eva's reds by going to one of the local bathhouses and sharing one of the private hot baths—which is, as they discovered several months ago, something that two women can do with relative impunity—they returned home and fucked heartily for most of the night, the dildo getting more than its fair share of use.

Not that they'd been entirely chaste throughout the week, mind you. Eva tried to abstain as usual, for her monthlies quite revolt her, but Mary Jane was not to be so easily dissuaded from intimacy. One night, when Eva was giving herself a wash before bed, she stepped in and took over the operation, working a damp washcloth between the self-conscious teen's thighs until she was barely able to stand.

"Oh, don't." Eva squirmed. "You're making it hot. We mustn't ..."

Ignoring that, Mary Jane sat her down in a chair and knelt before her. "Sshhh." She discarded the pretense of the washcloth. "Let me show you how much I love you."

Horrified, Eva yowled as Mary Jane's head dipped to her core. "Ohoo, you're never?!" She whimpered like a frightened kitten. "Don't it taste awful? However can you—"

She never finished that sentence. Not having had a spend in three days, she was too greedy for the pleasure, and Mary Jane was keen to get a taste of the letch that'd once earned one of her fellow harlots ten sovereigns in the Frenchwoman's house. Neither expected to do more, but at the conclusion of the oral operation, both were feeling thoroughly ruttish.

"I want a poke," Eva whispered softly, as if afraid the words were too wicked to be said out loud, and Mary Jane responded by strapping on her cock, only to be impeded before achieving the union of their bodies.

"Do you have doodle bonnet?" Eva held her off.

"What?" It took Mary Jane a moment to translate the question, recognizing that she was being asked for a French letter. "What the bleeding hell for? I can't get you in trouble."

"I don't want it up me without." Eva pouted. "If you do, I could never bear to put my mouth on it again. It's such a dirty business."

With a growl of frustration, Mary Jane backed off her and began a frantic search of every pocket in every item of clothing in Eva's room. Coming up empty, she strapped her cock to her thigh and pulled on her clothes. At that point, Eva offered to forget the matter and go to sleep, but Mary Jane wouldn't hear of it. She counted up the requisite number of coppers and hurried out, returning fifteen minutes later with a victorious grin on her lips. The next minute, her clothes were on the floor, her cock was sheathed, and they were united on the bed.

Of course, when morning came, Eva's modesty returned. She was desperately embarrassed, swore it would never happen again, and made Mary Jane promise not to tempt her. To that end, she laid a draft excluder along the length of the bed, effectively dividing it in the middle, and forced Mary Jane to keep to one side of it when sleeping. That worked to an extent, but the nights were cold. Eva always seemed to wake in Mary Jane's arms, with a hand up her nightdress, and the draft excluder was kicked out onto the floor.

It was a rotten way to spend their first week living as a proper couple, but Eva's enjoyed having Mary Jane to herself. With Joe out of the picture, they've been able to spend every free moment together—a delight marred only slightly by the spontaneous bouts of anxiety that have plagued Mary Jane with increasing frequency since her trip to Knightsbridge.

At their worst, these attacks—symptoms of a hysterical nervous condition called *delire émotif*, or

emotional delirium—caused them to abandon their plans to see a bonfire and fireworks on Guy Fawkes' Night, when Mary Jane collapsed in Whitechapel High Street. Rather than effigies of Guy Fawkes, people were parading along with those of Jack the Ripper, many wearing leather aprons splattered with animal blood and wielding butchers' knives.

Mary Jane slipped into a faint when a masked man leapt out in front of her, declared he was going to cut her up, and proceeded to thrash around with a blunted pocketknife clutched in his hand. She was able to stay on her feet just long enough for Eva to drag her into the recessed porch of a chandler's shop, where she slumped onto the ground and hyperventilated till she almost lost consciousness. When she'd calmed enough to manage the short walk home, Eva hurried her to Lolesworth and got her into bed, removing her clothes piece by piece while she sat in a dazed stupor, blank and unresponsive.

When asked what brought on this sudden case of the vapors, fright and timidity being an uncharacteristic quality in her, she would only say: "I was seen."

She refused to expound, and when Eva suggested she go to the police, she got testy.

"I already did." She snuggled up to Eva's chest. "They wanted nothing to do."

Knowing the people from Mary Jane's old life would do her great harm if they found her, Eva's been silently fretting for her welfare all week. Though at first skeptical about the offer of employment in Kent, she's now impatient for it to come to fruition.

"I've always wanted a garden," she muses, thinking about taking a barefoot stroll in the grounds of the guesthouse, feeling the cool, soft grass beneath her feet. "Do you think I could grow pansies there? I do so love pansies."

"Whatever makes you happy, love." Mary Jane smiles wearily.

The signs of fatigue have become apparent on her face in recent weeks. Even now, with the curtains closed, the room illuminated by only the firelight, Eva can see dark circles under her puffy lower lids. When she rises,

she'll conceal them with a dusting of rice powder, or zinc oxide. If she has any left, she'll use pearl powder—a precise mixture of chloride of bismuth and French chalk that she grew accustomed to buying in the West End, when money was in easy supply—but Eva knows she feels guilty for costing them the expense.

"Whatchu looking at?" Mary Jane catches her staring.

"You look tired." Eva tucks the cleaned phallus away beneath the sheets. "I worry for you."

"Don't be daft." Mary Jane squeezes her hand. "It's nothing a little powder can't fix."

"That ain't the point, Em." Eva sighs, frustrated by Mary Jane's tendency to paint over things rather than address the root cause. "This place is killing you."

"We'll be leaving it behind soon enough." Mary Jane yawns and stretches, considering getting out of bed. "I'm waiting to hear from Adel's land agent."

"So you've said." Eva balls up the washcloth and chucks it into the basin. "But how much longer is it gonna take?"

Mary Jane can't answer that. As much as she'd love to reassure Eva that everything's in hand, and that there's no need for her to continue working at the factory, she daren't. It simply wouldn't be prudent. The lack of word from Adel is worrisome, and on the off-chance this business takes a while to complete—or heaven forbid, falls through altogether—the factory will become their only source of steady income.

For the time being at least, all must go on as normal, so Mary Jane urges her to be just a little more patient and sends her off to work with a kiss and a smile, making plans to meet up on her dinner break. Nothing fancy, Eva warned her, determined to stretch Adel's five pounds out over at least a month. A meat pie would do. Maybe some sausages. She wouldn't say no to bacon. Or a piece of cake. Mmm, cake.

Feeling like a lame duck for lounging in bed while Eva's out earning an honest living, Mary Jane rises mid-morning and endeavors to be productive. In short order, she makes the bed, spruces up Eva's room, scavenges the

cupboard for some breakfast, and plans out the rest of her day, making Miller's Court the first stop on her list of chores.

She's been subletting her room to Maria for the last few nights, and is hoping to do so again this evening, but she's out of luck. When she gets there—the damp chilling her to the core, despite wearing her thick linsey-woolsey frock—she finds a note from Maria informing her that she's found permanent lodgings elsewhere on Dorset Street and won't be needing the bed. That's thruppence lost.

Resigning herself to some unfinished crochet work instead, her next stop is the chandler's shop run by her landlord, where she buys a farthing dip for light and receives a lecture about the non-payment of her rent.

"Over a pound owing." McCarthy shakes his rent book at her over the counter. "Do I look like a baby's arse to you?"

"Eh?" Mary Jane raises an eyebrow.

"Soft," he barks at her. "You must think I'm a bloody rug, the way you're walking all over me. I got my own bills, you know."

"That's all well and good, but what am I to do? You know my husband's left me." Mary Jane spins the truth. "I'm doing whatever I can, but I'm all alone these days."

"You're gonna get booted out on your ear if you're not careful."

"Oh, you ain't gonna give the poor girl her notice." Missus McCarthy steps in, backhanding her husband's shoulder. "I shan't see one of our tenants end up the way of them other unfortunates." She turns to Mary Jane, wagging a motherly finger. "Don't you go doing nothing to put yourself at risk. I don't want you out on these streets. Not with Jack about."

"Aye, he's a concern, isn't he?" Mary Jane picks at the frayed wick on the farthing dip, picturing Fleming looming over her, wielding a pocketknife. "I hear he's ripe in this quarter."

Dispirited by such morbid talk, she goes back to her room and crochets until her eyes are aching from the strain. When one o'clock thankfully rolls around, she

packs it in for the day and meets Eva outside the factory, swiftly whisking her off to a family-run coffeehouse on Brick Lane.

The quiet establishment displays a sprig of artificial violets in the front window, and as soon as they're inside—their love identified by the similar violet pinned to Mary Jane's bodice—they're shown through to a small room in the back. This private sitting area is concealed from the rest of the shop by a heavy velvet curtain, and within it, women are free to kiss, caress, and make love, stealing a few moments of precious affection with one another before returning to the drudgery of work, or home to their husbands.

"This is one of them places, ain't it?" Eva whispers excitedly, letting Mary Jane lead her by the hand. "We can be free here?"

"Absolutely, and they have bedrooms upstairs." Mary Jane chooses a rattan loveseat and pulls Eva down beside her. "So if you're feeling spreeish ..."

"Oh, hish! You'll stir me up and cause a bother in my drawers." Eva giggles, suitably excited by the proposition. "You make me think such wicked things."

"Don't think them," Mary Jane whispers, nuzzling her neck. "Do them."

Before she can suggest that they forego dinner and pay for a room of their own, some commotion erupts on the other side of the velvet curtain. A man tries to barge his way through, his intrusion blocked by the concerted efforts of several squealing waitresses and the matronly owner of the establishment, who threatens to send for the police.

Eva tenses up. "What was all that about?"

"Some arsehole trying to get a peep." Mary Jane shrugs. "Pay it no mind." She hooks Eva's chin on her finger and turns her into a kiss. "Relax. We're safe."

"This feels ever so naughty." Eva accepts Mary Jane's tongue in her mouth.

"It shouldn't in the least," Mary Jane says, breaking for breath. "Why ought we hide our love away? Besides, you're my wife, aintcha? Ought I be denied my wife's lips?"

629

Pinching her lower lip between her teeth, Eva unbuttons the top of her bodice and fishes some string out of her cleavage, the gold wedding band given to her by Mary Jane worn around her neck on a piece of thin twine. "I has it with me all the time." She clutches it proudly. "I likes having it near my heart."

Well up for fun, and willing to risk a sharp slap to the back of her hand, Mary Jane undoes another button, teasing the satin away from Eva's underclothes. "Are you sure I couldn't tempt you to get a room with me?" She slips her hand inside, fondling Eva's armored breast. "I'll give you such delicious pleasure."

Eva takes little convincing.

Minutes after making Eva's toes curl in a quiet bedroom above the coffeehouse, Mary Jane walks the giddy teen back to the cocoa factory. Flushed with endorphins, they part ways with a tender kiss and Mary Jane goes about the rest of her chores, gradually becoming aware of a man shadowing her every move.

When she's on Commercial Street, witnessing a fight between a young tart and her dissatisfied customer, he's there. When she's perusing the market stalls on Brick Lane, watching a small troupe of volunteers from the Whitechapel Vigilance Committee stick up posters offering a reward for the apprehension of Jack the Ripper, he's there. He keeps back several feet, always lingering in the periphery of her vision, and his presence is starting to unnerve her.

Though it's not wholly unusual for men to trail after her, working up the courage to engage her, there's something in his manner that sets her on edge. He has a military bearing about him, his clothes sharp and neat, his boots freshly polished. Despite walking with a limp

and the aid of a cane, he appears little impeded by his injury.

Continuing on to the post office on Whitechapel High Street, she finds two letters awaiting her: one from Adel, confirming an appointment with the land agent for tomorrow evening—what sweet relief!—and another from an old special, which she promptly discards. Though that particular gentleman has always been generous with his coin—paying a sovereign a time at least—she doesn't allow herself to be swayed by the lure of his deep pockets. That's not who she is. Not anymore.

Before leaving, she gets a good look at her shifty, beady-eyed leech through the post office window, observing that he's suffering from a bad case of the nervous fidgets. Still, there's nothing in his outward appearance to suggest arousal, and the only bulge in his trousers is in his pocket. Is he carrying a gun? Rather than risk a confrontation of some sort, she slips out quietly and tries to lose him, weaving left and right through the heavy foot traffic on Commercial Street and exploiting her intimate knowledge of the streets, but he doesn't shake easily.

Every increase in pace, he matches—albeit with some difficulty. When she turns left, he turns left. When she darts across a street, he darts after her, even at the risk of being hit by an oncoming hansom. No matter what she does, he keeps on her tail, so she picks up her skirts and runs. He simply can't keep up with that.

Never once looking behind her, she hightails it all the way back to Miller's Court and locks herself in her room. Panic is the enemy of weak lungs, which she well knows, having suffered from asthma as a child, but she can't control her nerves, nor shake off these morbid terrors.

Too fearful even to light the candle she bought, she sits in the dark in a state of melancholic dread. Not daring to make a sound, she listens to her neighbors' squealing, laughing, shrieking children playing with a ball in the court, flinching every time the ball gets kicked astray and hits the wall of her room.

A knock at the door goes ignored, though it was probably only one of her neighbors wanting to borrow her shawl, or some other such trifle. It may even have been someone seeking a bed.

Cursing herself for being so weak, her spirit thoroughly depleted, she opens her door and calls upon one of the older children. She needs courage, even if it is of a liquid variety.

"Come to me, girl." She pins her sights on a twelve-year-old fiery redhead, beckoning her over with the lure of a penny. "You know where the Blue Coat Boy is?"

The girl nods, used to running errands for other residents of the court.

"Good. I want some gin." Mary Jane hands her an empty jug from one trembling hand and shows her eightpence from the other. "I know well the measure eightpence fetches, so no skimming," she warns, wagging a finger in the face of the rosy-cheeked pre-teen. "If you bring it back proper, and fast, you'll get a penny for your trouble. Understand?"

More nodding, accompanied by a wide smile.

"Don't dally now." Mary Jane sends her off. "I shall be waiting."

Eager to claim the reward for her services, the girl rushes down the passage with Mary Jane's money and the empty jug, returning in under five minutes with a perfect eightpence measure, not a drop spilled or sipped.

"Well done." Mary Jane places a penny in her upturned palm and dismisses her, having no intention of requiring her services a second time.

Retreating to her room, she digs out her laudanum and adds a few unmeasured drops to the jug, hoping it will enhance the calmative effects of the booze, and then she begins to drink.

One glass.

Two.

Three ...

CHAPTER 53

A POUNDING ON THE DOOR JOLTS MARY JANE OUT OF A liquor and laudanum induced sleep. Momentarily disoriented, she sits bolt upright, having nodded off at the table after downing the whole jug of booze. Or was it two jugs? In either case, her swift movement triggers a throbbing pain that starts at the base of her skull and radiates down the back of her neck and she groans.

More pounding.

"Mary Jane?" a soft female voice calls out. "Are you in there?"

It's Eva! Leaping up much too fast, Mary Jane battles vertigo and a loss of peripheral vision, teetering on the brink of a faint. As she staggers against the table, she knocks over her empty gin glass, the cracked old tumbler rolling downward on the uneven table and slipping off the edge, shattering at her feet.

Hearing that, Eva drums on the door all the harder. "Em?! What was that noise? Is you all right?" She jiggles the knob. "Stop mucking about and let me in!"

Somewhat regaining her equilibrium, Mary Jane manages to unlock the door, clinging to it for support as she welcomes Eva inside. "I'm so glad you're here, my lovely."

"What's been going on?" Eva enters cautiously, tuppenceworth of fish and chips and a meat pie piled in her arms. "Whatchu doing sitting here in the dark?" She

glances around the gloomy room, fragments of glass crunching beneath her feet. "You didn't come to meet me after work and I've been ever so worried."

"Forgive me." Mary Jane rubs her eyes, stifling a yawn. "I must've fallen asleep."

"Oh, aye?" Eva sets their supper down on the table, noting the bottle of laudanum and sniffing the empty liquor jug, recognizing the smell of blue ruin. "Fell asleep, or passed out? Have you been on a drunk?" Her disappointment is palpable.

"I needed something to calm my nerves." Mary Jane sticks her head outside and peers down the narrow passage from Miller's Court onto Dorset Street, checking to make sure the strange man with the cane and the limp is nowhere to be seen. "The vapors came over me again."

"Why?" Eva pulls her in and locks the door. "What happened? You've got a queer look about you. Is your courses coming on? Is that why you took the laudanum?"

Still unsteady on her feet and afraid she might fall down, Mary Jane lowers herself back into her chair at the table. "A man's been following me."

Eva feels a chill ripple through her. "What man? Is he known to you?"

Mary Jane shakes her head. "Probably just some ruttish bastard who wants his whore-pipe draining." She forces a smile. "I'm being daft, I'm sure. Will you spend the night?"

Though she tries to minimize the potentially sinister experience, there's desperation in her voice and a splash of real fear in her eyes. She doesn't want to be alone.

"Course I will, you daft old thing." Eva cups Mary Jane's face, tilting her head up and thumbing her cheeks. "You don't have to ask."

"Thank you." Mary Jane pulls Eva onto her lap. "You're such a darling, and I'm sorry I've been such a wreck of late." She presses her face to Eva's bosom. "I need to be stronger. I ain't much use to you when I'm like this, am I?"

"Nobody's ever cared for me the way you do, Em. I love the way you love me." Eva kisses the top of her head, the reversal in their roles not escaping her. "Now let's get

us a fire going." She pries herself away. "It's bloody freezing in here. We'll catch our deaths."

Using nearly every bit of tinder in the scuttle, she coaxes a fire to catch and stokes it up with coke, suffusing the room in a warm glow and some much needed heat while Mary Jane digs a cracked plate and two forks out of the cupboard, cleaning them both on her apron.

"Don't fuss." Eva relieves her of them. "I likes taking care of you for a change, though I gets the feeling you ain't used to it." She sits Mary Jane down and dishes up the food, heaping it all together for them to share. "Ain't no-one ever been this way with you afore?"

"Not for a long time." Mary Jane stabs her fork into a piece of unidentifiable meat oozing from the broken shell of the pie. "But there was someone." She tears into the gristly, overcooked flesh. "My first woman."

"What was it like for you?" Eva drags up the other chair and starts attacking the plate. "How old was you? Did she teach you like you taught me?"

"I was sixteen—the same age as you when we met— but the first of me had already been claimed by a man, so I had no maidenhead to give her." Mary Jane fetches the bottle of vinegar she uses for douching and douses the chips with it. "I shall always regret that."

"Who was the fella?" Eva asks, her mouth full of fish.

"Billy Flanagan, a big brute of a bloke who ran with a bunch of Fenian roughs in Manchester." Mary Jane can't help sounding bitter. "It weren't long after my mam kicked me out. I was fifteen, petrified of a life on the street, and I thought he'd protect me so I stuck with him. He was easy twice my age, but I didn't care, and he was sweet to me in the beginning. By the time I realized what he was truly about, it was too late."

Shamefully, she recalls Billy taking her out and getting her mighty drunk. It was her first real taste of booze, and before she knew it, she could barely stand. He practically carried her back to his lodgings, laid her on the bed, and propped her legs open.

"Oh, Billy, don't." She squirmed. "I'm gonna be sick."

He didn't care. He told her to close her eyes and relax, and she felt a cool breeze on her inner thighs as he

yanked up her skirts and climbed on top of her. A moment later, something hard and thick was pressing at the entrance to her body.

"Is that your prick?" she mumbled, scowling as he slapped her mound with it. "Give it here." She reached out for it, ready to give it a tug as she'd done before. "I'll frig it off."

But it wasn't a tug he wanted. All of a sudden, he thrust forward and pierced her, a sharp pain shooting through her abdomen, followed by the heat of his intruding tool.

"Ahh!" she cried out, alarmed by the sudden friction. "Whatever have you done?!" She tried to sit up and look, but he pushed her down.

Aware then that she'd been breached, she wept. She wanted to fight him off, but her limbs were unresponsive. The bruises she found on her wrists in the morning led her to conclude that he'd pinned her down.

"Don't wet inside," she begged repeatedly, fearful of getting a swelling. "Please don't, Billy. Don't make a mess in me."

But he did wet inside. When he came, he made a point of ramming it hard up her, calling her his little spunk-emptier as he deposited his libation deep in her womb. Immediately after, he took her by the arm and heaved her off the bed, demanding that she wash.

"I thought I was meant to enjoy it, but I felt nothing," Mary Jane reflects on the experience, losing her appetite. "Nothing good anyway. Not that time, nor any time thereafter." She abandons her fork in the middle of a fish fillet. "Mercifully, he didn't do it to me often. He was heavy on drink and frequently came home so much the worse for it that he hadn't the energy for a shove."

"Was he the one who ..." Eva isn't sure how to ask. "The babe you had ... ?"

Mary Jane shakes her head. "He did put one in me once, but soon sorted it."

"How?" Eva grimaces, remembering a tale her mother once told her about a woman who relieved herself of her encumbrance with a fish hook trussed up to an old surgical probe thieved from the Whitechapel Infirmary.

"Pennyroyal tea." Mary Jane investigates the bottom of the liquor jug, finding it bone dry. "Between that and the hickery-pickery he put down my throat, it was a nasty business." She rubs a hand over her abdomen. "Damn near killed me, and I bled for a straight fortnight."

"How long was you with him?" Eva chases a pea around the plate.

"Six months or so. He fell out of work, we was hard up, and the pair of us got caught thieving. He had a record with the coppers already, so he was sentenced to Strangeways for a spell." Mary Jane helps herself to one more chip and gets up, moving over to the bed. "I never saw him again, and I'm lucky for that. The following year, I heard he got done for murdering his new paramour with a pocketknife. Nearly severed her head, he did. And he was a damned loon. Spent a few months in a lunatic hospital before I met him. The nasty old bastard was hanged in seventy-six, and good riddance it was."

"Bloody hell, Em." Eva claims her leftovers and polishes off the rest of the plate. "What happened to you after he got sent to the quod?"

"Being as I was so young, the magistrate took pity on me and sent me to a reformatory for wayward young Catholic girls, which is where I met Poppy." Mary Jane fluffs her under-stuffed pillows. "It was bloody dreadful. We had prayers six times a day, ate nothing but flummery, and the nuns had us all working our fingers to the bone." She flicks a wandering woodlouse off the palliasse. "I was trained as a seamstress there. It was either that, or work in the laundry."

"Poppy was your girl?" Eva wipes her mouth on the back of her hand and joins Mary Jane on the bed.

"Aye." Mary Jane smiles, receiving her. "We all slept in a large dormitory, although I can't say as too much sleeping got done. The hall was filled with sweet sighs of pleasure, which I never thought much of till the first time Poppy crawled into my bed."

Wistfully, she brings to mind that cold November night. The dormitory had no source of heat, and there was a thick layer of ice accumulating on the window panes like a sheet of warped glass. Each girl was only

given one blanket, so it made sense to bundle. Two girls in one cramped bed not only had each other's body heat, but then two blankets covering them.

"Cold, innit?" Poppy clambered in with Mary Jane, doubling up their blankets. "Much better to share. D'you mind?"

Mary Jane shook her head, used to bundling with her brothers and not giving a thought to the closeness. "I can't feel my toes no more."

Poppy clamped her feet around Mary Jane's and snuggled up. "I'll soon warm you."

All around them, there were soft gasps and faint moans. Two beds along, one of the other girls let out an exquisite whimper, her bedmate's head bobbing beneath their blankets, working at some operation between her thighs.

"D'you like listening to 'em?" Poppy asked, noting Mary Jane's interest.

"What's they doing?" Mary Jane peered through the darkness.

"Showing each other their things and having a lick." Poppy giggles. "You can see my precious bits if you like." She pulled her nightgown up to her neck, revealing herself without the slightest hint of diffidence.

"Oh, good Lordy ..." Mary Jane was transfixed.

Growing up with only brothers, this was her first intimate view of another young woman's body, and seventeen-year-old Poppy was beautifully made. Her mane was dark as coal, and hung in thick ringlets around her shoulders. Ornamenting her chest were two heavy breasts, the nipples large and prominent, her areolae dark and puffy.

Below her ribcage was her only imperfection—if you could call it that. She had a little paunch, and the pale skin of her soft belly was blemished with pink marks of stretching that were so dark they almost looked like scars. Lower still, and a thick, dense triangle of black pubic curls spread out from her core.

Seeing the direction of her gaze, Poppy brought a hand to her sex. "D'you like the hair on it?" She dragged

638

her fingers through the thicket. "Is there much hair on yours?"

Mary Jane hesitated. Her own downy outcrop had only recently sprouted, and she wasn't sure what to think of it. Billy told her it was a sign that she'd been made a full woman, and had declared himself the cause.

"Is you shy?" Poppy rightly guessed. "There honest ain't no need to be." She wriggled closer. "Will you show me?" She hooked her finger under the hem of Mary Jane's nightgown, easing it up. "I think it's nice to look."

Though Mary Jane didn't have the nerve to expose herself quite so readily, she let Poppy work the nightgown up over her hips, beyond her waist, and—at great length—above her breasts, putting her entirely on display.

"You have such pretty parts." Poppy took her by surprise and palmed one of her breasts.

The contact made her whine. Billy had never touched her like that. Indeed, nobody ever had. She'd always been clothed when he did his business to her, or in her nightgown at least. She'd never unveiled all her charms to him.

"D'you like that?" Poppy teased Mary Jane's nipple between her fingers, causing it to swell and stiffen. "You can do it to mine if you want."

Her body tingling with new sensations, Mary Jane reached tentatively for Poppy's breast, enveloping the warm, supple flesh with her cool, slender fingers. Feeling a spark of curiosity ignite within her, she gave the weighty orb a light squeeze and gasped when a tiny droplet of milk oozed from the nipple.

"Don't mind that." Poppy brushed it off. "I had a babe not long ago, but they took it from me. They said I ain't fit to care for it." She trailed her index finger down Mary Jane's body. "D'you like to be touched here?" She tickled her fingers through the blonde curls on Mary Jane's motte, finding her hidden treasure saturated with unrealized lust. "Shall we do it together?" She hooked one leg over Mary Jane's hip, opening herself up. "Put your hand to me."

Not so timidly this time, Mary Jane reciprocated Poppy's actions and explored the velvety crevices of her privy parts, inside and out, her unflinching enthusiasm for the operation quite taking them both by surprise. Minutes later, their lips were locked together and Poppy's tongue was in her mouth. Not long after that, Poppy stiffened, trembled, and Mary Jane felt a burst of hot, sticky fluid on her hand.

Her own paroxysm followed, and in the wake of it—invigorated by her first taste of pleasure—she pounced, flipping Poppy onto her back and crushing their bodies together.

"You done this afore?" Poppy mewled.

"Never," Mary Jane confessed. "But I like it."

Poppy later said that she'd been thrilled by Mary Jane's sudden exuberance for the delights of sapphic love. While it was true that most of the reformatory girls were amenable to a few kisses, the occasional tickle, or a bit of a lick—particularly on cold nights—it was merely a way of alleviating the boredom of convent life. Very few of them would seek out the company of a woman were there a man available to fill the void instead, and Poppy had been very lonely, always wanting more than what the other girls were willing to give.

"She taught me everything," Mary Jane remembers fondly. "I knew then why I wasn't stirred by a man, and why I hadn't never had a pleasure in all them months with Billy."

"How long was you and Poppy together?" Eva asks, curled against her chest.

"Not long enough." Mary Jane sighs, feeling a pang of loss. "When summer came, we ran off together, and Poppy did what she could to take care of me. She did what she had to, you understand, and I never begrudged her for it. We were happy."

"You loved her." Eva sounds sour.

"I did." Mary Jane rolls Eva over, cradling her. "She was my first love, and I know you know what that means, but you've no competition in my affections, darling." She caresses Eva's waist. "Poppy got sick." A lump forms in her throat. "She died."

Though she tries to suppress it, grief comes flooding back. "I wanted to get the money together for a proper burial. I knew I shouldn't, but I didn't tell no-one when she'd had her last breath. I kept her in our lodgings with me for a solid week, hoping I'd be able to do the right thing by her, but the stench of it ..." Mary Jane buries her face in the pillow. "It brought the landlady in, which brought the coppers in, and they took her from me. She's buried in a paupers' grave somewhere. I don't even know where. It ain't marked."

"Oh, Em, that's awful." Eva's jealousy melts into pity. "If the Lord took you from me like that, I reckon I'd—"

"If the Lord sees fit to call for me, then you're to take that savings book from my lockbox and make yourself a life with it." Mary Jane turns stern and motherly. "You're authorized to draw on the account, and I shan't leave you penniless. Not like I was after Poppy went." She wipes her eyes on a corner of the pillow. "I got evicted on account of all the back rent owed. There weren't no choice for me then but to go into a women's refuge. More nuns, more flummery."

"How old was you?"

Mary Jane shrugs. "Twenty or so. They gave me a character and helped me find a situation in a respectable house, so I became a housemaid for a while." A smile escapes. "The folks of the house had a daughter my age, and she proved to be a pleasant diversion, but her father ..." The smile wanes. "He was the one who did it." She clenches her jaw. "The rotten old bastard put his hands on me, and I let him do what he wanted—I was used to that."

"Is this why you was so frightened for me when I was working at Cavendish Square?" Eva puts two and two together. "You was always asking me questions about it."

"I'd been in your shoes." Mary Jane calls to mind the flutter of relief she'd felt every time she checked under Eva's skirts and found her virginity intact. "I know how people like that treat people like us, and I didn't want that for you." She beats her fist into the pillow. "I swear, if they'd laid a hand on you, I'd—"

641

"I was fine, Em." Eva settles her, coaxing her into an embrace. "Nobody hurt me."

"You were lucky." Mary Jane pulls her tight.

"Did the master of your house dismiss you after he did his damage? Like my mistress's maid who got in trouble with the first footman?" Eva pities the poor girl who got tossed out on her ear without so much as a thought. "I've heard that's how it so often goes."

"Aye, it is, but it were different for me." A little of Mary Jane's smile returns. "He caught me with my face between his daughter's thighs and ejected me that very night. I was sent off on my own with no character and a belly full."

Eva rubs Mary Jane's stomach, imagining it swollen with child. "He didn't help you?"

"Help?" Mary Jane snorts derisively. "He gave me a few quid, put me on a train back to Manchester, and told me to get rid."

"But you didn't?"

Mary Jane shakes her head. "I was too scared to give that hickery-pickery malarkey another go. I did a gin bath, but it had no effect, except to nearly drown me."

She recalls knocking back a pint of gin while sitting in a hot salt bath, then promptly falling asleep. When her head slipped under the water, she woke in a fright, gasping and spluttering for air.

"I heard it could be done with a hat pin or a knitting needle, by piercing the entrance to the womb," she muses. "But the thought of that put a fright in me n'all."

After some consideration, she opts against relating the horrific tale of a woman who accidentally poked a hole in her vaginal wall with a crochet hook while attempting that very procedure. The poor creature ended up dying of a dreadful infection that festered in her for three weeks before eventually killing her.

"It don't always work," Eva adds, well aware of the trick. "My mam tried it when she got one in her not long after my dadda died."

"I thought you was her last?" Mary Jane frowns.

"That's what she told people, but it weren't true." Eva sinks deeper into Mary Jane's arms. "After she

resorted to the bad life, as I know it was now, she was given a swelling by one of her friends and nuthin' worked to relieve her of it."

"What happened to the babe?"

"I ain't sure what was the matter with it." She thinks back, making sense of her memories as best she can. "I think it must've come out wrong, 'cause as soon as it was out of her, she wrapped it up in an old piece of cloth and tossed it on the fire. It never made a noise." She returns her hand to Mary Jane's belly. "Did yours come out all right?"

"I was in the workhouse when my time came," Mary Jane admits with shame. "That's where I ended up not long after being dismissed."

She remembers waking in the middle of the night, her abdomen cramping. She hadn't wanted to cause a fuss, so she lay there for five hours, biting her tongue against the pain, muffling the occasional wail in her pillow.

As the hours passed, the pain got worse, the cramping becoming ever more frequent. When she felt the sheets wet, a peculiar fluid dribbling from her sex, she knew she had to seek help. Rising from her dormitory bed, she hauled herself onto her feet, intending to alert the on-duty matron, but she never got further than the foot of the bed.

A contraction crippled her and she dropped into a squat, clutching the metal bedrail for support. Though she cried out, her yelp of pain echoing throughout the dormitory, no-one came to assist her. Not knowing what to do, she brought a hand to her core, feeling something protruding from her sex, blood dripping from her and onto the tiled floor as the emerging infant stretched and tore her perineum. Terrified, the next time a contraction came, she pushed hard, determined to expel the child from within her.

Once.

Twice.

On the third push, she felt the pressure give.

Reaching down, she caught the undernourished newborn in her hand, cradling its head and neck as its

bum slapped against the bloodied tiles and it began to cry.

"He was born and died in that wretched place, the poor soul." Mary Jane tears up again, her nipples aching at the thought of her lost child. "I ain't never told anyone that."

"Well, I'm glad you've told me." Eva tilts her head up and pecks Mary Jane's dry lips. "I want to know everything of you. What was it like in the 'house? Was it truly dreadful?"

"They had me picking oakum every daylight hour and beyond, till my fingers were black and bleeding." Mary Jane inspects a small scar on her right forefinger. "Me and the lad both come down with breathing troubles and spent a time in the infirmary. My sickness eventually shifted, but his didn't. He was a weak little thing." Her mind drifts. "Anyway, I had to get myself out of there, so I wrote to my cousin in Cardiff. She agreed to take me in, but I didn't know then that she was earning her living through immoral means."

"She was the one who steered you wrong?" Eva guesses.

"I went to the bad not long after," Mary Jane recounts the final step in her degradation. "She was content with that life, but I loathed it. There was money to be made in the West End, so I'd heard, and I thought we could pocket some pretty savings and do good for ourselves there. You know all the rest." She presses a kiss into Eva's chestnut locks. "I love you, Eva. I don't want no secrets from you, and I reckon now that you do truly know all there is to know of me."

Eva sucks on her lower lip, a confession of her own weighing on her mind. "I saw my uncle today." She keeps her eyes down. "He was waiting for me after work. He said he'd seen me in the street and recognized me directly. Whatever shall I do?"

Mary Jane makes a swift mental leap. First, there was the male intruder at the coffeehouse. Then, there was the strange man who followed her around Whitechapel. Could they be one and the same?

Pondering that, "Does your uncle happen to have a cane and a limp?"

"Uh-huh." Eva knits her brows. "How'd you come to reckon that?"

"He's the old cock who gave me such a fright this afternoon." Mary Jane laughs, relieved to have an explanation for his odd behavior. "He must've seen us together in the street."

"What if he tells my aunt?" Eva sits up in a panic. "What if he tells her where I am? You remember what she said to you? If she ever caught you near me—"

"It won't matter." Mary Jane hushes her. "I received a letter from Adel today, and all being well, we'll be leaving here on Lord Mayor's Day. Her man's coming to see me tomorrow night, and as soon as all the papers are signed, we can be on our way."

"Oh, Em! That's all I've wanted!" Eva flings herself into Mary Jane's arms. "Everything's gonna be proper and decent. We'll be so happy, and I'll be such a good wife to you. I swear I will."

"You already are, love." Mary Jane flips her onto her back. "But it doesn't hurt to practice your wifely duties." She trails a hand up Eva's leg, over her white stocking ...

CHAPTER 54

Thursday, November 8, 1888

THE TIP OF THE KNIFE PIERCES HER NECK, PUNCTURING HER carotid artery. Crimson fluid spurts from the wound, splashing on the wall beside the bed, and Mary Jane wakes up with a shriek. Attempting to escape from her invisible attacker, she kicks the bed covers away and scoots up to the headboard, hyperventilating and clutching her throat.

"It's all right." Eva bounds across and room and dives onto the bed, giving her a squeeze. "I'm here. You're safe." She pries Mary Jane's hands away from her neck, dropping soft kisses there. "It was just a bad dream." She pulls Mary Jane to her breast. "Was it the Ripper?"

Mary Jane nods, wheezing, struggling to catch her breath.

"You need to calm yourself." Eva strokes her tousled auburn mane. "Your poor old heart's gonna pack in if you keep this up." She presses her palm to Mary Jane's chest, feeling the overworked organ hammering beneath her ribcage. "You're in such a panic."

Despite the fire Eva started when she woke, the room's still chilly, much of the heat escaping through the two holes Mary Jane put in the window. Afraid that she'll catch her death, Eva tucks the blankets around Mary Jane's shoulders, covering her nude body.

"Keep warm." She rubs Mary Jane's back. "I don't want you falling ill."

"You're perfect." Mary Jane rests her forehead on Eva's shoulder, feeling utterly crapulent from last night's drinking. "I'm a shell of a woman, and you're so perfect."

"You'll be back to your old self in no time, I'm sure." Eva lifts her head up, beaming a warm, comforting smile. "Now what do you want for breakfast? I'm buying."

"With what?"

Fully dressed and ready to go, Eva digs three florins out of her pocket. "My uncle gived me these yesterday, so I can buy us breakfast, dinner, and supper."

"I'd wager he didn't want for you to spend that on me."

"Well, I don't give a fig what he wants." Eva pockets the money and gets up, snatching her hat down from one of the ceiling hooks. "I love you, and I shall care for you, just as you do for me." She pins the hat on top of her head and dons her coat, aware that Mary Jane's eyes are trained on her all the while. "Whatchu gawping at, Miss Kelly? You hoping to get a glimpse of my ankles?" She grabs a handful of her skirts, breaking into a grin as she hitches them up a few inches and bares her legs up to her calves.

"You're so grown up." Mary Jane admires her confidence. "When I met you, you were such a timorous, fearful young girl. I couldn't be more proud of the woman you've become."

"I wouldn't *be* the woman I am if it weren't for you showing me the way." Eva gives her a parting kiss. "I'd have died a lonely old spinster, or been married off by my aunt." One more kiss. "I'm lucky to have found you."

Mary Jane tries to pull her onto the bed. "Give me a tickle before you go."

"None of that." Eva giggles, grabbing up the empty jug from the table and blowing her a kiss from the door. "I'll be right back."

Rather than remain in bed awaiting her return, Mary Jane forces herself to rise. Not only has Eva gotten a fire going, but she's swept up the broken glass, cleaned off the table, and brought in fresh water. Feeling idle, Mary Jane hurries into her unflattering linsey-woolsey dress and

sets the table for breakfast, finding nothing but a stale lump of molding bread in the cupboard.

Peeking outside to check on dawn's progress, wondering what she ought to expect in the way of weather, she's greeted by a magpie pecking at her doorstep. That's never a good omen. According to Irish superstition, to find two magpies at your door is a sure sign of prosperity, but one ... well, that portends death.

Shortly, one of her neighbors—twenty-eight-year-old Elizabeth Prater—walks by on her way to the water pump. Though they seldom cross paths this early in the morning, Mary Jane quite often hears her rise and head out, for she isn't quiet about it. She's taken to barricading her door with a table, by way of protecting herself from the Ripper, and the dragging of wood against the floorboards is almost impossible to sleep through.

As usual, the odor of rum hangs on her like a stale perfume, betraying her recent return from the Ten Bells. No doubt she woke in a sweat, the onset of delirium tremens necessitating a quick trip to the pub for a top-up of liquor, and she'll soon settle herself back to sleep until the afternoon, when she must go out in search of money.

"Morning, Mary Jane." She flashes her neighbor a yellowed smile as she trundles by, jug in hand, her feet shuffling on the ground.

"Hello, my pretty." Mary Jane watches a small black kitten trail along behind her. "I hope I didn't wake you. I ain't been sleeping so good of late."

"No fear of that," Elizabeth grumbles. "I ain't yet been proper asleep me-self. All my worries been weighing on me dreadful."

Mary Jane doesn't doubt that. Though still relatively young, Elizabeth's features already bear the marks of dissipation. Her cheeks are gaunt and her skin is pasty, dark circles and bags under her eyes. She has the look of a woman who was once beautiful, but years of hard living—and even harder drinking—have robbed her of her radiance. For that, her husband is to blame. He deserted her some years ago, and she's been living an immoral life ever since, muddling on as best she can.

"I hear it's gonna be a dreary one today." She casts her eyes upward, tugging a ragged, moth-eaten shawl around her shoulders. "Bloody rain."

Mary Jane looks up at the lightening sky. "Well, it can do what it likes for the time being, but I hope it will be a fine day tomorrow. I want to go to the Lord Mayor's show."

As Elizabeth disappears around the corner to the pump, Eva returns with bacon, sausages, two fresh eggs, and a jug of milk.

"I thought we could fry these up." She holds the eggs delicately in her palm. "Do you fancy one? If not, I think I shall eat 'em both."

"I'm sure you will." Mary Jane steers her inside, not noticing Elizabeth's kitten sneaking in under her skirts. "I'll get the pan on."

Feeling something brush between her feet, Eva squeals, very nearly dropping both eggs and losing the jug of milk as the kitten bolts out from her skirts and disappears beneath the table.

"Clear off! What are you?!" She sets her load down and looks for the pest, swatting at him with a hanky when he jumps up onto the table and meows at her.

"That's Diddles." Mary Jane fetches two old cups for the milk. "He belongs to Missus Prater, the woman who lives above me."

Charmed by his inquisitive face and twitching whiskers, Eva reaches out to pet him behind the ears, but stops short when she sees a flea jump off his back and onto the table. "Ugh! The little blighter's got livestock!"

"It's not his fault." Mary Jane picks him up and shows him the door. "Ain't you ever had lice before? I bet you have, and I bet that's why your mam shaved off all your moss that time."

Eva colors up. "I had a frightful itch down there, but she never found nuthin'. I was clean as a button, and I come to reckon it was my drawers what was irritating me." She stands in strong defense of her vaginal cleanliness, affronted by the suggestion that she might be dirty. "I'd not long been wearing 'em, and I think my grummit needed an airing out."

Mary Jane pulls her backwards into a hug. "It's all right, love. I'm only jesting." She licks Eva's neck, trailing the tip of her tongue from the collar of the teen's dress to her ear. "Now where's that tickle I was promised?" She starts to pull up Eva's skirts, but is promptly halted.

"Oi! Not yet." Eva slaps her hands away, trying to remain stern, but succumbing to a smile. "Mind your manners." She wriggles free. "Let's eat first. And let's get some light in here." She leans over the table to draw the curtains back, deliberately jutting her bum out so that it rubs against Mary Jane's crotch.

"You tease." Mary Jane growls. "You wicked thing."

She gives Eva's rump a slap. Not the light tap she's given once or twice before, but a firm, playful smack, her open palm making a sharp clap as it strikes the teen's buttock.

"Oh!" Eva yelps, jerking upright and clasping a hand over her chastised bottom. "Whatever's the meaning of that?" She spins around. "You ain't never spanked me afore."

"Do you want me to?" There's a sinful glint in Mary Jane's eyes. "I have quite a reputation for it. In some quarters, I'm known as Mary Thrash, Queen of the Lash."

Eva covers her mouth to stifle a laugh. "Is that meant to be funny?"

"No, it bloody well ain't." Mary Jane scowls. "And no-one ever laughed when I was holding the whip, neither." She starts laying out the food.

"Wherever have you done such things?" Eva quizzes her, fascinated.

"Here and there." Mary Jane pours two cups of milk. "Do you know of Mary Jeffries? She's quite notorious. She runs brothels in Chelsea, Kensington, and elsewhere, including one that offers only flagellation, and another that specializes in other forms of pain and punishment."

"You worked for her?" Eva's jaw drops a little, having read all about Mary Jeffries in the paper when she was charged with running a disorderly house back in 1885.

"I was loaned out to her on occasion." Mary Jane cracks the eggs into a frying pan and cooks them on a

metal grill wedged over the fire in the small cast iron fireplace. "I was a favorite for men who had a particular letch to be spanked, whipped, beaten, and birched by a bushel-bubbied redhead wearing a black leather corset and very little else besides."

"Crikey." Eva pictures that as she returns to the curtains, opening them all the way to reveal Elizabeth Prater squatted by the water pump, her skirts rucked up, laddered cotton stockings bared, and a hand between her legs, rubbing vigorously.

That knocks all pleasurable thoughts of Mary Jane clean out of her head and she freezes, unable to take her eyes off the sight. "What is that woman doing?"

Mary Jane glances out and dishes up the eggs. "Having a wash."

"Can't she rinse out her grummit indoors like the rest of us?" Eva pulls a face.

"Be nice." Mary Jane suggests Eva into a chair out of Elizabeth's eyeline, for fear of her staring. "She's a lovely woman, and worse off than you or I."

Presently, another Miller's Court resident, Julia, comes out to fill a water jug at the pump. Seeing them at the window, she looks in and waves.

"Is she gonna do hers n'all?" Eva sneers.

"Hush." Mary Jane waves back. "Eat."

That's not an instruction Eva needs to receive twice. She tucks in, gulping her food down so fast Mary Jane frets she might choke.

"Steady on. It ain't gonna run away from you." She paces herself with her own helping. "There ain't no rush."

"I've got to hurry, for I'm late enough as it is." Eva guzzles some milk. "I nearly woke you earlier, but you was sleeping so soundly and I didn't have the heart. You needed the rest, and I weren't gonna let you wake up alone, but now it's coming up on ten o'clock."

"What's that got to do?" Mary Jane's heart sinks. "You're surely not going to work?"

"Before you say aught to dissuade me, it ain't for want of the money. I've got friends there, Em." Eva wipes her mouth on the back of her hand. "I want a chance to

say goodbye. Ain't there no-one you wanna say your goodbyes to afore we leave?"

"Maybe a few. I dunno. I can't say as I've given it a great deal of thought." Mary Jane picks at the last of her bacon. "In any case, I've got to be quiet about my goings on. I need to be shot of here before McCarthy realizes I've done a bunk. I owe him so much."

"So you ain't gonna tell no-one? Not even Maria?" Eva hardly dare hope that their leaving London might spell the end of Mary Jane's acquaintance with her former lover. "You won't want to keep up with her?"

"I reckon not." Mary Jane pushes her plate away. "Maria's been a true friend to me, but the lushy old girl does no good for my bad habits." She leans forward, resting her elbows on the table. "I'm not ignorant of my weakness, darling, and if I'm to be the right woman for you, then I'd best steer clear of such influences. I know well how you feel about my liking for drink, and I don't want there to be no reason for me to disappoint you."

Hearing Mary Jane make such a candid declaration stirs Eva's heart.

"I'm truly glad to hear you say such things." She leaves her chair and peeps through the window, checking to make sure the courtyard's free of prying eyes before hitching up her skirts and lowering herself onto Mary Jane's lap, straddling her thighs. "I'll make you happier than a cheap bottle of gin ever could," she promises, punctuating the sentiment with a deep kiss.

"I know you will." Mary Jane leans back, running her hands over Eva's waist, delighting in her shape. "Am I getting my tickle now?"

"No." Eva smirks, taking hold of one of Mary Jane's wandering hands. "I'm getting mine." She sucks Mary Jane's fore and middle fingers into her mouth, thoroughly wetting them before releasing them with a pop and maneuvering them under her skirts, directly to her core.

"Oh, love ..." Mary Jane caresses the lubricious valley between her plump labia, drawing the moisture up toward her hardened clitoris. "You need to come."

"Make it squeeze," Eva whispers against her lips, then kisses her. "Touch me inside."

A voluptuous sigh escapes her lips as Mary Jane seizes her firmly by the waist and penetrates her, her experienced body accommodating the intrusion with ease, Mary Jane's delicate manipulations bringing her to the brink of a spend in under two minutes.

"I love you," she mewls, beginning to quiver, a single tear spilling down her cheek. "Do I tell you that enough? Do you know how much I—unghh!" She throws her head back and grips Mary Jane's shoulder, her cunt in spasms.

At that moment, the Spitalfields church bell strikes ten. She ought to be leaving, but ...

"I don't have to go." She wraps her arms around Mary Jane's neck, her contractions subsiding. "If you want me to remain with you today, I shall."

Perfectly aware that Eva's only offering out of concern for her fragile mental state, Mary Jane salvages the last of her pride and feigns casual indifference. "I'll be all right, darling. You toddle along. There's no need to worry. Nothing bad's gonna happen."

Not sure if she entirely believes that, Eva rises and rearranges her skirts. "You'll spend the night with me, won't you? After your business is concluded."

"Of course I will," Mary Jane assures her. "You owe me a tickle."

"And you'll get it." Eva kisses her goodbye. "With interest." She heads for the door, stopping abruptly as a thought strikes her. "My uncle ... he didn't follow you all the way here, did he? He don't know where you live?"

"No," Mary Jane assures her without pause, not at all knowing whether she's telling the truth or a lie. "Why?"

"In case he told my aunt of us." Eva hovers in the doorway. "She used to put a right fear in me talking about what horrors she'd do to you if she ever caught you with me again."

Mary Jane gets up and pulls Eva into a hug, embracing her tightly. Words aren't necessary. She holds Eva to her breast, melting her fears away, their hearts beating together. Twenty-four more hours. That's all.

Parting from her with the deepest, painfully concealed reluctance, Mary Jane settles herself in to complete one last piece of crochet work, not wanting to waste the time already invested in it. As she sits there by her window, she watches life go on in the court. As residents wake and ready themselves for the day, they come and go from the water pump, dispose of the dust accumulated in their fire grates in the bins, and toss their slop buckets into one of the privies at the end of the court. Elizabeth Prater puts in one more appearance while on the hunt for her errant kitten, begging a saucer of milk off Mary Jane for the purpose of luring him back.

Whether that works or not, Mary Jane could not say. She finishes her crochet and delivers it for payment, busying herself with other loose ends here and there. When she runs into McCarthy on Dorset Street, she pleads poverty and promises him a few shillings in the morning, then returns to her room and organizes her few remaining possessions, everything of any value already removed to Eva's lodgings.

While on her knees in front of the cupboard, lining up empty ginger beer bottles so that she might return them for the deposits, Maria knocks on the door and invites herself in, a bundle of clothes stacked in her arms.

"What's all that?" Mary Jane frowns at the assorted heap. At a glance, she can see a white petticoat, a few shirts, a black overcoat, and a black crêpe bonnet with black satin strings.

"It's for you." Maria dumps it all on the table. "There's a couple men's shirts what might want a bit of a wash, but there's plenty life left in 'em." A button pops off the overcoat and rolls long the floor. "Oh, and this!" She digs a pawn ticket out of her pocket. "It's for a lovely gray shawl. Two bob's been lent on it, but it's worth a pretty penny more than that, I promise you."

"That's all very well, but what's you giving it me for?" Mary Jane inspects the ticket.

"You've been mighty decent to me of late, what with giving me a place to doss and that. I thought you could wear this nice bonnet on Lord Mayor's Day, 'cause I knows you don't own one." Maria models the bonnet on

655

her own head. "P'raps your girl might like the shawl, and your Joe would fit the coat for certain."

"He ain't my Joe," Mary Jane reminds her. "Not anymore."

Maria shrugs. "Sell it, then. That and the other bits is sure to get you a few pennies."

Struck by a sudden maudlin impulse, realizing that this might very well be the last time she sees her best friend, Mary Jane invites Maria to dinner. Dinner and a drink. Or in Maria's case, several drinks.

While Mary Jane nurses a pint of beer in the Britannia, followed by another in the Horn of Plenty—pausing in between for a quick tour of Maria's new lodgings—Maria manages to knock back enough to make her noticeably elevated, and dinner turns into an all-afternoon affair. By the time they call it quits, evening is upon them and Mary Jane leads the way back to Miller's Court, letting Maria use her as a crutch.

Emerging clumsily from the narrow passage, they bump into another resident of the court: Lizzie Alberge. She's a delicate young thing with a lathy body not unlike Eva's former svelte form, and she has a similar chestnut mane. The fresh-faced twenty-year-old hasn't lived there long, but she and Mary Jane struck up a friendship a short while ago, when they met in Crossingham's Lodging House across the street. Mary Jane was there on business with a special, and young Lizzie was cleaning the halls, as she frequently does to earn a bit extra here and there.

On Mary Jane's part, there was an immediate attraction. Eva was absent on the continent, her letters having ceased a week prior, and she was finding herself increasingly drawn to those in whom she saw Eva's likeness. Already half-screwed, having been treated to some cheap champagne by the fella she'd been entertaining, she wasn't shy to solicit Lizzie's company, and they spent the evening drinking together—indulging to excess, as had lately become her habit.

Rum, gin, brandy—anything and everything. Mary Jane introduced her to herbal cigarettes, which they smoked with Maria, and when the pubs closed, they

bought enough liquor to keep them going till the early hours of the morning, then stumbled home.

Waking up everyone within earshot, Mary Jane regaled Lizzie with Irish songs, and they continued to drink in Lizzie's room—one at the far end of the court, on the first floor—until their stock of booze was depleted.

"I ain't never been this screwed in me life." Lizzie flopped on the bed. "Me head's spinning and I feels all queer."

Mary Jane remained seated at the table, sipping at the last of the rum they'd been sharing. "I bet you feel nice."

"Eh?" Lizzie squinted at her. "Is you talking bawdy at me?"

"Maybe." Mary Jane's eyes wandered to Lizzie's ankles, exposed when she tumbled backwards onto the bed and her skirts flew up. "You've got such fine legs."

"Have I?" Lizzie peered down at herself, tugging her skirts up a few inches higher.

"Would I lie?" Mary Jane swigged the rum. "Show me more."

"More of me legs?" Lizzie pulled her skirts up to her shins. "D'you honest like 'em that much?" She stuck her pins straight out, scrutinizing their appearance.

"Let me see where you garter." Mary Jane pushed her luck.

"Oh, I knows what you're about now." Lizzie giggled. "You's one of them peculiar women, aintcha?" She bent her knees to the ceiling and let her skirts fall around her hips. "A sapphist." She whispered the word, as if anxious someone might hear.

"What if I am?" Mary Jane quirked an eyebrow. "Do you mind me looking?"

Lizzie shook her head. "It's nice to be seen."

"Are you a virgin?" Mary Jane gazed fixedly at her bare thighs, her stockings gartered below the knee.

More head shaking. More giggling. "I's got a fella. He's done it to me."

"Do you like it?"

"What?" Lizzie colored up beautifully, as Eva always did at the first hint of bawdy talk.

"Fucking." Mary Jane took another gulp of rum. "Do you like to be fucked?"

"Who don't?" Lizzie brought a hand to her sex, raking her fingers through the hair on her motte. "Feels nice when he puts his thing in. I likes the shoving, and the wetting he gives me."

Finishing the rum, Mary Jane moved over to the bed and raised Lizzie's skirts to her belly, watching her toy languidly with her sex.

"You've a lovely cunt." She stared at the thick blanket of brown curls covering Lizzie's parts, droplets of moisture clinging to them like dew.

"Your eyes is eating me up." Lizzie slipped her fingers lower, probing inside herself. "You's making me so randy all a sudden."

"Where's your man?" Mary Jane broke her eyes away, taking in enough of the room to ascertain a man's regular habitation of it.

"Away." Lizzie kept her fingers at work. "He ain't back till tomorra."

Saying that, she parted her legs wide, inviting Mary Jane into that hallowed space between her thighs, and Mary Jane knew she was ripe for the taking. Liquor had made her hot cunted, her passions aroused beyond all reason ... yet Mary Jane turned away. Suppressing temptation, she drooped her arms over the footboard and closed her eyes, alarmed by the degree of her lust, and by how precipitously it had been revealed.

"What's wrong?" Lizzie sat up.

"I want to fuck you." Mary Jane fought tears, ashamed of her weakness.

"Well, that's all right." Lizzie crawled to the foot of the bed and rubbed Mary Jane's tensed shoulders. "I wanna let ya." She touched a hand to Mary Jane's cheek, her fingers coated with amatory fluid, the smell intensifying Mary Jane's lust.

"Oh, God help me." Mary Jane captured her hand, kissing those fingers and sucking them clean. "It's been so long since I've tasted a woman."

Succumbing, she turned her eyes to Lizzie's lips and leant forward, pressing their mouths together. She was

ready to launch into a deep, erotic kiss, but the overture was met with no reciprocated desire. Instead, she felt a halting. There was a slight drawing away, limiting the duration of the intimacy, and she recognized it immediately: it was the very way she had reacted the first time her lips touched Billy Flanagan's.

What she interpreted then as her own foolish timidity was, she came to learn, merely the sudden, disappointing realization that it felt wrong. Not repulsive exactly, but thoroughly dulling. She was no more meant to kiss a man's lips than Lizzie was to kiss a woman's, and even in her drunken state, with her sex throbbing for attention, she knew it was a mistake and she withdrew. It brought sense to her. She was lonely, desperate, and clinging to any small shred of Eva she could find. Even in the figure of another woman.

"Let's go to sleep now," she suggested then, lying her exhausted body on the palliasse. "Before I make a further fool of myself."

That was the finish of it. From then on, all flirtation ceased. Mary Jane continued to see her at the lodging house, and continued to admire her beauty—particularly her likeness to Eva—but henceforth did so from an appropriate distance, their contact kept to a chaste hug and a friendly peck on the cheek.

Saddened by the thought of their friendship now coming to an end, Mary Jane disentangles herself from Maria and greets Lizzie with a squeeze. "You on your way to work?"

Lizzie nods. "It never ends."

"Oh, Gawd, me bladder's about to burst." Maria leans against the wall outside the door of number one and squats, peeing right there on the ground.

"Excuse her." Mary Jane apologizes to Lizzie on Maria's behalf. "She's lacking in manners and refinement." She shoves open the door to her room, budging it with her shoulder. "Come in and have a word a while, won't you? It's been an age since we've talked."

"Aye, I'll spare a minute." Lizzie follows her inside. "I ain't seen you round much of late." She takes off her

pelerine—a short woolen cape crocheted for her by Mary Jane—and sits herself at the table. "How's you been?"

"Had better days, had worse." Mary Jane sighs. "But I've got my health and a good woman to keep me warm at nights, so I mustn't grumble."

"I'll drink to that." Maria appears in the doorway, cupping her crotch so as to tuck the fabric of her underskirts against her privy parts, dabbing herself dry. "Who fancies a spree?"

"I can't, I've got work on." Mary Jane shuts her down. "Maybe some other night, eh?"

Maria blows a raspberry at her. "Well then, my Old Mare, I shall not see you this evening again." She turns in the direction of Dorset Street. "I shall go find me some money."

"Be careful, you lushy old tart." Mary Jane watches her walk away. "I love you."

Maria stops halfway down the passage, thinks hard about Mary Jane's words, then bursts into laughter. "Booze makes you maudlin, Mare. I'll see you tomorra."

"No, you won't." Mary Jane whispers after her and closes the door, forgetting that Lizzie's sitting within earshot.

"Is you going somewhere?" Lizzie asks innocently.

"Only the Lord Mayor's show." Mary Jane covers her slip-up. "Ain't got the money to go nowhere else, have I?"

"Where would you go if you did? If you could go anywhere in the world?"

"Ireland, I should think. I've got family there." Mary Jane folds the clothes Maria left strewn about the table. "It'd be nice to get away from the likes of men. Not that Joe's a bad bloke, but I ain't suited to him."

"I knows why that is." Lizzie snickers. "It's a wonder to me how you gets along in your work, given your partic'lar proclivities, but I s'pose it's a means to an end. To tell truth, if it weren't for Jack, I reckon I might have a go at it me-self. Beats scrubbing privies."

"Don't you dare." Mary Jane shakes her head disapprovingly. "My dear, sweet girl, don't sink to this life. Promise me." She crouches at Lizzie's feet, placing both hands on her knees. "Whatever you do, don't you do

no wrong and turn out as I have. You marry that young man of yours, and you be true to him. He'll take care of you."

"Who'll take care of you, Mare?"

Thinking of Eva, Mary Jane smiles. "Don't you worry about me, love." She pats Lizzie's lap. "Everything is as it's meant to be."

Just then, Joe comes thundering down the court and barges through the open door, angered by a fresh altercation with Maria. "That damned bitch of yours is talking her mouth off out there, saying you've been flat-cocking her all afternoon. Has she been in here with you again?" He spots Lizzie. "Lord take my bloody soul. Is this another one now?! I hope they's all paying ya."

"I'd best be off." Lizzie gets up. "I'm late as it is." She whispers her goodbyes to Mary Jane and slips away, bringing the door to behind her.

Once alone with her former keeper, Mary Jane folds her arms, staring him down. "Whatchu want?"

"Just wondering if you was free for a bit."

"I ain't never free, you know that." She keeps her arms folded, her body language closed. "Available maybe, but never free."

"I ain't got nuthin' to give ya, if that's what you're getting at." Joe takes off his hat, twirling it in his hands as he did when they first met. "I wish I did, but I'm flat broke."

"Then I ain't got nothing to give you, neither." Mary Jane starts to open the door, ready to usher him out, but he stops her.

"That ain't what I'm here for." He pulls her hand away from the latch. "I miss ya."

She believes that's true. He's been almost every day visiting her, giving her coin in dribs and drabs, never asking for anything in return. Not that it's getting him anywhere.

"I don't like being apart from ya," he goes on. "We was good together, and we can be so again, but you has to stop it with all these women." He flings his hat on the table and drops to his knees before her. "You quit them habits, and I'll make you my only woman. I swear to you I

will." He holds her by the hips. "I'll marry you proper if that's whatchu want."

"It's too late. I can't live like this no more." Mary Jane relaxes her arms, but offers him no comfort. "You're a good man, Joe Barnett, but you can't be *my* man."

He drops his head forward, burying his face in her skirts, his shoulders heaving with sobs. Pitying him, she urges him up and over to the bed.

"Here, lie down, you daft old boy." She settles him on the palliasse and retreats to the other side of the room, taking a long look at herself in the cracked mirror above her washstand before inserting her diaphragm and returning to him.

Perching on the edge of the bed, she rolls him onto his back and unbuttons his trousers, fishing inside for his flaccid cock.

"Whatchu—" he starts to ask, but she shushes him.

"Don't speak." She pulls his piercer free and takes it into her mouth, feeling blood rush into it directly she wraps her lips around the tip.

When he's stiff enough to accomplish a poke, she abandons the minette and tugs up her skirts, clambering onto her knees above him before lowering herself onto his pulsing prick, accepting him inside her for the last time. Her palms pressed flat to his chest, she begins to move, massaging his priapus as she grinds on him, doing nothing to hurry him and everything to please him, though she isn't entirely sure why.

In absolute silence, they fuck long and slow. At the moment of completion, he grits his teeth and jerks his hips up, thrusting into her, and she milks every drop from him. His libation as abundant as it's ever been, she swipes a hanky from her pocket, dismounts, and plugs her cavity, preventing any of his seminal muck from getting on her clothes, lest Eva should see it.

"What'd you do that for?" Joe sits up, catching his breath.

"I don't know." Mary Jane retreats to the foot of the bed and stares bleakly at the wall, holding a hand to her core to keep the hanky in place, making sure there's no spillage. "You get on your way now."

Understanding that he's being dismissed, Joe wipes his wilting prick on the bed sheets, puts himself away, and retrieves his hat, but dithers at the door.

Glancing back at the bed, "Tell me you love me."

The desperation in his voice is heartbreakingly palpable, yet Mary Jane says nothing. After a moment of expectant, hopeful silence, he leaves.

CHAPTER 55

Mary Jane adjusts Maria's donated bonnet, nudging it left and right, pulling it forwards and back, trying to get it just so. It's coming up on the prescribed time to meet Adel's land agent, and she wants to look respectable. When she has it suitably placed, she ties the satin strings beneath her chin and fixes it with a few hatpins. Not even a gale force wind could dislodge it.

As the church clock strikes nine, she puts on her jacket and smudges some of the rouge off her cheeks, considering her appearance passable. The linsey-woolsey dress she's been wearing for the past few days might not be pretty or elegant, and may indeed betray how sadly impecunious she's become, but it certainly keeps her from freezing on the cold winter streets. In any case, her better clothes are at Eva's.

Leaving Miller's Court—having arranged to meet the land agent near Aldgate East Station, where his train is due to arrive in fifteen minutes—she bumps into Elizabeth Prater. The bedraggled, rum-soaked woman, lacking either bonnet or coat, is shivering in the cold, peering up and down Dorset Street as if deciding in which direction she ought to go. Having been out since late afternoon, walking a hundred miles all around in search of money, she shifts her weight from one aching foot to the other, her worn boots providing little cushioning on the hard ground, or protection from the

elements. A hole in the toe of her left boot is plugged up with glazier's putty and the laces have snapped on the other, necessitating some hasty repair work with a piece of string and some old garter elastic.

She looks harrowed this evening, and Mary Jane can guess why. No woman wants to be forced out to work at this time of night. Not anymore.

"Heavy thoughts?" she inquires, buttoning her jacket up against the cold.

"I think it's set to rain." Elizabeth squints up at the cloudy sky, hugging her arms around her chest. "But I must find me money somehow."

"Me n'all." Mary Jane turns westward. "I mustn't dawdle. Keep yourself safe, my pretty."

While Elizabeth trundles off down Commercial Street, Mary Jane heads straight to the Essex: a public house near Aldgate High Street. She plans to wait for the land agent outside the establishment, as any decent lady would, but changes her mind when she spots a glimpse of a man who looks like Fleming loitering in a storage yard.

The sight of him triggers the first unpleasant twinges of anxiety in her chest and a tightness in her airway, her palms instantly clammy. One brandy won't hurt, she tells herself as she slips inside and takes a seat at the bar. Two will warm her nicely, she thinks, taking her bonnet off and getting comfortable. Three will dispel her nerves completely, and four ... well, when she gets to her fourth drink, she stops making excuses.

The latter is bought for her by a gentleman with unrealistic hopes, and upon asking him for the current time, she's shocked to learn that over an hour's gone by. Whatever could've gone wrong? Is the land agent's train late? Has he been waylaid? Moreover, what if he isn't coming? What will she tell Eva? Contemplating that, she orders up a fifth drink, and is in the midst of a premature mope when a well-dressed man with a curled mustache enters the pub behind her.

Standing out in an astrakhan-trimmed great coat, the dark-haired gent removes his black felt hat and glances around the room, paying particular interest to

any woman who appears to be seated alone, as if weighing his options.

Unsure of his intentions, Mary Jane refrains from making eye contact and observes him in the periphery of her vision, guessing him to be a few years her senior and decidedly better off. In his left hand, he clutches a leather-bound package which he sets on the bar as he moves into the empty space beside her, homing in on her curiosity and reciprocating it.

Without yet speaking, he hooks his finger on a heavy gold chain dangling from the fob pocket of his waistcoat and fishes out an elaborately engraved pocket watch, checking the time.

"Can I help you, sir?" She regards him with no small amount of suspicion and a dash of loathing, presuming— as she does with all men who look so intently at her—that he's interested in procuring her for services of a distinctly immoral nature.

"Unless I'm very much mistaken, I do believe you can," he responds with a smile, slipping the watch back into its pouch. "I'm seeking a woman."

Mary Jane snorts, expecting as much. "Well, you are mistaken indeed, sir." She angles her body away from him. "Even for a gent as fine as yourself, I'm afraid I ain't for sale—and I'm sure as I don't know what it is I've done to give you that impression—but if you wish, I should be glad to point you in the direction of a house that caters for such needs."

"Oh, my dear woman, you misunderstand me, and have painted me with the most wicked brush. I meant nothing whatsoever untoward." He presses a hand over his heart, stressing his sincerity. "I was engaged to meet a woman in this quarter an hour since, but I became very much delayed and missed the time of our appointment. When I saw you sitting here alone, I thought you might be that woman. I do apologize if I've offended you."

Mary Jane swivels back to him. "You're the agent of Missus Adella Adkins?"

"Indeed I am." He pulls a metal case from the inside pocket of his coat and withdraws a trade card, handing it to her with a flourish. "Arthur Halford at your service."

He extends his hand for a shake. "You are Miss Malone then, yes?"

"I am today." She accepts the introductory hand, suppressing a tremor of nerves and the unsteadiness of mild inebriation, wishing she'd had the sense to stop after the third drink. "Do forgive my being so abrupt with you. As a single woman, I very often find myself subjected to the most vulgar propositions one can imagine."

"I don't doubt it." Arthur plants himself on the stool beside her. "And it is I who should be begging your forgiveness, for having made you wait so long."

As he pulls open his coat to return the metal card case to its pocket, he reveals an artificial green carnation pinned inconspicuously on the left breast of his waistcoat.

"I like your flower," Mary Jane compliments him, knowing well that the green carnation is a floral symbol worn by homosexual men.

"And I like yours." He nods to the artificial violet on her bodice.

Now that they understand one another, they share a laugh, their initial misunderstanding forgotten and all tension dissolved.

Business is conducted swiftly then. Three copies of a tenancy agreement—already endorsed by Missus B——and Adel—are signed, and Mary Jane's copy is sealed for her in an envelope, along with instructions concerning how and where to collect the keys for the property upon her arrival in Kent.

In celebration, they share a small jug of rum, then Arthur escorts her back to Whitechapel. At least, he escorts her as far as she'll permit him to. Shame prevents her from allowing him any further than Dorset Street, so she walks the last few hundred yards alone, her heels clacking on the frozen ground, the gathering frost glistening like a thousand shards of shattered crystal under the city gaslights.

Disinclined to show up at Lolesworth stinking of booze, knowing she'd receive a nagging for it, she intends only a brief stop at Miller's Court to brush her teeth

before seeing Eva, but as the imminence of her departure starts to sink in, she regrets parting from Maria without a proper goodbye.

Now armed with an address to which Maria might write, she abandons the bonnet on the table, picks up her shawl, and heads out. Sadly, her best friend proves elusive. She's not at her lodgings, nor in the Blue Coat Boy, the Horn of Plenty, the Ten Bells, the Queen's Head, or the Britannia, though Mary Jane stops for a drink or two in each, chatting to other friends, passing acquaintances, and former customers, mentally preparing herself to leave them all behind.

When she finally gets up to leave the Britannia, ready to call it a night, having long given up on Maria, the world turns on its side like a listing ship and she pitches forward, steadying herself on the table.

"Oops." She waits for her vision to settle, until then not realizing how screwed she'd allowed herself to become. "A few too many for me, I think."

"I shall walk you to your lodgings," a ginger-haired man with a thick mustache and drink-reddened cheeks offers, swinging a full pot of ale in his hand. "It is my manly duty."

Recognizing him as an old customer—not a rich one, but a kind one—she feels safe enough in his company to indulge him ... with a caveat.

"I ain't taking no-one tonight," she warns him, tottering out into the street, promptly hit by a blast of freezing winter air. "I ain't working no more."

"I only want to see you out of harm's way, my love." He follows her outside and flings a heavy arm around her shoulders, leaning on her for support. "You can't be walking about here alone at this time of night. You don't know who's lurking about."

"Jack, you mean?" She blows a raspberry. "Ha! It's too late for old Jack. I'm leaving. Come tomorra, I won't be here, and he won't know where to find me."

Her senses numbed by drink, she leads the way to Miller's Court, unaware that they're being followed. Not just by a man in a dark coat with a hat pulled down low

on his brow and a red silk handkerchief in his pocket, but also by one of her neighbors: Mary Ann Cox.

They meet at the end of the passage, Mary Ann acknowledging her first.

"Goodnight, Mary Jane." The older woman's thin, cracked lips curl into something resembling a smile as she walks onward to her own room at the end of the court.

"Goodnight." Mary Jane gives the unlocked door a firm shove. "I think I'm going to have a song."

She leans on the doorjamb, beaming at her neighbor, but barely gets her slightly slurred words out before the man with the carroty mustache budges past her, grabs her by the waist, and pulls her inside, slamming the door closed behind them.

"Oi!" She squirms, wresting herself free. "Don't muck me about."

"Let's get some light on, eh?" Her uninvited guest plants himself in a chair, finds a cup, and pours some beer into it.

"Cheeky bastard." Mary Jane grabs another cup. "As long as you're staying, you're sharing." She helps herself to his beer as he helped himself to a seat, then lights a candle and slumps into the other chair, soon breaking into a rendition of *A Violet from Mother's Grave*.

Feeling disgustingly mawkish, still regretting her decision to leave London without telling Maria, she continues to sing on and off for the next hour, until the Spitalfields church bell strikes one o'clock, the pot of ale runs dry, and she begins to tire of the carroty man's presence.

"Ain't you got a wife to go home to?" She tries to send him on his way, but he's got a question on his mind and an expectant lump forming in the crotch of his trousers.

"Give us a look first." He scrounges up thruppence from his pockets and slaps the coins on the table. "I've got a stiff one rising."

Mary Jane doesn't budge. "Didn't I say I weren't taking no-one tonight?"

"Aye, but what's the harm in it?" He fumbles his prick out of his trousers. "Get yer grinder out and let me have a come afore me cods burst."

Lacking the energy to argue, Mary Jane hands him a tub of cold cream and drags her chair in front of him. "Don't make a mess of the place." She flings a hanky into his lap, sits down, and tugs up her skirts, baring herself to him with one foot propped on the table.

All in all, it's a rather pathetic affair that comes to an end in under two minutes. He empties himself into the hanky, thanks her, chucks the semenalized rag on the floor, and leaves. Throughout, Mary Jane sits there like a ragdoll, limp and uncaring, staring at the thruppence and wondering why she just allowed herself to be bought. In the end, she puts it down to habit. That, and drink. As her mother always used to say to her stepfather: when the drop is inside, the sense is outside.

Watching the carroty man's deposit trickle from the folds of the fabric and seep onto the floorboards, she begins to sob. Eva deserves better than a cheap paphian who shows off her commodity for a few coppers and a sip of beer.

Eva.

Oh, darling Eva.

Hungry, and hoping the ingestion of some starchy food might soak up the alcohol in her stomach—thus also having a sobering effect—she straightens her linsey frock, wraps herself up in her jacket and shawl, and sets out for the fish and chip shop on Thrawl Street, hurrying to get there before it closes at two o'clock.

It's raining now, and she keeps her shawl pulled up over her head, concealing herself from the elements and acknowledging no-one—or trying not to. A familiar voice arrests her as she passes Flower and Dean Street.

"Is that you, Mary Jane?"

The deep, gravelly voice belongs to a young man named George Hutchinson. They met three years ago, when she was working at the Ratcliffe bawdyhouse. He was barely twenty-one then, and she was his first whore. In fact, she was his first woman. He confessed his virginity when she—in an attempt to secure his

business—palmed his erection through his clothing and caused a most embarrassing eruption. Feeling the unexpected discharge gush onto her hand, she peered down and found his cock spewing copiously into his trousers, his ejaculation quite surprising her.

The poor man's cheeks were red with shame, and she took pity on him. She walked him back to his home and helped him wash his clothes before the rest of his family returned from work, then gave him a proper tug—gratis. Her hand soapy from the washbasin, she took hold of his standing prick—for it rose again the moment it was exposed to her—and frigged it till he spurted into the sudsy water.

He was sweet then, as most men are before they learn the cruel ways of manhood. As soon as he was able to afford her, he went to her at the Ratcliffe house and received his carnal introduction, and even became a little spoony on her for a while. He's seen other whores since, of course, and is now married, but she'll always be his favorite. His fondness for her predisposes him to be generous, which isn't something she's ever been shy to exploit, and tonight is no exception.

"Mister Hutchinson, whatchu doing skulking round these parts so late?" She stops, sheltering in the porch of a boot warehouse on the corner of Flower and Dean Street. "Being as you're here, make yourself useful and lend a girl a tanner." She winks, holding her palm out.

"I can't, love." George looks sincerely apologetic. "I spent all my money going down to Romford." He turns his trouser pockets inside out, proving his claim.

"Well, that's a true pity." Mary Jane hops off the porch and goes on her way. "I'll have to find me some money elsewhere now, won't I?" She teases him, knowing how much it'll eat at him to think he missed out on a poke.

Giving him no more thought than that, she carries on to Thrawl Street, refraining from looking up at Eva's window as she passes by the Lolesworth Buildings.

It pains her heart to think of Eva tucked up in bed alone, but if she were to turn up in her current state, it'd only cause a fight.

After using the carroty man's money to buy her supper, and donating the remainder of it to an elderly, shoeless vagrant because it disgusts her to keep it in her possession, she ambles back to Commercial Street. George is still there, but now standing under the porch light of the Queen's Head, staring at her. She tries to avoid him, but as she turns down Dorset Street, she hears him walking behind her, his footsteps matching hers. A moment later, he taps her on the shoulder, halting her at the mouth of the Miller's Court passage.

"How might I be of assistance to you, Mister Hutchinson?" She faces him, holding her shawl tightly around her chest. "I'm afraid it's much too late for you to obtain a bed at any of the good lodging houses round these parts."

Cold and wet, George looks up at the cloudy sky, both hands shoved in his pockets. "The weather's foul. Can I warm my bones in your lodgings?"

Mary Jane shakes her head, backing away. "I don't think so."

"Come on, old girl." He steps in front of the passage, blocking her avenue of retreat. "Take pity on a man. I've been lodging at the Victoria Home, only I ain't got a pass and they won't let me in."

Mary Jane knows that to be true. Tickets for beds are only issued from five o'clock until half-twelve, and all ticketed men must be on the premises by one o'clock. After that, entry is only permitted to those with a special pass, and if he doesn't possess one, then he's out of luck. The doors won't open again until four o'clock, when many of the men start leaving for work. Nevertheless, she doesn't want him in her room.

"I'm sorry, I can't help you." She spins on her heels, thinking to give Maria one more try by showing up at her lodgings in New Court, but before she takes a step, she spots a stern figure lurking on the porch of Crossingham's Lodging House opposite. His face is shrouded in the shadow cast by the wide brim of his hat, but she identifies him by the silk hanky sticking out of his pocket. The red silk hanky.

"Who is that man?" George follows her gaze. "Your bully?"

He refers to the practice of some men to procure prostitutes for themselves—often by violent means. These men make it their business to oversee the whore's work, stepping in to protect their merchandise when necessary, and ensuring that all men pay what they owe. Every penny she earns goes to him, and in return, he feeds and clothes her, sees that she has a warm bed at nights, keeps her in drink, and fucks her at whim.

"No man controls me," Mary Jane snarls, offended by suggestion.

"Friend of yours, then?" George returns Fleming's stare. "Likes to keep an eye, does he?"

"I wouldn't say friend, neither." Mary Jane adjusts her shawl, cutting Fleming out of her line of vision. "He has an interest in me that's not reciprocated. What of it?"

"He looks set to cause you some bother." George exploits Mary Jane's obvious discomfort to his own ends. "P'raps you'd best invite me in after all. He'll think you occupied for the night and move on."

"Oh, aye?" Mary Jane raises a disbelieving eyebrow. "And what of you?"

"I'll warm me-self and be on my way."

Though suspicious of his motives, what he says makes some sort of sense.

"All right, come along." She sighs, agreeing to a short visit. "I'll light a fire and you'll be comfortable."

Victorious, George gives her a spontaneous peck on the cheek. "My darling, you're an angel!" He puts his arm around her shoulders.

"Give over." Mary Jane shrugs his arm off and leads the way to her room.

Inside, she shakes off her drenched shawl and stokes up a fire. Since Eva used the last of her tinder that morning, she dumps her fish and chips onto a plate and uses the greasy paper to get a flame going, then throws some of Maria's donated clothing on it, starting with the girl's petticoat and a boy's shirt. For extra warmth, she takes the overcoat and rigs it up to the window as a

makeshift curtain, using forks to stab it into the rotting window frame.

That achieved, she sets her shawl and jacket to dry in front of the fire, draped over a chair, and sits down to eat while George warms himself, an awkward silence descending upon the pair. Much too late to do anything about it, she realizes the carroty man's used hanky is still on the floor, and it gives George the wrong impression.

"You oughtn't be alone at night." He eyes the oozing deposit. "It ain't safe."

Beginning to feel uneasy, Mary Jane finishes her supper and shows him the door. "I think you'd best leave now." She reaches for the latch, but he wrenches her away from it.

"Let's have a bit first." He lays his heavy hands on her waist and maneuvers her toward the bed. "My old woman's got one in her again and she won't give way."

"Neither will I, so get your grubby paws off me!" Unable to get free, she slaps him, striking his cheek with her open palm.

The return hit comes as a surprise. The back of his hand smacks the side of her face and she crumples like a paper doll. Still intoxicated, dizzy, and weak, she topples backwards, cracking her head on the bedpost.

In that instant, the world turns black.

CHAPTER 56

"Oh! murder!" mary jane regains consciousness on the bed, expecting to fight George off, but he's nowhere to be seen.

Alone, confused, and disoriented, with no clue as to how much time has passed, she clutches her sore head and eases herself into an upright position. Her legs have been placed wide apart, positioned for mounting, and her commodity is throbbing. Moreover, there's a wetness between her thighs. Is she bleeding? Hoping that's the case—hoping her courses have come on suddenly—she brings a hand to her sex, wincing as she dips her fingertips into the oozing slit, her labia inflamed from some recent friction.

She knows what that means.

She's been fucked.

"Bastard," she growls, grimacing at the pearly webs of seminal fluid dripping from her fingers, disgusted to find more semen splattered on the bodice of her linsey frock, and a slimy mess left behind on her skirt where he must've wiped himself off after he finished.

A fire is still burning in the hearth, but barely. She feeds it with the crusty hanky used by the carroty man, another of the shirts left by Maria, and the newspaper clippings she's been keeping hidden underneath her floorboards. Eva's been nagging her to get rid of the latter for weeks anyway. She blames them for contributing to

the morbid terrors that have been crippling her with episodes of intense fright and panic of late, and she's probably right.

Once the fire's stoked up, she heats some water in the kettle and gives herself a thorough wash—inside and out—before cleaning George's muck off her dress and laying it out to dry with her shawl and jacket.

Now fairly well sober, she wants nothing more than to see Eva. Since most of her other clothes are already at Lolesworth, she pulls the tin bath out from under her bed and rummages through it, the rusty bucket being used to store all the odd bits and bobs she no longer uses on a daily basis, including the old décolletage-baring outfit she wore when she was still walking the streets, and some particularly shabby clothes only worn on washday. From this limited assortment, she picks a dark skirt and a green velvet bodice—the warmest garments available—and gets ready to leave. Then, there's a faint knock on the door.

Since the light's out in the court, she deduces that it must be gone three o'clock. It's too early for her neighbor, Catherine Pickett, a flower seller, to be coming by to borrow her shawl—as she's in the habit of doing—and too late for any other of her neighbors to be calling on her. If the fire weren't giving her away, she'd pretend not to be home. As it is, she has no choice but to call out.

"Who is it?"

"I'm in need of a bed," a soft female voice replies.

The fact that it's a woman—albeit one she doesn't immediately recognize—puts her at ease and she opens the door, taken aback to find Joe's inferior Mary Jane lookalike standing on her doorstep, appearing somewhat bedraggled.

"I hate to call upon you like this." The woman stares at the ground, fearing rejection. "I know we ain't friends, and there ain't no reason on God's good Earth why you oughta help me, but I don't have nowhere else to go."

"No money for a doss?" Mary Jane guesses.

The woman shakes her head. "I've just been booted out of Crossingham's kitchen, and I can't bear to be on the streets tonight." She coughs and wheezes, her lungs

full of fluid. "I ain't got the nerve. I swear a man's been following me."

"Ain't our Joe been looking after you no more?"

More head shaking. More coughing. "He's a kind heart, ain't he? But I ain't seen him since the day he brung me here." She peers up at the inimitable original upon which her alterations were based. "I didn't know of you till then, but when I saw you ..." She returns her eyes to the ground. "I knew it weren't me he wanted."

"I'm sorry he led you on such a dance." Mary Jane pities her. "It was cruel of him." She holds the door open. "Now come in out the cold."

The woman hesitates to enter. "I ain't got no money to give ya."

"Let's not fret about that." Mary Jane pulls her through. "You can have my room for the rest of the night. I have somewhere else to be, and there's no sense in the bed going to waste."

As the woman rests her exhausted body on the bed, Mary Jane checks the state of her jacket, disappointed to find it still wet.

"Take mine if you like." The woman offers up hers. "It's quite dry, and I reckon it's yours anyway." She sneezes into a hanky. "Joe gived it to me."

"Arsehole said he pawned it." Mary Jane inspects the garment, determining it is indeed hers by initials MJK stitched into the lining under the collar.

"You can have it back if you want."

"Nah, you're all right." Mary Jane slips it on, tucking the tenancy papers into the inside pocket. "I'll bring it back to you in the morning." She points toward the fire. "There's some water in the kettle if you fancy some tea. See that the door locks behind me."

With that, she covers her head with her damp shawl and leaves Miller's Court, walking speedily in the direction of Thrawl Street. Along the way, she spots a man hovering in Dorset Street, but pays him no mind, not caring if it's George, Fleming, or some other lonely soul.

To surprise Eva, she takes a slight detour on her way to Lolesworth and stops at a pawn shop on Commercial

Street, catching them as they open and paying back the money lent on the pawn ticket given to her by Maria, hoping that the gift of a nice new shawl might lessen any anger Eva might be feeling at being left on her own all evening, or for being woken up.

As it happens, however, Eva isn't in the least bit angry. Seconds after Mary Jane knocks for her, the door flings open and the teen—fully dressed—bursts through it, leaping into her arms, both feet leaving the floor.

"Such exuberance!" Mary Jane catches her and carries her back over the threshold into the warm, fire-lit room, kicking the door closed behind them. "I hope you shall always be this excited to see me."

"Oh, Em. I ain't slept a wink waiting for you to come home to me." Eva clings on tight, as though Mary Jane might float away from her. "Where's you been?"

"Sorting things for us." Mary Jane lets her down but keeps her close, one hand on her waist and the other on her bum. "I was afraid I'd wake you."

Eva shakes her head. "I hates sleeping alone now. My bed feels so empty without you in it." She runs her fingers over the lapel of Mary Jane's borrowed jacket and glances down at her old, shabby skirt. "Whatchu wearing?"

"I got caught out in the rain." Mary Jane tells a half-truth. "I dug these out so as I could come to you right away."

"What's this?" Eva picks at a triangle of the gray shawl peeking out of her jacket pocket, pinching the smooth fabric between her fingers.

"It's for you." Mary Jane whisks it out of her pocket and wraps it around Eva's shoulders. "Do you like it?"

"It's proper silk, ain't it?" Eva inspects the intricate patterning and the soft tasseled edge. "Wherever's it from?"

"Maria gave it me as thanks for letting her doss in my room."

"I love the feel of it." Eva rubs it on her cheeks.

"I love the feel of you." Mary Jane draws her near. "Shall we go to bed?"

"Wait." Eva prevents her from moving in for a kiss. "What news do you bring?" Her eyes are wide with desperate expectation. "Is it done?"

"We have everything we need, darling." Mary Jane pulls the tenancy documents from the inside pocket of her jacket. "I can take care of you." She hands them over, encouraging Eva to look. "We don't own the place, of course, but it's ours to live in. *Ours*, Eva. Me and you."

"And the running of it?"

"I'm to manage that." Mary Jane starts undressing. "I shall hire the staff and see to it that things operate as they should." Down to her undergarments, she drops to her knees and puts her hands up Eva's skirts, divesting her of her drawers. "You'll want for nothing."

Eva casts her eyes over the pages, digesting what she can, though much of the legalize is well above her level of comprehension. "This is real?"

"All real and all for us." Mary Jane rises to her feet. "Didn't I tell you it'd all come good in the end?" She plucks the papers from Eva's trembling hands and lays them on the table. "I wish I'd got it using my brain instead of my madge, but beggars can't be choosers, eh?"

Tears flowing freely, Eva wraps her arms around Mary Jane's neck. "We don't have to speak of that no more. Not ever again." She crushes their bodies together, standing on tiptoe to tuck her head on Mary Jane's shoulder. "You're all mine now. Really truly."

Touched that Eva's excitement for this change in their circumstance focuses not on being kept, nor on the expansive Kent property they now get to call home—with its flushing toilets, hot and cold running water, and gas lighting—but simply on the fact that she no longer has to share her lover, Mary Jane becomes sympathetically teary.

"Oh, my sweet love." She pulls Eva to her chest. "This is our last night in London. How should we celebrate? You still owe me that tickle. Don't think I've forgotten."

"Best collect the debt from me, then." Eva backs herself toward the bed, unbuttoning her bodice as she goes. "I don't like to owe."

Still working on her poses, her ideas stolen from Mary Jane's bawdy picture book, Eva removes her clothing piece by piece, making Mary Jane watch from a distance. Clambering onto the bed, she lets down her hair and strips to her chemise, flaunting the divine curves of her body and inspiring Mary Jane's passions.

To finish, she rolls onto her front and lifts her chemise over her raised bum, giving it a playful wiggle, and Mary Jane pounces. She dives onto the bed, seizes Eva by the waist, and flips her over, stopping abruptly when she hears the crinkling of paper beneath the bed sheets.

"Whatchu been reading?" She searches for the source of the noise.

"It's one of yours." Eva turns coy. "I hopes you don't mind."

Mary Jane giggles. Judging by the sheepish, slightly flushed look on Eva's face, she hadn't been reading any of her few innocent titles such as *Oliver Twist: The Parish Boy's Progress*, or something educational, like *On the Origin of Species by Means of Natural Selection*, most of which would likely confound her. Indeed, as she expects, what she fishes out from under the covers is a copy of the erotic magazine *The Pearl*, opened to a story entitled *The Voluptuous Experiences of an Old Maid*.

"This was given to me by a bawdy old customer some years ago." She skims through it, refreshing her memory of its contents. "He thought I'd like it because ... well, because it contains some passages of the most explicit love between women. Did you read those parts?"

Eva's cheeks flare. "They likes the birching, don't they?"

Finding a second lump beneath the blankets, Mary Jane pulls out another title from her small collection of erotic material: *The Romance of Lust*.

"You've really been practicing your reading tonight." She winks. "I thought you wouldn't like this one so much, though." She peruses it. "It's full of men."

"Not the way I imagine it." Eva colors up. "I thinks of you with your doodle, the way you was in them lewd dreams I used to have."

Mary Jane feels a tingle in her loins. "You'd like it if I had a big cock under my dress?"

"Sometimes." Eva shrugs. "But I'd miss the other and your doodle is better. It comes and goes and ain't nearly so messy."

"Hiding anything else under here?" Mary Jane pats the covers, discovering *Memoirs of a Woman of Pleasure* tucked under a pillow. "Oh, now that's a filthy one."

"I didn't know." Eva snatches it from her. "I only picked it up to have a look, and it flopped open to this page." She demonstrates how the dog-eared book naturally parts to a section where the spine has been broken from repeated use, the pages of this portion especially creased, some corners folded down to mark favorite passages. "You've read this lots."

"I certainly have," Mary Jane declares frankly. "I find the text stimulating. Do you?"

"There's bits what reminds me of when we first knew each other." Eva flips through to the corresponding paragraphs, in which an older woman initiates an innocent teenage girl into the pleasures of fucking. "It's almost like it was when you first had me."

"Will you read it to me?" Mary Jane snuggles up behind her. "I shall enjoy hearing it from your lips."

Used to being asked to read aloud, for Mary Jane often insists that she practices her words this way, Eva clears her throat and begins, speaking slowly and with great care, making sure to get every word out right.

"She turned to me, embraced and kissed me with great eagerness. This was new, this was odd, but—" She squeals, her words cut short as Mary Jane acts them out.

In a single breath, she's swept up into Mary Jane's arms and bombarded with kisses upon her neck. Mary Jane's soft, moist lips trail down to her bare shoulder, biting and nipping, then reverse, a hot, wet tongue slithering up to her earlobe.

"Keep going, my darling," Mary Jane whispers, gripping her tightly. "Indulge me."

Eva turns her eyes back to the pages. "Her hands became extremely free and wandered over my whole body, with touches, squeezes, and pressures that rather

warmed and surprised me with their novelty than they either shocked or alarmed me." She gasps, feeling Mary Jane's hands traverse the contours of her body in rhythm with the words.

Touching.

Squeezing.

Such exquisite squeezing.

"More," Mary Jane urges, tucking herself to Eva's rump.

Swallowing hard, Eva continues. "I lay then all tame and passive as she could wish, whilst her freedom raised no other emotions but those of a strange, and till then unfelt, pleasure. Every part of me was open and exposed to the lie ... sent ..." She struggles with the next word.

"Licentious," Mary Jane fills in for her.

"Lice-en-shus courses of her hands"—Eva picks up and carries on—"which, like a lambent fire, ran over my whole body and thawed all coldness as they went."

Mary Jane drags her fingernails over Eva's belly. "What next?"

"My diddeys ..." Eva moans, her breasts engulfed in Mary Jane's hands. "They employed and amused her hands awhile, till, slipping down lower ..."

Mary Jane slides a hand from Eva's bosom to the small swell of her abdomen, and as her fingertips meet the bushy thatch of hair on Eva's pubic mound, causing Eva's capacity for coherent thought to diminish completely, she takes over the telling of the story.

"She could feel the soft, silky down that had, but a few months before, put forth and garnished the mount pleasant of those parts, and promised to spread a grateful shelter over the seat of the most exquisite sensation, which had been, till that instant, the seat of the most insensible innocence." She recites the text from memory. "Her fingers played and strove to twine in the young tendrils of that moss, but not contented with these outer posts, she began to twitch, to insinuate—and at length, to force—an introduction of a finger into the quick itself."

Eva groans, the book falling away from her as Mary Jane's fingers push inside her.

"Oh, what a charming creature thou art!" Mary Jane goes on. "You must not, my sweet girl, think to hide all these treasures from me. My sight must be feasted as well as my touch. I must devour with my eyes this springing bosom." She throws up Eva's chemise. "Suffer me to kiss it. I have not seen it enough. Let me kiss it once more." She dips her head, planting kisses all over Eva's snowy flesh. "What firm, smooth, white flesh is here! How deliciously shaped! Then this delicious down!" She drags her fingers through the thick curls on Eva's motte. "Oh, let me view the small, dear, tender cleft!" She unfurls Eva's folds. "This is too much. I cannot bear it! I must, I must ..."

Veering from the text, she dips her head and puts her mouth to work on Eva's parts.

CHAPTER 57

Friday, November 9, 1888

As THE SUN RISES AND A FIRE DIES IN THE HEARTH, MARY Jane lies awake in Eva's bed, propped on her elbow, watching the teen sleep. Her steamer trunk is open on the table, raided of all its bawdy literature, for when they were done with their impromptu performance of a few favorite passages from *Memoirs of a Woman of Pleasure*, they turned to other works.

From *The Pearl*, they played out a scene in which Mary Jane took the part of a French governess and Eva filled the role of her virtuous teenage charge. Though Eva couldn't quite bring herself to entertain the fancy of being birched, she consented to be spanked repeatedly before she received an altogether more tender education with Mary Jane's fingers and tongue.

At some point shortly thereafter, they enacted a wedding night. Mary Jane—ornamented with her glass cock—assumed the part of the groom, while Eva took the place of the virginal bride. The game was complete with Eva feigning fright and concern, followed by tentative acceptance of the foreign intrusion between her thighs and pain when it entered her, but as soon as their bodies were locked together, all pretense dissolved.

Memorized lines were forgotten, sham modesty was thrown to the wind, and much to Eva's delight, the routine ended with an attitude that was new to both of them. As Mary Jane lay supine, she reversed and lay

above her, face to crotch, their tongues working in unison, lapping feverishly at one another until they were both rewarded with a taste of the other's pleasure.

Their nocturnal antics concluded with some fun of their own design. To begin, Mary Jane took the mirror off the wall and propped it lengthways on the bed. Then, she got Eva on her knees and elbows and went up her from behind. In this variation of dog fashion, she lifted one of Eva's legs and hooked it over her hip, contorting the teen's body for deeper penetration and twisting her in such a way that she could see the phallus plunging up her on every thrust.

Never had they fucked so hard, and Eva enjoyed the novelty of it for the briefest of moments, then wilted in Mary Jane's arms. It was too much for her, and at the first hint of her discomfort, Mary Jane eased off, withdrew, and flipped her over, uniting them face to face.

"I do so like it when you take me this way," Eva cooed, gripping Mary Jane's rear. "But I can't hold meself back. You fetch me too quick."

"Too quick?" Mary Jane slid a hand beneath her rump, encouraging her to meet each thrust. "Is there such a thing?"

"I want it to last." Eva gripped tighter. "Do make it last."

To achieve that, Mary Jane harnessed restraint and adjusted her pace, easing off each time she felt Eva's body stiffen in anticipation of her climax, bringing her to the cusp of her peak over and over again, denying her the ultimate pinnacle of her pleasure until she was wound up like a coiled spring, her whole body quivering with need.

"Oh, do let me have it," she pled at last. "I want a come. Give me a come. Please do, Em!" She gripped Mary Jane's rump, attempting to direct the force and angle of her thrusts. "I need a pleasure." She jerked her hips up, stirring the phallus inside her depths.

Only then did Mary Jane allow the whimpering, mewling teen to have her release, which came with such a profusion of her amatory juices that they were both drenched by it.

Indeed, the palliasse is still damp. The sheets are cold and wet in the middle, causing the love-struck pair to huddle together near the edge, Eva on her back, claiming all the room, while Mary Jane—awake, and not in the least bit tired—is wedged against the wall.

Easing the covers down, she pores over Eva's nude body, remembering a time when, in the days of her innocence, this sweet young girl would've been thoroughly mortified to be so exposed. In admiration of her form, she trails a finger from Eva's collar bone, once around each nipple, over her ribs, passing her belly button, and sinking into the bed of dense curls covering her motte. There, she cups her hand around Eva's treasure, dipping one finger between her plump labia to caress her spent flesh.

The contact has a rousing effect. Eva wakes with a surprised gasp, followed by the spreading of her thighs.

"Good morning." Mary Jane bends to kiss her. "I couldn't resist you."

"Did you sleep at all?" Eva smiles up at her.

"Not a wink." Mary Jane draws her hand up, tracing invisible patterns on Eva's ribs. "I wanted to savor this feeling."

"What feeling's that?"

"Like everything is just about as perfect as it could ever be." She takes up Eva's left hand, admiring the ring which, at some point during their operations, had been torn from the string around her neck and placed upon her marriage finger.

"Have you ever gived someone a ring afore?" Eva hopes to hear that she's the only one. *Needing* to hear it, in fact, for Mary Jane has all her firsts, and she should like to claim at least one in return.

"Never," Mary Jane answers her hope. "For all that I am, I give to you, and all that I have, I share with you," she recites a few lines of some common marriage vows and steals a kiss.

"This is really happening, ain't it?" Eva beams, soaking up her devotion. "Show it me again." She looks around for the tenancy papers, knowing them to be

somewhere on the floor, in amongst the scattered array of bawdy literature.

Happy to oblige, Mary Jane clambers out of bed and retrieves them, presenting them to her for the umpteenth time. "This wouldn't mean anything without you." She perches herself on the edge of the palliasse, her arm around Eva's shoulders. "I don't believe I ever had a single moment of true happiness until the day we met."

"Nor I." Eva gazes at Mary Jane's inked signature. "When do we go?"

"After breakfast." Mary Jane rises, collecting her clothes from disorganized mound on one of the chairs. "You pack up your things while I run back to my old room to collect my dress." She wriggles into her petticoat. "I shall return with enough bacon to feed an army."

In preparation for the Lord Mayor's Day celebrations, which begin at ten o'clock, the streets are already crowded by the strike of eight. People are coming and going, hurrying from here to there, meeting friends and lovers. No doubt many of them are getting ready for a night of heavy drinking and much debauchery, doing their best to use this day of celebration to forget about the tragedies of recent months. If such a thing is possible.

Dressed in yesterday's rummagings from the tin bath, her shawl pulled around her shoulders, Mary Jane returns to Miller's Court and knocks on the door to her room, not wanting to walk in on her guest, lest she be in a state of undress.

She receives no response.

After a second knock goes unanswered, she tries the door, giving it a firm shove, but it doesn't budge. Thinking the woman to be a heavy sleeper, she traipses around the corner to unlatch the door through the

window—as she's done innumerous times since losing her key.

Thinking nothing of it, she hitches up her skirts and props her knee on the window ledge, bracing herself on the gutter pipe as she reaches her arm through the lower broken pane and fumbles for the latch, her view obstructed by the coat she pinned up there.

Rather disconcertingly, when she finally gets her fingers on the latch, she finds it wet to the touch. It's covered with something moist and sticky, like slowly drying paint.

"That best not be what I think it is," she grumbles, unlocking the door and retracting her arm, having a suspicion that it's some man's mucilage.

But it's not. When she peers down at her hand, she discovers that her fingertips are smeared, not with the pearly white gloop ejected from a man's ballocks, but with an altogether more disturbing fluid of a dark carmine hue: blood.

A bolt of fear courses through her. Wiping her fingers clean with a hanky, she approaches the unlocked door and nudges it open a crack.

"Hello?" she calls into the void, hearing nothing in return.

No sound at all, but the smell ...

Wet pennies. The stench wafts out from the enclosed room and hits her immediately. It's a pungent, coppery, slightly sweet odor, and she knows it well. The memory of it has been permanently lodged in her nostrils since her visits to the mortuary with Inspector Reid. The smell of blood. The smell of death.

Barely breathing, she pushes the door open wider, flinching when it unexpectedly knocks against the table beside the bed. So far, all looks relatively normal. The table by the window is as she left it—minus the bonnet left by Maria—and her linsey frock is draped over the chair in front of the smoldering fire, the embers hot, thick plumes of smoke drifting up the chimney. The remains of the bonnet are visible in the grate, burnt to cinders, and there's something on the floor.

A red silk hanky.

Summoning every last shred of courage she has left, she takes a step inside, the floorboards creaking beneath her feet. Not daring to turn fully into the room, she peeks around the door and glimpses the end of the bed, the sheets bundled up and pushed against the wall.

There's a foot.

It's a slender foot with polished nails.

There's no movement.

Taking one more step, she sees it all and staggers backwards, falling into the other chair and covering her mouth with her hand, stifling a scream. Staring back at her from the bed is the lifeless form of a woman, her features hacked beyond all recognition.

She's lying quite naked, her head turned on the left cheek, facing the door, as if positioned there by some design. Her clouded eyes are aimed directly at anyone who should enter, but the rest of her face has been obliterated by lacerations. Nose, cheeks, eyebrows, and ears are all partially dissevered from the head. The lips are cut apart at all angles, her chin and forehead similarly gashed with the frantic lashings of a madman's knife, flaps of skin falling away from the bone like peeling wallpaper.

At the top right corner of the palliasse, the sheets are saturated with blood, the shoddily constructed partition wall streaked with several spurts of crimson, the spillage continuing beneath the bed and pooling on the floor. Her hair color is indistinguishable. Loosely braided for bed, her long mane is coated in red ooze from root to tip.

In a posture so familiar to all who earn a living on their backs, her legs are propped wide apart. The left knee is bent at right angles to her body, lying flat to the palliasse, the inner thigh stripped of all flesh. The right knee is angled toward the ceiling, flopped slightly outward and resting on the bunched up blankets. The inner thigh of this leg completely denuded of all meat and muscle, the stark white of bone visible through the torn strips of flesh left dripping from what the remains of the upper limb.

Moreover, the woman's entire genital area, including part of her right buttock, has been cut away. This, along

with the flaps of the inner thighs, has been deposited on the bedside table, her privy parts facing upward, her motte bared, the petals of her sex splayed open. Much of the innards removed from her emptied abdominal cavity are slopped beneath these parts, dangling off the table: all the fat and tissue. The viscera are laid out elsewhere, and the mutilation continues above her waist.

Her left arm is draped across her hollowed abdomen, gashed from shoulder to wrist, chunks of flesh gouged jaggedly from the extremity, her hand superficially marked, indicating that some attempt to fend off her attack was made. The other arm is almost completely severed at the shoulder, her pale skin shredded by the work of a knife, her hand upturned, her fingers clenched. More horrific still, her breasts have been sliced clean from her ribcage by two circular cuts, and the pleural cavity is visible through the wounds.

One of her severed breasts has been planted by her right foot and the other is tucked underneath her head, along with her uterus and both kidneys. To finish, her intestines are heaped at her right side, her spleen by her left, and her liver is between her feet.

The cause of death is quite plain to see. Her neck is cut deeply, right down to the bone, bisecting her trachea and very nearly decapitating her, and the skin surrounding the slashes is bruised and discolored, indicating that she was alive when her throat was slit. Just like the others.

Unable to draw a steady breath, Mary Jane presses a hand to her chest. She needs to breathe. She needs clean air. She needs ... to vomit. At that moment, the poorly soldered kettle spout, melted from several hours spent above the fire, falls off. It drops into the grate, causing a sudden clatter, and she jumps from her chair as though shot.

The door slams behind her as she bolts from the room, and she only just makes it to the end of the Miller's Court passage before she collapses on the pavement and throws up in the Dorset Street gutter. Having nothing in her stomach but some ginger beer she drank before leaving Lolesworth, her retching brings up an acidic

mixture of beer and bile, leaving a greenish-yellow frothy puddle at the side of the street.

Shaking uncontrollably, she crawls to the edge of the pavement and picks herself up, using the building for support. While she's slumped against it, hunched over in fear that she might vomit again, the matronly deputy of the adjacent Crossingham's Lodging House passes.

"Hello, dear. Are you quite well?" She stops, a stack of plates balanced carefully in her arms, an empty milk jug atop them. "You look frightful ill. Do you have a sickness?"

"The horrors ..." Mary Jane fails to formulate an entire thought.

Misunderstanding her situation—in particular, the reason for the tremors in her hands—the deputy, Missus Maxwell, comes up with a prompt suggestion. "You should nip into Missus Ringer's and have yourself a glass of beer. That'll put you right."

Mary Jane shakes her head, about to set the well-meaning deputy straight, for it's the horrors of Jack's work that have her so affected, not the horrors of drink. But before any words leave her lips, she restrains herself from sharing the news of her discovery. It would only inflame panic. Besides, it's the police who ought to be informed.

Choosing then to go along with Missus Maxwell's assumption, she brushes the suggestion off. "I've already done so, but I brought it up." She points to her vomit in the gutter. "I've been drinking so much these last few days."

"Poor love." Missus Maxwell trundles on. "I do pity your feelings."

When she's well out of sight, Mary Jane staggers to Commercial Street, weak and faint. Reaching the Britannia, she pauses to regain control of herself, remaining there in a daze until a kindly market porter offers her assistance and walks her across the busy street. Where to go now? Commercial Street Police Station, to speak with Detective Constable Dew? Or Leman Street? Where to go, where to go, where to go ...

Mary Jane bangs furiously on the door to Inspector Reid's home. She's out of breath, having run the last few hundred yards, and her cheeks are flushed from the exertion. She doesn't need any rouge today. Impatient, she's about to rap on the door again when her first knock is responded to by Reid's wife, Emily, dressed up in her finest clothes for the Lord Mayor's Day celebrations.

"Please, Missus Reid." She leans on the doorjamb, her shawl hanging limply off one shoulder and trailing behind her, her hair half-fallen from its up-do. "Is your husband home?"

"My dear girl, you look a frightful state." Emily pries her away from the woodwork. "Do come inside." She takes Mary Jane by the elbow and leads her into the parlor. "Sit and rest yourself." She lowers her onto the sofa. "Mister Reid is upstairs. I shall fetch him for you."

On the verge of hysterics, Mary Jane props her elbows on her knees and buries her face in her hands, willing herself to wake up from this nightmare.

"Miss Kelly?" Reid appears, straightening his shirt cuffs.

"Inspector." She leaps to her feet at his arrival, standing much too fast and nearly succumbing to a faint, forced to grasp the arm of the sofa for support.

"What in heaven's name is the matter?" He rushes to her side, easing her back onto the sofa. "What's happened? Tell me."

"He's done it again," Mary Jane manages to rasp out. "He said he wouldn't, but he bloody well has—and in *my* bed!"

"Who's done what?" Reid kneels at her feet, holding her hands in her lap.

"*Him*," she hisses. "Who do you think? The bloody Ripper, that's who."

From the doorway, a gasp. Emily, standing there with her two children, covers the ears of her youngest, pressing the boy's head to her stomach. "Edmund?"

"Take the children." Reid rises to address her, passing her money from his pocket. "Buy them breakfast. I shall join you shortly." He sends her off with a kiss, waiting for the sound of the door before pressing Mary Jane for details.

Her body language concerns him. She rises from the sofa and paces back and forth in front of the fireplace, biting on her fingernails. He's never seen her so agitated.

"You say the Ripper has struck again." He pinches his furrowed brow. "How do you know this? I've heard no word of it."

"It's there on the floor. One of his red hankies." She paces, her chest heaving. "And the dear woman is lying there dead." She stops herself. "No, more than dead. She's destroyed."

"Who's dead?" Reid fetches her a small glass of brandy in the hope that it might calm her and unravel her ramblings. "You're making very little sense."

"Her name is not known to me." Mary Jane leans on the mantel, ashamed that she never thought to ask. "I've been letting out my room to all and sundry of late, for I've had no need of the bed, and she came to me last night."

"You let your room to strangers?" Reid hands her the glass.

"I let my room to those who need it." Mary Jane accepts the drink, knocking it back in a single gulp. "This particular woman I saw once before, after I had a falling out with the man who was keeping me. He threatened to procure himself another ... amusement, so I told him it was no concern of mine and that he ought to do as he pleased." She hands Reid the empty glass. "Next I know, he's at my lodgings with this cheap, bushel-bubbied, blue-eyed tart who's got her tresses all colored up the same as mine and ..." A horrifying thought occurs to her. "She looked like me. Did he think she *was* me? What might he do when he realizes his mistake? Oh, Lord, what if he already has?" Struck by a fright, her chest tightens. "He's utterly mad, you know. I saw the doctor's note in

his pocket. He has episodes of mania. He's a certified nutcase." She seizes Reid by the hand, imploring him. "What am I to do? He means to murder me."

"I've feared as much." Reid seats her in the nearest armchair. "When I came to you after the Mitre Square event, I was troubled by the escalation in his crimes. I could see in his work how difficult it was becoming for him to control his sickening impulse, as though he were teetering on the brink of some climactic event."

"You didn't say."

"You wouldn't let me." Reid crouches at her feet, clasping her trembling hands in his firm, steady grip. "Will you tell me now: Did he warn you off seeing me?"

Mary Jane nods. "The night of his last work. He promised he'd behave if I fell silent, but he's broken that promise now. He's killed again."

Reid tucks a fallen lock of hair behind her ear, running the tip of his thumb over her pierced earlobe and the silver earring dangling from it, contemplating a way forward. "How alike is this murdered woman to you?"

Mary Jane shrugs. "Alike enough for a man who wants to see something he likes, but what difference does that make now? I can assure you, she's quite unrecognizable. Not as herself, or me. Barely even as a woman at all."

"What do you mean?"

Struggling to answer, Mary Jane swallows hard, keeping her liquor down. "She has no face." Her voice comes out as a whisper. "Her eyes are all that remain. There's not a shred of anything else left of her."

Considering how such gruesomeness might be turned to their advantage, Reid formulates a plan. "Is there somewhere you can go? Somewhere you'll be safe? Away from here."

Mary Jane nods. "Eva and I are—"

"Then go." Reid cuts her off. "Tell no-one."

"And you?"

"I shall see to the rest." He holds his hand out, palm up. "Give me your earrings."

"Why?" Mary Jane doesn't move. "What is it that you intend to do? If this compromises you in any way, I shan't—"

"That's not your concern." He keeps his hand held out. "Your earrings, please. Not many women of your class are able to afford such ornaments. They're an identifying feature."

Chastised by his tone, Mary Jane tries to comply, but her fingers refuse to cooperate with the delicate task. Aiding her, Reid eases the thin French hooks from her lobes, his dexterous magician's hands making quick work of it.

"Why do you take such risks for me?" Mary Jane's voice cracks.

"It doesn't need saying." He pockets the paste emerald earrings and helps her out of the chair, showing her to the door. "Now please go. You and Miss Sullivan must leave the city at once. Do you have money for a train?"

"Yes, but—"

"There's nothing more to say." Reid shuts her down. "This must be done, and it must be done without hesitation. I know of no other way to keep you safe."

Mary Jane opens her mouth to object further, but the words are halted in her throat.

"Please, Miss Kelly." Reid makes one more attempt to send her on her way. "Trust me."

Though placing her trust in any man is a foreign concept to her, Mary Jane does exactly that. Accepting her dismissal, she hightails it from Reid's home to Lolesworth and barges through the door to Eva's room, flushed and out of breath, breaking in on her as she finishes packing up the last of their belongings.

"What took you?" Eva stuffs Mollie the doll into her trunk and looks up, disappointed to see that Mary Jane's hands are empty. "Where's the bacon?"

"We need to leave." Mary Jane pulls her to her feet. "Right now."

EPILOGUE

Monday, July 8, 1889
Eight months later ...

UP SINCE DAWN, MARY JANE STANDS AT THE EDGE OF A comfortable country bedroom, sipping her second cup of morning coffee. This new routine is taking some getting used to. Never a morning person, she now has to be up early to tend to the needs of the house. Does the milkman need paying? Are the maids up? Who's checking out today? Who's checking in?

Enjoying a rare moment of peace before breakfast, she admires the nude eighteen-year-old lying on her bed. Now fully blossomed into womanhood, Eva lies on her back with her legs akimbo, the plump pink lips of her core slightly parted, her small cleft almost completely concealed by a thick fringe of pubic curls. She's kicked the sheets off on account of the summer heat, and her curvaceous body is unabashedly on display, sprawled there as Mary Jane had left her some hours before, too exhausted to move post-fuck.

Windows on either side of the bed are open, letting a cool breeze circulate throughout the room, the net curtains billowing with every fresh gust, the scent of cut grass and fragrant flowers drifting in on the air. The world is virtually silent. Birds twitter to one another in the trees framing the guesthouse's modest back garden, over which the bedroom looks, and in the distance, a horse and cart can be heard trotting down the lane.

All around the room, there are mirrors. Entirely for Eva's pleasure, two large mirrors are suspended from the ceiling above the bed, and three cheval mirrors are positioned to reflect the bed from all angles. She does love to watch.

Catching her own reflection in one of the mirrors, Mary Jane has some difficulty recognizing the person she's become. Her features are still lightly painted—her cheeks rouged, her lips pinked, and her lashes and brows darkened—but her long auburn hair is now tightly pinned up. A few loose curls frame her face, and new silver teardrop earrings ornament her ears. The amethyst gems are still paste, but no-one would know it.

Her old clothes are long gone. In their place, she's wearing a plum-colored silk dress with black silk accents and black lace trims around the collar and cuffs. A small pouch on the lower left of her tight-fitting bodice holds a slender pocket watch—the first she's ever owned. She looks frightfully sophisticated.

The only decoration is an artificial violet pinned to her bodice, and a silver chatelaine that hangs at her right hip. On the chatelaine, keys dangle from thin chains of different lengths, granting her sole access to anything and everything with a lock: desks, chests of drawers, her private drawing room, the safe, and all the household cabinets—including one kept full of various devices of pleasure, all available for sale or rent to her paying guests.

Inspired to wake Eva up in the most loving way, she sets aside her coffee, hitches up her skirts, and clambers onto the foot of the bed, dipping her head between the teen's spread thighs to taste the dewy flesh of her exposed charms.

Feeling a burst of heat on her parts, Eva groans and stirs. "What time is it?"

"Almost ten o'clock." Mary Jane lavishes the valley of her sex with kisses. "Will you join me for a late breakfast?" She clamps her lips over Eva's clit and teases it with the tip of her tongue, coaxing it to stiffen, sucking gently. But that's where it ends.

A knock at the door brings a premature halt to her ministrations.

"Miss Mary Jane?" a female voice calls out. "There's a gentleman arrived to see you. He didn't give his name, but he reckons he knows you from Lunnon."

Eva sits up, panicked. "Who could it be? Ain't no-one from London meant to know that you've still got breath in your lungs."

"Don't fret, love." Mary Jane wipes her mouth and slides off the bed, suppressing her own anxiety for Eva's sake. "I'm sure he's mistaken." She straightens her clothes, flashing Eva the most reassuring smile she can muster. "Get dressed and meet me in the breakfast room. I'll have the cook fry up some extra bacon."

Feigning more confidence than she feels, she joins the young maid in the hall. "This gentleman asked for me by name?"

The maid shakes her head. "The proprietress, he said."

Encouraged by that, believing the man to be in error, Mary Jane makes her way to the lobby and enters quietly, finding a gent of middling age with short, steadily graying hair perusing a photographic portrait of herself and Eva on the wall, his back to her.

"You wish to speak with me, sir." She draws his attention from a safe distance away, ready to make a hasty retreat if necessary, but breathes an audible sigh of relief when he turns to face her.

It's Inspector Reid.

"How good it is to see you again, Miss Kelly." He whisks off his bowler hat, clutching it in the same hand he holds a briefcase and a rolled up copy of the local newspaper. "Or should I be calling you Miss Malone?"

"Call me Mary Jane, if you like." She greets him with a peck on the cheek. "However did you find me?" Though she did once send him a blank postcard from Ramsgate when she and Eva first took up residence in their new home, simply to let him know that she was all right, she'd never made any mention of the guesthouse.

Reid holds up the newspaper, opened to a page containing an advertisement for a private women's

retreat managed by Miss MJ Malone and her companion, Miss Eva Sullivan.

"You clever old cock." Mary Jane liberates the newspaper from him. "You ought to quit the force and become a private investigator."

"I might just do that." He looks around the foyer, spotting a nosey maid lurking by the reception desk, pretending to dust. "Is there somewhere private we can talk?"

"That sounds frightfully ominous, but of course." Mary Jane fumbles for a key on her chatelaine. "You may come through to my drawing room."

So that the privacy of her paying guests might be protected, this is the only room where male visitors are permitted. In it, an over-stuffed velvet sofa and two armchairs are positioned around a brochure-cluttered coffee table adorned with a large vase of violets. Among other modest items of furniture, there's also a small writing desk, a sideboard, and a large bookshelf built around the fireplace. It all conveys decency, with a touch of refinement, and Mary Jane appears to fit right in.

Reid runs his eyes over her, noting the healthy glow in her cheeks, her easy smile, and the effortless grace with which she glides in her expensive clothes, her deportment and carriage rivaling that of any well-bred lady.

"You look ..."

"Respectable?" She pre-empts the compliment.

"Well," he corrects her. "You look well, and you have a beautiful home."

"Not mine, more's the pity. Everything you see here is courtesy of my wealthy benefactors. This property, this business, and even this beautiful dress." She picks at her flounced skirts. "Would you like some brandy?"

Reid checks his pocket watch. "It's not yet eleven o'clock."

"Don't you start on me as well." She rolls her eyes and opens up the locked sideboard. "I get enough of all those temperance lectures from Eva." She pours two glasses of brandy from a decanter, her measures generous. "Besides, is this not a special occasion? Surely

you would not frown on me for a little indulgence with an old friend?"

As she passes off one of the glasses to him, he catches sight of a thin gold wedding band on the appropriate finger of her left hand.

"You're married?"

"As much as the law permits me to be." Mary Jane sinks into an armchair, inviting him to seat himself on the sofa. "If I could make it a legal union, I surely would." She twirls the ring on her finger. "Indeed, if I was able to do all that a man could, I would." Her thoughts drift, imagining Eva with a full belly. "So far as I can see, that is the one and only drawback of not being in possession of a fully-functioning priapic appendage." She crosses her legs at the knee, trapping the strapped-on and tied-down dildo between her thighs.

"Delicately put, as ever." Reid chuckles, glad to see that she hasn't changed quite so much. "How's business here?" He sets his briefcase at his feet, his hat on the arm of the sofa, and picks up a guesthouse advertising card from the coffee table, reading all about this oddly secretive haven for women of a delicate nature. "There are no signs on the road."

"We survive mostly by word of mouth." Mary Jane sips her brandy. "It has to be that way, since we cater exclusively to women of a very particular persuasion."

Reid looks blank.

"It's a quiet sanctuary for women to express themselves freely," she clarifies, pausing before adding, "With each other."

"Is it a brothel?"

"Heavens, no!" She laughs. "My house is certainly not disorderly. We're merely a discreet venue for the facilitation of intimate encounters between respectable women who wish for their private affairs to remain private."

Reid digests that, pondering where the line is drawn, and Mary Jane lets that topic of conversation ebb, anxious for him to shed light on the reason for his sudden visit.

"Why are you here?" she asks at last. "Why now? Has something happened?"

"I wish that were the case." Reid swirls the liquor in his glass. "I wish I could say the matter has been dealt with, but at this time, he remains ... elusive."

A frown creases Mary Jane's brow. "You don't know where he is?" Though she tries to conceal it, her voice is laced with fear.

"I shan't stop looking," Reid assures her. "I believe him to be living under an assumed name, staying in low lodging houses and never keeping to a job, but he shall not evade me for long. I have men on him. He will be unearthed."

"Men?" Mary Jane raises an eyebrow. "What sort of men?"

"Bad men," Reid admits, hesitating to divulge more. "The type of men who exist only in the shadows, hurting others for profit or personal gain."

"The gangs," Mary Jane infers. "The people who killed my friend Emma Smith."

"I'm putting their talents to good use." Reid knocks back his drink. "Whatever you think of my reasons for pursuing him, he deserves the rope. I'll make no apologies for my methods."

He expects her to castigate him for the unlawful approach, but she no longer has the inclination to do so. Not since she found a dead woman in her bed. Instead, she lets the thought settle on her mind, then chooses to ignore it.

"May I ask you something, Inspector?" She locks eyes with him. "The identification of the body. How did you do it?"

"Magic, Miss Kelly." He puts down his glass and withdraws a ha'penny from his pocket. "The simple art of illusion." He places the coin in the palm of one hand and makes it disappear. "The eyes are so easy to deceive." With a flourish, he opens up his other hand, revealing the apparently teleported coin, and goes on to describe how he arrived at Shoreditch mortuary, where the body lay.

For the benefit of those coming to identify it, it was concealed from the neck down, the hideously disfigured face stitched up as best it could be.

Jagged slivers of flesh had been sewn crudely back into place, and the nose was anchored in approximate position with a small hook. The lidless eyes, permanently fixed open, had pronounced postmortem changes. The irises were cloudy and dull, and the sclera had turned deep brown from exposure to the air.

"We surely can't allow anyone to see her like this. It's much too frightful." He directed the mortuary attendant's attention to her discolored eyes. "Can nothing be done? Is it not possible to replace them with glass prosthetics alike in color?"

While the mortuary attendant shuffled off to root through a jar of miscellaneous eyeballs, searching for a matching pair, Reid took one of his wife's sewing needles from his pocket and pierced the ears of the corpse. By the time Joe Barnett showed up for the identification, the minor enhancements were complete, and he needed only a little encouragement.

"Don't you recognize the eyes of the woman you love?" Reid gave him a mental nudge. "Haven't you looked into those eyes a hundred times?"

Joe leaned over the shell in which she was laid, squinting at her features. After some hesitation, he nodded. To strengthen his conviction, Reid produced Mary Jane's silver and paste emerald earrings and declared that they were found upon the body. That did the trick.

"People see what they expect to see," Reid explains, producing the earrings again now for Mary Jane, returning them to her. "It's all misdirection."

"Such a simple trick." Mary Jane lays the earrings out on her palm. "But Joe did always like to believe what he was told. What of the others? My friends? Maria? Lizzie? Catherine?" She lists off names of her close associates. "How about Missus Cox? Or Julia? And Missus Prater who lived upstairs? Were they all so easily convinced?"

705

"The women did but glance. I'm quite sure they had not the faintest idea what or who they were looking at, but they believed it with all their hearts."

"What of McCarthy?" Mary Jane inquires of her landlord.

"Men are susceptible to many forms of manipulation, as I'm sure you can attest to." Reid cracks a small smile. "Once you know his weakness, it can be exploited."

He relates leading John McCarthy into the mortuary and fixing his mind to the identification with one simple, seemingly off-hand comment: "If it does indeed prove to be your unfortunate tenant, perhaps some relatives will come forward and settle her arrears with you. I've heard her family are rather well-to-do."

That was all it took.

"Even stubborn men find their principles lacking when presented with the right persuasion," Reid goes on, recounting how Mary Jane's former customer, George Hutchinson, proved to be something of an annoyance.

"That ain't her," George had stated flatly, shaking his head. "I don't believe it."

To convince him otherwise, Reid set a crumpled five pound note in front of him and told him to look again. For a man out of work, as George then was, a hundred shillings was a windfall.

"If you're interested, I brought along a selection of newspaper clippings." Reid reaches into his briefcase, withdrawing a brown cardboard police file. "There was extensive press coverage at the time, as I'm sure you can imagine, and I didn't know if you'd be keeping abreast of all the goings on, so I saved them for you."

Mary Jane eyes the folder warily. "Eva forbid me to read of it, and I don't blame her. I was such a wreck when we left London." She downs the last of her drink, keen to change the subject. "Will you stay for dinner?"

"That's a kind offer, but I ought to be going." Reid plucks his hat off the arm of the sofa. "I'm on my annual leave, and my dear wife is waiting for me. We come to Kent every year, and I fancy that one day I shall retire here. It's where I'm from, after all."

"Then I shall be glad to have a friend nearby." Mary Jane rises to bid him goodbye and walks him to the front door. "We might reinstate our coffee visits."

"We might indeed." He dallies on the porch, hesitant to clamber back into the carriage waiting for him at the end of the driveway. "Although, if we're to remain friends, it occurs to me that you might now tell me the truth of you. I still don't know who you really are."

"What is there to say?" Mary Jane remains unnecessarily guarded. "I'm a woman who lost her way. I suffered misfortunes, as we all have, but I was made whole again by the love of a young girl who latched on to the last shred of a decent woman in me, and a friend who showed me respect, even when I had none for myself." She pauses. "Will that suffice?"

Accepting that he'll never know anything more than that, Reid kisses her cheek and departs. "Take care, Mary Jane. We will meet again."

In the wake of his departure, Mary Jane slinks back to her drawing room, pours herself another glass of brandy, and sits down to read the contents of the folder he left on her coffee table, finding a myriad of articles from more than a dozen papers, some less flattering than others. In many, she's referred to by the French variant of her name, often paired with the married name she invented: Marie Jeanette Davies née Kelly.

"Joe Barnett, you little turd," she grumbles, knowing such information could only have come from his mouth. "I bet you spat on my grave n'all."

In the Illustrated Police News, she discovers an illustration depicting her as a frumpy, over-plump woman with fat cheeks and black hair.

"Euggh." She grimaces at her unlikeness, crumpling up the offending page and tossing it in the general direction of a waste basket. "How rude."

In another paper, she reads how the killer removed the woman's heart. He reached up under her ribcage and cut it out of her. What he did with it, no-one knows, though Mary Jane suspects it went the same way as Annie Chapman's liver.

While in India, she heard accounts of men cannibalizing their dead enemies. To do so is to exact the greatest amount of dominance over a foe, and some even believe that consuming the organs of the dead imbues them with the power contained therein.

"Who was your visitor?" Eva strides in without knocking, concerned for Mary Jane's welfare after watching the man leave. "Is everything all right?"

She looks a picture in the blue silk dress Mary Jane bought for her eighteenth birthday. The pricey garment cost several pounds for the fabric, plus a little to have the draper cut it to her specifications, but it was worth every penny. To save on additional expenses, Mary Jane made the whole thing up herself, doing so during daylight hours, in a brightly lit conservatory, no need to squint by candlelight and work long into the night. It was a delight to do.

The first time Eva put it on, she spent ten minutes standing in front of the mirror, running her hands over the fabric, fussing over the expenditure, but Mary Jane assured her that every woman is deserving of at least one silk dress. Pierced ears came next, and now she wears a simple pair of silver earrings purchased in celebration of their most recent anniversary.

"Tell me, Em." She approaches the sofa, plucking the brandy glass out of Mary Jane's hand and confiscating it from her. "Who was that man?"

"Mister Reid. You remember him? He brought me some old news clippings from London."

Eva glances at the coffee table, turning her nose up at the unwelcome reminder. "What do you want to see all that ghastliness for?" She picks up the discarded article from the Illustrated Police News, pulling a face similar to the one Mary Jane made. "Who gave 'em that description? Looks like your head's stuffed with a tater." She turns her focus to the lower portion of the page, where a coffin is shown being removed from Miller's Court, and her mind turns to the unknown woman lying dead in the shell. "Do you ever wonder who she was?"

"All the time," Mary Jane answers solemnly. "It's my fault she's dead."

A heavy silence falls.

"Don't say that," Eva chastises her, ignorant of the facts. "And don't let's ruin the day over it." She tears the article into tiny pieces. "Dispose of all this nastiness and come to breakfast. I'm famished."

As she skips off to the breakfast room, Mary Jane flips through the remainder of the folder. At the bottom of the pile, there are some things that don't belong. The first is a clipping from the London Daily News, printed on June 5. The headline reads: Supposed Murder of a Woman. Discovery of Mutilated Remains. She skims the article.

"Early yesterday morning, and almost simultaneously, two packages containing portions of a woman's mutilated body were discovered on the foreshore of the Thames ..."

"Riverside workmen had been attracted to the spot, and they at once commenced to undo the parcel. They were horrified to discover that it contained the lower part of a woman's abdomen, cut in two pieces ..."

"While this ghastly parcel was being examined, news was received that another portion of a woman's body had been picked up from the Surrey side of the river, just by the Albert Bridge. In this case, the parcel contained the left leg and thigh of a woman who apparently in life was of good physical proportions ..."

"This limb had been wrapped up in the corresponding half piece of the pair of drawers to that used for enveloping the abdominal organs."

Another article identifies the woman as Elizabeth Jackson, a prostitute from Chelsea, and behind it, there's a note from Reid. It says simply: I think you're right.

ADDENDUM

Joseph Fleming
(aka James Evans)

He had a history of mental illness.

On May 23, 1888, he was admitted to the Whitechapel Union Infirmary under the assumed name of James Evans and remained there until June 27, 1888. He was declared to be of unsound mind.

On July 3, 1888, he was again admitted to the Whitechapel Union Infirmary as James Evans. He was declared insane, but was nevertheless released on July 9, 1888. Four weeks later, Martha Tabram was murdered.

On July 4, 1892, he was confined to the City of London Lunatic Asylum and declared a lunatic. The form of insanity from which he suffered was determined to be 'melancholia,' and he had delusions of being followed by men who intended to kill him.

In early 1893, he was very nearly released. He appeared, for a short time, to be free of his delusions, but upon being examined prior to his discharge, it was found that his delusions had returned. He was described as being 'peculiar, nervous, and irritable,' and frequently talked to himself. He was also prone to becoming abusive. By the latter part of that year, he became very incoherent and his delusions worsened.

On February 14, 1895, he was transferred to the London County Lunatic Asylum at Claybury. He died there on August 28, 1920. Cause of death was pulmonary tuberculosis.

Before his permanent confinement, he may have been responsible for the deaths of Alice McKenzie, a Whitechapel prostitute who was murdered on July 17, 1889, and Frances Coles, another Whitechapel prostitute, murdered on February 13, 1891.

Detective Inspector Edmund Reid

In 1896, he retired from the police force and moved to Herne, Kent.

That same year, he became a private investigator.

He died on December 5, 1917, aged 71.

Photograph taken circa 1896.
Origin unknown.

Mary Jane Kelly

What became of the real Mary Jane Kelly is not known.

A Lost Woman: Mary Kelly in Miller's Court.
From the Penny Illustrated newspaper, 1888.

Sketch of Mary Jane Kelly's funeral, circa 1888.
Origin unknown.

"What makes it so easy for him is that the women lead him, of their own free will, to the spot where they know interruption is least likely. It is not as if he has to wait for his chance; they make the chance for him. And then they are so miserable and so hopeless, so utterly lost to all that makes a person want to live, that for the sake of fourpence—enough to get drunk on—they will go in any man's company and run the risk that it is him. I tell many of them to go home, but they say they have no home. And when I try to frighten them and speak of the danger they run, they'll laugh and say, 'Oh, I know what you mean. I ain't afraid of him. It's the Ripper or the bridge with me. What's the odds?' And it's true, that's the worst of it."

– Chief Inspector Henry Moore (1848–1918)
Scotland Yard
Lead investigative officer, the Whitechapel murders

AUTHOR'S NOTE

I admit it: this book is rather large. Under normal circumstances, I've always felt that the more a streamlined a piece of work can be, the better. In this case, however, it was important to me to include as much detail as I possibly could because I felt I had a certain duty to the memory of Mary Jane Kelly. I wanted to give life to a woman who is only remembered for her death. To do that, I needed words. Lots of words.

The truth of the matter is that very little is known for certain about the woman called Mary Jane Kelly. Whether or not she was the woman found murdered and mutilated on Friday, November 9, 1888, in room number 13 at Miller's Court, is a topic of some debate, and having grown to love her very deeply over the last year, I'd rather like to think that she survived.

ABOUT THE AUTHOR

Keira Michelle Telford is an award-winning author with a love for the gruesome, the macabre, and the downright filthy. She writes historical and contemporary erotic sapphic romance, and other sapphic fiction.

Erotic Lesbian Romance
Cadence of My Heart
The Housemistress

Historical Lesbian Romance
The Ruin of Us
Never Come to Rest

Short Stories
Hoar & Rime
Evonnia & the Maiden
Falling Hard

Futanari
All the Devils (short story)
Come, My Pet

Website: www.keiramichelle.com
Twitter: @km_telford
Facebook: www.facebook.com/keiramichelletelford
Goodreads: www.goodreads.com/keiramichelle
Amazon: www.amazon.com/author/keiramichelle

www.ingramcontent.com/pod-product-compliance
Lightning Source LLC
Chambersburg PA
CBHW051053030726
47504CB00006B/1608